MW00395835

The Chaplet of Pearls

Charlotte M. Yonge

Alpha Editions

This edition published in 2021

ISBN : 9789354848803

Design and Setting By
Alpha Editions
www.alphaedis.com
Email – info@alphaedis.com

Contents

PREFACE

It is the fashion to call every story controversial that deals with times when controversy or a war of religion was raging; but it should be remembered that there are some which only attempt to portray human feelings as affected by the events that such warfare occasioned. 'Old Mortality' and 'Woodstock' are not controversial tales, and the 'Chaplet of Pearls' is so quite as little. It only aims at drawing certain scenes and certain characters as the convulsions of the sixteenth century may have affected them, and is, in fact, like all historical romance, the shaping of the conceptions that the imagination must necessarily form when dwelling upon the records of history. That faculty which might be called the passive fancy, and might almost be described in Portia's song,—

> 'It is engendered in the eyes,
>
> By READING fed—and there it dies,'—

that faculty, I say, has learnt to feed upon character and incident, and to require that the latter should be effective and exciting. Is it not reasonable to seek for this in the days when such things were not infrequent, and did not imply exceptional wickedness or misfortune in those engaged in them? This seems to me one plea for historical novel, to which I would add the opportunity that it gives for study of the times and delineation of characters. Shakespeare's Henry IV. and Henry V., Scott's Louis XI., Manzoni's Federigo Borromeo, Bulwer's Harold, James's Philip Augustus, are all real contributions to our comprehension of the men themselves, by calling the chronicles and memoirs into action. True, the picture cannot be exact, and is sometimes distorted—nay, sometimes praiseworthy efforts at correctness in the detail take away whatever might have been lifelike in the outline. Yet, acknowledging all this, I must still plead for the tales that presumptuously deal with days gone by, as enabling the young to realize history vividly—and, what is still more desirable, requiring an effort of the mind which to read of modern days does not. The details of Millais' Inquisition or of his Huguenot may be in error in spite of all his study and diligence, but they have brought before us for ever the horrors of the *auto-da-fe*, and the patient, steadfast heroism of the man who can smile aside his wife's endeavour to make him tacitly betray his faith to save his life. Surely it is well, by pen as by picture, to go back to the past for figures that will stir the heart like these, even though the details be as incorrect as those of the revolt of Liege or of La Ferrette in 'Quentin Durward' and 'Anne of Geierstein.'

Scott, however, willfully carved history to suit the purposes of his story; and in these days we have come to feel that a story must earn a certain amount of credibility by being in keeping with established facts, even if striking events have to be sacrificed, and that the order of time must be preserved. In Shakespeare's days, or even in Scott's, it might have been possible to bring Henry III. and his *mignons* to due punishment within the limits of a tale beginning with the Massacre of St. Bartholomew; but in 1868 the broad outlines of tragedy must be given up to keep within the bounds of historical verity.

How far this has been done, critics better read than myself must decide. I have endeavoured to speak fairly, to the best of my ability, of such classes of persons as fell in with the course of the narrative, according to such lights as the memoirs of the time afford. The Convent is scarcely a CLASS portrait, but the condition of it seems to be justified by hints in the Port Royal memoirs, respecting Maubuisson and others which Mere Angelique reformed. The intolerance of the ladies at Montauban is described in Madame Duplessis-Mornay's life; and if Berenger's education and opinions are looked on as not sufficiently alien from Roman Catholicism, a reference to Froude's 'History of Queen Elizabeth' will show both that the customs of the country clergy, and likewise that a broad distinction was made by the better informed among the French between Calvinism and Protestantism or Lutheranism, in which they included Anglicanism. The minister Gardon I do not consider as representing his class. He is a POSSIBILITY modified to serve the purposes of the story.

Into historical matters, however, I have only entered so far as my story became involved with them. And here I have to apologize for a few blunders, detected too late for alteration even in the volumes. Sir Francis Walsingham was a young rising statesman in 1572, instead of the elderly sage he is represented; his daughter Frances was a mere infant, and Sir Philip Sidney was not knighted till much later. For the rest, I have tried to show the scenes that shaped themselves before me as carefully as I could; though of course they must not be a presentiment of the times themselves, but of my notion of them.

C. M. Yonge

November 14th, 1868

CHAPTER I
THE BRIDAL OF THE WHITE
AND BLACK

Small was the ring, and small in truth the finger:

What then? the faith was large that dropped it down.

Aubrey De Vere, INFANT BRIDAL

Setting aside the consideration of the risk, the baby-weddings of the Middle Ages must have been very pretty sights.

So the Court of France thought the bridal of Henri Beranger Eustache de Ribaumont and of Marie Eustacie Rosalie de Rebaumont du Nid-de-Merle, when, amid the festivals that accompanied the signature of the treaty of Cateau-Cabresis, good-natured King Henri II. presided merrily at the union of the little pair, whose unite ages did not reach ten years.

There they stood under the portal of Notre-Dame, the little bridegroom in a white velvet coat, with puffed sleeves, slashed with scarlet satin, as were the short, also puffed breeches meeting his long white knitted silk stockings some way above the knee; large scarlet rosettes were in his white shoes, a scarlet knot adorned his little sword, and his velvet cap of the same colour bore a long white plume, and was encircled by a row of pearls of priceless value. They are no other than that garland of pearls which, after a night of personal combat before the walls of Calais, Edward III. of England took from his helmet and presented to Sir Eustache de Ribaumont, a knight of Picardy, bidding him say everywhere that it was a gift from the King of England to the bravest of knights.

The precious heirlooms were scarcely held with the respect due to an ornament so acquired. The manly garb for the first time assumed by his sturdy legs, and the possession of the little sword, were evidently the most interesting parts of the affair to the youthful husband, who seemed to find in them his only solace for the weary length of the ceremony. He was a fine, handsome little fellow, fair and rosy, with bright blue eyes, and hair like shining flax, unusually tall and strong-limbed for his age; and as he gave his hand to his little bride, and walked with her under a canopy up to kneel at the High Altar, for the marriage blessing and the mass, they looked like a full-grown couple seen through a diminishing-glass.

The little bride was perhaps a less beautiful child, but she had a splendid pair of black eyes, and a sweet little mouth, both set into the uncomprehending solemnity of baby gravity and contentment in fine clothes. In accordance with the vow indicated by her name of Marie, her dress was white and blue, turquoise forget-me-nots bound the little lace veil on her dark chestnut hair, the bosom of her white satin dress was sprinkled with the same azure jewel, and turquoises bordered every seam of the sweeping skirt with a train befitting a count's daughter, and meandered in gorgeous constellations round the hem. The little thing lisped her own vows forth without much notion of their sense, and indeed was sometimes prompted by her bridesmaid cousin, a pretty little girl a year older, who thrust in her assistance so glibly that the King, as well as others of the spectators, laughed, and observed that she would get herself married to the boy instead of her cousin.

There was, however, to be no doubt nor mistake about Beranger and Eustacie de Ribaumont being man and wife. Every ceremony, religious or domestic, that could render a marriage valid, was gone through with real earnestness, although with infinite gaiety, on the part of the court. Much depended on their union, and the reconcilement of the two branches of the family had long been a favourite scheme of King Henri II.

Both alike were descended from Anselme de Ribaumont, renowned in the first Crusade, and from the brave Picard who had received the pearls; but, in the miserable anarchy of Charles VI.'s reign, the elder brother had been on the Burgundian side—like most of the other nobles of Picardy— and had thus been brought into the English camp, where, regarding Henry V. as lawfully appointed to the succession, and much admiring him and his brother Nedford, he had become an ardent supporter of the English claim. He had married an English lady, and had received the grant if the castle of Leurre in Normandy by way of compensation for his ancestral one of Ribaumont in Picardy, which had been declared to be forfeited by his treason, and seized by his brother.

This brother had always been an Armagnac, and had risen and thriven with his party,—before the final peace between France and England obliged the elder line to submit to Charles VII. Since that time there had been a perpetual contention as to the restitution of Chateau Ribaumont, a strife which under Louis XI. had become an endless lawsuit; and in the days of dueling had occasioned a good many insults and private encounters. The younger branch, or Black Ribaumonts, had received a grant from Louis XI. of the lands of Nid-de-Merle, belonging to an unfortunate Angevin noble, who had fallen under the royal displeasure, and they had enjoyed court favour up to the present generation, when Henri II., either from opposition to his father, instinct for honesty, or both, had become a warm friend to the gay and brilliant young Baron de Ribaumont, head of the white or elder branch of the family.

The family contention seemed likely to wear out of its own accord, for the Count de Ribaumont was an elderly and childless man, and his brother, the Chevalier de Ribaumont, was, according to the usual lot of French juniors, a bachelor, so that it was expected that the whole inheritance would centre upon the elder family. However, to the general surprise, the Chevalier late in life married, and became the father of a son and daughter; but soon after calculations were still more thrown out by the birth of a little daughter in the old age of the Count.

Almost from the hour in which her sex was announced, the King had promised the Baron de Ribaumont that she should be the wife of his young son, and that all the possessions of the house should be settled upon the little couple, engaging to provide for the Chevalier's disappointed heir in some commandery of a religious order of knighthood.

The Baron's wife was English. He had, when on a visit to his English kindred, entirely turned the head of the lovely Annora Walwyn, and finding that her father, one of the gravest of Tudor statesmen, would not hear of her breaking her engagement to the honest Dorset squire Marmaduke Thistlewood, he had carried her off by a stolen marriage and *coup de main*, which, as her beauty, rank, and inheritance were all considerable, had won him great reputation at the gay court of Henri II.

Infants as the boy and girl were, the King had hurried on their marriage to secure its taking place in the lifetime of the Count. The Countess had died soon after the birth of the little girl, and if the arrangement were to take effect at all, it must be before she should fall under the guardianship of her uncle, the Chevalier. Therefore the King had caused her to be brought up from the cottage in Anjou, where she had been nursed, and in person superintended the brilliant wedding. He himself led off the dance with the tiny bride, conducting her through its mazes with fatherly kindliness and condescension; but Queen Catherine, who was strongly in the interests of the Angevin branch, and had always detested the Baron as her husband's intimate, excused herself from dancing with the bridegroom. He therefore fell to the share of the Dauphiness Queen of Scots, a lovely, bright-eyed, laughing girl, who so completely fascinated the little fellow, that he convulsed the court by observing that he should not have objected to be married to some one like her, instead of a little baby like Eustacie.

Amid all the mirth, it was not only the Chevalier and the Queen who bore displeased looks. In truth, both were too great adepts in court life to let their dissatisfaction appear. The gloomiest face was that of him whose triumph it was—the bridegroom's father, the Baron de Ribaumont. He had suffered severely from the sickness that prevailed in St. Quentin, when in the last August the Admiral de Coligny had been besieged there by the Spaniards, and all agreed that he had never been the same man since, either in health or in demeanour. When he came back from his captivity and found the King bent on crowning his return by the marriage of the children, he had hung back, spoken of scruples about such unconscious vows, and had finally only consented under stress of the personal friendship of the King, and on condition that he and his wife should at once have the sole custody of the little bride. Even then he moved about the gay scene with so distressed and morose an air that he was evidently either under the influence of a scruple of conscience or of a foreboding of evil.

No one doubted that it had been the latter, when, three days later, Henri II., in the prime of his strength and height of his spirits, encountered young Des Lorges in the lists, received the splinter of a lance in his eye, and died two days afterwards.

No sooner were his obsequies over than the Baron de Ribaumont set off with his wife and the little bridal pair for his castle of Leurre, in Normandy, nor was he ever seen at court again.

CHAPTER II
THE SEPARATION

Parted without the least regret,

Except that they had ever met.

*   *   *   *

Misses, the tale that I relate,

This lesson seems to carry:

Choose not alone a proper mate,

But proper time to marry!

COWPER, *PAIRING TIME ANTICIPATED*

'I will have it!'

'Thou shalt not have it!'

'Diane says it is mine.'

'Diane knows nothing about it.'

'Gentlemen always yield to ladies.'

'Wives ought to mind their husbands.'

'Then I will not be thy wife.'

'Thou canst not help it.'

'I will. I will tell my father what M. le Baron reads and sings, and then I know he will.'

'And welcome.'

Eustacie put out her lip, and began to cry.

The 'husband and wife,' now eight and seven years old, were in a large room hung with tapestry, representing the history of Tobit. A great state bed, curtained with piled velvet, stood on a sort of *dais* at the further end; there was a toilet-table adorned with curiously shaped boxes, and coloured Venetian glasses, and filagree pouncet-boxes, and with a small mirror whose frame was inlaid with gold and ivory. A large coffer, likewise inlaid, stood against the wall, and near it a cabinet, of Dutch workmanship, a combination of ebony, ivory, wood, and looking-glass, the centre retreating, and so arranged that by the help of most ingenious attention to perspective and reflection, it appeared like the entrance to a magnificent miniature cinque-cento palace, with steps up to a vestibule paved in black and white lozenges, and with three endless corridors diverging from it. So much for show; for use, this palace was a bewildering complication of secret drawers and pigeon-holes, all depending indeed upon one tiny gold key; but unless the use of that key were well understood, all it led to was certain outer receptacles of fragrant Spanish gloves, knots of ribbon, and kerchiefs strewn over with rose leaves and lavender. However, Eustacie had secured the key, and was now far beyond these mere superficial matters. Her youthful lord had just discovered her mounted on a chair, her small person decked out with a profusion of necklaces, jewels, bracelets, chains, and rings; and her fingers, as well as they could under their stiffening load, were opening the very penetralia of the cabinet, the inner chamber of the hall, where lay a case adorned with the Ribaumont arms and containing the far-famed chaplet of pearls. It was almost beyond her reach, but she had risen on tip-toe, and was stretching out her hand for it, when he, springing behind her on the chair, availed himself of his superior height and strength to shut the door of this Arcanum and turn the key. His mortifying permission to his wife to absent herself arose from pure love of teasing, but the next moment he added, still holding his hand on the key—'As to telling what my father reads, that would be treason. How shouldst thou know what it is?'

'Does thou think every one is an infant but thyself?'

'But who told thee that to talk of my father's books would get him into trouble?' continued the boy, as they still stood together on the high heavy wooden chair.

She tossed her pretty head, and pretended to pout.

'Was it Diane? I will know. Didst thou tell Diane?'

Instead of answering, now that his attention to the key was relaxed, Eustacie made a sudden dart, like a little wild cat, at the back of the chair and at the key. They chair over-balanced; Beranger caught at the front drawer of the cabinet, which, unlocked by Eustacie, came out in his hand, and chair, children, drawer, and curiosities all went rolling over together on the floor with a hubbub that brought all the household together, exclaiming and scolding. Madame de Ribaumont's displeasure at the rifling of her hoards knew no bounds; Eustacie, by way of defence, shrieked 'like twenty demons;' Beranger, too honourable to accuse her, underwent the same tempest; and at last both were soundly rapped over the knuckles with the long handle of Madame's fan, and consigned to two separate closets, to be dealt with on the return of M. le Baron, while Madame returned to her embroidery, lamenting the absence of that dear little Diane, whose late visit at the chateau had been marked by such unusual tranquility between the children.

Beranger, in his dark closet, comforted himself with the shrewd suspicion that his father was so employed as not to be expected at home till supper-time, and that his mother's wrath was by no means likely to be so enduring as to lead her to make complaints of the prisoners; and when he heard a trampling of horses in the court, he anticipated a speedy release and summons to show himself to the visitors. He waited long, however, before he heard the pattering of little feet; then a stool scraped along the floor, the button of his door was undone, the stool pushed back, and as he emerged, Eustacie stood before him with her finger to her lip. 'CHUT, Beranger! It is my father and uncle, and Narcisse, and, oh! so many *gens d'armes*. They are come to summon M. le Baron to go with them to disperse the *preche* by the Bac de l'Oie. And oh, Beranger, is he not there?'

'I do not know. He went out with his hawk, and I do not think he could have gone anywhere else. Did they say so to my mother?'

'Yes; but she never knows. And oh, Beranger, Narcisse told me—ah, was it to tease me?—that Diane has told them all they wanted to know, for that they sent her here on purpose to see if we were not all Huguenots.'

'Very likely, the little viper! Le me pass, Eustacie. I must go and tell my father.'

'Thou canst not get out that way; the court is full of men-at-arms. Hark, there's Narcisse calling me. He will come after me.'

There was not a moment to lose. Berenger flew along a corridor, and down a narrow winding stair, and across the kitchen; then snatching at the arm of a boy of his own age whom he met at the door, he gasped out, 'Come and help me catch Follet, Landry!' and still running across an orchard, he pulled down a couple of apples from the trees, and bounded into a paddock where a small rough Breton pony was feeding among the little tawny Norman cows. The animal knew his little master, and trotted towards him at his call of 'Follet, Follet. Now be a wise Follet, and play me no tricks. Thou and I, Follet, shall do good service, if thou wilt be steady.'

Follet made his advances, but with a coquettish eye and look, as if ready to start away at any moment.

'Soh, Follet. I have no bread for thee, only two apples; but, Follet, listen. There's my *beau-pere* the Count, and the Chevalier, all spite, and their whole troop of savage *gens d'armes*, come out to fall upon the poor Huguenots, who are doing no harm at all, only listening to a long dull sermon. And I am much afraid my father is there, for he went out his hawk on his wrist, and he never does take Ysonde for any real sport, as thou and I would do, Follet. He says it is all vanity of vanities. But thou know'st, if they caught him at the *preche* they would call it heresy and treason, and all sorts of horrors, and any way they would fall like demons on the poor Huguenots, Jacques and all—thine own Jacques, Follet. Come, be a loyal pony, Follet. Be at least as good as Eustacie.'

Follet was evidently attentive to this peroration, turning round his ear in a sensible attitude, and advancing his nose to the apples. As Beranger held them out to him, the other boy clutched his shaggy forelock so effectually that the start back did not shake him off, and the next moment Beranger was on his back.

'And I, Monsieur, what shall I do?'

'Thou, Landry? I know. Speed like a hare, lock the avenue gate, and hide the key. That will delay them a long time. Off now, Follet.'

Beranger and Follet understood one another far too well to care about such trifles as saddle and bridle, and off they went through green grassy balks dividing the fields, or across the stubble, till, about three miles from the castle, they came to a narrow valley, dipping so suddenly between the hills that it could hardly have been suspected by one unaware of its locality, and the sides were dotted with copsewood, which entirely hid the bottom. Beranger guided his pony to a winding path that led down the steep side of the valley, already hearing the cadence of a loud, chanting voice, throwing out its sounds over the assembly, whence arose assenting hums over an undercurrent of sobs, as though the excitable French assembly were strongly affected.

The thicket was so close that Beranger was almost among the congregation before he could see more than a passing glimpse of a sea of heads. Stout, ruddy, Norman peasants, and high white-capped women, mingled with a few soberly-clad townsfolk, almost all with the grave, steadfast cast of countenance imparted by unresisted persecution, stood gathered round the green mound that served as a natural pulpit for a Calvinist minister, who more the dress of a burgher, but entirely black. To Beranger's despair, he was in the act of inviting his hearers to join with him in singing one of Marot's psalms; and the boy, eager to lose not a moment, grasped the skirt of the outermost of the crowd. The man, an absorbed-looking stranger, merely said, 'Importune me not, child.'

'Listen!' said Beranger; 'it imports——'

'Peace,' was the stern answer; but a Norman farmer looked round at that moment, and Beranger exclaimed, 'Stop the singing! The *gens d'armes!*' The psalm broke off; the whisper circulated; the words 'from Leurre' were next conveyed from lip to lip, and, as it were in a moment, the dense human mass had broken up and vanished, stealing through the numerous paths in the brushwood, or along the brook, as it descended through tall sedges and bulrushes. The valley was soon as lonely as it had been populous; the pulpit remained a mere mossy bank, more suggestive or fairy dances than of Calvinist sermons, and no one remained on the scene save Beranger with his pony, Jacques the groom, a stout farmer, the preacher, and a tall thin figure in the plainest dark cloth dress that could be worn by a gentleman, a hawk on his wrist.

'Thou here, my boy!' he exclaimed, as Beranger came to his side; and as the little fellow replied in a few brief words, he took him by the hand, and said to the minister, 'Good Master Isaac, let me present my young son to you, who under Heaven hath been the means of saving many lives this day.'

Maitre Isaac Gardon, a noted preacher, looked kindly at the boy's fair face, and said, 'Bless thee, young sir. As thou hast been already a chosen instrument to save life, so mayest thou be ever after a champion of the truth.'

'Monsieur le Baron,' interposed Jacques, 'it were best to look to yourself. I already hear sounds upon the wind.'

'And you, good sir?' said the Baron.

'I will see to him,' said the farmer, grasping him as a sort of property. 'M. le Baron had best keep up the beck. Out on the moor there he may fly the hawk, and that will best divert suspicion.'

'Farewell, then,' said the Baron, wringing the minister's hand, and adding, almost to himself, 'Alas! I am weary of these shifts!' and weary indeed he seemed, for as the ground became so steep that the beck danced noisily down its channel, he could not keep up the needful speed, but paused, gasping for breath, with his hand on his side. 'Beranger was off his pony in an instant, assuring Follet that it ought to be proud to be ridden by his father, and exhaling his own exultant feelings in caresses to the animal as it gallantly breasted the hill. The little boy had never been so commended before! He loved his father exceedingly; but the Baron, while ever just towards him, was grave and strict to a degree that the ideas even of the sixteenth century regarded as severe. Little Eustacie with her lovely face, her irrepressible saucy grace and audacious coaxing, was the only creature to whom he ever showed much indulgence and tenderness, and even that seemed almost against his will and conscience. His son was always under rule, often blamed, and scarcely ever praised; but it was a hardy vigorous nature, and respectful love throve under the system that would have crushed or alienated a different disposition. It was not till the party had emerged from the wood upon a stubble field, where a covey of partridges flew up, and to Beranger's rapturous delight furnished a victim for Ysonde, that M. de Ribaumont dismounted from the pony, and walking towards home, called his son to his side, and asked him how he had learnt the intentions of the Count and the Chevalier. Beranger explained how Eustacie had come to warn him, and also told what she had said of Diane de Ribaumont, who had lately, by her father's request, spent a few weeks at the chateau with her cousins.

'My son,' said the Baron, 'it is hard to ask of babes caution and secrecy; but I must know from thee what thy cousin may have heard of our doings?'

'I cannot tell, father,' replied Beranger; 'we played more than we talked. Yet, Monsieur, you will not be angry with Eustacie if I tell you what she said to me to-day?'

'Assuredly not, my son.'

'She said that her father would take her away if he knew what M. le Baron read, and what he sung.'

'Thou hast done well to tell me, my son. Thinkest thou that this comes from Diane, or from one of the servants?'

'Oh, from Diane, my father; none of the servants would dare to say such a thing.'

'It is as I suspected then,' said the Baron. 'That child was sent amongst us as a spy.' Tell me, Beranger, had she any knowledge of our intended journey to England?'

'To England! But no, father, I did not even know it was intended. To England—to that Walwyn which my mother takes such pains to make us speak rightly. Are we then, going?'

'Listen, my son. Thou hast to-day proved thyself worthy of trust, and thou shalt hear. My son, ere yet I knew the truth I was a reckless disobedient youth, and I bore thy mother from her parents in England without their consent. Since, by Heaven's grace, I have come to a better mind, we have asked and obtained their forgiveness, and it has long been their desire to see again their daughter and her son. Moreover, since the accession of the present Queen, it has been a land where the light is free to shine forth; and though I verily believe what Maitre Gardon says, that persecution is a blessed means of grace, yet it is grievous to expose one's dearest thereto when they are in no state to count the cost. Therefore would I thither convey you all, and there amid thy mother's family would we openly abjure the errors in which we have been nurture. I have already sent to Paris to obtain from the Queen-mother the necessary permission to take my family to visit thy grand-father, and it must now be our endeavour to start immediately on the receipt of the reply, before the Chevalier's information can lead to any hindrance or detention of Eustacie.'

'Then Eustacie will go with us, Monsieur?'

'Certainly. Nothing is more important than that her faith should be the same as yours! But discretion, my son: not a word to the little one.'

'And Landry, father? I had rather Landry went than Eustacie. And Follet, dear father, pray take him.'

After M. de Ribaumont's grave confidence to his son and heir, he was a little scandalized at the comparative value that the boy's voice indicated for wife, foster-brother, and pony, and therefore received it in perfect silence, which silence continued until they reached the chateau, where the lady met them at the door with a burst of exclamations.

'Ah, there you are, safe, my dear Baron. I have been in despair. Here were the Count and his brother come to call on you to join them in dispersing a meeting of those poor Huguenots and they would not permit me to send out to call you in! I verily think they suspected that you were aware of it.'

M. de Ribaumont made no answer, but sat wearily down and asked for his little Eustacie.

'Little vixen!' exclaimed the Baroness, 'she is gone; her father took her away with him.' And as her husband looked extremely displeased, she added that Eustacie had been meddling with her jewel cabinet and had been put in penitence. Her first impulse on seeing her father had been to cling to him and poor out her complaints, whereupon he had declared that he should take her away with him at once, and had in effect caused her pony to be saddled, and he had ridden away with her to his old tower, leaving his brother, the Chevalier, to conduct the attack on the Huguenot conventicle.

'He had no power or right to remove her,' said the Baron. 'How could you let him do so in my absence? He had made over her wardship to me, and has no right to resume it!'

'Well, perhaps I might have insisted on his waiting till your return; but, you see, the children have never done anything but quarrel and fight, and always by Eustacie's fault; and if ever they are to endure each other, it must be by being separated now.'

'Madame,' said the Baron, gravely, 'you have done your utmost to ruin your son's chances of happiness.'

That same evening arrived the King's passport permitting the Baron de Ribaumont and his family to pay a visit to his wife's friends in England. The next morning the Baron was summoned to speak to one of his farmers, a Huguenot, who had come to inform him that, through the network of intelligence kept up by the members of the persecuted faith, it had become known that the Chevalier de Ribaumont had set off for court that night, and there was little doubt that his interference would lead to an immediate revocation of the sanction to the journey, if to no severer measures. At best, the Baron knew that if his own absence were permitted, it would be only on condition of leaving his son in the custody of either the Queen-mother or the Count. It had become impossible to reclaim Eustacie. Her father would at once have pleaded that she was being bred up in Huguenot errors. All that could be done was to hasten the departure ere the royal mandate could arrive. A little Norman sailing vessel was moored two evenings after in a lonely creek on the coast, and into it stepped M. de Ribaumont, with his Bible, Marot's Psalter, and Calvin's works, Beranger still tenderly kissing a lock of Follet's mane, and Madame mourning for the pearls, which her husband deemed too sacred an heirloom to carry away to a foreign land. Poor little Eustacie, with her cousin Diane, was in the convent of Bellaise in Anjou. If any one lamented her absence, it was her father-in-law.

CHAPTER III
THE FAMILY COUNCIL

He counsels a divorce

Shakespeare, *KING HENRY VIII.*

In the spring of the year 1572, a family council was assembled in Hurst Walwyn Hall. The scene was a wainscoted oriel chamber closed off by a screen from the great hall, and fitted on two sides by presses of books, surmounted the one by a terrestrial, the other by a celestial globe, the first 'with the addition of the Indies' in very eccentric geography, the second with enormous stars studding highly grotesque figures, regarded with great awe by most beholders.

A solid oaken table stood in the midst, laden with books and papers, and in a corner, near the open hearth, a carved desk, bearing on one slope the largest copy of the 'Bishops' Bible'; on the other, one of the Prayer-book. The ornaments of the oaken mantelpiece culminated in a shield bearing a cross *boutonnee*, i.e. with trefoil terminations. It was supported between a merman with a whelk shell and a mermaid with a comb, and another like Siren curled her tail on the top of the gaping baronial helmet above the shield, while two more upheld the main weight of the chimney-piece on either side of the glowing wood-fire.

In the seat of honour was an old gentleman, white-haired, and feeble of limb, but with noble features and a keen, acute eye. This was Sir William, Baron of Hurst Walwyn, a valiant knight at Guingate and Boulogne, a statesman of whom Wolsey had been jealous, and a ripe scholar who had shared the friendship of More and Erasmus. The lady who sat opposite to him was several years younger, still upright, brisk and active, though her hair was milk-white; but her eyes were of undimmed azure, and her complexion still retained a beauteous pink and white. She was highly educated, and had been the friend of Margaret Roper and her sisters, often sharing their walks in the bright Chelsea garden. Indeed, the musk-rose in her own favourite nook at Hurst Walwyn was cherished as the gift of Sir Thomas himself.

Near her sat sister, Cecily St. John, a professed nun at Romsey till her twenty-eight year, when, in the dispersion of convents, her sister's home had received her. There had she continued, never exposed to tests of opinion, but pursuing her quiet course according to her Benedictine rule, faithfully keeping her vows, and following the guidance of the chaplain, a college friend of Bishop Ridley, and rejoicing in the use of the vernacular prayers and Scriptures. When Queen Mary had sent for her to consider of the revival of convents, her views had been found to have so far diverged from those of the Queen that Lord Walwyn was thankful to have her safe at home again; and yet she fancied herself firm to old Romsey doctrine. She was not learned, like Lady Walwyn, but her knowledge in all needlework and confectionery was consummate, so that half the ladies in Dorset and Wilts longed to send their daughters to be educated at Hurst Walwyn. Her small figure and soft cheeks had the gentle contour of a dove's form, nor had she lost the conventual serenity of expression; indeed it was curious that, let Lady Walwyn array her as she would, whatever she wore bore a nunlike air. Her silken farthingales hung like serge robes, her ruffs looked like mufflers, her coifs like hoods, even necklaces seemed rosaries, and her scrupulous neatness enhanced the pure unearthly air of all belonging to her.

Eager and lively, fair and handsome, sat the Baronne de Ribaumont, or rather, since the higher title had been laid aside, Dame Annora Thistlewood. The health of M. de Ribaumont had been shattered at St. Quentin, and an inclement night of crossing the Channel had brought on an attack on the lungs, from which he only rallied enough to amaze his English friends at finding the gay dissipated young Frenchman they remembered, infinitely more strict and rigid than themselves. He was never able to leave the house again after his first arrival at Hurst Walwyn, and sank under the cold winds of the next spring, rejoicing to leave his wife and son, not indeed among such strict Puritans as he preferred, but at least where the pure faith could be openly avowed without danger.

Sir Marmaduke Thistlewood, the husband to whom Annora Walwyn had been destined before M. de Ribaumont had crossed her path, was about the same time left a widower with one son and daughter, and as soon as a suitable interval had passed, she became a far happier wife than she had been in either the Baron's gay or grave days. Her son had continued under the roof of his grandfather, to whose charge his father had specially committed him, and thus had been scarcely separated from his mother, since Combe Manor was not above three miles across the downs from Hurst Walwyn, and there was almost daily intercourse between the families. Lucy Thistlewood had been brought to Hurst Walwyn to be something between a maid of honour and a pupil to the ladies there, and her brother Philip, so soon as he was old enough, daily rode thither to share with Berenger the instructions of the chaplain, Mr. Adderley, who on the present occasion formed one of the conclave, sitting a little apart as not quite familiar, though highly esteemed.

With an elbow on the table, and one hand toying with his long riding-whip, sat, booted and spurred, the jovial figure of Sir Marmaduke, who called out, in his hearty voice, 'A good riddance of an outlandish Papist, say I! Read the letter, Berenger lad. No, no, no! English it! I know nothing of your mincing French! 'Tis the worst fault I know in you, boy, to be half a Frenchman, and have a French name'—a fault that good Sir Marmaduke did his best to remedy by always terming his step-son Berenger or Berry Ribmount, and we will so far follow his example as henceforth to give the youth the English form of his Christian name. He was by this time a tall lad of eighteen, with straight features, honest deep blue eyes, very fair hair cut short and brushed up to a crest upon the middle of his head, a complexion of red and white that all the air of the downs and the sea failed to embrown, and that peculiar openness and candour of expression which seems so much an English birthright, that the only trace of his French origin was, that he betrayed no unbecoming awkwardness in the somewhat embarrassing position in which he was placed, literally standing, according to the respectful discipline of the time, as the subject of discussion, before the circle of his elders. His colour was indeed, deepened, but his attitude was easy and graceful, and he used no stiff rigidity nor restless movements to mask his anxiety. At Sir Marmaduke's desire, he could not but redden a good deal more, but with a clear, unhesitating voice, he translated, the letter that he had received from the Chevalier de Ribaumont, who, by the Count's death, had become Eustacie's guardian. It was a request in the name of Eustacie and her deceased father, that Monsieur le Baron de Ribaumont— who, it was understood, had embraced the English heresy—would concur with his spouse in demanding from his Holiness the Pope a decree annulling the childish marriage, which could easily be declared void, both on account of the consanguinity of the parties and the discrepancy of their faith; and which would leave each of them free to marry again.

'Nothing can be better,' exclaimed his mother. 'How I have longed to free him from that little shrew, whose tricks were the plague of my life! Now there is nothing between him and a worthy match!'

'We can make an Englishman of him now to the backbone,' added Sir Marmaduke, 'and it is well that it should be the lady herself who wants first to be off with it, so that none can say he has played her a scurvy trick.'

'What say you, Berenger?' said Lord Walwyn. 'Listen to me, fair nephew. You know that all my remnant of hope is fixed upon you, and that I have looked to setting you in the room of the son of my own; and I think that under our good Queen you will find it easier to lead a quiet God-fearing life than in your father's vexed country, where the Reformed religion lies under persecution. Natheless, being a born liegeman of the King of France, and heir to estates in his kingdom, meseemeth that before you are come to years of discretion it were well that you should visit them, and become better able to judge for yourself how to deal in this matter when you shall have attained full age, and may be able to dispose of them by sale, thus freeing yourself from allegiance to a foreign prince. And at the same time you can take measures, in concert with this young lady, for loosing the wedlock so unhappily contracted.'

'O sir, sir!' cried Lady Thistlewood, 'send him not to France to be burnt by the Papists!'

'Peace, daughter,' returned her mother. 'Know you not that there is friendship between the court party and the Huguenots, and that the peace is to be sealed by the marriage of the King's sister with the King of Navarre? This is the most suitable time at which he could go.'

'Then, madam,' proceeded the lady, 'he will be running about to all the preachings on every bleak moor and wet morass he can find, catching his death with rheums, like his poor father.'

There was a general smile, and Sir Marmaduke laughed outright.

'Nay, dame,' he said, 'have you marked such a greed of sermons in our Berry that you should fear his so untowardly running after them?'

'Tilly-vally, Sir Duke,' quoth Dame Annora, with a flirt of her fan, learnt at the French court. 'Men will run after a preacher in a marshy bog out of pure forwardness, when they will nod at a godly homily on a well-stuffed bench between four walls.'

'I shall commit that matter to Mr. Adderley, who is good enough to accompany him,' said Lord Walwyn, 'and by whose counsel I trust that he will steer the middle course between the pope and Calvin.'

Mr. Adderley bowed in answer, saying he hoped that he should be enable to keep his pupil's mind clear between the allurements of Popery and the errors of the Reformed; but meanwhile Lady Thistlewood's mind had taken a leap, and she exclaimed,—

'And, son, whatever you do, bring home the chaplet of pearls! I know they have set their minds upon it. They wanted me to deck Eustacie with it on that unlucky bridal-day, but I would not hear of trusting her with it, and now will it rarely become our Lucy on your real wedding-day.'

'You travel swiftly, daughter,' said Lord Walwyn. 'Nor have we yet heard the thoughts of one who ever thinks wisely. Sister,' he added, turning to Cecily St. John, 'hold not you with us in this matter?'

'I scarce comprehend it, my Lord,' was the gentle reply. 'I knew not that it was possible to dissolve the tie of wedlock.'

'The Pope's decree will suffice,' said Lord Walwyn.

'Yet, sir,' still said the ex-nun, 'methought you had shown me that the Holly Father exceeded his power in the annulling of vows.'

'Using mine own lessons against me, sweet sister?' said Lord Walwyn, smiling; 'yet, remember, the contract was rashly made between two ignorant babes; and, bred up as they have severally been, it were surely best for them to be set free from vows made without their true will or knowledge.'

'And yet,' said Cecily, perplexed, 'when I saw my niece here wedded to Sir Marmaduke, was it not with the words, 'What God hath joined let no man put asunder'?'

'Good lack! aunt,' cried Lady Thistlewood, 'you would not have that poor lad wedded to a pert, saucy, ill-tempered little moppet, bred up that den of iniquity, Queen Catherine's court, where my poor Baron never trusted me after he fell in with the religion, and had heard of King Antony's calling me the Swan of England.'

At that moment there was a loud shriek, half-laugh, half-fright, coming through the window, and Lady Thistlewood, starting up, exclaimed, 'The child will be drowned! Box their ears, Berenger, and bring them in directly.'

Berenger, at her bidding, hurried out of the room into the hall, and thence down a flight of steps leading into a square walled garden, with a couple of stone male and female marine divinities accommodating their fishy extremities as best they might on the corners of the wall. The square contained a bowling-green of exquisitely-kept turf, that looked as if cut out of green velvet, and was edged on its four sides by a raised broad-paved walk, with a trimming of flower-beds, where the earliest blossoms were showing themselves. In the centre of each side another paved path intersected the green lawn, and the meeting of these two diameters was at a circular stone basin, presided over by another merman, blowing a conch on the top of a pile of rocks. On the gravelled margin stood two distressed little damsels of seven and six years old, remonstrating with all their might against the proceedings of a roguish-looking boy of fourteen of fifteen, who had perched their junior—a fat, fair, kitten-like element of mischief, aged about five—*en croupe* on the merman, and was about, according to her delighted request, to make her a bower of water, by extracting the plug and setting the fountain to play; but as the fountain had been still all the winter, the plug was hard of extraction, especially to a young gentleman who stood insecurely, with his feet wide apart upon pointed and slippery point of rock-work; and Berenger had time to hurry up, exclaiming, 'Giddy pate! Dolly would Berenger drenched to the skin.'

'And she has on her best blue, made out of mother's French farthingale,' cried the discreet Annora.

'Do you know, Dolly, I've orders to box your ears, and send you in?' added Berenger, as he lifted his half-sister from her perilous position, speaking, as he did so, without a shade of foreign accent, though with much more rapid utterance than was usual in England. She clung to him without much alarm, and retaliated by an endeavour to box his ears, while Philip, slowly making his way back to the mainland, exclaimed, 'Ah there's no chance now! Here comes demure Mistress Lucy, and she is the worst mar-sport of all.'

A gentle girl of seventeen was drawing near, her fair delicately-tinted complexion suiting well with her pale golden hair. It was a sweet face, and was well set off by the sky-blue of the farthingale, which, with her white lace coif and white ruff, gave her something the air of a speedwell flower, more especially as her expression seemed to have caught much of Cecily's air of self-restrained contentment. She held a basketful of the orange pistils of crocuses, and at once seeing that some riot had taken place, she said to the eldest little girl, 'Ah, Nan, you had been safer gathering saffron with me.'

'Nay, brother Berry came and made all well,' said Annora; 'and he had been shut up so long in the library that he must have been very glad to get out.'

'And what came of it?' cried Philip. 'Are you to go and get yourself unmarried?'

'Unmarried!' burst out the sisters Annora and Elizabeth.

'What, laughed Philip, 'you knew not that this is an ancient husband, married years before your father and mother?'

'But, why? said Elizabeth, rather inclined to cry. 'What has poor Lucy done that you should get yourself unmarried from her?'

There was a laugh from both brothers; but Berenger, seeing Lucy's blushes, restrained himself, and said. 'Mine was not such good luck, Bess, but they gave me a little French wife, younger than Dolly, and saucier still; and as she seems to wish to be quit of me, why, I shall be rid of her.'

'See there, Dolly,' said Philip, in a warning voice, 'that is the way you'll be served if you do not mend your ways.'

'But I thought,' said Annora gravely, 'that people were married once for all, and it could not be undone.'

'So said Aunt Cecily, but my Lord was proving to her out of all law that a contract between such a couple of babes went for nought,' said Berenger.

'And shall you, indeed, see Paris, and all the braveries there?' asked Philip. 'I thought my Lord would never have trusted you out of his sight.'

'And now it is to be only with Mr. Adderley,' said Berenger; 'but there will be rare doings to be seen at this royal wedding, and maybe I shall break a lance there in your honour, Lucy.'

'And you'll bring me a French fan?' cried Bess.

'And me a pouncet-box?' added Annora.

'And me a French puppet dressed Paris fashion?' said Dolly.

'And what shall he bring Lucy?' added Bess.

'I know,' said Annora; 'the pearls that mother is always talking about! I heard her say that Lucy should wear them on her wedding-day.'

'Hush!' interposed Lucy, 'don't you see my father yonder on the step, beckoning to you?'

The children flew towards Sir Marmaduke, leaving Berenger and Lucy together.

'Not a word to wish me good speed, Lucy, now I have my wish?' said Berenger.

'Oh, yes,' said Lucy, 'I am glad you should see all those brave French gentlemen of whom you used to tell me.'

'Yes, they will be all at court, and the good Admiral is said to be in high favour. He will surely remember my father.'

'And shall you see the lady?' asked Lucy, under her breath.

'Eustacie? Probably; but that will make no change. I have heard too much of *l'escadron de la Reine-mere* to endure the thought of a wife from thence, were she the Queen of Beauty herself. And my mother says that Eustacie would lose all her beauty as she grew up—like black-eyed Sue on the down; nor did I ever think her brown skin and fierce black eyes to compare with you, Lucy. I could be well content never to see her more; but,' and here he lowered his voice to a tone of confidence, 'my father, when near his death, called me, and told me that he feared my marriage would be a cause of trouble and temptation to me, and that I must deal with it after my conscience when I was able to judge in the matter. Something, too, he said of the treaty of marriage being a burthen on his soul, but I know not what he meant. If ever I saw Eustacie again, I was to give her his own copy of Clement Marot's Psalter, and to tell her that he had ever loved and prayed for her as a daughter; and moreover, my father added,' said Berenger, much moved at the remembrance it brought across him, 'that if this matter proved a burthen and perplexity to me, I was to pardon him as one who repented of it as a thing done ere he had learnt to weigh the whole world against a soul.'

'Yes, you must see her,' said Lucy.

'Well, what more were you going to say, Lucy?'

'I was only thinking,' said Lucy, as she raised her eyes to him, 'how sorry she will be that she let them write that letter.'

Berenger laughed, pleased with the simplicity of Lucy's admiration, but with modesty and common sense enough to answer, 'No fear of that, Lucy, for an heiress, with all the court gallants of France at her feet.'

'Ah, but you!'

'I am all very well here, when you have never seen anybody but lubberly Dorset squires that never went to London, nor Oxford, nor beyond their own furrows,' said Berenger; 'but depend upon it, she has been bred up to care for all the airs and graces that are all the fashion at Paris now, and will be as glad to be rid of an honest man and a Protestant as I shall to be quit of a court puppet and a Papist. Shall you have finished my point-cuffs next week, Lucy? Depend upon it, no gentleman of them all will wear such dainty lace of such a fancy as those will be.'

And Lucy smiled, well pleased.

Coming from the companionship of Eustacie to that of gentle Lucy had been to Berenger a change from perpetual warfareto perfect supremacy, and his preference to his little sister, as he had been taught to call her from the first, had been loudly expressed. Brother and sister they had ever since considered themselves, and only within the last few months had possibilities been discussed among the elders of the family, which oozing out in some mysterious manner, had become felt rather than known among the young people, yet without altering the habitual terms that existed between them. Both were so young that love was the merest, vaguest dream to them; and Lucy, in her quiet faith that Berenger was the most beautiful, excellent, and accomplished cavalier the earth could afford, was little troubled about her own future share in him. She seemed to be promoted to belong to him just as she had grown up to curl her hair and wear ruffs and farthingales. And to Berenger Lucy was a very pleasant feature in that English home, where he had been far happier than in the uncertainties of Chateau Leurre, between his naughty playfellow, his capricious mother, and morose father. If in England his lot was to be cast, Lucy was acquiesced in willingly as a portion of that lot.

CHAPTER IV
TITHONUS

A youth came riding towards a palace gate,

And from the palace came a child of sin

And took him by the curls and led him in!

Where sat a company with heated eyes.

Tennyson, *A VISION OF SIN*

It was in the month of June that Berenger de Ribaumont first came in sight of Paris. His grandfather had himself begun by taking him to London and presenting him to Queen Elizabeth, from whom the lad's good mien procured him a most favourable reception. She willingly promised that on which Lord Walwyn's heart was set, namely, that his title and rank should be continued to his grandson; and an ample store of letter of recommendation to Sir Francis Walsingham, the Ambassador, and all others who could be of service in the French court, were to do their utmost to provide him with a favourable reception there.

Then, with Mr. Adderley and four or five servants, he had crossed the Channel, and had gone first to Chateau Leurre, where he was rapturously welcomed by the old steward Osbert. The old man had trained up his son Landry, Berenger's foster-brother, to become his valet, and had him taught all the arts of hair-dressing and surgery that were part of the profession of a gentleman's body-servant; and the youth, a smart, acuter young Norman, became a valuable addition to the suite, the guidance of which, through a foreign country, their young master did not find very easy. Mr. Adderley thought he knew French very well, through books, but the language he spoke was not available, and he soon fell into a state of bewilderment rather hard on his pupil, who, though a very good boy, and crammed very full of learning, was still nothing more than a lad of eighteen in all matters of prudence and discretion.

Lord Walwyn was, as we have seen, one of those whose Church principles had altered very little and very gradually; and in the utter diversity of practice that prevailed in the early years of Queen Elizabeth, his chaplain as well as the rector of the parish had altered no more than was absolutely enjoined of the old ceremonial. If the poor Baron de Ribaumont had ever been well enough to go to church on a Sunday, he would perhaps have thought himself still in the realms of what he considered as darkness; but as he had never openly broken with the Gallic Church, Berenger had gone at once from mass at Leurre to the Combe Walwyn service. Therefore when he spent a Sunday at Rouen, and attended a Calvinist service in the building that the Huguenots were permitted outside the town, he was much disappointed in it; he thought its very fervour familiar and irreverent, and felt himself much more at home in the cathedral into which he strayed in the afternoon. And, on the Sunday he was at Leurre, he went, as a part of his old home-habits, to mass at the old round-arched church, where he and Eustacie had played each other so many teasing tricks at his mother's feet, and had received so many admonitory nips and strokes of her fan. All he saw there was not congenial to him, but he liked it vastly better than the Huguenot meeting, and was not prepared to understand or enter into Mr. Adderley's vexation, when the tutor assured him that the reverent gestures that came naturally to him were regarded by the Protestants as idolatry, and that he would be viewed as a recreants from his faith. All Mr. Adderley hoped was that no one would hear of it: and in this he felt himself disappointed, when, in the midst of his lecture, there walked into the room a little, withered, brown, dark-eyed man, in a gorgeous dress of green and gold, who doffing a hat with an umbrageous plume, precipitated himself, as far as he could reach, towards Berenger's neck, calling him fair cousin and dear baron. The lad stood taken by surprise for a moment, thinking that Tithonus must have looked just like this, and skipped like this, just as he became a grasshopper; then he recollected that this must be the Chevalier de Ribaumont, and tried to make up for his want of cordiality. The old man had, it appeared, come out of Picardy, where he lived on *soupe maigre* in a corner of the ancestral castle, while his son and daughter were at court, the one in Monsieur's suite, the other in that of the Queen-mother. He had come purely to meet his dear young cousin, and render him all the assistance is his power, conduct him to Paris, and give him introductions.

Berenger, who had begun to find six Englishmen a troublesome charge in France, was rather relieved at not being the only French scholar of the party, and the Chevalier also hinted to him that he spoke with a dreadful Norman accent that would never be tolerated at court, even if it were understood by the way. Moreover, the Chevalier studied him all over, and talked of Paris tailors and posture-masters, and, though the pink of politeness, made it evident that there was immensely too much of him. 'It might be the custom in England to be so tall; here no one was of anything like such a height, but the Duke of Guise. He, in his position, with his air, could carry it off, but we must adapt ourselves as best we can.'

And his shrug and look of concern made Berenger for a moment almost ashamed of that superfluous height of which they were all so proud at home. Then he recollected himself, and asked, 'And why should not I be tall as well as M. de Guise?'

'We shall see, fair cousin,' he answered, with an odd satirical bow; 'we are as Heaven made us. All lies in the management and if you had the advantages of training, PERHAPS you could even turn your height into a grace.'

'Am I such a great lubber?' wondered Berenger; 'they did not think so at home. No; nor did the Queen. She said I was a proper stripling! Well, it matters the less, as I shall not stay long to need their favour; and I'll show them there is some use in my inches in the tilt-yard. But if they think me such a lout, what would they say to honest Philip?'

The Chevalier seemed willing to take on him the whole management of his 'fair cousin.' He inquired into the amount of the rents and dues which old Osbert had collected and held ready to meet the young Baron's exigencies; and which would, it seemed, be all needed to make his dress any way presentable at court. The pearls, too, were inquired for, and handed over by Osbert to his young Lord's keeping, with the significant intimation that they had been demanded when the young Madame la Baronne went to court; but that he had buried them in the orchard, and made answer that they were not in the chateau. The contract of marriage, which Berenger could just remember signing, and seeing signed by his father, the King, and the Count, was not forthcoming; and the Chevalier explained that it was in the hands of a notary at Paris. For this Berenger was not sorry. His grandfather had desired him to master the contents, and he thought he had thus escaped a very dry and useless study.

He did not exactly dislike the old Chevalier de Ribaumont. The system on which he had been brought up had not been indulgent, so that compliments and admiration were an agreeable surprise to him; and rebuffs and rebukes from his elders had been so common, that hints, in the delicate dressing of the old knight, came on him almost like gracious civilities. There was no love lost between the Chevalier and the chaplain, that was plain; but how could there be between an ancient French courtier and a sober English divine? However, to Mr. Adderley's great relief, no attempts were made on Berenger's faith, his kinsman even was disposed to promote his attendance at such Calvinist places of worship as they passed on the road, and treated him in all things as a mere guest, to be patronized indeed, but as much an alien as if he had been born in England. And yet there was a certain deference to him as head of the family, and a friendliness of manner that made the boy feel him a real relation, and all through the journey it came naturally that he should be the entire manager, and Berenger the paymaster on a liberal scale.

Thus had the travellers reached the neighbourhood of Paris, when a jingling of chains and a trampling of horses announced the advance of riders, and several gentlemen with a troop of servants came in sight.

All were gaily dressed, with feathered hats, and short Spanish cloaks jauntily disposed over one shoulder; and their horses were trapped with bright silvered ornaments. As they advanced, the Chevalier exclaimed: 'Ah! It is my son! I knew he would come to meet me.' And, simultaneously, father and son leapt from their horses, and rushed into each other's arms. Berenger felt it only courteous to dismount and exchange embraces with his cousin, but with a certain sense of repulsion at the cloud of perfume that seemed to surround the younger Chevalier de Ribaumont; the ear-rings in his ears; the general air of delicate research about his riding-dress, and the elaborate attention paid to a small, dark, sallow face and figure, in which the only tolerable feature was an intensely black and piercing pair of eyes.

'Cousin, I am enchanted to welcome you.'

'Cousin, I thank you.'

'Allow me to present you.' And Berenger bowed low in succession several times in reply to salutations, as his cousin Narcisse named M. d'O, M. de la Valette, M. de Pibrac, M. l'Abbe de Mericour, who had done him the honour to accompany him in coming out to meet his father and M. le Baron. Then the two cousins remounted, something was said to the Chevalier of the devoirs of the demoiselles, and they rode on together bandying news and repartee so fast, that Berenger felt that his ears had become too much accustomed to the more deliberate English speech to enter at once into what caused so much excitement, gesture, and wit. The royal marriage seemed doubtful—the Pope refused his sanction; nay, but means would be found—the King would not be impeded by the Pope; Spanish influence—nay, the King had thrown himself at the head of the Reformed—he was bewitched with the grim old Coligny—if order were not soon taken, the Louvre itself would become a temple.

Then one of the party turned suddenly and said, 'But I forget, Monsieur is a Huguenot?'

'I am a Protestant of the English Church,' said Berenger, rather stiffly, in the formula of his day.

'Well, you have come at the right moment, 'Tis all for the sermon now. If the little Abbe there wished to sail with a fair wind, he should throw away his breviary and study his Calvin.'

Berenger's attention was thus attracted to the Abbe de Mericour, a young man of about twenty, whose dress was darker than that of the rest, and his hat of a clerical cut, though in other respects he was equipped with the same point-device elegance.

'Calvin would never give him the rich abbey of Selicy,' said another; 'the breviary is the safer speculation.'

'Ah! M. de Ribaumont can tell you that abbeys are no such securities in these days. Let yonder Admiral get the upper hand, and we shall see Mericour, the happy cadet of eight brothers and sisters, turned adrift from their convents. What a fatherly spectacle M. le Marquis will present!'

Here the Chevalier beckoned to Berenger, who, riding forward, learnt that Narcisse had engaged lodgings for him and his suite at one of the great inns, and Berenger returned his thanks, and a proposal to the Chevalier to become his guest. They were by this time entering the city, where the extreme narrowness and dirt of the streets contrasted with the grandeur of the palatial courts that could be partly seen through their archways. At the hostel they rode under such an arch, and found themselves in a paved yard that would have been grand had it been clean. Privacy had scarcely been invented, and the party were not at all surprised to find that the apartment prepared for them was to serve both day and night for Berenger, the Chevalier, and Mr. Adderley, besides having a truckle-bed on the floor for Osbert. Meals were taken in public, and it was now one o'clock—just dinner-time; so after a hasty toilette the three gentlemen descended, the rest of the party having ridden off to their quarters, either as attendants of Monsieur or to their families. It was a sumptuous meal, at which a great number of gentlemen were present, coming in from rooms hired over shops, &c—all, as it seemed, assembled at Paris for the marriage festivities; but Berenger began to gather that they were for the most part adherents of the Guise party, and far from friendly to the Huguenot interest. Some of them appeared hardly to tolerate Mr. Adderley's presence at the table; and Berenger, though his kinsman's patronage secured civil treatment, felt much out of his element, confused, unable to take part in the conversation, and sure that he was where those at home did not wish to see him.

No sooner was the dinner over than he rose and expressed his intention of delivering his letters of introduction in person to the English ambassador and to the Admiral de Coligny, whom, as his father's old friend and the hero of his boyhood, he was most anxious to see. The Chevalier demurred to this. Were it not better to take measures at once for making himself presentable, and Narcisse had already supplied him with directions to the fashionable hair-cutter, &c. It would be taken amiss if he went to the Admiral before going to present himself to the King.

'And I cannot see my cousins till I go to court?' asked Berenger.

'Most emphatically No. Have I not told you that the one is in the suite of the young Queen, the other in that of the Queen-mother? I will myself present you, if only you will give me the honour of your guidance.'

'With all thanks, Monsieur,' said Berenger; 'my grandfather's desire was that I should lose no time in going to his friend Sir Francis Walsingham, and I had best submit myself to his judgment as to my appearance at court.'

On this point Berenger was resolute, though the Chevalier recurred to the danger of any proceeding that might be unacceptable at court. Berenger, harassed and impatient, repeated that he did not care about the court, and wished merely to fulfil his purpose and return, at which his kinsman shook his head and shrugged his shoulders, and muttered to himself, 'Ah, what does he know! He will regret it when too late; but I have done my best.'

Berenger paid little attention to this, but calling Landry Osbert, and a couple of his men, he bade them take their swords and bucklers, and escort him in his walk through Paris. He set off with a sense of escape, but before he had made many steps, he was obliged to turn and warn Humfrey and Jack that they were not to walk swaggering along the streets, with hand on sword, as if every Frenchman they saw was the natural foe of their master.

Very tall were the houses, very close and extremely filthy the streets, very miserable the beggars; and yet here and there was to be seen the open front of a most brilliant shop, and the thoroughfares were crowded with richly-dressed gallants. Even the wider streets gave little space for the career of the gay horsemen who rode along them, still less for the great, cumbrous, though gaily-decked coaches, in which ladies appeared glittering with jewels and fan in hand, with tiny white dogs on their knees.

The persons of whom Berenger inquired the way all uncapped most respectfully, and replied with much courtesy; but when the hotel of the English ambassador had been pointed out to him, he hardly believed it, so foul and squalid was the street, where a large nail-studded door occupied a wide archway. Here was a heavy iron knocker, to which Osbert applied himself. A little door was at once opened by a large, powerful John Bull of a porter, whose looks expanded into friendly welcome when he heard the English tongue of the visitor. Inside, the scene was very unlike that without. The hotel was built round a paved court, adorned with statues and stone vases, with yews and cypresses in them, and a grand flight of steps led up to the grand centre of the house, around which were collected a number of attendants, wearing the Walsingham colours. Among these Berenger left his two Englishmen, well content to have fallen into an English colony. Landry followed him to announce the visitor, Berenger waiting to know whether the Ambassador would be at liberty to see him.

Almost immediately the door was re-opened, and a keen-looking gentleman, about six-and-thirty years of age, rather short in stature, but nevertheless very dignified-looking, came forward with out-stretched hands—'Greet you well, my Lord de Ribaumont. We expected your coming. Welcome, mine honoured friend's grandson.'

And as Berenger bent low in reverent greeting, Sir Francis took his hand and kissed his brow, saying, 'Come in, my young friend; we are but sitting over our wine and comfits after dinner. Have you dined?'

Berenger explained that he had dined at the inn, where he had taken lodgings.

'Nay, but that must not be. My Lord Walwyn's grandson here, and not my guest! You do me wrong, sir, in not having ridden hither at once.'

'Truly, my Lord, I ventured not. They sent me forth with quite a company—my tutor and six grooms.'

'Our chaplain will gladly welcome his reverend brother,' said Sir Francis; and as to the grooms, one of my fellows shall go and bring them and their horses up. What!' rather gravely, as Berenger still hesitated. 'I have letters for you here, which methinks will make your grandfather's wish clear to you.'

Berenger saw the Ambassador was displeased with his reluctance, and answered quickly, 'In sooth, my Lord, I would esteem myself only too happy to be thus honoured, but in sooth——' he repeated himself, and faltered.

'In sooth, you expected more freedom than in my grave house,' said Walsingham, displeased.

'Not so, my Lord: it would be all that I could desire; but I have done hastily. A kinsman of mine has come up to Paris with me, and I have made him my guest. I know not how to break with him—the Chevalier de Ribaumont.'

'What, the young ruffler in Monsieur's suite?'

'No, my Lord; his father. He comes on my business. He is an old man, and can ill bear the cost, and I could scarce throw him over.'

Berenger spoke with such earnest, bright, open simplicity, and look so boyish and confiding, that Sir Francis's heart was won, and he smiled as he said, 'Right, lad, you are a considerate youth. It were not well to cast off your kinsman; but when you have read your letters, you may well plead your grandfather's desires, to say nothing of a hint from her Grace to have an eye to you. And for the rest, you can acquit yourself gracefully to the gentleman, by asking him to occupy the lodging that you had taken.'

Berenger's face brightened up in a manner that spoke for his sincerity; and Sir Francis added, 'And where be these lodgings?'

'At the Croix de Lorraine.'

'Ha! Your kinsman has taken you into a nest of Guisards. But come, let me present you to my wife and my other guests, then will I give you your letters, and you shall return and make your excuses to Monsieur le Chevalier.'

Berenger seemed to himself to be on familiar ground again as his host thus assumed the direction of him and ushered him into a large dining-hall, where the table had been forsaken in favour of a lesser table placed in the ample window, round which sat assembled some six or eight persons, with fruit, wine, and conserves before them, a few little dogs at their feet or on their laps, and a lute lying on the knee of one of the young gentlemen. Sir Francis presented the young Lord de Ribaumont, their expected guest, to Lady Walsingham, from whom he received a cordial welcome, and her two little daughter, Frances and Elizabeth, and likewise to the gentleman with the lute, a youth about a year older than Berenger, and of very striking and prepossessing countenance, who was named as Mr. Sidney, the son of the Lord Deputy of Ireland. A couple of gentlemen who would in these times have been termed *attaches*, a couple of lady attendants upon Lady Walsingham, and the chaplain made up the party, which on this day chanced only to include, besides the household, the young traveller, Sidney. Berenger was at once seated, and accepted a welcoming-cup of wine (i.e. a long slender glass with a beautifully twisted stem), responded to friendly inquiries about his relatives at home, and acknowledged the healths that were drunk in honour of their names; after which Lady Walsingham begged that Mr. Sidney would sing the madrigal he had before promised: afterwards a glee was sung by Sidney, one of the gentlemen, and Lady Walsingham; and it was discovered that Mr. de Ribaumont had a trained ear, and the very voice that was wanting to the Italian song they were practising. And so sped a happy hour, till a booted and spurred messenger came in with letters for his Excellency, who being thus roused from his dreamy enjoyment of the music, carried young Ribaumont off with him to his cabinet, and there made over to him a packet, with good news from home, and orders that made it clear that he could do no other than accept the hospitality of the Embassy. Thus armed with authority, he returned to the Croix de Lorraine, where Mr. Adderley could not contain his joy at the change to quarters not only so much more congenial, buts so much safer;

and the Chevalier, after some polite demur, consented to remain in possession of the rooms, being in fact well satisfied with the arrangement.

'Let him steep himself up to the lips among the English,' said Tithonus to his son. 'Thus will he peaceably relinquish to you all that should have been yours from the first, and at court will only be looked on as an overgrown English page.'

The change to the Ambassador's made Berenger happy at once. He was not French enough in breeding, or even constitution, to feel the society of the Croix de Lorraine congenial; and, kind as the Chevalier showed himself, it was with a wonderful sense of relief that Berenger shook himself free from both his fawning and his patronizing. There was a constant sense of not understanding the old gentleman's aims, whereas in Walsingham's house all was as clear, easy, and open as at home.

And though Berenger had been educated in the country, it had been in the same tone as that of his new friends. He was greatly approved by Sir Francis as a stripling of parts and modesty. Mr. Sidney made him a companion, and the young matron, Lady Walsingham, treated him as neither lout nor lubber. Yet he could not be at ease in his state between curiosity and repulsion towards the wife who was to be discarded by mutual consent. The sight of the scenes of his early childhood had stirred up warmer recollections of the pretty little playful torment, who through the vista of years assumed the air of a tricksy elf rather than the little vixen he used to think her. His curiosity had been further stimulated by the sight of his rival, Narcisse, whose effeminate ornaments, small stature, and seat on horseback filled Sir Marmaduke's pupil with inquisitive disdain as to the woman who could prefer anything so unmanly.

Sidney was to be presented at the after-dinner reception at the Louvre the next day, and Sir Francis proposed to take young Ribaumont with him. Berenger coloured, and spoke of his equipment, and Sidney good-naturedly offered to come and inspect. That young gentleman was one of the daintiest in apparel of his day; but he was amazed that the suit in which Berenger had paid his devoir to Queen Elizabeth should have been set aside—it was of pearl-grey velvet, slashed with rose-coloured satin, and in shape and fashion point-device—unless, as the Ambassador said good-humouredly, 'my young Lord Ribaumont wished to be one of Monsieur's clique.' Thus arrayed, then, and with the chaplet of pearls bound round the small cap, with a heron-plume that sat jauntily on one side of his fair curled head, Berenger took his seat beside the hazel-eyed, brown-haired Sidney, in his white satin and crimson, and with the Ambassador and his attendants were rolled off in the great state-coach drawn by eight horses, which had no sinecure in dragging the ponderous machine through the unsavoury *debris* of the streets.

Royalty fed in public. The sumptuous banqueting-room contained a barrier, partitioning off a space where Charles IX. sat alone at his table, as a State spectacle. He was a sallow, unhealthy-looking youth, with large prominent dark eyes and a melancholy dreaminess of expression, as if the whole ceremony, not to say the world itself, were distasteful. Now and then, as though endeavouring to cast off the mood, he would call to some gentleman and exchange a rough jest, generally fortified with a tremendous oath, that startled Berenger's innocent ears. He scarcely tasted what was put on his plate, but drank largely of sherbet, and seemed to be trying to linger through the space allotted for the ceremony.

Silence was observed, but not so absolute that Walsingham could not point out to his young companions the notabilities present. The lofty figure of Henri, Duke of Guise, towered high above all around him, and his grand features, proud lip, and stern eye claimed such natural superiority that Berenger for a moment felt a glow on his cheek as he remembered his challenge of his right to rival that splendid stature. And yet Guise was very little older than himself; but he walked, a prince of men, among a crowd of gentlemen, attendants on him rather than on the King. The elegant but indolent-looking Duke de Montmorency had a much more attractive air, and seemed to hold a kind of neutral ground between Guise on the one hand, and the Reformed, who mustered at the other end of the apartment. Almost by intuition, Berenger knew the fine calm features of the gray-haired Admiral de Coligny before he heard him so addressed by the King's loud, rough voice. When the King rose from table the presentations took place, but as Charles heard the name of the Baron de Ribaumont, he exclaimed, 'What, Monsieur, are you presented here by our good sister's representative?'

Walsingham answered for him, alluding to the negotiations for Queen Elizabeth's marriage with one of the French princes—'Sire, in the present happy conjuncture, it needs not be a less loyal Frenchman to have an inheritance in the lands of my royal mistress.'

'What say you, Monsieur?' sharply demanded the King: 'are you come here to renounce your country, religion—and love, as I have been told?'

'I hope, Sire, never to be unfaithful where I owe faith,' said Berenger, heated, startled, and driven to extremity.

'Not ill answered for the English giant,' said Charles aside to an attendant: then turning eagerly to Sidney, whose transcendent accomplishments had already become renowned, Charles welcomed him to court, and began to discuss Ronsard's last sonnet, showing no small taste and knowledge of poetry. Greatly attracted by Sidney, the King detained the whole English party by an invitation to Walsingham to hear music in the Queen-mother's apartments; and Berenger, following in the wake of his friends, found himself in a spacious hall, with a raised gallery at one end for the musicians, the walls decorated with the glorious paintings collected by Francois I., Greek and Roman statues clustered at the angles, and cabinets with gems and antiques disposed at intervals. Not that Berenger beheld much of this: he was absolutely dazzled with the brilliant assembly into which he was admitted. There moved the most beautiful women in France, in every lovely-coloured tint that dress could assume: their bosoms, arms, and hair sparkling with jewels; their gossamer ruffs surrounding their necks like fairy wings; their light laugh mingling with the music, as they sat, stood, or walked in graceful attitudes conversing with one another or with the cavaliers, whose brilliant velvet and jewels fifty mixed with their bright array. These were the sirens he had heard of, the 'squadron of the Queen-mother,' the dangerous beings against whom he was to steel himself. And which of them was the child he had played with, to whom his vows had been plighted? It was like some of the enchanting dreams of romance merely to look at these fair creatures; and he stood as if gazing into a magic-glass till Sir Francis Walsingham, looking round for him, said, 'Come, then, my young friend, you must do your devoirs to the Queens. Sidney, I see, is as usual in his element; the King has seized upon him.'

Catherine de Medicis was seated on a large velvet chair, conversing with the German ambassador. Never beautiful, she appeared to more advantage in her mature years than in her girlhood, and there was all the dignity of a lifetime of rule in demeanour and gestures, the bearing of her head, and motion of her exquisite hands. Her eyes were like her son's, prominent, and gave the sense of seeing all round at once, and her smile was to the highest degree engaging. She received the young Baron de Ribaumont far more graciously than Charles has done, held out her hand to be kissed, and observed 'that the young gentleman was like Madame *sa mere* whom she well remembered as much admired. Was it true that she was married in England?'

Berenger bowed assent.

'Ah! You English make good spouses,' she said, with a smile. 'Ever satisfied with home! But, your Excellency,' added she, turning to Walsingham, 'what stones would best please my good sister for the setting of the jewel my son would send her with his portrait? He is all for emeralds, for the hue of hope; but I call it the colour of jealousy.'

Walsingham made a sign that Berenger had better retreat from hearing the solemn coquetting carried on by the maiden Queen through her gravest ambassadors. He fell back, and remained watching the brilliant throng, trying in vain to discover the bright merry eyes and velvet cheek he remembered of old. Presently a kind salutation interrupted him, and a gentleman who perceived him to be a stranger began to try to set him at ease, pointed out to him the handsome, foppishly-dressed Duke of Anjou, and his ugly, spiteful little brother of Alengon, then designated as Queen Elizabeth's future husband, who was saying something to a lady that made her colour and bite her lips. 'Is that the younger Queen?' asked Berenger, as his eye fell on a sallow, dark-complexioned, sad-looking little creature in deep mourning, and with three or four such stately-looking, black-robed, Spanish-looking duennas round her as to prove her to be a person of high consequence.

'That? Oh no; that is Madame Catherine of Navarre, who has resided here ever since her mother's death, awaiting her brother, our royal bridegroom. See, here is the bride, Madame Marguerite, conversing with M. de Guise.'

Berenger paid but little heed to Marguerite's showy but already rather coarse beauty, and still asked where was the young Queen Elizabeth of Austria. She was unwell, and not in presence. 'Ah! then,' he said, 'her ladies will not be here.'

'That is not certain. Are you wishing to see any one of them?'

'I would like to see——' He could not help colouring till his cheeks rivaled the colour of his sword-knot. 'I want just to know if she is here. I know not if she be called Madame or Mademoiselle de Ribaumont.'

'The fair Ribaumont! Assuredly; see, she is looking at you. Shall I present you?'

A pair of exceedingly brilliant dark eyes were fixed on Berenger with a sort of haughty curiosity and half-recognition. The face was handsome and brilliant, but he felt indignant at not perceiving a particle of a blush at encountering him, indeed rather a look of amusement at the deep glow which his fair complexion rendered so apparent. He would fain have escaped from so public an interview, but her eye was upon him, and there was no avoiding the meeting. As he moved nearer he saw what a beautiful person she was, her rich primrose-coloured dress setting off her brunette complexion and her stately presence. She looked older than he had expected; but this was a hotbed where every one grew up early, and the expression and manner made him feel that an old intimacy was here renewed, and that they were no strangers.

'We need no introduction, cousin,' she said, giving a hand to be saluted. 'I knew you instantly. It is the old face of Chateau Leurre, only gone up so high and become so handsome.'

'Cousins,' thought he. 'Well, it makes things easier! but what audacity to be so much at her ease, when Lucy would have sunk into the earth with shame.' His bow had saved him the necessity of answering in words, and the lady continued:

'And Madame *votre mere*. Is she well? She was very good to me.'

Berenger did not think that kindness to Eustacie had been her chief perfection, but he answered that she was well and sent her commendations, which the young lady acknowledged by a magnificent curtsey. 'And as beautiful as ever?' she asked.

'Quite as beautiful,' he said, 'only somewhat more *embonpoint.*'

'Ah!' she said, smiling graciously, and raising her splendid eyes to his face, 'I understand better what that famous beauty was now, and the fairness that caused her to be called the Swan.'

It was so personal that the colour rushed again into his cheek. No one had ever so presumed to admire him; and with a degree gratified and surprised, and sensible more and more of the extreme beauty of the lady, there was a sort of alarm about him as if this were the very fascination he had been warned against, and as if she were casting a net about him, which, wife as she was, it would be impossible to him to break.

'Nay, Monsieur,' she laughed, 'is a word from one so near too much for your modesty? Is it possible that no one has yet told you of your good mien? Or do they not appreciate Greek noses and blue eyes in the land of fat Englishmen? How have you ever lived *en province?* Our princes are ready to hang themselves at the thought of being in such banishment, even at court—indeed, Monsieur has contrived to transfer the noose to M. d'Alengon. Have you been at court, cousin?'

'I have been presented to the Queen.'

She then proceeded to ask questions about the chief personages with a rapid intelligence that surprised him as well as alarmed him, for he felt more and more in the power of a very clever as well as beautiful woman, and the attraction she exercised made him long the more to escape; but she smiled and signed away several cavaliers who would have gained her attention. She spoke of Queen Mary of Scotland, then in the fifth years of her captivity, and asked if he did not feel bound to her service by having been once her partner. Did not he remember that dance?

'I have heard my mother speak of it far too often to forget it,' said Berenger, glowing again for her who could speak of that occasion without a blush.

'You wish to gloss over your first inconstancy, sir,' she said, archly; but he was spared from further reply by Philip Sidney's coming to tell him that the Ambassador was ready to return home. He took leave with an alacrity that redoubled his courtesy so much that he desired to be commended to his cousin Diane, whom he had not seen.

'To Diane?' said the lady, inquiringly.

'To Mademoiselle Diane de Ribaumont,' he corrected himself, ashamed of his English rusticity. 'I beg pardon if I spoke too familiarly of her.'

'She should be flattered by M. le Baron's slightest recollection,' said the lady, with an ironical tone that there was no time to analyze, and with a mutual gesture of courtesy he followed Sidney to where Sir Francis awaited them.

'Well, what think you of the French court?' asked Sidney, so soon as the young men were in private.

'I only know that you may bless your good fortune that you stand in no danger from a wife from thence.'

'Ha!' cried Sidney, laughing, 'you found your lawful owner. Why did you not present me?'

'I was ashamed of her bold visage.'

'What!—was she the beauteous demoiselle I found you gallanting,' said Philip Sidney, a good deal entertained, 'who was gazing at you with such visible admiration in her languishing black eyes?'

'The foul fiend seize their impudence!'

'Fie! for shame! thus to speak of your own wife,' said the mischievous Sidney, 'and the fairest——'

'Go to, Sidney. Were she fairer than Venus, with a kingdom to her dower, I would none of a woman without a blush.'

'What, in converse with her wedded husband,' said Sidney. 'Were not that over-shamefastness?'

'Nay, now, Sidney, in good sooth give me your opinion. Should she set her fancy on me, even in this hour, am I bound in honour to hold by this accursed wedlock—lock, as it may well be called?'

'I know no remedy,' said Sidney, gravely, 'save the two enchanted founts of love and hate. They cannot be far away, since it was at the siege of Paris that Rinaldo and Orlando drank thereof.'

Another question that Berenger would fain have asked Sidney, but could not for very shame and dread of mockery, was, whether he himself were so dangerously handsome as the lady had given him to understand. With a sense of shame, he caught up the little mirror in his casket, and could not but allow to himself that the features he there saw were symmetrical—the eyes azure, the complexion of a delicate fairness, such as he had not seen equaled, except in those splendid Lorraine princes; nor could he judge of the further effect of his open-faced frank simplicity and sweetness of expression—contemptible, perhaps, to the astute, but most winning to the world-weary. He shook his head at the fair reflection, smiled as he saw the colour rising at his own sensation of being a fool, and then threw it aside, vexed with himself for being unable not to feel attracted by the first woman who had shown herself struck by his personal graces, and yet aware that this was the very thing he had been warned against, and determined to make all the resistance in his power to a creature whose very beauty and enchantment gave him a sense of discomfort.

CHAPTER V
THE CONVENT BIRD

Young knight, whatever that dost armes professe,

And through long labours huntest after fame,

Beware of fraud, beware of ficklenesse,

In choice and change of thy beloved dame.

Spenser, FAERY QUEENE

Berenger' mind was relieved, even while his vanity was mortified, when the Chevalier and his son came the next day to bring him the formal letter requesting the Pope's annulment of his marriage. After he had signed it, it was to be taken to Eustacie, and so soon as he should attain his twenty-first year he was to dispose of Chateau Leurre, as well as of his claim to the ancestral castle in Picardy, to his cousin Narcisse, and thus become entirely free to transfer his allegiance to the Queen of England.

It was a very good thing—that he well knew; and he had a strong sense of virtue and obedience, as he formed with his pen the words in all their fullness, Henri Beranger Eustache, Baron de Ribaumont et Seigneur de Leurre. He could not help wondering whether the lady who looked at him so admiringly really preferred such a mean-looking little fop as Narcisse, whether she were afraid of his English home and breeding, or whether all this open coquetry were really the court manners of ladies towards gentlemen, and he had been an absolute simpleton to be flattered. Any way, she would have been a most undesirable wife, and he was well quit of her; but he did feel a certain lurking desire that, since the bonds were cut and he was no longer in danger from her, he might see her again, carry home a mental inventory of the splendid beauties he had renounced, and decide what was the motive that actuated her in rejecting his own handsome self. Meantime, he proceeded to enjoy the amusements and advantage of his sojourn at Paris, of which by no means the least was the society of Philip Sidney, and the charm his brilliant genius imparted to every pursuit they shared. Books at the University, fencing and dancing from the best professors, Italian poetry, French sonnets, Latin epigrams; nothing came amiss to Sidney, the flower of English youth: and Berenger had taste, intelligence, and cultivation enough to enter into all in which Sidney led the way. The good tutor, after all his miseries on the journey, was delighted to write to Lord Walwyn, that, far from being a risk and temptation, this visit was a school in all that was virtuous and comely.

If the good man had any cause of dissatisfaction, it was with the Calvinistic tendencies of the Ambassador's household. Walsingham was always on the Puritanical side of Elizabeth's court, and such an atmosphere as that of Paris, where the Roman Catholic system was at that time showing more corruption than it has ever done before or since in any other place, naturally threw him into sympathy with the Reformed. The reaction that half a century later filled the Gallican Church with saintliness had not set in; her ecclesiastics were the tools of a wicked and bloodthirsty court, who hated virtue as much as schism in the men whom they persecuted. The Huguenots were for the most part men whose instincts for truth and virtue had recoiled from the popular system, and thus it was indeed as if piety and morality were arrayed on one side, and superstition and debauchery on the other. Mr. Adderley thus found the tone of the Ambassador's chaplain that of far more complete fellowship with the Reformed pastors than he himself was disposed to admit. There were a large number of these gathered at Paris; for the lull in persecution that had followed the battle of Moncontour had given hopes of a final accommodation between the two parties, and many had come up to consult with the numerous lay nobility who had congregated to witness the King of Navarre's wedding. Among them, Berenger met his father's old friend Isaac Gardon, who had come to Paris for the purpose of giving his only surviving son in marriage to the daughter of a watchmaker to whom he had for many years been betrothed. By him the youth, with his innocent face and gracious respectful manners, was watched with delight, as fulfilling the fairest hopes of the poor Baron, but the old minister would have been sorely disappointed had he known how little Berenger felt inclined towards his party.

The royal one of course Berenger could not love, but the rigid bareness, and, as he thought, irreverence of the Calvinist, and the want of all forms, jarred upon one used to a ritual which retained much of the ancient form. In the early years of Elizabeth, every possible diversity prevailed in parish churches, according to the predilections of rector and squire; from forms scarcely altered from those of old times, down to the baldest, rudest neglect of all rites; and Berenger, in his country home, had been used to the first extreme. He could not believe that what he heard and saw among the *Sacrementaires*, as they were called, was what his father had prized; and he greatly scandalized Sidney, the pupil of Hubert Languet, by openly expressing his distaste and dismay when he found their worship viewed by both Walsingham and Sidney as a model to which the English Protestants ought to be brought.

However, Sidney excused all this as more boyish distaste to sermons and love of externals, and Berenger himself reflected little on the subject. The aspect of the venerable Coligny, his father's friend, did far more towards making him a Huguenot than any discussion of doctrine. The good old Admiral received him affectionately, and talked to him warmly of his father, and the grave, noble countenance and kind manner won his heart. Great projects were on foot, and were much relished by the young King, for raising an army and striking a blow at Spain by aiding the Reformed in the Netherlands; and Coligny was as ardent as a youth in the cause, hoping at once to aid his brethren, to free the young King from evil influences, and to strike one good stroke against the old national enemy. He talked eagerly to Sidney of alliances with England, and then lamented over the loss of so promising a youth as young Ribaumont to the Reformed cause in France. If the marriage with the heiress could have taken effect, he would have obtained estates near enough to some of the main Huguenot strongholds to be very important, and these would now remain under the power of Narcisse de Ribaumont, a determined ally of the Guise faction. It was a pity, but the Admiral could not blame the youth for obeying the wish of his guardian grandfather; and he owned, with a sigh, that England was a more peaceful land than his own beloved country. Berenger was a little nettled at this implication, and began to talk of joining the French standard in a campaign in their present home and described the conversation, Walsingham said,—

'The Admiral's favourite project! He would do wisely not to brag of it so openly. The King of Spain has too many in his interest in this place not to be warned, and to be thus further egged on to compass the ruin of Coligny.'

'I should have thought,' said Sidney. 'that nothing could add to his hatred of the Reformed.'

'Scarcely,' said Walsingham; 'save that it is they who hinder the Duke of Guise from being a good Frenchman, and a foe to Spain.'

Politics had not developed themselves in Berenger's mind, and he listened inattentively while Walsingham talked over with Sidney the state of parties in France, where natural national enmity to Spain was balanced by the need felt by the Queen-mother of the support of that great Roman Catholic power against the Huguenots; whom Walsingham believed her to dread and hate less for their own sake than from the fear of loss of influence over her son. He believed Charles IX. himself to have much leaning towards the Reformed, but the late victories has thrown the whole court entirely into the power of the Guises, the truly unscrupulous partisans of Rome. They were further inflamed against the Huguenots by the assassination of the last Duke of Guise, and by the violences that had been committed by some of the Reformed party, in especial a massacre of prisoners at *Nerac*.

Sidney exclaimed that the Huguenots had suffered far worse cruelties.

'That is true,' replied Sir Francis, 'but, my young friend, you will find, in all matters of reprisals, that a party has no memory for what it may commit, only for what it may receive.'

The conversation was interrupted by an invitation to the Ambassador's family and guests to a tilting-match and subsequent ball at the Louvre. In the first Berenger did his part with credit; to the second he went feeling full of that strange attraction of repulsion. He knew gentlemen enough in Coligny's suite for it to be likely that he might remain unperceived among them, and he knew this would be prudent, but he found himself unexpectedly near the ranks of ladies, and smile and gesture absolutely drew him towards his semi-spouse, so that he had no alternative but to lead her out to dance.

The stately measure was trod in silence as usual, but he felt the dark eyes studying him all the time. However, he could bear it better now that the deed was done, and she had voluntarily made him less to her than any gallant parading or mincing about the room.

'So you bear the pearls, sir?' she said, as the dance finished.

'The only heirloom I shall take with me,' he said.

'Is a look at them too great a favour to ask from their jealous guardian?' she asked.

He smiled, half ashamed of his own annoyance at being obliged to place them in her hands. He was sure she would try to cajole him out of them, and by way of asserting his property in them he did not detach them from the band of his black velvet cap, but gave it with them into her hand. She looked at each one, and counted them wistfully.

'Seventeen!' she said;' and how beautiful! I never saw them so near before. They are so becoming to that fair cheek that I suppose no offer from my—my uncle, on our behalf, would induce you to part with them?'

An impulse of open-handed gallantry would have made him answer, 'No offer from your uncle, but a simple request from you;' but he thought in time of the absurdity of returning without them, and merely answered, 'I have no right to yield them, fair lady. They are the witness to my forefather's fame and prowess.'

'Yes, sir, and to those of mine also,' she replied. 'And you would take them over to the enemy from whom that prowess extorted them?'

'The country which honoured and rewarded that prowess!' replied Berenger.

She looked at him with an interrogative glance of surprise at the readiness of his answer; then, with half a sigh, said, 'There are your pearls, sir; I cannot establish our right, though I verily believe it was the cause of our last quarrel;' and she smiled archly.

'I believe it was,' he said, gravely; but added, in the moment of relief at recovering the precious heirloom, 'though it was Diane who inspired you to seize upon them.'

'Ah! poor Diane! you sometimes recollect her then? If I remember right, you used to agree with her better than with your little spouse, cousin!'

'If I quarrelled with her less, I liked her less,' answered Berenger—who, since the act of separation, had not been so guarded in his demeanour, and began to give way to his natural frankness.

'Indeed! Diane would be less gratified than I ought to be. And why, may I ask?'

'Diane was more caressing, but she had no truth.'

'Truth! that was what *feu* M. le Baron ever talked of; what Huguenots weary one with.'

'And the only thing worth seeking, the real pearl,' said Berenger, 'without which all else is worthless.'

'Ah!' she said, 'who would have thought that soft, youthful face could be so severe! You would never forgive a deceit?'

'Never,' he said, with the crystal hardness of youth; 'or rather I might forgive; I could never esteem.'

'What a bare, rude world yours must be,' she said, shivering. 'And no weak ones in it! Only the strong can dare to be true.'

'Truth is strength!' said Berenger. 'For example: I see yonder a face without bodily strength, perhaps, but with perfect candour.'

'Ah! some Huguenot girl of Madame Catherine's, no doubt—from the depths of Languedoc, and dressed like a fright.'

'No, no; the young girl behind the pale, yellow-haired lady.'

'Comment, Monsieur. Do you not yet know the young Queen?'

'But who is the young demoiselle!—she with the superb black eyes, and the ruby rose in her black hair?'

'Take care, sir, do you not know I have still a right to be jealous?' she said, blushing, bridling, and laughing.

But this pull on the cords made him the more resolved; he would not be turned from his purpose. 'Who is she?' he repeated; 'have I ever seen her before? I am sure I remember that innocent look of *espieglerie*.'

'You may see it on any child's face fresh out of the convent; it does not last a month!' was the still displeased, rather jealous answer. 'That little thing—I believe they call her Nid-de-Merle—she has only just been brought from her nunnery to wait on the young Queen. Ah! your gaze was perilous, it is bringing on you one of the jests of Madame Marguerite.'

With laughter and gaiety, a troop of gentlemen descended on M. de Ribaumont, and told him that Madame Marguerite desired that he should be presented to her. The princess was standing by her pale sister-in-law, Elizabeth of Austria, who looked grave and annoyed at the mischievous mirth flashing in Marguerite's dark eyes.

'M. de Ribaumont,' said the latter, her very neck heaving with suppressed fun, 'I see I cannot do you a greater favour than by giving you Mademoiselle de Nid-de-Merle for your partner.'

Berenger was covered with confusion to find that he had been guilty of such a fixed stare as to bring all this upon the poor girl. He feared that his vague sense of recognition had made his gaze more open than he knew, and he was really and deeply ashamed of this as his worst act of provincial ill-breeding.

Poor little convent maid, with crimson cheeks, flashing eyes, panting bosom, and a neck evidently aching with proud dignity and passion, she received his low bow with a sweeping curtsey, as lofty as her little person would permit.

His cheeks burnt like fire, and he would have found words to apologize, but she cut him short by saying, hastily and low, 'Not a word, Monsieur! Let us go through it at once. No one shall make game of us.'

He hardly durst look at her again; but as he went through his own elaborate paces he knew that the little creature opposite was swimming, bending, turning, bounding with the fluttering fierceness of an angry little bird, and that the superb eyes were casting flashes on him that seemed to carry him back to days of early boyhood.

Once he caught a mortified, pleading, wistful glance that made him feel as if he had inflicted a cruel injury by his thoughtless gaze, and he resolved to plead the sense of recognition in excuse; but no sooner was the performance over than she prevented all conversation by saying, 'Lead me back at once to the Queen, sir; she is about to retire.' They were already so near that there was no time to say anything; he could only hold as lightly as possible the tiny fingers that he felt burning and quivering in his hand, and then, after bringing her to the side of the chair of state, he was forced to release her with the mere whisper of 'Pardon, Mademoiselle;' and the request was not replied to, save by the additional stateliness of her curtsey.

It was already late, and the party was breaking up; but his head and heart were still in a whirl when he found himself seated in the ambassadorial coach, hearing Lady Walsingham's well-pleased rehearsal of all the compliments she had received on the distinguished appearance of both her young guests. Sidney, as the betrothed of her daughter, was property of her own; but she also exulted in the praises of the young Lord de Ribaumont, as proving the excellence of the masters whom she had recommended to remove the rustic clownishness of which he had been accused.

'Nay,' said Sir Francis; 'whoever called him too clownish for court spake with design.'

The brief sentence added to Berenger's confused sense of being in a mist of false play. Could his kinsman be bent on keeping him from court? Could Narcisse be jealous of him? Mademoiselle de Ribaumont was evidently inclined to seek him, and her cousin might easily think her lands safer in his absence. He would have been willing to hold aloof as much as his uncle and cousin could wish, save for an angry dislike to being duped and cajoled; and, moreover, a strong curiosity to hear and see more of that little passionate bird, fresh from the convent cage. Her gesture and her eyes irresistibly carried him back to old times, though whether to an angry blackbird in the yew-tree alleys at Leurre, or to the eager face that had warned him to save his father, he could not remember with any distinctness. At any rate, he was surprised to find himself thinking so little in comparison about the splendid beauty and winning manners of his discarded spouse, though he quite believed that, now her captive was beyond her grasp, she was disposed to catch at him again, and try to retain him, or, as his titillated vanity might whisper, his personal graces might make her regret the family resolution which she had obeyed.

CHAPTER VI
FOULLY COZENED

I was the more deceived.—HAMLET

The unhappy Charles IX. had a disposition that in good hands might have achieved great nobleness; and though cruelly bound and trained to evil, was no sooner allowed to follow its natural bent than it reached out eagerly towards excellence. At this moment, it was his mother's policy to appear to leave the ascendancy to the Huguenot party, and he was therefore allowed to contract friendships which deceived the intended victims the more completely, because his admiration and attachment were spontaneous and sincere. Philip Sidney's varied accomplishment and pure lofty character greatly attracted the young King, who had leant on his arm conversing during great part of the ball, and the next morning sent a royal messenger to invite the two young gentlemen to a part at pall-mall in the Tuileries gardens.

Pall-mall was either croquet or its nearest relative, and was so much the fashion that games were given in order to keep up political influence, perhaps, because the freedom of a garden pastime among groves and bowers afforded opportunities for those seductive arts on which Queen Catherine placed so much dependence. The formal gardens, with their squares of level turf and clipped alleys, afforded excellent scope both for players and spectators, and numerous games had been set on foot, from all of which, however, Berenger contrived to exclude himself, in his restless determination to find out the little Demoiselle de Nid-de-Merle, or, at least, to discover whether any intercourse in early youth accounted for his undefined sense of remembrance.

He interrogated the first disengaged person he could find, but it was only the young Abbe de Mericour, who had been newly brought up from Dauphine by his elder brother to solicit a benefice, and who knew nobody. To him ladies were only bright phantoms such as his books had taught him to regard like the temptations of St. Anthony, but whom he actually saw treated with as free admiration by the ecclesiastic as by the layman.

Suddenly a clamour of voices arose on the other side of the closely-clipped wall of limes by which the two youths were walking. There were the clear tones of a young maiden expostulating in indignant distress, and the bantering, indolent determination of a male annoyer.

'Hark!' exclaimed Berenger; 'this must be seen to.'

'Have a care,' returned Mericour; 'I have heard that a man needs look twice are meddling.'

Scarcely hearing, Berenger strode on as he had done at the last village wake, when he had rescued Cis of the Down from the impertinence of a Dorchester scrivener. It was a like case, he saw, when breaking through the arch of clipped limed he beheld the little Demoiselle de Nid-de-Merle, driven into a corner and standing at bay, with glowing cheeks, flashing eyes, and hands clasped over her breast, while a young man, dressed in the extreme of foppery, was assuring her that she was the only lady who had not granted him a token—that he could not allow such *pensionnaire* airs, and that now he had caught her he would have his revenge, and win her rose-coloured break-knot. Another gentleman stood by, laughing, and keeping guard in the walk that led to the more frequented part of the gardens.

'Hold!' thundered Berenger.

The assailant had just mastered the poor girl's hand, but she took advantage of his surprise to wrench it away and gather herself up as for a spring, but the Abbe in dismay, the attendant in anger, cried out, 'Stay—it is Monsieur.'

'Monsieur; be he who he may,' exclaimed Berenger, 'no honest man can see a lady insulted.'

'Are you mad? It is Monsieur the Duke of Anjou,' said Mericour, pouncing on his arm.

'Shall we have him to the guardhouse?' added the attendant, coming up on the other side; but Henri de Valois waved them both back, and burst into a derisive laugh. 'No, no; do you not see who it is? Monsieur the English Baron still holds the end of the halter. His sale is not yet made. Come away, D'O, he will soon have enough on his hands without us. Farewell, fair lady, another time you will be free of your jealous giant.'

So saying, the Duke of Anjou strolled off, feigning indifference and contempt, and scarcely heeding that he had been traversed in one of the malicious adventures which he delighted to recount in public before the discomfited victim herself, often with shameful exaggeration.

The girl clasped her hands over her brow with a gesture of dismay, and cried, 'Oh! if you have only not touched your sword.'

'Let me have the honour of reconducting you, Mademoiselle,' said Berenger, offering his hand; but after the first sigh of relief, a tempestuous access seized her. She seemed about to dash away his hand, her bosom swelled with resentment, and with a voice striving for dignity, though choked with strangled tears, she exclaimed, 'No, indeed! Had not M. le

Baron forsaken me, I had never been thus treated!' and her eyes flashed through their moisture.

'Eustacie! You are Eutacie!'

'Whom would you have me to be otherwise? I have the honour to wish M. le Baron a good morning.'

'Eustacie! Stay! Hear me! It concerns my honour. I see it is you—but whom have I seen? Who was she?' he cried, half wild with dismay and confusion. 'Was it Diane?'

'You have seen and danced with Diane de Ribaumont,' answered Eustacie, still coldly; 'but what of that? Let me go, Monsieur; you have cast me off already.'

'I! when all this has been of your own seeking?'

'Mine?' cried Eustacie, panting with the struggle between her dignity and her passionate tears. 'I meddled not. I heard that M. le Baron was gone to a strange land, and had written to break off old ties.' Her face was in a flame, and her efforts for composure absolute pain.

'I!' again exclaimed Berenger. 'The first letter came from your uncle, declaring that it was your wish!' And as her face changed rapidly, 'Then it was not true! He has not had your consent?'

'What! would I hold to one who despised me—who came here and never even asked to see this hated spouse!'

I did! I entreated to see you. I would not sign the application till—Oh, there has been treachery! And have they made you too sign it!'

When they showed me your name they were welcome to mine.'

Berenger struck his forehead with wrath and perplexity, then cried, joyfully, 'It will not stand for moment. So foul a cheat can be at once exposed. Eutacie, you know—you understand, that it was not you but Diane whom I saw and detested; and no wonder, when she was acting such a cruel treason!'

'Oh no, Diane would never so treat me,' cried Eustacie. 'I see how it was! You did not know that my father was latterly called Marquis de Nid-de-Merle, and when they brought me here, they WOULD call me after him: they said a maid of honour must be Demoiselle, and my uncle said there was only one way in which I could remain Madame de Ribaumont! And the name must have deceived you. Thou wast always a great dull boy,' she added, with a sudden assumption of childish intimacy that annihilated the nine years since their parting.

- 47 -

'Had I seen thee, I had not mistaken for an instant. This little face stirred my heart; hers repelled me. And she deceived me wittingly, Eustacie, for I asked after her by name.'

'Ah, she wished to spare my embarrassment. And then her brother must have dealt with her.'

'I see,' exclaimed Berenger, 'I am to be palmed off thus that thou mayest be reserved for Narcisse. Tell me, Eustacie, wast thou willing?'

'I hate Narcisse!' she cried. 'But oh, I am lingering too long. Monsieur will make some hateful tale! I never fell into his way before, my Queen and Madame la Comtesse are so careful. Only to-day, as I was attending her alone, the King came and gave her his arm, and I had to drop behind. I must find her; I shall be missed,' she added, in sudden alarm. 'Oh, what will they say?'

'No blame for being with thy husband,' he answered, clasping her hand. 'Thou art mine henceforth. I will soon cut our way out of the web thy treacherous kindred have woven. Meantime——'

'Hush! There are voices,' cried Eustacie in terror, and, guided by something he could not discern, she fled with the swiftness of a bird down the alley. Following, with the utmost speed that might not bear the appearance of pursuit, he found that on coming to the turn she had moderated her pace, and was more tranquilly advancing to a bevy of ladies, who sat perched on the stone steps like great butterflies sunning themselves, watching the game, and receiving the attentions of their cavaliers. He saw her absorbed into the group, and then began to prowl round it, in the alleys, in a tumult of amazement and indignation. He had been shamefully deceived and cheated, and justice he would have! He had been deprived of a thing of his own, and he would assert his right. He had been made to injure and disown the creature he was bound to protect, and he must console her and compensate to her, were it only to redeem his honour. He never even thought whether he loved her; he merely felt furious at the wrong he had suffered and been made to commit, and hotly bent on recovering what belonged to him. He might even have plunged down among the ladies and claimed her as his wife, if the young Abbe de Mericour, who was two years older than he, and far less of a boy for his years, had not joined him in his agitated walk. He then learnt that all the court knew that the daughter of the late Marquis de Nid-de-Merle, Comte de Ribaumont, was called by his chief title, but that her marriage to himself had been forgotten by some and unknown to others, and thus that the first error between the cousins had not been wonderful in a stranger, since the Chevalier's daughter had always been Mdlle. de Ribaumont. The error once made, Berenger's distaste to Diane had been so convenient that it had been carefully encouraged, and the desire to keep him at a distance from court and throw him into the background was accounted for. The Abbe was almost as indignant as Berenger, and assured him both of his sympathy and his discretion.

'I see no need for discretion,' said Berenger. 'I shall claim my wife in the face of the sun.'

'Take counsel first, I entreat,' exclaimed Mericour. 'The Ribaumonts have much influence with the Guise family, and now you have offended Monsieur.'

'Ah! Where are those traitorous kinsmen?' cried Berenger.

'Fortunately all are gone on an expedition with the Queen-mother. You will have time to think. I have heard my brother say no one ever prospered who offended the meanest follower of the house of Lorraine.'

'I do not want prosperity, I only want my wife. I hope I shall never see Paris and its deceivers again.'

'Ah! But is it true that you have applied to have the marriage annulled at Rome?'

'We were both shamefully deceivers. That can be nothing.'

'A decree of his Holiness: you a Huguenot; she an heiress. All is against you. My friend, be cautions, exclaimed the young ecclesiastic, alarmed by his passionate gestures. 'To break forth now and be accused of brawling in the palace precincts would be fatal—fatal—most fatal!'

'I am as calm as possible,' returned Berenger. 'I mean to act most reasonably. I shall stand before the King and tell him openly how I have been tamperes with, demanding my wife before the whole court.'

'Long before you could get so far the ushers would have dragged you away for brawling, or for maligning an honour-able gentlemen. You would have to finish your speech in the Bastille, and it would be well if even your English friends could get you out alive.'

'Why, what a place is this!' began Berenger; but again Mericour entreated him to curb himself; and his English education had taught him to credit the house of Guide with so much mysterious power and wickedness, that he allowed himself to be silenced, and promised to take no open measures till he had consulted the Ambassador.

'He could not obtain another glimpse of Eustacie, and the hours passed tardily till the break up of the party. Charles could scarcely release Sidney from his side, and only let him go on condition that he should join the next day in an expedition to the hunting chateau of Montpipeau, to which the King seemed to look forward as a great holiday and breathing time.

When at length the two youths did return, Sir Francis Walsingham was completely surprised by the usually tractable, well-behaved stripling, whose praises he had been writing to his old friend, bursting in on him with the outcry, 'Sir, sir, I entreat your counsel! I have been foully cozened.'

'Of how much?' said Sir Francis, in a tone of reprobation.

'Of my wife. Of mine honour. Sir, your Excellency, I crave pardon, if I spoke too hotly,' said Berenger, collecting himself; 'but it is enough to drive a man to frenzy.'

'Sit down, my Lord de Ribaumont. Take breath, and let me know what is this coil. What hath thus moved him, Mr. Sidney?'

'It is as he says, sir,' replied Sidney, who had beard all as they returned; 'he has been greatly wronged. The Chevalier de Ribaumont not only writ to propose the separation without the lady's knowledge, but imposed his own daughter on our friend as the wife he had not seen since infancy.'

'There, sir,' broke forth Berenger; 'surely if I claim mine own in the face of day, no man can withhold her from me!'

'Hold!' said Sir Francis. 'What mean this passion, young sir? Methought you came hither convinced that both the religion and the habits in which the young lady had been bred up rendered your infantine contract most unsuitable. What hath fallen out to make this change in your mind?'

'That I was cheated, sir. The lady who palmed herself off on me as my wife was a mere impostor, the Chevalier's own daughter!'

'That may be; but what known you of this other lady? Has she been bred up in faith or manners such as your parents would have your wife?'

'She is my wife,' reiterated Berenger. 'My faith is plighted to her. That is enough for me.'

Sir Francis made a gesture of despair. 'He has seen her, I suppose,' said he to Sidney.

'Yes truly, sir,' answered Berenger; 'and found that she had been as greatly deceived as myself.'

'Then mutual consent is wanting,' said the statesman, gravely musing.

'That is even as I say,' began Berenger, but Walsingham help up his hand, and desired that he would make his full statement in the presence of his tutor. Then sounding a little whistle, the Ambassador despatched a page to request the attendance of Mr. Adderley, and recommended young Ribaumont in the meantime to compose himself.

Used to being under authority as Berenger was, the somewhat severe tone did much to allay his excitement, and remind him that right and reason were so entirely on his side, that he had only to be cool and rational to make them prevail. He was thus able to give a collected and coherent account of his discovery that the part of his wife had been assumed by her cousin Diane, and that the signature of both the young pair to the application to the Pope had been obtained on false pretences. That he had, as Sidney said, been foully cozened, in both senses of the word, was as clear as daylight; but he was much angered and disappointed to find that neither the Ambassador nor his tutor could see that Eustacie's worthiness was proved by the iniquity of her relation, or that any one of the weighty reasons for the expediency of dissolving the marriage was remove. The whole affair had been in such good train a little before, that Mr. Adderley was much distressed that it should thus have been crossed, and thought the new phase of affairs would be far from acceptable at Combe Walwyn.

'Whatever is just and honourable must be acceptable to my grandfather,' said Berenger.

'Even so,' said Walsingham; 'but it were well to consider whether justice and honour require you to overthrow the purpose wherewith he sent you hither.'

'Surely, sir, justice and require me to fulfil a contract to which the other party is constant,' said Berenger, feeling very wise and prudent for calling that wistful, indignant creature the other party.

'That is also true,' said the Ambassador, 'provided she be constant; but you own that she signed the requisition for the dissolution.'

'She did so, but under the same deception as myself, and further mortified and aggrieved at my seeming faithlessness.'

'So it may easily be represented,' muttered Walsingham.

'How, sir?' cried Berenger, impetuously; 'do you doubt her truth?'

'Heaven forefend,' said Sir Francis, 'that I should discuss any fair lady's sincerity! The question is how far you are bound. Have I understood you that you are veritably wedded, not by a mere contract of espousal?'

'Berenger could produce no documents, for they had been left at Chateau Leurre, and on his father's death the Chevalier had claimed the custody of them; but he remembered enough of the ceremonial to prove that the wedding had been a veritable one, and that only the papal intervention could annul it.

Indeed an Englishman, going by English law, would own no power in the Pope, nor any one on earth, to sever the sacred tie of wedlock; but French courts of law would probably ignore the mode of application, and would certainly endeavour to separate between a Catholic and a heretic.

'I am English, sir, in heart and faith,' said Berenger, earnestly. 'Look upon me as such, and tell me, am I married or single at this moment?'

'Married assuredly. More's the pity,' said Sir Francis.

'And no law of God or man divides us without our own consent.' There was no denying that the mutual consent of the young pair at their present age was all that was wanting to complete the inviolability of their marriage contract.

Berenger was indeed only eighteen, and Eustacie more than a year younger, but there was nothing in their present age to invalidate their marriage, for persons of their rank were usually wedded quite as young or younger. Walsingham was only concerned at his old friend's disappointment, and at the danger of the young man running headlong into a connection probably no more suitable than that with Diane de Ribaumont would have been. But it was not convenient to argue against the expediency of a man's loving his own wife; and when Berenger boldly declared he was not talking of love but of justice, it was only possible to insist that he should pause and see where true justice lay.

And thus the much-perplexed Ambassador broke up the conference with his hot and angry young guest.

'And Mistress Lucy——?' sighed Mr. Adderley, in rather an *inapropos* fashion it must be owned; but then he had been fretted beyond endurance by his pupil striding up and down his room, reviling Diane, and describing Eustacie, while he was trying to write these uncomfortable tidings to Lord Walwyn.

'Lucy! What makes you bring her up to me?' exclaimed Berenger. 'Little Dolly would be as much to the purpose!'

'Only, sir, no resident at Hurst Walwyn could fail to know that has been planned and desired.'

'Pshaw!' cries Berenger; 'have you not heard that it was a mere figment, and that I could scarce have wedded Lucy safely, even had this matter gone as you wish? This is the luckiest chance that could have befallen her.'

'That may be,' said Mr. Adderley; 'I wish she may think so—sweet young lady!'

'I tell you, Mr. Adderley, you should know better! Lucy has more sense. My aunt, whom she follows more than any other creature, ever silenced the very sport or semblance of love passages between us even as children, by calling them unseemly in one wedded as I am. Brother and sister we have ever been, and have loved as such—ay, and shall! I know of late some schemes have crossed my mother's mind——'

'Yea, and that of others.'

'But they have not ruffled Lucy's quiet nature—trust me! And for the rest? What doth she need me in comparison of this poor child? She—like a bit of her own gray lavender in the shadiest nook of the walled garden, tranquil there—sure not to be taken there, save to company with fine linen in some trim scented coffer, whilst this fresh glowing rosebud has grown up pure and precious in the very midst of the foulest corruption Christendom can show, and if I snatch her not from it, I, the innocence and sweetness, what is to be her fate? The very pity of a Christian, the honour of a gentleman, would urge me, even if it were not my most urgent duty!'

'Mr. Adderley argued no more. When Berenger came to his duty in the matter he was invincible, and moreover all the more provoking, because he mentioned it with a sort of fiery sound of relish, and looked so very boyish all the time. Poor Mr. Adderley!' feeling as if his trust were betrayed, loathing the very idea of a French court lady, saw that his pupil had been allured into a headlong passion to his own misery, and that of all whose hopes were set on him, yet preached to by this stripling scholar about duties and sacred obligations! Well might he rue the day he ever set foot in Paris.

Then, to his further annoyance, came a royal messenger to invite the Baron de Ribaumont to join the expedition to Montpipeau. Of course he must go, and his tutor must be left behind, and who could tell into what mischief he might not be tempted!

Here, however, Sidney gave the poor chaplain some comfort. He believed that no ladies were to be of the party, and that the gentlemen were chiefly of the King's new friends among the Huguenots, such as Coligny, his son-in-law Teligny, Rochefoucauld, and the like, among whom the young gentleman could not fall into any very serious harm, and might very possibly be influenced against a Roman Catholic wife. At any rate, he would be out of the way, and unable to take any dangerous steps.

This same consideration so annoyed Berenger that he would have declined the invitation, if royal invitations could have been declined. And in the morning, before setting out, he dressed himself point device, and with

Osbert behind him marched down to the Croix de Larraine, to call upon the Chevalier de Ribaumont. He had a very fine speech at his tongue's end when he set out, but a good deal of it had evaporated when he reached the hotel, and perhaps he was not very sorry not to find the old gentleman within.

On his return, he indited a note to the Chevalier, explaining that he had now seen his wife, Madame la Baronne de Ribaumont, and had come to an understanding with her, by which he found that it was under a mistake that the application to the Pope had been signed, and that they should, therefore, follow it up with a protest, and act as if no such letter had been sent.

Berenger showed this letter to Walsingham, who, though much concerned, could not forbid his sending it. 'Poor lad,' he said to the tutor; ''tis an excellently writ billet for one so young. I would it were in a wiser cause. But he has fairly the bit between his teeth, and there is no checking him while he has this show of right on his side.'

And poor Mr. Adderley could only beseech Mr. Sidney to take care of him.

CHAPTER VII
THE QUEEN'S PASTORAL

Either very gravely gay,

Or very gaily grave,

> —*W. M. PRAED*

Montpipeau, though in the present day a suburb of Paris, was in the sixteenth century far enough from the city to form a sylvan retreat, where Charles IX, could snatch a short respite from the intrigues of his court, under pretext of enjoying his favourite sport. Surrounded with his favoured associates of the Huguenot party, he seemed to breathe a purer atmosphere, and to yield himself up to enjoyment greater than perhaps his sad life had ever known.

He rode among his gentlemen, and the brilliant cavalcade passed through poplar-shaded roads, clattered through villages, and threaded their way through bits of forest still left for the royal chase. The people thronged out of their houses, and shouted not only 'Vive le Roy,' but 'Vive l'Amiral,' and more than once the cry was added, 'Spanish war, or civil war!' The heart of France was, if not with the Reformed, at least against Spain and the Lorrainers, and Sidney perceived, from the conversation of the gentlemen round him, that the present expedition had been devised less for the sake of the sport, than to enable the King to take measures for emancipating himself from the thraldom of his mother, and engaging the country in a war against Philip II. Sidney listened, but Berenger chafed, feeling only that he was being further carried out of reach of his explanation with his kindred. And thus they arrived at Montpipeau, a tower, tall and narrow, like all French designs, but expanded on the ground floor by wooden buildings capable of containing the numerous train of a royal hunter, and surrounded by an extent of waste land, without fine trees, though with covert for deer, boars, and wolves sufficient for sport to royalty and death to peasantry. Charles seemed to sit more erect in his saddle, and to drink in joy with every breath of the thyme-scented breeze, from the moment his horse bounded on the hollow-sounding turf; and when he leapt to the ground, with the elastic spring of youth, he held out his hands to Sidney and to Teligny, crying 'Welcome, my friends. Here I am indeed a king!'

It was a lovely summer evening, early in August, and Charles bade the supper to be spread under the elms that shaded a green lawn in front of the chateau. Etiquette was here so far relaxed as to permit the sovereign to dine with his suite, and tables, chairs, and benches were brought out, drapery festooned in the trees to keep off sun and wind, the King lay down in the fern and let his happy dogs fondle him, and as a hers-girl passed along a vista in the distance, driving her goats before her, Philip Sidney marvelled whether it was not even thus in Arcadia.

Presently there was a sound of horses trampling, wheels moving, a party of gaily gilded archers of the guard jingled up, and in their midst was a coach. Berenger's heart seemed to leap at once to his lips, as a glimpse of ruffs, hats, and silks dawned on him through the windows.

The king rose from his lair among the fern, the Admiral stood forward, all heads were bared, and from the coach-door alighted the young Queen; no longer pale, subdued, and indifferent, but with a face shining with girlish delight, as she held out her hand to the Admiral. 'Ah! This is well, this is beautiful,' she exclaimed; 'it is like our happy chases in the Tyrol. Ah, Sire!' to the King, 'how I thank you for letting me be with you.'

After her Majesty descended her gentleman-usher. Then came the lady-in-waiting, Madame de Sauve, the wife of the state secretary in attendance on Charles, and a triumphant, coquettish beauty, than a fat, good-humoured Austrian dame, always called Madame la Comtesse, because her German name was unpronounceable, and without whom the Queen never stirred, and lastly a little figure, rounded yet slight, slender yet soft and plump, with a kitten-like alertness and grace of motion, as she sprang out, collected the Queen's properties of fan, kerchief, pouncet-box, mantle, &c., and disappeared in to the chateau, without Berenger's being sure of anything but that her little black hat had a rose-coloured feather in it.

The Queen was led to a chair placed under one of the largest trees, and there Charles presented to her such of his gentlemen as she was not yet acquainted with, the Baron de Ribaumont among the rest.

'I have heard of M. de Ribaumont,' she said, in a tone that made the colour mantle in his fair cheek; and with a sign of her hand she detained him at her side till the King had strolled away with Madame la Sauve, and no one remained near but her German countess. Then changing her tone to one of confidence, which the high-bred homeliness of her Austrian manner rendered inexpressibly engaging, she said, 'I must apologize, Monsieur, for the giddiness of my sister-in-law, which I fear caused you some embarrassment.'

'Ah, Madame,' said Berenger, kneeling on one knee as she addressed him, and his heart bounding with wild, undefined hope, 'I cannot be grateful enough. It was that which led to my being undeceived.'

'It was true, then, that you were mistaken?' said the Queen.

'Treacherously deceived, Madame, by those whose interest it is to keep us apart,' said Berenger, colouring with indignation; 'they imposed my other cousin on me as my wife, and caused her to think me cruelly neglectful.'

'I know,' said the Queen. 'Yet Mdlle. de Ribaumont is far more admired than my little blackbird.'

'That may be, Madame, but not by me.'

'Yet is it true that you came to break off the marriage?'

'Yes, Madame,' said Berenger, honestly, 'but I had not seen her.'

'And now?' said the Queen, smiling.

'I would rather die than give her up,' said Berenger. 'Oh, Madame, help us of your grace. Every one is trying to part us, every one is arguing against us, but she is my own true wedded wife, and if you will but give her to me, all will be well.'

'I like you, M. de Ribaumont,' said the Queen, looking him full in the face. 'You are like our own honest Germans at my home, and I think you mean all you say. I had much rather my dear little Nid de Merle were with you than left here, to become like all the others. She is a good little *Liegling*,—how do you call it in French? She has told me all, and truly I would help you with all my heart, but it is not as if I were the Queen-mother. You must have recourse to the King, who loves you well, and at my request included you in the hunting-party.'

Berenger could only kiss her hand in token of earnest thanks before the repast was announced, and the King came to lead her to the table spread beneath the trees. The whole party supped together, but Berenger could have only a distant view of his little wife, looking very demure and grave by the side of the Admiral.

But when the meal was ended, there was a loitering in the woodland paths, amid healthy openings or glades trimmed into discreet wildness fit for royal rusticity; the sun set in parting glory on one horizon, the moon rising in crimson majesty on the other. A musician at intervals touched the guitar, and sang Spanish or Italian airs, whose soft or quaint melody came dreamily through the trees. Then it was that with beating heart Berenger stole up to the maiden as she stood behind the Queen, and ventured to whisper her name and clasp her hand.

She turned, their eyes met, and she let him lead her apart into the wood. It was not like a lover's tryst, it was more like the continuation of their old childish terms, only that he treated her as a thing of his own, that he was bound to secure and to guard, and she received him as her own lawful but tardy protector, to be treated with perfect reliance but with a certain playful resentment.

'You will not run away from me now,' he said, making full prize of her hand and arm.

'Ah! is not she the dearest and best of queens?' and the large eyes were lifted up to him in such frank seeking of sympathy that he could see into the depths of their clear darkness.

'It is her doing then. Though, Eustacie, when I knew the truth, not flood nor fire should keep me long from you, my heart, my love, my wife.'

'What! wife in spite of those villainous letter?' she said, trying to pout.

'Wife for ever, inseparably! Only you must be able to swear that you knew nothing of the one that brought me here.'

'Poor me! No, indeed! There was Celine carried off at fourteen, Madame de Blanchet a bride at fifteen; all marrying hither and thither; and I—' she pulled a face irresistibly droll—'I growing old enough to dress St. Catherine's hair, and wondering where was M. le Baron.'

'They thought me too young,' said Berenger, 'to take on me the cares of life.'

'So they were left to me?'

'Cares! What cares have you but finding the Queen's fan?'

'Little you know!' she said, half contemptuous, half mortified.

'Nay, pardon me, *ma mie*. Who has troubled you?'

'Ah! you would call it nothing to be beset by Narcisse; to be told one's husband is faithless, till one half believes it; to be looked at by ugly eyes; to be liable to be teased any day by Monsieur, or worse, by that mocking ape, M. d'Alecon, and to have nobody who can or will hinder it.'

She was sobbing by this time, and he exclaimed, 'Ah, would that I could revenge all! Never, never shall it be again! What blessed grace has guarded you through all?'

'Did I not belong to you?' she said exultingly. 'And had not Sister Monique, yes, and M. le Baron, striven hard to make me good? Ah, how kind he was!'

'My father? Yes, Eustacie, he loved you to the last. He bade me, on his deathbed, give you his own Book of Psalms, and tell you he had always loved and prayed for you.'

'Ah! his Psalms! I shall love them! Even at Bellaise, when first we came there, we used to sing them, but the Mother Abbess went out visiting, and when she came back she said they were heretical. And Soeur Monique would not let me say the texts he taught me, but I WOULD not forget them. I say them often in my heart.'

'Then,' he cried joyfully, 'you will willingly embrace my religion?'

'Be a Huguenot?' she said distastefully.

'I am not precisely a Huguenot; I do not love them,' he answered hastily; 'but all shall be made clear to you at my home in England.'

'England!' she said. 'Must we live in England? Away from every one?'

'Ah, they will love so much! I shall make you so happy there,' he answered. 'There you will see what it is to be true and trustworthy.'

'I had rather live at Chateau Leurre, or my own Nid de Merle,' she replied. 'There I should see Soeur Monique, and my aunt, the Abbess, and we would have the peasants to dance in the castle court. Oh! if you could but see the orchards at Le Bocage, you would never want to go away. And we could come now and then to see my dear Queen.

'I am glad at least you would not live at court.'

'Oh, no, I have been more unhappy here than ever I knew could be borne.'

And a very few words from him drew out all that had happened to her since they parted. Her father had sent her to Bellaise, a convent founded by the first of the Angevin branch, which was presided over by his sister, and where Diane was also educated. The good sister Monique had been mistress of the *pensionnaires*, and had evidently taken much pains to keep her charge innocent and devout. Diane had been taken to court about two years before, but Eustacie had remained at the convent till some three months since, when she had been appointed maid of honour to the recently-married Queen; and her uncle had fetched her from Anjou, and had informed her at the same time that her young husband had turned Englishman and heretic, and that after a few formalities had been complied with, she would become the wife of her cousin Narcisse. Now there was no person whom she so much dreaded as Narcisse, and when Berenger spoke of him as a feeble fop, she shuddered as though she knew him to have something of the tiger.

'Do you remember Benoit?' she said; 'poor Benoit, who came to Normandy as my *laquais*? When I went back to Anjou he married a girl from Leurre, and went to aid his father at the farm. The poor fellow had imbibed the Baron's doctrine—he spread it. It was reported that there was a nest of Huguenots on the estate. My cousin came to break it up with his *gens d'armes* O Berenger, he would hear no entreaties, he had no mercy; he let them assemble on Sunday, that they might be all together. He fired the house; shot down those who escaped; if a prisoner were made, gave him up to the Bishop's Court. Benoit, my poor good Benoit, who used to lead my palfrey, was first wounded, then tried, and burnt—burnt in the PLACE at Lucon! I heard Narcisse laugh—laugh as he talked of the cries of the poor creatures in the conventicler. My own people, who loved me! I was but twelve years old, but even then the wretch would pay me a half-mocking courtesy, as one destined to him; and the more I disdained him and said I belonged to you, the more both he and my aunt, the Abbess, smiled, as though they had their bird in a cage; but they left me in peace till my uncle brought me to court, and then all began again: and when they said you gave me up, I had no hope, not even of a convent. But ah, it is all over now, and I am so happy! You are grown so gentle and so beautiful, Berenger, and so much taller than I ever figured you to myself, and you look as if you could take me up in your arms, and let no harm happen to me.'

'Never, never shall it!' said Berenger, felling all manhood, strength, and love stir within him, and growing many years in heart in that happy moment. 'My sweet little faithful wife, never fear again now you are mine.'

Alas! poor children. They were a good way from the security they had begun to fancy for themselves. Early the next morning, Berenger went in his straightforward way to the King, thanked him, and requested his sanction for at once producing themselves to the court as Monsieur le Baron and Madame la Baronne de Ribaumont.

At this Charles swore a great oath, as one in perplexity, and bade him not go so fast.

'See here,' said he, with the rude expletives only too habitual with him; 'she is a pretty little girl, and she and her lands are much better with an honest man like you than with that *pendard* of a cousin; but you see he is bent on having her, and he belongs to a cut-throat crew that halt at nothing. I would not answer for your life, if you tempted him so strongly to rid himself of you.'

'My own sword, Sire, can guard my life.'

'Plague upon your sword! What does the foolish youth think it would do against half-a-dozen poniards and pistols in a lane black as hell's mouth?'

The foolish young WAS thinking how could a king so full of fiery words and strange oaths bear to make such an avowal respecting his own capital and his own courtiers. All he could do was to bow and reply, 'Nevertheless, Sire, at whatever risk, I cannot relinquish my wife; I would take her at one to the Ambassador's.'

'How, sir!' interrupted Charles, haughtily and angrily, 'if you forget that you are a French nobleman still, I should remember it! The Ambassador may protect his own countrymen-none else.'

'I entreat your Majesty's pardon,' said Berenger, anxious to retract his false step. 'It was your goodness and the gracious Queen's that made me hope for your sanction.'

'All the sanction Charles de Valois can give is yours, and welcome,' said the King, hastily. 'The sanction of the King of France is another matter! To say the truth, I see no way out of the affair but an elopement.' 'Sire!' exclaimed the astonished Berenger, whose strictly-disciplined education had little prepared him for such counsel.

'Look you! if I made you known as a wedded pair, the Chevalier and his son would not only assassinate you, but down on me would come my brother, and my mother, and M. de Guise and all their crew, veritably for giving the prize out of the mouth of their satellite, but nominally for disregarding the Pope, favouring a heretical marriage, and I know not what, but, as things go here, I should assuredly get the worst of it; and if you made safely off with your prize, no one could gainsay you—I need know nothing about it—and lady and lands would be your without dispute. You might ride off from the skirts of the forest; I would lead the hunt that way, and the three days' riding would bring you to Normady, for you had best cross to England immediately. When she is one there, owned by your kindred, Monsieur le cousin may gnash his teeth as he will, he must make the best of it for the sake of the honour of his house, and you can safely come back and raise her people and yours to follow the Oriflamme when it takes the field against Spain. What! you are still discontented? Speak out! Plain speaking is a treat not often reserved for me.'

'Sire, I am most grateful for your kindness, but I should greatly prefer going straightforward.'

'Peste! Well is it said that a blundering Englishman goes always right before him! There, then! As your King on the one hand, as the friend who has brought you and your wife together, sir, it is my command that you do not compromise me and embroil greater matters than you can understand by publicly claiming this girl. Privately I will aid you to the best of my ability; publicly, I command you, for my sake, if you heed not your own, to be silent!'

Berenger sought out Sidney, who smiled at his surprise.

'Do you not see,' he said, 'that the King is your friend, and would be very glad to save the lady's lands from the Guisards, but that he cannot say so; he can only befriend a Huguenot by stealth.'

'I would not be such a king for worlds!'

However, Eustacie was enchanted. It was like a prince and princess in Mere Perinne's fairy tales. Could they go like a shepherd and shepherdess? She had no fears-no scruples. Would she not be with her husband? It was the most charming frolic in the world. So the King seemed to think it, though he was determined to call it all the Queen's doing—the first intrigue of her own, making her like all the rest of us—the Queen's little comedy. He undertook to lead the chase as far as possible in the direction of Normandy, when the young pair might ride on to an inn, meet fresh horses, and proceed to Chateau Leurre, and thence to England. He would himself provide a safe-conduct, which, as Berenger suggested, would represent them as a young Englishman taking home his young wife. Eustacie wanted at least to masquerade as an Englishwoman, and played off all the fragments of the language she had caught as a child, but Berenger only laughed at her, and said they just fitted the French bride. It was very pretty to laugh at Eustacie; she made such a droll pretence at pouting with her rosebud lips, and her merry velvety eyes belied them so drolly.

Such was to be the Queen's pastoral; but when Elisabeth found the responsibility so entirely thrown on her, she began to look grave and frightened. It was no doubt much more than she had intended when she brought about the meeting between the young people, and the King, who had planned the elopement, seemed still resolved to make all appear her affair. She looked all day more like the grave, spiritless being she was at court than like the bright young rural queen of the evening before, and she was long in her little oratory chapel in the evening. Berenger, who was waiting in the hall with the other Huguenot gentlemen, thought her devotions interminable since they delayed all her ladies. At length, however, a page came up to him, and said in a low voice, 'The Queen desires the presence of M. le Baron de Ribaumont.'

He followed the messenger, and found himself in the little chapel, before a gaily-adorned altar, and numerous little shrines and niches round. Sidney would have dreaded a surreptitious attempt to make him conform, but Berenger had no notion of such perils,—he only saw that Eustacie was standing by the Queen's chair, and a kindly-looking Austrian priest, the Queen's confessor, held a book in his hand.

The Queen came to meet him. 'For my sake,' she said, with all her sweetness, 'to ease my mind, I should like to see my little Eustacie made entirely your own ere you go. Father Meinhard tells me it is safer that, when the parties were under twelve years old, the troth should be again exchanged. No other ceremony is needed.'

'I desire nothing but to have her made indissolubly my own,' said Berenger, bowing.

'And the King permits,' added Elisabeth.

The King growled out, 'It is your comedy, Madame; I meddle not.'

The Austrian priest had no common language with Berenger but Latin. He asked a few questions, and on hearing the answers, declared that the sacrament of marriage had been complete, but that—as was often done in such cases—he would once more hear the troth-plight of the young pair. The brief formula was therefore at once exchanged—the King, when the Queen looked entreatingly at him, rousing himself to make the bride over to Berenger. As soon as the vows had been made, in the briefest manner, the King broke in boisterously: 'There, you are twice marred, to please Madame there; but hold your tongues all of you about this scene in the play.'

Then almost pushing Eustacie over to Berenger, he added, 'There she is! Take your wife, sir; but mind, she was as much yours before as she is now.'

But for all Berenger had said about 'his wife,' it was only now that he really FELT her his own, and became husband rather than lover-man instead of boy. She was entirely his own now, and he only desired to be away with her; but some days' delay was necessary. A chase on the scale of the one that was to favour their evasion could not be got up without some notice; and, moreover, it was necessary to procure money, for neither Sidney nor Ribaumont had more than enough with them for the needful liberalities to the King's servants and huntsmen. Indeed Berenger had spent all that remained in his purse upon the wares of an Italian pedlar whom he and Eustacie met in the woods, and whose gloves 'as sweet as fragrant posies,' fans, scent-boxes, pocket mirrors, Genoa wire, Venice chains, and other toys, afforded him the mean of making up the gifts that he wished to carry home to his sisters; and Eustacie's counsel was merrily given in the choice. And when the vendor began with a meaning smile to recommend to the young pair themselves a little silver-netted heart as a love-token, and it turned out that all Berenger's money was gone, so that it could not be bought without giving up the scented casket destined for Lucy, Eustacie turned with her sweetest, proudest smile, and said, 'No, no; I will not have it; what do we two want with love-tokens now?'

Sidney had taken the youthful and romantic view of the case, and considered himself to be taking the best possible bare of is young friend, by enabling him to deal honourably with so charming a little wife as Eustacie. Ambassador and tutor would doubtless be very angry; but Sidney could judge for himself of the lady, and he therefore threw himself into her interests, and sent his servant back to Paris to procure the necessary sum for the journey of Master Henry Berenger and Mistress Mary, his wife. Sidney was, on his return alone to Paris, to explain all to the elders, and pacify them as best he could; and his servant was already the bearer of a letter from Berenger that was to be sent at once to England with Walsingham's dispatches, to prepare Lord Walwyn for the arrival of the runaways. The poor boy laboured to be impressively calm and reasonable in his explanation of the misrepresentation, and of his strong grounds for assuming his rights, with his persuasion that his wife would readily join the English church—a consideration that he knew would greatly smooth the way for her. Indeed, his own position was impregnable: nobody could blame him for taking his own wife to himself, and he was so sure of her charms, that he troubled himself very little about the impression she might make on his kindred. If they loved her, it was all right; if not, he could take her back to his own castle, and win fame and honour under the banner of France in the Low Countries. As the Lucy Thistlewood, she was far too discreet to feel any disappointment or displeasure; or if she should, it was her own fault and that of his mother, for all her life she had known him to be married. So he finished his letter with a message that the bells should be ready to ring, and that when Philip heard three guns fired on the coast, he might light the big beacon pile above the Combe.

Meantime 'the Queen's Pastoral' was much relished by all the spectators. The state of things was only avowed to Charles, Elisabeth, and Philip Sidney, and even the last did not know of the renewed troth which the King chose to treat as such a secret; but no one had any doubt of the mutual relations of M. de Ribaumont and Mdlle. de Nid de Merle, and their dream of bliss was like a pastoral for the special diversion of the holiday of Montpipeau. The transparency of their indifference in company, their meeting eyes, their trysts with the secrecy of an ostrich, were the subjects of constant amusement to the elders, more especially as the shyness, blushes, and caution were much more on the side of the young husband than on that of the lady. Fresh from her convent, simple with childishness and innocence, it was to her only the natural completion of her life to be altogether Berenger's, and the brief concealment of their full union added a certain romantic enchantment, which added to her exultation in her victory over her cruel kindred. She had been upon her own mind, poor child, for her few weeks of court life. She had been upon her own mind, poor child, for her few weeks of court life, but not long enough to make her grow older, though just so long as to make the sense of her having her own protector with her doubly precious. He, on the other hand, though full of happiness, did also feel constantly deepening on him the sense of the charge and responsibility he had assumed, hardly knowing how. The more dear Eustacie became to him, the more she rested on him and became entirely his, the more his boyhood and INSOUCIANCE drifted away behind him; and while he could hardly bear to heave his darling a moment out of his sight, the less he could endure any remark or jest upon his affection for her. His home had been a refined one, where Cecile's convent purity seemed to diffuse an atmosphere of modest reserve such as did not prevail in the court of the Maiden Queen herself, and the lad of eighteen had not seem enough of the outer world to have rubbed off any of that grace. His seniority to his little wife seemed to show itself chiefly in his being put out of countenance for her, when she was too innocent and too proud of her secret matronhood to understand or resent the wit.

Little did he know that this was the ballet-like interlude in a great and terrible tragedy, whose first act was being played out on the stage where they schemed and sported, like their own little drama, which was all the world to them, and noting to the others. Berenger knew indeed that the Admiral was greatly rejoiced that the Nid de Merle estates should go into Protestant hands, and that the old gentleman lost no opportunity of impressing on him that they were a heavy trust, to be used for the benefit of 'the Religion,' and for the support of the King in his better mind. But it may be feared that he did not give a very attentive ear to all this. He did not like to think of those estates; he would gladly have left them all the Narcisse, so that he might have their lady, and though quite willing to win his spurs under Charles and Coligny against the Spaniard, his heart and head were far too full to take in the web of politics. Sooth to say, the elopement in prospect seemed to him infinitely more important than Pope or Spaniard, Guise or Huguenot, and Coligny observed with a sigh to Teligny that he was a good boy, but nothing but the merest boy, with eyes open only to himself.

When Charles undertook to rehearse their escape with them, and the Queen drove out in a little high-wheeled litter with Mne. la Comtesse, while Mme. De Sauve and Eustacie were mounted on gay palfreys with the pommelled side-saddle lately invented by the Queen-mother, Berenger, as he watched the fearless horsemanship and graceful bearing of his newly-won wife, had no speculations to spend on the thoughtful face of the Admiral. And when at the outskirts of the wood the King's bewildering hunting-horn—sounding as it were now here, now there, now low, now high—called every attendant to hasten to its summons, leaving the young squire and damsel errant with a long winding high-banked lane before them, they reckoned the dispersion to be all for their sakes, and did not note, as did Sidney's clear eye, that when the entire company had come straggling him, it was the King who came up with Mme. De Sauve almost the last; and a short space after, as if not to appear to have been with him, appeared the Admiral and his son-in-law.

Sidney also missed one of the Admiral's most trusted attendants, and from this and other symptoms he formed his conclusions that the King had scattered his followers as much for the sake of an unobserved conference with Coligny as for the convenience of the lovers, and that letters had been dispatched in consequence of that meeting.

Those letters were indeed of a kind to change the face of affairs in France. Marshal Strozzi, then commanding in the south-west, was bidden to embark at La Rochelle in the last week of August, to hasten to the succour of the Prince of Orange against Spain, and letters were dispatched by Coligny to all the Huguenot partisans bidding them assemble at Melun on the third of September, when they would be in the immediate neighbourhood of the court, which was bound for Fontainebleau. Was the star of the Guises indeed waning? Was Charles about to escape from their hands, and commit himself to an honest, high-minded policy, in which he might have been able to purify his national Church, and wind back to her those whom her corruptions had driven to seek truth and morality beyond her pale?

Alas! there was a bright pair of eyes that saw more than Philip Sidney's, a pair of ears that heard more, a tongue and pen less faithful to guard a secret.

CHAPTER VIII
'LE BROUILON'

But never more the same two sister pearls

Ran down the silken thread to kiss each other.

—Tennyson

Berenger was obliged to crave permission from the King to spend some hours in riding with Osbert to the first hostel on their way, to make arrangements for the relay of horses that was to meet them there, and for the reception of Veronique, Eustacie's maid, who was to be sent off very early in the morning on a pillion behind Osbert, taking with her the articles of dress that would be wanted to change her mistress from the huntress maid of honour to the English dame.

It was not long after he had been gone that a sound of wheels and trampling horses was heard in one of the forest drives. Charles, who was amusing himself with shooting at a mark together with Sidney and Teligny, handed his weapon to an attendant, and came up with looks of restless anxiety to his Queen, who was placed in her chair under the tree, with the Admiral and her ladies round her, as judges of the prize.

'Here is *le brouillon*,' he muttered. 'I thought we had been left in peace too long.'

Elisabeth, who Brantome says was water, while her husband was fire, tried to murmur some hopeful suggestion; and poor little Eustacie, clasping her hands, could scarcely refrain from uttering the cry, 'Oh, it is my uncle! Do not let him take me!'

The next minute there appeared four horses greatly heated and jaded, drawing one of the court coaches; and as it stopped at the castle gate, two ladies became visible within it—the portly form of Queen Catherine, and on the back seat the graceful figure of Diane de Ribaumont.

Charles swore a great oath under his breath. He made a step forward, but then his glance falling on Eustacie's face, which had flushed to the rosiest hue of the carnation, he put his finger upon his lip with a menacing air, and then advanced to greet his mother, followed by his gentlemen.

'Fear not, my dear child,' said the young Queen, taking Eustacie's arm as she rose for the same purpose. 'Obey the King, and he will take care that all goes well.'

The gentle Elisabeth was, however, the least regarded member of the royal family. Her mother-in-law had not even waited to greet her, but had hurried the King into his cabinet, with a precipitation that made the young Queen's tender heart conclude that some dreadful disaster had occurred, and before Mademoiselle de Ribaumont had had time to make her reverence, she exclaimed, breathlessly, 'Oh, is it ill news? Not from Vienna?'

'No, no, Madame; reassure yourself,' replied Diane; 'it is merely that her Majesty, being on the way to Monceaux with Mesdames, turned out of her road to make a flying visit to your graces, and endeavour to persuade you to make her party complete.'

Elisabeth looked as if questioning with herself if this would possibly be the whole explanation. Monceaux was a castle belonging to the Queen Dowager at no great distance from Montpipeau, but there had been no intention of leaving Paris before the wedding, which was fixed for the seventeenth of August, and the bridegroom was daily expected. She asked who was the party at Monceaux, and was told that Madame de Nemours had gone thither the evening before, with her son, M. de Guise, to make ready; and that Monsieur was escorting thither his two sisters, Madame de Lorraine and Madame Marguerite. The Queen-mother had set out before them very early in the morning.

'You must have made great speed,' said Elisabeth; 'it is scarcely two o'clock.'

'Truly we did, Madame; two of our horses even died upon the road; but the Queen was anxious to find the King ere he should set off on one of his long chases.'

Diane, at every spare moment, kept her eyes interrogatively fixed on her cousin, and evidently expected that the taciturn Queen, to whom a long conversation, in any language but Spanish, was always a grievance, would soon dismiss them both; and Eustacie did not know whether to be thankful or impatient, as Elisabeth, with tardy, hesitating, mentally-translated speech, inquired into every circumstance of the death of the poor horses, and then into all the court gossip, which she was currently supposed neither to hear nor understand; and then bethought herself that this good Mademoiselle de Ribaumont could teach her that embroidery stitch she had so long wished to learn. Taking her arm, she entered the hall, and produced her work, so as effectually to prevent any communication between the cousins; Eustacie, meanwhile her heart clinging to her friend, felt her eyes filling with tears at the thoughts of how unkind her morrow's flight would seem without one word of farewell or of confidence, and was already devising tokens of tenderness to be left behind for Diane's consolation, when the door of the cabinet opened, and Catherine sailed down the stairs, with her peculiar gliding step and sweep of dignity. The King followed her with a face of irresolution and distress. He was evidently under her displeasure; but she advanced to the young Queen with much graciousness, and an air of matronly solicitude.

'My daughter,' she said, 'I have just assured the King that I cannot leave you in these damp forests. I could not be responsible for the results of the exposure any longer. It is for him to make his own arrangements, but I brought my coach empty on purpose to transport you and your ladies to Monceaux.

The women may follow with the mails. You can be ready as soon as the horses are harnessed.'

Elisabeth was used to passiveness. She turned one inquiring look to her husband, but he looked sullen, and, evidently cowed by his mother, uttered not a word. She could only submit, and Catherine herself add that there was room for Madame de Sauve and Mademoiselle de Nid de Merle. Madame la Comtesse should follow! It was self-evident that propriety would not admit of the only demoiselle being left behind among the gentlemen. Poor Eustacie, she looked mutely round as if she hoped to escape! What was the other unkindness to this? And ever under the eyes of Diane too, who followed her to their chamber, when she went to prepare, so that she could not even leave a token for him where he would have been most certain to find it. Moments were few; but at the very last, while the queens were being handed in the carriage, she caught the eye of Philip Sidney. He saw the appealing look, and came near. She tried to laugh. 'Here is my gage, Monsieur Sidney,' she said, and held out a rose-coloured knot of ribbon; then, as he came near enough, she whispered imploringly three of her few English words—

'Give to HIM.'

'I take the gage as it is meant,' said Sidney, putting a knee to the ground, and kissing the trembling fingers, ere he handed her into the carriage. He smiled and waved his hand as he met her earnest eyes. One bow contained a scrap of paper pricked with needle-holes. Sidney would not have made out those pricks for the whole world, even had he been able to do more than hastily secure the token, before the unhappy King, with a paroxysm of violent interjections, demanded of him whether the Queen of England, woman though she were, ever were so beset, and never allowed a moment to herself; then, without giving time for an answer, he flung away to his cabinet, and might be heard pacing up and down there in a tempest of perplexity. He came forth only to order his horse, and desire M. de Sauve and a few grooms to be ready instantly to ride with him. His face was full of pitiable perplexity—the smallest obstacle was met with a savage oath; and he was evidently in all the misery of a weak yet passionate nature, struggling with impotent violence against a yoke that evidently mastered it.

He flung a word to his guests that he should return ere night, and they thus perceived that he did not intend their dismissal.

'Poor youth,' said Coligny, mildly, 'he will be another being when we have him in our camp with the King of Navarre for his companion.'

And then the Admiral repaired to his chamber to write one of his many fond letters to the young wife of his old age; while his son-in-law and Philip Sidney agreed to ride on, so as to met poor young Ribaumont, and prepare him for the blow that had befallen him personally, while they anxiously debated what this sudden descent of the Queen-mother might portend. Teligny was ready to believe in any evil intention on her part, but he thought himself certain of the King's real sentiments, and in truth Charles had never treated any man with such confidence as this young Huguenot noble, to whom he had told his opinion of each of his counsellors, and his complete distrust of all. That pitying affection which clings to those who cling to it, as well as a true French loyalty of heart, made Teligny fully believe that however Catherine might struggle to regain her ascendancy, and whatever apparent relapses might be caused by Charles's habitual subjection to her, yet the high aspirations and strong sense of justice inherent in the King were asserting themselves as his youth was passing into manhood; and that the much-desired war would enable him to develop all his higher qualities. Sidney listened, partially agreed, talked of caution, and mused within himself whether violence might not sometimes be mistaken for vigour.

Ere long, the merry cadence of an old English song fell with a homelike sound upon Sidney's ear, and in another moment they were in sight of Berenger, trotting joyously along, with a bouquet of crimson and white heather-blossoms in his hand, and his bright young face full of exultation in his arrangements. He shouted gaily as he saw them, calling out, 'I thought I should meet you! but I wondered not to have heard the King's bugle-horn. Where are the rest of the hunters?'

'Unfortunately we have had another sort of hunt to-day,' said Sidney, who had ridden forward to meet him; 'and one that I fear, will disquiet you greatly.'

'How! Not her uncle?' exclaimed Berenger.

'No, cheer up, my friend, it was not she who was the object of the chase; it was this unlucky King,' he added, speaking English, 'who has been run to earth by his mother.'

'Nay, but what is that to me?' said Berenger, with impatient superiority to the affairs of the nation. 'How does it touch us?'

Sidney related the abstraction of the young Queen and her ladies, and then handed over the rose-coloured token, which Berenger took with vehement ardour; then his features quivered as he read the needle-pricked words-two that he had playfully insisted on her speaking and spelling after him in his adopted tongue, then not vulgarized, but the tenderest in the language, 'Sweet heart.' That was all, but to him they conveyed constancy to him and his, whatever might betide, and an entreaty not to leave her to her fate.

'My dearest! never!' he muttered; then turning hastily as he put the precious token into his bosom, he exclaimed, 'Are their women yet gone?' and being assured that they were not departed when the two friends had set out, he pushed his horse on at speed, so as to be able to send a reply by Veronique. He was barely in time: the clumsy wagon-like conveyance of the waiting-women stood at the door of the castle, in course of being packed with the Queen's wardrobe, amid the janglings of lackeys, and expostulating cries of *femmes de chambre*, all in the worst possible humour at being crowded up with their natural enemies, the household of the Queen-mother.

Veronique, a round-faced Angevin girl—who, like her lady, had not parted with all her rustic simplicity and honesty, and who had been necessarily taken into their confidence—was standing apart from the whirl of confusion, holding the leashes of two or three little dogs that had been confided to her care, that their keepers might with more ease throw themselves into the *melee*. Her face lighted up as she saw the Baron de Ribaumont arrive.

'Ah, sir, Madame will be so happy that I have seen Monsieur once more,' she exclaimed under her breath, as he approached her.

'Alas! there is not a moment to write,' he said, looking at the vehicle, already fast filling, 'but give her these flowers; they were gathered for her; give her ten thousand thanks for her token. Tell her to hold firm, and that neither king nor queen, bolt nor bar, shall keep me from her. Tell her, our watchword is HOPE.'

The sharp eyes of the duenna of the Queen's household, a rigid Spanish dame, were already searching for stray members of her flock, and Veronique had to hurry to her place, while Berenger remained to hatch new plans, each wilder than the last, and torment himself with guesses whether his project had been discovered. Indeed, there were moments when he fancied the frustration of his purpose the special object of Queen

Catherine's journey, but he had the wisdom to keep any such suggestion to himself.

The King came back by supper-time, looking no longer in a state of indecision, but pale and morose. He spoke to no one as he entered, and afterwards took his place at the head of the supper-table in silence, which he did not break till the meal was nearly over. Then he said abruptly, 'Gentlemen, our party has been broken up, and I imagine that after our great hunt tomorrow, no one will have any objection to return to Paris. We shall have merrier sport at Fontainebleau when this most troublesome of weddings is over.'

There was nothing to be done but to bow acquiescence, and the King again became grimly silent. After supper he challenged Coligny to a game of chess, and not a word passed during the protracted contest, either from the combatants or any other person in the hall. It was as if the light had suddenly gone out to others besides the disappointed and anxious Berenger, and a dull shadow had fallen on the place only yesterday so lively, joyous, and hopeful.

Berenger, chained by the etiquette of the royal presence, sat like a statue, his back against the wall, his arms crossed on his breast, his eyes fixed, chewing the cud of the memories of his dream of bliss, or striving to frame the future to his will, and to decide what was the next reasonable step he could take, or whether his irrepressible longing to ride straight off to Monceaux, claim his wife, and take her on horseback behind him, were a mere impracticable vision.

The King, having been checkmated twice out of three times by the Admiral, too honest a man not truly to accept his declaration of not wanting courtly play, pushed away the board, and was attended by them all to his COUCHER, which was usually made in public; and the Queen being absent, the gentlemen were required to stand around him till he was ready to fall asleep. He did not seem disposed to talk, but begged Sidney to fetch his lute, and sing to him some English airs that had taken his fancy much when sung by Sidney and Berenger together.

Berenger felt as if they would choke him in his present turbid state of resentful uncertainty; but even as the unhappy young King spoke, it was with a heavy, restless groan, as he added, 'If you know any lullaby that will give rest to a wretch tormented beyond bearing, let us have it.'

'Alas, Sire!' said the Admiral, seeing that no perilous ears remained in the room; 'there are better and more soothing words than any mundane melody.'

'*Peste*! My good father,' said the King, petulantly, 'has not old Phlipote, my nurse, rocked me to the sound of your Marot's Psalms, and crooned her texts over me? I tell you I do not want to think. I want what will drive thought away—to dull——'

'Alas! what dulls slays,' said the Admiral.

'Let it. Nothing can be worse than the present,' said the wretched Charles; then, as if wishing to break away from Coligny, he threw himself round towards Berenger, and said, 'Here; stoop down, Ribaumont; a word with you. Your matters have gone up the mountains, as the Italians say, with mine. But never fear. Keep silence, and you shall have the bird in your hand, only you must be patient. Hold! I will make you and Monsieur Sidney gentlemen of my bed-chamber, which will give you the *entree* of the Louvre; and if you cannot get her out of it without an *eclat*, then you must be a much duller fellow than half my court. Only that it is not their own wives that they abstract.'

With this Berenger must needs content himself; and the certainty of the poor King's good-will did enable him to do his part with Sidney in the songs that endeavoured to soothe the torments of the evil spirit which had on that day effected a fresh lodgment in that weak, unwilling heart.

It was not till the memoirs of the secret actors in this tragedy were brought to light that the key to these doings was discovered. M. de Sauve, Charles's secretary, had disclosed his proceedings to his wife; she, flattered by the attentions of the Duke of Anjou, betrayed them to him; and the Queen-mother, terrified at the change of policy, and the loss of the power she had enjoyed for so many years, had hurried to the spot.

Her influence over her son resembled the fascination of a snake: once within her reach he was unable to resist her; and when in their *tete-a-tete* she reproached him with ill-faith towards her, prophesied the overthrow of the Church, the desertion of his allies, the ruin of his throne, and finally announced her intention of hiding her head in her own hereditary estates in Auvergne, begging, as a last favour, that he would give his brother time to quit France instead of involving him in his own ruin, the poor young man's whole soul was in commotion. His mother knew her strength, left the poison to work, and withdrew in displeasure to Monceaux, sure that, as in effect happened, he would not be long in following her, imploring her not to abandon him, and making an unconditional surrender of himself, his conscience, and his friends into her hands. Duplicity was so entirely the element of the court, that, even while thus yielding himself, it was as one checked, but continuing the game; he still continued his connection with the Huguenots, hoping to succeed in his aims by some future counter-intrigue; and his real hatred of the court policy, and the genuine desire to make common cause with them, served his mother's purpose completely, since his cajolery thus became sincere. Her purpose was, probably, not yet formed. It was power that she loved, and hoped to secure by the intrigues she had played off all her life; but she herself was in the hands of an infinitely more bloodthirsty and zealous faction, who could easily accomplish their ends by working on the womanly terrors of an unscrupulous mind.

CHAPTER IX
THE WEDDING WITH CRIMSON FAVOURS

And trust me not at all or all in all.

.—*TENNYSON*

So extensive was the Louvre, so widely separated the different suites of apartments, that Diane and Eustacie had not met after the pall-mall party till they sat opposite to their several queens in the coach driving through the woods, the elder cousin curiously watching the eyes of the younger, so wistfully gazing at the window, and now and then rapidly winking as though to force back a rebellious tear.

The cousins had been bred up together in the convent at Bellaise, and had only been separated by Diane's having been brought to court two years sooner than Eustacie. They had always been on very kindly, affectionate terms; Diane treating her little cousin with the patronage of an elder sister, and greatly contributing to shield her from the temptations of the court. The elder cousin was so much the more handsome, brilliant, and admired, that no notion of rivalry had crossed her mind; and Eustacie's inheritance was regarded by her as reserved for her brother, and the means of aggradizement an prosperity for herself and her father. She looked upon the child as a sort of piece of property of the family, to be guarded and watched over for her brother; and when she had first discovered the error that the young baron was making between the two daughters of the house, it was partly in kindness to Eustacie, partly to carry out her father's plans, and partly from her own pleasure in conversing with anything so candid and fresh as Berenger, that she had maintained the delusion. Her father believed himself to have placed Berenger so entirely in the background, that he would hardly be at court long enough to discover the imposition; and Diane was not devoid of a strong hope of winning his affection and bending his will so as to induce him to become her husband, and become a French courtier for her sake—a wild dream, but a better castle in the air than she had ever yet indulged in.

This arrangement was, however, disconcerted by the King's passion for Sidney's society, which brought young Ribaumont also to court; and at the time of the mischievous introduction by Madame Marguerite, Diane had perceived that the mistake would soon be found out, and that she should no longer be able to amuse herself with the fresh-coloured, open-faced boy who was unlike all her former acquaintance; but the magnetism that shows a woman when she produces an effect had been experienced by her, and she had been sure that a few efforts more would warm and mould the wax in her fingers. That he should prefer a little brown thing, whose beauty was so inferior to her own, had never crossed her mind; she did not even know that he was invited to the pall-mall party, and was greatly taken by surprise when her father sought an interview with her, accused her of betraying their interests, and told her that this foolish young fellow declared that he had been mistaken, and having now discovered his veritable wife, protested against resigning her.

By that time the whole party were gone to Montpipeau, but that the Baron was among them was not known at the Louvre until Queen Catherine, who had always treated Diane as rather a favoured, quick-witted *protegee*, commanded her attendance, and on her way let her know that Madame de Sauve had reported that, among all the follies that were being perpetrated at the hunting-seat, the young Queen was absolutely throwing the little Nid-de-Merle into the arms of her Huguenot husband, and that if measures were not promptly taken all the great estates in the Bocage would be lost to the young Chevalier, and be carried over to the Huguenot interest.

Still Diane could not believe that it was so much a matter of love as that the young had begun to relish court favour and to value the inheritance, and she could quite believe her little cousin had been flattered by a few attentions that had no meaning in them. She was not prepared to find that Eustacie shrank from her, and tried to avoid a private interview. In truth, the poor child had received such injunctions from the Queen, and so stern a warning look from the King, that she durst not utter a syllable of the evening that had sealed her lot, and was so happy with her secret, so used to tell everything to Diane, so longing to talk of her husband, that she was afraid of betraying herself if once they were alone together. Yet Diane, knowing that her father trusted to her to learn how far things had gone, and piqued at seeing the transparent little creature, now glowing and smiling with inward bliss, now pale, pensive, sighing, and anxious, and scorning her as too childish for the love that she seemed to affect, was resolved on obtaining confidence from her.

And when the whole female court had sat down to the silk embroidery in which Catherine de Medicis excelled, Diane seated herself in the recess of a window and beckoned her cousin to her side, so that it was not possible to disobey.

'Little one,' she said, 'why have you cast off your poor cousin? There, sit down'—for Eustacie stood, with her silk in her hand, as if meaning instantly to return to her former place; and now, her cheeks in a flame, she answered in an indignant whisper, 'You know, Diane! How could you try to keep him from me?'

'Because it was better for thee, my child, than to be pestered with an adventurer,' she said, smiling, though bitterly.

'My husband!' returned Eustacie proudly.

'Bah! You know better than that!' Then, as Eustacie was about to speak, but checked herself, Diane added, 'Yes, my poor friend, he has a something engaging about him, and we all would have hindered you from the pain and embarrassment of a meeting with him.'

Eustacie smiled a little saucy smile, as though infinitely superior to them all.

'*Pauvre petite*,' said Diane, nettled; 'she actually believes in his love.'

'I will not hear a word against my husband!' said Eustacie, stepping back, as if to return to her place, but Diane rose and laid her hand on hers. 'My dear,' she said, 'we must no part thus. I only wish to know what touches my darling so nearly. I thought she loved and clung to us; why should she have turned from me for the sake of one who forgot her for half his life? What can he have done to master this silly little heart?'

'I cannot tell you, Diane,' said Eustacie, simply; and though she looked down, the colour on her face was more of a happy glow than a conscious blush. 'I love him too much; only we understand each other now, and it is of no use to try to separate us.'

'Ah, poor little thing, so she thinks,' said Diane; and as Eustacie again smiled as one incapable of being shaken in her conviction, she added, 'And how do you know that he loves you?'

Diane was startled by the bright eyes that flashed on her and the bright colour that made Eustacie perfectly beautiful, as she answered, 'Because I am his wife! That is enough!' Then, before her cousin could speak again, 'But, Diane, I promised not to speak of it. I know he would despise me if I broke my word, so I will not talk to you till I have leave to tell you all, and I am going back to help Gabrielle de Limeuil with her shepherdess.'

Mademoiselle de Ribaumont felt her attempt most unsatisfactory, but she knew of old that Eustacie was very determined—all Bellaise know that to oppose the tiny Baronne was to make her headstrong in her resolution; and if she suspected that she was coaxed, she only became more obstinate. To make any discoveries, Diane must take the line of most cautious caresses, such as to throw her cousin off her guard; and this she was forced to confess to her father when he sought an interview with her on the day of her return to Paris. He shook his head. She must be on the watch, he said, and get quickly into the silly girl's confidence. What! had she not found out that the young villain had been on the point of eloping with her? If such a thing as that should succeed, the whole family was lost, and she was the only person who could prevent it. He trusted to her.

The Chevalier had evidently come to regard his niece as his son's lawful property, and the Baron as the troublesome meddler; and Diane had much the same feeling, enhanced by sore jealousy at Eustacie's triumph over her, and curiosity as to whether it could be indeed well founded. She had an opportunity of judging the same evening—mere habit always caused Eustacie to keep under her wing, if she could not be near the Queen, whenever there was a reception, and to that reception of course Berenger came, armed with his right as gentleman of the bedchamber. Eustacie was colouring and fluttering, as if by the instinct of his presence, even before the tall fair head became visible, moving forward as well as the crowd would permit, and seeking about with anxious eyes. The glances of the blue and the black eyes met at last, and a satisfied radiance illuminated each young face; then the young man steered his way through the throng, but was caught midway by Coligny, and led up to be presented to a hook-nosed, dark-haired, lively-looking young man, in a suit of black richly laced with silver. It was the King of Navarre, the royal bridegroom, who had entered Paris in state that afternoon. Eustacie tried to be proud of the preferment, but oh! she thought it mistimed, and was gratified to mark certain wandering of the eye even while the gracious King was speaking. Then the Admiral said something that brought the girlish rosy flush up to the very roots of the short curls of flaxen hair, and made the young King's white teeth flash out in a mirthful, good-natured laugh, and thereupon the way opened, and Berenger was beside the two ladies, kissing Eustacie's hand, but merely bowing to Diane.

She was ready to take the initiative.

'My cousins deem me unpardonable,' she said; 'yet I am going to purchase their pardon. See this cabinet of porcelain *a le Reine*, and Italian vases and gems, behind this curtain. There is all the siege of Troy, which M. le Baron will not doubt explain to Mademoiselle, while I shall sit on this cushion, and endure the siege of St. Quentin from the *bon* Sieur de Selinville.'

Monsieur de Selinville was the court bore, who had been in every battle from Pavia to Montcontour, and gave as full memoirs of each as did Blaise de Monluc, only *viva voce* instead of in writing. Diane was rather a favourite of his; she knew her way through all his adventures. So soon as she had heard the description of the King of Navarre's entry into Paris that afternoon, and the old gentleman's lamentation that his own two nephews were among the three hundred Huguenot gentleman who had formed the escort, she had only to observe whether his reminiscences had gone to Italy or to Flanders in order to be able to put in the appropriate remarks at each pause, while she listened all the while to the murmurs behind the curtain. Yet it was not easy, with all her court breeding, to appear indifferent, and solely absorbed in hearing of the bad lodgings that had fallen to the share of the royal troops at Brescia, when such sounds were reaching her. It was not so much the actual words she heard, though these were the phrases— '*mon ange*, my heart, my love;' those were common, and Diane had lived in the Queen-mother's squadron long enough to despise those who uttered them only less than those who believed them. It was the full depth of tenderness and earnestness, in the subdued tones of the voice, that gave her a sense of quiet force and reality beyond all she had ever known. She had heard and overheard men pour out frantic ravings of passion, but never had listened to anything like the sweet protecting tenderness of voice that seemed to embrace and shelter its object. Diane had no doubts now; he had never so spoken to her; nay, perhaps he had had no such cadences in his voice before. It was quite certain that Eustacie was everything to him, she herself nothing; she who might have had any gallant in the court at her feet, but had never seen one whom she could believe in, whose sense of esteem had been first awakened by this stranger lad who despised her. Surely he was loving this foolish child simply as his duty; his belonging, as his right he might struggle hard for her, and if he gained her, be greatly disappointed; for how could Eustacie appreciate him, little empty-headed, silly thing, who would be amused and satisfied by any court flatterer?

However, Diane held out and played her part, caught scraps of the conversation, and pieced them together, yet avoided all appearance of inattention to M. de Selinville, and finally dismissed him, and manoeuvred first Eustacie, and after a safe interval Berenger, out of the cabinet. The latter bowed as he bade her good night, and said, with the most open and cordial of smiles, 'Cousin, I thank you with all my heart.'

The bright look seemed to her another shaft. 'What happiness!' said she to herself. 'Can I overthrow it? Bah! it will crumble of its own accord, even if I did nothing! And my father and brother!'

Communication with her father and brother was not always easy to Diane, for she lived among the Queen-mother's ladies. Her brother was quartered in a sort of barrack among the gentlemen of Monsieur's suite, and the old Chevalier was living in the room Berenger had taken for him at the Croix de Lorraine, and it was only on the most public days that they attended at the palace. Such a day, however, there was on the ensuing

Sunday, when Henry of Navarre and Marguerite of France were to be wedded. Their dispensation was come, but, to the great relief of Eustacie, there was no answer with it to the application for the CASSATION of her marriage. In fact, this dispensation had never emanated from the Pope at all. Rome would not sanction the union of a daughter of France with a Huguenot prince; and Charles had forged the document, probably with his mother's knowledge, in the hope of spreading her toils more completely round her prey, while he trusted that the victims might prove too strong for her, and destroy her web, and in breaking forth might release himself.

Strange was the pageant of that wedding on Sunday, the 17th of August, 1572. The outward seeming was magnificent, when all that was princely in France stood on the splendidly decked platform in front of Notre-Dame, around the bridegroom in the bright promise of his kingly endowments, and the bride in her peerless beauty. Brave, noble-hearted, and devoted were the gallant following of the one, splendid and highly gifted the attendants of the other; and their union seemed to promise peace to a long distracted kingdom.

Yet what an abyss lay beneath those trappings! The bridegroom and his comrades were as lions in the toils of the hunter, and the lure that had enticed them thither was the bride, herself so unwilling a victim that her lips refused to utter the espousal vows, and her head as force forward by her brother into a sign of consent; while the favoured lover of her whole lifetime agreed to the sacrifice in order to purchase the vengeance for which he thirsted, and her mother, the corrupter of her own children, looked complacently on at her ready-dug pit of treachery and bloodshed.

Among the many who played unconscious on the surface of that gulf of destruction, were the young creatures whose chief thought in the pageant was the glance and smile from the gallery of the Queen's ladies to the long procession of the English ambassador's train, as they tried to remember their own marriage there; Berenger with clear recollection of his father's grave, anxious face, and Eustacie chiefly remembering her own white satin and turquoise dress, which indeed she had seen on every great festival-day as the best raiment of the image of Notre Dame de Bellaise. She remained in the choir during mass, but Berenger accompanied the rest of the Protestants with the bridegroom at their head into the nave, where Coligny beguiled the time with walking about, looking at the banners that had been taken from himself and Conde at Montcontour and Jarnac, saying that he hoped soon to see them taken down and replaced by Spanish banners. Berenger had followed because he felt the need of doing as Walsingham and Sidney thought right, but he had not been in London long enough to become hardened to the desecration of churches by frequenting 'Paul's Walk.' He remained bareheaded, and stood as near as he could to the choir, listening to the notes that floated from the priests and acolytes at the high altar, longing from the time when he and Eustacie should be one in their prayers, and lost in a reverie, till a grave old nobleman passing near him reproved him for dallying with the worship of Rimmon. But his listening attitude had not passed unobserved by others besides Huguenot observers.

The wedding was followed by a ball at the Louvre, from which, however, all the stricter Huguenots absented themselves out of respect to Sunday, and among them the family and guests of the English Ambassador, who were in the meantime attending the divine service that had been postponed on account of the morning's ceremony. Neither was the Duke of Guise present at the entertainment; for though he had some months previously been piqued and entrapped into a marriage with Catherine of Cleves, yet his passion for Marguerite was still so strong that he could not bear to join in the festivities of her wedding with another. The absence of so many distinguished persons caused the admission of many less constantly privileged, and thus it was that Diane there met both her father and brother, who eagerly drew her into a window, and demanded what she had to tell them, laughing too at the simplicity of the youth, who had left for the Chevalier a formal announcement that he had dispatched his protest to Rome, and considered himself as free to obtain his wife by any means in his power.

'Where is *la petite*?' Narcisse demanded. Behind her Queen, as usual?'

'The young Queen keeps her room to-night,' returned Diane. 'Nor do I advise you, brother, to thrust yourself in the way of *la petite entetee* just at present.'

'What, is she so besotted with the peach face? He shall pay for it!'

'Brother, no duel. Father, remind him that she would never forgive him.'

'Fear not, daughter,' said the Chevalier; 'this folly can be ended by much quieter modes, only you must first give us information.'

'She tells me nothing,' said Diane; 'she is in one of her own humours— high and mighty.'

'*Peste*! where is your vaunt of winding the little one round your finger?'

'With time, I said,' replied Diane. Curiously enough, she had no compunction in worming secrets from Eustacie and betraying them, but she could not bear to think of the trap she had set for the unsuspecting youth, and how ingenuously he had thanked her, little knowing how she had listened to his inmost secrets.

'Time is everything,' said her father; 'delay will be our ruin. Your inheritance will slip through your fingers, my son. The youth will soon win favour by abjuring his heresy; he will play the same game with the King as his father did with King Henri. You will have nothing but your sword, and for you, my poor girl, there is nothing but to throw yourself on the kindness of your aunt at Bellaise, if she can receive the vows of a dowerless maiden.'

'It will never be,' said Narcisse. 'My rapier will soon dispose of a big rustic like that, who knows just enough of fencing to make him an easy prey. What! I verily believe the great of entreaty. 'And yet the fine fellow was willing enough to break the marriage when he took her for the bride.'

'Nay, my son,' argued the Chevalier, will apparently to spare his daughter from the sting of mortification, 'as I said, all can be done without danger of bloodshed on either side, were we but aware of any renewed project of elopement. The pretty pair would be easily waylaid, the girl safely lodged at Bellaise, the boy sent off to digest his pride in England.'

'Unhurt?' murmured Diane.

Her father checked Narcisse's mockery at her solicitude, as he added, 'Unhurt? Yes. He is a liberal-hearted, gracious, fine young man, whom I should much grieve to harm; but if you know of any plan of elopement and conceal it, my daughter, then upon you will lie either the ruin and disgrace of your family, or the death of one or both of the youths.'

Diane saw that her question had betrayed her knowledge. She spoke faintly. 'Something I did overhear, but I know not how to utter a treason.'

'There is no treason where there is no trust, daughter,' said the Chevalier, in the tone of a moral sage. 'Speak!'

Diane never disobeyed her father, and faltered, 'Wednesday; it is for Wednesday. They mean to leave the palace in the midst of the masque; there is a market-boat from Leurre to meet them on the river; his servants will be in it.'

'On Wednesday!' Father and son looked at each other.

'That shall be remedied,' said Narcisse.

'Child,' added her father, turning kindly to Diane, 'you have saved our fortunes. There is put one thing more that you must do. Make her obtain the pearls from him.'

'Ah!' sighed Diane, half shocked, half revengeful, as she thought how he had withheld them from her.

'It is necessary,' said the Chevalier. 'The heirloom of our house must not be risked. Secure the pearls, child, and you will have done good service, and earned the marriage that shall reward you.'

When he was gone, Diane pressed her hands together with a strange sense of misery. He, who had shrunk from the memory of little Diane's untruthfulness, what would he think of the present Diane's treachery? Yet it was to save his life and that of her brother—and for the assertion of her victory over the little robber, Eustacie.

CHAPTER X
MONSIEUR'S BALLET.

The Styx had fast bound her

Nine times around her.

—POPE, ODE ON ST.CECILIA'S DAY

Early on Monday morning came a message to Mademoiselle Nid de Merle that she was to prepare to act the part of a nymph of Paradise in the King's masque on Wednesday night, and must dress at once to rehearse her part in the ballet specially designed by Monsieur.

Her first impulse was to hurry to her own Queen, whom she entreated to find some mode of exempting her. But Elisabeth, who was still in bed, looked distressed and frightened, made signs of caution, and when the weeping girl was on the point of telling her of the project that would thus be ruined, silenced her by saying, 'Hush! my poor child, I have but meddled too much already. Our Lady grant that I have not done you more harm than good! Tell me no more.'

'Ah! Madame, I will be discreet, I will tell you nothing; but if you would only interfere to spare me from this ballet! It is Monsieur's contrivance! Ah! Madame, could you but speak to the King!'

'Impossible, child,' said the Queen. 'Things are not her as they were at happy Montpipeau.'

And the poor young Queen turned her face in to her pillow, and wept.

Every one who was not in a dream of bliss like poor little Eustacie knew that the King had been in so savage a mood ever since his return that no one durst ask anything from him a little while since, he had laughed at his gentle wife for letting herself, and Emperor's daughter, be trampled on where his brother Francis's Queen, from her trumpery, beggarly realm, had held up her head, and put down *la belle Mere*; he had amused himself with Elisabeth's pretty little patronage of the young Ribaumonts as a promising commencement in intriguing like other people; but now he was absolutely violent at any endeavour to make him withstand his mother, and had driven his wife back into that cold, listless, indifferent shell of apathy from which affection and hope had begun to rouse her. She knew it would only make it the worse for her little Nid de Merle for her to interpose when Monsieur had made the choice.

And Eustacie was more afraid of Monsieur than even of Narcisse, and her Berenger could not be there to protect her. However, there was protection in numbers. With twelve nymphs, and cavaliers to match, even the Duke of Anjou could not accomplish the being very insulting. Eustacie—light, agile, and fairy-like—gained considerable credit for ready comprehension and graceful evolutions. She had never been so much complimented before, and was much cheered by praise. Diane showed herself highly pleased with her little cousin's success, embraced her, and told her she was finding her true level at court. She would be the prettiest of all the nymphs, who were all small, since fairies rather than Amazons were wanted in their position. 'And, Eustacie,' she added, 'you should wear the pearls.'

'The pearls!' said Eustacie. 'Ah! but HE always wears them. I like to see them on his bonnet—they are hardly whiter than his forehead.'

'Foolish little thing!' said Diane, 'I shall think little of his love if he cares to see himself in them more than you.'

The shaft seemed carelessly shot, but Diane knew that it would work, and so it did. Eustacie wanted to prove her husband's love, not to herself, but to her cousin.

He made his way to her in the gardens of the Louvre that evening, greatly dismayed at the report that had reached him that she was to figure as a nymph of Elysium. She would thus be in sight as a prominent figure the whole evening, even till an hour so late that the market boat which Osbert had arranged for their escape could not wait for them without exciting suspicion, and besides, his delicate English feelings were revolted at the notion of her forming a part of such a spectacle. She could not understand his displeasure. If they could not go on Wednesday, they could go on Saturday; and as to her acting, half the noblest ladies in the court would be in piece, and if English husbands did not like it, they must be the tyrants she had always heard of.

'To be a gazing-stock——' began Berenger.

'Hush! Monsieur, I will hear no more, or I shall take care how I put myself in your power.'

'That has been done for you, sweetheart,' he said, smiling with perhaps a shade too much superiority; 'you are mine entirely now.'

'That is not kind,' she pouted, almost crying—for between flattery, excitement, and disappointment she was not like herself that day, and she was too proud to like to be reminded that she was in any one's power.

'I thought,' said Berenger, with the gentleness that always made him manly in dealing with her, 'I thought you like to own yourself mine.'

'Yes, sir, when you are good, and do not try to hector me for what I cannot avoid.'

Berenger was candid enough to recollect that royal commands did not brook disobedience, and, being thoroughly enamoured besides of his little wife, he hastened to make his peace by saying, 'True, *ma mie*, this cannot be helped. I was a wretch to find fault. Think of it no more.'

'You forgive me?' she said, softened instantly.

'Forgive you? What for, pretty one? For my forgetting that you are still a slave to a hateful Court?'

'Ah! then, if you forgive me, let me wear the pearls.'

'The poor pearls,' said Berenger, taken aback for a moment, 'the meed of our forefather's valour, to form part of the pageant and mummery? But never mind, sweetheart,' for he could not bear to vex her again: 'you shall have them to-night: only take care of them. My mother would look back on me if she knew I had let them out of my care, but you and I are one after all.'

Berenger could not bear to leave his wife near the Duke of Anjou and Narcisse, and he offered himself to the King as an actor in the masque, much as he detested all he heard of its subject. The King nodded comprehension, and told him it was open to him either to be a demon in a tight suit of black cloth, with cloven-hoof shoes, a long tail, and a trident; or one of the Huguenots who were to be repulsed from Paradise for the edification of the spectators. As these last were to wear suits of knightly armour, Berenger much preferred making one of them in spite of their doom.

The masque was given at the hall of the Hotel de Bourbon, where a noble gallery accommodated the audience, and left full space beneath for the actors. Down the centre of the stage flowed a stream, broad enough to contain a boat, which was plied by the Abbe de Mericour—transformed by a gray beard and hair and dismal mask into Charon.

But so unused to navigation was he, so crazy and ill-trimmed his craft, that his first performance would have been his submersion in the Styx had not Berenger, better accustomed to boats than any of the *dramatis personoe*, caught him by the arms as he was about to step in, pointed out the perils, weighted the frail vessel, and given him a lesson in paddling it to and fro, with such a masterly hand, that, had there been time for a change of dress, the part of Charon would have been unanimously transferred to him; but the delay could not be suffered, and poor Mericour, in fear of a ducking, or worse, of ridicule, balanced himself, pole in hand, in the midst of the river. To the right of the river was Elysium—a circular island revolving on a wheel which was an absolute orrery, representing in concentric circles the skies, with the sun, moon, the seven planets, twelve signs, and the fixed stars, all illuminated with small lamps. The island itself was covered with verdure, in which, among bowers woven of gay flowers, reposed twelve nymphs of Paradise, of whom Eustacie was one.

On the other side of the stream was another wheel, whose grisly emblems were reminders of Dante's infernal circles, and were lighted by lurid flames, while little bells were hung round so as to make a harsh jangling sound, and all of the court who had any turn for buffoonery were leaping and dancing about as demons beneath it, and uttering wild shouts.

King Charles and his two brothers stood on the margin of the Elysian lake. King Henry, the Prince of Conde, and a selection of the younger and gayer Huguenots, were the assailants,—storming Paradise to gain possession of the nymphs. It was a very illusive armour that they wore, thin scales of gold or silver as cuirasses over their satin doublets, and the swords and lances of festive combat in that court had been of the bluntest foil ever since the father of these princes had died beneath Montgomery's spear. And when the King and his brothers, one of them a puny crooked boy, were the champions, the battle must needs be the merest show, though there were lookers-on who thought that, judging by appearances, the assailants ought to have the best chance of victory, both literal and allegorical.

However, these three guardian angels had choice allies in the shape of the infernal company, who, as fast as the Huguenots crossed swords or shivered lances with their royal opponents, encircled them with their long black arms, and dragged them struggling away to Tartarus. Henry of Navarre yielded himself with a good-will to the horse-play with which this was performed, resisting just enough to give his demoniacal captors a good deal of trouble, while yielding all the time, and taking them by surprise by agile efforts, that showed that if he were excluded from Paradise it was only by his own consent, and that he heartily enjoyed the merriment. Most of his comrades, in especial the young Count de Rochefoucauld, entered into the sport with the same heartiness, but the Prince of Conde submitted to his fate with a gloomy, disgusted countenance, that added much to the general mirth; and Berenger, with Eustacie before his eyes, looking pale, distressed, and ill at ease, was a great deal too much in earnest. He had so veritable an impulse to leap forward and snatch her from that giddy revolving prison, that he struck against the sword of Monsieur with a hearty good-will. His silvered lath snapped in his hand, and at that moment he was seized round the waist, and, when his furious struggle was felt to be in earnest, he was pulled over on his back, while yells and shouts of discordant laughter rang round him, as demons pinioned him hand and foot.

He thought he heard a faint cry from Eustacie, and, with a sudden, unexpected struggle, started into a sitting posture; but a derisive voice, that well he knew, cried, 'Ha, the deadly sin of pride! Monsieur thinks his painted face pleases the ladies. To the depths with him—' and therewith one imp pulled him backwards again, while others danced a war-dance round him, pointing their forks at him; and the prime tormentor, whom he perfectly recognized, not only leapt over him, but spurned at his face with a cloven foot, giving a blow, not of gay French malice, but of malignity. It was too much for the boy's forbearance. He struggled free, dashing his adversaries aside fiercely, and as they again gathered about him, with the leader shouting, 'Rage, too, rage! To the prey, imps—' he clenched his fist, and dealt the foremost foe such a blow in the chest as to level him at once with the ground.

'Monsieur forgets,' said a voice, friendly yet reproachful, 'that this is but sport.'

It was Henry of Navarre himself who spoke, and bent to give a hand to the fallen imp. A flush of shame rushed over Berenger's face, already red with passion. He felt that he had done wrong to use his strength at such a moment, and that, though there had been spite in is assailant, he had not been therefore justified. He was glad to see Narcisse rise lightly to his feet, evidently unhurt, and, with the frankness with which he had often made it up with Philip Thistlewood or his other English comrades after a sharp tussle, he held out his hand, saying, 'Good demon, your pardon. You roused my spirit, and I forgot myself.'

'Demons forget not,' was the reply. 'At him, imps!' And a whole circle of hobgoblins closed upon with their tridents, forks, and other horrible implements, to drive him back within two tall barred gates, which, illuminated by red flames, were to form the ghastly prison of the vanquished. Perhaps fresh indignities would have been attempted, had not the King of Navarre thrown himself on his side, shared with him the brunt of all the grotesque weapons, and battled them off with infinite spirit and address, shielding him as it were from their rude insults by his own dexterity and inviolability, though retreating all the time till the infernal gates were closed on both.

Then Henry of Navarre, who never forgot a face, held out his hand, saying, 'Tartarus is no region of good omen for friendships, M. de Ribaumont, but, for lack of yonder devil's claw, here is mine. I like to meet a comrade who can strike a hearty blow, and ask a hearty pardon.'

'I was too hot, Sire,' confessed Berenger, with one of his ingenuous blushes, 'but he enraged me.'

'He means mischief.' said Henry. 'Remember, if you are molested respecting this matter, that you have here a witness that you did the part of a gentleman.'

Berenger bowed his thanks, and began something about the honour, but his eye anxiously followed the circuit on which Eustacie was carried and the glance was quickly remarked.

'How? Your heart is spinning in that Mahometan paradise, and that is what put such force into your fists. Which of the houris is it? The little one with the wistful eyes, who looked so deadly white, and shrieked out when the devilry overturned you? Eh! Monsieur, you are a happy man.'

'I should be, Sire;' and Berenger was on the point of confiding the situation of his affairs to this most engaging of princes, when a fresh supply of prisoners, chased with wild antics and fiendish yells by the devils, came headlong in on them; and immediately, completing, as Henry said, the galimatias of mythology, a pasteboard cloud was propelled on the stage, and disclosed the deities Mercury and Cupid, who made a complimentary address to the three princely brothers, inciting them to claim the nymphs whom their valour had defended, and lead them through the mazes of a choric celestial dance.

This dance had been the special device of Monsieur and the ballet-master, and during the last three days the houris had been almost danced off their legs with rehearsing it morning, noon, and night, but one at least of them was scarcely in a condition for its performance. Eustacie, dizzied at the first minute by the whirl of her Elysian merry-go-round, had immediately after become conscious of that which she had been too childish to estimate merely in prospect, the exposure to universal gaze. Strange staring eyes, glaring lights, frightful imps seemed to wheel round her in an intolerable delirious succession. Her only refuge was in closing her eyes, but even this could not long be persevered in, so necessary a part of the pageant was she; and besides, she had Berenger to look for, Berenger, whom she had foolishly laughed at for knowing how dreadful it would be. But of course the endeavour to seek for one object with her eyes made the dizziness even more dreadful; and when, at length, she beheld him dragged down by the demoniacal creatures, whose horrors were magnified by her confused senses, and the next moment she was twirled out of sight, her cry of distracted alarm was irrepressible. Carried round again and again, on a wheel that to her was far more like Ixion's than that of the spheres, she never cleared her perceptions as to where he was, and only was half-maddened by the fantastic whirl of incongruous imagery, while she barely sat out Mercury's lengthy harangue; and when her wheel stood still, and she was released, she could not stand, and was indebted to Charon and one of her fellow-nymphs for supporting her to a chair in the back of the scene. Kind Charon hurried to bring her wine, the lady revived her with essences, and the ballet-master clamoured for his performers.

Ill or well, royal ballets must be danced. One long sob, one gaze round at the refreshing sight of a room no longer in motion, one wistful look at the gates of Tartarus, and the misery of the throbbing, aching head must be disregarded. The ballet-master touched the white cheeks with rouge, and she stepped forward just in time, for Monsieur himself was coming angrily forward to learn the cause of the delay.

Spectators said the windings of that dance were exquisitely graceful. It was well that Eustacie's drilling had been so complete, for she moved through it blindly, senselessly, and when it was over was led back between the two Demoiselles de Limeuil to the apartment that served as a green-room, drooping and almost fainting. They seated her in a chair, and consulted round her, and her cousin Narcisse was among the first to approach; but no sooner had she caught sight of his devilish trim than with a little shriek she shut her eyes, and flung herself to the other side of the chair.

'My fair cousin,' he said, opening his black vizard, 'do you not see me? I am no demon, remember! I am your cousin.'

'That makes it no better,' said Eustacie, too much disordered and confused to be on her guard, and hiding her face with her hands. 'Go, go, I entreat.'

In fact he had already done this, and the ladies added their counsel; for indeed the poor child could scarcely hold up her head, but she said, 'I should like to stay, if I could: a little, a little longer. Will they not open those dreadful bars?' she added, presently.

'They are even now opening them,' said Mdlle. de Limeuil. 'Hark! they are going to fight *en melle*. Mdlle. de Nid de Merle is better now?'

'Oh yes; let not detain you.'

Eustacie would have risen, but the two sisters had fluttered back, impatient to lose nothing of the sports; and her cousin in his grim disguise stood full before her. 'No haste, cousin,' he said; 'you are not fit to move.'

'Oh, then go,' said Eustacie, suffering too much not to be petulant. 'You make me worse.'

'And why? It was not always thus,' began Narcisse, so eager to seize an opportunity as to have little consideration for her condition; but she was unable to bear any more, and broke out: 'Yes, it was; I always detested you more than ever, since you deceived me so cruelly. Oh, do but leave me!'

'You scorn me, then! You prefer to me—who have loved you so long— that childish new-comer, who was ready enough to cast you off.'

'Prefer! He is my husband! It is an insult for any one else to speak to me thus!' said Eustacie, drawing herself up, and rising to her feet; but she was forced to hold by the back of her chair, and Diane and her father appearing at that moment, she tottered towards the former, and becoming quite passive under the influence of violent dizziness and headache, made no objection to being half led, half carried, through galleries that connected the Hotel de Bourbon with the Louvre.

And thus it was that when Berenger had fought out his part in the *melle* of the prisoners released, and had maintained the honours of the rose-coloured token in his helmet, he found that his lady-love had been obliged by indisposition to return home; and while he stood, folding his arms to restrain their strong inclination to take Narcisse by the throat and demand whether this were another of his deceptions, a train of fireworks suddenly exploded in the middle of the Styx—a last surprise, especially contrived by King Charles, and so effectual that half the ladies were shrieking, and imagining that they and the whole hall had blown up together.

A long supper, full of revelry, succeeded, and at length Sidney ad Ribaumont walked home together in the midst of their armed servants bearing torches. All the way home Berenger was bitter in vituperation of the hateful pageant and all its details.

'Yea, truly,' replied Sidney; 'methought that it betokens disease in the mind of a nation when their festive revelry is thus ghastly, rendering the most awful secrets made known by our God in order to warm man from sin into a mere antic laughing-stock. Laughter should be moved by what is fair and laughter-worthy—even like such sports as our own "Midsummer Night's Dream." I have read that the bloody temper of Rome fed itself in gladiator shows, and verily, what we beheld to-night betokens something at once grisly and light-minded in the mood of this country.'

Sidney thought so the more when on the second ensuing morning the Admiral de Coligny was shot through both hands by an assassin generally known to have been posted by the Duke of Guise, yet often called by the sinister sobriquet of *Le Tueur de Roi.*

CHAPTER XI
THE KING'S TRAGEDY.

The night is come, no fears disturb

The sleep of innocence

They trust in kingly faith, and kingly oath.

They sleep, alas! they sleep

Go to the palace, wouldst thou know

How hideous night can be;

Eye is not closed in those accursed walls,

Nor heart is quiet there!

—Southey, BARTHOLOMEW'S EVE

'Young gentlemen,' said Sir Francis Walsingham, as he rose from dinner on the Saturday, 'are you bound for the palace this evening?'

'I am, so please your Excellency,' returned Berenger.

'I would have you both to understand that you must have a care of yourselves,' said the Ambassador. 'The Admiral's wound has justly caused much alarm, and I hear that the Protestants are going vapouring about in so noisy and incautious a manner, crying out for justice, that it is but too likely that the party of the Queen-mother and the Guise will be moved to strong measures.'

'They will never dare lay a finger upon us!' said Sidney.

'In a terror-stricken fray men are no respecters of persons,' replied Sir Francis. 'This house is, of course, inviolable; and, whatever the madness of the people, we have stout hearts enough here to enforce respect thereto; but I cannot answer even for an Englishman's life beyond its precincts; and you, Ribaumont, whom I cannot even claim as my Queen's subject—I greatly fear to trust you beyond its bounds.'

'I cannot help it, sir. Nay, with the most grateful thanks for all your goodness to me, I must pray you not to take either alarm or offence if I return not this night.'

'No more, my friend,' said Walsingham, quickly; 'let me know nothing of your purposes, but take care of yourself. I would you were safe at home again, though the desire may seem inhospitable. The sooner the better with whatever you have to do.'

'Is the danger so imminent?' asked Sidney.

'I know nothing, Philip. All I can tell is that, as I have read that dogs and cattle scent an earthquake in the air, so man and women seem to breathe a sense of danger in this city. And to me the graciousness with which the Huguenots have been of late treated wears a strangely suspicious air. Sudden and secret is the blow like to be, and we cannot be too much on our guard. Therefore remember, my young friends both, that your danger or death would fall heavily on those ye love and honour at home.'

So saying, he left the two youths, unwilling to seek further confidence, and Berenger held his last consultation with Sidney, to whom he gave directions for making full explanation to Walsingham in his absence, and expediting Mr. Adderley's return to England. Osbert alone was to go to the Louvre with him, after having seen the five English grooms on board the little decked market-vessel on the Seine, which was to await the fugitives. Berenger was to present himself in the palace as in his ordinary court attendance, and, contriving to elude notice among the throng who were there lodged, was to take up his station at the foot of the stairs leading to the apartments of ladies, whence Eustacie was to descend at about eleven o'clock, with her maid Veronique. Landry Osbert was to join them from the lackey's hall below, where he had a friend, and the connivance of the porter at the postern opening towards the Seine had been secured.

Sidney wished much to accompany him to the palace, if his presence could be any aid or protection, but on consideration it was decided that his being at the Louvre was likely to attract notice to Ribaumont's delaying there. The two young men therefore shook hands and parted, as youths who trusted that they had begun a lifelong friendship, with mutual promises to write to one another—the one, the adventures of his flight; the other, the astonishment it would excite. And auguries were exchanged of merry meetings in London, and of the admiration the lovely little wife would excite at Queen Elizabeth's court.

Then, with an embrace such as English friends then gave, they separated at the gate; and Sidney stood watching, as Berenger walked free and bold down the street, his sword at his side, his cloak over one shoulder, his feathered cap on one side, showing his bright curling hair, a sunshiny picture of a victorious bridegroom—such a picture as sent Philip Sidney's wits back to Arcadia.

It was not a day of special state, but the palace was greatly crowded. The Huguenots were in an excited mood, inclined to rally round Henry of

Navarre, whose royal title made him be looked on as is a manner their monarch, though his kingdom had been swallowed by Spain, and he was no more than a French duke distantly related to royalty in the male line, and more nearly through his grandmother and bride. The eight hundred gentlemen he had brought with him swarmed about his apartments, making their lodging on staircases and in passages; and to Berenger it seemed as if the King's guards and Monsieur's gentlemen must have come in in equal numbers to balance them. Narcisse was there, and Berenger kept cautiously amid his Huguenot acquaintance, resolved not to have a quarrel thrust on him which he could not honourably desert. It was late before he could work his way to the young Queen's reception-room, where he found Eustacie. She looked almost as white as at the masque; but there was a graver, less childish expression in her face than he had ever seen before, and her eyes glanced confidence when they met his.

Behind the Queen's chair a few words could be spoken.

'*Ma mie,* art thou well again? Canst bear this journey now?'

'Quite well, now! quite ready. Oh that we may never have masques in England!'

He smiled—'Never such as this!'

'Ah! thou knowest best. I am glad I am thine already; I am so silly, thou wouldest never have chosen me! But thou wilt teach me, and I will strive to be very good! And oh! let me but give one farewell to Diane.'

'It is too hard to deny thee aught to-night, sweetheart, but judge for thyself. Think of the perils, and decide.'

Before Eustacie could answer, a rough voice came near, the King making noisy sport with the Count de Rochefoucauld and others. He was louder and ruder than Berenger had ever yet seen him, almost giving the notion of intoxication; but neither he nor his brother Henry ever tasted wine, though both had a strange pleasure in being present at the orgies of their companions: the King, it was generally said, from love of the self-forgetfulness of excitement—the Duke of Anjou, because his cool brain there collected men's secrets to serve afterwards for his spiteful diversion.

Berenger would willingly have escaped notice, but his bright face and sunny hair always made him conspicuous, and the King suddenly strode up to him: 'You here, sir? I thought you would have managed your affairs so as to be gone long ago!' then before Berenger could reply, 'However, since here you are, come along with me to my bedchamber! We are to have a carouse there to-night that will ring through all Paris! Yes, and shake

Rochefoucauld out of his bed at midnight! You will be one of us, Ribaumont? I command it!'

And without waiting for reply he turned away with an arm round Rochefoucauld's neck, and boisterously addressed another of the company, almost as wildly as if he were in the mood that Scots call 'fey.'

'Royalty seems determined to frustrate our plans,' said Berenger, as soon as the King was out of hearing.

'But you will not go! His comrades drink till—oh! two, three in the morning. We should never get away.'

'No, I must risk his displeasure. We shall soon be beyond his reach. But at least I may make his invitation a reason for remaining in the Louvre. People are departing! Soon wilt thou be my own.'

'As soon as the Queen's COUCHER is over! I have but to change to a traveling dress.'

'At the foot of the winding stair. Sweetest be brave!'

'I fear nothing with thee to guard me. See, the Queen is rising.'

Elizabeth was in effect rising to make her respectful progress to the rooms of the Queen-mother, to bid her good night; and Eustacie must follow. Would Diane be there? Oh that the command to judge between her heart and her caution had not been given! Cruel kindness!

Diane was there, straight as a poplar, cold as marble, with fixed eyes. Eustacie stole up to her, and touched her. She turned with a start. 'Cousin, you have been very good to me!' Diane started again, as if stung. You will love me still, whatever you hear?'

'Is this meant for farewell?' said Diane, grasping her wrist.

'Do not ask me, Diane. I may not.'

'Where there is no trust there is no treason,' said Diane, dreamily. 'No, answer me not, little one, there will be time for that another day. Where is he?'

'In the *oeil-de-boeuf*, between the King's and Queen's suites of rooms. I must go. There is the Queen going. Diane, one loving word.'

'Silly child, you shall have plenty another time,' said Diane, breaking away. 'Follow thy Queen now!'

Catherine, who sat between her daughters Claude and Marguerite, looked pre-occupied, and summarily dismissed her daughter-in-law, Elizabeth, whom Eustacie was obliged to follow to her own state-room.

There all the forms of the COUCHER were tediously gone through; every pin had its own ceremony, and even when her Majesty was safely deposited under her blue satin coverlet the ladies still stood round till she felt disposed to fall asleep. Elisabeth was both a sleepy and a considerate person, so that this was not so protracted a vigil as was sometimes exacted by the more wakeful princesses; but Eustacie could not escape from it till it was already almost midnight, the period for her tryst.

Her heart was very full. It was not the usual flutter and terror of an eloping girl. Eustacie was a fearless little being, and her conscience had no alarms; her affections were wholly with Berenger, and her transient glimpses of him had been as of something come out of a region higher, tenderer, stronger, purer, more trustworthy than that where she had dwelt. She was proud of belonging to him. She had felt upheld by the consciousness through years of waiting, and now he more than realized her hopes, and she could have wept for exulting joy. Yet it was a strange, stealthy break with all she had to leave behind. The light to which he belonged seemed strange, chill, dazzling light, and she shivered at the thought of it, as if the new world, new ideas, and new requirements could only be endured with him to shield her and help her on. And withal, there seemed to her a shudder over the whole place on that night. The King's eyes looked wild and startled, the Queen-mother's calm was strained, the Duchess of Lorraine was evidently in a state of strong nervous excitement; there were strange sounds, strange people moving about, a weight on everything, as if they were under the shadow of a thunder-cloud. 'Could it be only her own fancy?' she said to herself, because this was to be the great event of her life, for surely all these great people could not know or heed that little Eustacie de Ribaumont was to make her escape that night!

The trains of royalty were not sumptuously lodged. France never has cared so much for comfort as for display. The waiting-lady of the bedchamber slept in the ante-room of her mistress; the others, however high their rank, were closely herded together up a winding stair leading to a small passage, with tiny, cell-like recesses, wherein the demoiselles slept, often with their maids, and then dressed themselves in the space afforded by the passage. Eustacie's cell was nearly at the end of the gallery, and exchanging 'good-nights' with her companions, she proceeded to her recess, where she expected to find Veronique ready to adjust her dress. Veronique, however, was missing; but anxious to lose no time, she had taken off her delicate white satin farthingale to change it for an unobtrusive dark woolen kirtle, when, to her surprise and dismay, a loud creaking, growling sound made itself heard outside the door at the other end. Half-a-dozen heads came out of their cells; half-a-dozen voices asked and answered the question, 'What is it?' 'They are bolting our door outside.' But only Eustacie sped like lightning along the passage, pulled at the door, and cried, 'Open! Open, I say!' No answer, but the other bolt creaked.

'You mistake, CONCIERGE! We are never bolted in! My maid is shut out.'

No answer, but the step retreated. Eustacie clasped her hands with a cry that she could hardly have repressed, but which she regretted the next moment.

Gabrielle de Limeuil laughed. 'What, Mademoiselle, are you afraid they will not let us out to-morrow?'

'My maid!' murmured Eustacie, recollecting that she must give a colour to her distress.

'Ah! perhaps she will summon old Pierre to open for us.'

This suggestion somewhat consoled Eustacie, and she stood intently listening for Veronique's step, wishing that her companions would hold their peace; but the adventure amused them, and they discussed whether it were a blunder of the CONCIERGE, or a piece of prudery of Madame la Comtesse, or, after all, a precaution. The palace so full of strange people, who could say what might happen? And there was a talk of a conspiracy of the Huguenots. At any rate, every one was too much frightened to go to sleep, and, some sitting on the floor, some on a chest, some on a bed, the girls huddled together in Gabrielle de Limeuil's recess, the nearest to the door, and one after another related horrible tales of blood, murder, and vengeance—then, alas! Only too frequent occurrences in their unhappy land—each bringing some frightful contribution from her own province, each enhancing upon the last-told story, and ever and anon pausing with bated breath at some fancied sound, or supposed start of one of the others; then clinging close together, and renewing the ghastly anecdote, at first in a hushed voice that grew louder with the interest of the story. Eustacie alone would not join the cluster. Her cloak round her shoulders, she stood with her back against the door, ready to profit by the slightest indication outside of a step that might lead to her release, or at least enable her to communicate with Veronique; longing ardently that her companions would go to bed, yet unable to avoid listening with the like dreadful fascination to each of the terrible histories, which added each moment to the nervous horror of the whole party. Only one, a dull and composed girl, felt the influence of weariness, and dozed with her head in her companion's lap; but she was awakened by one general shudder and suppressed cry when the hoarse clang of a bell struck on the ears of the already terrified, excited maidens.

'The tocsin! The bell of St. Germain! Fire! No, a Huguenot rising! Fire! Oh, let us out! Let us out! The window! Where is the fire? Nowhere! See the lights! Hark, that was a shot! It was in the palace! A heretic rising! Ah! there was to be a slaughter of the heretics! I heard it whispered. Oh, let us out! Open the door!'

But nobody heard: nobody opened. There was one who stood without word or cry, close to the door—her eyes dilated, her cheek colourless, her whole person, soul and body alike, concentrated in that one impulse to spring forward the first moment the bolt should be drawn. But still the door remained fast shut!

CHAPTER XII
THE PALACE OF SLAUGHTER

A human shambles with blood-reeking floor.

MISS SWANWICK, Esch. Agamemnon

The door was opened at last, but not till full daylight. It found Eustacie as ready to rush forth, past all resistance, as she had been the night before, and she was already in the doorway when her maid Veronique, her face swollen with weeping, caught her by the hands and implored her to turn back and listen.

And words about a rising of the Huguenots, a general destruction, corpses lying in the court, were already passing between the other maidens and the CONCIERGE. Eustacie turned upon her servant: 'Veronique, what means it? Where is he?'

'Alas! alas! Ah! Mademoiselle, do but lie down! Woe is me! I saw it all! Lie down, and I will tell you.'

'Tell! I will not move till you have told me where my husband is,' said Eustacie, gazing with eyes that seemed to Veronique turned to stone.

'Ah! my lady—my dear lady! I was on the turn of the stairs, and saw all. The traitor—the Chevalier Narcisse—came on him, cloaked like you— and—shot him dead—with, oh, such cruel words of mockery! Oh! woe the day! Stay, stay, dear lady, the place is all blood—they are slaying them all— all the Huguenots! Will no one stop her?—Mademoiselle—ma'm'selle!—'

For Eustacie no sooner gathered the sense of Veronique's words than she darted suddenly forwards, and was in a few seconds more at the foot of the stairs. There, indeed, lay a pool of dark gore, and almost in it Berenger's black velvet cap, with the heron plume. Eustacie, with a low cry, snatched it up, continued her headlong course along the corridor, swiftly as a bird, Veronique following, and vainly shrieking to her to stop. Diane, appearing at the other end of the gallery, saw but for a moment the little figure, with the cloak gathered round her neck, and floating behind her, understood Veronique's cry and joined in the chase across hall and gallery, where more stains were to be seen, even down to the marble stairs, every step slippery with blood. Others there were who saw and stood aghast, not understanding the apparition that flitted on so swiftly, never pausing till at the great door at the foot of the stairs she encountered a gigantic Scottish archer, armed to the teeth. She touched his arm, and standing with folder arms, looked up and said, 'Good soldier, kill me! I am a Huguenots!'

'Stop her! bring her back!' cried Diane from behind. 'It is Mdlle. De Nil-de-Merle!'

'No, no! My husband is Huguenot! I am a Huguenot! Let them kill me, I say!'—struggling with Diane, who had now come up with her, and was trying to draw her back.

'Puir lassie!' muttered the stout Scotsman to himself, 'this fearsome night has driven her demented.'

But, like a true sentinel, he moved neither hand nor foot to interfere, as shaking herself loose from Diane, she was springing down the steps into the court, when at that moment the young Abbe de Mericour was seen advancing, pale, breathless, horrorstruck, and to him Diane shrieked to arrest the headlong course. He obeyed, seeing the wild distraction of the white face and widely glaring eyes, took her by both hands, and held her in a firm grasp, saying, 'Alas, lady, you cannot go out. It is no sight for any one.'

'They are killing the Protestants,' she said; 'I am one! Let me find them and die.'

A strong effort to free herself ensued, but it was so suddenly succeeded by a swoon that the Abbe could scarcely save her from dropping on the steps. Diane begged him to carry her in, since they were in full view of men-at-arms in the court, and, frightful to say, of some of the ladies of the palace, who, in the frenzy of that dreadful time, had actually come down to examine the half-stripped corpses of the men with whom they had jested not twelve hours before.

'Ah! it is no wonder,' said the youthful Abbe, as he tenderly lifted the inanimate figure. 'This has been a night of horrors. I was coming in haste to know whether the King knows of this frightful plot of M. de Guise, and the bloody work that is passing in Paris.'

'The King!' exclaimed Diane. 'M. l'Abbe, do you know where he is now? In the balcony overlooking the river, taking aim at the fugitives! Take care! Even your *soutane* would not save you if M. d'O and his crew heard you. But I must pray you to aid me with this poor child! I dread that her wild cries should be heard.'

The Abbe, struck dumb with horror, silently obeyed Mdlle. De Ribaumont, and brought the still insensible Eustacie to the chamber, now deserted by all the young ladies. He laid her on her bed, and finding he could do no more, left her to her cousin and her maid.

The poor child had been unwell and feverish ever since the masque, and the suspense of these few days with the tension of that horrible night had prostrated her. She only awoke from her swoon to turn her head from the light and refuse to be spoken to.

'But, Eustacie, child, listen; this is all in vain—he lives,' said Diane.

'Weary me not with falsehoods,' faintly said Eustacie.

'No! no! no! They meant to hinder your flight, but——'

'They knew of it?' cried Eustacie, sitting up suddenly. 'Then you told them. Go—go; let me never see you more! You have been his death!'

'Listen! I am sure he lives! What! would they injure one whom my father loved? I heard my father say he would not have him hurt. Depend upon it, he is safe on his way to England.'

Eustacie gave a short but frightful hysterical laugh, and pointed to Veronique. 'She saw it,' she said; 'ask her.'

'Saw what?' said Diane, turning fiercely on Veronique. 'What vile deceit have you half killed your lady with?'

'Alas! Mademoiselle, I did but tell her what I had seen,' sighed Veronique, trembling.

'Tell me!' said Diane, passionately.

'Yes, everything,' said Eustacie, sitting up.

'Ah! Mademoiselle, it will make you ill again.'

'I WILL be ill—I WILL die! Heaven's slaying is better than man's. Tell her how you saw Narcisse.'

'False girl!' burst out Diane.

'No, no,' cried Veronique. 'Oh, pardon me, Mademoiselle, I could not help it.'

In spite of her reluctance, she was forced to tell that she had found herself locked out of her mistress's room, and after losing much time in searching for the CONCIERGE, learnt that the ladies were locked up by order of the Queen-mother, and was strongly advised not to be running about the passages. After a time, however, while sitting with the CONCIERGE'S wife, she heard such frightful whispers from men with white badges, who were admitted one by one by the porter, and all led silently to a small lower room, that she resolved on seeking out the Baron's servant, and sending him to warn his master, while she would take up her station at her lady's door. She found Osbert, and with him was ascending a narrow spiral leading from the offices—she, unfortunately, the foremost. As she came to the top, a scuffle was going on—four men had thrown themselves upon one, and a torch distinctly showed her the younger Chevalier holding a pistol to the cheek of the fallen man, and she heard the worlds, '*Le baiser d'Eustacie! Jet e barbouillerai ce chien de visage,*" and at the same moment the pistol was discharged. She sprang back, oversetting, as she believed, Osbert, and fled shrieking to the room of the CONCIERGE, who shut her in till morning.

'And how—how,' stammered Diane, 'should you know it was the Baron?'

Eustacie, with a death-like look, showed for a moment what even in her swoon she had held clenched to her bosom, the velvet cap soaked with blood.

'Besides,' added Veronique, resolved to defend her assertion, 'whom else would the words suit? Besides, are not all the heretic gentlemen dead? Why, as I sat there in the porter's room, I heard M. d'O call each one of them by name, one after the other, into the court, and there the white-sleeves cut them down or pistolled them like sheep for the slaughter. They lie all out there on the terrace like so many carcases at market ready for winter salting.'

'All slain?' said Eustacie, dreamily.

'All, except those that the King called into his own *garde robe.*'

'Then, I slew him!' Eustacie sank back.

'I tell you, child,' said Diane, almost angrily, 'he lives. Not a hair of his head was to be hurt! The girl deceives you.'

But Eustacie had again become insensible, and awoke delirious, entreating to have the door opened, and fancying herself still on the revolving elysium, 'Oh, demons, have pity!' was her cry.

Diane's soothings were like speaking to the winds; and at last she saw the necessity of calling in further aid; but afraid of the scandal that the poor girl's raving accusations might create, she would not send for the Huguenots surgeon, Ambroise Pare, whom the King had carefully secured in his own apartments, but employed one of the barber valets of the Queen-mother's household. Poor Eustacie was well pleased to see her blood flowing, and sank back on her pillow murmuring that she had confessed her husband's faith, and would soon be one with him, and Diane feared for a moment lest the swoon should indeed be death.

The bleeding was so far effectual that it diminished the fever, and Eustacie became rational again when she had dozed and wakened, but she was little able or willing to speak, and would not so much as listen to Diane's asseverations that Veronique had made a frightful error, and that the Baron would prove to be alive. Whether it were that the admission that Diane had known of the project for preventing the elopement that invalidated her words, or whether the sufferer's instinct made her believe Veronique's testimony rather than her cousin's assurances, it was all 'cramming words into her ear against the stomach of her sense,' and she turned away from them with a piteous, petulant hopelessness: 'Could they not even let her alone to die in peace!'

Diane was almost angered at this little silly child being in such an agony of sorrow—she, who could never have known how to love him. And after all this persistent grief was willfully thrown away. For Diane spoke in perfect sincerity when she taxed Veronique with an injurious, barbarous mistake. She knew her father's strong aversion to violence, and the real predilection that Berenger's good mien, respectful manners, and liberal usage had won from him, and she believed he had much rather the youth lived, provided he were inoffensive. No doubt a little force had been necessary to kidnap one so tall, active, and determined, and Veronique had made up her horrible tale after the usual custom of waiting-maids.

Nothing else SHOULD be true. Did she think otherwise, she should be even more frantic than Eustacie! Why, it would be her own doing! She had betrayed the day of the escape—she had held aloof from warning. There was pleasure in securing Nid-de-Merle for her brother, pleasure in balking the foolish child who had won the heart that disregarded her. Nay, there might have been even pleasure in the destruction of the scorner of her charms—the foe of her house—there might have been pride in receiving Queen Catherine's dexterous hint that she had been an apt pupil, if the young Baron had only been something different—something less fair, gracious, bright, and pure. One bright angel seemed to have flitted across her path, and nothing should induce her to believe she had destroyed him.

The stripped corpses of the murdered Huguenots of the palace had been laid in a line on the terrace, and the ladies who had laughed with them the night before went to inspect them in death. A few remnants of Soeur Monique's influence would have withheld Diane, but that a frenzy of suspense was growing on her. She must see for herself. If it were so, she must secure a fragment of the shining flaxen hair, if only as a token that anything so pure and bright had walked the earth.

She went on the horrible quest, shrinking where others stared. For it was a pitiless time, and the squadron of the Queen-mother were as lost to womanhood as the fishwomen of two centuries later. But Diane saw no corpse at once so tall, so young, and so fair, though blond Normans and blue-blooded Franks, lads scarce sixteen and stalwart warriors, lay in one melancholy rank. She at least bore away the certainly that the English Ribaumont was not there; and if not, he MUST be safe! She could obtain no further certainty, for she knew that she must not expect to see either her father or brother. There was a panic throughout the city. All Paris imagined that the Huguenots were on the point of rising and slaying all the Catholics, and, with the savagery of alarmed cowardice, the citizens and the mob were assisting the armed bands of the Dukes of Anjou and Guise to complete the slaughter, dragging their lodgers from their hiding-places, and denouncing all whom they suspected of reluctance to mass and confession. But on the Monday, Diane was able to send an urgent message to her father that he must come to speak with her, for Mdlle. De Nid-de-Merle was extremely ill. She would meet him in the garden after morning mass.

There accordingly, when she stepped forth pale, rigid, but stately, with her large fan in her hand to serve as a parasol, she met both him and her brother. She was for a moment sorry, for she had much power over her father, while she was afraid of her brother's sarcastic tongue and eye; she knew he never scrupled to sting her wherever she was most sensitive, and she would have been able to extract much more from her father in his absence. France has never been without a tendency to produce the tiger-monkey, or ferocious fop; and the GENUS was in its full ascendancy under the sons of Catherine de Medicis, when the dregs of Francois the First's PSEUDO-chivalry were not extinct—when horrible, retaliating civil wars of extermination had made life cheap; nefarious persecutions had hardened the heart and steeled the eye, and the licentiousness promoted by the shifty Queen as one of her instruments of government had darkened the whole understanding. The most hateful heights of perfidy, effeminacy, and hypocrisy were not reached till poor Charles IX., who only committed crimes on compulsion, was in his grave, and Henry III. on the throne; but Narcisse de Ribaumont was one of the choice companions of the latter, and after the night and day of murder now stood before his sister with scented hair and handkerchief—the last, laced, delicately held by a hand in an embroidered glove—emerald pendants in his ears, a moustache twisted into sharp points and turned up like an eternal sardonic smile, and he led a little white poodle by a rose-coloured ribbon.

'Well, sister,' he said, as he went, through the motions of kissing her hand, and she embraced her father; 'so you don't know how to deal with megrims and transports?'

'Father,' said Diane, not vouchsafing any attention, 'unless you can send her some assurance of his life, I will not answer for the consequences.'

Narcisse laughed: 'Take her this dog, with my compliments. That is the way to deal with such a child as that.'

'You do not know what you say, brother,' answered Diane with dignity. 'It goes deeper than that.'

'The deeper it goes, child,' said the elder Chevalier, 'the better it is that she should be undeceived as soon as possible. She will recover, and be amenable the sooner.'

'Then he lives, father?' exclaimed Diane. 'He lives, though she is not to hear it—say——'

'What know I?' said the old man, evasively. 'On a night of confusion many mischances are sure to occur! Lurking in the palace at the very moment when there was a search for the conspirators, it would have been a miracle had the poor young man escaped.'

Diane turned still whiter. 'Then,' she said, 'that was why you made Monsieur put Eustacie into the ballet, that they might not go on Wednesday!'

'It was well hinted by you, daughter. We could not have effectually stopped them on Wednesday without making a scandal.'

'Once more,' said Diane, gasping, though still resolute; 'is not the story told by Eustacie's woman false—that she saw him—pistolled—by you, brother?'

'*Peste!*' cried Narcisse. 'Was the prying wench there? I thought the little one might be satisfied that he had neighbour's fare. No matter; what is done for one's *beaux yeux* is easily pardoned—and if not, why, I have her all the same!'

'Nevertheless, daughter,' said the Chevalier, gravely, 'the woman must be silenced. Either she must be sent home, or taught so to swear to having been mistaken, that *la petite* may acquit your brother! But what now, my daughter?'

'She is livid!' exclaimed Narcisse, with his sneer. 'What, sir, did not you know she was smitten with the peach on the top of a pole?'

'Enough, brother,' said Diane, recovering herself enough to speak hoarsely, but with hard dignity. 'You have slain—you need not insult, one whom you have lost the power of understanding!'

'Shallow schoolboys certainly form no part of my study, save to kick them down-stairs when they grow impudent,' said Narcisse, coolly. 'It is only women who think what is long must be grand.'

'Come, children, no disputes,' said the Chevalier. 'Of course we regret that so fine a youth mixed himself up with the enemies of the kingdom, like the stork among the sparrows. Both Diane and I are sorry for the necessity; but remember, child, that when he was interfering between your brother and his just right of inheritance and destined wife, he could not but draw such a fate on himself. Now all is smooth, the estates will be united in their true head, and you—you too, my child, will be provided for as suits your name. All that is needed is to soothe the little one, so as to hinder her from making an outcry—and silence the maid; my child will do her best for her father's sake, and that of her family.'

Diane was less demonstrative than most of her countrywomen. She had had time to recollect the uselessness of giving vent to her indignant anguish, and her brother's derisive look held her back. The family tactics, from force of habit, recurred to her; she made no further objection to her father's commands; but when her father and brother parted with her, she tottered into the now empty chapel, threw herself down, with her burning forehead on the stone step, and so lay for hours. It was not in prayer. It was because it was the only place where she could be alone. To her, heaven above and earth below seemed alike full of despair, darkness, and cruel habitations, and she lay like one sick with misery and repugnance to the life and world that lay before her—the hard world that had quenched that one fair light and mocked her pity. It was a misery of solitude, and yet no thought crossed her of going to weep and sympathize with the other sufferer. No; rivalry and jealousy came in there! Eustacie viewed herself as his wife, and the very thought that she had been deliberately preferred and had enjoyed her triumph hardened Diane's heart against her. Nay, the open violence and abandonment of her grief seemed to the more restrained and concentrated nature of her elder a sign of shallowness and want of durability; and in a certain contemptuous envy at her professing a right to mourn, Diane never even reconsidered her own resolution to play out her father's game, consign Eustacie to her husband's murdered, and leave her to console herself with bridal splendours and a choice of admirers from all the court.

However, for the present Diane would rather stay away as much as possible from the sick-bed of the poor girl; and when an approaching step forced her to rouse herself and hurry away by the other door of the chapel, she did indeed mount to the ladies' bed-chamber, but only to beckon Veronique out of hearing and ask for her mistress.

Just the same still, only sleeping to have feverish dreams of the revolving wheel or the demons grappling her husband, refusing all food but a little drink, and lying silent except for a few moans, heedless who spoke or looked at her.

Diane explained that in that case it was needless to come to her, but added, with the *vraisemblance* of falsehood in which she had graduated in Catherine's school, 'Veronique, as I told you, you were mistaken.'

'Ah, Mademoiselle, if M. le Baron lives, she will be cured at once.'

'Silly girl,' said Diane, giving relief to her pent-up feeling by asperity of manner, 'how could he live when you and your intrigues got him into the palace on such a night? Dead he is, OF COURSE; but it was your own treacherous, mischievous fancy that laid it on my brother. He was far away with M. de Guise at the attack on the Admiral. It was some of Monsieur's grooms you saw. You remember she had brought him into a scrape with Monsieur, and it was sure to be remembered. And look you, if you repeat the other tale, and do not drive it out of her head, you need not look to be long with her—no, nor at home. My father will have no one there to cause a scandal by an evil tongue.'

That threat convinced Veronique that she had been right; but she, too, had learnt lessons at the Louvre, and she was too diplomatic not to ask pardon for her blunder, promise to contradict it when her mistress could listen, and express her satisfaction that it was not the Chevalier Narcisse— for such things were not pleasant, as she justly observed, in families.

About noon on the Tuesday the Louvre was unusually tranquil. All the world had gone forth to a procession to Notre Dame, headed by the King and all the royal family, to offer thanksgiving for the deliverance of the country from the atrocious conspiracy of the Huguenots. Eustacie's chamber was freed from the bustle of all the maids of honour arraying themselves, and adjusting curls, feathers, ruffs and jewels; and such relief as she was capable of experiencing she felt in the quiet.

Veronique hoped she would sleep, and watched like a dragon to guard against any disturbance, springing out with upraised finger when a soft gliding step and rustling of brocade was heard. 'Does she sleep?' said a low voice; and Veronique, in the pale thin face with tear-swollen eyes and light yellow hair, recognized the young Queen. 'My good girl,' said Elisabeth, with almost a beseeching gesture, 'let me see her. I do not know when again I may be able.'

Veronique stood aside, with the lowest possible of curtseys, just as her mistress with a feeble, weary voice murmured, 'Oh, make them let me alone!'

'My poor, poor child,' said the Queen, bending over Eustacie, while her brimming eyes let the tears fall fast, 'I will not disturb you long, but I could not help it.'

'Her Majesty!' exclaimed Eustacie, opening wide her eyes in amazement.

'My dear, suffer me here a little moment,' said the meek Elisabeth, seating herself so as to bring her face near to Eustacie's; 'I could not rest till I had seen how it was with you and wept with you.'

'Ah, Madame, you can weep,' said Eustacie slowly, looking at the Queen's heavy tearful eyes almost with wonder; 'but I do not weep because I am dying, and that is better.'

'My dear, my dear, do not so speak!' exclaimed the gentle but rather dull Queen.

'Is it wrong? Nay, so much the better—then I shall be with HIM,' said Eustacie in the same feeble dreamy manner, as if she did not understand herself, but a little roused by seeing she had shocked her visitor. 'I would not be wicked. He was all bright goodness and truth: but his does not seem to be goodness that brings to heaven, and I do not want to be in the heaven of these cruel false men—I think it would go round and round.' She shut her eyes as if to steady herself, and that moment seemed to give her more self-recollection, for looking at the weeping, troubled visitor, she exclaimed, with more energy, 'Oh! Madame, it must be a dreadful fancy! Good men like him cannot be shut into those fiery gates with the torturing devils.'

'Heaven forbid!' exclaimed the Queen. 'My poor, poor child, grieve not yourself thus. At my home, my Austrian home, we do not speak in this dreadful way. My father loves and honours his loyal Protestants, and he trusts that the good God accepts their holy lives in His unseen Church, even though outwardly they are separate from us. My German confessor ever said so. Oh! Child, it would be too frightful if we deemed that all those souls as well as bodies perished in these frightful days. Myself, I believe that they have their reward for their truth and constancy.'

Eustacie caught the Queen's hand, and fondled it with delight, as though those words had veritably opened the gates of heaven to her husband. The Queen went on in her slow gentle manner, the very tone of which was inexpressibly soothing and sympathetic: 'Yes, and all will be clear there. No more violence. At home our good men think so, and the King will think the same when these cruel counselors will leave him to himself; and I pray, I pray day and night, that God will not lay this sin to his account, but open his eyes to repent. Forgive him, Eustacie, and pray for him too.'

'The King would have saved my husband, Madame,' returned Eustacie. 'He bade him to his room. It was I, unhappy I, who detained him, lest our flight should have been hindered.'

The Queen in her turn kissed Eustacie's forehead with eager gratitude. 'Oh, little one, you have brought a drop of comfort to a heavy heart. Alas! I could sometimes feel you to be a happier wife than I, with your perfect trust in the brave pure-spirited youth, unwarped by these wicked cruel advisers. I loved to look at his open brow; it was so like our bravest German Junkers. And, child, we thought, both of us, to have brought about your happiness; but, ah! it has but caused all this misery.'

'No, no, dearest Queen,' said Eustacie, 'this month with all its woe has been joy—life! Oh! I had rather lie here and die for his loss than be as I was before he came. And NOW—now, you have given him to me for all eternity—if but I am fit to be with him!'

Eustacie had revived so much during the interview that the Queen could not believe her to be in a dying state; but she continued very ill, the low fever still hanging about her, and the faintness continual. The close room, the turmoil of its many inhabitants, and the impossibility of quiet also harassed her greatly, and Elisabeth had little or no power of making any other arrangements for her in the palace. Ladies when ill were taken home, and this poor child had no home. The other maids of honour were a gentler, simpler set than Catherine's squadron, and were far from unkind; but between them and her, who had so lately been the brightest child of them all, there now lay that great gulf. *Ich habe gelebt und geliebet.*' That the little blackbird, as they used to call her, should have been on the verge of running away with her own husband was a half understood, amusing mystery discussed in exaggerating prattle. This was hushed, indeed, in the presence of that crushed, prostrate, silent sorrow; but there was still an utter incapacity of true sympathy, that made the very presence of so many oppressive, even when they were not in murmurs discussing the ghastly tidings of massacres in other cities, and the fate of acquaintances.

On that same day, the Queen sent for Diane to consult her about the sufferer. Elisabeth longed to place her in her own cabinet and attend on her herself; but she was afraid to do this, as the unhappy King was in such a frenzied mood, and so constantly excited by his brother and Guise, that it was possible that some half-delirious complaint from poor Eustacie might lead to serious consequences. Indeed, Elisabeth, though in no state to bear agitation, was absorbed in her endeavour to prevent him from adding blood to blood, and a few days later actually saved the lives of the King of Navarre and Prince of Conde, by throwing herself before him half-dressed, and tearing his weapon from his hand. Her only hope was that if she should give him a son, her influence for mercy would revive with his joy. Meantime she was powerless, and she could only devise the sending the poor little sufferer to a convent, where the nuns might tend her till she was restored to health and composure. Diane acquiesced, but proposed sending for her father, and he was accordingly summoned. Diane saw him first alone, and both agreed that he had better take Eustacie to Bellaise, where her aunt would take good care of her, and in a few months she would no doubt be weary enough of the country to be in raptures to return to Paris on any terms.

Yet even as Diane said this, a sort of longing for the solitude of the woods of Nid-de-Merle came over her, a recollection of the good Sister Monique, at whose knee she had breathed somewhat of the free pure air that her murdered cousin had brought with him; a sense that there she could pour forth her sorrow. She offered herself at once to go with Eustacie.

'No, no, my daughter,' said the Chevalier, 'that is unnecessary. There is pleasanter employment for you. I told you that your position was secured. Here is a brilliant offer—M. de Selinville,'

Le bonhomme de Selinville!" exclaimed Diane, feeling rather as if the compensation were like the little dog offered to Eustacie.

'Know ye not that his two heretic nephews perished the other night. He is now the head of his name, the Marquis, the only one left of his house.'

'He begins early,' said Diane.

'An old soldier, my daughter, scarce stays to count the fallen. He has no time to lose. He is sixty, with a damaged constitution. It will be but the affair of a few years, and then will my beautiful Marquise be free to choose for herself. I shall go from the young Queen to obtain permission from the Queen-mother.'

No question was asked. Diane never even thought objection possible. It was a close to that present life which she had begun to loathe; it gave comparative liberty. It would dull and confuse her heart-sick pain, and give her a certain superiority to her brother. Moreover, it would satisfy the old father, whom she really loved. Marriage with a worn-out old man was a simple step to full display for young ladies without fortune.

The Chevalier told Queen Elisabeth his purpose of placing his niece in the family convent, under the care of her aunt, the Abbess, in a foundation endowed by her own family on the borders of her own estate. Elisabeth would have liked to keep her nearer, but could not but own that the change to the scenes of her childhood might be more beneficial than a residence in a nunnery at Paris, and the Chevalier spoke of his niece with a tender solicitude that gained the Queen's heart. She consented, only stipulating that Eustacie's real wishes should be ascertained, and herself again made the exertion of visiting the patient for the purpose.

Eustacie had been partly dressed, and was lying as near as she could to the narrow window. The Queen would not let her move, but took her damp languid hand, and detailed her uncle's proposal. It was plain that it was not utterly distasteful. 'Soeur Monique,' she said, 'Soeur Monique would sing hymns to me, and then I should not see the imps at night.'

'Poor child! And you would like to go? You could bear the journey?'

'It would be in the air! And then I should not smell blood—blood!' And her cheeks became whiter again, if possible.

'Then you would not rather be at the Carmelites, or Maubuisson, near me?'

'Ah! Madame, there would not be Soeur Monique. If the journey would only make me die, as soon as I came, with Soeur Monique to hush me, and keep off dreadful images!'

'Dear child, you should put away the thought of dying. Maybe you are to live, that your prayers may win salvation for the soul of him you love.'

'Oh, then! I should like to go into a convent so strict—so strict, cried Eustacie, with renewed vigour. 'Bellaise is nothing like strict enough. Does your Majesty indeed think that my prayers will aid him?'

'Alas! what hope could we have but in praying?' said Elisabeth, with tears in her eyes. 'Little one, we will be joined at least in our prayers and intercessions: thou wilt not forget in thine one who yet lives, unhappier than all!'

'And, oh, my good, my holy Queen, will you indeed pray for him—my husband? He was so good, his faith can surely not long be reckoned against him. He did not believe in Purgatory! Perhaps——' Then frowning with a difficulty far beyond a fever-clouded brain, she concluded—'At least, orisons may aid him! It is doing something for him! Oh, where are my beads?—I can begin at once.'

The Queen put her arm round her, and together they said the *De profundis*,—the Queen understood every word far more for the living than the dead. Again Elisabeth had given new life to Eustacie. The intercession for her husband was something to live for, and the severest convent was coveted, until she was assured that she would not be allowed to enter on any rule till she had time to recover her health, and show the constancy of her purpose by a residence at Bellaise.

Ere parting, however, the Queen bent over her, and colouring, as if much ashamed of what she said, whispered—'Child, not a word of the ceremony at Montpipeau!—you understand? The King was always averse; it would bring him and me into dreadful trouble with THOSE OTHERS, and alas! It makes no difference now. You will be silent?'

And Eustacie signed her acquiescence, as indeed no difficulty was made in her being regarded as the widow of the Baron de Ribaumont, when she further insisted on procuring a widow's dress before she quitted her room, and declared, with much dignity, that she should esteem no person her friend who called her Mademoiselle de Nid-de-Merle. To this the Chevalier de Ribaumont was willing to give way; he did not care whether Narcisse married her as Berenger's widow or as the separated maiden wife, and he thought her vehement opposition and dislike would die away the faster the fewer impediments were placed in her way. Both he and Diane strongly discouraged any attempt on Narcisse's widow part at a farewell interview; and thus unmolested, and under the constant soothing influence of reciting her prayers, in the trust that they were availing her husband, Eustacie rallied so much that about ten day after the dreadful St. Batholomew, in the early morning, she was half-led half-carried down the stairs between her uncle and Veronique. Her face was close muffled in her thick black veil, but when she came to the foot of the first stairs where she had found Berenger's cap, a terrible shuddering came on her; she again murmured something about the smell of blood, and fell into a swoon.

'Carry her on at once,' said Diane, who was following,—'there will be not end to it if you do not remove her immediately.'

And thus shielded from the sight of Marcisse's intended passionate gesture of farewell at the palace-door, Eustecie was laid at full length on the seat of the great ponderous family coach, where Veronique hardly wished to revive her till the eight horses should have dragged her beyond the streets of Paris, with their terrible associations, and the gibbets still hung with the limbs of the murdered.

CHAPTER XIII
THE BRIDEGROOM'S ARRIVAL

The starling flew to his mother's window stane,

It whistled and it sang,

And aye, the ower word of the tune

Was 'Johnnie tarries lang.'

—JOHNNIE OF BREDISLEE

There had been distrust and dissatisfaction at home for many a day past. Berenger could hardly be censured for loving his own wife, and yet his family were by not means gratified by the prospect of his bringing home a little French Papist, of whom Lady Thistlewood remembered nothing good.

Lucy was indignantly fetched home by her stepmother, who insisted on treating her with extreme pity as a deserted maiden, and thus counteracting Aunt Cecily's wise representations, that there never should, and therefore never could, have been anything save fraternal affection between the young people, and that pity was almost an insult to Lucy. The good girl herself was made very uncomfortable by there demonstrations, and avoided them as much as possible, chiefly striving in her own gentle way to prepare her little sisters to expect numerous charms in brother Berenger's wife, and heartily agreeing with Philip that Berenger knew his own mind best.

'And at any rate,' quoth Philip, 'we'll have the best bonfire that ever was seen in the country! Lucy, you'll coax my father to give us a tar-barrel!'

The tar-barrel presided over a monstrous pile of fagots, and the fisher-boys were promised a tester to whoever should first bring word to Master Philip that the young lord and lady were in the creek.

Philip gave his pony no rest, between the lock-out on the downs and the borders of the creek; but day after day passed, and still the smacks from Jersey held no person worth mentioning; and still the sense of expectation kept Lucy starting at every sound, and hating herself for her own folly.

At last Philip burst into Combe Manor, fiery red with riding and consternation. 'Oh! father, father, Paul Duval's boat is come in, and he says that the villain Papists have butchered every Protestant in France.'

Sir Marmaduke's asseveration was of the strongest, that he did not believe a word of it. Nevertheless, he took his horse and rode down to interrogate Paul Duval, and charge him not to spread the report was in the air. He went to the Hall, and the butler met him with a grave face, and took him to the study, where Lord Walwyn was sitting over letter newly received from London, giving hints from the Low Countries of bloody work in France. And when he returned to his home, his wife burst out upon him in despair. Here had they been certainly killing her poor buy. Not a doubt that he was dead. All from this miserable going to France, that had been quite against her will.

Stoutly did Sir Marmaduke persevere in his disbelief; but every day some fresh wave of tidings floated in. Murder wholesale had surely been perpetrated. Now came stories of death-bells at Rouen from the fishermen on the coast; now markets and petty sessions discussed the foul slaughter of the Ambassador and his household; truly related how the Queen had put on mourning, and falsely that she had hung the French Ambassador, La Mothe Feneon. And Burleigh wrote to his old friend from London, that some horrible carnage had assuredly taken place, and that no news had yet been received of Sir Francis Walsingham or of his suite.

All these days seems so many years taken from the vital power of Lord Walwyn. Not only had his hopes and affections would themselves closely around his grandson, but he reproached himself severely with having trusted him in his youth and inexperience among the seductive perils of Paris. The old man grieved over the promising young life cut off, and charged on himself the loss and grief to the women, whose stay he had trusted Berenger would have been. He said little, but his hand and head grew more trembling; he scarcely ate or slept, and seemed to waste from a vigorous elder to a feeble being in the extremity of old age, till Lady Walwyn had almost ceased to think of her grandson in her anxiety for her husband.

Letters came at last. The messenger despatched by Sir Francis Walsingham had not been able to proceed till the ways had become safe, and he had then been delayed; but on his arrival his tidings were sent down. There were letters both from Sir Francis Walsingham and from heart-broken Mr. Adderley, both to the same effect, with all possible praises of the young Baron de Ribaumont, all possible reproach to themselves for having let him be betrayed, without even a possibility of recovering his remains for honourable burial. Poor Mr. Adderley further said that Mr. Sidney, who was inconsolable for the loss of his friend, had offered to escort him to the Low Countries, whence he would make his way to England, and would present himself at Hurst Walwyn, if his Lordship could endure the sight of his creature who had so miserably failed in his trust.

Lord Walwyn read both letters twice through before he spoke. Then he took off his spectacles, laid them down, and said calmly, 'God's will be done. I thank God that my boy was blameless. Better they slew him than sent him home tainted with their vices.'

The certainty, such as it was, seemed like repose after the suspense. They knew to what to resign themselves, and even Lady Thistlewood's tempestuous grief had so spent itself that late in the evening the family sat round the fire in the hall, the old lord dozing as one worn out with sorrow, the others talking in hushed tones of that bright boyhood, that joyous light quenched in the night of carnage.

The butler slowly entered the hall, and approached Sir Marmaduke, cautiously. 'Can I speak with you, sir?'

'What is it, Davy?' demanded the lady, who first caught the words. 'What did you say?'

'Madam, it is Humfrey Holt!'

Humfrey Holt was the head of the grooms who had gone with Berenger; and there was a general start and suppressed exclamation. 'Humfrey Hold!' said Lord Walwyn, feebly drawing himself to sit upright, 'hath he, then, escaped?'

'Yea, my Lord,' said Davy, 'and he brings news of my young Lord'

'Alack! Davy,' said Lady Walwyn, 'such news had been precious a while ago.'

'Nay, so please your Ladyship, it is better than you deem. Humfley says my young Lord is yet living.'

'Living! shrieked Lady Thistlewood, starting up. 'Living! My son! and where?'

'They are bearing him home, my Lady,' said the butler; 'but I fear me, by what Humfley says, that it is but in woeful case.'

'Bringing him home! Which way?' Philip darted off like an arrow from the bow. Sir Marmaduke hastily demanded if aid were wanted; and Lady Walwyn, interpreting the almost inaudible voice of her husband, bade that Humfley should be called in to tell his own story.

Hands were held out in greeting, and blessings murmured, as the groom entered, looking battered and worn, and bowing low in confusion at being thus unusually conspicuous, and having to tell his story to the head and body, and slashed about the face so as it is a shame to see. Nor hath he done aught these three weary weeks but moan from time to time so as it is enough to break one's heart to hear him; and I fear me 'tis but bringing him home to die.'

'Even so, God be thanked; and you too, honest Humfley,' said Lady Walwyn.' 'Let us hear when and how this deed was done.'

'Why, that, my Lord, I can't so well say, being that I was not with him; more's the pity, or I'd have known the reason why, or even they laid a finger on him. But when Master Landry, his French foster-brother, comes, he will resolve you in his own tongue. I can't parleyvoo with him, but he's an honest rogue for a Frenchman, and 'twas he brought off my young Lord. You see we were all told to be abroad the little French craft.

Master Landry took me down and settled it all with the master, a French farmer fellow that came a horse-dealing to Paris. I knew what my young Lord was after, but none of the other varlets did; and I went down and made as decent a place as I could between decks. My Lord and Master Landry were gone down to the court meantime, and we were to lie off till we heard a whistle like a mavis on the bank, then come and take them aboard. Well, we waited and waited, and all the lights were out, and not a sound did we hear till just an hour after midnight. Then a big bell rang out, not like a decent Christianable bell, but a great clash, then another, and a lot of strokes enough to take away one's breath. Then half the windows were lighted up, and we heard shots, and screeches, and splashes, till, as I said to Jack Smithers, 'twas as if one half the place was murthering the other. The farmer got frightened, and would have been off; but when I saw what he was at, "No," says I, "not an inch do we budge without news of my Lord." So Jack stood by the rope, and let them see that 'twas as much as their life was worth to try to unmoor. Mercy, what a night it was! Shrieks and shouts, and shots and howls, here, there, and everywhere, and splashes into the rive; and by and by we saw the poor murthered creatures come floating by. The farmer, he had some words with one of the boats near, and I heard somewhat of Huguenot and Hereteek, and I knew that was what they called good Protestants. Then up comes the farmer with his sons looking mighty ugly at us, and signing that unless we let them be off 'twould be set ashore for us; and we began to think as how we had best be set ashore, and go down the five of us to see if we could stand by my young Lord in some strait, or give notice to my Lord Ambassador.'

'God reward you!' exclaimed Lady Walwyn.

'Twas only our duty, my Lady,' gruffly answered Humfrey; 'but just as Hal had got on the quay, what should I see but Master Landry coming down the street with my young Lord in his back! I can tell you he was well-nigh spent; and just then half a dozen butcherly villains came out on him, bawling, "Tu-y! tu-y!" which it seems means "kill, kill." He turned about

- 116 -

and showed them that he had got a white sleeve and white cross in his bonnet, like them, the rascals, giving them to understand that he was only going to throw the corpse into the river. I doubted him then myself; but he caught sight of us, and in his fashion of talk with us, called out to us to help, for there was life still. So two of us took my Lord, and the other three gave the beggarly French cut-throats as good as they meant for us; while Landry shouted to the farmer to wait, and we got aboard, and made right away down the river. But never a word has the poor young gentleman spoken, though Master Landry has done all a barber or a sick-nurse could do; and he got us past the cities by showing the papers in my Lord's pocket, so that we got safe to the farmer's place. There we lay till we could get a boat to Jersey, and thence again home; and maybe my young Lord will mend now Mistress Cecily will have the handing of him.'

'That is it the wisest Hands, good Humfrey,' said Lord Walwyn, as the tears of feeble age flowed down his cheeks. 'May He who hath brought the lad safely so far spare him yet, and raise him up. But whether he live or die, you son and daughter Thistlewood will look that the faithfulness of Humfrey Holt and his comrades be never forgotten or unrewarded.'

Humfrey again muttered something about no more than his duty; but by this time sounds were heard betokening the approach of the melancholy procession, who, having been relieved by a relay of servants sent at once from the house, were bearing home the wounded youth. Philip first of all dashed in hurrying and stumbling. He had been unprepared by hearing Humfrey's account, and, impetuous and affectionate as he was, was entirely unrestrained, and flinging himself on his knees with the half-audible words, 'Oh! Lucy! Lucy! He is as good as dead!' hid his face between his arms on his sister's lap, and sobbed with the abandonment of a child, and with all his youthful strength; so much adding to the consternation and confusion, that, finding all Lucy's gentle entreaties vain, his father at last roughly pulled up his face by main force, and said, 'Philip, hold your tongue! Are we to have you on our hands as well as my Lady? I shall send you home this moment! Let your sister go.'

This threat reduced the boy to silence. Lucy, who was wanted to assist in preparing Berenger's room, disengaged herself; but he remained in the same posture, his head buried on the seat of the chair, and the loud weeping only forcibly stifled by forcing his handkerchief into his mouth, as if he had been in violent bodily pain. Nor did he venture again to look up as the cause of all his distress was slowly carried into the hall, corpse-like indeed. The bearers had changed several times, all but a tall, fair Norman youth, who through the whole transit had supported the head, endeavouring to guard it from shocks. When the mother and the rest came forward, he made a gesture to conceal the face, saying in French, 'Ah! Mesdames; this is no sight for you.'

Indeed the head and face were almost entirely hidden by bandages, and it was not till Berenger had been safely deposited on a large carved bed that the anxious relatives were permitted to perceive the number and extent of his hurts; and truly it was only by the breath, the vital warmth, and the heavy moans when he was disturbed, or the dressings of the wounds were touched, that showed him still to be a living man. There proved to be no less than four wounds—a shot through the right shoulder, the right arm also broken with a terrible blow with a sword, a broad gash from the left temple to the right ear, and worse than all, *'le baiser d'Eustacie,''* a bullet wound where the muzzle of the pistol had absolutely been so close as to have burnt and blackened the cheek; so that his life was, as Osbert averred, chiefly owing to the assassin's jealousy of his personal beauty, which had directed his shot to the cheek rather than the head; and thus, though the bullet had terribly shattered the upper jaw and roof of the mouth, and had passed out through the back of the head, there was a hope that it had not penetrated the seat of life or reason. The other gash on the face was but a sword-wound, and though frightful to look at, was unimportant, compared with the first wound with the pistol-shot in the shoulder, with the arm broken and further injured by having served to suspend him round Osbert's neck; but it was altogether so appalling a sight, that it was no wonder that Sis Marmaduke muttered low but deep curses on the cowardly ruffians; while his wife wept in grief as violent, though more silent, than her stepson's, and only Cecily gathered the faintest ray of hope. The wounds had been well cared for, the arm had been set, the hair cut away, and lint and bandages applied with a skill that surprised her, till she remembered that Landry Osbert had been bred up in preparation to be Berenger's valet, and thus to practise those minor arts of surgery then required in a superior body-servant. For his part, though his eyes looked red, and his whole person exhausted by unceasing watching, he seemed unable to relinquish the care of his master for a moment, and her nunnery French would not have perceived her tender touch and ready skill. These were what made him consent to leave his post even for a short meal, and so soon as he had eaten it he was called to Lord Walwyn to supply the further account which Humfley had been unable to give. He had waited, he explained, with a lackey, a friend of his in the palace, till he became alarmed by the influx of armed men, wearing white crosses and shirt-sleeves on their left arms, but his friend had assured him that his master had been summoned to the royal bedchamber, where he would be as safe as in church; and obtaining from Landry Osbert himself a perfectly true assurance of being a good Catholic, had supplied him with the badges that were needful for security. It was just then that Madame's maid crept down to his waiting-place with the intelligence that her mistress had been bolted in, and after a short consultation they agreed to go and see whether M. le Baron were indeed waiting, and, if he were, to warn him of the suspicious state of the lower regions of the palace.

They were just in time to see, but not to prevent the attack upon their young master; and while Veronique fled, screaming, Landry Osbert, who had been thrown back on the stairs in her sudden flight, recovered himself and hastened to his master. The murderers, after their blows had been struck, had hurried along the corridor to join the body of assassins, whose work they had in effect somewhat anticipated. Landry, full of rage and despair, was resolved at least to save his foster-brother's corpse from further insult, and bore it down-stairs in his arms. On the way, he perceived that life was not yet extinct, and resolving to become doubly cautious, he sought in the pocket for the purse that had been well filled for the flight, and by the persuasive argument of gold crowns, obtained egress from the door-keeper of the postern, where Berenger hoped to have emerged in a far different manner. It was a favourable moment, for the main body of the murderers were at that time being poster in the court by the captain of the guard, ready to massacre the gentlemen of the King of Navarre's suite, and he was therefore unmolested by any claimant of the plunders of the apparent corpse he bore on his shoulders. The citizens of Paris who had been engaged in their share of the murders for more than an hour before the tragedy began in the Louvre, frequently beset him on his way to the quay, and but for the timely aid of his English comrades, he would hardly have brought off his foster-brother safely.

The pass with which King Charles had provided Berenger for himself and his followers when his elopement was first planned, enabled Osbert to carry his whole crew safely past all the stations where passports were demanded. He had much wished to procure surgical aid at Rouen, but learning from the boatmen on the river that the like bloody scenes were there being enacted, he had decide on going on to his master's English home as soon as possible, merely trusting to his own skill by the way; and though it was the slightest possible hope, yet the healthy state of the wounds, and the mere fact of life continuing, had given him some faint trust that there might be a partial recovery.

Lord Walwyn repeated his agitated thanks and praises for such devotion to his grandson.

Osbert bower, laid his hand on his heart, and replied—'Monseigneur is good, but what say I? Monsieur le Baron is my foster-brother! Say that, and all is said in one word.'

He was then dismissed, with orders to take some rest, but he obstinately refused all commands in French or English to go to bed, and was found some time after fast asleep.

CHAPTER XIV
SWEET HEART

Ye hae marred a bonnier face than your ain.

DYING WORDS OF THE BONNIE EARL OF MORAY

One room at Hurst Walwyn, though large, wainscoted, and well furnished, bore as pertinaciously the air of a cell as the appearance of Sister Cecily St. John continued like that of a nun. There was a large sunny oriel, in which a thrush sang merrily in a wicker cage; and yet the very central point and leading feature of the room was the altar-like table, covered with rich needlework, with a carved ebony crucifix placed on it, and on the wall above, quaint and stiff, but lovely-featured, delicately tinted pictures of Our Lady in the centre, and of St. Anne and St. Cecilia on either side, with skies behind of most ethereal blue, and robes tenderly trimmed with gold. A little shrine of purple spar, with a crystal front, contained a fragment of sacred bone; a silver shell help holy water, perpetuated from some blessed by Bishop Ridley.

'With velvet bound and broidered o'er,

Her breviary book'

Lay open at 'Sext,' and there, too, lay with its three marks at the Daily Lessons, the Bishop's Bible, and the Common Prayer beside it.

The elder Baron de Ribaumont had never pardoned Cecily his single glance at that table, and had seriously remonstrated with his father-in-law for permitting its existence, quoting Rachel, Achan, and Maachah. Yet he never knew of the hair-cloth smock, the discipline, the cord and sack-cloth that lay stored in the large carved awmry, and were secretly in use on every fast or vigil, not with any notion of merit, but of simple obedience, and with even deeper comprehension and enjoyment of their spiritual significance, of which, in her cloister life, she had comprehended little.

It was not she, however, who knelt with bowed head and clasped hands before the altar-table, the winter sunbeams making the shadows of the ivy sprays dance upon the deep mourning dress and pale cheek. The eyelashes were heavy with tear-drops, and veiled eyes that had not yet attained to the region of calm, like the light quivering of the lips showed that here was the beginning of the course of trial through which serenity might be won, and for ever.

By and by the latch was raise, and Cecily came forward. Lucy rose quickly to her feet, and while giving and returning a fond embrace, asked with her eyes the question that Cecily answered, 'Still in the same lethargy. The only shade of sense that I have seen is an unclosing of the eyes, a wistful look whenever the door opened, and a shiver through all his frame whenever the great bell rings, till my Lord forbade it to be sounded.'

'That frightful bell that the men told us of,' said Lucy, shuddering; 'oh, what a heart that murderess must have had!'

'Hold, Lucy! How should we judge her, who may at this moment be weeping in desolation?'

Lucy looked up astonished. 'Aunt,' she said, 'you have been so long shut up with him that you hardly can have heard all-how she played fast and loose, and for the sake of a mere pageant put off the flight from the time when it would have been secure even until that dreadful eve!'

'I know it,' said Cecily. 'I fear me much that her sin has been great; yet, Lucy, it were better to pray for her than to talk wildly against her.'

'Alas!' murmured Lucy, 'I could bear it and glory in it when it seemed death for the faith's sake, but,' and the tears burst out, 'to find he was only trapped and slain for the sake of a faithless girl—and that he should love her still.'

'She is his wife,' said Cecily. 'Child, from my soul I grieve for you, but none the less must I, if no other will, keep before your eyes that our Berenger's faith belongs solely to her.'

'You—you never would have let me forget it,' said Lucy. 'Indeed I am more maidenly when not alone with you! I know verily that he is loyal, and that my hatred to her is more than is meet. I will—I will pray for her, but I would that you were in your convent still, and that I could hide me there.'

'That were scarce enough,' said Cecily. 'One sister we had who had fled to our house to hide her sorrows for her betrothed had wedded another. She took her sorrows for her vocation, strove to hurry on her vows, and when they were taken, she chafed and fretted under them. It was she who wrote to the commissioner the letter that led to the visitation of our house, and, moreover, she was the only one of us who married.'

'To her own lover?'

'No, to a brewer at Winchester! I say not that you could ever be like poor sister Bridget, but only that the cloister has no charm to still the heart—prayer and duty can do as much without as within.'

'When we deemed her worthy, I was glad of his happiness,' said Lucy, thoughtfully.

'You did, my dear, and I rejoiced. Think now how grievous it must be with her, if she, as I fear she may, yielded her heart to those who told her that to ensnare him was her duty, or if indeed she were as much deceived as he.'

'Then she will soon be comforted,' said Lucy, still with some bitterness in her voice; bitterness of which she herself was perhaps conscious, for suddenly dropping in her knees, she hid her face, and cried. 'Oh, help me to pray for her, Aunt Cecily, and that I may do her wrong no more!'

And Cecily, in her low conventual chant, sang, almost under her breath, the noonday Latin hymn, the words of which, long familiar to Lucy, had never as yet so come home to her.

> 'Quench Thou the fires of heat and strife,
>
> The wasting fever of the heart;
>
> From perils guard our feeble life,
>
> And to our souls Thy help impart.'

Cecily's judgment would have been thought weakly charitable by all the rest of the family. Mr. Adderley had been forwarded by Sir Francis Walsingham like a bale of goods, and arriving in a mood of such self-reproach as would be deemed abject, by persons used to the modern relations between noblemen and their chaplains, was exhilarated by the unlooked-for comfort of finding his young charge at least living, and in his grandfather's house. From his narrative, Walsingham's letter, and Osbert's account, Lord Walwyn saw no reason to doubt that the Black Ribaumonts had thought that massacre a favourable moment for sweeping the only survivor of the White or elder branch away, and that not only had royalty lent itself to the cruel project, but that as Diane de Ribaumont had failed as a bait, the young espoused wife had herself been employed to draw him into the snare, and secure his presence at the slaughter-house, away from his safe asylum at the Ambassador's or even in the King's garde-robe. It was an unspeakably frightful view to take of the case, yet scarcely worse than the reality of many of the dealings of those with whom the poor young girl had been associated: certainly not worse than the crimes, the suspicion of which was resting on the last dowager Queen of France; and all that could be felt by the sorrowing family, was comfort that at least corruption of mind had either not been part of the game, or had been unsuccessful, and, by all testimony, the victim was still the same innocent boy. This was all their relief, while for days, for weeks, Berenger de Ribaumont lay in a trance or torpor between life and death. Sometimes, as Cecily had said, his eyes turned with a startled wistfulness towards the door, and the sound of a bell seemed to thrill him with a start of agony; but for the most part he neither appeared to see or hear, and a few moans were the only sounds that escaped him. The Queen, in her affection for her old friend, and her strong feeling for the victims of the massacre, sent down the court physician, who turned him about, and elicited sundry heavy groans, but could do no more than enjoin patient waiting on the beneficent powers of nature in early youth. His visit produced one benefit, namely, the strengthening of Cecily St. John's hands against the charms, elixirs, and nostrums with which Lady Thistlewood's friends supplied her,—plasters from the cunning women of Lyme Regis, made of powder of giant's bones, and snakes prayed into stone by St. Aldhelm, pills of live woodlice, and fomentations of living earthworms and spiders. Great was the censure incurred by Lady Walwyn for refusing to let such remedies be tried on HER grandson. And he was so much more her child than his mother's, that Dame Annora durst do no more than maunder.

In this perfect rest, it seemed as if after a time 'the powers of nature' did begin to rally, there were appearances of healing about the wounds, the difference between sleeping and waking became more evident, the eyes lost the painful, half-closed, vacant look, but were either shut or opened with languid recognition. The injuries were such as to exclude him from almost every means of expression, the wound in his mouth made speech impossible, and his right arm was not available for signs. It was only the clearness of his eyes, and their response to what was said, that showed that his mind was recovering tone, and then he seemed only alive to the present, and to perceive nothing but what related to his suffering and its alleviations. The wistfulness that had shown itself at first was gone, and even when he improved enough to establish a language of signs with eye, lip, or left hand, Cecily became convinced that he has little or no memory of recent occurrences, and that finding himself at home among familiar faces, his still dormant perceptions demanded no further explanation.

This blank was the most favourable state for his peace and for his recovery, and it was of long duration, lasting even till he had made so much progress that he could leave his bed, and even speak a few words, though his weakness was much prolonged by the great difficulty with which he could take nourishment. About two winters before, Cecily had successfully nursed him through a severe attack of small-pox, and she thought that he confounded his present state with the former illness, when he had had nearly the same attendants and surroundings as at present; and that his faculties were not yet roused enough to perceive the incongruity.

Once or twice he showed surprise at visits from his mother or Philip, who had then been entirely kept away from him, and about Christmas he brightened so much, and awoke to things about him so much more fully, that Cecily thought the time of recollection could not be much longer deferred. Any noise, however, seemed so painful to him, that the Christmas festivities were held at Combe Manor instead of Hurst Walwyn; only after church, Sir Marmaduke and Lady Thistlewood came in to make him a visit, as he sat in a large easy-chair by his bedroom-fire, resting after having gone through as much of the rites of the day as he was able for, with Mr. Adderlay. The room looked very cheerful with the bright wood-fire on the open hearth, shining on the gay tapestry hangings, and the dark wood of the carved bed. The evergreen-decked window shimmered with sun shine, and even the patient, leaning back among crimson cushions, though his face and head were ghastly enough wherever they were not covered with patches and bandages, still had a pleasant smile with lip and eye to thank his stepfather for his cheery wishes of 'a merry Christmas, at least one better in health.'

'I did not bring the little wenches, Berenger, lest they should weary you,' said his mother.

Berenger looked alarmed, and said with the indistinctness with which he always spoke, 'Have they caught it? Are they marked?'

'No, no, not like you, may boy,' said Sir Marmaduke, sufficiently aware of Berenger's belief to be glad to keep it up, and yet obliged to walk to the window to hide his diversion at the notion of his little girls catching the contagion of sword-gashes and bullet-wounds. Dame Annora prattled on, 'But they have sent you their Christmas gifts by me. Poor children, they have long been busied with them, and I fancy Lucy did half herself. See, this kerchief is hemmed by little Dolly, and here are a pair of bands and cuffs to match, that Nanny and Bessy have been broidering with their choicest stitchery.'

Berenger smile, took, expressed admiration by gesture, and then said in a dreamy, uncertain manner, 'Methought I had some gifts for them;' then looking round the room, his eye fell on a small brass-bound casket which had travelled with him to hold his valuables; he pointed to it with a pleased look, as Sir Marmaduke lifted it and placed it on a chair by his side. The key, a small ornamental brass one, was in his purse, not far off, and Lady Thistlewood was full of exceeding satisfaction at the unpacking not only of foreign gifts, but, as she hoped, of the pearls; Cecily meantime stole quietly in, to watch that her patient was not over-wearied.

He was resuming the use of his right arm, though it was still weak and stiff, and he evidently had an instinct against letting any one deal with that box but himself; he tried himself to unlock it, and though forced to leave this to Sir Marmaduke, still leant over it when opened, as if to prevent his mother's curious glances from penetrating its recesses, and allowed no hands near it but his own. He first brought out a pretty feather fan, saying as he held it to his mother, 'For Nan, I promised it. It was bought at the Halles,' he added, more dreamily.

Then again he dived, and brought out a wax medallion of Our Lady guarded by angels, and made the sign that always brought Cecily to him. He held it up to her with a puzzled smile, saying, 'They thought me a mere Papist for buying it—M. de Teligny, I think it was.'

They had heard how the good and beloved Teligny had been shot down on the roof of his father-in-law's house, by rabid assassins, strangers to his person, when all who knew him had spared him, from love to his gentle nature; and the name gave a strange thrill.

He muttered something about 'Pedlar,—Montpipeau,'—and still continued. Then came a small silver casket, diffusing an odour of attar of roses—he leant back in his chair—and his mother would have taken it from him, supposing him overcome by the scent, but he held it fast and shook his head, saying, 'For Lucy,—but she must give it herself. She gave up any gift for herself for it—she said we needed no love-tokens.' And he closed his eyes. Dame Annora plunged into the unpacking, and brought out a pocket-mirror with enamelled cupids in the corner, addressed to herself; and then came upon Berenger's own.

Again came a fringed pair of gloves among the personal jewellery such as gentlemen were wont to wear, the rings, clasps and brooches he had carried from home. Dame Annora's impatience at last found vent in the exclamation, 'The pearls, son; I do not see the chaplet of pearls.'

'She had them,' answered Berenger, in a matter-of-fact tone, 'to wear at the masque.'

'She——'

Sir Marmaduke's great hand choked, as it were, the query on his wife's lips, unseen by her son, who, as if the words had touched some chord, was more eagerly seeking in the box, and presently drew out a bow of carnation ribbon with a small piece of paper full of pin-holes attached to it. At once he carried it to his lips, kissed it fervently, and then, sinking back in his chair, seemed to be trying to gather up the memory that had prompted the impulse, knitted his brows together, and then suddenly exclaimed, 'Where is she?'

His mother tried the last antecedent. 'Lucy? She shall come and thank you to-morrow.'

He shook his head with a vehement negative, beckoned Cecily impatiently, and said earnestly, 'Is it the contagion? Is she sick? I will go to her.'

Cecily and Sir Marmaduke both replied with a 'No, no!' and were thankful, though in much suspense at the momentary pause, while again he leant back on the cushions, looked steadily at the pin-holes, that formed themselves into the word 'Sweet heart,' then suddenly began to draw up the loose sleeve of his wrapping-gown and unbutton the wristband of his right sleeve. His mother tried to help him, asking if he had hurt or tired his arm. They would have been almost glad to hear that it was so, but he shook her off impatiently, and the next moment had a view of the freshly skinned over, but still wide and gaping gash on his arm. He looked for a brief space, and said, 'It is a sword-cut.'

'Truly it is, lad,' said Sir Marmaduke, 'and a very bad one, happily whole! Is this the first time you have seen it?'

He did not answer, but covered his eyes with his hand, and presently burst out again, 'Then it is no dream? Sir—have I been to France?'

'Yes, my son, you have,' said Sir Marmaduke, gently, and with more tenderness than could have been looked for; 'but what passed there is much better viewed as a dream, and cast behind your back.'

Berenger had, while he spoke, taken up the same little mirror where he had once admired himself; and as he beheld the scar and plaster that disfigured his face, with a fresh start of recollection, muttered over, '"Barbouiller ce chien de visage"'—ay, so he said. I felt the pistol's muzzle touch! Narcisse! Has God had mercy on me? I prayed Him. Ah! "le baiser d'Eustacie"—so he said. I was waiting in the dark. Why did he come instead of her? Oh! father, where is she?'

It was a sore task, but Sir Marmaduke went bravely and bluntly, though far from unkindly, to the point: 'She remains with her friends in France.'

There the youth's look of utter horror and misery shocked and startled them all, and he groaned rather than said, 'Left there! Left to them! What have I done to leave her there?'

'Come, Berenger, this will not serve,' said his mother, trying to rouse and cheer him. 'You should rather be thankful that when you had been so foully ensnared by their wiles, good Osbert brought you off with your life away from those bloody doings. Yes, you may thank Heaven and Osbert, for you are the only one of them living now.'

'Of whom, mother?'

'Of all the poor Protestants that like you were deluded by the pack of murderers over there. What,'—fancying it would exhilarate him to hear of his own escape—'you knew not that the bloody Guise and the Paris cut-throats rose and slew every Huguenot they could lay hands on? Why, did not the false wench put off your foolish runaway project for the very purpose of getting you into the trap on the night of the massacre?'

He looked with a piteous, appealing glance from her to Cecily and Sir Marmaduke, as if in hopes that they would contradict.

'Too true, my lad,' said Sir Marmaduke. 'It is Heaven's good mercy that Osbert carried you out alive. No other Protestant left the palace alive but the King of Navarre and his cousin, who turned renegades.'

'And she is left there?' he repeated.

'Heed her not, my dear boy,' began his mother; 'you are safe, and must forget her ill-faith and——'

Berenger seemed scarcely to hear this speech—he held out his hands as if stunned and dizzied, and only said, or rather indicated, 'Let me lie down.'

His stepfather almost carried him across the room, and laid him on his bed, where he turned away from the light and shut his eyes; but the knot of ribbon and the pin-pricked word was still in his hand, and his mother longed to take away the token of this false love, as she believed it. The great clock struck the hour for her to go. 'Leave him quiet,' said Cecily, gently; 'he can bear no more now. I will send over in the evening to let you know how he fares.'

'But that he should be so set on the little bloodthirsty baggage,' sighed Lady Thistlewood; and then going up to her son, she poured out her explanation of being unable to stay, as her parents were already at the Manor, with no better entertainers than Lucy, Philip, and the children. She thanked him for the gifts, which she would take to them with his love. All this passed by him as though he heard it not, but when leaning down, she kissed his forehead, and at the same time tried to withdraw the knot of ribbon: his fingers closed on it with a grasp like steel, so cold were they, yet so fast.

Sir Masmaduke lingered a few moments behind her, and Berenger opening his eyes, as if to see whether solitude had been achieved, found the kind-hearted knight gazing at him with eyes full of tears. 'Berry, my lad,' he said, 'bear it like a man. I know how hard it is. There's not a woman of them all that an honest, plain Englishman has a chance with, when a smooth-tongued Frenchman comes round her! But a man may live a true and honest life however sore his heart may be, and God Almighty makes it up to him if he faces it out manfully.'

Good Sir Marmaduke in his sympathy had utterly forgotten both Berenger's French blood, and that he was the son of the very smooth-tongued interloper who had robbed his life of its first bloom. Berenger was altogether unequal to do more than murmur, as he held out his hand in response to the kindness, 'You do not know her.'

'Ah! Poor lad.' Sir Marmaduke shook his head and left him to Cecily.

After the first shock, Berenger never rested till he had made Osbert, Mr. Adderley, and Cecily tell him all they knew, and asked by name after those whom he had known best at Paris. Alas! of all those, save such as had been in the Ambassador's house, there was but one account to give. Venerable warrior, noble-hearted youth, devoted pastor, all alike had perished!

This frightful part of the story was altogether new to him. He had been probably the earliest victim in the Louvre, as being the special object of private malice, which had contrived to involve him in the general catastrophe; and his own recollections carried him only to the flitting of lights and ringing of bells, that has made him imagine that an alarm of fire would afford a good opportunity of escape if SHE would but come. A cloaked figure had approached,—he had held out his arms—met that deadly stroke—heard the words hissed in his ear.

He owned that for some time past strange recollections had been flitting though his mind—a perpetual unsatisfied longing for and expectation of his wife, and confused impressions of scenes and people had harassed him perpetually, even when he could not discern between dreams and reality; but knowing that he had been very ill, he had endeavoured to account for everything as delirious fancies, but had become increasingly distressed by their vividness, confusion, and want of outward confirmation. At last these solid tokens and pledges from that time had brought certainty back, and with it the harmony and clearness of his memory: and the strong affection, that even his oblivion had not extinguished, now recurred in all its warmth to its object.

Four months had passed, as he now discovered, since that night when he had hoped to have met Euctacie, and she must be believing him dead. His first measure on the following day when he had been dressed and seated in his chair was to send for his casket, and with his slow stiff arm write thus:—

'Mon Coeur, My own sweetheart,—Hast thou thought me dead, and thyself deserted? Osbert will tell thee all, and why I can scarce write. Trust thyself to him to bring to me. I shall be whole seeing thee. Or if thou canst not come with him, write or send me the least token by him, and I will come and bear thee home so soon as I can put foot in stirrup. Would that I could write all that is in my heart!

'Thy Husband.'

It was all that either head or hand would enable him to say, but he had the fullest confidence in Landry Osbert, who was one of the few who understood him at half a word. He desired Osbert to seek the lady out wherever she might be, whether still at court or in a convent, convey the letter to her if possible, and, if she could by any means escape, obtain from Chateau Leurre such an escort as she could come to England with. If, as was too much to be feared, she was under too close restraint, Osbert should send intelligence home, as he could readily do through the Ambassador's household, and Berenger trusted by that time to be able to take measures for claiming her in person.

Osbert readily undertook everything, but supplies for his journey were needed, and there was an absolute commotion in the house when it was known that Berenger had been writing to his faithless spouse, and wishing to send for her. Lord Walwyn came up to visit his grandson, and explain to him with much pity and consideration that he considered such a step as vain, and only likely to lead to further insult. Berenger's respect forced him to listen without interruption, and though he panted to answer, it was a matter of much difficulty, for the old lord was becoming deaf, and could not catch the indistinct, agitated words—

'My Lord, she is innocent as day.'

'Ah! Anan, boy.'

'I pledge my life on her love and innocence.'

'Love! Yes, my poor boy; but if she be unworthy?—Eh? Cecily, what says he?'

'He is sure of her innocence, sir?'

'That is of course. But, my dear lad, you will soon learn that even a gentle, good woman who has a conscience-keeper is too apt to think her very sense of right ought to be sacrificed to what she calls her religion.— What is it, what is he telling you, Cecily?'

'She was ready to be one of us,' Berenger said, with a great effort to make it clear.

'Ah, a further snare. Poor child! The very softest of them become the worst deceivers, and the kindred who have had the charge of her all their life could no doubt bend her will.'

'Sir,' said Berenger, finding argument impossible, 'if you will but let me dispatch Osbert, her answer will prove to you what she is.'

'There is something in that,' said Lord Walwyn, when he had heard it repeated by Cecily. 'It is, of course, needful that both she and her relations should be aware of Berenger's life, and I trow nothing but the reply will convince him.'

'Convince him!' muttered Berenger. 'Oh that I could make him understand. What a wretch I am to have no voice to defend her!'

'What?' said the old lord again.

'Only that I could speak, sir; you should know why it is sacrilege to doubt her.'

'Ah! well, we will not wound you, my son, while talk is vain. You shall have the means of sending your groom, if thus you will set your mind at rest, though I had rather have trusted to Walsingham's dealing. I will myself give him a letter to Sir Francis, to forward him on his way; and should the young lady prove willing to hold to her contract and come to you here, I will pray him to do everything to aid her that may be consistent with his duty in his post.'

This was a great and wonderful concession for Lord Walwyn, and Berenger was forced to be contented with it, though it galled him terribly to have Eustacie distrusted, and be unable to make his vindication even heard or understood, as well as to be forced to leave her rescue, and even his own explanation to her, to a mere servant.

This revival of his memory had not at all conduced to his progress in recovery. His brain was in no state for excitement or agitation, and pain and confusion were the consequence, and were counteracted, after the practice of the time, by profuse bleedings, which prolonged his weakness. The splintered state of the jaw and roof of the moth likewise produced effects that made him suffer severely, and deprived him at times even of the small power of speech that he usually possessed; and though he had set his heart upon being able to start for Paris so soon as Osbert's answer should arrive, each little imprudence he committed, in order to convince himself of his progress, threw him back so seriously, that he was barely able to walk down-stairs to the hall, and sit watching—watching, so that it was piteous to see him—the gates of the courtyard, but the time that, on a cold March day, a booted and spurred courier (not Osbert) entered by them.

He sprang up, and faster than he had yet attempted to move, met the man in the hall, and demanded the packet. It was a large one, done up in canvas, and addressed to the Right Honourable and Worshipful Sir William,

Baron Walwyn of Hurst Walwyn, and he had further to endure the delay of carrying it to his grandfather's library, which he entered with far less delay and ceremony than was his wont. 'Sit down, Berenger,' said the old man, while addressing himself to the fastenings; and the permission was needed, for he could hardly have stood another minute. The covering contained a letter to Lord Walwyn himself, and a packet addressed to the Baron de Ribaumont which his trembling fingers could scarcely succeed in cutting and tearing open.

How shall it be told what the contents of the packet were? Lord Walwyn reading on with much concern, but little surprise, was nevertheless startled by the fierce shout with which Berenger broke out:

'A lie! A lie forged in hell!' And then seizing the parchment, was about to rend it with all the force of passion, when his grandfather, seizing his hand, said, in his calm, authoritative voice, 'Patience, my poor son.'

'How, how should I have patience when they send me such poisoned lies as these of my wife, and she is in the power of the villains? Grandfather, I must go instantly——'

'Let me know what you have heard,' said Lord Walwyn, holding him feebly indeed, but with all the impressive power and gravity of his years.

'Falsehoods,' said Berenger, pushing the whole mass of papers over to him, and then hiding his head between his arms on the table.

Lord Walwyn finished his own letter first. Walsingham wrote with much kind compassion, but quite decisively. He had no doubt that the Ribaumont family had acted as one wheel in the great plot that had destroyed all the heads of Protestant families and swept away among others, as they had hoped, the only scion of the rival house. The old Chevalier de Ribaumont had, he said, begun by expressing sorrow for the mischance that had exposed his brave young cousin to be lost in the general catastrophe, and he had professed proportionate satisfaction on hearing of the young man's safety. But the Ambassador believed him to have been privy to his son's designs; and whether Mdlle. de Nid de Merle herself had been a willing agent or not, she certainly had remained in the hands of the family. The decree annulling the marriage had been published, the lady was in a convent in Anjou, and Narcisse de Ribaumont had just been permitted to assume the title of Marquis de Nid de Merle, and was gone into Anjou to espouse her. Sir Francis added a message of commiseration for the young Baron, but could not help congratulating his old friend on having his grandson safe and free from these inconvenient ties.

Berenger's own packet contained, in the first place, a copy of the cassation of the marriage, on the ground of its having been contracted when the parties were of too tender age to give their legal consent, and its having been unsatisfied since they had reached ecclesiastical years for lawful contraction of wedlock.

The second was one of the old Chevalier's polite productions. He was perfectly able to ignore Berenger's revocation of his application for the separation, since the first letter had remained unanswered, and the King's peremptory commands had prevented Berenger from taking any open measures after his return from Montpipeau. Thus the old gentleman, after expressing due rejoicing at his dear young cousin's recovery, and regret at the unfortunate mischance that had led to his confounded with the many suspected Huguenots, proceeded as if matters stood exactly as they had been before the pall-mall party, and as if the decree that he enclosed were obtained in accordance with the young Baron's intentions. He had caused it to be duly registered, and both parties were at liberty to enter upon other contracts of matrimony. The further arrangements which Berenger had undertaken to sell his lands in Normandy, and his claim on the ancestral castle in Picardy, should be carried out, and deeds sent for his signature so soon as he should be of age. In the meantime, the Chevalier courteously imparted to his fair cousin the marriage of his daughter, Mademoiselle Diane de Ribaumont with M. le Comte de Selinville, which had taken place on the last St. Martin's day, and of his niece, Mademoiselle Eustacie de Ribaumont de Nid de Merle with his son, who had received permission to take her father's title of Marquis de Nid de Merle. The wedding was to take place at Bellaise before the end of the Cardinal, and would be concluded before this letter came to hand.

Lastly, there was an ill written and spelt letter, running somewhat thus—

'Monseigneur,—Your faithful servant hopes that Monsieur le Baron will forgive him for not returning, since I have been assured by good priests that it is not possible to save my soul in a country of heretics. I have done everything as Monsieur commanded, I have gone down into Anjou, and have had the honour to see the young lady to whom Monsieur le Baron charged me with a commission, and I delivered to her his letter, whereupon the lady replied that she thanked M. le Baron for the honour he had done her, but that being on the point of marriage to M. le Marquis de Nid de Merle, she did not deem it fitting to write to him, nor had she any tokens to send him, save what he had received on the St. Barthelemy midnight; they might further his suit elsewhere. These, Monsieur, were her words, and she laughed as she said them, so gaily that I thought her fairer than ever. I have prevailed with her to take me into her service as intendant of the Chateau de Nid de Merle, knowing as she does my fidelity to the name of Ribaumont. And so, trusting Monseigneur will pardon me for what I do solely for the good of my soul, I will ever pray for his welfare, and remain,

'His faithful menial and valet,

'LANDRY OSBERT.'

The result was only what Lord Walwyn had anticipated, but he was nevertheless shocked at the crushing weight of the blow. His heart was full of compassion for the youth so cruelly treated in these his first years of life, and as much torn in his affections as mangled in person. After a pause, while he gathered up the sense of the letters, he laid his hand kindly on his grandson's arm, and said, 'This is a woeful budget, my poor son; we will do our best to help you to bear it.'

'The only way to bear it,' said Berenger, lifting up his face, 'is for me to take horse and make for Anjou instantly. She will hold out bravely, and I may yet save her.'

'Madness,' said his grandfather; 'you have then not read your fellow's letter?'

'I read no letter from fellow of mine. Yonder is a vile forgery. Narcisse's own, most likely. No one else would have so profaned her as to put such words into her mouth! My dear faithful foster-brother—have they murdered him?'

'Can you point to any proof that it is forged?' said Lord Walwyn, aware that handwriting was too difficult an art, and far too crabbed, among persons of Osbert's class, for there to be any individuality of penmanship.

'It is all forged,' said Berenger. 'It is as false that she could frame such a message as that poor Osbert would leave me.'

'These priests have much power over the conscience,' began Lord Walwyn; but Berenger, interrupting his grandfather for the first time in his life, cried, 'No priest could change her whole nature. Oh! my wife! my darling! what may they not be inflicting on her now! Sir, I must go. She may be saved! The deadly sin may be prevented!'

'This is mere raving, Berenger,' said Lord Walwyn, not catching half what he said, and understanding little more than his resolution to hasten in quest of the lady. 'You, who have not mounted a horse, nor walked across the pleasance yet!'

'My limbs should serve me to rescue her, or they are worth nothing to me.'

Lord Walwyn would have argued that he need not regret his incapacity to move, since it was no doubt already too late, but Berenger burst forth— 'She will resist; she will resist to the utmost, even if she deems me dead.

Tortures will not shake her when she knows I live. I must prepare.' And he started to his feet.

'Grandson,' said Lord Walwyn, laying a hand on his arm, 'listen to me. You are in not state to judge for yourself. I therefore command you to desist from this mad purpose.'

He spoke gravely, but Berenger was disobedient for the first time. 'My Lord,' he said, 'you are but my grandfather. She is my wife. My duty is to her.'

He had plucked his sleeve away and was gone, before Lord Walwyn had been able to reason with him that there was no wife in the case, a conclusion at which the old statesman would not have arrived had he known of the ceremony at Montpipeau, and all that had there passed; but not only did Berenger deem himself bound to respect the King's secret, but conversation was so difficult to him that he had told very little of his adventures, and less to Lord Walwyn than any one else. In effect, his grandfather considered this resolution of going to France as mere frenzy, and so it almost was, not only on the score of health and danger, but because as a ward, he was still so entirely under subjection, that his journey could have been hindered by absolutely forcible detention; and to this Lord Walwyn intended to resort, unless the poor youth either came to a more rational mind, or became absolutely unable to travel.

The last—as he had apprehended—came to pass only too surely. The very attempt to argue and to defend Eustacie was too much for the injured head; and long before night Berenger full believed himself on the journey, acted over its incidents, and struggled wildly with difficulties, all the time lying on his bed, with the old servants holding him down, and Cecily listening tearfully to his ravings.

For weeks longer he was to lie there in greater danger than ever. He only seemed soothed into quiet when Cecily chanted those old Latin hymns of her Benedictine rule, and then—when he could speak at all—he showed himself to be in imagination praying in Eustacie's convent chapel, sure to speak to her when the service should be over.

CHAPTER XV
NOTRE-DAME DE BELLAISE*

There came a man by middle day, He spied his sport and went away, And brought the king that very night, And brake my bower and slew my knight. The Border Widow's Lament

*[footnote: Bellaise is not meant for a type of all nunneries, but of the condition to which many of the lesser ones had come before the general reaction and purification of the seventeenth century.]

That same Latin hymn which Cecily St. John daily chanted in her own chamber was due from the choir of Cistercian sisters in the chapel of the Convent of Our Lady at Bellaise, in the Bocage of Anjou; but there was a convenient practice of lumping together the entire night and forenoon hours at nine o'clock in the morning, and all the evening ones at Compline, so that the sisters might have undisturbed sleep at night and entertainment by day. Bellaise was a very comfortable little nunnery, which only received richly dowered inmates, and was therefore able to maintain them in much ease, though without giving occasion to a breath of scandal. Founded by a daughter of the first Angevin Ribaumont, it had become a sort of appanage for the superfluous daughters of the house, and nothing would more have amazed its present head, Eustacie Barbe de Ribaumont,—conventually known as La Mere Marie Seraphine de St.-Louis, and to the world as Madame de Bellaise,—than to be accused of not fulfilling the intentions of the Bienheureuse Barbe, the foundress, or of her patron St. Bernard.

Madame de Bellaise was a fine-looking woman of forty, in a high state of preservation, owing to the healthy life she had led. Her eyes were of brilliant, beautiful black her complexion had a glow, her hair—for she wore it visibly—formed crisp rolls of jetty ringlets on her temples, almost hiding her close white cap. The heavy thick veil was tucked back beneath the furred purple silk hood that fastened under her chin. The white robes of her order were not of serge, but of the finest cloth, and were almost hidden by a short purple cloak with sleeves, likewise lined and edged with fur, and fastened on the bosom with a gold brooch. Her fingers, bearing more rings than the signet of her house, were concealed in embroidered gauntlets of Spanish leather. One of them held an ivory-handled riding-rod, the other the reins of the well-fed jennet, on which the lady, on a fine afternoon, late in the Carnival, was cantering home through the lanes of the Bocage, after a successful morning's hawking among the wheat-ears. She was attended by a pair of sisters, arrayed somewhat in the same style, and by a pair of mounted grooms, the falconer with his charge having gone home by a footway.

The sound of horses' feet approaching made her look towards a long lane that came down at right angles to that along which she was riding, and slacken her pace before coming to its opening. And as she arrived at the intersection, she beheld advancing, mounted on a little rough pony, the spare figure of her brother the Chevalier, in his home suit, so greasy and frayed, that only his plumed hat (and a rusty plume it was) and the old sword at his side showed his high degree.

He waved his hand to her as a sign to halt, and rode quickly up, scarcely giving time for a greeting ere he said, 'Sister the little one is not out with you.'

'No, truly, the little mad thing, she is stricter and more head-strong than ever was her preceptress. Poor Monique! I had hoped that we should be at rest when that *cass-tete* had carried off her scruples to Ste.-Claire, at Lucon, but here is this little droll far beyond her, without being even a nun!'

'Assuredly not. The business must be concluded at once. She must be married before Lent.'

'That will scarce be—in her present frame.'

'It must be. Listen, sister. Here is this miserable alive!'

'Her spouse!'

'Folly about her spouse! The decree from Rome has annulled the foolish mummery of her infancy. It came a week after the Protestant conspiracy, and was registered when the Norman peasants at Chateau Leurre showed contumacy. It was well; for, behold, our gallant is among his English friends, recovering, and even writing a billet. Anon he will be upon our hands in person. By the best fortune, Gillot fell in with his messenger this morning, prowling about on his way to the convent, and brought him to me to be examined. I laid him fat in ward, and sent Gillot off to ride day and night to bring my son down to secure the girl at once.'

'You will never obtain her consent. She is distractedly in love with his memory! Let her guess at his life, and——'

'Precisely. Therefore must we be speedy. All Paris knows it by this time, for the fellow went straight to the English Ambassador; and I trust my son has been wise enough to set off already; for should we wait till after Lent, Monsieur le Baron himself might be upon us.'

'Poor child! You men little heed how you make a woman suffer.'

'How, Reverend Mother! you pleading for a heretic marriage, that would give our rights to a Huguenot—what say I?—an English renegade!'

'I plead not, brother. The injustice towards you must be repaired; but I have a certain love for my niece, and I fear she will be heartbroken when she learns the truth, the poor child.'

'Bah! The Abbess should rejoice in thus saving her soul! How if her heretic treated Bellaise like the convents of England?'

'No threats, brother. As a daughter of Ribaumont and a mother of the Church will I stand by you,' said the Abbess with dignity.

'And now tell me how it has been with the child. I have not seen her since we agreed that the request did but aggravate her. You said her health was better since her nurse had been so often with her, and that she had ceased from her austerities.'

'Not entirely; for when first she came, in her transports of despair and grief on finding Soeur Monique removed, she extorted from Father Bonami a sort of hope that she might yet save her husband's, I mean the Baron's soul. Then, truly, it was a frenzy of fasts and prayers. Father Bonami has made his profit, and so have the fathers of Chollet—all her money has gone in masses, and in alms to purchase the prayers of the poor, and she herself fasting on bread and water, kneeling barefooted in the chapel till she was transfixed with cold. No *chaufferette*, not she! Obstinate to the last degree! Tell her she would die—it was the best news one could bring; all her desire, to be in a more rigid house with Soeur Monique at Lucon. At length, Mere Perrine and Veronique found her actually fainting and powerless with cold on the chapel-floor; and since that time she has been more reasonable. There are prayers as much as ever; but the fancy to kill herself with fasting has passed. She begins to recover her looks, nay, sometimes I have thought she had an air of hope in her eyes and lips; but what know I? I have much to occupy me, and she persists in shutting herself up with her woman.'

'You have not allowed her any communication from without?'

'Mere Perrine has come and gone freely; but she is nothing. No, the child could have no correspondence. She did, indeed, write a letter to the Queen, as you know, brother, six weeks ago; but that has never been answered, nor could any letters have harmed you, since it is only now that this young man is known to be living.'

'You are right, sister. No harm can have been done. All will go well. The child must be wearied with her frenzy of grief and devotion! She will catch gladly at an excuse for change. A scene or two, and she will readily yield!'

'It is true,' said the Abbess, thoughtfully, 'that she has walked and ridden out lately. She has asked questions about her Chateaux, and their garrisons. I have heard nothing of the stricter convent for many weeks; but still, brother, you must go warily to work.'

'And you, sister, must show no relenting. Let her not fancy she can work upon you.'

By this time the brother and sister were at the gateway of the convent; a lay sister presided there, but there was no *cloture*, as the strict seclusion of a nunnery was called, and the Chevalier rode into the cloistered quadrangle as naturally as if he had been entering a secular Chateau, dismounted at the porch of the hall, and followed Madame de Bellaise to the parlour, while she dispatched a request that her niece would attend her there.

The parlour had no grating to divide it, but was merely a large room furnished with tapestry, carved chests, chairs, and cushions, much like other reception-rooms. A large, cheerful wood-fire blazed upon the hearth, and there was a certain air of preparation, as indeed an ecclesiastical dignity from Saumur was expected to sup with the ladies that evening.

After some interval, spent by the Chevalier in warming himself, a low voice at the door was heard, saying, '*Deus vobiscum.*' The Abbess answered, '*Et cum spiritu tuo*;' and on this monastic substitute for a knock and 'come in,' there appeared a figure draped and veiled from head to foot in heavy black, so as to look almost like a sable moving cone. She made an obeisance as she entered, saying, 'You commanded my presence, Madame?'

'Your uncle would speak to you, daughter, on affairs of moment.'

'At his service. I, too, would speak to him.'

'First, then, my dear friend,' said the Chevalier, 'let me see you. That face must not be muffled any longer from those who love you.'

She made no movement of obedience, until her aunt peremptorily bade her turn back her veil. She did so, and disclosed the little face, so well known to her uncle, but less childish in its form, and the dark eyes sparkling, though at once softer and more resolute.

'Ah! my fair niece,' said the Chevalier, 'this is no visage to be hidden! I am glad to see it re-embellished, and it will be lovelier than ever when you have cast off this disguised.'

'That will never be,' said Eustacie.

'Ah! we know better! My daughter is sending down a counterpart of her own wedding-dress for your bride of the *Mardi-Gras*.'

'And who may that bride be?' said Eustacie, endeavouring to speak as though it were nothing to her.

'Nay, *ma petite*! it is too long to play the ignorant when the bridegroom is on his way from Paris.'

'Madame,' said Eustacie, turning to her aunt, 'you cannot suffer this scandal. The meanest peasant may weep her first year of widowhood in peace.'

'Listen, child. There are weighty reasons. The Duke of Anjou is a candidate for the throne of Poland, and my son is to accompany him thither. He must go as Marquis de Nid de Merle, in full possession of your estates.'

'Let him take them,' began Eustacie, 'who first commits a cowardly murder, and then forces himself on the widow he has made?'

'Folly, child, folly,' said the Chevalier, who supposed her ignorant of the circumstances of her husband's assassination; and the Abbess, who was really ignorant, exclaimed—'*Fid donc* niece; you know not what you say.'

'I know, Madame—I know from an eye-witness,' said Eustacie, firmly. 'I know the brutal words that embittered my husband's death; and were there no other cause, they would render wedlock with him who spoke them sacrilege.' Resolutely and steadily did the young wife speak, looking at them with the dry fixed eye to which tears had been denied ever since that eventful night.'

'Poor child,' said the Chevalier to his sister. 'She is under the delusion still. Husband! There is none in the case.' Then waving his hand as Eustacie's face grew crimson, and her eyes flashed indignation, while her lips parted, 'It was her own folly that rendered it needful to put an end to the boy's presumption. Had she been less willful and more obedient, instead of turning the poor lad's head by playing at madame, we could have let him return to his island fogs; but when SHE encouraged him in contemplating the carrying her away, and alienating her and her lands from the true faith, there was but one remedy—to let him perish with the rest. My son is willing to forgive her childish pleasure in a boy's passing homage, and has obtained the King's sanction to an immediate marriage.'

'Which, to spare you, my dear,' added the aunt, 'shall take place in our chapel.'

'It shall never take place anywhere,' said Eustacie, quietly, though with a quiver in her voice; 'no priest will wed me when he has heard me.'

'The dispensation will overcome all scruples,' said the Abbess. 'Hear me, niece. I am sorry for you, but it is best that you should know at once that there is nothing in heaven or earth to aid you in resisting your duty.'

Eustacie made no answer, but there was a strange half-smile on her lip, and a light in her eye which gave her an air not so much of entreaty as of defiance. She glanced from one to the other, as if considering, but then slightly shook her head. 'What does she mean?' asked the Chevalier and the Abbess one of another, as, with a dignified gesture, she moved to leave the room.

'Follow her. Convince her that she has no hope,' said the uncle; and the Abbess, moving faster than her wont, came up with her at the archway whence one corridor led to the chapel, another to her own apartments. Her veil was down again, but her aunt roughly withdrew it, saying, 'Look at me, Eustacie. I come to warn you that you need not look to tamper with the sisters. Not one will aid you in your headstrong folly. If you cast not off ere supper-time this mockery of mourning, you shall taste of that discipline you used to sigh for. We have borne with your fancy long enough—you, who are no more a widow than I—nor wife.'

'Wife and widow am I in the sight of Him who will protect me,' said Eustacie, standing her ground.

'Insolent! Why, did I not excuse this as a childish delusion, should I not spurn one who durst love—what say I—not a heretic merely, but the foe of her father's house?'

'He!' cried Eustacie; 'what had he ever done?'

'He inherited the blood of the traitor Baron,' returned her aunt. 'Ever have that recreant line injured us! My nephew's sword avenged the wrongs of many generations.'

'Then,' said Eustacie, looking at her with a steady, fixed look of inquire, 'you, Madame l'Abbesse, would have neither mercy nor pity for the most innocent offspring of the elder line?'

'Girl, what folly is this to talk to me of innocence. That is not the question. The question is—obey willingly as my dear daughter, or compulsion must be used.'

'My question is answered,' said Eustacie, on her side. 'I see that there is neither pity nor hope from you.'

And with another obeisance, she turned to ascend the stairs. Madame paced back to her brother.

'What,' he said; 'you have not yet dealt with her?'

'No, brother, I never saw a like mood. She seems neither to fear nor to struggle. I knew she was too true a Ribaumont for weak tears and entreaties; but, fiery little being as once she was, I looked to see her force spend itself in passion, and that then the victory would have been easy; but no, she ever looks as if she had some inward resource—some security—and therefore could be calm. I should deem it some Huguenot fanaticism, but she is a very saint as to the prayers of the Church, the very torment of our lives.'

'Could she escape?' exclaimed the Chevalier, who had been considering while his sister was speaking.

'Impossible! Besides, where could she go? But the gates shall be closed. I will warn the portress to let none pass out without my permission.'

'The Chevalier took a turn up and down the room; then exclaimed, 'It was very ill-advised to let her women have access to her! Let us have Veronique summoned instantly.'

At that moment, however, the ponderous carriage of Monseigneur, with out-riders, both lay and clerical, came trampling up to the archway, and the Abbess hurried off to her own apartment to divest herself of her hunting-gear ere she received her guest; and the orders to one of the nuns to keep a watch on her niece were oddly mixed with those to the cook, confectioner, and butterer.

La Mere Marie Saraphine was not a cruel or an unkind woman. She had been very fond of her pretty little niece in her childhood, but had deeply resented the arrangement which had removed her from her own superintendence to that of the Englishwoman, besides the uniting to the young Baron one whom she deemed the absolute right of Narcisse. She had received Eustacie on her first return with great joy, and had always treated her with much indulgence, and when the drooping, broken-hearted girl came back once more to the shelter of her convent, the good-humoured Abbess only wished to make her happy again.

But Eustacie's misery was far beyond the ken of her aunt, and the jovial turn of these consolations did but deepen her agony. To be congratulated on her release from the heretic, assured of future happiness with her cousin, and, above all, to hear Berenger abused with all the bitterness of rival family and rival religion, tore up the lacerated spirit. Ill, dejected, and broken down, too subdued to fire up in defence, and only longing for the power of indulging in silent grief, Eustacie had shrunk from her, and wrapped herself up in the ceaseless round of masses and prayers, in which she was allowed to perceive a glimmering of hope for her husband's soul. The Abbess, ever busy with affairs of her convent or matters of pleasure, soon relinquished the vain attempt to console where she could not sympathize, trusted that the fever of devotion would wear itself out, and left her niece to herself. Of the seven nuns, two were decorously gay, like their Mother Abbess; one was a prodigious worker of tapestry, two were unrivalled save by one another as confectioners. Eustacie had been their pet in her younger days; now she was out of their reach, they tried in turn to comfort her; and when she would not be comforted, they, too, felt aggrieved by the presence of one whose austerity reproached their own laxity; they resented her disappointment at Soeur Monique's having been transferred to Lucon, and they, too, left her to the only persons whose presence she had ever seemed to relish,—namely, her maid Veronique, and Veronique's mother, her old nurse Perrine, wife of a farmer about two miles off. The woman had been Eustacie's foster-mother, and continued to exert over her much of the caressing care of a nurse.

After parting with her aunt, Eustacie for a moment looked towards the chapel, then, clasping her hands, murmured to herself, 'No! no! speed is my best hope;' and at once mounted the stairs, and entered a room, where the large stone crucifix, a waxen Madonna, and the holy water font gave a cell-like aspect to the room; and a straw pallet covered with sackcloth was on the floor, a richly curtained couch driven into the rear, as unused.

She knelt for a moment before the Madonna; 'Ave Maria, be with me and mine. Oh! blessed Lady, thou hadst to fly with thy Holy One from cruel men. Have thou pity on the fatherless!'

Then going to the door, she clapped her hands; and, as Veronique entered, she bade her shut and bolt the door, and at the same moment began in nervous haste to throw off her veil and unfasten her dress.

'Make haste, Veronique. A dress of thine——'

'All is known, then!' cried Veronique, throwing up her arms.

'No, but he is coming—Narcisse—to marry me at once—*Marde-Gras*——'

'*Et quoi?* Madame has but to speak the word, and it is impossible.'

'And after what my aunt has said, I would die a thousand deaths ere speaking that word. I asked her, Veronique! She would have vengeance on the most guiltless—the most guiltless—do you hear?—of the Norman house. Never, never shall she have the chance! Come, thy striped petticoat!'

'But, oh! what will Madame do? Where would she go? Oh! it is impossible.'

'First to thy father's. Yes, I know. He has once called it a madness to think of rallying my vassals to protect their lady. That was when he heard of it from thee—thou faint of heart—and thy mother. I shall speak to him in person now. Make haste, I tell thee, girl. I must be out of this place before I am watched or guarded,' she added breathlessly. 'I feel as if each moment I lost might have death upon it;' and she looked about her like a startled deer.

'To my father's. Ah! there it is not so ill! But the twilights, the length of way,' sobbed Veronique, in grievous distress and perplexity. 'Oh! Madame, I cannot see you go. The Mother Abbess is good. She must have pity. Oh, trust to her!'

'Trust! Did I not trust to my cousin Diane? Never! Nothing will kill me but remaining in their hands.'

Veronique argued and implored in vain. Ever since, in the height of those vehement austerities by which the bereaved and shattered sufferer strove to appease her wretchedness by the utmost endeavour to save her husband's soul, the old foster-mother had made known to her that she might thus sacrifice another than herself. Eustacie's elastic heart had begun to revive, with all its dauntless strength of will. What to her women seemed only a fear, was to her only a hope.

Frank and confiding as was her nature, however, the cruel deceptions already practiced on her by her own kindred, together with the harsh words with which the Abbess spoke of Berenger, had made her aware that no comfort must be looked for in that quarter. It was, after all, perhaps her won instinct, and the aunt's want of sympathy, that withheld her from seeking counsel of any save Perrine and her daughter, at any rate till she could communicate with the kind young Queen. To her, then, Eustacie had written, entreating that a royal mandate would recall her in time to bestow herself in some trustworthy hands, or even in her husband's won Norman castle, where his heir would be both safe and welcome. But time has passed—the whole space that she had reckoned as needful for the going and coming of her messenger—allowing for all the obstructions of winter roads—nay, he had come back; she knew letter was delivered, but answer there was none. It might yet come—perhaps a royal carriage and escort— and day after day had she waited and hoped, only tardily admitting the conviction that Elisabeth of Austria was as powerless as Eustacie de Ribaumont, and meantime revolving and proposing many a scheme that could only have entered the brain of a brave-spirited child as she was. To appeal to her vassals, garrison with them a ruinous old tower in the woods, and thence send for aid to the Montmorencys; to ride to Saumur, and claim the protection of the governor of the province; to make her way to the coast and sail for England; to start for Paris, and throw herself in person on the Queen's protection,—all had occurred to her, and been discussed with her two *confidantes*; but the hope of the Queen's interference, together with the exceeding difficulty of acting, had hitherto prevented her from taking any steps, since no suspicion had arisen in the minds of those about her. Veronique, caring infinitely more for her mistress's health and well-being than for the object of Eustacie's anxieties, had always secretly trusted that delay would last till action was impossible, and that the discovery would be made, only without her being accused of treason. In the present stress of danger, she could but lament and entreat, for Eustacie's resolution bore her down; and besides, as she said to herself, her Lady was after all going to her foster-father and mother, who would make her hear reason, and bring her back at once, and then there would be no anger nor disgrace incurred. The dark muddy length of walk would be the worst of it—and, bah! most likely Madame would be convinced by it, and return of her own accord.

So Veronique, though not intermitting her protests, adjusted her own dress upon her mistress,—short striped petticoat, black bodice, winged turban-like white cap, and a great muffling gray cloth cloak and hook over the head and shoulders—the costume in which Veronique was wont to run to her home in the twilight on various errands, chiefly to carry her mistress's linen; for starching Eustacie's plain bands and cuffs was Mere Perrine's special pride. The wonted bundle, therefore, now contained a few garments, and the money and jewels, especially the chaplet of pearls, which Eustacie regarded as a trust.

Sobbing, and still protesting, Veronique, however, engaged that if her Lady succeeded in safely crossing the kitchen in the twilight, and in leaving the convent, she would keep the secret of her escape as long as possible, reporting her refusal to appear at supper, and making such excuses as might very probably prevent the discovery of her flight till next day.

'And then,' said Eustacie, 'I will send for thee, either to Saumur or to the old tower! Adieu, dear Veronique, do not be frightened. Thou dost not know how glad I am that the time for doing something is come! To-morrow!'

'To-morrow!' thought Veronique, as she shut the door; 'before that you will be back here again, my poor little Lady, trembling, weeping, in dire need of being comforted. But I will make up a good fire, and shake out the bed. I'll let her have no more of that villainous palliasse. No, no, let her try her own way, and repent of it; then, when this matter is over, she will turn her mind to Chevalier Narcisse, and there will be no more languishing in this miserable hole.'

CHAPTER XVI
THE HEARTHS AND THICKETS OF
THE BOCAGE.

I winna spare for his tender age,   Nor yet for his hie kin;

But soon as ever he born is,

He shall mount the gallow's pin.—Fause Foodrage.

Dusk was closing in, but lamps had not yet been lighted, when with a trembling, yet almost a bounding heart, Eustacie stole down the stone staircase, leading to a back-door—an utterly uncanonical appendage to a nunnery, but one much used among the domestic establishment of Bellaise.

A gleam of red light spread across the passage from the half-open kitchen door, whence issued the savoury steam of the supper preparing for Monseigneur. Eustacie had just cautiously traversed it, when the voice of the presiding lay-sister called out, 'Veronique, is that you?'

'Sister!' returned Eustacie, with as much of the Angevin twang as she could assume.

'Where are you going?'

'To the Orchard Farm with this linen.'

'Ah! it must be. But there are strict orders come from Madame about nobody going out unreported, and you may chance to find the door locked if you do not come back in good time. Oh! and I had well-night forgot; tell your mother to be here early to-morrow, Madame would speak with her.'

Eustacie assented, half stifled by the great throb of her fluttering heart at the sense that she had indeed seized the last moment. Forth then she stepped. How dark, waste, and lonely the open field looked! But her heart did not fail her; she could only feel that a captivity was over, and the most vague and terrible of her anxieties soothed, as she made her way into one of the long shady lanes of the Bocage. It was nearly dark, and very muddy, but she had all the familiarity of a native with the way, and the farm, where she had trotted about in her infancy like a peasant's child, always seemed like home to her. It had been a prime treat to visit it during her time of education at the convent, and there was an association of pleasure in treading the path that seemed to bear her up, and give her enjoyment in the mere adventure and feeling of escape and liberty. She had no fear of the dark, nor of the distant barking of dogs, but the mire was deep, and it was plodding work in those heavy *sabots*, up the lane that led from the convent; and the poor child was sorely weary long before she came to the top of the low hill that she used scarcely to know to be rising round at all. The stars had come out; and as she sat for a few moments to rest on a large stone, she saw the lights of the cottage fires in the village below, and looking round could also see the many gleams in the convent windows, the read fire-light in her own room among them. She shivered a little as she thought of its glowing comfort, but turned her back resolutely, tightened her cloak over her head, looked up to a glimmer in the watch-tower of her own castle far above her on the hill and closed against her; and then smiled to herself with hope at the sparkle of a window in a lonely farmhouse among the fields.

With fresh vigour she rose, and found her way through lane and field-path to the paddock where she had so often played. Here a couple of huge dogs dashed forward with an explosion of barks, dying away into low growls as she spoke to them by their names, and called aloud on 'Blaise!' and 'Mere Perrine!' The cottage door was opened, the light streamed forth, and a man's head in a broad had appeared. 'Veronique, girl, is this an hour to be gadding abroad?'

'Blaise, do you not know me?'

'It is our Lady. Ah!'

The next moment the wanderer was seated in the ample wooden chair of the head of the family, the farmer and his two stout sons standing before her as their liege Lady, and Mere Perrine hanging over her, in great anxiety, not wholly dispelled by her low girlish laugh, partly of exultation at her successful evasion, partly of amusement at their wonder, and partly, too, because it was so natural to her to enjoy herself at that hearth that she could not help it. A savoury mess from the great caldron that was for ever stewing over the fire was at once fished out for her, before she was allowed to explain herself; and as she ate with the carved spoon and from the earthenware crock that had been called Mademoiselle's ever since her baby-days, Perrine chafed and warmed her feet, fondled her, and assured her, as if she were still their spoiled child, that they would do all she wished.

Pierre and Tiennot, the two sons, were sent out to fodder the cattle, and keep careful watch for any sounds of pursuers from the convent; and Blaise, in the plenitude of his respects and deference, would have followed them, but Eustacie desired him to remain to give her counsel.

Her first inquire was after the watch-tower. She did not care for any discomfort if her vassals would be faithful, and hold it out for her, till she could send for help to the allies of her husband's house, and her eyes glanced as she spoke.

But Blaise shook his head. He had looked at the tower as Madame bade, but it was all in ruins, crumbling away, and, moreover, M. le Chevalier had put a forester there—a grim, bad subject, who had been in the Italian wars, and cared neither for saint nor devil, except Chevalier Narcisse. Indeed, even if he had not been there, the place was untenable, it would only be getting into a trap.

'Count Hebert held it out for twelve days against the English!' said Eustacie, proudly.

'Ah! ah! but there were none of your falconets, or what call you those cannons then. No; if Madame would present herself as a choice morsel for Monsieur le Chevalier to snap up, that is the place.'

Then came the other plan of getting an escort of the peasants together, and riding with them towards the Huguenot territories around La Rochelle, where, for her husband's sake, Eustacie could hardly fail to obtain friends. It was the more practicable expedient, but Blaise groaned over it, wondered how many of the farmers could be trusted, or brought together, and finally expressed his intention of going to consult Martin, his staunch friend, at the next farm. Meantime, Madame had better lie down and sleep. And Madame did sleep, in Perrine's huge box-bedstead, with a sweet, calm, childlike slumber, whilst her nurse sat watching her with eyes full of tears of pity and distress; the poor young thing's buoyant hopefulness and absence of all fear seemed to the old woman especially sad, and like a sort of want of comprehension of the full peril in which she stood.

Not till near dawn was Eustacie startled from her rest by approaching steps. 'Nurse, is all ready?' she cried. 'Can we set off? Are the horses there?'

'No, my child; it is but my good man and Martin who would speak with you. Do not hasten. There is nothing amiss as yet.'

'Oh, nurse,' cried Eustacie, as she quickly arranged the dress in which she had lain down, 'the dear old farm always makes me sleep well. This is the first time I have had no dream of the whirling wheel and fiery gates! Oh, is it a token that HE is indeed at rest? I am so well, so strong. I can ride anywhere now. Let them come in and tell me.'

Martin was a younger, brisker, cleverer man than Blaise, and besides being a vassal of the young Lady, was a sort of agent to whom the Abbess instructed many of the matters of husbandry regarding the convent lands. He stood, like Blaise, bareheaded as he talked to little Lady, and heard her somewhat peremptorily demand why they had not brought the horses and men for her escort.

It was impossible that night, explained Martin. Time was needed to bring in the farm-horses, and summon the other peasants, without whom the roads were unsafe in these times of disorder. He and Blaise must go round and warn them to be ready. A man could not be ready in a wink of the eye, as Madame seemed to think, and the two peasants looked impenetrable in stolidity.

'Laggards that you are!' cried Eustacie, petulantly, clasping her hands; 'and meantime all will be lost. They will be upon me!'

'Not so, Madame. It is therefore that I came here,' said Martin, deferentially, to the little fuming impatient creature; 'Madame will be far safer close at hand while the pursuit and search are going on. But she must not stay here. This farm is the first place they will come to, while they will never suspect mine, and my good woman Lucette will be proud to keep watch for her. Madame knows that the place is full of shrubs and thickets, where one half of an army might spend a fine day in looking for the other.'

'And at night you will get together the men and convoy me?' asked Eustacie, eagerly.

'All in good time, Madame. Now she must be off, ere the holy mothers be astir. I have brought an ass for her to ride.'

Eustacie had no choice but compliance. None of the Orchard family could go with her, as it was needful that they should stay at home and appear as unconcerned as possible; but they promised to meet her at the hour and place to be appointed, ad if possible to bring Veronique.

Eating a piece of rye-bread as she went, Eustacie, in her gray cloak, rode under Martin's guardianship along the deep lanes, just budding with spring, in the chill dewiness before sunrise. She was silent, and just a little sullen, for she had found stout shrewd Martin less easy to talk over than the admiring Blaise, and her spirit was excessively chafed by the tardiness of her retainers. But the sun rose and cleared away all clouds of temper, the cocks crew, the sheep bleated, and fresh morning sounds met her ear, and seemed to cheer and fill her with hope; and in some compunction for her want of graciousness, she thanked Martin, and praised his ass with a pretty cordiality that would have fully compensated for her displeasure, even if the honest man had been sensible of it.

He halted under the lee of a barn, and gave a low whistle. At the sound, Lucette, a brown, sturdy young woman with a red handkerchief over her head, and another over her shoulders, came running round the corner of the barn, and whispered eagerly under her breath, 'Ah! Madame, Madame, what an honour!' kissing Eustacie's hand with all her might as she spoke; 'but, alas! I fear Madame cannot come into the house. The questing Brother Francois—plague upon him!—has taken it into his head to drop in to breakfast. I longed to give him the cold shoulder, but it might have brought suspicion down.'

'Right, good woman,' said Martin; 'but what shall Madame do? It is broad way, and no longer safe to run the lanes!'

'Give me a distaff,' said Eustacie, rising to the occasion; 'I will go to that bushy field, and herd the cows.'

Madame was right, the husband and wife unwillingly agreed. There, in her peasant dress, in the remote field, sloping up into a thick wood, she was unlikely to attract attention; and though the field was bordered on one side by the lane leading to the road to Paris, it was separated from it by a steep bank, crowned by one of the thick hedgerows characteristic of the Bocage.

Here, then, they were forced to leave her, seated on a stone beneath a thorn-bush, distaff in hand, with bread, cheese, and a pitcher of milk for her provisions, and three or four cows grazing before her. From the higher ground below the wood of ash and hazel, she could see the undulating fields and orchards, a few houses, and that inhospitable castle of her own.

She had spent many a drearier day in the convent than this, in the free sun and air, with the feeling of liberty, and unbounded hopes founded on this first success. She told her beads diligently, trusting that the tale of devotions for her husband's spirit would be equally made up in the field as in the church, and intently all day were her ears and eyes on the alert. Once Lucette visited her, to bring her a basin of porridge, and to tell her that all the world at the convent was in confusion, that messengers had been sent out in all directions, and that M. le Chevalier had ridden out himself in pursuit; but they should soon hear all about it, for Martin was pretending to be amongst the busiest, and he would know how to turn them away. Again, much later in the day, Martin came striding across the field, and had just reached her, as she sat in the hedgerow, when the great dog who followed him pricked his ears, and a tramping and jingling was audible in the distance in the lane. Eustacie held up her finger, her eyes dilating.

'It must be M. le Chevalier returning. Madame must wait a little longer. I must be at home, or they may send out to seek me here, and that would be ruin. I will return as soon as it is safe, if Madame will hide herself in the hedgerow.'

Into the hedgerow accordingly crept Eustacie, cowering close to a holly-tree at the very summit of the bank, and led by a strange fascination to choose a spot where, unseen herself, she could gaze down on the party who came clanking along the hollow road beneath. Nearer, nearer, they came; and she shuddered with more of passion than of fear, as she beheld, not only her uncle in his best well-preserved green suit, but Narcisse, muddy with riding, though in his court braveries. Suddenly they came to a halt close beneath her! Was she detected? Ah! just below was the spot where the road to the convent parted from the road to the farm; and, as Martin had apprehended, they were stopping for him. The Chevalier ordered one of the armed men behind him to ride up to the farm and summon Martin to speak with him; and then he and his son, while waiting under the holly-bush, continued their conversation.

'So that is the state of things! A fine overthrow!' quoth Narcisse.

'Bah! not at all. She will soon be in our hands again. I have spoken with, or written to, every governor of the cities she must pass through, and not one will abet the little runaway. At the first barrier she is ours.'

'Et puis?'

'Oh, we shall have her mild as a sheep.' (Eustacie set her teeth.) 'Every one will be in the same story, that her marriage was a nullity; she cannot choose but believe, and can only be thankful that we overlook the escapade and rehabilitate her.'

'Thank you, my good uncle,' almost uttered his unseen auditor.

'Well! There is too much land down here to throw away; but the affair has become horribly complicated and distasteful.'

'No such thing. All the easier. She can no longer play the spotless saint—get weak-minded priests on her side—be all for strict convents. No, no; her time for that is past! Shut her up with trustworthy persons from whom she will hear nothing from without, and she will understand her case. The child? It will scarce be born alive, or at any rate she need not know whether it is. Then, with no resource, no hope, what can she do but be too thankful for pardon, and as glad to conceal the past as we could wish?'

Eustacie clenched her fist. Had a pistol been within her reach, the speaker's tenure of life had been short! She was no chastened, self-restrained, forgiving saint, the poor little thing, only a hot-tempered, generous, keenly-sensitive being, well-nigh a child in years and in impulses, though with the instincts of a mother awakening within her, and of a mother who heard the life of her unborn babe plotted against. She was absolutely forced to hold her lips together, to repress the sobbing scream of fury that came to her throat; and the struggles with her gasping breath, the surging of the blood in her ears, hindered her from hearing or seeing anything for some seconds, though she kept her station. By the time her perceptions had cleared themselves, Martin, cap in hand, was in the lane below, listening deferentially to the two gentlemen, who were assuring him that inquiry had been made, and a guard carefully set at the fugitive could have passed those, or be able to do so. She must certainly be hidden somewhere near home, and Martin had better warn all his friends against hiding her, unless they wished to be hung up on the thresholds of their burning farm-steads. Martin bowed, and thought the fellows would know their own interest and Mademoiselle's better.

'Well,' said the Chevalier, 'we must begin without loss of time. My son has brought down a set of fellows here, who are trained to ferret out heretics. Not a runaway weasel cold escape them! We will set them on as soon as ever they have taken a bit of supper up there at the Chateau; and do you come up with us just to show them the way across to Leonard's. That's no unlikely place for her to lurk in, as you said this morning, good fellow.'

It was the most remote farm from that of Martin, and Eustacie felt how great were his services, even while she flushed with anger to hear him speaking of her as Mademoiselle. He was promising to follow immediately to the castle, to meet *ces Messieurs* there almost as soon as they could arrive, but excusing himself from accompanying them, by the need of driving home the big bull, whom no one else could manage.

They consented, and rode on. Martin watched them out of sight, then sprang up by some stepping-stones in the bank, a little below where Eustacie sat, and came crackling through the boughs to where she was crouching down, with fierce glittering eyes and panting breath, like a wild animal ready to spring.

'Madame has heard,' said Martin, under his breath.

'If I have heard! Oh that I were a man, to slay them where they stood! Martin, Martin! you will not betray me. Some day WE will reward you.'

'Madame need not have said THAT to me,' said Martin, rather hurt. 'I am only thinking what she can do. Alas! I fear that she must remain in this covert till it is dark, for these men's eyes are all on the alert. At dark, I or Lucette will come and find a shelter for her for the night.'

Long, long, then, did Eustacie sit, muffled in her gray cloak, shrinking together to shelter herself from the sunset chill of early spring, but shuddering more with horror than with cold as the cruel cold-blooded words she had heard recurred to her, and feeling as if she were fast within a net, every outlet guarded against her, and search everywhere; yet still with the indomitable determination to dare and suffer to the utmost ere that which was dearer than her own life should come into peril from her enemies.

The twilight closed in, the stars came out, sounds of life died away, and still she sat on, becoming almost torpid in the cold darkness, until at length she heard the low call of Lucette, 'MADAME! AH!*la pauvre Madame.*' She started up, so stiff that she could hardly more, and only guided by the voice to feel her way through the hedgerow in the right direction. Another moment, and Lucette's warn arms had received her; and she was guided, scarce knowing how or where, in cautious silence to the farmyard, and into the house, where a most welcome sight, a huge fire, blazed cheerfully on the hearth, and Martin himself held open the door for her. The other occupants of the kitchen were the sleeping child in its wooden cradle, some cocks and hens upon the rafters, and a big sheep-dog before the fire.

The warmth, and the chicken that Lucette had killed and dressed, brought the colour back to the exhausted wanderer's cheek, and enabled her again to hold council for her safety. It was plain, as Martin had found in conversation with the men-at-arms, that precautions had been taken against her escaping in any of the directions where she might hope to have reached friends. Alone she could not go, and any escort sufficient to protect her would assuredly be stopped at the first town; besides which, collecting it in secret was impossible under present circumstances, and it would be sure to be at once overtaken and demolished by the Chevalier Narcisse's well-armed followers. Martin, therefore, saw no alternative but for her to lurk about in such hiding-places as her faithful vassals could afford her, until the search should blow over, and the vigilance of her uncle and cousin relax. Hope, the high-spirited hope of early youth, looked beyond to indefinite but infinite possibility. Anything was better than the shame and horror of yielding, and Eustacie trusted herself with all her heart for the present, fancying, she knew not what, the future.

Indeed, the Vendean fidelity has often been tested, and she made full proof of it among the lanes, copses, and homesteads of her own broad lands. The whole country was a network of deep lanes, sunk between impenetrable hedgerows, inclosing small fields, orchards, and thickets, and gently undulating in low hills and shallow valleys, interspersed with tall wasp-waisted windmills airily waving their arms on the top of lofty masts. It was partitioned into small farms, inhabited by a simple-hearted peasantry, religious and diligent, with a fair amount of rural wealth and comfort. Their love for their lords was loyally warm, and Eustacie monopolized it, from their detestation of her uncle's exactions; they would risk any of the savage punishments with which they were threatened for concealing her; and as one by one it was needful to take them into the secret, so as to disarm suspicion, and she was passed from one farm to another, each proved his faithful attachment, and though himself repaid by her thankful smile and confiding manner.

The Chevalier and his son searched vigorously. On the slightest suspicion, they came down to the farm, closed up the outlets, threatened the owners, turned out the house, and the very place they had last searched would become her quarters on the next night! Messages always had warned her in time. Intelligence was obtained by Martin, who contrived to remain a confidential agent, and warnings were dispatched to her by many a strange messenger—by little children, by old women, or even by the village innocent.

The most alarming days were those when she was not the avowed object of the chase, but when the pursuit of game rendered the coverts in the woods and fields unsafe, and the hounds might lead to her discovery. On one of these occasions Martin locked her up in the great hayloft of the convent, where she could actually hear the chants in the chapel, and distinguish the chatter of the lay-sisters in the yard. Another time, in conjunction with the sacristan, he bestowed her in the great seigneurial tribune (or squire's pew) in the village church, a tall carved box, where she was completely hidden; and the only time when she had failed to obtain warning beforehand, she stood kneading bread at a tub in Martin's cottage, while the hunt passed by, and a man-at-arms looked in and questioned the master on the last traces of the runaway.

It was seldom possible to see Mere Perrine, who was carefully watched, under the conviction that she must know where her nursling was; but one evening Veronique ventured up to Martin's farm, trusting to tidings that the gentlemen had been Eustacie's only secure harbour; and when, in a bright evening gleam of the setting sun from beneath the clouds, Veronique came in sight of her Lady, the Queen's favourite, it was to see her leading by a string a little shaggy cow, with a bell round its neck, her gray cloak huddled round her, though dank with wet, a long lock of black hair streaming over her brow, her garments clinging with damp, her bare ankles scratched with thorns, her heavy SABOTS covered with mire, her cheeks pale with cold and wet.

The contrast overwhelmed poor Veronique. She dropped on her knees, sobbing as if her heart would break, and declaring that this was what the Abbess had feared; her Lady was fast killing herself.

'Hush! Veronique,' said Eustacie; 'that is all folly. I am wet and weary now, but oh! if you knew how much sweeter to me life is now than it was, shut up down there, with my fears. See,' and she held up a bunch of purple pasque-flowers and wood-sorrel, 'this is what I found in the wood, growing out of a rugged old dead root; and just by, sheltered by the threefold leaves of the alleluia-flower, was a bird's nest, the mother-bird on her eggs, watching me with the wise black eye that saw I would not hurt her. And it brought back the words I had heard long ago, of the good God caring for the sparrows; and I knew He would care the more for me and mine, because I have not where to lay my head.'

'Alas!' sobbed Veronique, 'now she is getting to be a saint outright. She will be sure to die! Ah, Madame—dear Madame! do but listen to me. If you did but know how Madame de Bellaise is afflicting herself on your account! She sent for me—ah! do not be angry, dear Lady?'

'I wish to hear nothing about her,' said Eustacie.

'Nay, listen, *de grace*—one moment, Madame! She has wept, she has feared for you, all the lay-sisters say so. She takes no pleasure in hawking, nor in visiting; and she did not eat more than six of Soeur Bernardine's best conserves. She does nothing but watch for tidings of Madame. And she sent for me, as I told you, and conjured me, if I knew where you were, or had any means of finding out, to implore you to trust to her. She will swear on all the relics in the chapel never to give a hint to Messieurs les Chevaliers if only you would trust her, and not slay yourself with all this dreadful wandering.'

'Never!' said Eustacie; 'she said too much!'

'Ah! but she declares that, had she known the truth, she never would have said that. Ah, yes, Madame, the Abbess is good!' And Veronique, holding her mistress's cloak to secure a hearing, detailed the Abbess' plan for lodging her niece in secret apartments within the thickness of the convent walls, where Mere Perrine could be with her, and every sacred pledge should be given that could remove her fears.

'And could they make me believe them, so that the doubt and dread would not kill me in themselves?' said Eustacie.

'But it is death—certain death, as it is. Oh, if Madame would hear reason!—but she is headstrong! She will grieve when it is too late!'

'Listen, Veronique. I have a far better plan. The sacristan has a sister who weaves red handkerchiefs at Chollet. She will receive me, and keep me as long as there is need. Martin is to take me in his cart when he carries the hay to the garrison. I shall be well hidden, and within reach of your mother. And then, when my son is once come—then all will be well! The peasants will rise in behalf of their young Lord, though not for a poor helpless woman. No one will dare to dispute his claim, when I have appealed to the King; and then, Veronique, you shall come back to me, and all will be well!'

Veronique only began to wail aloud at her mistress' obstinacy. Martin came up, and rudely silenced her, and said afterwards to his wife, 'Have a care! That girl has—I verily believe—betrayed her Lady once; and if she do not do so again, from pure pity and faintness of heart, I shall be much surprised.'

CHAPTER XVII
THE GHOSTS OF THE TEMPLARS

'Tis said, as through the aisles they passed,

They heard strange voices on the blast,

And through the cloister galleries small,

Which at mid-height thread the chancel wall,

Loud sobs and laughter louder ran,

And voices unlike the voice of man,

As if the fiends kept holiday.

Scott, *LAY OF THE LAST MINSTREL*

'Ill news, Martin, I see by your look!' cried Eustacie, starting to her feet from the heap of straw on which she was sitting in his cowhouse, one early April day, about seven weeks since her evasion from the convent.

'Not so, I hope, Madame, but I do not feel at ease. Monsieur has not sent for me, nor told me his plans for the morrow, and I much doubt me whether that bode not a search here. Now I see a plan, provided Madame would trust herself to a Huguenot.'

'They would guard me for my husband's sake.'

'And could Madame walk half a league, as far as the Grange du Temple? There live Matthieu Rotrou and his wife, who have, they say, baffled a hundred times the gendarmes who sought their ministers. No one ever found a pastor, they say, when Rotrou had been of the congregation; and if they can do so much for an old preacher with a long tongue, surely they can for a sweet young lady; and if they could shelter her just for tomorrow, till the suspicion is over, then would I come for Madame with my cart, and carry her into Chollet among the trusses of hay, as we had fixed.'

Eustacie was already tying her cloak, and asking for Lucette; but she was grieved to hear that Martin had sent her to vespers to disarm suspicion, and moreover that he meant not to tell her of his new device. 'The creature is honest enough,' he said, 'but the way to be safe with women is not to let them know.'

He cut short all messages and expressions of gratitude, and leading Eustacie to a small stream, he made her creep along its course, with her feet in the water so as to be sheltered by the boughs that hung over the banks, while he used his ling strides to enable him to double back and enter into conversation with passers-by, quite of the track of the Grange du Temple, but always telling her where he should join her again, and leaving with her the great dog, whom she had come to regard as a friend and protector. Leaving the brook, he conducted her beneath hedges and by lonely woodland paths beyond the confines of her own property, to a secluded valley, so shut in by wooded hills that she had not been aware of its existence. Through an extensive orchard, she at length, when nearly spent with the walk, beheld the cluster of stone buildings, substantial as the erections of religious orders were wont to be.

Martin found a seat for her, where she might wait while he went on alone to the house, and presently returned with both the good people of the farm. They were more offhand and less deferential than were her own people, but were full of kindliness. They were middle-aged folk, most neatly clad, and with a grave, thoughtful look about them, as if life were a much heavier charge to them than to their light-hearted neighbours.

'A fair day to you, Madame,' said the farmer, doffing his wide-flapped hat. 'I am glad to serve a sufferer for the truth's sake.'

'My husband was,' faltered Eustacie.

'AH! *la pauvre*,' cried the good woman, pressing forward as she saw how faint, heated, and exhausted was the wanderer. 'Come in, *ma pauvrette*. Only a bride at the Bartholomew! Alas! There, lean on me, my dear.'

To be *tutoyee* by the Fermiere Rotrou was a shock; yet the kind manner was comfortable, and Eustacie suffered herself to be led into the farm-house, where, as the dame observed, she need not fear chance-comers, for they lived much to themselves, and no one would be about till their boy Robinet came in with the cows. She might rest and eat there in security, and after that they would find a hiding-place for her—safe as the horns of the altar—for a night or two; only for two nights at most.

'Nor do I ask more,' said Eustacie. 'Then Martin will come for me.'

'Ah, I or Blaise, or whichever of us can do it with least suspicion.'

'She shall meet you here,' added Rotrou.

'All right, good man; I understand; it is best I should not know where you hide her. Those rogues have tricks that make it as well to know nothing. Farewell, Madame, I commend you to all the saints till I come for you on Monday morning.'

Eustacie gave him her hand to kiss, and tried to thank him, but somehow her heart sank, and she felt more lonely than ever, when entirely cast loose among these absolute strangers, than amongst her own vassals. Even the farm-kitchen, large, stone-built, and scrupulously clean, seemed strange and dreary after the little, smoky, earth-built living-rooms in which her peasantry were content to live, and she never had seemed to herself so completely desolate; but all the time she was so wearied out with her long and painful walk, that she had no sooner taken some food than she began to doze in her chair.

'Father,' said the good wife, 'we had better take *la pauvrette* to her rest at once.'

'Ah! must I go any farther?' sighed Eustacie.

'It is but a few fields beyond the yard, *ma petite*,' said the good woman consolingly; 'and it will be safer to take you there ere we need a light.'

The sun had just set on a beautiful evening of a spring that happily for Eustacie had been unusually warm and mild, when they set forth, the dame having loaded her husband with a roll of bedding, and herself taking a pitcher of mild and a loaf of bread, whilst Eustacie, as usual, carried her own small parcel of clothes and jewels. The way was certainly not long to any one less exhausted than she; it was along a couple of fields, and then through a piece of thicket, where Rotrou held back the boughs and his wife almost dragged her on with kind encouraging words, till they came up to a stone ivy-covered wall, and coasting along it to a tower, evidently a staircase turret. Here Rotrou, holding aside an enormous bush of ivy, showed the foot of a winding staircase, and his wife assured her that she would not have far to climb.

She knew where she was now. She had heard of the old Refectory of the Knights Templars. Partly demolished by the hatred of the people upon the abolition of the Order, it had ever since lain waste, and had become the centre of all the ghostly traditions of the country; the locality of all the most horrid tales of REVENANTS told under the breath at Dame Perrine's hearth or at recreation hour at Bellaise. Her courage was not proof against spiritual terrors. She panted and leant against the wall, as she faintly exclaimed, 'The Temple—there—and alone!'

'Nay, Lady, methought as *Monsieur votre mari* knew the true light, you would fear no vain terror nor power of darkness.'

Should these peasants—these villeins—be bold, and see the descendant of the 'bravest of knights,' the daughter of the house of Ribaumont, afraid? She rallied herself, and replied manfully, 'I FEAR not, no!' but then, womanfully, 'But it is the Temple! It is haunted! Tell me what I must expect.'

'I tell you truly, Madame,' said Rotrou; 'none whom I have sheltered here have seen aught. On the faith of a Christian, no evil spirit—no ghost—has ever alarmed them; but they were fortified by prayer and psalm.'

'I do pray! I have a psalm-book,' said Eustacie, and she added to herself, 'No, they shall never see that I fear. After all, REVENANTS can do nothing worse than scare one; they cannot touch one; the saints and angels will not let them—and my uncle would do much worse.'

But to climb those winding stairs, and resign herself to be left alone with the Templars for the night, was by far the severest trial that had yet befallen the poor young fugitive. As her tire feet dragged up the crumbling steps, her memory reverted to the many tales of the sounds heard by night within those walls—church chants turning into diabolical songs, and bewildered travelers into thickets and morasses, where they had been found in the morning, shuddering as they told of a huge white monk, with clanking weapons, and a burning cross of fire printed on his shoulder and breast, who stood on the walls and hurled a shrieking babe into the abyss. Were such spectacles awaiting her? Must she bear them? And could her endurance hold out? Our Lady be her aid, and spare her in her need!

At the top of the stairs she found Rotrou's hand, ready to help her out on a stone floor, quite dark, but thickly covered, as she felt and smelt, with trusses of hay, between which a glimmering light showed a narrow passage. A few steps, guided by Rotrou's hand, brought her out into light again, and she found herself in a large chamber, with the stone floor broken away in some places, and with a circular window, thickly veiled with ivy, but still admitting a good deal of evening light.

It was in fact a chamber over the vaulted refectory of the knights. The walls and vaults still standing in their massive solidity, must have tempted some peasant, or mayhap some adventurer, rudely to cover in the roof (which had of course been stripped of its leading), and thus in the unsuspected space to secure a hiding-place, often for less innocent commodities than the salt, which the iniquitous and oppressive *gabelle* had always led the French peasant to smuggle, ever since the days of the first Valois. The room had a certain appearance of comfort; there was a partition across it, a hearth with some remains of wood-ashes, a shelf, holding a plate, cup, lamp, and a few other necessaries; and altogether the aspect of the place was so unlike what Eustacie had expected, that she almost forgot the Templar as she saw the dame begin to arrange a comfortable-looking couch for her wearied limbs. Yet she felt very unwilling to let them depart, and even ventured on faltering out the inquiry whether the good woman could not stay with her,—she would reward her largely.

'It is for the love of Heaven, Madame, not for gain,' said Nanon Rotrou, rather stiffly. 'If you were ill, or needed me, all must then give way; but for me to be absent this evening would soon be reported around the village down there, for there are many who would find occasion against us.' But, by way of consolation, they gave her a whistle, and showed her that the window of their cottage was much nearer to a loophole-slit looking towards the east than she had fancied. The whistle perpetrated a mist unearthly screech, a good deal like that of an owl, but more discordant, and Nanon assured her that the sound would assuredly break her slumbers, and bring her in a few minutes at any moment of need. In fact, the noise was so like the best authenticated accounts of the shrieks indulged in by the spirits of the Temple, that Eustacie had wit enough to suspect that it might be the foundation of some of the stories; and with that solace to her alarms, she endured the departure of her hosts, Nanon promising a visit in the early morning.

The poor child was too weary to indulge in many terrors, the beneficent torpor of excessive fatigue was upon her, happily bringing slumberous oblivion instead of feverish restlessness. She strove to repeat her accustomed orisons; but sleep was too strong for her, and she was soon lying dreamlessly upon the clean homely couch prepared for her.

When she awoke, it was with a start. The moon was shining in through the circular window, making strange white shapes on the floor, all quivering with the shadows of the ivy sprays. It looked strange and eerie enough at the moment, but she understood it the next, and would have been reassured if she had not become aware that there was a low sound, a tramp, tramp, below her. 'Gracious saints! The Templar! Have mercy on me! Oh! I was too sleepy to pray! Guard me from being driven wild by fright!' She sat upright, with wide-spread eyes, and, finding that she herself was in the moonlight, through some opening in the roof, she took refuge in the darkest corner, though aware as she crouched there, that if this were indeed the Templar, concealment would be vain, and remembering suddenly that she was out of reach of the loophole-window.

And therewith there was a tired sound in the tread, as if the Templar found his weird a very length one; then a long heavy breath, with something so essentially human in its sound that the fluttering heart beat more steadily. If reason told her that the living were more perilous to her than the dead, yet feeling infinitely preferred them! It might be Nanon Rotrou after all; then how foolish to be crouching there in a fright! It was rustling through the hay. No-no Nanon; it is a male figure, it has a long cloak on. Ah! it is in the moonlight-silver hair—silver beard. The Templar! Fascinated with dismay, yet calling to mind that no ghost has power unless addressed, she sat still, crossing herself in silence, but unable to call to mind any prayer or invocation save a continuous 'Ave Mary,' and trying to restrain her gasping breath, lest, if he were not the Templar after all, he might discover her presence.

He moved about, took off his cloak, laid it down near the hay, then his cap, not a helmet after all, and there was no fiery cross.

He was in the gloom again, and she heard him moving much as though he were pulling down the hay to form a bed. Did ghosts ever do anything so sensible? If he were an embodied spirit, would it be possible to creep past him and escape while he lay asleep? She was almost becoming familiarized with the presence, and the supernatural terror was passing off into a consideration of resources, when, behold, he was beginning to sing. To sing was the very way the ghosts began ere they came to their devilish outcries. 'Our Lady keep it from bringing frenzy. But hark! hark!' It was not one of the chants, it was a tune and words heard in older times of her life; it was the evening hymn, that the little husband and wife had been wont to sing to the Baron in the Chateau de Leurre—Marot's version of the 4th Psalm.

> *Plus de joie m'est donnee*
>
> *Par ce moyen, O Dieu Tres-Haut,*
>
> *Que n'ont ceux qui ont grand annee*
>
> *De froment et bonne vinee,*
>
> *D'huile et tout ce qu'il leur faut.'*

If it had indeed been the ghostly chant, perhaps Eustacie would not have been able to help joining it. As it was, the familiar home words irresistibly impelled her to mingle her voice, scarce knowing what she did, in the verse—

> *'Si qu'en paix et surete bonne*
>
> *Coucherai et reposerai;*
>
> *Car, Seigneur, ta bonte tout ordonne*
>
> *Et elle seule espoir me donne*
>
> *Que sur et seul regnant serai.'*

The hymn died away in its low cadence, and then, ere Eustacie had had time to think of the consequences of thus raising her voice, the new-comer demanded:

'Is there then another wanderer here?'

'Ah! sir, pardon me!' she exclaimed. 'I will not long importune you, but only till morning light—only till the Fermiere Rotrou comes.'

'If Matthieu and Anne Rotrou placed you here, then all is well,' replied the stranger. 'Fear not, daughter, but tell me. Are you one of my scattered flock, or one whose parents are known to me?' Then, as she hesitated, 'I am Isaac Gardon—escaped, alas! alone, from the slaughter of the Barthelemy.'

'Master Gardon!' cried Eustacie. 'Oh, I know! O sir, my husband loved and honoured you.'

'Your husband?'

'Yes, sir, le Baron de Ribaumont.'

'That fair and godly youth! My dear old patron's son! You—you! But—' with a shade of doubt, almost of dismay, 'the boy was wedded—wedded to the heiress——'

'Yes, yes, I am that unhappy one! We were to have fled together on that dreadful night. He came to meet me to the Louvre—to his doom!' she gasped out, nearer to tears than she had ever been since that time, such a novelty was it to her to hear Berenger spoken of in kind or tender terms; and in her warmth of feeling, she came out of her corner, and held our her hand to him.

'Alas! poor thing!' said the minister, compassionately, 'Heaven has tried you sorely. Had I known of your presence here, I would not have entered; but I have been absent long, and stole into my lair here without disturbing the good people below. Forgive the intrusion, Madame.'

The minister replied warmly that surely persecution was a brotherhood, even had she not been the window of one he had loved and lamented.

'Ah! sir, it does me good to hear you say so.'

And therewith Eustacie remembered the hospitalities of her loft. She perceived by the tones of the old man's voice that he was tired, and probably fasting, and she felt about for the milk and bread with which she had been supplied. It was a most welcome refreshment, though he only partook sparingly; and while he ate, the two, so strangely met, came to a fuller knowledge of one another's circumstances.

Master Isaac Gardon had, it appeared, been residing at Paris, in the house of the watchmaker whose daughter had been newly married to his son; but on the fatal eve of St. Bartholomew, he had been sent for to pray with a sick person in another quarter of the city. The Catholic friends of the invalid were humane, and when the horrors began, not only concealed their kinsman, but almost forcibly shut up the minister in the same cellar with him. And thus, most reluctantly, had he been spared from the fate that overtook his son and daughter-in-law. A lone and well-night broken-hearted man, he had been smuggled out of the city, and had since that time been wandering from one to another of the many scattered settlements of Huguenots in the northern part of France, who, being left pastorless, welcomed visits from the minister of their religion, and passed him on from one place to another, as his stay in each began to be suspected by the authorities. He was now on his way along the west side of France, with no fixed purpose, except so far as, since Heaven had spared his life when all that made it dear had been taken from him, he resigned himself to believe that there was yet some duty left for him to fulfil.

Meantime the old man was wearied out; and after due courtesies had passed between him and the lady in the dark, he prayed long and fervently, as Eustacie could judge from the intensity of the low murmurs she heard; and then she heard him, with a heavy irrepressible sigh, lie down on the couch of hay he had already prepared for himself, and soon his regular breathings announced his sound slumbers. She was already on the bed she had so precipitately quitted, and not a thought more did she give to the Templars, living or dead, even though she heard an extraordinary snapping and hissing, and in the dawn of the morning saw a white weird thing, like a huge moth, flit in through the circular window, take up its station on a beam above the hay, and look down with the brightest, roundest eyes she had ever beheld. Let owls and bats come where they would, she was happier than she had been for months. Compassion for herself was plentiful enough, but to have heard Berenger spoken of with love and admiration seemed to quiet the worst ache of her lonely heart.

CHAPTER XVIII
THE MOONBEAM

She wandered east, she wandered west,

She wandered out and in;

And at last into the very swine's stythe

The queen brought forth a son.—Fause Foodrage

The morrow was Sunday, and in the old refectory, in the late afternoon, a few Huguenots, warned by messages from the farm, met to profit by one of their scanty secret opportunities for public worship. The hum of the prayer, and discourse of the pastor, rose up through the broken vaulting to Eustacie, still lying on her bed; for she had been much shaken by the fatigues of the day and alarm of the night, and bitterly grieved, too, by a message which Nanon conveyed to her, that poor Martin was in no state to come for her in the next day; but he and his wife having been seized upon by Narcisse and his men, and so savagely beaten in order to force from them a confession of her hiding-place, that both were lying helpless on their bed; and could only send an entreaty by the trustworthy fool, that Rotrou would find means of conveying Madame into Chollet in some cart of hay or corn, in which she could be taken past the barriers.

But this was not to be. Good Nanon had sacrificed the sermon to creep up to Eustacie, and when the congregation were dispersing in the dusk, she stole down the stairs to her husband; and a few seconds after he was hurrying as fast as *detours* would allow him to Blaise's farm. An hour and a half later, Dame Perrine, closely blindfolded for the last mile, was dragged up the spiral staircase, and ere the bandage was removed heard Eustacie's voice, with a certain cheeriness, say, 'Oh! nurse; my son will soon come!'

The full moon gave her light, and the woman durst not have any other, save from the wood-fire that Nanon had cautiously lighted and screened. The moonshine was still supreme, when some time later a certain ominous silence and half-whisper between the two women at the hearth made Eustacie, with a low cry of terror, exclaim, 'Nurse, nurse, what means this? Oh! He lives! I know he lives! Perrine, I command you tell me!'

'Living! Oh, yes, my love, my Lady,' answered Perrine, returning towards her; 'fair and perfect as the day. Be not disquieted for a moment.'

'I will—I will disquiet myself,' panted Eustacie, 'unless you tell me what is amiss.'

'Nothing amiss,' said Nanon, gruffly. 'Madame will give thanks for this fair gift of a daughter.'

It must be owned the words felt chill. She had never thought of this! It was as if the being for whom she had dared and suffered so much, in the trust that he would be Berenger's representative and avenger, had failed her and disappointed her. No defender, no paladin, no so to be proud of! Her heart and courage sank down in her weakness as they had never done before; and, without speaking, she turned her head away towards the darkness, feeling as if had been for nothing, and she might as well sink away in her exhaustion. Mere Perrine was more angry with Nanon than conscious of her Lady's weakness. 'Woman, you speak as if you knew not the blow to this family, and to all who hoped for better days. What, that my Lady, the heiress, who ought to be in a bed of state, with velvet curtains, lace pillows, gold caudle-cups, should be here in a vile ruin, among owls and bats, like any beggar, and all for the sake, not of a young Lord to raise up the family, but of a miserable little girl! Had I known how it would turn out, I had never meddled in this mad scheme.'

Before Nanon could express her indignation, Eustacie had turned her head opened her eyes, and called out, 'Miserable! Oh! what do you mean? Oh, it is true, Nanon? is it well with her?

'As well as heart could wish,' answered Nanon, cheerily. 'Small, but a perfect little piece of sugar. There, Lady, she shall speak for herself.'

And as Nanon laid the babe on the young mother's bosom, the thrilling touch at once put an end to all the repinings of the heiress, and awoke far other instincts.

'My child! my little one, my poor little orphan—all cruel to her! Oh, no welcome even from thy mother! Babe, babe, pardon me, I will make it up to thee; indeed I will! Oh! let me see her! Do not take her away, dear good woman, only hold her in the moonlight!'

The full rays of the moon, shining through the gable window, streamed down very near where Eustacie lay, and by a slight movement Dame Rotrou was able to render the little face as distinctly visible to her as if it had been daylight, save that the blanching light was somewhat embellishing to the new-born complexion, and increased that curious resemblance so often borne for the first few hours of life to the future self. Eustacie's cry at once was, 'Himself, himself—his very face! Let me have her, my own moonbeam—his child—my joy!'

The tears, so long denied, rushed down like summer rain as she clasped the child in her arms. Dame Perrine wandered to and fro, like one beside herself, not only at her Lady's wretched accommodations, but at the ill omens of the moonlight illumination, of the owls who snapped and hissed incessantly over the hay, and above all the tears over the babe's face. She tried to remonstrate with Eustacie, but was answered only, 'Let me weep! Oh, let me weep! It eases my heart! It cannot hurt my little one! She cannot weep for her father herself, so I must weep for her.'

The weeping was gentle, not violent; and Dame Rotrou thought it did good rather than harm. She was chiefly anxious to be quit of Perrine, who, however faithful to the Lady of Ribaumont, must not be trusted to learn the way to this Huguenot asylum, and must be escorted back by Rotrou ere peep of dawn. The old woman knew that her own absence from home would be suspicious, and with many grumblings submitted; but first she took the child from Eustacie's reluctant arms, promising to restore her in a few moments, after finishing dressing her in the lace-edged swaddling bands so carefully preserved ever since Eustacie's own baby hood. In these moments she had taken them all by surprise, without asking any questions, sprinkling the babe with water, and baptizing her by the hereditary name of Berangere, the feminine of the only name Eustacie had always declared her son should bear. Such baptisms were not unfrequently performed by French nurses, but Eustacie exclaimed with a sound half dismay, half indignation.

'*Eh quoi*!' said Perrine, 'it is only *ondoyee*. You can have all the ceremonies if ever time shall fit; but do you think I could leave my Lady's child—mere girl though it be—alone with owls, and *follets*, and REVENANTS, and heretics, and she unbaptized? She would be a changeling long ere morning, I trow.'

'Come, good woman,' said Rotrou, from between the trusses of hay at the entrance; 'you and I must begin our Colin-Mail-lard again, or it may be the worse for us both.'

And with the promise of being conducted to Eustacie again in three nights' time, if she would meet her guide at the cross-roads after dark, Perrine was forced to take her leave. She had never suspected that all this time Maitre Gardon had been hidden in the refectory below, and still less did she guess that soon after her departure the old man was installed as her Lady's chief attendant. It was impossible that Nanon should stay with Eustacie; she had her day's work to attend to, and her absence would have excited suspicion. He, therefore, came partly up the stairs, and calling to Nanon, proffered himself to sit with '*cette pauvre*,' and make a signal in case Nanon should be wanted. The good woman was thus relieved of a great care. She would not have dared to ask it of him, but with a low reverence, she owned that it was an act of great charity towards the poor lady, who, she hoped, was falling into a tranquil sleep, but who she would hardly have dared to leave. The pastor, though hardships, battles, and persecutions had left him childless, had been the father of a large family; and perhaps he was drawn the more strongly towards the mother and child, because he almost felt as if, in fulfilling the part of a father towards the widow of Berenger de Ribaumont, he was taking her in the stead of the widow of his own Theodore.

Had the little Baronne de Ribaumont been lodged in a tapes-tried chamber, between curtains of velvet and gold, with a *beauffet* by her side glistening with gold and silver plate, as would have befitted her station, instead of lying on a bed of straw, with no hangings to the walls save cobwebs and hay, and wallflowers, no *beauffet* but the old rickety table, no attendants but Nanon and M. Gardon, no visitors but the two white owls, no provisions save the homely fare that rustic mothers lived upon—neither she nor her babe could have thriven better, and probably not half so well. She had been used to a hardy, out-of-door life, like the peasant women; and she was young and strong, so that she recovered as they did. If the April shower beat in at the window, or the hole in the roof, they made a screen of canvas, covered her with cloaks, and heaped them with hay, and she took no harm; and the pure open air that blew in was soft with all the southern sweetness of early spring-tide, and the little one throve in it like the puff-ball owlets in the hayloft, or the little ring-doves in the ivy, whose parent's cooing voice was Eustacie's favourite music. Almost as good as these her fellow-nestlings was the little Moonbeam, *la petite Rayonette*, as Eustacie fondly called this light that had come back to her from the sunshine she had lost. Had she cried or been heard, the sounds would probably have passed for the wailings of the ghostly victims of the Templars, but she exercised an exemplary forbearance in that respect, for which Eustacie thought she could not be sufficiently admired.

Like the child she was, Eustacie seemed to have put care from her, and to be solely taken up with the baby, and the amusement of watching the owl family.

There was a lull in the search at this moment, for the Chevalier had been recalled to Paris by the fatal illness of his son-in-law, M. de Selinvine. The old soldier, after living half his life on bread and salad, that he might keep up a grand appearance at Paris, had, on coming into the wealth of the family, and marrying a beautiful wife, returned to the luxuries he had been wont only to enjoy for a few weeks at a time, with in military occupation of some Italian town. Three months of festivities had been enough to cause his death; and the Chevalier was summoned to assist his daughter in providing for his obsequies, and in taking possession of the huge endowments which, as the last of his race, he had been able to bequeath to her. Such was the news brought by the old nurse Perrine, who took advantage of the slackening vigilance of the enemy to come to see Eustacie. The old woman was highly satisfied; for one of the peasants' wives had—as if on purpose to oblige her Lady—given birth to twins, one of whom had died almost immediately; and the parents had consented to conceal their loss, and at once take the little Demoiselle de Ribaumont as their own— guarding the secret till her mother should be able to claim her. It was so entirely the practice, under the most favourable circumstances, for French mothers to send their infants to be nursed in cottages, that Perrine was amazed by the cry of angry refusal that burst from Eustacie: 'Part with my child! leave her to her enemies!—never! never! Hold your tongue, Perrine! I will not hear of such a thing!'

'But, Madame, hear reason. She will pass for one of Simonette's!'

'She shall pass for none but mine!—I part with thee, indeed! All that is left me of thy father!—the poor little orphaned innocent, that no one loves but her mother!'

'Madame—Mademoiselle, this is not common sense! Why, how can you hide yourself? how travel with a baby on your neck, whose crying may betray you?'

'She never cries—never, never! And better I were betrayed than she.'

'If it were a boy——' began Perrine.

'If it were a boy, there would be plenty to care for it. I should not care for it half so much. As for my poor little lonely girl, whom every one wishes away but her mother—ah! yes, baby, thy mother will go through fire and water for thee yet. Never fear, thou shalt not leave her!'

'No nurse can go with Madame. Simonette could not leave her home.'

'What needs a nurse when she has me?'

'But, Madame,' proceeded the old woman, out of patience, 'you are beside yourself! What noble lady ever nursed her babe?'

'I don't care noble ladies—I care for my child,' said the vehement, petulant little thing.

'And how—what good will Madame's caring for it do? What knows she of infants? How can she take care of it?'

'Our Lady will teach me,' said Eustacie, still pressing the child passionately to her heart; 'and see—the owl—the ring-dove—can take care of their little ones; the good God shows them how—He will tell me how!'

Perrine regarded her Lady much as if she were in a naughty fit, refusing unreasonably to part with a new toy, and Nanon Rotrou was much of the same mind; but it was evident that if at the moment they attempted to carry off the babe, the other would put herself into an agony of passion, that they durst not call forth; and they found it needful to do their best to soothe her out of the deluge of agitated tears that fell from her eyes, as she grasped the child so convulsively that she might almost have stifled it at once. They assured her that they would not take it away now—not now, at any rate; and when the latent meaning made her fiercely insist that it was to leave her neither now nor ever, Perrine made pacifying declarations that it should be just as she pleased—promises that she knew well, when in that coaxing voice, meant nothing at all. Nothing calmed her till Perrine had been conducted away; and even then Nanon could not hush her into anything like repose, and at last called in the minister, in despair.

'Ah! sir, you are a wise man; can you find how to quiet the poor little thing? Her nurse has nearly driven her distracted with talking of the foster-parents she has found for the child.'

'Not found!' cried Eustacie. 'No, for she shall never go!'

'There!' lamented Nanon—'so she agitates herself, when it is but spoken of. And surely she had better make up her mind, for there is no other choice.'

'Nay, Nanon,' said M. Gardon, 'wherefore should she part with the charge that God has laid on her?'

Eustacie gave a little cry of grateful joy. 'Oh, sir, come nearer! Do you, indeed, say that they have no right to tear her from me?'

'Surely not, Lady. It is you whose duty it is to shield and guard her.'

'Oh, sir, tell me again! Yours is the right religion. Oh, you are the minister for me! If you will tell me I ought to keep my child, then I will believe everything else. I will do just as you tell me.' And she stretched out both hands to him, with vehement eagerness.

'Poor thing! This is no matter of one religion or another,' said the minister; 'it is rather the duty that the Almighty hath imposed, and that He hath made an eternal joy.'

'Truly,' said Nanon, ashamed at having taken the other side: 'the good *pasteur* says what is according to nature. It would have gone hard with me if any one had wished to part me from Robin or Sara; but these fine ladies, and, for that matter, BOURGEOISES too, always do put out their babes; and it seemed to me that Madame would find it hard to contrive for herself—let alone the little one.'

'Ah! but what would be the use of contriving for myself, without her?' said Eustacie.

If all had gone well and prosperously with Madame de Ribaumont, probably she would have surrendered an infant born in purple and in pall to the ordinary lot of its contemporaries; but the exertions and suffering she had undergone on behalf of her child, its orphanhood, her own loneliness, and even the general disappointment in its sex, had given it a hold on her vehement, determined heart, that intensified to the utmost the instincts of motherhood; and she listened as if to an angle's voice as Maitre Gardon replied to Nanon—

'I say not that it is not the custom; nay, that my blessed wife and myself have not followed it; but we have so oft had cause to repent the necessity, that far be it from me ever to bid a woman forsake her sucking child.'

'Is that Scripture?' asked Eustacie. 'Ah! sir, sir, tell me more! You are giving me all—all—my child! I will be—I am—a Huguenot like her father! and, when my vassals come, I will make them ride with you to La Rochelle, and fight in your cause!'

'Nay,' said Maitre Gardon, taken by surprise; 'but, Lady, your vassals are Catholic.'

'What matters it? In my cause they shall fight!' said the feudal Lady, 'for me and my daughter!'

And as the pastor uttered a sound of interrogative astonishment, she continued—

'As soon as I am well enough, Blaise will send out messages, and they will meet me at midnight at the cross-roads, Martin and all, for dear good Martin is quite well now, and we shall ride across country, avoiding towns, wherever I choose to lead them. I had thought of Chantilly, for I know M. de Montmorency would stand my friend against a Guisard; but now, now I know you, sir, let me escort you to La Rochelle, and do your cause service worthy of Nid de Merle and Ribaumont!' And as she sat up on her bed, she held up her little proud head, and waved her right hand with the grace and dignity of a queen offering an alliance of her realm.

Maitre Gardon, who had hitherto seen her as a childish though cheerful and patient sufferer, was greatly amazed, but he could not regard her project as practicable, or in his conscience approve it; and after a moment's consideration he answered, 'I am a man of peace, Lady, and seldom side with armed men, nor would I lightly make one of those who enroll themselves against the King.'

'Not after all the Queen-mother had done!' cried Eustacie.

'Martyrdom is better than rebellion,' quietly answered the old man, folding his hands. Then he added 'Far be it from me to blame those who have drawn the sword for the faith; yet, Lady, it would not be even thus with your peasants; they might not follow you.'

'Then,' said Eustacie, with flashing eyes, 'they would be traitors.'

'Not to the King,' said the pastor, gently. 'Also, Lady, how will it be with their homes and families—the hearths that have given you such faithful shelter?'

'The women would take to the woods,' readily answered she; 'it is summer-time, and they should be willing to bear something for my sake. I should grieve indeed,' she added, 'if my uncle misused them. They have been very good to me, but then they belong to me.'

'Ah! Lady, put from you that hardening belief of seigneurs. Think what their fidelity deserves from their Lady.'

'I will be good to them! I do love them! I will be their very good mistress,' said Eustacie, her eyes filling.

'The question is rather of forbearing than of doing,' said the minister.

'But what would you have me do?' asked Eustacie, petulantly.

'This, Lady. I gather that you would not return to your relations.'

'Never! never! They would rend my babe from me; they would kill her, or at least hide her for ever in a convent—they would force me into this abhorrent marriage. No—no—no—my child and I would die a hundred deaths together rather than fall into the hands of Narcisse.'

'Calm yourself, Lady; there is no present fear, but I deem that the safest course for the little one would be to place her in England. She must be heiress to lands and estates there; is she not?'

'Yes; and in Normandy.'

'And your husband's mother lives? Wherefore then should you not take me for your guide, and make your way—more secretly than would be possible with a peasant escort—to one of your Huguenot towns on the coast, whence you could escape with the child to England?'

'My *belle-mere* has re-married! She has children! I would not bring the daughter of Ribaumont as a suppliant to be scorned!' said Eustacie, pouting. 'She has lands enough of her own.'

'There is no need to discuss the question now,' said M. Gardon, gravely; for a most kind offer, involving much peril and inconvenience to himself, was thus petulantly flouted. 'Madame will think at her leisure of what would have been the wishes of Monsieur le Baron for his child.'

He then held himself aloof, knowing that it was not well for her health, mental or bodily, to talk any more, and a good deal perplexed himself by the moods of his strange little impetuous convert, if convert she could be termed. He himself was a deeply learned scholar, who had studied all the bearings of the controversy; and, though bound to the French Reformers who would gladly have come to terms with the Catholics at the Conference of Plassy, and regretted the more decided Calvinism that his party had since professed, and in which the Day of St. Bartholomew confirmed them. He had a strong sense of the grievous losses they suffered by their disunion from the Church. The Reformed were less and less what his ardent youthful hopes had trusted to see them; and in his old age he was a sorrow-stricken man, as much for the cause of religion as for personal bereavements. He had little desire to win proselytes, but rather laid his hand to build up true religion where he found it suffering shocks in these unsettled, neglected times; and his present wish was rather to form and guide this little willful warm-hearted mother—whom he could not help regarding with as much affection as pity—to find a home in the Church that had been her husband's, than to gain her to his own party. And most assuredly he would never let her involve herself, as she was ready to do, in the civil war, without even knowing the doctrine which grave and earnest men had preferred to their loyalty.

He could hear her murmuring to her baby, 'No, no, little one, we are not fallen so low as to beg our bread among strangers.' To live upon her own vassals had seemed to her only claiming her just rights, but it galled her to think of being beholden to stranger Huguenots; and England and her mother-in-law, without Berenger, were utterly foreign and distasteful to her.

Her mood was variable. Messages from Blaise and Martin came and went, and it became known that her intended shelter at Chollet, together with all the adjacent houses, had been closely searched by the younger Ribaumont in conjunction with the governor; so that it was plain that some treachery must exist, and that she only owed her present freedom to her detention in the ruined temple; and it would be necessary to leave that as soon as it was possible for her to attempt the journey.

The plan that seemed most feasible to the vassals was, that Rotrou should convey her in a cart of fagots as far as possible on the road to Paris; that there his men should meet her by different roads, riding their farm-horses—and Martin even hoped to be able to convey her own palfrey to her from the monastery stable, and thence, taking a long stretch across country, they trusted to be able to reach the lands of a dependant of the house of Montmorency, who would not readily yield her up to a Guise's man. But, whether instigated by Perrine, or by their own judgment, the vassals declared that, though Madame should be conducted wherever she desired, it was impossible to encumber themselves with the infant. Concealment would be impossible; rough, hasty rides would be retarded, her difficulties would be tenfold increased, and the little one would become a means of tracing her. There was no choice but to leave it with Simonette.

Angrily and haughtily did Eustacie always reject this alternative, and send fresh commands back by her messenger, to meet the same reply in another form. The strong will and practical resolution of the stout farmers, who were about to make a terrible venture for her, and might reasonably think they had a right to prescribe the terms that they thought best. All this time Maitre Gardon felt it impossible to leave her, still weak and convalescent, alone in the desolate ruin with her young child; though still her pride would not bend again to seek the counsel that she had so much detested, nor to ask for the instruction that was to make her 'believe like her husband.' If she might not fight for the Reformed, it seemed as if she would none of their doctrine!

But, true lady that she was, she sunk the differences in her intercourse with him. She was always prettily and affectionately grateful for every service that he rendered her, and as graciously polite as though she had been keeping house in the halls of Ribaumont. Then her intense love for her child was so beautiful, and there was so much sweetness in the cheerful patience with which she endured the many hardships of her situation, that he could not help being strongly interested in the willful, spirited little being.

And thus time passed, until one night, when Martin ventured over the farm with a report so serious that Rotrou, at all risks, brought him up to communicate his own tidings. Some one had given information, Veronique he suspected, and the two Chevaliers were certainly coming the next day to search with fire the old buildings of the temple. It was already dawning towards morning, and it would be impossible to do more at present than to let Rotrou build up the lady in a vault, some little way off, whence, after the search was over, she could be released, and join her vassals the next night according to the original design. As to the child, her presence in the vault

z

- 173 -

was impossible, and Martin had actually brought her intended nurse, Simonette, to Rotrou's cottage to receive her.

'Never!' was all Eustacie answered. 'Save both of us, or neither.'

'Lady,' said M. Gardon as she looked towards him, 'I go my way with my staff.'

'And you—you more faithful than her vassals—will let me take her?'

'Assuredly.'

'Then, sir, even to the world's end will I go with you'

Martin would have argued, have asked, but she would not listen to him. It was Maitre Gardon who made him understand the project. There was what in later times has been termed an underground railway amid the persecuted Calvinists, and M. Gardon knew his ground well enough to have little doubt of being able to conduct the lady safely to some town on the coast, whence she might reach her friends in England. The plan highly satisfied Martin. It relieved him and his neighbours from the necessity of provoking perilous wrath, and it was far safer for her herself than endeavouing to force her way with an escort too large not to attract notice, yet not warlike enough for efficient defence. He offered no further opposition, but augured that after all she would come back a fine lady, and right them all.

Eustacie, recovering from her anger, and recollecting his services, gave him her hand to kiss, and bade him farewell with a sudden effusion of gratitude and affection that warmed the honest fellow's heart. Rewards could not be given, lest they should become a clue for her uncle; and perhaps they would have wounded both him and their kind hosts, who did their best to assist her in their departure. A hasty meal was provided by Nanon, and a basket so stored as to obviate the need of entering a village, on that day at least, to purchase provisions; Eustacie's money and jewels again formed the nucleus of the bundle of clothes and spare swaddling-banks of her babe; her peasant dress was carefully arranged—a stout striped cloth skit and black bodice, the latter covered by a scarlet Chollet kerchief. The winged white cap entirely hid her hair; a gray cloak with a hood could either fold round her and her child or be strapped on her shoulders. Her *sabots* were hung on her shoulder, for she had learnt to go barefoot, and walked much more lightly thus; and her little bundle was slung on a staff on the back of Maitre Gardon, who in his great peasant's hat and coat looked so like a picture of St. Joseph, that Eustacie, as the light of the rising sun fell on his white beard and hair, was reminded of the Flight into Egypt, and came close to him, saying shyly, 'Our Blessed Lady will bless and feel for my baby. She knows what this journey is.'

'The Son of the Blessed Mary assuredly knows and blesses,' he answered.

CHAPTER XIX
LA RUE DES TROIS FEES

And round the baby fast and close Her trembling grasp she folds. And with a strong convulsive grasp The little infant holds.—SOUTHEY.

A wild storm had raged all the afternoon, hail and rain had careered on the wings of the wind along the narrow street of the Three Fairies, at the little Huguenot bourg of La Sablerie; torrents of rain had poached the unpaved soil into a depth of mud, and thunder had reverberated over the chimney-tops, and growled far away over the Atlantic, whose angry waves were tossing on the low sandy coast about two miles from the town.

The evening had closed in with a chill, misty drizzle, and, almost May though it were, the Widow Noemi Laurent gladly closed the shutters of her unglazed window, where small cakes and other delicate confections were displayed, and felt the genial warmth of the little fire with which she heated her tiny oven. She was the widow of a pastor who had suffered for his faith in the last open persecution, and being the daughter of a baker, the authorities of the town had permitted her to support herself and her son by carrying on a trade in the more delicate 'subtilties' of the art, which were greatly relished at the civic feasts. Noemi was a grave, sad woman, very lonely ever since she had saved enough to send her son to study for the ministry in Switzerland, and with an aching heart that longed to be at rest from the toil that she looked on as a steep ladder on her way to a better home. She occupied two tiny rooms on the ground-floor of a tall house; and she had just arranged her few articles of furniture with the utmost neatness, when there was a low knock at her door, a knock that the persecuted well understood, and as she lifted the latch, a voice she had known of old spoke the scriptural salutation, 'Peace be with this house.'

'*Eh quoi*, Master Issac, is it thou? Come in—in a good hour—ah!'

As, dripping all round his broad hat and from every thread of his gray mantle, the aged traveller drew into the house a female figure whom he had been supporting on his other arm, muffled head and shoulders in a soaked cloak, with a petticoat streaming with wet, and feet and ankles covered with mire, 'Here we are, my child,' he said tenderly, as he almost carried her to Noemi's chair. Noemi, with kind exclamations of '*La pauvre! la pauvre!*' helped the trembling cold hand to open the wet cloak, and then cried out with fresh surprise and pity at the sight of the fresh little infant face, nestled warm and snug under all the wrappings in those weary arms.

'See,' said the poor wanderer, looking up to the old man, with a faint smile; 'she is well—she is warm—it hurts her not.'

'Can you take us in?' added M. Gardon, hastily; 'have you room?'

'Oh yes; if you can sleep on the floor here, I will take this poor dear to my own bed directly,' said Noemi. '*Tenez*,' opening a chest; 'you will find dry clothes there, of my husband's. And thou,' helping Eustacie up with her strong arm, and trying to take the little one, 'let me warm and dry thee within.'

Too much worn out to make resistance, almost past speaking, knowing merely that she had reached the goal that had been promised her throughout these weary days, feeling warmth, and hearing kind tones, Eustacie submitted to be led into the inner room; and when the good widow returned again, it was in haste to fetch some of the warm *potage* she had already been cooking over the fire, and hastily bade M. Gardon help himself to the rest. She came back again with the babe, to wash and dress it in the warmth of her oven fire. Maitre Gardon, in the black suit of a Calvinist pastor, had eaten his *potage*, and was anxiously awaiting her report. 'Ah! *la pauvre*, with His blessing she will sleep! she will do well. But how far did you come to-day?'

'From Sainte Lucie. From the Grange du Temple since Monday.'

'Ah! is it possible? The poor child! And this little one—sure, it is scarce four weeks old?'

'Four weeks this coming Sunday.'

'Ah! the poor thing. The blessing of Heaven must have been with you to bear her through. And what a lovely infant—how white—what beauteous little limbs! Truly, she has sped well. Little did I think, good friend, that you had this comfort left, or that our poor Theodore's young wife had escaped.'

'Alas! no, Noemi; this is no child of Theodore's. His wife shared his martyrdom. It is I who am escaped alone to tell thee. But, nevertheless, this babe is an orphan of that same day. Her father was the son of the pious Baron de Ribaumont, the patron of your husband, and of myself in earlier days.'

'Ah!' exclaimed Noemi, startled. 'Then the poor young mother—is she—can she be the lost Demoiselle de Nid de Merle?'

'Is the thing known here? The will of Heaven be done; but she can send to her husband's kindred in England.'

- 176 -

'She might rest safely enough, if others beside myself believed in her being your son's widow,' said Noemi. 'Wherefore should she not be thought so?'

'Poor Esperance! She would willingly have lent her name to guard another,' said Master Gardon, thoughtfully; 'and, for the sake of the child, my little lady may endure it. Ah! there is the making of a faithful and noble woman in that poor young thing. Bravely, patiently, cheerfully, hath she plodded this weary way; and, verily, she hath grown like my own daughter to me—as I never thought to love earthly thing again; and had this been indeed my Theodore's child, I could hardly care for it more.'

And as he related how he had fallen in with the forlorn Lady of Ribaumont, and all that she had dared, done, and left undone for the sake of her little daughter, good Noemi Laurent wept, and agreed with him that a special providence must have directed them to his care, and that some good work must await one who had been carried through so much. His project was to remain here for a short time, to visit the flock who had lost their pastor on the day of the massacre, and to recruit his own strength; for he, too, had suffered severely from the long travelling, and the exposure during many nights, especially since all that was warm and sheltered had been devoted to Eustacie. And after this he proposed to go to La Rochelle, and make inquiries for a trusty messenger who could be sent to England to seek out the family of the Baron de Ribaumont, or, mayhap, a sufficient escort with whom the lady could travel; though he had nearly made up his mind that he would not relinquish the care of her until he had safely delivered her to her husband's mother.

Health and life were very vigorous in Eustacie; and though at first she had been completely worn out, a few days of comfort, entire rest, and good nursing restored her. Noemi dressed her much like herself, in a black gown, prim little white starched ruff, and white cap,—a thorough Calvinist dress, and befitting a minister's widow. Eustacie winced a little at hearing of the character that had been fastened upon her; she disliked for her child, still more than for herself, to take this *bourgeois* name of Gardon; but there was no help for it, since, though he chief personages of the town were Huguenot, there could be no safety for her if the report were once allowed to arise that the Baronne de Ribaumont had taken refuge there.

It was best that she should be as little noticed as possible; nor, indeed, had good Noemi many visitors. The sad and sorrowful woman had always shut herself up with her Bible and her meditations, and sought no sympathy from her neighbours, nor encourage gossip in her shop. In the first days, when purchasers lingered to ask if it were true that Maitre Gardon had brought his daughter-in-law and grandchild, her stern-faced, almost grim answer, that '*la pauvre* was ill at ease,' silenced them, and forced them to carry off their curiosity unsatisfied; but it became less easy to arrange when Eustacie herself was on foot again—refreshed, active, and with an irrepressible spring of energy and eagerness that could hardly be caged down in the Widow Laurent's tiny rooms. Poor child, had she not been ill and prostrate at first, and fastened herself on the tender side of the good woman's heart by the sweetness of an unselfish and buoyant nature in illness, Noemi could hardly have endured such an inmate, not even half a Huguenot, full of little Catholic observances like second nature to her; listening indeed to the Bible for the short time, but always, when it was expounded, either asleep, or finding some amusement indispensable for her baby; eager for the least variety, and above all spoilt by Maitre Gardon to a degree absolutely perplexing to the grave woman.

He would not bid her lay aside the observances that, to Noemi, seemed almost worship of the beast. He rather reverted to the piety which originated them; and argued with his old friend that it was better to build than to destroy, and that, before the fabric of truth, superstition would crumble away of itself. The little he taught her sounded to Noemi's puzzled ears mere Christianity instead of controversial Calvinism. And, moreover, he never blamed her for wicked worldliness when she yawned; but even devised opportunities for taking her out for a walk, to see as much life as might be on a market-day. He could certainly not forget—as much as would have been prudent—that she was a high-born lady; and even seemed taken aback when he found her with her sleeves turned up over her shapely-delicate arms, and a thick apron before her, with her hands in Veuve Laurent's flour, showing her some of those special mysterious arts of confectionery in which she had been initiated by Soeur Bernardine, when, not three years ago, she had been the pet of the convent at Bellaise. At first it was half sport and the desire of occupation, but the produce of her manipulations was so excellent as to excite quite a sensation in La Sablerie, and the echevins and baillis sent in quite considerable orders for the cakes and patties of Maitre Gardon's Paris-bred daughter-in-law.

Maitre Gardon hesitated. Noemi Laurent told him she cared little for the gain—Heaven knew it was nothing to her—but that she thought it wrong and inconsistent in him to wish to spare the poor child's pride, which was unchristian enough already. 'Nay,' he said sadly, 'mortifications from without do little to tame pride; nor did I mean to bring her here that she should turn cook and confectioner to pamper the appetite of Baillis La Grasse.'

But Eustacie's first view was a bright pleasure in the triumph of her skill; and when her considerate guardian endeavoured to impress on her that there was no necessity for vexing herself with the task, she turned round on him with the exclamation, 'Nay, dear father, do you not see it is my great satisfaction to be able to do something for our good hostess, so that my daughter and I be not a burden to her?'

'Well spoken, my Lady,' said the pastor; 'there is real nobility in that way of thinking. Yet, remember, Noemi is not without means; she feels not the burden. And the flock contribute enough for the shepherd's support, and yours likewise.'

'Then let her give it to the poor creatures who so often come in begging, and saying they have been burned out of house and home by one party or the other,' said Eustacie. 'Let me have my way, dear sir; Soeur Bernadine always said I should be a prime *menagere*. I like it so much.'

And Madame de Ribaumont mixed sugar and dough, and twisted quaint shapes, and felt important and almost light-hearted, and sang over her work and over her child songs that were not always Marot's psalms; and that gave the more umbrage to Noemi, because she feared that Maitre Gardon actually like to hear them, though, should their echo reach the street, why it would be a peril, and still worse, a horrible scandal that out of that sober, afflicted household should proceed profane tunes such as court ladies sang.

CHAPTER XX
THE ABBE.

By the day and night her sorrows fall

  Where miscreant hands and rude

Have stained her pure, ethereal pall

  With many a martyr's blood.

And yearns not her maternal heart

  To hear their secret sighs,

Upon whose doubting way apart

  Bewildering shadows rise?—KEBLE

It was in the summer twilight that Eustacie, sitting on the doorstep between the two rooms, with her baby on her knees, was dreamily humming to her a tune, without even words, but one that she loved, because she had first learnt to sing it with Berenger and his friend Sidney to the lute of the latter; and its notes always brought before her eyes the woods of Montpipeau. Then it was that, low and soft as was the voice, that befell which Noemi had feared: a worn, ragged-looking young man, who had been bargaining at the door for a morsel of bread in exchange for a handkerchief, started at the sound, and moved so as to like into the house.

Noemi was at the moment not attending, being absorbed in the study of the handkerchief, which was of such fine, delicate texture that an idea of its having been stolen possessed her; and she sought the corner where, as she expected, a coat-of-arms was embroidered. Just as she was looking up to demand explanation, the stranger, with a sudden cry of 'Good heavens, it is she!' pushed past her into the house, and falling on his knee before Eustacie, exclaimed, 'O Lady, Lady, is it thus that I see you?'

Eustacie had started up in dismay, crying out, 'Ah! M. l'Abbe, as you are a gentleman, betray me not. Oh! have they sent you to find me? Have pity on us! You loved my husband!'

'You have nothing to fear from me, Lady,' said the young man, still kneeling; 'if you are indeed a distressed fugitive—so am I. If you have shelter and friends—I have none.'

'Is it indeed so?' said Eustacie, wistfully, yet scarce reassured. 'You are truly not come from my uncle. Indeed, Monsieur, I would not doubt you, but you see I have so much at stake. I have my little one here, and they mean so cruelly by her.'

'Madame, I swear by the honour of a nobleman—nay, by all that is sacred—that I know nothing of your uncle. I have been a wanderer for many weeks past; proscribed and hunted down because I wished to seek into the truth.'

'Ah!' said Eustacie, with a sound of relief, and of apology, 'pardon me, sir; indeed, I know you were good. You loved my husband;' and she reached out her hand to raise him, when he kissed it reverently. Little *bourgeoise* and worn mendicant as they were in dress, the air of the Louvre breathed round them; and there was all its grace and dignity as the lady turned round to her astonished hosts, saying, 'Good sir, kind mother, this gentleman is, indeed, what you took me for, a fugitive for the truth. Permit me to present to you, Monsieur l'Abbe de Mericour—at least, so he was, when last I had the honour to see him.'

The last time HE had seen her, poor Eustacie had been incapable of seeing anything save that bloody pool at the foot of the stairs.

Mericour now turned and explained. 'Good friends,' he said courteously, but with the *fierete* of the noble not quite out of his tone, 'I beg your grace. I would not have used so little ceremony, if I had not been out of myself at recognizing a voice and a tune that could belong to none but Madame—'

'Sit down, sir,' said Noemi, a little coldly and stiffly—for Mericour was a terrible name to Huguenots ears; 'a true friend to this lady must needs be welcome, above all if he comes in Heaven's name.'

'Sit down and eat, sir,' added Gardon, much more heartily; 'and forgive us for not having been more hospitable—but the times have taught us to be cautious, and in that lady we have a precious charge. Rest; for you look both weary and hungry.'

Eustacie added an invitation, understanding that he would not sit without her permission, and then, as he dropped into a chair, she exclaimed, 'Ah! sir, you are faint, but you are famished.'

'It will pass,' he said; 'I have not eaten to-day.'

Instantly a meal was set before him, and ere long he revived; and as the shutters were closed, and shelter for the night promised to him by a Huguenot family lodging in the same house, he began to answer Eustacie's anxious questions, as well as to learn from her in return what had brought her into her present situation.

Then it was that she recollected that it had been he who, at her cousin Diane's call, had seized her when she was rushing out of the palace in her first frenzy of grief, and had carried her back to the women's apartments.

'It was that day which brought me here,' he said.

And he told how, bred up in his own distant province, by a pious and excellent tutor, he had devoutly believed in the extreme wickedness of the Reformers; but in his seclusion he had been trained to such purity of faith and morals, that, when his brother summoned him to court to solicit a benefice, he had been appalled at the aspect of vice, and had, at the same time, been struck by the pure lives of the Huguenots; for truly, as things then were at the French court, crime seemed to have arrayed itself on the side of the orthodox party, all virtue on that of the schismatics.

De Mericour consulted spiritual advisers, who told him that none but Catholics could be truly holy, and that what he admired were merely heathen virtues that the devil permitted the Huguenots to display in order to delude the unwary. With this explanation he had striven to be satisfied, though eyes unblended by guilt and a pure heart continued to be revolted at the practices which his Church, scared at the evil times, and forgetful of her own true strength, left undenounced in her partisans. And the more that the Huguenot gentlemen thronged the court, and the young Abbe was thrown into intercourse with them, and the more he perplexed himself how the truth, the faith, the uprightness, the forbearance, the purity that they evinced could indeed be wanting in the zeal that made them acceptable. Then came the frightful morning when carnage reigned in every street, and the men who had been treated as favourite boon companions were hunted down like wild beasts in every street. He had endeavoured to save life, but would have speedily been slaughtered himself except for his soutane; and in all good faith he had hurried to the Louvre, to inform royalty of the horrors that, as he thought, a fanatic passion was causing the populace to commit.

He found the palace become shambles—the King himself, wrought up to frenzy, firing on the fugitives. And the next day, while his brain still seemed frozen with horror, he was called on to join in the procession of thanksgiving for the King's deliverance from a dangerous plot. Surely, if the plot were genuine, he thought, the procession should have savoured of penance and humiliation rather than of barbarous exultation! Yet these might be only the individual crimes of the Queen-mother, and of the Guises seeking to mask themselves under the semblance of zeal; and the infallible head of the visible Church would disown the slaughter, and cast it from the Church with loathing as a blood-stained garment. Behold, Rome was full of rejoicing, and sent sanction and commendation of the pious zeal of the King! Had the voice of Holy Church become indeed as the voice of the bloodhound? Was this indeed her call?

The young man, whose life from infancy had been marked out for the service of the Church—so destined by his parents as securing a wealthy provision for a younger son, but educated by his good tutor with more real sense of his obligations—felt the question in its full import. He was under no vows; he had, indeed, received the tonsure, but was otherwise unpledged, and he was bent on proving all things. The gaieties in which he had at first mingled had become abhorrent to him, and he studied with the earnestness of a newly-awakened mind in search of true light. The very face of study and inquiry, in one of such a family as that of his brother the Duke de Mericour, was enough to excite suspicion of Huguenot inclinations. The elder brother tried to quash the folly of the younger, by insisting on his sharing the debaucheries which, whether as priest or monk, or simply as Christian man, it would be his duty to abjure; and at length, by way of bringing things to a test, insisted on his making one of a party who were about to break up and destroy a Huguenot assembly. Unable, in his present mood, to endure the thought of further cruelty, the young Abbe fled, gave secret warning to the endangered congregation, and hastened to the old castle in Brittany, where he had been brought up, to pour out his perplexities, and seek the counsel of the good old chaplain who had educated him. Whether the kind, learned, simple-hearted tutor could have settled his mind, he had no time to discover, for he had scarcely unfolded his troubles before warnings came down that he had better secure himself—his brother, as head of the family, had obtained the royal assent to the imprisonment of the rebellious junior, so as to bring him to a better mind, and cure him of the Huguenot inclinations, which in the poor lad were simply undeveloped. But in all the Catholic eyes he was a tainted man, and his almost inevitable course was to take refuge with some Huguenot relations. There he was eagerly welcome; instruction was poured in on him; but as he showed a disposition to inquire and examine, and needed time to look into what they taught him, as one who feared to break his link with the Church, and still longed to find her blameless and glorious, the righteous nation that keepeth the truth, they turned on him and regarded him as a traitor and a spy, who had come among them on false pretences.

All the poor lad wanted was time to think, time to examine, time to consult authorities, living and dead. The Catholics called this treason to the Church, the Huguenots called it halting between two opinions; and between them he was a proscribed, distrusted vagabond, branded on one side as a recreant, and on the other as a traitor. He had asked for a few months of quiet, and where could they be had? His grand-mother had been the daughter of a Scottish nobleman in the French service, and he had once seen a nephew of hers who had come to Paris during the time of Queen Mary's residence there. He imagined that if he were once out of this distracted land of France, he might find respite for study, for which he longed; and utterly ignorant of the real state of Scotland, he had determined to make his way to his kindred there; and he had struggled on the way to La Rochelle, cheated out of the small remains of his money, selling his last jewels and all the clothing that was not indispensable, and becoming so utterly unable to pay his passage to England, that he could only trust to Providence to find him some means of reaching his present goal.

He had been listened to with kindness, and a sympathy such as M. Gardon's large mind enable him to bestow, where his brethren had been incapable of comprehending that a man could sincerely doubt between them and Rome. When the history was finished, Eustacie exclaimed, turning to Maitre Gardon, 'Ah! sir, is not this just what we sought? If this gentleman would but convey a letter to my mother-in-law——'

M. Gardon smiled. 'Scotland and England are by no means the same place, Lady,' he said.

'Whatever this lady would command, wherever she would send me, I am at her service,' cried the Abbe, fervently.

And, after a little further debate, it was decided that it might really be the best course, for him as for Madame de Ribaumont, to become the bearer of a letter and token from her, entreating her mother-in-law to notify her pleasure whether she should bring her child to England. She had means enough to advance a sufficient sum to pay Mericour's passage, and he accepted it most punctiliously as a loan, intending, so soon as her despatches were ready, to go on to La Rochelle, and make inquiry for a ship.

Chance, however, seemed unusually propitious, for the next day there was an apparition in the streets of La Sablerie of four or five weather-beaten, rollicking-looking men, their dress profusely adorned with ribbons, and their language full of strange oaths. They were well known at La Sablerie as sailors belonging to a ship of the fleet of the Count de Montgomery, the unfortunate knight whose lance had caused the death of King Henry II., and who, proscribed by the mortal hatred of Catherine de Medicis, had become the admiral of a piratical fleet in the Calvinist interest, so far winked at the Queen Elizabeth that it had its head-quarters in the Channel Islands, and thence was a most formidable foe to merchant vessels on the northern and eastern coasts of France; and often indulged in descents on the coast, when the sailors—being in general the scum of the nation—were apt to comport themselves more like American buccaneers than like champions of any form of religion.

La Sablerie was a Huguenot town, so they used no violence, but only swaggered about, demanding from Bailli La Grasse, in the name of their gallant Captain Latouche, contributions and provisions, and giving him to understand that if he did not comply to the uttermost it should be the worse for him. Their ship, it appeared, had been forced to put into the harbour, about two miles off, and Maitre Gardon and the young Abbe decided on walking thither to see it, and to have an interview with the captain, so as to secure a passage for Mericour at least. Indeed Maitre Gardon had, in consultation with Eustacie, resolved, if he found things suitable, to arrange for their all going together. She would be far safer out of France; and, although the Abbe alone could not have escorted her, yet Maitre Gardon would gladly have secured for her the additional protection of a young, strong, and spirited man; and Eustacie, who was no scribe, was absolutely relieved to have the voyage set before her as an alternative to the dreadful operation of composing a letter to the *belle-mere*, whom she had not seen since she had been seven years old, and of whose present English name she had the most indistinct ideas.

However, the first sight of the ship overthrew all such ideas. It was a wretched single-decked vessel, carrying far more sail than experienced nautical eyes would have deemed safe, and with no accommodation fit for a woman and child, even had the aspect of captain or crew been more satisfactory—for the ruffianly appearance and language of the former fully rivaled that of his sailors. It would have been mere madness to think of trusting the lady in such hands; and, without a word to each other, Gardon and Mericour resolved to give no hint even that she and her jewels were in La Sablerie. Mericour, however, made his bargain with the captain, who understood to transport him as far as Guernsey, whence he might easily make his way to Dorsetshire, where M. Gardon knew that Berenger's English home had been.

So Eustacie, with no small trouble and consideration, indited her letter—telling of her escape, the birth of her daughter, the dangers that threatened her child—and begging that its grand-mother would give it a safe home in England, and love it for the sake of its father. An answer would find her at the Widow Noemi Laurent's, Rue des Trois Fees, La Sablerie. She could not bring herself to speak of the name of Eserance Gardon which had been saddled upon her; and even M. de Mericour remained in ignorance of her bearing this disguise. She recommended him to the kindness of her mother-in-law; and M. Gardon added another letter to the lady, on behalf of the charge to whom he promised to devote himself until he should see them safe in friendly hands. Both letters were addressed, as best they might be, between Eustacie's dim comprehension of the word

Thistlewood, and M. Gardon's notion of spelling. 'Jadis, Baronne de Ribaumont' was the securest part of the direction.

And for a token, Eustacie looked over her jewels to find one that would serve for a token; but the only ones she knew would be recognized, were the brooch that had fastened the plume in Berenger's bloody cap, and the chaplet of pearls. To part with the first, or to risk the second in the pirate-ship, was impossible, but Eustacie at last decided upon detaching the pear-shaped pearl which was nearest the clasp, and which was so remarkable in form and tint that there was no doubt of its being well known.

CHAPTER XXI
UNDER THE WALNUT-TREE

Mistress Jean was making the elder-flower wine—

'And what brings the

Laird at sic a like time?'

LADY NAIRN, THE LAIRD OF COCKPEN

Summer was nearly ended, and Lucy Thistlewood was presiding in the great kitchen of the Manor-house, standing under the latticed window near the large oak-table, a white apron over her dress, presiding over the collecting of elder-berries for the brew of household-wine for the winter. The maids stood round her with an array of beechen bowls or red and yellow crocks, while barefooted, bareheaded children came thronging in with rush or wicker baskets of the crimson fruit, which the maids poured in sanguine cascades into their earthenware; and Lucy requited with substantial slices of bread and cheese, and stout homely garment mostly of her own sewing.

Lucy was altogether an inmate of her father's house. She had not even been at Hurst Walwyn for many months; for her step-mother's reiterated hopes that Berenger would make her his consolation for all he had suffered from his French spouse rendered it impossible to her to meet him with sisterly unconsciousness; and she therefore kept out of the way, and made herself so useful at home, that Dame Annora only wondered how it had been possible to spare her so long, and always wound up her praises by saying, that Berenger would learn in time how lucky he had been to lose the French puppet, and win the good English housewife.

If only tidings would have come that the puppet was safe married. That was the crisis which all the family desired yet feared for Berenger, since nothing else they saw would so detach his thoughts from the past as the leave him free to begin life again. The relapse brought on by the cruel reply to Osbert's message had been very formidable: he was long insensible or delirious and then came a state of annihilated thought, then of frightfully sensitive organs, when light, sound, movement, or scent were alike agony; and when he slowly revived, it was with such sunken spirits, that his silence was as much from depression as from difficulty of speech. His brain was weak, his limbs feeble, the wound in his mouth never painless; and all this necessarily added to his listless indifference and weariness, as though all youthful hope and pleasure were extinct in him. He had ceased to refer to the past. Perhaps he had thought it over, and seen that the deferred escape, the request for the pearls, the tryst at the palace, and detention from the king's chamber, made an uglier case against Eustacie than he could endure to own even to himself. If his heart trusted, his mind could not argue out her defence, and his tongue would not serve him for discussion with his grandfather, the only person who could act for him. Perhaps the stunned condition of his mind made the suspense just within the bounds of endurance, while trust in his wife's innocence rendered his inability to come to her aid well-nigh intolerable; and doubt of her seemed both profanity and misery unspeakable. He could do nothing. He had shot his only shaft by sending Landry Osbert, and had found that to endeavour to induce his grandfather to use further measures was worse than useless, and was treated as mere infatuation. He knew that all he had to do was to endeavour for what patience he could win from Cecily's sweet influence and guidance, and to wait till either certainty should come—that dreadful, miserable certainty that all looked for, and his very helplessness might be bringing about—or till he should regain strength to be again effective.

And miserably slow work was this recovery. No one had surgical skill to deal with so severe a wound as that which Narcisse had inflicted; and the daily pain and inconvenience it caused led to innumerable drawbacks that often—even after he had come as far as the garden—brought him back to his bed in a dark room, to blood-letting, and to speechlessness. No one knew much of his mind—Cecily perhaps the most; and next to her, Philip—who, from the time he had been admitted to his step-brother's presence, had been most assiduous in tending him—seemed to understand his least sign, and to lay aside all his boisterous roughness in his eager desire to do him service. The lads had loved each other from the moment they had met as children, but never so apparently as now, when all the rude horse-play of healthy youths was over—and one was dependent, the other considerate. And if Berenger had made on one else believe in Eustacie, he had taught Philip to view her as the 'Queen's men' viewed Mary of Scotland. Philip had told Lucy the rough but wholesome truth, that 'Mother talks mere folly. Eustacie is no more to be spoken of with you than a pheasant with old brown Partlet; and Berry waits but to be well to bring her off from all her foes. And I'll go with him.'

It was on Philip's arm that Berenger first crept round the bowling-green, and with Philip at his rein that he first endured to ride along the avenue on Lord Walwyn's smooth-paced palfrey; and it was Philip who interrupted Lucy's household cares by rushing in and shouting, 'Sister, here! I have wiled him to ride over the down, and he is sitting under the walnut-tree quite spent, and the three little wenches are standing in a row, weeping like so many little mermaids. Come, I say!'

Lucy at once followed him through the house, through the deep porch to the court, which was shaded by a noble walnut-tree, where Sir Marmaduke loved to sit among his dogs. There not sat Berenger, resting against the trunk, overcome by the heat and exertion of his ride. His cloak and hat lay on the ground; the dogs fawned round him, eager for the wonted caress, and his three little sisters stood a little aloof, clinging to one another and crying piteously.

It was their first sight of him; and it seemed to them as if he were behind a frightful mask. Even Lucy was not without a sensation of the kind, of this effect in the change from the girlish, rosy complexion to extreme paleness, on which was visible, in ghastly red and purple, the great scar left by Narcisse, from the temple on the one side to the ear on the other.

The far more serious would on the cheek was covered with a black patch, and the hair had almost entirely disappeared from the head, only a few light brown locks still hanging round the neck and temples, so that the bald brow gave a strange look of age; and the disfigurement was terrible, enhanced as it was by the wasting effect of nearly a year of sickness. Lucy was so much shocked, that she could hardly steady her voice to chide the children for not giving a better welcome to their brother. They would have clung round her, but she shook them off, and sent Annora in haste for her mother's fan; while Philip arriving with a slice of diet-bread and a cup of sack, the one fanned him, and the other fed him with morsels of the cake soaked in the wine, till he revived, looked up with eyes that were unchanged, and thanked them with a few faltering words, scarcely intelligible to Lucy. The little girls came nearer, and curiously regarded him but when he held out his hand to his favourite Dolly, she shrank back in reluctance.

'Do not chide her,' he said wearily. 'May she never become used to such marks!'

'What, would you have her live among cowards?' exclaimed Philip; but Berenger, instead of answering, looked up at the front of the house, one of those fine Tudor facades that seem all carved timber and glass lattice, and asked, so abruptly that Lucy doubted whether she heard him alright,— 'How many windows are there in this front?'

'I never counted,' said Philip.

'I have,' said Annora; 'there are seven and thirty, besides the two little ones in the porch.'

'None shall make them afraid,' he muttered. 'Who would dare build such a defenceless house over yonder?'—pointing south.

'Our hearts are guarded now,' said Philip, proudly. Berenger half smiled, as he was wont to do when he meant more than he could conveniently utter, and presently he asked, in the same languid, musing tone, 'Lucy, were you ever really affrighted?'

Lucy questioned whether he could be really in his right mind, as if the bewilderment of his brain was again returning; and while she paused, Annora exclaimed, 'Yes, when we were gathering cowslips, and the brindled cow ran at us, and Lucy could not run because she had Dolly in her arm. Oh! we were frightened then, till you came, brother.'

'Yes,' added Bessie; 'and last winter too, when the owl shrieked at the window——'

'And,' added Berenger, 'sister, what was your greatest time of revelry?'

Annora again put in her word. 'I know, brother; you remember the fair-day, when my Lady Grandame was angered because you and Lucy went on dancing when we and all then gentry had ceased. And when Lucy said she had not seen that you were left alone, Aunt Cecily said it was because the eyes of discretion were lacking.'

'Oh, the Christmas feast was far grander,' said Bessie. 'Then Lucy had her first satin farthingale, and three gallants, besides my brother, wanted to dance with her.'

Blushing deeply, Lucy tried to hush the little ones, much perplexed by the questions, and confused by the answers. Could he be contrasting the life where a vicious cow had been the most alarming object, a greensward dance with a step-brother the greatest gaiety, dye of the elder juice the deepest stain, with the temptations and perils that had beset one equally young? Resting his head on his hand, his elbow on his knee, he seemed to be musing in a reverie that he could hardly brook, as his young brow was knitted by care and despondency.

Suddenly, the sounds in the village rose from the quiet sleepy summer hum into a fierce yell of derisive vituperation, causing Philip at once to leap up, and run across the court to the entrance-gate, while Lucy called after him some vain sisterly warning against mingling in a fray.

It seemed as if his interposition had a good effect, for the uproar lulled almost as soon as he had hurried to the scene of action; and presently he reappeared, eager and breathless. 'I told them to bring him up here,' he said; 'they would have flogged him at the cart's-tail, the rogues, just because my father is out of the way. I could not make out his jargon, but you can, brother; and make that rascal Spinks let him go.'

'What should I have to do with it?' said Berenger, shrinking from the sudden exposure of his scarred face and maimed speech. 'I am no magistrate.'

'But you can understand him; he is French, the poor rogue something abut a letter, and wanting to ask his way. Ah! I thought that would touch you, and it will cost you little pains, and slouching it over his face, rose, and, leaning upon Annora's shoulder, stepped forward, just as the big burly blacksmith-constable and small shriveled cobbler advanced, dragging along, by a cord round the wrists, a slight figure with a red woolen sailor's shirt, ragged black hosen, bare head, and almost bare feet.

Doffing their caps, the men began an awkward salutation to the young Lord on his recovery, but he only touched his beaver in return, and demanded, 'How now! what have you bound him for?'

'You see, my Lord,' began the constable, 'there have been a sort of vagrants of late, and I'll be bound' twas no four-legged fox as took Gaffer Shepherd's lamb.'

The peroration was broken off, for with a start as if he had been shot, Berenger cried aloud, 'Mericour! the Abbe!'

'Ah, Monsieur, if you know me,' cried the young man, raising his head, 'free me from this shame—aid me in my mission!'

'Loose him, fellows,' shouted Berenger; 'Philip, a knife—Lucy, those scissors.'

'Tis my duty, my Lord,' said Spinks, gruffly. 'All vagabonds to be apprehended and flogged at the cart's-tail, by her Grace's special commands. How is it to be answered to his Honour, Sir Marmaduke?'

'Oaf!' cried Philip, 'you durst not have used such violence had my father been at home! Don't you see my brother knows him?'

With hands trembling with haste, Berenger had seized the scissors that, house-wife like, hung at Lucy's waist, and was cutting the rope, exclaiming in French, 'Pardon, pardon, friend, for so shameful a reception.'

'Sir,' was the reply, without a sign of recognition, 'if, indeed, you know my name, I entreat you to direct me to the chateau of Le Sieur Tistefote, whose lady was once Baronne de Ribaumont.'

'My mother! Ah, my friend, my friend! what would you?' he cried in a tone of tremulous hope and fear, laying one hand on Mericour's shoulder, and about to embrace him.

Mericour retreated from him; but the high-spirited young man crossed his arms on his breast, and gazing at the group with indignant scorn, made answer, 'My message is from her who deems herself a widow, to the mother of the husband whom she little imagines to be not only alive, but consoled.'

'Faithful! Faithful!' burst out Berenger, with a wild, exultant, strangely-ringing shout. 'Woe, woe to those who would have had me doubt her! Philip—Lucy—hear! Her truth is clear to all the world!' Then changing back again to French, 'Ten thousand blessings on you, Mericour! You have seen her! Where—how?'

Mericour still spoke with frigid politeness. 'I had the honour to part with Madame la Baronne de Ribaumont in the town of La Sablerie, among humble, Huguenot guardians, to whom she had fled, to save her infant's life—when no aid came.'

He was obliged to break off, for Berenger, stunned by the sudden rush of emotion, reeled as he stood, and would have fallen but for the prompt support of Lucy, who was near enough to guide him back to rest upon the bench, saying resentfully in French as she did so, 'My brother is still very ill. I pray you, sir, have a care.'

She had not half understood the rapid words of the two young men, Philip comprehended them far less, and the constable and his crew of course not at all; and Spinks pushed forward among the group as he saw Berenger sink back on the bench; and once more collaring his prisoner, exclaimed almost angrily to Philip, 'There now, sir, you've had enough of the vagabond. We'll keep him tight ere he bewitches any more of you.'

This rude interference proved an instant restorative. Berenger sprang up at once, and seizing Spink's arm, exclaimed, 'Hands off, fellow! This is my friend—a gentleman. He brings me tidings of infinite gladness. Who insults him, insults me.'

Spinks scarcely withdrew his hand from Mericour's neck; and scowling, said, 'Very odd gentleman—very queer tidings, Master Berenger, to fell you like an ox. I must be answerable for the fellow till his Honour comes.'

'Ah! *Eh quoi*, wherefore not show the *canaille* your sword?' said Mericour, impatiently.

'It may not be here, in England,' said Berenger (who fortunately was not wearing his weapon). 'And in good time here comes my step-father,' as the gate swung back, and Sir Marmaduke and Lady Thistlewood rode through it, the former sending his voice far before him to demand the meaning of the hurly-burly that filled his court.

Philip was the first to spring to his rein, exclaiming, 'Father, it is a Frenchman whom Spinks would have flogged at the cart's-tail; but it seems he is a friend of Berenger's, and has brought him tidings. I know not what—about his wife, I believe—any way he is beside himself with joy.'

'Sir, your Honour,' shouted Spinks, again seizing Mericour, and striving to drag him forward, 'I would know whether the law is to be hindered from taking its course because my young Lord there is a Frenchman and bewitched.'

'Ah,' shrieked Lady Thistlewood, 'I knew it. They will have sent secret poison to finish him. Keep the fellow safe. He will cast it in the air.'

'Ay, ay, my Lady,' said Spinks, 'there are plenty of us to testify that he made my young Lord fall back as in a swoon, and reel like one distraught. Pray Heaven it have not gone further.'

'Sir,' exclaimed Berenger, who on the other side held his friend's hand tight, 'this is a noble gentleman—the brother of the Duke de Mericour. He has come at great risk to bring me tidings of my dear and true wife. And not one word will these demented rascals let me hear with their senseless clamour.'

'Berenger! You here, my boy!' exclaimed Sir Marmaduke, more amazed by this than all the rest.

'He touches him—he holds him! Ah! will no one tear him away?' screamed Lady Thistlewood. Nor would Spinks have been slow in obeying her if Sir Marmaduke had not swung his substantial form to the ground, and stepping up to the prisoner, rudely clawed on one side by Spinks, and affectionately grasped on the other side by Berenger, shouted—

'Let go, both!' does he speak English? Peace, dame! If the lad be bewitched, it is the right way. He looks like the other man. Eh, lad, what does your friend say for himself?'

'Sir,' said Berenger, interpreting Mericour's words as they were spoken, 'he has been robbed and misused at sea by Montgomery's pirate crews. He fled from court for the religion's sake; he met her—my wife' (the voice was scarcely intelligible, so tremulously was it spoken), 'in hiding among the Huguenots—he brings a letter and a token from her to my mother.'

'Ha! And you know him? You avouch him to be what he represents himself?'

'I knew him at court. I know him well. Father, make these fellows cease their insults! I have heard nothing yet. See here!' holding out what Mericour had put into his hand; 'this you cannot doubt, mother.'

'Parted the pearls! Ah, the little minx!' cried the lady, as she recognized the jewels.

'I thought he had been robbed?' added Sir Marmaduke.

'The gentleman doubts?' said Mericour, catching some of the words. 'He should know that what is confided in a French gentleman is only taken from him with his life. Much did I lose; but the pearl I kept hidden in my mouth.'

Therewith he produced the letter. Lady Thistlewood pronounced that no power on earth should induce her to open it, and drew off herself and her little girls to a safe distance from the secret poison she fancied it contained; while Sir Marmaduke was rating the constables for taking advantage of his absence to interpret the Queen's Vagrant Act in their own violent fashion; ending, however, by sending them round to the buttery-hatch to drink the young Lord's health. For the messeger, the good knight heartily grasped his hand, welcoming him and thanking him for having 'brought comfort to you poor lad's heart.'

But there Sir Marmaduke paused, doubting whether the letter had indeed brought comfort; for Berenger, who had seized on it, when it was refused by his mother, was sitting under the tree—turning away indeed, but not able to conceal that his tears were gushing down like rain. The anxious exclamation of his step-father roused him at length, but he scarce found power or voice to utter, as he thrust the letter into the knight's hand, 'Ah! see what has she not suffered for me! me, whom you would have had believed her faithless!'

He then grasped his friend's arm, and with him disappeared into the house, leaving Sir Marmaduke holding the letter in a state of the utmost bewilderment, and calling by turns on his wife and daughter to read and explain it to him.

And as Lucy read the letter, with her mother could not yet prevail on herself to touch, she felt at each word more grateful to the good Aunt Cecily, whose influence had taught her always to view Berenger as a brother, and not to condemn unheard the poor young wife. If she had not been thus guarded, what distress might not this day of joy to Berenger have brought to Lucy! Indeed, Lady Thistlewood was vexed enough as it was, and ready to carry her incredulity to the most inconsistent lengths. 'It was all a trick for getting the poor boy back, that they might make an end of him altogether. Tell her they thought him dead.—Tilley-valley! It was a mere attempt on her own good-nature, to get a little French impostor on her hands. Let Sir Duke look well to it, and take care that her poor boy was not decoyed among them. The Frenchman might be cutting his throat at that moment! Where was he? Had Sir Duke been so lost as to let them out of sight together? No one had either pity or prudence now that her poor father was gone;' and she began to weep.

'No great fear on that score, dame,' laughed the knight. 'Did you not hear the lad shouting for 'Phil, Phil!' almost in a voice like old times? It does one good to hear it.'

Just at twilight, Berenger came down the steps, conducting a graceful gentleman in black, to whom Lady Thistlewood's instinct impelled her to make a low courtesy, before Berenger had said, 'Madam, allow me to present to you my friend, the Abbe de Mericour.'

'Is it the same?' whispered Bessie to Annora. 'Surely he is translated!'

'Only into Philip's old mourning suit. I know it by the stain on the knee.

'Then it is translated too. Never did it look so well on Philip! See, our mother is quite gracious to him; she speaks to him as though he were some noble visitor to my Lord.'

Therewith Sir Marmaduke came forward, shook Mericour with all his might by the hand, shouted to him his hearty thanks for the good he had done his poor lad and assured him of a welcome from the very bottom of his heart. The good knight would fain have kept both Berenger and his friend at the Manor, but Berenger was far too impatient to carry home his joy, and only begged the loan of a horse for Mericour. For himself, he felt as if fatigue or dejection would never touch him again, and he kissed his mother and his sisters, including Lucy, all round, with an effusion of delight.

'Is that indeed your step-father?' said Mericour, as they rode away together. 'And the young man, is he your half-brother?'

'Brother wholly in dear love,' said Berenger; 'no blood relation. The little girls are my mother's children.'

'Ah! so large a family all one? All at home? None in convents?'

'We have no convents.'

'Ah, no, but all at home! All at peace! This is a strange place, your England.'

CHAPTER XXII
DEPARTURE

It is my mistress!

Since she is living, let the time run on

To good or bad.—CYMBELINE

Mericour found the welcome at Hurst Walwyn kindly and more polished than that at Combe Manor. He was more readily understood, and found himself at his natural element. Lord Walwyn, in especial, took much notice of him, and conversed with him long and earnestly; while Berenger, too happy and too weary to exert himself to say many words, sat as near Cecily as he could, treating her as though she, who had never contradicted in his trust in Eustacie, were the only person who could worthily share his infinite relief, peace, and thankfulness.

Lord Walwyn said scarcely anything to his grandson that night, only when Berenger, as usual, bent his knee to ask his blessing on parting for the night, he said, gravely, 'Son, I am glad of your joy; I fear me you have somewhat to pardon your grandsire. Come to my library so soon as morning prayers be over; we will speak then. Not now, my dear lad,' he added, as Berenger, with tears in his eyes, kissed his hand, and would have begun; 'you are too much worn and spent to make my dear ears hear. Sleep, and take my blessing with you.'

It was a delight to see the young face freed from the haggard, dejected expression that had been sadder than the outward wound; and yet it was so questionable how far the French connection was acceptable to the family, that when Berenger requested Mr. Adderley to make mention of the mercy vouch-safed to him in the morning devotions, the chaplain bowed, indeed, but took care to ascertain that his so doing would be agreeable to my Lord and my Lady.

He found that if Lady Walwyn was still inclined to regret that the Frenchwoman was so entirely a wife, and thought Berenger had been very hasty and imprudent, yet that the old Lord was chiefly distressed at the cruel injustice he had so long been doing this poor youth thing. A strong sense of justice, and long habit of dignified self-restraint, alone prevented Lord Walwyn from severely censuring Mr. Adderley for misrepresentations; but the old nobleman recollected that Walsingham had been in the same story, and was too upright to visit his own vexation on the honestly-mistaken tutor.

However, when Berenger made his appearance in the study, looking as if not one right, but weeks, had been spent in recovering health and spirit, the old man's first word was a gentle rebuke for his having been left unaware of how far matters had gone; but he cut short the attempted reply, but saying he knew it was chiefly owing to his own over-hasty conclusion, and fear of letting his grandson injure himself by vainly discussing the subject. Now, however, he examined Berenger closely on all the proceedings Paris and at Montpipeau, and soon understood that the ceremony had been renewed, ratifying the vows taken in infancy. The old statesman's face cleared up at once; for, as he explained, he had now no anxieties as to the validity of the marriage by English law, at least, in spite of the decree from Rome, which, as he pointed out to his grandson, was wholly contingent on the absence of subsequent consent, since the parties had come to an age for free-will. Had he known of this, the re-marriage, he said, he should certainly have been less supine. Why had Berenger been silent?

'I was commanded, sir. I fear I have transgressed the command by mentioning it now. I must pray you to be secret.'

'Secret, foolish lad. Know you not that the rights of your wife and your children rest upon it?' and as the change in Berenger's looks showed that he had not comprehended the full importance of the second ceremony as nullifying the papal sentence, which could only quash the first on the ground of want of mutual consent, he proceeded, 'Command, quotha? Who there had any right to command you, boy?'

'Only one, sir.'

'Come, this no moment for lover's folly. It was not the girl, then? Then it could no other than the miserable King—was it so?'

'Yes, sir,' said Berenger. 'He bade me as king, and requested me as the friend who gave her to me. I could do no otherwise, and I thought it would be but a matter of a few days, and that our original marriage was the only important one.'

'Have you any parchment to prove it?'

'No, sir. It passed but as a ceremony to satisfy the Queen's scruples ere she gave my wife to me to take home. I even think the King was displeased at her requiring it.'

'Was Mr. Sidney a witness?'

'No, sir. None was present, save the King and Queen, her German countess, and the German priest.'

'The day?'

'Lammas-day.'

'The 1st of August of the year of grace 1572. I will write to Walsingham to obtain the testimony, if possible, of king or of priest; but belike they will deny it all. It was part of the trick. Shame upon it that a king should dig pits for so small a game as you, my poor lad!'

'Verily, my Lord,' said Berenger, 'I think the King meant us kindly, and would gladly have sped us well away. Methought he felt his bondage bitterly, and would fain have dared to be a true king. Even at the last, he bade me to his *garde-robe*, and all there were unhurt.'

'And wherefore obeyed you not?'

'The carouse would have kept me too late for our flight.'

'King's behests may not lightly be disregarded,' said the old courtier, with a smile. 'However, since he showed such seeming favour to you, surely you might send a petition to him privately, through Sir Francis Walsingham, to let the priest testify to your renewal of contract, engaging not to use it to his detriment in France.'

'I will do so, sir. Meanwhile,' he added, as one who felt he had earned a right to be heard in his turn, 'I have your permission to hasten to bring home my wife?'

Lord Walwyn was startled at this demand from one still so far from recovered as Berenger. Even this talk, eager as the youth was, had not been carried on without much difficulty, repetitions, and altered phrases, when he could not pronounce distinctly enough to be understood and the effort brought lines of pain into his brow. He could take little solid food, had hardly any strength for walking or riding; and, though all his wounds were whole, except that one unmanageable shot in the mouth, he looked entirely unfit to venture on a long journey in the very country that had sent him home a year before scarcely alive. Lord Walwyn had already devised what he thought a far more practicable arrangement; namely, to send Mr. Adderley and some of my Lady's women by sea, under the charge of Master Hobbs, a shipmaster at Weymouth, who traded with Bordeaux for wine, and could easily put in near La Sablerie, and bring off the lady and child, and, if she wished it, the pastor to whom such a debt of gratitude was owing.

Berenger was delighted with the notion of the sea rather than the land journey; but he pointed out at once that this would remove all objection to his going in person. He had often been out whole nights with the fishermen, and knew that a sea-voyage would be better for his health than anything,—certainly better than pining and languishing at home, as he had done for months. He could not bear to think of separation from Eustacie an hour longer than needful; nay, she had been cruelly entreated enough already; and as long as he could keep his feet, it was absolutely due to her that he should not let others, instead of himself, go in search of her. It would be almost death to him to stay at home.

Lord Walwyn looked at the pallid, wasted face, with all its marks of suffering and intense eagerness of expression, increased by the difficulty of utterance and need of subduing agitation. He felt that the long-misunderstood patience and endurance had earned something; and he knew, too, that for all his grandson's submission and respect, the boy, as a husband and father, had rights and duties that would assert themselves manfully if opposed. It was true that the sea-voyage obviated many difficulties, and it was better to consent with a good grace than drive one hitherto so dutiful to rebellion. He did then consent, and was rewarded by the lightning flash of joy and gratitude in the bright blue eyes, and the fervent pressure and kiss of his hand, as Berenger exclaimed, 'Ah! sir, Eustacie will be such a daughter to you. You should have seen how the Admiral liked her!'

The news of Lord Walwyn's consent raised much commotion in the family. Dame Annora was sure her poor son would be murdered outright this time, and that nobody cared because he was only HER son; and she strove hard to stir up Sir Marmaduke to remonstrate with her father; but the good knight had never disputed a judgment of 'my Lord's' in his whole life, and had even received his first wife from his hands, when forsaken by the gay Annora. So she could only ride over the Combe, be silenced by her father, as effectually as if Jupiter had nodded, and bewail and murmur to her mother till she lashed Lady Walwyn up into finding every possible reason why Berenger should and must sail. Then she went home, was very sharp with Lucy, and was reckoned by saucy little Nan to have nineteen times exclaimed 'Tilley-valley' in the course of one day.

The effect upon Philip was a vehement insistence on going with his brother. He was sure no one else would see to Berry half as well; and as to letting Berry go to be murdered again without him, he would not hear of it; he must go, he would not stay at home; he should not study; no, no, he should be ready to hang himself for vexation, and thinking what they were doing to his brother. And thus he extorted from his kind-hearted father an avowal that he should be easier a bout the lad if Phil were there, and that he might go, provided Berry would have him, and my Lord saw no objection. The first point was soon settled; and as to the second, there was no reason at all that Philip should not go where his brother did. In fact, excepting for Berenger's state of health, there was hardly any risk about the matter. Master Hobbs, to whom Philip rode down ecstatically to request him to come and speak to my Lord, was a stout, honest, experienced seaman, who was perfectly at home in the Bay of Biscay, and had so strong a feudal feeling for the house of Walwyn, that he placed himself and his best ship, the THROSTLE, entirely at his disposal. The THROSTLE was a capital sailer, and carried arms quite sufficient in English hands to protect her against Algerine corsairs or Spanish pirates. He only asked for a week to make her cabin ready for the reception of a lady, and this time was spent in sending a post to London, to obtain for Berenger the permit from the Queen, and the passport from the French Ambassador, without which he could not safely have gone; and, as a further precaution, letters were requested from some of the secret agents of the Huguenots to facilitate his admission into La Sablerie.

In the meantime, poor Mr. Adderley had submitted meekly to the decree that sentenced him to weeks of misery on board the THROSTLE, but to his infinite relief, an inspection of the cabins proved the space so small, that Berenger represented to him grandfather that the excellent tutor would be only an incumbrance to himself and every one else, and that with Philip he should need no one. Indeed, he had made such a start into vigour and alertness during the last few days that there was far less anxiety about him, though with several sighs for poor Osbert. Cecily initiated Philip into her simple rules for her patient's treatment in case of the return of his more painful symptoms. The notion of sending female attendants for Eustacie was also abandoned: her husband's presence rendered them unnecessary, or they might be procured at La Sablerie; and thus it happened that the only servants whom Berenger was to take with him were Humfrey Holt and John Smithers, the same honest fellows whose steadiness had so much conduced to his rescue at Paris.

Claude de Mericour had in the meantime been treated as an honoured guest at Combe Walwyn, and was in good esteem with its master. He would have set forth at once on his journey to Scotland, but that Lord Walwyn advised him to wait and ascertain the condition of his relatives there before throwing himself on them. Berenger had, accordingly, when writing to Sidney by the messenger above mentioned, begged him to find out from Sir Robert Melville, the Scottish Envoy, all he could about the family whose designation he wrote down at a venture from Mericour's lips.

Sidney returned a most affectionate answer, saying that he had never been able to believe the little shepherdess a traitor and was charmed that she had proved herself a heroine; he should endeavour to greet her with all his best powers as a poet, when she should brighten the English court; but his friend, Master Spenser, alone was fit to celebrate such constancy. As to M. l'Abbe de Mericour's friends, Sir Robert Melville had recognized their name at once, and had pronounced them to be fierce Catholics and Queensmen, so sorely pressed by the Douglases, that it was believed they would soon fly the country altogether; and Sidney added, what Lord Walwyn had already said, that to seek Scotland rather than France as a resting-place in which to weigh between Calvinism and Catholicism, was only trebly hot and fanatical. His counsel was that M. de Mericour should so far conform himself to the English Church as to obtain admission to one of the universities, and, through his uncle of Leicester, he could obtain for him an opening at Oxford, where he might fully study the subject.

There was much to incline Mericour to accept this counsel. He had had much conversation with Mr. Adderley, and had attended his ministrations in the chapel, and both satisfied him far better than what he had seen among the French Calninists; and the peace and family affection of the two houses were like a new world to him. But he had not yet made up his mind to that absolute disavowal of his own branch of the Church, which alone could have rendered him eligible for any foundation at Oxford. His attainments in classics would, Mr. Adderley thought, reach such a standard as to gain one of the very few scholarships open to foreigners; and his noble blood revolted at becoming a pensioner of Leicester's, or of any other nobleman.

Lord Walwyn, upon this, made an earnest offer of his hospitality, and entreated the young man to remain at Hurst Walwyn till the return of Berenger and Philip, during which time he might study under the directions of Mr. Adderley, and come to a decision whether to seek reconciliation with his native Church and his brother, or to remain in England. In this latter case, he might perhaps accompany both the youths to Oxford, for, in spite of Berenger's marriage, his education was still not supposed to be complete. And when Mericour still demurred with reluctance to become a burden on the bounty of the noble house, he was reminded gracefully of the debt of gratitude that the family owed to him for the relief he had brought to Berenger; and, moreover, Dame Annora giggled out that, 'if he would teach Nan and Bess to speak and read French and Italian, it would be worth something to them.' The others of the family would have hushed up this uncalled-for proposal; but Mericour caught at it as the most congenial mode of returning the obligation. Every morning he undertook to walk or ride over to the Manor, and there gave his lessons to the young ladies, with whom he was extremely popular. He was a far more brilliant teacher than Lucy, and ten thousand times preferable to Mr. Adderley, who had once begun to teach Annora her accidence with lamentable want of success.

CHAPTER XXIII
THE EMPTY CRADLE

Eager to know

The worst, and with that fatal certainty

To terminate intolerable dread,

He spurred his courser forward—all his fears

Too surely are fulfilled.—SOUTHEY

Contrary winds made the voyage of the THROSTLE much more tardy than had been reckoned on by Berenger's impatience; but hope was before him, and he often remembered his days in the little vessel as much happier than he had known them to be at the time.

It was in the calm days of right October that Captain Hobbs at length was putting into the little harbour nearest to La Sablerie. Berenger, on that morning, had for the first time been seized by a fit of anxiety as to the impression his face would make, with its terrible purple scar, great patch, and bald forehead, and had brought out a little black velvet mask, called a *tour de nez*, often used in riding to protect the complexion, intending to prepare Eustacie for his disfigurement. He had fastened on a carnation-coloured sword-knot, would a scarf of the same colour across his shoulder, clasped a long ostrich plume into his broad Spanish hat, and looked out his deeply-fringed Spanish gloves; and Philip was laughing merrily, not to say rudely, at him, for trying to deck himself out so bravely.

'See, Master Hobbs,' cried the boy in his high spirits, as he followed his brother on deck, 'you did not know you had so fine a gallant on board. Here be braveries for my Lady.'

'Hush, Phil,' broke in Berenger, who had hitherto taken all the raillery in perfect good part. 'What is amiss, Master Hobbs?'

'I cannot justly say, sir,' returned Master Hobbs, without taking his gaze off the coast, 'but by yonder banks and creeks this should be the Sables d'Olonne; and I do not see the steeple of La Sablerie, which has always been the landmark for the harbour of St. Julien.'

'What do you understand by that?' asked Berenger, more struck by his manner than his words.

'Well, sir, if I am right, a steeple that has stood three or four hundred years does not vanish out of sight like a cloud of smoke for nothing. I may be lightning, to be sure; or the Protestants may have had it down for Popery; but methinks they would have too much Christian regard for poor mariners than to knock down the only landmark on this coast till you come to Nissard spire.' Then he hailed the man at the mast-head, demanding if he saw the steeple of La Sablerie. 'No, no, sir.' But as other portions of the land became clearer, there was no doubt that the THROSTLE was right in her bearings; so the skipper gave orders to cast anchor and lower a boat. The passengers would have pressed him with inquiries as to what he thought the absence of his landmark could portend; but he hurried about, and shouted orders, with the deaf despotism of a nautical commander; and only when all was made ready, turned round and said, 'Now, sir, maybe you had best let me go ashore first, and find out how the land lies.'

'Never!' said Berenger, in an agony of impatience.

'I thought so,' said the captain. 'Well, then, sir, are your fellows ready? Armed? All right.'

So Berenger descended to the boat, followed by Philip; next came the captain, and then the two serving-men. Six of the crew were ready to row them to the shore, and were bidden by their captain to return at once to the vessel, and only return on a signal from him. the surging rush of intense anxiety, sure to precede the destined moment of the consummation of hope long deferred, kept Berenger silent, choked by something between fear and prayer; but Philip, less engrossed, asked Master Hobbs if it were not strange that none of the inhabitants of the squalid little huts on the shore had not put out to greet them in some of the boats that were drawn up on the beach.

'Poor wretches,' said Hobbs; 'they scarce know friend from foe, and are slow to run their heads into the lion's mouth. Strange fellows have the impudence to sail under our flag at times.'

However, as they neared the low, flat, sandy shore, a few red caps peeped out at the cottage-doors, and then, apparently gaining confidence from the survey, some wiry, active figures appeared, and were hailed by Hobbs. His Bordeaux trade had rendered him master of the coast language; and a few incomprehensible shouts between him and the natives resulted in a line being thrown to them, and the boat dragged as near as possible to the landing-place, when half a dozen ran up, splashing with their bare legs, to offer their shoulders for the transport of the passengers, both of whom were seized upon before they were aware, Philip struggling with all his might, till a call from Captain Hobbs warned him to resign himself; and then he became almost helpless with laughter at the figure cut by the long-legged Berenger upon a small fisherman's back.

They were landed. Could it be that Berenger was only two miles—only half an hour's walk form Eustacie? The bound his heart gave as he touched the shore seemed to stifle him. He could not believe it. Yet he knew how fully he had believed it, the next moment, when he listened to what the fishermen were saying to Captain Hobbs.

'Did Monsieur wish to go to La Sablerie? Ah! then he did not know what had happened. The soldiers had been there; there had been a great burning. They had been out in their boats at sea, but they had seen the sky red—red as a furnace, all night; and the steeple was down. Surely, Monsieur had missed the steeple that was a guide to all poor seafarers; and now they had to go all the way to Brancour to sell their fish.'

'And the townspeople?' Hobbs asked.

'Ah! poor things; 'twas pity of them, for they were honest folk to deal with, even if they were heretics. They loved fish at other seasons if not in Lent; and it seemed but a fair return to go up and bury as many of them as were not burnt to nothing in their church; and Dom Colombeau, the good priest of Nissard, has said it was a pious work; and he was a saint, if any one was.'

'Alack, sir,' said Hobbs, laying his hand on the arm of Berenger, who seemed neither to have breathed nor moved while the man was speaking: 'I feared that there had been some such bloody work when I missed the steeple. But take heart yet: your lady is very like to have been out of the way. We might make for La Rochelle, and there learn!' Then, again to the fisherman, 'None escaped, fellow?'

'Not one,' replied the man. 'They say that one of the great folks was in a special rage with them for sheltering the lady he should have wedded, but who had broken convent and turned heretic; and they had victualled Montgomery's pirates too.'

'And the lady?' continued Hobbs, ever trying to get a more supporting hold of his young charge, in case the rigid tension of his limbs should suddenly relax.'

'I cannot tell, sir. I am a poor fisher; but I could guide you to the place where old Gillot is always poking about. He listened to their preachings, and knows more than we do.'

'Let us go,' said Berenger, at once beginning to stride along in his heavy boots through the deep sand. Philip, who had hardly understood a word of the *patois*, caught hold of him, and begged to be told what had happened;

but Master Hobbs drew the boy off, and explained to him and to the two men what were the dreadful tidings that had wrought such a change in Berenger's demeanour. The way over the shifting sands was toilsome enough to all the rest of the party; but Berenger scarcely seemed to feel the deep plunge at every step as they almost ploughed their way along for the weary two miles, before a few green bushes and half-choked trees showed that they were reaching the confines of the sandy waste. Berenger had not uttered a word the whole time, and his silence hushed the others. The ground began to rise, grass was seen still struggling to grow, and presently a large straggling mass of black and gray ruins revealed themselves, with the remains of a once well-trodden road leading to them. But the road led to a gate-way choked by a fallen jamb and barred door, and the guide led them round the ruins of the wall to the opening where the breach had been. The sand was already blowing in, and no doubt veiled much; for the streets were scarcely traceable through remnants of houses more or less dilapidated, with shreds of broken or burnt household furniture within them.

'Ask him for *la rue des Trois Fées*,' hoarsely whispered Berenger.

The fisherman nodded, but soon seemed at fault; and an old man, followed by a few children, soon appearing, laden with piece of fuel, he appealed to him as Father Gillot, and asked whether he could find the street. The old man seemed at home in the ruins, and led the way readily. 'Did he know the Widow Laurent's house?'

'Mademoiselle [footnote: This was the title of *bourgeoise* wives, for many years, in France.] Laurent! Full well he knew her; a good pious soul was she, always ready to die for the truth,' he added, as he read sympathy in the faces round; 'and no doubt she had witnessed a good confession.'

'Knew he aught of the lady she had lodged?'

'He knew nothing of ladies. Something he had heard of the good widow having sheltered that shining light, Isaac Gardon, quenched, no doubt, in the same destruction; but for his part, he had a daughter in one of the isles out there, who always sent for him if she suspected danger here on the mainland, and he had only returned to his poor farm a day or two after Michael-mas.' So saying, he led them to the threshold of a ruinous building, in the very centre, as it were, of the desolation, and said, 'That, gentlemen, is where the poor honest widow kept her little shop.'

Black, burnt, dreary, lay the hospitable abode. The building had fallen, but the beams of the upper floor had fallen aslant, so as to shelter a portion of the lower room, where the red-tile pavement, the hearth with the gray ashes of the harmless home-fire, some unbroken crocks, a chain, and a *sabot*, were still visible, making the contrast of dreariness doubly mournful.

Berenger had stepped over the threshold, with his hat in his hand, as if the ruin were a sacred place to him, and stood gazing in a transfixed, deadened way. The captain asked where the remains were.

'Our people,' said the old man and the fisher, 'laid them by night in the earth near the church.'

Just then Berenger's gaze fell on something half hidden under the fallen timbers. He instantly sprang forward, and used all his strength to drag it out in so headlong a manner that all the rest hurried to prevent his reckless proceedings from bringing the heavy beams down on his head. When brought to light, the object proved to be one of the dark, heavy, wooden cradles used by the French peasantry, shining with age, but untouched by fire.

'Look in,' Berenger signed to Philip, his own eyes averted, his mouth set.

The cradle was empty, totally empty, save for a woolen covering, a little mattress, and a string of small yellow shells threaded.

Berenger held out his hand, grasped the baby-play thing convulsively, then dropped upon his knees, clasping his hands over his ashy face, the string of shells still wound among his fingers. Perhaps he had hitherto hardly realized the existence of his child, and was solely wrapped up in the thought of his wife; but the wooden cradle, the homely toy, stirred up fresh depths of feelings; he saw Eustacie wither tender sweetness as a mother, he beheld the little likeness of her in the cradle; and oh! that this should have been the end! Unable to repress a moan of anguish from a bursting heart, he laid his face against the senseless wood, and kissed it again and again, then lay motionless against it save for the long-drawn gasps and sobs that shook his frame. Philip, torn to the heart, would have almost forcibly drawn him away; but Master Hobbs, with tears running down his honest cheeks, withheld the boy. 'Don't ye, Master Thistlewood, 'twill do him good. Poor young gentleman! I know how it was when I came home and found our first little lad, that we had thought so much on, had been take. But then he was safe laid in his own churchyard, and his mother was there to meet me; while your poor brother——Ah! God comfort him!'

'*Le pauvre Monsieur!*' exclaimed the old peasant, struck at the sight of his grief, 'was it then his child? And he, no doubt, lying wounded elsewhere while God's hand was heavy on this place. Yet he might hear more. They said the priest came down and carried off the little ones to be bred up in convents.'

'Who?—where?' asked Berenger, raising his head as if catching at a straw in this drowning of all his hopes.

''Tis true,' added the fisherman. 'It was the holy priest of Nissard, for he send down to St. Julien for a woman to nurse the babes.'

'To Nissard, then,' said Berenger, rising.

'It is but a chance,' said the old Huguenot; 'many of the innocents were with their mothers in yonder church. Better for them to perish like the babes of Bethlehem than to be bred up in the house of Baal; but perhaps Monsieur is English, and if so he might yet obtain the child. Yet he must not hope too much.'

'No, for there was many a little corpse among those we buried,' said the fisher. 'Will the gentleman see the place?'

'Oh, no!' exclaimed Philip, understanding the actions, and indeed many of the words; 'this place will kill him.'

'To the grave,' said Berenger, as if he heard nothing.

'See,' added Philip, 'there are better things than graves,' and he pointed to a young green sucker of a vine, which, stimulated by the burnt soil, had shot up between the tiles of the floor. 'Look, there is hope to meet you even here.'

Berenger merely answered by gathering a leaf from the vine and putting it into his bosom; and Philip, whom only extreme need could have thus inspired, perceived that he accepted it as the augury of hope.

Berenger turned to bid the two men bear the cradle with them, and then followed the old man out into the PLACE, once a pleasant open paved square, now grass-grown and forlorn. On one side lay the remains of the church. The Huguenots had been so predominant at La Sablerie as to have engrossed the building, and it had therefore shared the general destruction, and lay in utter, desolate ruin, a mere shell, and the once noble spire, the mariner's guiding star, blown up with gun-cruel that ever desolated the country. Beyond lay the burial-ground, in unspeakable dreariness. The crossed of the Catholic dead had been levelled by the fanaticism of the Huguenots, and though a great dominant stone cross raised on steps had been re-erected, it stood uneven, tottering and desolate among nettles, weeds, and briers. There seemed to have been a few deep trenches dug to receive the bodies of the many victims of the siege, and only rudely and slightly filled in with loose earth, on which Philippe treading had nearly sunk in, so much to his horror that he could hardly endure the long contemplation in which his brother stood gazing on the dismal scene, as if to bear it away with him. Did the fair being he had left in a king's palace sleep her last sleep her last sleep amid the tangled grass, the thistles and briers that grew so close that it was hardly possible to keep from stumbling over them, where all memorials of friend or foe were alike obliterated? Was a resting-place among these nameless graves the best he could hope for the wife whose eyes he had hoped by this time would be answering his own— was this her shelter from foe, from sword, famine, and fire?

A great sea-bird, swooping along with broad wings and wild wailing cry, completed the weird dismay that had seized on Philip, and clutching at his brother's cloak, he exclaimed, 'Berry, Berry, let us be gone, or we shall both be distraught!'

Berenger yielded passively, but when the ruins of the town had been again crossed, and the sad little party, after amply rewarding the old man, were about to return to St. Julien, he stood still, saying, 'Which is the way to Nissard?' and, as the men pointed to the south, he added, 'Show me the way thither.'

Captain Hobbs now interfered. He knew the position of Nissard, among dangerous sandbanks, between which a boat could only venture at the higher tides, and by daylight. To go the six miles thither at present would make it almost impossible to return to the THROSTLE that night, and it was absolutely necessary that he at least should do this. He therefore wished the young gentleman to return with him on board, sleep there, and be put ashore at Nissard as soon as it should be possible in the morning. But Berenger shook his head. He could not rest for a moment till he had ascertained the fate of Eustacie's child. Action alone could quench the horror of what he had recognized as her own lot, and the very pursuit of this one thread of hope seemed needful to him to make it substantial. He would hear of nothing but walking at once to Nissard; and Captain Hobbs, finding it impossible to debate the point with one so dazed and crushed with grief, and learning from the fishermen that not only was the priest one of the kindest and most hospitable men living, but that there was a tolerable *caberet* not far from the house, selected from the loiterers who had accompanied them from St. Julien a trustworthy-looking, active lad as a guide, and agreed with the high tide on the morrow, either to concert measures for obtaining possession of the lost infant, or, if all were in vain, to fetch them off. Then he, with the mass of stragglers from St. Julien, went off direct for the coast, while the two young brothers, their two attendants, and the fishermen, turned southwards along the summit of the dreary sandbanks.

CHAPTER XXIV
THE GOOD PRIEST OF NISSARD

Till at the set of sun all tracks and ways In darkness lay enshrouded. And e'en thus The utmost limit of the great profound At length we reach'd, where in dark gloom and mist Cimmeria's people and their city lie Enveloped ever.—ODYSSEY (MUSGROVE)

The October afternoon had set in before the brothers were the way to Nissard; and in spite of Berenger's excited mood, the walk through the soft, sinking sand could not be speedily performed. It was that peculiar sand-drift which is the curse of so many coasts, slowly, silently, irresistibly flowing, blowing, creeping in, and gradually choking all vegetation and habitation. Soft and almost impalpable, it lay heaped in banks yielding as air, and yet far more than deep enough to swallow up man and horse. Nay, tops of trees, summits of chimneys, told what it had already swallowed. The whole scene far and wide presented nothing but the lone, tame undulations, liable to be changed by every wind, and solitary beyond expression—a few rabbits scudding hither and thither, or a sea-gull floating with white, ghostly wings in the air, being the only living things visible. On the one hand a dim, purple horizon showed that the inhabited country lay miles inland; on the other lay the pale, gray, misty expanse of sea, on which Philip's eyes could lovingly discern the THROSTLE'S masts.

That view was Philip's chief comfort. The boy was feeling more eerie and uncomfortable than ever he had been before as he plodded along, sinking deep with every step almost up to his ankles in the sand, on which the bare-footed guide ran lightly, and Berenger, though sinking no less deeply, seemed insensible to all inconveniences. This desolateness was well-nigh unbearable; no one dared to speak while Berenger thus moved on in the unapproachableness of his great grief, and Philip presently began to feel a dreamy sense that they had all thus been moving for years, that this was the world's end, the land of shadows, and that his brother was a ghost already. Besides vague alarms like these, there was the dismal English and Protestant prejudice in full force in Philip's mind, which regarded the resent ground as necessarily hostile, and all Frenchmen, above all French priests, as in league to cut off every Englishman and Protestant. He believed himself in a country full of murderers, and was walking on with the one determination that his brother should not rush on danger without him, and that the Popish rogues should be kept in mind that there was an English ship in sight. Alas! that consolation was soon lost, for a dense gray mist was slowly creeping in from the sea, and blotted out the vessel, then gathered in closer, and obliterated all landmarks. Gradually it turned to a heavy rain, and about the same time the ground on which they walked became no longer loose sand-hills, but smooth and level. It was harder likewise from the wet, and this afforded better walking, but there lay upon it fragments of weed and shell, as though it were liable to be covered by the sea, and there was a low, languid plash of the tide, which could not be seen. Twilight began to deepen the mist. The guide was evidently uneasy; he sidled up to Philip, and began to ask what he—hitherto obstinately deaf and contemptuous to French—was very slow to comprehend. At last he found it was a question how near it was to All Soul's day; and then came an equally amazing query whether the gentlemen's babe had been baptized; for it appeared that on All Soul's day the spirits of unchristened infants had the power of rising from the sands in a bewildering mist, and leading wayfarers into the sea. And the poor guide, white and drenched, vowed he never would have undertaken this walk if he had only thought of this. These slaughters of heretics must so much have augmented the number of the poor little spirits; and no doubt Monsieur would be specially bewildered by one so nearly concerned with him. Philip, half frightened, could not help stepping forward and pulling Berenger by the cloak to make him aware of this strange peril; but he did not get much comfort. 'Baptized? Yes; you know she was, by the old nurse. Let me alone, I say. I would follow her wherever she called me, the innocent, and glad—the sooner the better.'

And he shook his brother off with a sadness and impatience so utterly unapproachable, that Philip, poor boy, could only watch his tall figure in the wide cloak and slouched hat, stalking on ever more indistinct in the gloom, while his much confused mind tried to settle the theological point whether the old nurse's baptism were valid enough to prevent poor little Berangere from becoming one of these mischievous deluders; and all this was varied by the notion of Captain Hobbs picking up their corpses on the beach, and of Sir Marmaduke bewailing his only son.

At last a strange muffled sound made him start in the dead silence, but the guide hailed the sound with a joyful cry——

'Hola! Blessings on Notre-Dame and holy Father Colombeau, now are we saved!' and on Philip's hasty interrogation, he explained that it was from the bells of Nissard, which the good priest always caused to be rung during these sea-fogs, to disperse all evil beings, and guide the wanderers.

The guide strode on manfully, as the sound became clearer and nearer, and Philip was infinitely relived to be free from all supernatural anxieties, and to have merely to guard against the wiles of a Polish priest, a being almost as fabulously endowed in his imagination as poor little Berangere's soul could be in that of the fisherman.

The drenching Atlantic mist had wetted them all to the skin, and closed round them so like a solid wall, that they had almost lost sight of each other, and had nothing but the bells' voices to comfort them, till quite suddenly there was a light upon the mist, a hazy reddish gleam—a window seemed close to them. The guide, heartily thanking Our Lady and St. Julian, knocked at a door, which opened at once into a warm, bright, superior sort of kitchen, where a neatly-dressed elderly peasant woman exclaimed, 'Welcome, poor souls! Enter, then. Here, good Father, are some bewildered creatures. Eh! wrecked are you, good folks, or lost in the fog?'

At the same moment there came from behind the screen that shut off the fire from the door, a benignant-looking, hale old man in a cassock, with long white hair on his shoulders, and a cheerful face, ruddy from sea-wind.

'Welcome, my friends,' he said. 'Thanks to the saints who have guided you safely. You are drenched. Come to the fire at once.'

And as they moved on into the full light of the fire and the rude iron lamp by which he had been reading, and he saw the draggled plumes and other appurtenances that marked the two youths as gentlemen, he added, 'Are you wrecked, Messieurs? We will do our poor best for your accommodation;' and while both mechanically murmured a word of thanks, and removed their soaked hats, the good man exclaimed, as he beheld Berenger's ashy face, with the sunken eyes and deep scars, 'Monsieur should come to bed at once. He is apparently recovering from a severe wound. This way, sir; Jolitte shall make you some hot tisane.'

'Wait, sir,' said Berenger, very slowly, and his voice sounding hollow from exhaustion; 'they say that you can tell me of my child. Let me hear.'

'Monsieur's child!' exclaimed the bewildered curate, looking from him to Philip, and then to the guide, who poured out a whole stream of explanation before Philip had arranged three words of French.

'You hear, sir,' said Berenger, as the man finished: 'I came hither to seek my wife, the Lady of Ribaumont.'

'Eh!' exclaimed the *cure*, 'do I then see M. le Marquis de Nid de Merle?'

'No!' cried Berenger; 'no, I am not that *scelerat*! I am her true husband, the Baron de Ribaumont.'

'The Baron de Ribaumont perished at the St. Bartholomew,' said the *cure*, fixing his eyes on him, as though to confute an impostor.

'Ah, would that I had!' said Berenger. 'I was barely saved with the life that is but misery now. I came to seek her—I found what you know. They told me that you saved the children. Ah, tell me where mine is!—all that is left me.'

'A few poor babes I was permitted to rescue, but very few. But let me understand to whom I speak,' he added, much perplexed. 'You, sir——'

'I am her husband, married at five years old—contract renewed last year. It was he whom you call Nid de Merle who fell on me, and left me for dead. A faithful servant saved my life, but I have lain sick in England till now, when her letter to my mother brought me to La Sablerie, to find—to find THIS. Oh, sir, have pity on me! Tell me if you know anything of her, or if you can give me her child.'

'The orphans I was able to save are—the boys at nurse here, the girls with the good nuns at Lucon,' said the priest, with infinite pity in his look. 'Should you know it, sir?'

'I would—I should,' said Berenger. 'But it is a girl. Ah, would that it were here! But you—you, sir—you know more than these fellows. Is there no—no hope of herself?'

'Alas! I fear I can give you none,' said the priest; 'but I will tell all I know; only I would fain see you eat, rest, and be dried.'

'How can I?' gasped he, allowing himself, however, to sink into a chair; and the priest spoke:

'Perhaps you know, sir, that the poor lady fled from her friends, and threw herself upon the Huguenots. All trace had been lost, when, at a banquet given by the mayor of Lucon, there appeared some *patisseries*, which some ecclesiastic, who had enjoyed the hospitality of Bellaise, recognized as peculiar to the convent there, where she had been brought up. They were presented to the mayor by his friend, Bailli la Grasse, who had boasted of the excellent *confitures* of the heretic pastor's daughter that lodged in the town of La Sablerie. The place was in disgrace for having afforded shelter and supplies to Montgomery's pirate crews, and there were narrations of outrages committed on Catholics. The army were enraged by their failure before La Rochelle; in effect, it was resolved to make an example, when, on M. de Nid de Merle's summons, all knowledge of the lady was denied. Is it possible that she was indeed not there?'

Berenger shook his head. 'She was indeed there,' he said, with an irrepressible groan. 'Was there no mercy—none?'

'Ask not, sir,' said the compassionate priest; 'the flesh shrinks, though there may be righteous justice. A pillaged town, when men are enraged, is like a place of devils unchained. I reached it only after it had been taken by assault, when all was flame and blood. Ask me no more; it would be worse for you to hear than me to tell,' he concluded, shuddering, but laying his hand kindly on Berenger's arm. 'At least it is ended now and God is more merciful than men. Many died by the bombs cast into to city, and she for whom you ask certainly fell not alive into the hands of those who sought her. Take comfort, sir; there is One who watches and takes count of our griefs. Sir, turning to Philip, 'this gentleman is too much spent with sorrow to bear this cold and damp. Aid me, I entreat, to persuade him to lie down.'

Philip understood the priest's French far better than that of the peasants, and added persuasions that Berenger was far too much exhausted and stunned to resist. To spend a night in a Popish priest's house would once have seemed to Philip a shocking alternative, yet here he was, heartily assisting in removing the wet garments in which his brother had sat only too long, and was heartily relieved to lay him down in the priest's own bed, even though there was an image over the head, which, indeed, the boy never saw. He only saw his brother turn away from the light with a low, heavy moan, as if he would fain be left alone with his sorrow and his crushed hopes.

Nothing could be kinder than Dome Colombeau, the priest of Nissard. He saw to the whole of his guests being put into some sort of dry habiliments before they sat round his table to eat of the savoury mess in the great *pot-au-feu*, which had, since their arrival, received additional ingredients, and moreover sundry villagers had crept into the house. Whenever the good Father supped at home, any of his flock were welcome to drop in to enjoy his hospitability. After a cup of hot cider round, they carried off the fisherman to ledge in one of their cottages. Shake-downs were found for the others, and Philip, wondering what was to become of the good host himself, gathered that he meant to spend such part of the night on the kitchen floor as he did not pass in prayer in the church for the poor young gentleman, who was in such affliction. Philip was not certain whether to resent this as an impertinence or an attack on their Protestant principles; but he was not sure, either, that the priest was aware what was their religion, and was still less certain of his own comprehension of these pious intentions: he decided that, any way, it was better not to make a fool of himself. Still, the notion of the mischievousness of priests was so rooted in his head, that he consulted Humfrey on the expedience of keeping watch all night, but was sagaciously answered that 'these French rogues don't do any hurt unless they be brought up to it, and the place was as safe as old Hurst.'

In fact, Philip's vigilance would have been strongly against nature. He never awoke till full daylight and morning sun were streaming through the vine-leaves round the window, and then, to his dismay, he saw that Berenger had left his bed, and was gone. Suspicions of foul play coming over him in full force as he gazed round on much that he considered as 'Popish furniture,' he threw on his clothes, and hastened to open the door, when, to his great relief, he saw Berenger hastily writing at a table under the window, and Smithers standing by waiting for the billet.

'I am sending Smithers on board, to ask Hobbs to bring our cloak bags,' said Berenger, as his brother entered. 'We must go on to Lucon.'

He spoke briefly and decidedly, and Philip was satisfied to see him quite calm and collected—white indeed, and with the old haggard look, and the great scar very purple instead of red, which was always a bad sign with him. He was not disposed to answer questions; he shortly said, 'He had slept not less than usual,' which Philip knew meant very little; and he had evidently made up his mind, and was resolved not to let himself give way. If his beacon of hope had been so suddenly, frightfully quenched, he still was kept from utter darkness by straining his eyes and forcing his steps to follow the tiny, flickering spark that remained.

The priest was at his morning mass; and so soon as Berenger had given his note to Smithers, and sent him off with a fisherman to the THROSTLE, he took up his hat, and went out upon the beach, that lay glistening in the morning sun, then turned straight towards the tall spire of the church, with had been their last night's guide. Philip caught his cloak.

'You are never going there, Berenger?'

'Vex me not now,' was all the reply he got. 'There the dead and living meet together.'

'But, brother, they will take you for one of their own sort.'

'Let them.'

Philip was right that it was neither a prudent nor consistent proceeding, but Berenger had little power of reflection, and his impulse at present bore him into the church belonging to his native faith and land, without any defined felling, save that it was peace to kneel there among the scattered worshippers, who came and went with their fish-baskets in their hands, and to hear the low chant of the priest and his assistant from within the screen.

Philip meantime marched up and down outside in much annoyance, until the priest and his brother came out, when the first thing he heard the good Colombeau say was, 'I would have called upon you before, my son, but that I feared you were a Huguenot.'

'I am an English Protestant,' said Berenger; 'but, ah! sir, I needed comfort too much to stay away from prayer.'

Pere Colombeau looked at him in perplexity, thinking perhaps that here might be a promising convert, if there were only time to work on him; but Berenger quitted the subject at once, asking the distance to Lucon.

'A full day's journey,' answered Pere Colombeau, and added, 'I am sorry you are indeed a Huguenot. It was what I feared last night, but I feared to add to your grief. The nuns are not permitted to deliver up children to Huguenot relations.'

'I am her father!' exclaimed Berenger, indignantly.

'That goes for nothing, according to the rules of the Church,' said the priest. 'The Church cannot yield her children to heresy.'

'But we in England and not Calvinists,' cried Berenger. 'We are not like your Huguenots.'

'The Church would make no difference,' said the priest. 'Stay, sir,' as Berenger stuck his own forehead, and was about to utter a fierce invective. 'Remember that if your child lives, it is owing to the pity of the good nuns. You seem not far from the bosom of the Church. Did you but return——'

'It is vain to speak of that,' said Berenger, quickly. 'Say, sir, would an order from the King avail to open these doors?'

'Of course it would, if you have the influence to obtain one.'

'I have, I have,' cried Berenger, eagerly. 'The King has been my good friend already. Moreover, my English grandfather will deal with the Queen. The heiress of our house cannot be left in a foreign nunnery. Say, sir,' he added, turning to the priest, 'if I went to Lucon at once know your name, and refuse all dealings with you.'

'She could not do so, if I brought an order from the King.'

'Certainly not.'

'Then to Paris!' And laying his hand on Philip's shoulder, he asked the boy whether he had understood, ad explained that he must go at once to Paris—riding post—and obtain the order from the King.

'To Paris—to be murdered again!' said Philip, in dismay.

'They do not spend their time there in murder,' said Berenger. 'And now is the time, while the savage villain Narcisse is with his master in Poland. I cannot but go, Philip; we both waste words. You shall take home a letter to my Lord.'

'I—I go not home without you,' said Philip, doggedly.

'I cannot take you, Phil; I have no warrant.'

'I have warrant for going, though. My father said he was easier about you with me at your side. Where you go, I go.'

The brothers understood each other's ways so well, that Berenger knew the intonation in Philip's voice that meant that nothing should make him give way. He persuaded no more, only took measures for the journey, in which the kind priest gave him friendly advice. There was no doubt that the good man pitied him sincerely, and wished him success more than perhaps he strictly ought to have done, unless as a possible convert. Of money for the journey there was no lack, for Berenger had brought a considerable sum, intending to reward all who had befriended Eustacie, as well as to fit her out for the voyage; and this, perhaps, with his papers, he had brought ashore to facilitate his entrance into La Sablerie,—that entrance which, alas! he had found only too easy. He had therefore only to obtain horses and a guide, and this could be done at la Motte-Achard, where the party could easily be guided on foot, or conveyed in a boat if the fog should not set in again, but all the coast-line of Nissard was dangerous in autumn and winter; nay, even this very August an old man, with his daughter, her infant, and a donkey, had been found bewildered between the creeks on a sandbank, where they stood still and patient, like a picture of the Flight into Egypt, when an old fisherman found them, and brought them to the beneficent shelter of the Presbytere.

Stories of this kind were told at the meal that was something partaking of the nature of both breakfast and early dinner, but where Berenger ate little and spoke less. Philip watched him anxiously; the boy thought the journey a perilous experiment every way, but, boyishly, was resolved neither to own his fears of it nor to leave his brother. External perils he was quite ready to face, and he fancied that his English birth would give him some power of protecting Berenger, but he was more reasonably in dread of the present shock bringing on such an illness as the last relapse; and if Berenger lost his senses again, what should they do? He even ventured to hint at this danger, but Berenger answered, 'That will scarce happen again. My head is stronger now. Besides, it was doing nothing, and hearing her truth profaned, that crazed me. No one at least will do that again. But if you wish to drive me frantic again, the way would be to let Hobbs carry me home without seeking her child.'

Philip bore this in mind, when, with flood-tide, Master Hobbs landed, and showed himself utterly dismayed at the turn affairs had taken. He saw the needlessness of going to Lucon without royal authority; indeed, he thought it possible that the very application there might give the alarm, and cause all tokens of the child's identity to be destroyed, in order to save her from her heretic relations. But he did not at all approve of the young gentlemen going off to Paris at once. It was against his orders. He felt bound to take them home as he has brought them, and they might then make a fresh start if it so pleased them; but how could he return to my Lord and Sir Duke without them? 'Mr. Ribaumont might be right—it was not for him to say a father ought not to look after his child—yet he was but a stripling himself, and my Lord had said, 'Master Hobbs, I trust him to you.'' He would clearly have liked to have called in a boat's crew, mastered the young gentlemen, and carried them on board as captives; but as this was out of his power, he was obliged to yield the point. He disconsolately accepted the letters in which Berenger had explained all, and in which he promised to go at once to Sir Francis Walsingham's at Paris, to run into no needless danger, and to watch carefully over Philip; and craved pardon, in a respectful but yet manly and determined tone, for placing his duty to his lost, deserted child above his submission to his grandfather. Then engaging to look out for a signal on the coast if he should said to Bordeaux in January, to touch and take the passengers off, Captain Hobbs took leave, and the brothers were left to their own resources.

CHAPTER XXV
THE VELVET COACH

No, my good Lord, Diana—

ALL'S WELL THAT ENDS WELL

A late autumn journey from the west coast to Paris was a more serious undertaking in the sixteenth century than the good seaman Master Hobbs was aware of, or he would have used stronger dissuasive measures against such an undertaking by the two youths, when the elder was in so frail a state of health; but there had been a certain deceptive strength and vigour about young Ribaumont while under strong excitement and determination, and the whole party fancied him far fitter to meet the hardships than was really the case. Philip Thistlewood always recollected that journey as the most distressing period of his life.

They were out of the ordinary highways, and therefore found the hiring of horses often extremely difficult. They had intended to purchase, but found no animals that, as Philip said, they would have accepted as a gift, though at every wretched inn where they had to wait while the country was scoured for the miserable jades, their proposed requirements fell lower and lower. Dens of smoke, dirt, and boorishness were the great proportion of those inns, where they were compelled to take refuge by the breaking down of one or other of the beasts, or by stress of weather. Snow, rain, thaw and frost alternated, each variety rendering the roads impassable; and at the best, the beasts could seldom be urged beyond a walk, fetlock-deep in mire or water. Worse than all, Berenger, far from recovered, and under the heavy oppression of a heartrending grief, could hardly fail to lose the ground that he had gained under the influence of hope. The cold seemed to fix itself on the wound on his cheek, terrible pain and swelling set in, depriving him entirely of sleep, permitting him to take no nourishment but fragments of soft crumbs soaked in wine or broth—when the inns afforded any such fare—and rendering speech excessively painful, and at last unintelligible.

Happily this was not until Philip and Humfrey both had picked up all the most indispensable words to serve their needs, and storming could be done in any language. Besides, they had fallen in at La Motte-Achard with a sharp fellow named Guibert, who had been at sea, and knew a little English, was a Norman by birth, knew who the Baron de Ribaumont was, and was able to make himself generally useful, though ill supplying the place of poor Osbert, who would have been invaluable in the present predicament. Nothing was so much dreaded by any of the party as that their chief should become utterly unable to proceed. Once let him be laid up at one of these little *auberges*, and Philip felt as if all would be over with him; and he himself was always the most restlessly eager to push on, and seemed to suffer less even in the biting wind and sleet than on the dirty pallets or in the smoky, noisy kitchens of the inns. That there was no wavering of consciousness was the only comfort, and Philip trusted to prevent this by bleeding him whenever his head seemed aching or heated; and under this well-meant surgery it was no wonder that he grew weaker every day, in spite of the most affectionate and assiduous watching on his brother's part.

Nearly six weeks had been spent in struggling along the cross-roads, or rather in endless delays; and when at last they came on more frequented ways, with better inns, well-paved *chaussees*, and horses more fit for use, Berenger was almost beyond feeling the improvement. At their last halt, even Philip was for waiting and sending on to Paris to inform Sir Francis Walsingham of their situation; but Berenger only shook his head, dressed himself, and imperatively signed to go on. It was a bright morning, with a clear frost, and the towers and steeples of Paris presently began to appear above the poplars that bordered the way; but by this time Berenger was reeling in his saddle, and he presently became so faint and dizzy, that Philip and Humfrey were obliged to lift him from his horse, and lay him under an elm-tree that stood a little back from the road.

'Look up, sir, it is but a league further,' quoth Humfrey; 'I can see the roof of the big church they call Notre-Dame.'

'He does not open his eyes, he is swooning,' said Philip. 'He must have some cordial, ere he can sit his horse. Can you think of no lace where we could get a drop of wine or strong waters?'

'Not I, Master Philip. We passed a convent wall but now, but 'twas a nunnery, as good as a grave against poor travelers. I would ride on, and get some of Sir Francis's folk to bring a litter or coach, but I doubt me if I could get past the barrier without my young Lord's safe-conduct.'

Berenger, hearing all, here made an effort to raise himself, but sank back against Philip's shoulder. Just then, a trampling and lumbering became audible, and on the road behind appeared first three horsemen riding abreast, streaming with black and white ribbons; then eight pair of black horses, a man walking at the crested heads of each couple, and behind these a coach, shaped like an urn reversed, and with a coronet on the top, silvered, while the vehicle itself was, melon-like, fluted, alternately black, with silver figures, and white with black landscapes; and with white draperies, embroidered with black and silver, floating from the windows.

Four lacqueys, in the same magpie-colouring, stood behind, and outriders followed; but as the cavalcade approached the group by the road-side, one of the horsemen paused, saying lightly, 'Over near the walls from an affair of honour! Has he caught it badly? Who was the other?'

Ere Guibert could answer, the curtains were thrust aside, the coach stopped, a lady's head and hand appeared, and a female voice exclaimed, in much alarm, 'Halt! Ho, you there, in our colours, come here. What is it? My brother here? Is he wounded?'

'It is no wound, Madame,' said Guibert, shoved forward by his English comrades, 'it is M. le Baron de Ribaumont who is taken ill, and—ah! here is Monsieur Philippe.'

For Philip, seeing a thick black veil put back from the face of the most beautiful lady who had ever appeared to him, stepped forward, hat in hand, as she exclaimed, 'Le Baron de Ribaumont! Can it be true? What means this? What ails him?'

'It is his wound, Madame,' said Philip, in his best French; 'it has broken out again, and he has almost dropped from his horse from *defaillance*.'

'Ah, bring him here—lay him on the cushions, we will have the honour of transporting him,' cried the lady; and, regardless of the wet road, she sprang out of the coach, with her essences in her hand, followed by at least three women, two pages, and two little white dogs which ran barking towards the prostrate figure, but were caught up by their pages. 'Ah, cousin, how dreadful,' she cried, as she knelt down beside him, and held her essences towards him. Voice and scent revived him, and with a bewildered look and gesture half of thanks, half of refusal, he gazed round him, then rose to his feet without assistance, bent his head, and making a sign that he was unable to speak, turned towards his horse.

'Cousin, cousin,' exclaimed the lady, in whose fine black eyes tears were standing, 'you will let me take you into the city—you cannot refuse.'

'Berry, indeed you cannot ride,' entreated Philip; 'you must take her offer. Are you getting crazed at last?'

Berenger hesitated for a moment, but he felt himself again dizzy; the exertion of springing into his saddle was quite beyond him, and bending his head he submitted passively to be helped into the black and white coach. Humfrey, however, clutched Philip's arm, and said impressively, 'Have a care, sir; this is no other than the fine lady, sister to the murderous villain that set upon him. If you would save his life, don't quit him, nor let her take him elsewhere than to our Ambassador's. I'll not leave the coach-door, and as soon as we are past the barriers, I'll send Jack Smithers to make known we are coming.'

Philip, without further ceremony, followed the lady into the coach, where he found her insisting that Berenger, who had sunk back in a corner, should lay his length of limb, muddy boots and all, upon the white velvet cushions richly worked in black and silver, with devices and mottoes, in which the crescent moon, and eclipsed or setting suns, made a great figure. The original inmates seemed to have disposed of themselves in various nooks of the ample conveyance, and Philip, rather at a loss to explain his intrusion, perched himself awkwardly on the edge of the cushions in front of his brother, thinking that Humfrey was an officious, suspicious fellow, to distrust this lovely lady, who seemed so exceedingly shocked and grieved at Berenger's condition. 'Ah! I never guessed it had been so frightful as this. I should not have known him. Ah! had I imagined——' She leant back, covered her face, and wept, as one overpowered; then, after a few seconds, she bent forward, and would have taken the hand that hung listlessly down, but it was at once withdrawn, and folded with the other on his breast.

'Can you be more at ease? Do you suffer much?' she asked, with sympathy and tenderness that went to Philip's heart, and he explained. 'He cannot speak, Madame; the shot in his cheek' (the lady shuddered, and put her handkerchief to her eyes) 'from time to time cases this horrible swelling and torture. After that he will be better.'

'Frightful, frightful,' she sighed, 'but we will do our best to make up. You, sir, must be his *trucheman.*'

Philip, not catching the last word, and wondering what kind of man that might be, made answer, 'I am his brother, Madame.'

'*Eh! Monsieur son frere.* Had *Madame sa mere* a son so old?'

'I am Philip Thistlewood, her husband's son, at your service, Madame,' said Philip, colouring up to the ears; 'I came with him for he is too weak to be alone.'

'Great confidence must be reposed in you, sir,' she said, with a not unflattering surprise. 'But whence are you come? I little looked to see Monsieur here.'

'We came from Anjou, Madame. We went to La Sablerie,' and he broke off.

'I understand. Ah! let us say no more! It rends the heart;' and again she wiped away tear. 'And now——'

'We are coming to the Ambassador's to obtain'—he stopped, for Berenger gave him a touch of peremptory warning, but the lady saved his embarrassment by exclaiming that she could not let her dear cousin go to the Ambassador's when he was among his own kindred. Perhaps Monsieur did not know her; she must present herself as Madame de Selinville, *nee* de Ribaumont, a poor cousin of *ce cher Baron*, 'and even a little to you, *M. le frere*, if you will own me,' and she held out a hand, which he ought to have kissed, but not knowing how, he only shook it. She further explained that her brother was at Cracow with Monsieur, now King of Poland, but that her father lived with her at her hotel, and would be enchanted to see his dear cousin, only that he, like herself, would be desolated at the effects of that most miserable of errors. She had been returning from her Advent retreat at a convent, where she had been praying for the soul of the late M. de Selinville, when a true Providence had made her remark the colours of her family. And now, nothing would serve her, but that this dear Baron should be carried at once to their hotel, which was much nearer than that of the Ambassador, and where every comfort should await him. She clasped her hands in earnest entreaty, and Philip, greatly touched by her kindness and perceiving that every jolt of the splendid by springless vehicle caused Berenger's head a shoot of anguish, was almost acceding to her offer, when he was checked by one of the most imperative of those silent negatives. Hitherto, Master Thistlewood had been rather proud of his bad French, and as long as he could be understood, considered trampling on genders, tenses, and moods as a manful assertion of Englishry, but he would just now have given a great deal for the command of any language but a horseboy's, to use to this beautiful gracious personage. '*Merci, Madame, nous ne fallons pas, nous avons passe notre parole d'aller droit a l'Ambassadeur's et pas ou else*,' did not sound very right to his ears; he coloured up to the roots of his hair, and knew that if Berry had had a smile left in him, poor fellow, he would have smiled now. But this most charming and polite of ladies never betrayed it, if it were ever such bad French; she only bowed her head, and said something very pretty—if only he could make it out—of being the slave of one's word, and went on persuading. Nor did it make the conversation easier, that she inquired after Berenger, and mourned over his injuries as if he were unconscious, while Philip knew, nay, was reminded every instant, that he was aware of all that was passing, most anxious that as little as possible should be said, and determined against being taken to her hotel. So unreasonable a prejudice did this seem to Philip, that had it not been for Humfrey's words, he would have doubted whether, in spite of all his bleeding, his brother's brain were not wandering.

However, what with Humfrey without, and Berenger within, the turn to the Ambassador's hotel was duly taken, and in process of time a hearty greeting passed between Humfrey and the porter; and by the time the carriage drew up, half the household were assembled on the steps, including Sir Francis himself, who had already heard more than a fortnight back from Lord Walwyn, and had become uneasy at the non-arrival of his two young guests. On Smithers's appearance, all had been made ready; and as Berenger, with feeble, tardy movements, made courteous gestures of thanks to the lady, and alighted form the coach, he was absolutely received into the dignified arms of the Ambassador. 'Welcome, my poor lad, I am glad to see you here again, though in such different guise. Your chamber is ready for you, and I have sent my secretary to see if Maitre Par be at home, so we will, with God's help, have you better at ease anon.'

Even Philip's fascination by Madame de Selinville could not hold out against the comfort of hearing English voices all round him, and of seeing his brother's anxious brow expand, and his hand and eyes return no constrained thanks. Civilities were exchanged on both sides; the Ambassador thanked the lady for the assistance she had rendered to his young friend and guest; she answered with a shade of stiffness, that she left her kinsman in good hands, and said she should send to inquire that evening, and her father would call on the morrow; then, as Lady Walsingham did not ask her in, the black and white coach drove away.

The lady threw herself back in one corner, covered her face, and spoke no word. Her coach pursued its way through the streets, and turned at length into another great courtyard, surrounded with buildings, where she alighted, and stepped across a wide but dirty hall, where ranks of servants stoop up and bowed as she passed; then she ascended a wide carved staircase, opened a small private door, and entered a tiny wainscoted room hardly large enough for her farthingale to turn round in. 'You, Veronique, come in—only you,' she said, at the door; and a waiting-woman, who had been in the carriage, obeyed, no longer clad in the Angevin costume, but in the richer and less characteristic dress of the ordinary Parisian *femme de chambre*.

'Undo my mantle in haste!' gasped Madame de Selinville. 'O Veronique—you saw—what destruction!'

'Ah! if my sweet young lady only known how frightful he had become, she had never sacrificed herself,' sighed Veronique.

'Frightful! What, with the grave blue eyes that seem like the steady avenging judgment of St. Michael in his triumph in the picture at the Louvre?' murmured Madame de Selinville; then she added quickly, 'Yes, yes, it is well. She and you, Veronique, may see him frightful and welcome. There are other eyes—make haste, girl. There—another handerchief. Follow me not.'

And Madame de Selinville moved out of the room, past the great state bedroom and the *salle* beyond, to another chamber where more servants waited and rose at her entrance.

'Is any one with my father?'

'No, Madame;' and a page knocking, opened the door and announced, 'Madame la Comtesse.'

The Chevalier, in easy *deshabille*, with a flask of good wine, iced water, and delicate cakes and *confitures* before him, a witty and licentious epigrammatic poem close under his hand, sat lazily enjoying the luxuries that it had been his daughter's satisfaction to procure for him ever since her marriage. He sprang up to meet her with a grace and deference that showed how different a person was the Comtesse de Selinville from Diane de Ribaumont.

'Ah! *ma belle*, my sweet,' as there was a mutual kissing of hands, 'thou art returned. Had I known thine hour, I had gone down for thy first embrace. But thou lookest fair, my child; the convent has made thee lovelier than ever.'

'Father, who think you is here? It is he—the Baron.'

'The Baron? Eh, father!' she cried impetuously. 'Who could it be but one?'

'My child, you are mistaken! That young hot-head can never be thrusting himself here again.'

'But he is, father; I brought him into Paris in my coach! I left him at the Ambassador's.'

'Thou shouldest have brought him here. There will be ten thousand fresh imbroglios.'

'I could not; he is as immovable as ever, though unable to speak! Oh, father, he is very ill, he suffers terribly. Oh, Narcisse! Ah! may I never see him again!'

'But what brings him blundering her again?' exclaimed the Chevalier. 'Speak intelligibly, child! I thought we had guarded against that! He knows nothing of the survivance.'

'I cannot tell much. He could not open his mouth, and his half-brother, a big dull English boy, stammered out a few words of shocking French against his will. But I believe they had heard of *la pauvre petite* at La Sablerie, came over for her, and finding the ruin my brother makes wherever he goes, are returning seeking intelligence and succour for HIM.'

'That may be,' said the Chevalier, thoughtfully. 'It is well thy brother is in Poland. I would not see him suffer any more; and we may get him back to England ere my son learns that he is here.'

'Father, there is a better way! Give him my hand.'

'*Eh quoi*, child; if thou art tired of devotion, there are a thousand better marriages.'

'No, father, none so good for this family. See, I bring him all—all that I was sold for. As the price of that, he resigns for ever all his claims to the ancestral castle—to La Leurre, and above all, that claim to Nid de Merle as Eustacie's widower, which, should he ever discover the original contract, will lead to endless warfare.'

'His marriage with Eustacie was annulled. Yet—yet there might be doubts. There was the protest; and who knows whether they formally renewed their vows when so much went wrong at Montpipeau. Child, it is a horrible perplexity. I often could wish we had had no warning, and the poor things had made off together. We could have cried shame till we forced out a provision for thy brother; and my poor little Eustacie—' He had tears in his eyes as he broke off.

Diane made an impatient gesture. 'She would have died of tedium in England, or broken forth so as to have a true scandal. That is all over, father, now; weigh my proposal! Nothing else will save my brother from all that his cruel hand merits! You will win infinite credit at court. The King loved him more than you thought safe.'

'The King has not a year to live, child, and he has personally offended the King of Poland. Besides, this youth is heretic.'

'Only by education. Have I not heard you say that he had by an abjuration. And as to Monsieur's enmity, if it be not forgotten, the glory of bringing about a conversion would end that at once.'

'Then, daughter, thou shouldst not have let him bury himself among the English.'

'It was unavoidable, father, and perhaps if he were here he would live in an untamable state of distrust, whereas we may now win him gradually. You will go and see him to-morrow, my dear father.'

'I must have time to think of this thy sudden device.'

'Nay, he is in no condition to hear of it at present. I did but speak now, that you might not regard it as sudden when the fit moment comes. It is the fixed purpose of my mind. I am no girl now, and I could act for myself if I would; but as it is for your interest and that of my brother thus to dispose of me, it is better that you should act for me.'

'Child, headstrong child, thou wilt make no scandal,' said the Chevalier, looking up at his daughter's handsome head drawn up proudly with determination.

'Certainly not, sir, if you will act for me.' And Diane sailed away in her sweeping folds of black brocade.

In a few moments more she was kneeling with hands locked together before a much-gilded little waxem figure of St. Eustacie with his cross-bearing stag by his side, which stood in a curtained recess in the alcove where her stately bed was placed.

'Monseigneur St. Eustache, ten wax candles everyday to your shrine at Bellaise, so he recovers; ten more if he listen favourably and loves me. Nay, all—all the Selinville jewels to make you a shrine. All—all, so he will only let me love him;' and then, while taking up the beads, and pronouncing the repeated devotions attached to each, her mind darted back to the day when, as young children, she had played unfairly, defrauded Landry Osbert, and denied it; how Berenger, though himself uninjured, had refused to speak to her all that day—how she had hated him then—how she had thought she had hated him throughout their brief intercourse in the previous year; how she had played into her brother's hands; and when she thought to triumph over the man who had scorned her, found her soul all blank desolation, and light gone out from the earth! Reckless and weary, she had let herself be united to M. de Selinville, and in her bridal honours and amusements had tried to crowd out the sense of dreariness and lose herself in excitement. Then came the illness and death of her husband, and almost at the same time the knowledge of Berenger's existence. She sought excitement again that feverish form of devotion then in vogue at Paris, and which resulted in the League. She had hitherto stunned herself as it were with penances, processions, and sermons, for which the host of religious orders then at Paris had given ample scope; and she was constantly devising new extravagances. Even at this moment she wore sackcloth beneath her brocade, and her rosary was of death's heads. She was living on the outward husk of the Roman Church not penetrating into its living power, and the phase of religion which fostered Henry III. and the League offered her no more.

All, all had melted away beneath the sad but steadfast glance of those two eyes, the only feature still unchanged in the marred, wrecked countenance. That honest, quiet refusal, that look which came from a higher atmosphere, had filled her heart with passionate beatings and aspirations once more, and more consciously than ever. Womanly feeling for suffering, and a deep longing to compensate to him, and earn his love, nay wrest it from him by the benefits she would heap upon him, were all at work; but the primary sense was the longing to rest on the only perfect truth she had ever known in man, and thus with passionate ardour she poured forth her entreaties to St. Eustache, a married saint, who had known love, and could feel for her, and could surely not object to the affection to which she completely gave way for one whose hand was now as free as her own.

But St. Eustache was not Diane's only hope. That evening she sent Veronique to Rene of Milan, the court-perfumer, but also called by the malicious, *l'empoisonneur de le Reine*, to obtain from him the most infallible charm and love potion in his whole repertory.

CHAPTER XXVI
THE CHEVALIER'S EXPIATION

Next, Sirs, did he marry?

And whom, Sirs, did he marry? One like himself, Though doubtless graced

with many virtues, young, And erring, and in nothing more astray Than in

this marriage.—TAYLOR, EDWIN THE FAIR.

Nothing could be kinder than the Ambassador's family, and Philip found himself at once at home there, at least in his brother's room, which was all the world to him. fortunately, Ambroise Pare, the most skillful surgeon of his day, had stolen a day from his attendance of King Charles, at St. Germain, to visit his Paris patients, and, though unwilling to add to the list of cases, when he heard from Walsingham's secretary who the suffer was, and when injured, he came at once to afford his aid.

He found, however, that there was little scope for present treatment, he could only set his chief assistant to watch the patient and to inform him when the crisis should be nearer; but remarking the uneasy, anxious expression in Berenger's eyes, he desired to know whether any care on his mind might be interfering with his recovery. A Huguenot, and perfectly trustworthy, he was one who Walsingham knew might safely hear the whole, and after hearing all, he at once returned to his patient, and leaning over him, said, 'Vex not yourself, sir; your illness is probably serving you better than health could do.'

Sir Francis thought this quite probable, since Charles was so unwell and so beset with his mother's creatures that no open audience could be obtained from him, and Pare, who always had access to him, might act when no one else could reach him. Meantime the Ambassador rejoiced to hear of the instinctive caution that had made Berenger silence Philip on the object of the journey to Paris, since if the hostile family guessed at the residence of the poor infant, they would have full opportunity for obliterating all the scanty traces of her. Poor persecuted little thing! the uncertain hope of her existence seemed really the only thread that still bound Berenger to life. He had spent eighteen months in hope deferred, and constant bodily pain; and when the frightful disappointment met him at La Sablerie, it was not wonder that his heart and hope seemed buried in the black scorched ruins where all he cared for had perished. He was scarcely nineteen, but the life before him seemed full of nothing but one ghastly recollection, and, as he said in the short sad little letter which he wrote to his grandfather from his bed, he only desired to live long enough to save Eustacie's child from being a nameless orphan maintained for charity in a convent, and to see her safe in Aunt Cecily's care; and then he should be content to have done with this world for ever.

The thought that no one except himself could save the child, seemed to give him the resolution to battle for life that often bears the patient through illness, though now he as suffering more severely and consciously than ever he had done before; and Lady Walsingham often gave up hopes of him. He was tenderly cared for by her and her women; but Philip was the most constant nurse, and his unfailing assiduity and readiness amazed the household, who had begun by thinking him ungainly, loutish, and fit for nothing but country sports.

The Chevalier de Ribaumont came daily to inquire; and the first time he was admitted actually burst into tears at the sight of the swollen disfigured face, and the long mark on the arm which lay half-uncovered. Presents of delicacies, ointments, and cooling drinks were frequently sent from him and from the Countess de Selinville; but Lady Walsingham distrusted these, and kept her guest strictly to the regimen appointed by Pare. Now and then, billets would likewise come. The first brought a vivid crimson into Berenger's face, and both it and all its successors he instantly tore into the smallest fragments, without letting any one see them.

On the day of the Carnival, the young men of the household had asked Master Thistlewood to come out with them and see the procession of the *Boeuf Gras*; but before it could take place, reports were flying about that put the city in commotion, caused the Ambassador to forbid all going out, and made Philip expect another Huguenot massacre. The Duke of Alencon and the King of Navarre had been detected, it was said, in a conspiracy for overthrowing the power of the Queen-mother, bringing in the Huguenots, and securing the crown to Alencon on the King's death. Down-stairs, the Ambassador and his secretaries sat anxiously striving to sift the various contradictory reports; up-stairs, Philip and Lady Walsingham were anxiously watching Berenger in what seemed the long-expected crisis, and Philip was feeling as if all the French court were welcome to murder one another so that they would only let Ambroise Pare come to his brother's relief. And it was impossible even to send!

At last, however, when Ash-Wednesday was half over, there was a quiet movement, and a small pale man in black was at the bedside, without Philip's having ever seen his entrance. He looked at his exhausted patient, and said, 'It is well; I could not have done you any good before.'

And when he had set Berenger more at ease, he told how great had been the confusion at St. Germain when the plot had become known to the Queen-mother. The poor King had been wakened at two o'clock in the morning, and carried to his litter, when Pare and his old nurse had tended him. He only said, 'Can they not let me die in peace?' and his weakness had been so great on arriving, that the surgeon could hardly have left him for M. de Ribaumont, save by his own desire. 'Yes, sir,' added Pare, seeing Berenger attending to him, 'we must have you well quickly; his Majesty knows all about you, and is anxious to see you.'

In spite of these good wishes, the recovery was very slow; for, as the surgeon had suspected, the want of skill in those who had had the charge of Berenger at the first had been the cause of much of his protracted suffering. Pare, the inventor of trephining, was, perhaps, the only man in Europe who could have dealt with the fracture in the back of the head, and he likewise extracted the remaining splinters of the jaw, though at the cost of much severe handling and almost intolerable pain: but by Easter, Berenger found the good surgeon's encouragement verified, and himself on the way to a far more effectual cure than he had hitherto thought possible. Sleep had come back to him, he experienced the luxury of being free from all pain, he could eat without difficulty; and Pare, always an enemy to wine, assured him that half the severe headaches for which he had been almost bled to death, were the consequence of his living on bread soaked in sack instead of solid food; and he was forbidden henceforth to inflame his brain with anything stronger than sherbet. His speech, too, was much improved; he still could not utter all the consonants perfectly, and could not speak distinctly without articulating very slowly, but all the discomfort and pain were gone; and though still very weak, he told Philip that now all his course seemed clear towards his child, instead of being like a dull, distraught dream. His plan was to write to have a vessel sent from Weymouth, to lie off the coast till his signal should be seen from la Motte-Achard, and then to take in the whole party and the little yearling daughter, whom he declared he should trust to no one but himself. Lady Walsingham remonstrated a little at the wonderful plans hatched by the two lads together, and yet she was too glad to see a beginning of brightening on his face to make many objections. It was only too sand to think how likely he was again to be disappointed.

He was dressed, but had not left his room, and was lying on cushions in the ample window overlooking the garden, while Frances and Elizabeth Walsingham in charge of their mother tried to amuse him by their childish airs and sports, when a message was brought that M. le Chevalier de Ribaumont prayed to be admitted to see him privily.

'What bodes that?' he languidly said.

'Mischief, no doubt,' said Philip Walsingham. 'Send him word that you are seriously employed.'

'Nay, that could scarce be, when he must have heard the children's voices,' said Lady Walsingham. 'Come away, little ones.'

The ladies took the hint and vanished, but Philip remained till the Chevalier had entered, more resplendent than ever, in a brown velvet suit slashed with green satin, and sparkling with gold lace-a contrast to the deep mourning habit in which Berenger was dressed. After inquiries for his health, the Chevalier looked at Philip, and expressed his desire of speaking with his cousin alone.

'If it be of business,' said Berenger, much on his guard, 'my head is still weak, and I would wish to have the presence of the Ambassador or one of his secretaries.'

'This is not so much a matte of business as of family,' said the Chevalier, still looking so uneasily at Philip that Berenger felt constrained to advise him to join the young ladies in the garden; but instead of doing this, the boy paced the corridors like a restless dog waiting for his master, and no sooner heard the old gentleman bow himself out than he hurried back again, to find Berenger heated, panting, agitated as by a sharp encounter.

'Brother, what is it—what has the old rogue done to you?'

'Nothing,' said Berenger, tardily and wearily; and for some minutes he did not attempt to speak, while Philip devoured his curiosity as best he might. At last he said, 'He was always beyond me. What think you? Now he wants me to turn French courtier and marry his daughter.'

'His daughter!' exclaimed Philip, 'that beautiful lady I saw in the coach?'

A nod of assent.

'I only wish it were I.'

'Philip,' half angrily, 'how can you be such a fool?'

'Of course, I know it can't be,' said Philip sheepishly, but a little offended. 'But she's the fairest woman my eyes ever beheld.'

'And the falsest.'

'My father says all women are false; only they can't help it, and don't mean it.'

'Only some do mean it,' said Berenger, dryly.

'Brother!' cried Philip, fiercely, as if ready to break a lance, 'what right have you to accuse that kindly, lovely dame of falsehood?'

'It skills not going through all,' said Berenger, wearily. 'I know her of old. She began by passing herself off on me as my wife.'

'And you were not transported?'

'I am not such a gull as you.'

'How very beautiful your wife must have been!' said Philip, with gruff amazement overpowering his consideration.

'Much you know about it,' returned Berenger, turning his face away.

There was a long silence, first broken by Philip, asking more cautiously, 'And what did you say to him?'

'I said whatever could show it was most impossible. Even I said the brother's handwriting was too plain on my face for me to offer myself to the sister. But it seems all that is to be passed over as an unlucky mistake. I wish I could guess what the old fellow is aiming at.'

'I am sure the lady looked at you as if she loved you.'

'Simpleton! She looked to see how she could beguile me. Love! They do nothing for love here, you foolish boy, save *par amour*. If she loved me, her father was the last person she would have sent me. No, no; 'tis a new stratagem, if I could only seen my way into it. Perhaps Sir Francis will when he can spend an hour on me.'

Though full of occupation, Sir Francis never failed daily to look in upon his convalescent guest, and when he heard of the Chevalier's interview, he took care that Berenger should have full time to consult him; and, of course, he inquired a good deal more into the particulars of the proposal than Philip had done. When he learnt that the Chevalier had offered all the very considerable riches and lands that Diane enjoyed in right of her late husband as an equivalent for Berenger's resignation of all claims upon the Nid-de-Merle property, he noted it on his tables, and desired to know what these claims might be. 'I cannot tell,' said Berenger. 'You may remember, sir, the parchments with our contract of marriage had been taken away from Chateau Leurre, and I have never seen them.'

'Then,' said the Ambassador, 'you may hold it as certain that those parchments give you some advantage which he hears, since he is willing to purchase it at so heavy a price. Otherwise he himself would be the natural heir of those lands.'

'After my child,' said Berenger, hastily.

'Were you on your guard against mentioning your trust in your child's life?' said Sir Francis.

The long scar turned deeper purple than ever. 'Only so far as that I said there still be rights I had no power to resign,' said Berenger. 'And then he began to prove to me——what I had no mind to hear' (and his voice trembled) '——all that I know but too well.'

'Hum! you must not be left alone again to cope with him,' said Walsingham. 'Did he make any question of the validity of your marriage?'

'No, sir, it was never touched on. I would not let him take her name into his lips.'

Walsingham considered for some minutes, and then said, 'It is clear, then, that he believes that the marriage can be sufficiently established to enable you to disturb him in his possession of some part, at least, of the Angevin inheritance, or he would not endeavour to purchase your renunciation of it by the hand of a daughter so richly endowed.'

'I would willingly renounce it if that were all! I never sought it; only I cannot give up her child's rights.'

'And that you almost declared,' proceeded Walsingham; 'so that the Chevalier has by his negotiation gathered from you that you have not given up hope that the infant lives. Do your men know where you believe she is?'

'My Englishmen know it, of course,' said Berenger; 'but there is no fear of them. The Chevalier speaks no English, and they scarcely any French; and, besides, I believe they deem him equally my butcher with his son. The other fellow I only picked up after I was on my way to Paris, and I doubt his knowing my purpose.'

'The Chevalier must have had speech with him, though,' said Philip; 'for it was he who brought word that the old rogue wished to speak with you.'

'It would be well to be quit yourself of the fellow ere leaving Paris,' said Walsingham.

'Then, sir,' said Berenger, with an anxious voice, 'do you indeed think I have betrayed aught that can peril the poor little one?'

Sir Francis smiled. 'We do not set lads of your age to cope with old foxes,' he answered; 'and it seems to me that you used far discretion in the encounter. The mere belief that the child lives does not show him where she may be. In effect, it would seem likely to most that the babe would be nursed in some cottage, and thus not be in the city of La Sablerie at all. He might, mayhap, thus be put on a false scent.'

'Oh no,' exclaimed Berenger, startled; 'that might bring the death of some other person's child on my soul.'

'That shall be guarded against,' said Sir Francis. 'In the meantime, my fair youth, keep your matters as silent as may be——do not admit the Chevalier again in my absence; and, as to this man Guibert, I will confer with my steward whether he knows too much, and whether it be safer to keep of dismiss him!'

'If only I could see the King, and leave Paris,' sighed Berenger.

And Walsingham, though unwilling to grieve the poor youth further, bethought himself that this was the most difficult and hopeless matter of all. As young Ribaumont grew better, the King grew worse; he himself only saw Charles on rare occasions, surrounded by a host of watchful eyes and ears, and every time he marked the progress of disease; and though such a hint could be given by an Ambassador, he thought that by far the best chance of recovery of the child lay in the confusion that might probably follow the death of Charles IX. in the absence of his next heir.

Berenger reckoned on the influence of Elisabeth of Austria, who had been the real worker in his union with Eutacie; but he was told that it was vain to expect assistance from her. In the first year of her marriage, she had fondly hoped to enjoy her husband's confidence, and take her natural place in his court; but she was of no mould to struggle with Catherine de Medicis, and after a time had totally desisted. Even at the time of the St. Bartholomew, she had endeavoured to uplift her voice on the side of mercy, and had actually saved the lives of the King of Navarre and Prince of Conde; and her father, the good Maximilian II., had written in the strongest terms to Charles IX. expressing his horror of the massacre. Six weeks later, the first hour after the birth of her first and only child, she had interceded with her husband for the lives of two Huguenots who had been taken alive, and failing then either through his want of will or want of power, she had collapsed and yielded up the endeavour. She ceased to listen to petitions from those who had hoped for her assistance, as if to save both them and herself useless pain, and seemed to lapse into a sort of apathy to all public interests. She hardly spoke, mechanically fulfilled her few offices in the court, and seemed to have turned her entire hope and trust into prayer for her husband. Her German confessor had been sent home, and a Jesuit given her in his stead, but she had made no resistance; she seemed to the outer world a dull, weary stranger, obstinate in leading a conventual life; but those who knew her best——and of these few was the Huguenot surgeon Pare——knew that her heart had been broken two guilty lives, or to make her husband free himself from his bondage to bloody counsels. To pray for him was all that remained to her——and unwearied had been those prayers. Since his health had declined, she had been equally indefatigable in attending on him, and did not seem to have a single interest beyond his sick chamber.

- 234 -

As to the King of Navarre, for whose help Berenger had hoped, he had been all these months in the dishonouable thraldom of Catherine de Medicis, and was more powerless than ever at this juncture, having been implicated in Alencon's plot, and imprisoned at Vincennes.

And thus, the more Berenger heard of the state of things, the less hopeful did his cause appear, till he could almost have believed his best chance lay in Philip's plan of persuading the Huguenots to storm the convent.

CHAPTER XXVII
THE DYING KING

Die in terror of thy guiltiness,

Dream on, dream on of bloody deeds and death, Fainting, despair,

despairing yield thy breath

KING RICHARD III.

A few days later, when Berenger had sent out Philip, under the keeping of the secretaries, to see the Queen-mother represent Royalty in one of the grand processions of Rogation-tide, the gentle knock came to his door that always announced the arrival of his good surgeon.

'You look stronger, M. le Baron; have you yet left your room?'

'I have walked round the gallery above the hall,' said Berenger. 'I have not gone down-stairs; that is for to-morrow.'

'What would M. le Baron say if his chirurgeon took him not merely down-stairs, but up on flight at the Louvre?'

'Ha!' cried Berenger; 'to the King?'

'It is well-nigh the last chance, Monsieur; the Queen-mother and all her suite are occupied with services and sermons this week; and next week private access to the King will be far more difficult. I have waited as long as I could that you might gain strength to support the fatigue.'

'Hope cancels fatigue,' said Berenger, already at the other end of the room searching for his long-disused cloak, sword, gloves, hat, and mask.

'Not the sword,' said Pare, 'so please you. M. le Baron must condescend to obtain entrance as my assistant—the plain black doublet—yes, that is admirable; but I did not know that Monsieur was so tall,' he added, in some consternation, as, for the first time, he saw his patient standing up at his full height—unusual even in England, and more so in France. Indeed, Berenger had grown during his year of illness, and being, of course, extremely thin, looked all the taller, so as to be a very inconvenient subject to smuggle into to palace unobserved.

However, Ambroise had made up his mind to the risk, and merely assisted Berenger in assuming his few equipments, then gave him his arm to go down the stairs. Meeting Guibert on the way, Berenger left word with him that he was going out to take the air with Maitre Pare; and on the man's offering to attend him, refused the proposal.

Pare carriage waited in the court, and Berenger, seated in its depths, rolled unseen through the streets, till he found himself at the little postern of the Louvre, the very door whence he was to have led off his poor Eustacie. Here Ambroise made him take off his small black mask, in spite of all danger of his scars being remarked, since masks were not etiquette in the palace, and, putting into his arms a small brass-bound case of instruments, asked his pardon for preceding him, and alighted from the carriage.

This was Ambroise's usual entrance, and it was merely guarded by a Scottish archer, who probably observed nothing. They then mounted the stone stair, the same where Osbert had dragged down his insensible master; and as, at the summit, the window appeared where Berenger had waited those weary hours, and heard the first notes of the bell of St.-Germain-l'Auxerrois, his breath came in such hurried sobs, that Pare would fain have given him time to recover himself, but he gasped, 'Not here—not here;' and Pare, seeing that he could still move on, turned, not to the corridor leading to the King's old apartments, now too full of dreadful associations for poor Charles, but towards those of the young Queen. Avoiding the ante-room, where no doubt waited pages, users, and attendants, Pare presently knocked at a small door, so hidden in the wain-scoting of the passage that only a *habitue* could have found it without strict search. It was at once opened, and the withered, motherly face of an old woman, with keen black eyes under a formal tight white cap, looked out.

'Eh! Maitre Pare,' she said, 'you have brought the poor young gentleman? On my faith, he looks scarcely able to walk! Come in, sir, and rest a while in my chamber while Maitre Ambroise goes on to announce you to the King. He is more at ease to-day, the poor child, and will relish some fresh talk.

Berenger knew this to be Philippe, the old Huguenot nurse, whom Charles IX. loved most fondly, and in whom he found his greatest comfort. He was very glad to sink into the seat she placed for him, the only one is her small, bare room and recover breath there while Pare passed on to the King, and she talked as one delighted to have a hearer.

'Ah, yes, rest yourself—stay; I will give you a few spoonfuls of the cordial potage I have here for the King; it will comfort your heart. Ah! you have been cruelly mauled—but he would have saved you if he could.

'Yes, good mother, I know that; the King has been my very good lord.

'Ah! blessings on you if you say so from your heart, Monsieur; you know me for one of your poor Reformed. And I tell you—I who saw him born, who nursed him from his birth—that, suffer as you may, you can never suffer as he does. Maitre Ambroise may talk of his illness coming from blowing too much on his horn; I know better. But, ah! to be here at night would make a stone shed tears of blood. The Queen and I know it; but we say nothing, we only pray.

The sight of a Huguenot was so great a treat to the old woman in her isolated life, that her tongue ran thus freely while Berenger sat, scarce daring to speak or breathe in the strange boding atmosphere of the palace, where the nurse and surgeon moved as tolerated, privileged persons, in virtue of the necessity of the one to the King—of the other to all the world. After all brief interval Pare returned and beckoned to Berenger, who followed him across a large state-bedroom to a much smaller one, which he entered from under a heavy blue velvet curtain, and found himself in an atmosphere heavy with warmth and perfume, and strangely oppressed besides. On one side of the large fire sat the young Queen, faded, wan, and with all animation or energy departed, only gazing with a silent, wistful intentness at her husband. He was opposite to her in a pillowed chair, his feet on a stool, with a deadly white, padded, puffy cheek, and his great black eyes, always prominent, now with a glassy look, and strained wide, as though always gazing after some horrible sight. 'Madame la Comtesse stood in her old, wooden, automaton fashion behind the Queen; otherwise, no one was present save Pare, who, as he held up the curtain, stood back to let M. de Ribaumont advance. He stood still, however, merely bowing low, awaiting an invitation to come forward, and trying to repress the startled tear called up by the very shock of pity at the mournful aspect of the young King and Queen.

Elisabeth, absorbed in her husband, and indifferent to all besides, did not even turn her head as he entered; but Charles signed to him to approach, holding out a yellow, dropsical-looking hand; and as he dropped on one knee and kissed it fervently, the King said, 'Here he is, Madame, the Baron de Ribaumont, the same whose little pleasure-boat was sucked down in our whirlpool.

All Elisabeth's memories seemed to have been blotted out in that whirlpool, for she only bowed her head formally, and gave no look of recognition, though she, too, allowed Berenger to salute her listless, dejected hand. 'One would hardly have known him again, continued the King, in a low husky voice; 'but I hope, sir, I see you recovering.

'Thanks, Sire, to Heaven's goodness, and to your goodness in sparing to me the services of Maitre Pare.

'Ah! there is none like Pare for curing a wound OUTSIDE,' said Charles, then leant back silent; and Berenger, still kneeling, was considering whether he ought to proffer his petition, when the King continued, 'How fares your friend Sidney, M. le Baron?

'Right well, Sire. The Queen has made him one of her gentlemen.'

'Not after this fashion,' said Charles, as with his finger he traced the long scar on Berenger's face. 'Our sister of England has different badges of merit from ours for her good subjects. Ha! what say they of us in England, Baron?

'I have lain sick at home, Sire, and have neither seen nor heard, said Berenger.

'Ah! one day more at Montpipeau had served your turn,' said the King; 'but you are one who has floated up again. One—one at least whose blood is not on my head.

The Queen looked up uneasy and imploring, as Charles continued: 'Would that more of you would come in this way! They have scored you deep, but know you what is gashed deeper still? Your King's heart! Ah! you will not come, as Coligny does, from his gibbet, with his two bleeding hands. My father was haunted to his dying day by the face of one Huguenot tailor. Why, I see a score, night by night! You are solid; let me feel you, man.

'M. Pare,' exclaimed the poor Queen, 'take him away.

'No, Madame,' said the King, holding tight in his hot grasp Berenger's hand, which was as pale as his own, long, thin, and wasted, but cold from strong emotion; 'take not away the only welcome sight I have seen for well-nigh two years.' He coughed, and the handkerchief he put to his lips had blood on it; but he did not quit his hold of his visitor, and presently said in a feeble whisper, 'Tell me, how did you escape?

Pare, over the King's head, signed to him to make his narrative take time; and indeed his speech was of necessity so slow, that by the time he had related how Osbert had brought him safely to England, the King had recovered himself so as to say, 'See what it is to have a faithful servant. Which of those they have left me would do as much for me? And now, being once away with your life, what brings you back to this realm of ours, after your last welcome?

'I left my wife here, Sire.

'Ha! and the cousin would have married her—obtained permission to call himself Nid de Merle—but she slipped through his clumsy fingers; did she not? Did you know anything of her, Madame?

'No,' said the Queen, looking up. 'She wrote to me once from her convent; but I knew I could do nothing for her but bring her enemies' notice on her; so I made no answer.

Berenger could hardly conceal his start of indignation—less at the absolute omission, than at the weary indifference of the Queen's confession. Perhaps the King saw it, for he added, 'So it is, Ribaumont; the kindest service we can do our friends is to let them alone; and, after all, it was not the worse for her. She did evade her enemies?

'Yes, Sire,' said Berenger, commanding and steadying his voice with great difficulty, 'she escaped in time to give birth to our child in the ruined loft of an old grange of the Templars, under the care of a Huguenot farmer, and a pastor who had known my father. Then she took refuge in La Sablerie, and wrote to my mother, deeming me dead. I was just well enough to go in quest of her. I came—ah! Sire, I found only charred ruins. Your Majesty knows how Huguenot bourgs are dealt with.

'And she——?

Berenger answered but by a look.

'Why did you come to tell me this?' said the King, passionately. 'Do you not know that they have killed me already? I thought you came because there was still some one I could aid.

'There is, there is, Sire,' said Berenger, for once interrupting royalty. 'None save you can give me my child. It is almost certain that a good priest saved it; but it is in a convent, and only with a royal order can one of my religion either obtain it, or even have my questions answered.

'Nor with one in Paris,' said the King dryly; 'but in the country the good mothers may still honour their King's hand. Here, Ambroise, take pen and ink, and write the order. To whom?

'To the Mother Prioress of the Ursulines at Lucon, so please our Majesty,' said Berenger, 'to let me have possession of my daughter.

'Eh! is it only a little girl?

'Yes, Sire; but my heart yearns for her all the more,' said Berenger, with glistening eyes.

'You are right,' said the poor King. 'Mine, too, is a little girl; and I bless God daily that she is no son—to be the most wretched thing the France.

Let her come in, Madame. She is little older than my friend's daughter. I would show her to him.

The Queen signed to Madame la Comtesse to fetch the child, and Berenger added, 'Sire, you could do a further benefit to my poor little one. One more signature of yours would attest that ratification of my marriage which took place in your Majesty's presence.

'Ah! I remember,' said Charles. 'You may have any name of mine that can help you to oust that villain Narcisse; only wait to use it—spare me any more storms. It will serve your turn as well when I am beyond they, and you will make your claim good. What,' seeing Berenger's interrogative look, 'do you not know that by the marriage-contract the lands of each were settled on the survivor?

'No, Sire; I have never seen the marriage-contract.

'Your kinsman knew it well,' said Charles.

Just then, Madame la Comtesse returned, leading the little Princess by the long ribbons at her waist; Charles bent forward, calling, 'Here, *ma petite*, come here. Here is one who loves thy father. Look well at him, that thou mayest know him.

The little Madame Elisabeth so far understood, that, with a certain lofty condescension, she extended her hand for the stranger to kiss, and thus drew from the King the first smile that Berenger had seen. She was more than half a year older than the Berangere on whom his hopes were set, and whom he trusted to find not such a pale, feeble, tottering little creature as this poor young daughter of France, whose round black eyes gazed wonderingly at his scar; but she was very precocious, and even already too much of a royal lady to indulge in any awkward personal observation.

By the time she had been rewarded for her good behaviour by one of the dried plums in her father's comfit-box, the order had been written by Pare, and Berenger had prepared the certificate for the King's signature, according to the form given him by his grandfather.

'Your writing shakes nearly as much as mine,' said the poor King, as he wrote his name to this latter. 'Now, Madame, you had better sign it also; and tell this gentleman where to find Father Meinhard in Austria. He was a little too true for us, do you see—would not give thanks for shedding innocent blood. Ah!'—and with a gasp of mournful longing, the King sank back, while Elisabeth, at his bidding, added her name to the certificate, and murmured the name of a convent in Vienna, where her late confessor could be found.

'I cannot thank you Majesty enough,' said Berenger; 'My child's rights are now secure in England at least, and this'—as he held the other paper for the King—'will give her to me.

'Ah! take it for what it is worth,' said the King, as he scrawled his 'CHARLES' upon it. 'This order must be used promptly, or it will avail you nothing. Write to Ambroise how you speed; that is, if it will bring me one breath of good news.' And as Berenger kissed his hand with tearful, inarticulate thanks, he proceeded, 'Save for that cause, I would ask you to come to me again. It does me good. It is like a breath from Montpipeau— the last days of hope—before the frenzy—the misery.

'Whenever your Majesty does me the honour——' began Berenger, forgetting all except the dying man.

'I am not so senseless,' interrupted the King sharply; 'it would be losing the only chance of undoing one wrong. Only, Ribaumont,' he added fervently, 'for once let me hear that one man has pardoned me.

'Sire, Sire,' sobbed Berenger, totally overcome, 'how can I speak the word? How feel aught but love, loyalty, gratitude?

Charles half smiled again as he said in sad meditation—'Ah! it was in me to have been a good king if they had let me. Think of me, bid your friend Sidney think of me, as I would have been—not as I have been—and pray, pray for me.' Then hiding his face in his handkerchief, in a paroxysm of grief and horror, he murmured in a stifled tone, 'Blood, blood, deliver me, good Lord!

In effect, there was so sudden a gush of blood from mouth and nose that Berenger sprang to his feet in dismay, and was *bona fide* performing the part of assistant to the surgeon, when, at the Queen's cry, not only the nurse Philippe hurried in, but with her a very dark, keen-looking man, who at once began applying strong essences to the King's face, as Berenger supported his head. In a few moments Pare looked up at Berenger, and setting him free, intimated to him, between sign and whisper, to go into Philippe's room and wait there; and it was high time, for though the youth had felt nothing in the stress of the moment, he was almost swooning when he reached the little chamber, and lay back in the nurse's chair, with closed eyes, scarcely conscious how time went, or even where he was, till he was partly aroused by hearing steps returning.

'The poor young man,' said Philippe's kind voice, 'he is fainting. Ah! no wonder it overcame any kind heart.

'How is the King?' Berenger tried to say, but his own voice still sounded unnatural and far away.

'He is better for the time, and will sleep,' said Pare, administering to his other patient some cordial drops as he spoke. 'There, sir; you will soon be able to return to the carriage. This has been a sore trial to your strength.

'But I have gained all—all I could hope,' said Berenger, looking at his precious papers. 'But, alas! the poor King!

'You will never, never let a word of blame pass against him,' cried Philippe earnestly. 'It is well that one of our people should have seen how it really is with him. All I regret is that Maitre Rene thrust himself in and saw you.

'Who?' said Berenger, who had been too much engrossed to perceive any one.

'Maitre Rene of Milan, the Queen-mother's perfume. He came with some plea of bringing a pouncet-box from her, but I wager it was as a spy. I was doing my best to walk him gently off, when the Queen's cry called me, and he must needs come in after me.

'I saw him not,' said Berenger; 'perhaps he marked not me in the confusion.

'I fear,' said Pare gravely, 'he was more likely to have his senses about him than you. M. le Baron; these bleedings of the King's are not so new to us familiars to the palace. The best thing now to be done is to have you to the carriage, if you can move.

Berenger, now quite recovered, stood up, and gave his warm thanks to the old nurse for her kindness to him.

'Ah! sir,' she said, 'you are one of us. Pray, pray that God will have mercy on my poor child! He has the truth in his heart. Pray that it may save him at the last.

Ambroise, knowing that she would never cease speaking while there was any one to hear her, almost dragged Berenger out at the little secret door, conveyed him safely down the stairs, and placed him again in the carriage. Neither spoke till the surgeon said, 'You have seen a sad sight, Monsieur le Baron: I need not bid you be discreet.

'There are some things that go too deep for speech,' sighed the almost English Berenger; then, after a pause, 'Is there no hope for him? Is he indeed dying?

'Without a miracle, he cannot live a month. He is as truly slain by the St. Bartholomew as ever its martyrs were,' said Pare, moved out of his usual cautious reserve towards one who had seen so much and felt so truly. 'I tell you, sir, that his mother hath as truly slain her sons, as if she had sent Rene there to them with his drugs. According as they have consciences and hearts, so they pine and perish under her rule.

Berenger shuddered, and almost sobbed, 'And hath he no better hope, no comforter?' he asked.

'None save good old Flipote. As you heard, the Queen-mother will not suffer his own Church to speak to him in her true voice. No confessor but one chosen by the Cardinal of Lorraine may come near him; and with him all is mere ceremony. But if at the last he opens his ear and heart to take in the true hope of salvation, it will be from the voice of poor old Philippe.

And so it was! It was Philippe, who heard him in the night sobbing over the piteous words, 'My God, what horrors, what blood!' and, as she took from his tear-drenched handkerchief, spoke to him of the Blood that speaketh better things than the blood of Abel; and it was she who, in the final agony, heard and treasured these last words, 'If the Lord Jesus will indeed receive me into the company of the blest!' Surely, never was repentance deeper than that of Charles IX.—and these, his parting words, were such as to inspire the trust that it was not remorse.

All-important as Berenger's expedition had been, he still could think of little but the poor King; and, wearied out as he was, he made very little reply to the astonished friends who gathered round him on his return. He merely told Philip that he had succeeded, and then lay almost without speaking on his bed till the Ambassador made his evening visit, when he showed him the two papers. Sir Francis could hardly believe his good fortune in having obtained this full attestation of the marriage, and promised to send to the English Ambassador in Germany, to obtain the like from Father Meinhard. The document itself he advised Berenger not to expose to the dangers of the French journey, but to leave it with him to be forwarded direct to Lord Walwyn. It was most important, both as obviating any dispute on the legitimacy of the child, if she lived; or, if not, it would establish those rights of Berenger to the Nid de Merle estates, of which he had heard from the King. This information explained what were the claims that the Chevalier was so anxious to hush up by a marriage with Madame de Selinville. Berenger, as his wife's heir, was by this contract the true owner of the estates seized by the Chevalier and his son, and could only be ousted, either by his enemies proving his contract to Eustacie invalid and to be unfulfilled, or by his own voluntary resignation. The whole scheme was clear to Walsingham, and he wasted advice upon unheeding ears, as to how Berenger should act to obtain restitution so soon as he should be of age, and how he should try to find out the notary who had drawn up the contract. If Berenger cared at all, it was rather for the sake of punishing and balking Narcisse, than with any desire of the inheritance; and even for righteous indignation he was just now too weary and too sad. He could not discuss his rights to Nid de Merle, if they passed over the rights of Eustacie's child, round whom his affection were winding themselves as his sole hope.

The next evening Pare came in quest of Berenger, and after a calm, refreshing, hopeful Ascension-day, which had been a real balm to the weary spirit, found him enjoying the sweet May sunshine under a tree in the garden. 'I am glad to find you out of doors,' he said; 'I fear I must hasten your departure.

'I burn to lose no time,' cried Berenger. 'Prithee tell them I may safely go! They all call it madness to think of setting out.

'Ordinarily it would be,' said Pare; 'but Rene of Milan has sent his underlings to see who is my new, tall assistant. He will report all to the Queen-mother; and though in this house you could scarcely suffer personal harm, yet the purpose of your journey might be frustrated, and the King might have to undergo another of those *bourrasques* which he may well dread.

'I will go this very night,' said Berenger, starting up; 'where is Philip?— where is Sir Francis?

Even that very night Pare thought not too soon, and the Ascension-tide illuminations brought so many persons abroad that it would be easy to go unnoticed; and in the general festivity, when every one was coming and going from the country to gaze or worship at the shrines and the images decked in every church, it would be easy for the barriers to be passed without observation. Then the brothers would sleep at a large hostel, the first on the road to England, where Walsingham's couriers and guest always baited, and the next morning he would send out to them their attendants, with houses for their further journey back into Anjou. If any enemies were on the watch, this would probably put them off the scent, and it only remained further to be debated, whether the Norman Guibert had better be dismissed at once or taken with them. There was always soft place in Berenger's heart for a Norman, and the man was really useful; moreover, he would certainly be safer employed and in their company, than turned loose to tell the Chevalier all he might have picked up in the Hotel d'Angleterre. It was therefore decided that he should be the attendant of the two young men, and he received immediate orders that night to pack up their garments, and hold himself ready.

Nevertheless, before the hour of departure, Guibert had stolen out, had an interview with the Chevalier de Ribaumont at the Hotel de Selinville, and came back with more than one good French crown in his pocket, and hopes of more.

CHAPTER XXVIII
THE ORPHANS OF LA SABLERIE

The cream tarts with pepper in them.—ARABIAN NIGHTS.

Hope, spring, and recovery carried the young Baronde Ribaumont on his journey infinitely better than his companions had dared to expect. He dreaded nothing so much as being overtaken by those tidings which would make King Charles's order mere waste paper; and therefore pressed on with little regard to his own fatigue, although happily with increasing strength, which carried him a further stage every day.

Lucon was a closely-guarded, thoroughly Catholic city, and his safe-conduct was jealously demanded; but the name of Ribaumont silenced all doubt. 'A relation, apparently, of M. de Nid de Merle,' said the officer on guard, and politely invited him to dinner and bed at the castle; but these he thought it prudent to decline, explaining that he brought a letter from the King to the Mother Prioress.

The convent walls were pointed out to him, and he only delayed at the inn long enough to arrange his dress as might appear to the Abbess most respectful, and, poor boy, be least likely to startle the babe on whom his heart was set. At almost every inn, the little children had shrieked and run from his white and gashed face, and his tall, lank figure in deep black; and it was very sadly that he said to Philip, 'You must come with me. If she turns from me as an ogre, your bright ruddy face will win her.

The men were left at the inn with charge to let Guibert speak for them, and to avoid showing their nationality. The three months of Paris, and the tailors there, had rendered Philip much less conspicuous than formerly; but still people looked at him narrowly as he followed his brother along the street. The two lads had made up their minds to encumber themselves with no nurses, or womanfolk. The child should be carried, fondled, and fed by her boy-father alone. He believed that, when he once held her in his arms, he should scarcely even wish to give her up to any one else; and, in his concentration of mind, had hardly thought of all the inconveniences and absurdities that would arise; but, really, was chiefly occupied by the fear that she would not at first let him take her in his arms, and hold her to his heart.

Philip, a little more alive to the probabilities, nevertheless was disposed to regard them as 'fun and pastime.' He had had many a frolic with his baby-sisters, and this would be only a prolonged one; besides, it was 'Berry's' one hope, and to rescue any creature from a convent was a good work, in his Protestant eyes, which had not become a whit less prejudiced at Paris. So he was quite prepared to take his full share of his niece, or more, if she should object to her father's looks, and he only suggested halting at an old woman's stall to buy some sweetmeats by way of propitiation—a proceeding which much amazed the gazing population of Lucon. Two reports were going about, one that the King had vowed a silver image of himself to St. Ursula, if her Prioress would obtain his recovery by their prayers; the other that he was going to translate her to the royal Abbey of Fontevrault to take charge of his daughter, Madame Elisabeth. Any way, high honour by a royal messenger must be intended to the Prioress, Mere Monique, and the Luconnais were proud of her sanctity.

The portress had already heard the report, and opened her wicket even before the bell could be rung, then eagerly ushered him into the parlour, the barest and most ascetic-looking of rooms, with a boarded partition across, unenlivened except by a grated hollow, and the outer portion empty, save of a table, three chairs, and a rugged woodcut of a very tall St. Ursula, with a crowd of pigmy virgins, not reaching higher than the ample hem of her petticoat.

'Did Aunt Cecily live in such a place as this?' exclaimed Philip, gazing round; 'or do they live on the fat among down cushions inside there?'

'Hush—sh,' said Berenger, frowning with anxiety; for a rustling was heard behind the screen, and presently a black veil and white scapulary appeared, and a sweet calm voice said, 'Peace be with you, sir; what are your commands?'

Berenger bowed low, and replied, 'Thanks, reverend Lady; I bring a letter from the King, to request your aid in a matter that touches me nearly.

'His Majesty shall be obeyed. Come you from him?

He was forced to reply to her inquiries after the poor King's health before she opened the letter, taking it under her veil to read it; so that as he stood, trembling, almost sickening with anxiety, and scarcely able to breathe, he could see nothing but the black folds; and at her low murmured exclamation he started as if at a cannon-shot.

'De Ribaumont!' she said; 'can it be—the child—of—of—out poor dear little *pensionnaire* at Bellaise?

'It is—it is!' cried Berenger. 'O Madame, you knew her at Bellaise?

'Even so,' replied the Prioress, who was in fact the Soeur Monique so loved and regretted by Eustacie. 'I loved and prayed for her with all my heart when she was claimed by the world. Heaven's will be done; but the poor little thing loved me, and I have often thought that had I been still at

Bellaise when she returned she would not have fled. But of this child I have no knowledge.

'You took charge of the babes of La Sablerie, Madame,' said Berenger, almost under his breath.

'Her infant among those poor orphans!' exclaimed the Prioress, more and more startled and amazed.

'If it be anywhere in this life, it is in your good keeping, Madame,' said Berenger, with tears in his eyes. 'Oh! I entreat, withhold her no longer.

'But,' exclaimed the bewildered nun, 'who would you then be, sir?

'I—her husband—widower of Eustacie—father of her orphan!' cried Berenger. 'She cannot be detained from me, either by right or law.

'Her husband,' still hesitated Monique. 'But he is dead. The poor little one—Heaven have mercy on her soul—wrote me a piteous entreaty, and gave large alms for prayers and masses for his soul.

The sob in his throat almost strangled his speech. 'She mourned me to the last as dead. I was borne away senseless and desperately wounded; and when I recovered power to seek her it was too late! O Madame! have pity— let me see all she has left to me.

'Is it possible?' said the nun. 'We would not learn the parentage of our nurslings since all alike become children of Mother Church. Then, suddenly bethinking herself, 'But, surely, Monsieur cannot be a Huguenot.

It was no doubt the first time she had been brought in contact with a schismatic, and she could not believe that such respectful courtesy could come from one. He saw he must curb himself, and explain. 'I am neither Calvinist nor Sacrementaire, Madame. I was bred in England, where we love our own Church. My aunt is a Benedictine Sister, who keeps her rule strictly, though her convent is destroyed; and it is to her that I shall carry my daughter. Ah, Lady, did you but know my heart's hunger for her!

The Prioress, better read in the lives of the saints than in the sects of heretics, did not know whether this meant that he was of her own faith or not; and her woman's heart being much moved by his pleadings, she said, 'I will heartily give your daughter to you, sir, as indeed I must, if she be here; but you have never seen her?

'No; only her empty cradle in the burnt house. But I MUST know her. She is a year old.

'We have two babes of that age; but I fear me you will scarce see much likeness in either of them to any one you knew,' said the Prioress, thoughtfully. 'However, there are two girls old enough to remember the parentage of their companions, though we forbade them to mention it. Would you see them, sir?

'And the infants, so please you, reverend Mother,' exclaimed Berenger.

She desired him to wait, and after an interval of suspense there was a pattering of little *sabots* behind the partition, and through the grating he beheld six little girls in blue serge frocks and tight white caps. Of the two infants, one with a puny, wizen, pinched face was in the arms of the Prioress; the other, a big, stout, coarse child, with hard brown cheeks and staring black-eyes, was on its own feet, but with a great basket-work frame round its head to save it from falls. There were two much more prepossessing children of three or four, and two intelligent-looking girls of perhaps eight and ten, to the elder of whom the Prioress turned, saying, 'Agathe, I release you from my command not to speak of your former life, and desire you to tell this gentleman if you know who were the parents of these two little ones.

'Yes, reverend Mother,' said Agathe, readily; 'the old name of Claire' (touching the larger baby) 'was Salome Potier: her mother was the washerwoman; and Nannonciade, I don't know what her name was, but her father worked for Maitre Brassier who made the kettles.'

Philip felt relieved to be free from all doubt about these very uninviting little ones, but Berenger, though sighing heavily, asked quickly, 'Permit me, Madame, a few questions.—Little maid, did you ever hear of Isaac Gardon?

'Maitre Isaac! Oh yes, sir. We used to hear him preach at the church, and sometimes he catechized us,' she said, and her lip quivered.

'He was a heretic, and I abjure him,' added the other girl, perking up her head.

'Was he in the town? What became of him?' exclaimed Berenger.

'He would not be in the town,' said the elder girl. 'My poor father had sent him word to go away.

'*Eh quoi?*

'Our father was Bailli la Grasse,' interposed the younger girl, consequentially. 'Our names were Marthe and Lucie la Grasse, but Agathe and Eulalie are much prettier.

'But Maitre Gardon?' still asked Berenger.

'He ought to be take and burnt,' said the new Eulalie; 'he brought it all on us.

'How was it? Was my wife with him—Madame de Ribaumont? Speak, my child.

'That was the name,' said one girl.

'But Maitre Gardon had no great lady with him,' said the other, 'only his son's widow and her baby, and they lodged with Noemi Laurent, who made the *patisserie*.

'Ah!' cried Berenger, lighting up with the new ray of hope. 'Tell me, my dear, that they fled with him, and where.

'I do not know of their going,' said Agathe, confused and overborne by his eagerness.

'Curb yourself, sir,' said the Prioress, 'they will recollect themselves and tell you what they can.

'It was the little cakes with lemoned sugar,' suggested the younger girl. 'Maitre Tressan always said there would be a judgment on us for our daintiness. Ah! he was very cross about them, and after all it was the Maitre of Lucon who ate fifteen of them all at once; but then he is not a heretic.

Happily for Berenger, Agathe unraveled this speech.

'Mademoiselle Gardon made the sugar-lemoned cakes, and the Mayor of Lucon, one day when he supped with us, was so delighted with them that he carried one away to show his wife, and afterwards he sent over to order some more. Then, after a time, he sent secretly to my father to ask him if Maitre Gardon was there; for there was a great outcry about the lemon cakes, and the Duke of Alencon's army were coming to demand his daughter-in-law; because it seems she was a great lady, and the only person who could make the cakes.

'Agathe!' exclaimed the Prioress.

'I understand,' said Berenger. 'The Cure of Nissard told me that she was traced through cakes, the secret of which was only known at Bellaise.

'That might be,' said Mere Monique. 'I remember there was something of pride in the cakes of Bellaise, though I always tried to know nothing of them.

'Well, little one, continue,' entreated Berenger. 'You are giving me life and hope.

'I heard my father and mother talk about it,' said Agathe, gaining courage. 'He said he knew nothing of great people, and would give nobody up to the Catholics, but as to Maitre Isaac, he should let him know that the Catholic army were coming, and that it would be the better for us if we had no pastor within our walls; and that there was a cry that his daughter's lemon cakes were made by the lady that was lost.

'And they escaped! Ah! would that I could thank the good man!

'Surely yes, sir, I never saw them again. Maitre Tressan the elder prayed with us. And when the cruel soldiers came and demanded the lady and Maitre Isaac, and all obstinate Calvinists, our mayor and my father and the rest made answer that they had no knowledge of the lady, and did not know where Maitre Gardon was; and as to Huguenots, we were all one as obstinate as the other, but that we would pay any fine within our means so they would spare our lives. Then the man in the fine coat said, it was the lady they wanted, not the fine; and a great deal he said besides, I know not what but my father said, 'It is our life's blood that they want,' and he put on his breastplate and kissed us all, and went away. Then came horrible noises and firing of cannon, and the neighbours ran in and said that the enemy were battering down the old crumbly bit of wall where the monastery was burnt; and just then our man Joseph ran back all pale, and staring, to tell us my father was lying badly hurt in the street. My mother hurried out, and locked the door to keep us from following.

The poor child broke down in tears, and her sister went on. 'Oh, we were so frightened—such frightful sounds came close, and people ran by all blood and shrieking—and there was a glare in the sky—and nobody came home—till at last it grew so dreadful that we hid in the cellar to hear and see nothing. Only it grew hotter and hotter, and the light through the little grating was red. And at last there was a noise louder than thunder, and, oh, such a shaking—for it was the house falling down. But we did not know that; we tried to open the door, and could not; then we cried and called for father and mother—and no one heard—and we sat still for fear, till we slept—and then it was all dark, and we were very hungry. I don't know how time went, but at last, when I was daylight again, there was a talking above, a little baby crying, and a kind voice too; and then we called out, 'Oh, take us out and give us bread.' Then a face looked down the grating. Oh, it was like the face of an angel to us, with all the white hair flying round. It was the holy priest of Nissard; and when one of the cruel men said we were only little heretics who ought to die like rats in a hole, he said we were but innocents who did not know the difference.

'Ah! we did,' said the elder girl. 'You are younger, sister, you forget more;' and then, holding out her hands to Berenger, she exclaimed, 'Ah! sir, take us away with you.

'My child!' exclaimed the Prioress, 'you told me you were happy to be in the good course.

'Oh yes!' cried the poor child; 'but I don't want to be happy! I am forgetting all my poor father and mother used to say. I can't help it, and they would be so grieved. Oh, take me away, sir!

'Take care, Agathe, you will be a relapsed heretic,' said her sister, solemnly. 'For me, I am a true Catholic. I love the beautiful images and the processions.

'Ah! but what would our mother have said!' cried poor Agathe, weeping more bitterly.

'Poor child, her old recollections have been renewed,' said the Prioress, with unchanged sweetness; 'but it will pass. My dear, the gentleman will tell you that it is as impossible for him to take you as it is for me to let you go.

'It is so, truly, little one,' said Berenger. 'The only little girl I cold have taken with me would have been my own;' and as her eyes looked at him wistfully, he added, 'No doubt, if your poor mother could, she would thank this good Mother-prioress for teaching you to serve God and be a good child.

'Monsieur speaks well and kindly,' said the Prioress; 'and now, Agathe, make your curtsey, and take away the little ones.

'Let me ask one question more, reverend Mother,' said Berenger. 'Ah! children, did you ever see her whom you call Isaac Gardon's daughter-in-law?

'No, sir,' said the children; 'but mother did, and she promised one day to take us to see the baby, for it was so pretty—so white, that she had never seen the like.

'So white!' repeated Berenger to himself; and the Prioress, struck, perhaps, by the almost flaxen locks that sparsely waved on his temples, and the hue of the ungloved hand that rested on the edge of the *grille*, said, smiling, 'You come of a fair family, Monsieur.

'The White Ribaumonts,' said Berenger, 'and, moreover, my mother was called the Swan of England; my little sisters have skins like snow. Ah! Madame, though I have failed, I go away far happier than if I had succeeded.

'And reveal the true faith,' began the nun; but Philip in the meantime was nudging his brother, and whispering in English, 'No Popish prayers, I say! Stay, give these poor little prisoners one feast of the sweetmeats we brought.

Of this last hint Berenger was glad, and the Prioress readily consented to a distribution of the dainties among the orphans. He wished to leave a more lasting token of his gratitude to the little maiden whose father had perhaps saved Eustacie's life, and recollecting that he had about him a great gold coin, bearing the heads of Philip and Mary, he begged leave to offer it to Agathe, and found that it was received by good Mere Monique almost in the light of a relic, as bearing the head of so pious a queen.

Then, to complete Philip's disgust he said, 'I took with me my aunt's blessing when I set out; let me take yours with me also, reverend Mother.

When they were in the street again, Philip railed at him as though he had subjected himself to a spell.

'She is almost a saint,' answered Berenger.

'And have we not saints enough of our own, without running after Popish ones behind grates? Brother, if ever the good old days come back of invading France, I'll march straight hither, and deliver the poor little wretches so scandalously mewed up here, and true Protestants all the time!

'Hush! People are noticing the sound of your English.

'Let them! I never thanked Heaven properly before that I have not a drop of French——' Here Berenger almost shook him by the shoulder, as men turned at his broad tones and foreign words, and he walked on in silence, while Berenger at his side felt as one treading on air, so infinite was the burden taken off his mind. Though for the present absolutely at sea as to where to seek Eustacie, the relief from acquiescence in the horrible fate that had seemed to be hers was such, that a flood of unspeakable happiness seemed to rush in on him, and bear him up with a new infusion of life, buoyancy, and thankfulness.

CHAPTER XXIX
IN THE KING'S NAME

'Under which king, Bezonian? speak or die.

'Under King Harry.

—KING HENRY IV.

'One bird in the hand is not always worth two in the bush, assuredly,' said Philip, when Berenger was calm enough to hold council on what he called this most blessed discovery; 'but where to seek them?'

'I have no fears now,' returned Berenger. 'We have not been bore through so much not to be brought together at last. Soon, soon shall we have her! A minister so distinguished as Isaac Gardon is sure to be heard of either at La Rochelle, Montauban, or Nimes, their great gathering places.'

'For Rochelle, then?' said Philip.

'Even so. We will be off early to-morrow, and from thence, if we do not find her there, as I expected, we shall be able to write the thrice happy news to those at home.

Accordingly, the little cavalcade started in good time, in the cool of the morning of the bright long day of early June, while apple petal floated down on them in the lanes like snow, and nightingales in every hedge seemed to give voice and tune to Berenger's eager, yearning hopes.

Suddenly there was a sound of horse's feet in the road before them, and as they drew aside to make way, a little troop of gendarmes filled the narrow lane. The officer, a rough, harsh-looking man, laid his hand on Berenger's bridle, with the words, 'In the name of the King!

Philip began to draw his sword with one hand, and with the other to urge his horse between the officer and his brother, but Berenger called out, 'Back! This gentleman mistakes my person. I am the Baron de Ribaumont, and have a safe-conduct from the King.

'What king?' demanded the officer.

'From King Charles.

'I arrest you,' said the officer, 'in the name of King Henry III, and of the Queen Regent Catherine.

'The King dead?' Exclaimed Berenger.

'On the 30th of May. Now, sir.

'Your warrant—your cause?' still demanded Berenger.

'There will be time enough for that when you are safely lodged, said the captain, roughly pulling at the rein, which he had held all the time.

'What, no warrant?' shouted Philip, 'he is a mere robber!' and with drawn sword he was precipitating himself on the captain, when another gendarme, who had been on the watch, grappled with him, and dragged him off his horse before he could strike a blow. The other two English, Humfrey Holt and John Smithers, strong full-grown men, rode in fiercely to the rescue, and Berenger himself struggled furiously to loose himself from the captain, and deliver his brother. Suddenly there was the report of a pistol: poor Smithers fell, there was a moment of standing aghast, and in that moment the one man and the two youths were each pounced on by three or four gendarmes, thrown down and pinioned.

'Is this usage for gentlemen?' exclaimed Berenger, as he was roughly raised to his feet.

'The King's power has been resisted,' was all the answer; and when he would have been to see how it was with poor Smithers, one of the men-at-arms kicked over the body with sickening brutality, saying, 'Dead enough, heretic and English carrion!

Philip uttered a cry of loathing horror, and turned white; Berenger, above all else, felt a sort of frenzied despair as he thought of the peril of the boy who had been trusted to him.

'Have you had enough, sir?' said the captain. 'Mount and come.

They could only let themselves be lifted to their horses, and their hands were then set free to use their bridles, each being guarded by a soldier on each side of him. Philip attempted but once to speak, and that in English: 'Next time I shall take my pistol.

He was rudely silenced, and rode on with wide-open stolid eyes and dogged face, steadfastly resolved that no Frenchman should see him flinch, and vexed that Berenger had his riding mask on so that his face could not be studied; while he, on his side, was revolving all causes possible for his arrest, and all means of enforcing he liberation, if not of himself at least of Philip and Humfrey. He looked round for Guibert, but could not see him.

They rode on through the intricate lanes till the sun was high and scorching, and Berenger felt how far he was from perfect recovery. At last, however, some little time past noon, the gendarmes halted at a stone fountain, outside a village, and disposing a sufficient guard around his captives, the officer permitted them to dismount and rest, while he, with the rest of the troop and the horses, went to the village CABARET. Philip would have asked his brother what it meant, and what was to be done, but Berenger shook his head, and intimated that silence was safest as present, since they might be listened to; and Philip, who so much imagined treachery and iniquity to be the order of the day in France that he was scarcely surprised at the present disaster, resigned himself to the same sullen endurance. Provisions and liquor were presently sent up from the inn, but Berenger could taste nothing but the cold water of the fountain, which trickled out cool and fresh beneath an arch surmounted by a figure of Our Lady. He bathed his face and head in the refreshing spring, and lay down on a cloak in the shade, Philip keeping a constant change of drenched kerchiefs on his brow, and hoping that he slept, till at the end to two or three hours the captain returned, gave the word to horse, and the party rode on through intricate lanes, blossoming with hawthorn, and ringing with songs of birds that spoke a very different language now to Berenger's heart from what they had said in the hopeful morning.

A convent bell was ringing to evensong, when passing its gateway; the escort turned up a low hill, on the summit of which stood a chateau, covering a considerable extent of ground, with a circuit of wall, whitewashed so as perfectly to glare in the evening sun; at every angle a round, slim turret, crowned by a brilliant red-tiled extinguisher-like cap; and the whole surmounted by a tall old keep in the centre. There was a square projection containing an arched gateway, with heavy doorways, which were thrown open as the party approached. Philip looked up as he rode in, and over the doorway beheld the familiar fretted shield, with the leopard in the corner, and '*A moi Ribaumont*" round it. Could it then be Berenger's own castle, and was it thus that he was approaching it? He himself had not looked up; he was utterly spent with fatigue, dejection, and the severe headache brought on by the heat of the sun, and was only intent on rallying his powers for the crisis of fate that was probably approaching; and thus scarcely took note of the court into which he rode, lying between the gateway and the *corps de logis*, a building erected when comfort demanded more space than was afforded by the old keep, against which one end leant; but still, though inclosed in a court, the lower windows were small and iron-barred, and all air of luxury was reserved for the mullioned casements of the upper storey. The court was flagged, but grass shot up between the stones, and the trim air of ease and inhabited comfort to which the brothers were used at home was utterly wanting. Berenger was hustled off his horse, and roughly pushed through a deep porch, where the first thing he heard was the Chevalier de Ribaumont's voice in displeasure.

'How now, sir; hands off! Is this the way you conduct my nephew?

'He resisted, sir.

'Sir,' said Berenger, advancing into the hall, 'I know not the meaning of this. I am peacefully traveling with a passport from the King, when I am set upon, no warrant shown me, my faithful servant slain, myself and my brother, an English subject, shamefully handled.

'The violence shall be visited on whatever rascal durst insult a gentleman and my nephew,' said the Chevalier. 'For release, it shall be looked to; but unfortunately it is too true that there are orders from the Queen in Council for your apprehension, and it was only on my special entreaty for the honour of the family, and the affection I bear you, that I was allowed to receive you here instead of your being sent to an ordinary prison.

'On what pretext?' demanded Berenger.

'It is known that you have letters in your possession from escaped traitors now in England, to La Noue, Duplessis Mornay, and other heretics.

'That is easily explained,' said Berenger. 'You know well, sir, that they were to facilitate my search at La Sablerie. You shall see them yourself, sir.

'That I must assuredly do,' replied the Chevalier, 'for it is the order of her Majesty, I regret to say, that your person and baggage be searched;' then, as indignant colour rushed into Berenger's face, and an angry exclamation was beginning, he added, 'Nay, I understand, my dear cousin, it is very painful, but we would spare you as much as possible. It will be quite enough if the search is made by myself in the presence of this gentleman, who will only stand by for form's sake. I have no doubt it will enable us quickly to clear up matters, and set you free again. Do me the honour to follow me to the chamber destined for you.

'Let me see the order for my arrest,' said Berenger, holding his head high.

'The English scruple must be gratified,' said the Chevalier. And accordingly the gendarme captain unfolded before him a paper, which was evidently a distinct order to arrest and examine the person of Henri Beranger Eustache, Baron de Ribaumont and Sieur de Leurre, suspected of treasonable practices—and it bore the signature of Catherine.

'There is nothing here said of my step-father's son, Philip Thistlewood, nor of my servant, Humfrey Holt,' said Berenger, gathering the sense with his dizzy eyes as best he could. 'They cannot be detained, being born subjects of the Queen of England.

'They intercepted the justice of the King,' said the captain, laying his hand on Philip's shoulder. 'I shall have them off with me to the garrison of Lugon, and deal with them there.

'Wait!' said the Chevalier, interposing before Berenger's fierce, horror-struck expostulation could break forth; 'this is an honourable young gentleman, son of a chevalier of good reputation in England, and he need not be so harshly dealt with. You will not separate either him or the poor groom from my nephew, so the Queen's authority be now rightly acknowledged.

The captain shrugged his shoulders, as if displeased; and the Chevalier, turning to Berenger, said, 'You understand, nephew, the lot of you all depends on your not giving umbrage to these officers of her Majesty. I will do my poor best for you; but submission is first needed.

Berenger knew enough of his native country to be aware that *la justice du Roi* was a terrible thing, and that Philip's resistance had really put him in so much danger that it was needful to be most careful not further to offend the functionary of Government; and abhorrent as the proposed search was to him, he made no further objection, but taking Philip's arm, lest they should be separated, he prepared to follow wherever he was to be conducted. The Chevalier led the way along a narrow stone passage, with loophole-windows here and there; and Philip, for all his proud, indifferent bearing, felt his flesh creep as he looked for a stair descending into the bowels of the earth. A stair there was, but it went up instead of down, and after mounting this, and going through a sort of ante-room, a door was opened into a tolerably spacious apartment, evidently in the old keep; for the two windows on opposite sides were in an immensely massive wall, and the floor above and vaulting below were of stone; but otherwise there was nothing repulsive in the appearance of the room. There was a wood fire on the hearth; the sun, setting far to the north, peeped in aslant at one window; a mat was on the floor, tapestry on the lower part of the walls; a table and chairs, and a walnut chest, with a chess-board and a few books on it, were as much furniture as was to be seen in almost any living-room of the day. Humfrey and Guibert, too, were already there, with the small riding valises they and poor Smithers had had in charge. These were at one opened, but contained merely clothes and linen, nothing else that was noticed, except three books, at which the captain looked with a stupid air; and the Chevalier did not seem capable of discovering more than that all three were Latin—one, he believed, the Bible.

'Yes, sir, the Vulgate—a copy older than the Reformation, so not liable to be called an heretical version,' said Berenger, to whom a copy had been given by Lady Walwyn, as more likely to be saved if his baggage were searched. 'The other is the Office and Psalter after our English rite; and this last is not mine, but Mr. Sidney's—a copy of Virgilius Maro, which he had left behind at Paris.

The Chevalier, not willing to confess that he had taken the English Prayer-book for Latin, hastily said, 'Nothing wrong there—no, no, nothing that will hurt the State; may it only be so with what you carry on your person, fair cousin. Stand back, gentleman, this is gear for myself alone. Now, fair nephew,' he added, 'not a hand shall be laid on you, if you will give me your honourable word, as a nobleman, that you are laying before me all that you carry about you.

An instant's thought convinced Berenger that resistance would save nothing, and merely lead to indignity to himself and danger to Philip; and therefore he gave the promise to show everything about him, without compulsion. Accordingly, he produced his purse for current expenses, poor King Charles's safe-conduct, and other articles of no consequence, from his pockets; then reluctantly opened his doublet, and took off the belt containing his store of gold, which had been replenished at Walsingham's. This was greedily eyed by the captain, but the Chevalier at once made it over to Philip's keeping, graciously saying, 'We do no more than duty requires;' but at the same time he made a gesture towards another small purse that hung round Berenger's neck by a black ribbon.

'On my sacred word and honour,' said Berenger, 'it contains nothing important to any save myself.

'Alas! my bounden duty,' urged the Chevalier.

An angry reply died on Berenger's lip. At the thought of Philip, he opened the purse, and held out the contents on his palm: a tiny gold ring, a tress of black hair, a fragment of carnation-ribbon pricked with pin-holes, a string of small worthless yellow shells, and, threaded with them, a large pear-shaped pearl of countless price. Even the Chevalier was touched at the sight of this treasury, resting on the blanched palm of the thin, trembling hand, and jealously watched by eyes glistening with sudden moisture, though the lips were firm set. 'Alas! my poor young cousin,' he said, 'you loved her well.

'Not loved, but love,' muttered Berenger to himself, as if having recourse to the only cordial that could support him through the present suffering; and he was closing his fingers again over his precious hoard, when the Chevalier added, 'Stay! Nephew—that pearl?

'Is one of the chaplet; the token she sent to England,' he answered.

'*Pauvre petite!* Then, at least a fragment remains of the reward of our ancestor's courage,' said the Chevalier.

And Berenger did not feel it needful to yield up that still better possession, stored within his heart, that *la petite* and her pearls were safe together. It was less unendurable to produce the leather case from a secret pocket within his doublet, since, unwilling as he was that any eye should scan the letters it contained, there was nothing in them that could give any clue towards tracing her. Nothing had been written or received since his interview with the children at Lucon. There was, indeed, Eustacie's letter to his mother, a few received at Paris from Lord Walwyn, reluctantly consenting to his journey in quest of his child, his English passport, the unfortunate letters to La Noue; and what evidently startled the Chevalier more than all the rest, the copy of the certificate of the ratification of the marriage; but his consternation was so arranged as to appear to be all on behalf of his young kinsman. 'This is serious!' he said, striking his forehead; 'you will be accused of forging the late King's name.

'This is but a copy,' said Berenger, pointing to the heading; 'the original has been sent with our Ambassador's dispatches to England.

'It is a pity,' said the Chevalier, looking thoroughly vexed, 'that you should have brought fresh difficulties on yourself for a mere piece of waste paper to be affected by the validity of your marriage. Dear cousin,'—he glanced at the officer and lowered his voice,—'let me tear this paper; it would only do you harm, and the Papal decree annuls it.

'I have given my word,' said Berenger, 'that all that could do me harm should be delivered up! Besides,' he added, 'even had I the feeling for my own honour and that of my wife and child, living or dead, the harm, it seems to me, would be to those who withhold her lands from me.

'Ah, fair nephew! you have fallen among designing persons who have filled your head with absurd claims; but I will not argue the point now, since it becomes a family, not a State matter. These papers'—and he took them into his hand—'must be examined, and to-morrow Captain Delarue will take them to Paris, with any explanation you may desire to offer. Meantime you and your companions remain my guest, at full liberty, provided you will give me your parole to attempt no escape.

'No, sir,' said Berenger, hotly, 'we will not become our own jailers, nor acquiesce in this unjust detention. I warn you that I am a naturalized Englishman, acknowledged by the Queen as my grandfather's heir, and the English Ambassador will inform the court what Queen Elizabeth thinks of such dealings with her subjects.

'Well said,' exclaimed Philip, and drawing himself up, he added, 'I refuse my parole, and warn you that it is at your peril that you imprison an Englishman.

'Very well, gentlemen,' said the Chevalier; 'the difference will be that I shall unwillingly be forced to let Captain Delarue post guards at the outlets of this tower. A room beneath is prepared for your grooms, and the court is likewise free to you. I will endeavour to make your detention as little irksome as you will permit, and meantime allow me to show you your sleeping chamber. He then politely, as if he had been ushering a prince to his apartment, led the way, pointing to the door through which they had entered the keep, and saying, 'This is the only present communication with the dwelling-house. Two gendarmes will always be on the outside.' He conducted the young men up a stone spiral stair to another room, over that which they had already seen, and furnished as fairly as ordinary sleeping chambers were wont to be.

Here, said their compulsory host, he would leave them to prepare for supper, when they would do him the honour to join him in the eating-hall on their summons by the steward.

His departing bow was duly returned by Berenger, but no sooner did his steps die away on the stairs than the young man threw himself down on his bed, in a paroxysm of suffering both mental and bodily.

'Berry, Berry, what is this? Speak to me. What does it all mean? cried Philip.

'How can I tell?' said Berenger, showing his face for a moment, covered with tears; 'only that my only friend is dead, and some villainous trick has seized me, just—just as I might have found her. And I've been the death of my poor groom, and got you into the power of these vile dastards! Oh, would that I had come alone! Would that they had had the sense to aim direct!

'Brother, brother, anything but this!' cried Philip. 'The rogues are not worth it. Sir Francis will have us out in no time, or know the reason why. I'd scorn to let them wring a tear from me.

'I hope they never may, dear Phil, nor anything worse.

'Now,' continued Philip, 'the way will be to go down to supper, since they will have it so, and sit and eat at one's ease as if one cared for them no more than cat and dog. Hark! there's the steward speaking to Guibert. Come, Berry, wash your face and come.

'I—my head aches far too much, were there nothing else.

'What! it is nothing but the sun,' said Philip. 'Put a bold face on it, man, and show them how little you heed.

'How LITTLE I heed!' bitterly repeated Berenger, turning his face away, utterly unnerved between disappointment, fatigue, and pain; and Philip at that moment had little mercy. Dismayed and vaguely terrified, yet too resolute in national pride to betray his own feelings, he gave vent to his vexation by impatience with a temperament more visibly sensitive than his own: 'I never thought you so mere a Frenchman,' he said contemptuously. 'If you weep and wail so like a sick wench, they will soon have their will of you! I'd have let them kill me before they searched me.

''Tis bad enough without this from you, Phil,' said Berenger, faintly, for he was far too much spent for resentment or self-defence, and had only kept up before the Chevalier by dint of strong effort. Philip was somewhat aghast, both at the involuntary gesture of pain, and at finding there was not even spirit to be angry with him: but his very dismay served at the moment only to feed his displeasure; and he tramped off in his heavy boots, which he chose to wear as a proof of disdain for his companions. He explained that M. de Ribaumont was too much fatigued to come to supper, and he was accordingly marched along the corridor, with the steward before him bearing a lighted torch, and two gendarmes with halberds behind him. And in his walk he had ample time for, first, the resolution that illness, and not dejection, should have all the credit of Berenger's absence; then for recollecting of how short standing had been his brother's convalescence; and lastly, for a fury of self-execration for his own unkindness, rude taunts, and neglect of the recurring illness. He would have turned about and gone back at once, but the two gendarmes were close behind, and he knew Humfrey would attend to his brother; so he walked on to the hall—a handsome chamber, hung with armour and spoils of hunting, with a few pictures on the panels, and a great carved music-gallery at one end. The table was laid out somewhat luxuriously for four, according to the innovation which was beginning to separate the meals of the grandees from those of their household.

Great concern was expressed by the Chevalier, as Philip, in French, much improved since the time of his conversation with Madame de Selinville, spoke of his brother's indisposition, saying with emphasis, as he glared at Captain Delarue, that Maitre Pare had forbidden all exposure to mid-day heat, and that all their journeys had been made in morning or evening coolness. 'My young friend,' as his host called him, 'should, he was assured, have mentioned this, since Captain Delarue had no desire but to make his situation as little painful as possible.' And the Chevalier sent his steward at once to offer everything the house contained that his prisoner could relish for supper; and then anxiously questioned Philip on his health and diet, obtaining very short and glum answers. The Chevalier and the captain glanced at each other with little shrugs; and Philip, becoming conscious of his shock hair, splashed doublet, and dirty boots, had vague doubts whether his English dignity were not being regarded as English lubberliness; but, of course, he hated the two Frenchmen all the more, and received their civility with greater gruffness. They asked him the present object of his journey—though, probably, the Chevalier knew it before, and he told of the hope that they had of finding the child at Lucon.

'Vain, of course?' said the Chevalier. 'Poor infant! It is well for itself, as for the rest of us, that its troubles were ended long ago.'

Philip started indignantly.

'Does your brother still nurture any vain hope?' said the Chevalier.

'Not vain, I trust,' said Philip.

'Indeed! Who can foolishly have so inspired him with a hope that merely wears out his youth, and leads him into danger?'

Philip held his tongue, resolved to be impenetrable; and he was so far successful, that the Chevalier merely became convinced that the brothers were not simply riding to La Rochelle to embark for England, but had some hope and purpose in view; though as to what that might be, Philip's bluff replies and stubborn silence were baffling.

After the meal, the Chevalier insisted on coming to see how his guest fared; and Philip could not prevent him. They found Berenger sitting on the side of his bed, having evidently just started up on hearing their approach. Otherwise he did not seem to have moved since Philip left him; he had not attempted to undress; and Humfrey told Philip that not a word had been extracted from him, but commands to let him alone.

However, he had rallied his forces to meet the Chevalier, and answered manfully to his excuses for the broiling ride to which he had been exposed, that it mattered not, the effect would pass, it was a mere chance; and refused all offers of medicaments, potions, and TISANES, till his host at length left the room with a most correct exchange of good nights.

'Berry, Berry, what a brute I have been!' cried Philip.

'Foolish lad!' and Berenger half smiled. 'Now help me to bed, for the room turns round!'

CHAPTER XXX
CAGED IN THE BLACKBIRD'S NEST

Let him shun castles;

Safer shall he be on the sandy plain Than where castles mounted

stand.—KING HENRY VI.

While Berenger slept a heavy morning's sleep after a resless night, Philip explored the narrow domain above and below. The keep and its little court had evidently been the original castle, built when the oddly-nicknamed Fulkes and Geoffreys of Anjou had been at daggers drawn with the Dukes of Normandy and Brittany, but it had since, like most other such ancient feudal fortresses, become the nucleus of walls and buildings for use, defence, or ornament, that lay beneath him like a spider's web, when he had gained the roof of the keep, garnished with pepper-box turrets at each of the four angles. Beyond lay the green copses and orchards of the Bocage, for it was true, as he had at first suspected, that this was the chateau de Nid de Merle, and that Berenger was a captive in his wife's own castle.

Chances of escape were the lad's chief thought, but the building on which he stood went sheer down for a considerable way. Then on the north side there came out the sharp, high-pitched, tiled roof of the *corps du logis*; on the south, another roof, surmounted by a cross at the gable, and evidently belonging to the chapel; on the other two sides lay courts—that to the east, a stable-yard; that to the west, a small narrow, chilly-looking, paved inclosure, with enormously-massive walls, the doorway walled up, and looking like a true prison-yard. Beyond this wall—indeed, on every side—extended offices, servants' houses, stables, untidy desolate-looking gardens, and the whole was inclosed by the white wall with flanking red-tiled turrets, whose gaudy appearance had last night made Philip regard the whole as a flimsy, Frenchchified erection, but he now saw it to be of extremely solid stone and lime, and with no entrance but the great barbican gateway they had entered by; moreover, with a yawning dry moat all round. Wherever he looked he saw these tall, pointed red caps, resembling, he thought, those worn by the victims of an *auto-de-fe*, as one of Walsingham's secretaries had described them to him; and he ground his teeth at them, as thought they grinned at him like emissaries of the Inquisition.

Descending, he found Berenger dressing in haste to avoid receiving an invalid visit from the Chevalier, looking indeed greatly shaken, but hardly so as would have been detected by eyes that had not seen him during his weeks of hope and recovery. He was as resolved as Philip could wish against any sign of weakness before his enemy, and altogether disclaimed illness, refusing the stock of cooling drinks, cordials, and febrifuges, which the Chevalier said had been sent by his sister the Abbess of Bellaise. He put the subject of his health aside, only asking if this were the day that the gendarme-captain would return to Paris, and then begging to see that officer, so as to have a distinct understanding of the grounds of his imprisonment. The captain had, however, been a mere instrument; and when Philip clamoured to be taken before the next justice of the peace, even Berenger smiled at him for thinking that such a being existed in France. The only cause alleged was the vague but dangerous suspicion of conveying correspondence between England and the heretics, and this might become extremely perilous to one undeniably half English, regarded as whole Huguenot, caught on the way to La Rochelle with a letter to La Noue in his pocket; and, moreover, to one who had had a personal affray with a king famous for storing up petty offences, whom the last poor king had favoured, and who, in fine, had claims to estates that could not spared to the Huguenot interest.

He was really not sure that there was not some truth in the professions of the Chevalier being anxious to protect him from the Queen-mother and the Guises; he had never been able to divest himself of a certain trust in his old kinsman's friendliness, and he was obliged to be beholden to him for the forms in which to couch his defence. At the same time he wrote to Sir Francis Walsingham, and to his grandfather, but with great caution, lest his letters should be inspected by his enemies, and with the less hope of their availing him because it was probable that the Ambassador would return home on the king's death. No answer could be expected for at least a fortnight, and even then it was possible that the Queen-mother might choose to refer the cause to King Henry, who was then in Poland.

Berenger wrote these letters with much thought and care, but when they were once sealed, he collapsed again into despair and impatience, and frantically paced the little court as if he would dash himself against the walls that detained him from Eustacie; then threw himself moodily into a chair, hid his face in his crossed arms, and fell a prey to all the wretched visions called up by an excited brain.

However, he was equally alive with Philip to the high-spirited resolution that his enemies should not perceive or triumph in his dejection. He showed himself at the noon-day dinner, before Captain Delarue departed, grave and silent, but betraying no agitation; and he roused himself from his sad musings at the supper-hour, to arrange his hair, and assume the ordinary dress of gentlemen in the evening; though Philip laughed at the roses adorning his shoes, and his fresh ruff, as needless attentions to an old ruffian like the Chevalier. However, Philip started when he entered the hall, and beheld, not the Chevalier alone, but with him the beautiful lady of the velvet coach, and another stately, extremely handsome dame, no longer in her first youth, and in costly black and white garments. When the Chevalier called her his sister, Madame de Bellaise, Philip had no notion that she was anything but a widow, living a secular life; and though a couple of nuns attended her, their dress was so much less conventual than Cecily's that he did not at first find them out. It was explained that Madame de Selinville was residing with her aunt, and that, having come to visit her father, he had detained the ladies to supper, hoping to enliven the sojourn of his *beaux cousins*.

Madame de Selinville, looking anxiously at Berenger, hoped she saw him in better health. He replied, stiffly, that he was perfectly well; and then, by way of safety, repaired to the society of the Abbess, who immediately began plying him with questions about England, its court, and especially the secret marriage of Queen Elisabeth and '*ce* Comte de Dudley,' on which she was so minutely informed as to put him to the blush. Then she was very curious about the dispersed convents, and how many of the nuns had married; and she seemed altogether delighted to have secured the attention of a youth from the outer world. His soul at first recoiled from her as one of Eustacie's oppressors, and from her unconvent-like talk; and yet he could not but think her a good-natured person, and wonder if she could really have been hard upon his poor little wife. And she, who had told Eustacie she would strangle with her own hands the scion of the rival house!—she, like most women, was much more bitter against an unseen being out of reach, than towards a courteously-mannered, pale, suffering-looking youth close beside her. She had enough affection for Eustacie to have grieved much at her wanderings and at her fate; and now the sorrow-stricken look that by no effort could be concealed really moved her towards the youth bereaved husband. Besides, were not all feuds on the point of being made up by the excellent device concocted between her brother and her niece?

Meantime, Philip was in raptures with the kindness of the beautiful Madame de Selinville. He, whom the Mistresses Walsingham treated as a mere clumsy boy, was promoted by her manner to be a man and a cavalier. He blushed up to the roots of his hair and looked sheepish whenever one of her entrancing smiles lit upon him; but then she inquired after his brother so cordially, she told him so openly how brilliant had been Berenger's career at the court, she regretted so heartily their present danger and detention, and promised so warmly to use her interest with Queen Catherine, that in the delight of being so talked to, he forgot his awkwardness and spoke freely and confidentially, maybe too confidentially, for he caught Berenger frowning at him, and made a sudden halt in his narrative, disconcerted but very angry with his brother for his distrust.

When the ladies had ridden away to the convent in the summer evening, and the two brothers had returned to their prison, Philip would have begun to rave about Madame de Selinville, but his mouth was stopped at once with 'Don't be such a fool, Phil!' and when Perrine shut his eyes, leant back, and folded his arms together, there was no more use in talking to him.

This exceeding defection continued for a day or two, while Berenger's whole spirit chafed in agony at his helplessness, and like demons there ever haunted him the thoughts of what might betide Eustacie, young, fair, forsaken, and believing herself a widow. Proudly defiant as he showed himself to all eyes beyond his tower, he seemed to be fast gnawing and pining himself away in the anguish he suffered through these long days of captivity.

Perhaps it was Philip's excitement about any chance of meeting Madame de Selinville that first roused him from the contemplation of his own misery. It struck him that if he did not rouse himself to exert his influence, the boy, left to no companionship save what he could make for himself, might be led away by intercourse with the gendarmes, or by the blandishments of Diane, whatever might be her game. He must be watched over, and returned to Sir Marmaduke the same true-hearted honest lad who had left home. Nor had Berenger lain so long under Cecily St. John's tender watching without bearing away some notes of patience, trust, and dutifulness that returned upon him as his mind recovered tone after the first shock. The whispers that had bidden him tarry the Lord's leisure, be strong, and commit his way to Him who could bring it to pass, and could save Eustacie as she had already been saved, returned to him once more: he chid himself for his faintness of heart, rallied his powers, and determined that cheerfulness, dutifulness, and care for Philip should no longer fail.

So he reviewed his resources, and in the first place arranged for a brief daily worship with his two English fellow-prisoners, corresponding to the home hours of chapel service. Then he proposed to Philip to spend an hour every day over the study of the Latin Bible; and when Philip showed himself reluctant to give up his habit of staring over the battlements, he represented that an attack on their faith was not so improbable but that they ought to be prepared for it.

'I'm quite prepared,' quoth Philip; 'I shall not listen to a word they say.'

However, he submitted to this, but was more contumacious as to Berenger's other proposal of profiting by Sidney's copy of Virgil. Here at least he was away from Mr. Adderley and study, and it passed endurance to have Latin and captivity both at once. He was more obliged for Berenger's offer to impart to him the instruction in fencing he had received during his first visit to Paris; the Chevalier made no difficulty about lending them foils, and their little court became the scene of numerous encounters, as well as of other games and exercises. More sedentary sports were at their service, chess, tables, dice, or cards, but Philip detested these, and they were only played in the evening, or on a rainy afternoon, by Berenger and the Chevalier.

It was clearly no part of the old gentleman's plan to break their health or spirits. He insisted on taking them out riding frequently, though always with four gendarmes with loaded arquebuses, so as to preclude all attempt at escape, or conversation with the peasants. The rides were hateful to both youths, but Berenger knew that so many hours of tedium were thus disposed of, and hoped also to acquire some knowledge of the country; indeed, he looked at every cottage and every peasant with affectionate eyes, as probably having sheltered Eustacie; and Philip, after one visit paid to the convent at Bellaise, was always in hopes of making such another. His boyish admiration of Madame de Selinville was his chief distraction, coming on in accesses whenever there was a hope of seeing her, and often diverting Berenger by its absurdities, even though at other times he feared that the lad might be led away by it, or dissension sown between them. Meetings were rare—now and then Madame de Selinville would appear at dinner or at supper as her father's guest; and more rarely, the Chevalier would turn his horse's head in the direction of Bellaise, and the three gentlemen would be received in the unpartitioned parlour, and there treated to such lemon cakes as had been the ruin of La Sablerie; but in general the castle and the convent had little intercourse, or only just enough to whet the appetite of the prisoners for what constituted their only variety.

Six weeks had lagged by before any answer from Paris was received, and then there was no reply from Walsingham, who had, it appeared, returned home immediately after King Charles's funeral. The letter from the Council bore that the Queen-mother was ready to accept the Baron de Ribaumont's excuses in good part, and to consider his youth; and she had no doubt of his being treated with the like indulgence by the King, provided he would prove himself a loyal subject, by embracing the Catholic faith, renouncing all his illegitimate claims to the estates of Nid de Merle, and, in pledge of his sincerity, wedding his cousin, the Countess de Selinville, so soon as a dispensation should have been procured. On no other consideration could he be pardoned or set at liberty.

'Then,' said Berenger, slowly, 'a prisoner I must remain until it be the will of Heaven to open the doors.'

'Fair nephew!' exclaimed the Chevalier, 'make no rash replies. Bethink you to what you expose yourself by obstinacy; I may no longer be able to protect you when the King returns. And he further went on to represent that, by renouncing voluntarily all possible claims on the Nid de Merle estates, the Baron would save the honour of poor Eustacie (which indeed equally concerned the rest of the family), since they then would gladly drop all dispute of the validity of the marriage; and the lands of Selinville would be an ample equivalent for these, as well as for all expectations in England.

'Sir, it is impossible!' said Berenger. 'My wife lives.'

'Comment! when you wear mourning for her.'

'I wear black because I have been able to procure nothing else since I have been convinced that she did not perish at La Sablerie. I was on my way to seek her when I was seized and detained here.'

'Where would you have sought her, my poor cousin?' compassionately asked the Chevalier.

'That I know not. She may be in England by this time; but that she escaped from La Sablerie, I am well assured.'

'Alas! my poor friend, you feed on delusion. I have surer evidence—you shall see the man yourself—one of my son's people, who was actually at the assault, and had strict orders to seek and save her. Would that I could feel the least hope left!'

'Is the man here? Let me see him,' said Berenger, hastily.

He was at once sent for, and proved to be one of the stable servants, a rough, soldierly-looking man, who made no difficulty in telling that M. de Nid de Merle had bidden his own troop to use every effort to reach the Widow Laurent's house, and secure the lady. They had made for it, but missed the way, and met with various obstacles; and when they reached it, it was already in flames, and he had seen for a moment Mademoiselle de Nid de Merle, whom he well knew by sight, with an infant in her arms at an upper window. He had called to her by name, and was about to send for a ladder, when recognizing the Ribaumont colours, she had turned back, and thrown herself and her child into the flames. M. de Nid de Merle was frantic when he heard of it, and they had searched for the remains among the ruins; but, bah! it was like a lime-kiln, nothing was to be found—all was calcined.

'No fragment left?' said Berenger; 'not a corner of tile or beam?'

'Not so much wood as you could boil an egg with; I will swear it on the Mass.'

- 269 -

'That is needless,' said Berenger. 'I have seen the spot myself. That is all I desired to ask.'

The Chevalier would have taken his hand and condoled with him over the horrible story; but he drew back, repeating that he had seen Widow Laurent's house, and that he saw that some parts of the man's story were so much falsified that he could not believe the rest. Moreover, he knew that Eustacie had not been in the town at the time of the siege.

Now the Chevalier *bona fide* believed the man's story, so far as that he never doubted that Eustacie had perished, and he looked on Berenger's refusal to accept the tale as the mournful last clinging to a vain hope. In his eyes, the actual sight of Eustacie, and the total destruction of the house, were mere matters of embellishment, possibly untrue, but not invalidating the main fact. He only said, 'Well, my friend, I will not press you while the pain of this narration is still fresh.'

'Thank you, sir; but this is not pain, for I believe not a word of it; therefore it is impossible for me to entertain the proposal, even if I could forsake my faith or my English kindred. You remember, sir, that I returned this same answer at Paris, when I had no hope that my wife survived.'

'True, my fair cousin, but I fear time will convince you that this constancy is unhappily misplaced. You shall have time to consider; and when it is proved to you that my poor niece is out of the reach of your fidelity, and when you have become better acquainted with the claims of the Church to your allegiance, then may it only prove that your conversion does not come too late. I have the honour to take my leave.'

'One moment more, sir. Is there no answer as to my brother?'

'None, cousin. As I told you, your country has at present no Ambassador; but, of course, on your fulfillment of the conditions, he would be released with you.'

'So,' said Philip, when the old knight had quitted the room, 'of course you cannot marry while Eustacie lives; but if——'

'Not another word, profane boy!' angrily cried Berenger.

'I was only going to say, it is a pity of one so goodly not to bring her over to the true faith, and take her to England.'

'Much would she be beholden to you!' said Berenger. 'So!' he added, sighing, 'I had little hope but that it would be thus. I believe it is all a web of this old plotter's weaving, and that the Queen-mother acts in it at his request. He wants only to buy me off with his daughter's estates from asserting my claim to this castle and lands; and I trow he will never rise up here till—till——'

'Till when, Berry?'

'Till mayhap my grandfather can move the Queen to do something for us; or till Madame de Selinville sees a face she likes better than her brother's carving; or, what can I tell? till malice is tired out, and Heaven's will sets us free. May Eustacie only have reached home! But I'm sorry for you, my poor Phil.'

'Never heed, brother,' said Philip; 'what is prison to me, so that I can now and then see those lovely eyes?'

And the languishing air of the clumsy lad was so comical as to beguile Berenger into a laugh. Yet Berenger's own feeling would go back to his first meeting with Diane; and as he thought of the eyes then fixed on him, he felt that he was under a trial that might become more severe.

CHAPTER XXXI
THE DARK POOL OF THE FUTURE

Triumph, triumph, only she

That knit his bonds can set him free.

—SOUTHEY

No change was made in the life of the captives of Nid de Merle after the answer from Paris, except that Pere Bonami, who had already once or twice dined at the Chevalier's table, was requested to make formal exposition of the errors of the Reformers and of the tenets of his own Church to the Baron de Ribaumont.

Philip took such good care not to be deluded that, though he sat by to see fair play, yet it was always with his elbows on the table and his fingers in his ears, regardless of appearing to the priest in the character of the deaf adder. After all, he was not the object, and good Pere Bonami at first thought the day his own, when he found that almost all his arguments against Calvinism were equally impressed upon Berenger's mind, but the differences soon revealed themselves; and the priest, though a good man, was not a very happily-chosen champion, for he was one of the old-fashioned, scantily-instructed country priests, who were more numerous before the Jesuit revival of learning, and knew nothing of controversy save that adapted to the doctrines of Calvin; so that in dealing with an Anglican of the school of Ridley and Hooker, it was like bow ad arrow against sword. And tin those days of change, controversial reading was one of the primary studies even of young laymen, and Lord Walwyn, with a view to his grandson's peculiar position, had taken care that he should be well instructed, so that he was not at all unequal to the contest. Moreover, apart from argument, he clung as a point of honour to the Church as to the wife that he had accepted in his childhood; and often tried to recall the sketch that Philip Sidney had once given him of a tale that a friend of his designed to turn into a poem, like Ariosto's, in *terza rima*, of a Red Cross knight separated from his Una as the true faith, and tempted by a treacherous Duessa, who impersonated at once Falsehood and Rome. And he knew so well that the last relaxation of his almost terrified resistance would make him so entirely succumb to Diane's beauty and brilliancy, that he kept himself stiffly frigid and reserved.

Diane never openly alluded to the terms on which he stood, but he often found gifts from unknown hands placed in his room. The books which he had found there were changed when he had had time to study them; and marks were placed in some of the most striking passages. They were of the class that turned the brain of the Knight of La Mancha, but with a predominance of the pastoral, such as Diane of George of Montemayor and his numerous imitators—which Philip thought horrible stuff—enduring nothing but a few of the combats of Amadis de Gaul or Palmerin of England, until he found that Madame de Selinville prodigiously admired the 'silly swains more silly than their sheep,' and was very anxious that M. le Baron should be touched by their beauties; whereupon honest Philip made desperate efforts to swallow them in his brother's stead, but was always found fast asleep in the very middle of arguments between Damon and Thyrsis upon the *devoirs* of love, or the mournings of some disconsolate nymph over her jealousies of a favoured rival.

One day, a beautiful ivory box, exhaling sweet perfume, appeared in the prison chamber, and therewith a sealed letter in verse, containing an affecting description of how Corydon had been cruelly torn by the lions in endeavouring to bear away Sylvie from her cavern, how Sylvie had been rent from him and lost, and how vainly he continued to bewail her, and disregard the loving lament of Daphne, who had ever mourned and pined for him as she kept her flock, made the rivulets, the brooks, the mountains re-echo with her sighs and plaints, and had wandered through the hills and valleys, gathering simples wherewith she had compounded a balsam that might do away with the scars that the claws of the lions had left, so that he might again appear with the glowing cheeks and radiant locks that had excited the envy of the god of day.

Berenger burst out laughing over the practical part of this poetical performance, and laughed the more at Philip's hurt, injured air at his mirth. Philip, who would have been the first to see the absurdity in any other Daphne, thought this a passing pleasant device, and considered it very unkind in his brother not even to make experiment of the balsam of simples, but to declare that he had much rather keep his scars for Eustacie's sake than wear a smooth face to please Diane.

Still Berenger's natural courtesy stood in his way. He could not help being respectful and attentive to the old Chevalier, when their terms were, apparently at least, those of host and guest; and to a lady he COULD not be rude and repellant, though he could be reserved. So, when the kinsfolk met, no stranger would have discovered that one was a prisoner and the others his captors.

One August day, when Madame de Selinville and her lady attendants were supping at the castle at the early hour of six, a servant brought in word that an Italian pedlar craved leave to display his wares. He was welcome, both for need's sake and for amusement, and was readily admitted. He was a handsome olive-faced Italian, and was followed by a little boy with a skin of almost Moorish dye—and great was the display at once made on the tables, of

> 'Lawn as white as driven snow,
>
> Cyprus, black as e'er was crow;
>
> Gloves as sweet as fragrant posies,
>
> Masks for faces and for noses;'

and there was a good deal of the eager, desultory bargaining that naturally took place where purchasing was an unusual excitement and novelty, and was to form a whole evening's amusement. Berenger, while supplying the defects of his scanty traveling wardrobe, was trying to make out whether he had seen the man before, wondering if he were the same whom he had met in the forest of Montipipeau, though a few differences in dress, hair, and beard made him somewhat doubtful.

'Perfumes? Yes, lady, I have store of perfumes: ambergris and violet dew, and the Turkish essence distilled from roses; yea, and the finest spirit of the Venus myrtle-tree, the secret known to the Roman dames of old, whereby they secured perpetual beauty and love—though truly Madame should need no such essence. That which nature has bestowed on her secures to her all hearts—and one valued more than all.'

'Enough,' said Diane, blushing somewhat, though with an effort at laughing off his words; 'these are the tricks of your trade.'

'Madame is incredulous; yet, lady, I have been in the East. Yonder boy comes from the land where there are spells that make known the secrets of lives.'

The old Chevalier, who had hitherto been taken up with the abstruse calculation—derived from his past days of economy—how much ribbon would be needed to retrim his murrey *just-au-corps*, here began to lend an ear, though saying nothing. Philip looked on in open-eyed wonder, and nudged his brother, who muttered in return, 'Jugglery!'

'Ah, the fair company are all slow to believe,' said the pedlar. 'Hola, Alessio!' and taking a glove that Philip had left on the table, he held it to the boy. A few unintelligible words passed between them; then the boy pointed direct to Philip, and waved his hand northwards. 'He says the gentleman who owns this glove comes from the North, from far away,' interpreted the Italian; then as the boy made the gesture of walking in chains, 'that he is a captive.'

'Ay,' cried Philip, 'right, lad; and can he tell how long I shall be so?'

'Things yet to come,' said the mountebank, 'are only revealed after long preparation. For them must he gaze into the dark poor of the future. The present and the past he can divine by the mere touch of what has belonged to the person.'

'It is passing strange,' said Philip to Madame de Selinville. 'You credit it, Madame?'

'Ah, have we not seen the wonders come to pass that a like diviner fortold to the Queen-mother?' said Diane: 'her sons should be all kings— that was told her when the eldest was yet Dauphin.'

'And there is only one yet to come,' said Philip, awe-struck. 'But see, what has he now?'

'Veronique's kerchief,' returned Madame de Selinville, as the Italian began to interpret the boy's gesture.

'Pretty maidens, he says, serve fair ladies—bear tokens for them. This damsel has once been the bearer of a bouquet of heather of the pink and white, whose bells were to ring hope.'

'Eh, eh, Madame, it is true?' cried Veronique, crimson with surprise and alarm. 'M. le Baron knows it is true.'

Berenger had started at this revelation, and uttered an inarticulate exclamation; but at that moment the boy, in whose hand his master had placed a crown from the money newly paid, began to make vehement gestures, which the main interpreted. '*Le Balafre*, he says, pardon me, gentlemen, *le Balafre* could reveal even a deeper scar of the heart than of the visage'—and the boy's brown hand was pressed on his heart—'yet truly there is yet hope (*esperance*) to be found. Yes'—as the boy put his hand to his neck—'he bears a pearl, parted from its sister pearls. Where they are, there is hope. Who can miss Hope, who has sought it at a royal death-bed?'

'Ah, where is it?' Berenger could not help exclaiming.

'Sir,' said the pedlar, 'as I told Messieurs and Mesdames before, the spirits that cast the lights of the future on the dark pool need invocation. Ere he can answer M. le Baron's demands, he and I must have time and seclusion. If Monsieur le Chevalier will grant us an empty room, there will we answer all queries on which the spirits will throw light.'

'And how am I to know that you will not bring the devil to shatter the castle, my friend?' demanded the Chevalier. 'Or more likely still, that you are not laughing all the time at these credulous boys and ladies?'

'Of that, sir, you may here convince yourself,' said the mountebank, putting into his hand a sort of credential in Italian, signed by Renato di Milano, the Queen's perfumer, testifying to the skill of his compatriot Ercole Stizzito both in perfumery, cosmetics, and in the secrets of occult sciences.

The Chevalier was no Italian scholar, and his daughter interpreted the scroll to him, in a rapid low voice, adding, 'I have had many dealings with Rene of Milan, father. I know he speaks sooth. There can be no harm in letting the poor man play out his play—all the castle servants will be frantic to have their fortunes told.'

'I must speak with the fellow first, daughter,' said the Chevalier. 'He must satisfy me that he has no unlawful dealings that could bring the Church down on us.' And he looked meaningly at the mountebank, who replied by a whole muster-roll of ecclesiastics, male and female, who had heard and approved his predictions.

'A few more words with thee, fellow,' said the Chevalier, pointing the way to one of the rooms opening out of the hall. 'As master of the house I must be convinced of his honesty,' he added. 'If I am satisfied, then who will may seek to hear their fortune.'

Chevalier, man and boy disappeared, and Philip was the first to exclaim, 'A strange fellow! What will he tell us? Madame, shall you hear him?'

'That depends on my father's report,' she said. 'And yet,' sadly and pensively, 'my future is dark and void enough. Why should I vex myself with hearing it?'

'Nay, it may brighten,' said Philip.

'Scarcely, while hearts are hard,' she murmured with a slight shake of the head, that Philip thought indescribably touching; but Berenger was gathering his purchases together, and did not see. 'And you, brother,' said Philip, 'you mean to prove him?'

'No,' said Berenger. 'Have you forgotten, Phil, the anger we met with, when we dealt with the gipsy at Hurst Fair?'

'Pshaw, Berry, we are past flogging now.'

'Out of reach, Phil, of the rod, but scarce of the teaching it struck into us.'

'What?' said Philip, sulkily.

'That divining is either cozening manor forsaking God, Phil. Either it is falsehood, or it is a lying wonder of the devil.'

'But, Berry, this man is not cheat.'

'Then he is worse.'

'Only, turn not away, brother. How should he have known things that even I know not?—the heather.'

'No marvel in that,' said Berenger. 'This is the very man I bought Annora's fan from; he was prowling round Montpipeau, and my heather was given to Veronique with little secrecy. And as to the royal deathbed, it was Rene, his master, who met me there.'

'Then you think it mere cozeing? If so, we should find it out.'

'I don't reckon myself keener than an accomplished Italian mountebank,' said Berenger, dryly.

Further conference was cut short by the return of the Chevalier, saying, in his paternal genial way, 'Well, children, I have examined the fellow and his credentials, and for those who have enough youth and hope to care to have the future made known to them, bah! it is well.'

'Is it sorcery, sir?' asked Philip, anxiously.

The Chevalier shrugged his shoulders. 'What know I?' he said. 'For those who have a fine nose for brimstone there may be, but he assures me it is but the white magic practiced in Egypt, and the boy is Christian!'

'Did you try this secret, father?' inquired Madame de Selinville.

'I, my daughter? An old man's fortune is in his children. What have I to ask?'

'I—I scarcely like to be the first!' said the lady, eager but hesitating. 'Veronique, you would have your fortune told?'

'I will be the first,' said Philip, stepping forward manfully. 'I will prove him for you, lady, and tell you whether he be a cozener or not, or if his magic be fit for you to deal with.'

And confident in the inherent intuition of a plain Englishman, as well as satisfied to exercise his resolution for once in opposition to Berenger's opinion, Master Thistlewood stepped towards the closet where the Italian awaited his clients, and Berenger knew that it would be worse than useless to endeavour to withhold him. He only chafed at the smile which passed between father and daughter at this doughty self-assertion.

There was a long silence. Berenger sat with his eyes fixed on the window where the twilight horizon was still soft and bright with the pearly gold of the late sunset, thinking with an intensity of yearning what it would be could he truly become certain of Eustacie's present doings; questioning whether he would try to satisfy that longing by the doubtful auguries of the diviner, and then recollecting how he had heard from wrecked sailors that to seek to delude their thirst with sea-water did but aggravate their misery. He knew that whatever he might hear would be unworthy of confidence. Either it merely framed to soothe and please him—or, were it a genuine oracle, he had no faith in the instinct that was to perceive it, but what he HAD faith in was the Divine protection over his lost ones. 'No,' he thought to himself, 'I will not by a presumptuous sin, in my own impatience, risk incurring woes on them that deal with familiar spirits and wizards that peep and mutter. If ever I am to hear of Eustacie again, it shall be by God's will, not the devil's.'

Diane de Selinville had been watching his face all the time, and now said, with that almost timid air of gaiety that she wore when addressing him: 'You too, cousin, are awaiting Monsieur Philippe's report to decide whether to look into the pool of mystery.'

'Not at all, Madame,' said Berenger, gravely. 'I do not understand white magic.'

'Our good cousin has been too well bred among the Reformers to condescend to our little wickednesses, daughter,' said the Chevalier; and the sneer—much like that which would await a person now who scrupled at joining in table-turning or any form of spiritualism—purpled Berenger's scar, now his only manner of blushing; but he instantly perceived that it was the Chevalier's desire that he should consult the conjurer, and therefore became the more resolved against running into a trap.

'I am sure,' said Madame de Selinville, earnestly, though with an affectation of lightness, 'a little wickedness is fair when there is a great deal at stake. For my part, I would not hesitate long, to find out how soon the King will relent towards my fair cousin here!'

'That, Madame,' said Berenger, with the same grave dryness, 'is likely to be better known to other persons than this wandering Greek boy.'

Here Philip's step was heard returning hastily. He was pale, and looked a good deal excited, so that Madame de Selinville uttered a little cry, and exclaimed, 'Ah! is it so dreadful then?'

'No, no, Madame,' said Philip, turning round, with a fervour and confidence he had never before shown. 'On my word, there is nothing formidable. You see nothing—nothing but the Italia and the boy. The boy gazes into a vessel of some black liquid, and sees—sees there all you would have revealed. Ah!'

'Then you believe?' asked Madame de Selinville.

'It cannot be false,' answered Philip; 'he told me everything. Things he could not have known. My very home, my father's house, passed in review before that strange little blackamoor's eyes; where I—though I would have given worlds to see it—beheld only the lamp mirrored in the dark pool.'

'How do you know it was your father's house?' said Berenger.

'I could not doubt. Just to test the fellow, I bade him ask for my native place. The little boy gazed, smiled, babbled his gibberish, pointed. The man said he spoke of a fair mansion among green fields and hills, "a grand *cavalier embonpoint*,"—those were his very words,—at the door, with a tankard in one hand. Ah! my dear father, why could not I see him too? But who could mistake him or the Manor?'

'And did he speak of future as well as past?' said Diane.

'Yes, yes, yes,' said Philip, with more agitation. 'Lady, that will you know for yourself.'

'It was not dreadful?' she said, rising.

'Oh no!' and Philip had become crimson, and hesitated; 'certes, not dreadful. But—-I must not say more.'

'Save good night,' said Berenger, rising; 'See, our gendarmes are again looking as if we had long exceeded their patience. It is an hour later than we are wont to retire.'

'If it be your desire to consult this mysterious fellow now you have heard your brother's report, my dear Baron,' said the Chevalier, 'the gendarmes may devour their impatience a little longer.'

'Thanks, sir,' said Berenger; 'but I am not tempted,' and he gave the usual signal to the gendarmes, who, during meals, used to stand as sentries at the great door of the hall.

'It might settle your mind,' muttered Philip, hesitating. 'And yet—yet——'

But he used no persuasions, and permitted himself to be escorted with his brother along the passages to their own chamber, where he threw himself into a chair with a long sigh, and did not speak. Berenger meantime opened the Bible, glanced over the few verses he meant to read, found the place in the Prayer-book, and was going to the stairs to call Humfrey, when Philip broke forth: 'Wait, Berry; don't be in such haste.'

'What, you want time to lose the taste of your dealings with the devil?' said Berenger, smiling.

'Pshaw! No devil in the matter,' testily said Philip. 'No, I was only wishing you had not had a Puritan fit, and seen and heard for yourself. Then I should not have had to tell you,' and he sighed.

'I have no desire to be told,' said Berenger, who had become more fixed in the conviction that it was an imposture.

'No desire! Ah! I have none when I knew what it was. But you ought to know.'

'Well,' said Berenger, 'you will burst anon if I open not my ears.'

'Dear Berry, speak not thus. It will be the worse for you when you do hear. Alack, Berenger, all ours have been vain hopes. I asked for HER— and the boy fell well-nigh into convulsions of terror as he gazed; spoke of flames and falling houses. That was wherefore I pressed you not again—it would have wrung your heart too much. The boy fairly wept and writhed himself, crying out in his tongue for pity on the fair lady and the little babe in the burning house. Alack! brother,' said Philip, a little hurt that his brother had not changed countenance.

'This is the lying tale of the man-at-arms which our own eyes contradicted,' said Berenger; 'and no doubt was likewise inspired by the Chevalier.'

'See the boy, brother! How should he have heard the Chevalier? Nay, you might hug your own belief, but it is hard that we should both be in durance for your mere dream that she lives.'

'Come, Phil, it will be the devil indeed that sows dissension between us,' said Berenger. 'You know well enough that were it indeed with my poor Eustacie as they would fain have us believe, rather than give up her fair name I would not in prison for life. Or would you have me renounce my faith, or wed Madame de Selinville upon the witness of a pool of ink that I am a widower?' he added, almost laughing.

'For that matter,' muttered Philip, a good deal ashamed and half affronted, 'you know I value the Protestant faith so that I never heard a word from the will old priest. Nevertheless, the boy, when I asked of our release, saw the gates set open by Love.'

'What did Love look like in the pool? Had he wings like the Cupids in the ballets at the Louvre?' asked Berenger provokingly.

'I tell you I saw nothing,' said Philip, tartly: 'this was the Italian's interpretation of the boy's gesture. It was to be by means of love, he said, and of a lady who——he made it plain enough who she was,' added the boy, colouring.

'No doubt, as the Chevalier have instructed him to say that I—I—' he hesitated, 'that my—my love—I mean that he saw my shield per pale with the field fretty and the sable leopard.'

'Oh! it is to be my daughter, is it?' said Berenger, laughing; 'I am very happy to entertain your proposals for her.'

'Berenger, what mocking fiend has possessed you?' cried Philip, half angrily, half pitifully. 'How can you so speak of that poor child?'

'Because the more they try to force on me the story of her fate, the plainer it is to me that they do not believe it. I shall find her yet, and then, Phil, you shall have the first chance.'

Philip growled.

'Well, Phil,' said his brother, good-humouredly, 'any way, till this Love comes that is to let us out, don't let Moor or fiend come between us. Let me keep my credence for the honest Bailli's daughters at Lucon; and remember I would give my life to free you, but I cannot give away my faith.' Philip bent his head. He was of too stubborn a mould to express contrition or affection, but he mused for five minutes, then called Humfrey, and at the last moment, as the heavy tread came up-stairs, he turned round and said, 'You're in the right on't there, Berry. Hap what hap, the foul fiend may carry off the conjurer before I murmur at you again! Still I wish you had seen him. You would know 'tis sooth.'

While Berenger, in his prison chamber, with the lamplight beaming on his high white brow and clear eye, stood before his two comrades in captivity, their true-hearted faces composed to reverence, and as he read, 'I have hated them that hold of superstitious vanities, and my trust hath been in the Lord. I will be glad and rejoice in Thy mercy, for Thou hast considered my trouble and hast known my soul in adversities,' feeling that here was the oracle by which he was willing to abide—Diane de Selinville was entering the cabinet where the secrets of the future were to be unveiled.

There she stood—the beautiful court lady—her lace coif (of the Mary of Scotland type) well framed the beautiful oval of her face, and set of the clear olive of her complexion, softened by short jetty curls at the temples, and lighted splendid dark eyes, and by the smiles of a perfect pair of lips. A transparent veil hung back over the ruff like frostwork-formed fairy wings, and over the white silk bodice and sleeves laced with violet, and the violet skirt that fell in ample folds on the ground; only, however, in the dim light revealing by an occasional gleam that it was not black. It was a stately presence, yet withal there was a tremor, a quiver of the downcast eyelids, and a trembling of the fair hand, as though she were ill at ease; even though it was by no means the first time she had trafficked with the dealers in mysterious arts who swarmed around Catherine de Medicis. There were words lately uttered that weighed with her in their simplicity, and she could not forget them in that gloomy light, as she gazed on the brown face of the Italian, Ercole, faultless in outline as a classical mask, but the black depths of the eyes sparkling with intensity of observation, as if they were everywhere at once and gazed through and through. He wore his national dress, with the short cloak over one shoulder; but the little boy, who stood at the table, had been fantastically arrayed in a sort of semi-Albanian garb, a red cap with a long tassel, a dark, gold-embroidered velvet jacket sitting close to his body, and a white kilt over his legs, bare except for buskins stiff with gold. The poor little fellow looked pale in spite of his tawny hue, his enormous black eyes were heavy and weary, and he seemed to be trying to keep aloof from the small brazen vessel formed by the coils of two serpents that held the inky liquid of which Philip had spoken.

No doubt of the veritable nature of the charm crossed Diane; her doubt was of its lawfulness, her dread of the supernatural region she was invading. She hesitated before she ventured on her first question, and started as the Italian first spoke,—'What would the Eccelentissima? Ladies often hesitate to speak the question nearest their hearts. Yet is it ever the same. But the lady must be pleased to form it herself in words, or the lad will not see her vision.'

'Where, then, is my brother?' said Diane, still reluctant to come direct to the point.

The boy gazed intently into the black pool, his great eyes dilating till they seemed like black wells, and after a long time, that Diane could have counted by the throbs of her heart, he began to close his fingers, perform the action over the other arm of one playing on the lute, throw his head back, close his eyes, and appear to be singing a lullaby. Then he spoke a few words to his master quickly.

'He see,' said Ercole, 'a gentleman touching the lute, seated in a bedroom, where lies, on a rich pillow, another gentleman,'—and as the boy stroked his face, and pointed to his hands—'wearing a mask and gloves. It is, he says, in my own land, in Italy,' and as the boy made the action of rowing, 'in the territory of Venice.'

'It is well,' said Madame de Selinville, who knew that nothing was more probable than that her brother should be playing the King to his sleep in the medicated mask and gloves that cherished the royal complexion, and, moreover, that Henry was lingering to take his pastime in Italy to the great inconvenience of his kingdom.

Her next question came nearer her heat—'You saw the gentleman with a scar. Will he leave this castle?'

The boy gazed, then made gestures of throwing his arms wide, and of passing out; and as he added his few words, the master explained: 'He sees the gentleman leaving the castle, through open gate, in full day, on horseback; and—and it is Madame who is with them,' he added, as the lad pointed decidedly to her, 'it is Madame who opens their prison.'

Diane's face lighted with gladness for a moment; then she said, faltering (most women of her day would not have been even thus reserved), 'Then I shall marry again?'

The boy gazed and knitted his brow; then, without any pantomime, looked up and spoke. 'The Eccellentissima shall be a bride once more, he says,' explained the man, 'but after a sort he cannot understand. It is exhausting, lady, thus to gaze into the invisible future; the boy becomes confused and exhausted ere long.'

'Once more—I will only ask of the past. My cousin, is he married or a widower?'

The boy clasped his hands and looked imploringly, shaking his head at the dark pool, as he murmured an entreating word to his master. 'Ah! Madame,' said the Italian, 'that question hath already been demanded by the young Inglese. The poor child has been so terrified by the scene it called up, that he implored he may not see it again. A sacked and burning town, a lady in a flaming house——'

'Enough, enough,' said de; 'I could as little bear to hear as he to see. It is what we have ever known and feared. And now'—she blushed as she spoke—'sir, you will leave me one of those potions that Signor Renato is wont to compound.'

'*Capisco!*' said Ercole; 'but the Eccellentissima shall be obeyed if she will supply the means, for the expense will be heavy.'

The bargain was agreed upon, and a considerable sum advanced for a philter, compounded of strange Eastern plants and mystic jewels; and then Diane, with a shudder of relief, passed into the full light of the hall, bade her father good night, and was handed by him into the litter that had long been awaiting her at the door.

The Chevalier, then, with care on his brow, bent his steps towards the apartment where the Italian still remained counting the money he had received.

'So!' he said as he entered, 'so, fellow, I have not hindered your gains, and you have been true to your agreement?'

'Illustrissimo, yes. The pool of vision mirrored the flames, but nothing beyond—nothing—nothing.'

'They asked you then no more of those words you threw out of Esperance?'

'Only the English youth, sir; and there were plenty of other hopes to dance before the eyes of such a lad! With M. le Baron it will be needful to be more guarded.'

'M. le Baron shall not have the opportunity,' said the Chevalier. 'He may abide by his decision, and what the younger one may tell him. Fear not, good man, it shall be made good to you, if you obey my commands. I have other work for you. But first repeat to me more fully what you told me before. Where was it that you saw this unhappy girl under the name of Esperance?'

'At a hostel, sir, at Charente, where she was attending on an old heretic teacher of the name of Gardon, who had fallen sick there, being pinched by the fiend with rheumatic pains after his deserts. She bore the name of Esperance Gardon, and passed for his son's widow.'

'And by what means did you know her not to be the mean creature she pretended?' said the Chevalier, with a gesture of scornful horror.

'Illustrissimo, I never forget a face. I had seen this lady with M. le Baron when they made purchases of various trinkets at Montpipeau; and I saw her full again. I had the honour to purchase from her certain jewels, that the Eccellenza will probably redeem; and even—pardon, sir—I cut off and bought of her, her hair.'

'Her hair!' exclaimed the Chevalier, in horror. 'The miserable girl to have fallen so low! Is it with you, fellow?'

'Surely, Illustrissimo. Such tresses—so shining, so silky, so well kept,—I reserved to adorn the heads of Signor Renato's most princely customers', said the man, unpacking from the inmost recesses of one of his most ingeniously arranged packages, a parcel which contained the rich mass of beautiful black tresses. 'Ah! her head looked so noble,' he added, 'that I felt it profane to let my scissors touch those locks; but she said that she could never wear them openly more, and that they did but take up her time, and were useless to her child and her father—as she called him; and she much needed the medicaments for the old man that I gave her in exchange.'

'Heavens! A daughter of Ribaumont!' sighed the Chevalier, clenching his hand. 'And now, man, let me see the jewels with which the besotted child parted.'

The jewels were not many, nor remarkable. No one but a member of the family would have identified them, and not one of the pearls was there; and the Chevalier refrained from inquiring after them, lest, by putting the Italian on the scent of anything so exceptionally valuable, he should defeat his own object, and lead to the man's securing the pearls and running away with them. But Ercole understood his glance, with the quickness of a man whose trade forced him to read countenances. 'The Eccellenza is looking for the pearls of Ribaumont? The lady made no offer of them to me.'

'Do you believe that she has them still?'

'I am certain of it, sir. I know that she has jewels—though she said not what they were—which she preserved at the expense of her hair. It was thus. The old man had, it seems, been for weeks on the rack with pains caught by a chill when they fled from La Sablerie, and, though the fever had left him, he was still so stiff in the joints as to be unable to move. I prescribed for him unguents of balm and Indian spice, which, as the Eccellenza knows, are worth far more than their weight in gold; nor did these jewels make up the cost of these, together with the warm cloak for him, and the linen for her child that she had been purchasing. I tell you, sir, the babe must have no linen but the finest fabric of Cambrai—yes, and even carnation-coloured ribbons—though, for herself, I saw the homespun she was sewing. As she mused over what she could throw back, I asked if she had no other gauds to make up the price, and she said, almost within herself, "They are my child's, not mine." Then remembering that I had been buying the hair of the peasant maidens, she suddenly offered me her tresses. But I could yet secure the pearls, if Eccellenza would.'

'Do you then believe her to be in any positive want or distress?' said the Chevalier.

'Signor, no. The heretical households among whom she travels gladly support the families of their teachers, and at Catholic inns they pay their way. I understood them to be on their way to a synod of Satan at the nest of heretics, Montauban, where doubtless the old miscreant would obtain an appointment to some village.'

'When did you thus full in with them?'

'It was on one of the days of the week of Pentecost,' said Ercole. 'It is at that time I frequent fairs in those parts, to gather my little harvest on the maidens' heads.'

'*Parbleu*! class not my niece with those sordid beings, man,' said the Chevalier, angrily. 'Here is your price'—tossing a heavy purse on the table—'and as much more shall await you when you bring me sure intelligence where to find my niece. You understand; and mark, not one word of the gentleman you saw here. You say she believes him dead?'

'The Illustrissimo must remember that she never dropped her disguise with me, but I fully think that she supposed herself a widow. And I understand the Eccellenza, she is still to think so. I may be depended on.'

'You understand,' repeated the Chevalier, 'this sum shall reward you when you have informed me where to find her—as a man like you can easily trace her from Montauban. If you have any traffickings with her, it shall be made worth your while to secure the pearls for the family; but, remember, the first object is herself, and that she should be ignorant of the existence of him whom she fancied her husband.'

'I see, Signor; and not a word, of course, of my having come from you. I will discover her, and leave her noble family to deal with her. Has the Illustrissimo any further commands?'

'None,' began the Chevalier; then, suddenly, 'This unhappy infant—is it healthy? Did it need any of your treatment?'

'Signor, no. It was a fair, healthy bambina of a year old, and I heard the mother boasting that it had never had a day's illness.'

'Ah, the less a child has to do in the world, the more is it bent on living,' said the Chevalier with a sigh; and then, with a parting greeting, he dismissed the Italian, but only to sup under the careful surveillance of the steward, and then to be conveyed by early morning light beyond the territory where the affairs of Ribaumont were interesting.

But the Chevalier went through a sleepless night. Long did he pace up and down his chamber, grind his teeth, clench his fist and point them at his head, and make gestures of tearing his thin gray locks; and many a military oath did he swear under his breath as he thought to what a pass things had come. His brother's daughter waiting on an old Huguenot *bourgeois*, making sugar-cakes, selling her hair! And what next? Here was she alive after all, alive and disgracing herself; alive—yes, both she and her husband—to perplex the Chevalier, and force him either to new crimes or to beggar his son! Why could not the one have really died on the St. Bartholomew, or the other at La Sablerie, instead of putting the poor Chevalier in the wrong by coming to live again?

What had he done to be thus forced to peril his soul at his age? Ah, had he but known what he should bring on himself when he wrote the unlucky letter, pretending that the silly little child wished to dissolve the marriage! How should he have known that the lad would come meddling over? And then, when he had dexterously brought about that each should be offended with the other, and consent to the separation, why must royalty step in and throw them together again? Yes, and he surely had a right to feel ill-used, since it was in ignorance of the ratification of the marriage that he had arranged the frustration of the elopement, and that he had forced on the wedding with Narcisse, so as to drive Eustacie to flight from the convent— in ignorance again of her life that he had imprisoned Berenger, and tried to buy off his clams to Nid de Merle with Diane's hand. Circumstances had used him cruelly, and he shrank from fairly contemplating the next step.

He knew well enough what it must be. Without loss of time a letter must be sent to Rome, backed by strong interest, so as to make it appear that the ceremony at Montpipeau, irregular, and between a Huguenot and Catholic, had been a defiance of the Papal decree, and must therefore be nullified. This would probably be attainable, though he did not feel absolutely secure of it. Pending this, Eustacie must be secluded in a convent; and, while still believing herself a widow, must immediately on the arrival of the decree and dispensation, be forced into the marriage with Narcisse before she heard of Berenger's being still alive. And then Berenger would have no longer any excuse for holding out. His claims would be disposed of, and he might be either sent to England, or he might be won upon by Madame de Selinville's constancy.

And this, as the Chevalier believed, was the only chance of saving a life that he was unwilling to sacrifice, for his captive's patience and courtesy had gained so much upon his heart that he was resolved to do all that shuffling and temporizing could do to save the lad from Narcisse's hatred and to secure him Diane's love.

As to telling the truth and arranging his escape, that scarcely ever crossed the old man's mind. It would have been to resign the lands of Nid de Merle, to return to the makeshift life he knew but too well, and, what was worse, to ruin and degrade his son, and incur his resentment. It would probably be easy to obtain a promise from Berenger, in his first joy and gratitude, of yielding up all pretensions of his own or his wife's; but, however honourably meant, such a promise would be worth very little, and would be utterly scorned by Narcisse. Besides, how could he thwart the love of his daughter and the ambition of his son both at once?

No; the only security for the possession of Nid de Merle lay in either the death of the young baron and his child or else in his acquiescence in the invalidity of his marriage, and therefore in the illegitimacy of the child.

And it was within the bounds of possibility that, in his seclusion, he might at length learn to believe in the story of the destruction at La Sablerie, and, wearying of captivity, might yield at length to the persuasions of Diane and her father, and become so far involved with them as to be unable to draw back, or else be so stung by Eustacie's desertion as to accept her rival willingly.

It was a forlorn hope, but it was the only medium that lay between either the death or the release of the captive; and therefore the old man clung to it as almost praiseworthy, and did his best to bring it about by keeping his daughter ignorant that Eustacie lived, and writing to his son that the Baron was on the point of becoming a Catholic and marrying his sister: and thus that all family danger and scandal would be avoided, provided the matter were properly represented at Rome.

CHAPTER XXXII
'JAM SATIS'

You may go walk, and give me leave a while,

My lessons make no music in three parts.

TAMING OF THE SHREW

Whether the dark pool really showed Sir Marmaduke Thistlewood or not, at the moment that his son desired that his image should be called up, the good knight was, in effect, sitting nodding over the tankard of sack with which his supper was always concluded, while the rest of the family, lured out of the sunny hall by the charms of a fresh summer evening, had dispersed into the gardens or hall.

Presently a movement in the neighbourhood made him think it incumbent on him to open his eyes wide, and exclaim, 'I'm not asleep.'

'Oh no! you never are asleep when there's anything you ought to see!' returned Dame Annora, who was standing by him with her hand on his chair.

'How now? Any tidings of the lads?' he exclaimed.

'Of the lads? No, indeed; but there will be bad tidings for the lads if you do not see to it! Where do you think your daughter is, Sir Duke?'

'Where? How should I know? She went out to give her sisters some strawberries, I thought.'

'See here,' said Lady Thistlewood, leading the way to the north end of the hall, where a door opened into what was called the Yew-tree Grove. This consisted of five rows of yew-trees, planted at regular intervals, and their natural mode of growth so interfered with by constant cutting, that their ruddy trunks had been obliged to rise branchless, till about twelve feet above ground they had been allowed to spread out their limbs in the form of ordinary forest trees; and, altogether, their foliage became a thick, unbroken, dark, evergreen roof, impervious to sunshine, and almost impervious to rain, while below their trunks were like columns forming five arcades, floored only by that dark red crusty earth and green lichen growth that seems peculiar to the shelter of yew-trees. The depth of the shade and the stillness of the place made it something peculiarly soothing and quiet, more especially when, as now, the sunset light came below the branches, richly tinted the russet pillars, cast long shadows, and gleamed into all the recesses of the interlacing boughs and polished leafage above.

'Do you see, Sir Duke?' demanded his lady.

'I see my little maids making a rare feast under the trees upon their strawberries set out on leaves. Bless their little hearts! what a pretty fairy feast they've made of it, with the dogs looking on as grave as judges! It takes me young again to get a smack of the haut-bois your mother brought from Chelsea Gardens.'

'Haut-bois! He'd never see if the house ere afire overhead. What's that beyond?'

'No fire, my dear, but the sky all aglow with sunset, and the red cow standing up against the light, chewing her cud, and looking as well pleased as though she knew there wasn't her match in Dorset.'

Lady Thistlewood fairly stamped, and pointed with her fan, like a pistol, down a side aisle of the grove, where two figures were slowly moving along.

'Eh! what? Lucy with her apron full of rose-leaves, letting them float away while she cons the children's lesson for the morrow with Merrycourt? They be no great loss, when the place is full of roses. Or why could you not call to the wench to take better heed of them, instead of making all this pother?'

'A pretty sort of lesson it is like to be! A pretty sort of return for my poor son, unless you take the better heed!'

'Would that I saw any return at all for either of the poor dear lads,' sighed the knight wearily; 'but what you may be driving at I cannot perceive.'

'What! When 'tis before your very eyes, how yonder smooth-tongued French impostor, after luring him back to his ruin beyond seas, is supplanting him even here, and your daughter giving herself over to the wily viper!'

'The man is a popish priest,' said Sir Marmaduke; 'no more given to love than Mr. Adderley or Friar Rogers.'

The dame gave a snort of derision:' Prithee, how many popish priests be now wedded parsons? Nor, indeed, even if his story be true, do I believe he is a priest at all. I have seen many a young abbe, as they call themselves, clerk only in name, loitering at court, free to throw off the cassock any moment they chose, and as insolent as the rest. Why, the Abbe de Lorraine, cardinal that is now, said of my complexion——'

'No vows, quotha!' muttered Sir Marmaduke, well aware of the Cardinal de Lorraine's opinion of his lady's complexion. 'So much the better; he is too good a young fellow to be forced to mope single, and yet I hate men's breaking their word.'

'And that's all you have to say!' angrily cried her ladyship. 'No one save myself ever thinks how it is to be with my poor dear wounded, heart-broken son, when he comes home, to find himself so scurvily used by that faithless girl of yours, ready——'

'Hold, madam,' said Sir Marmaduke, with real sternness; 'nothing rash against my daughter. How should she be faithless to a man who has been wedded ever since she knew him?'

'He is free now,' said Lady Thistlewood, beginning to cry (for the last letters received from Berenger had been those from Paris, while he still believed Eustacie to have perished at La Sablerie); 'and I do say it is very hard that just when he is rid of the French baggage, the bane of his life, and is coming home, maybe with a child upon his hands, and all wounded, scarred, and blurred, the only wench he would or should have married should throw herself away on a French vagabond beggar, and you aiding and abetting.'

'Come, come, Dame Nan,' said Sir Marmaduke, 'who told you I was aiding and abetting?'

'Tell me not, Sir Duke, you that see them a courting under your very eyes, and will not stir a finger to hinder it. If you like to see your daughter take up with a foreign adventurer, why, she's no child of mine, thank Heaven! And I've nought to do with it.'

'Pshaw, dame, there's no taking up in the case; and if there were, sure it is not you that should be hard on Lucy.'

Whereupon Annora fell into such a flood of tears at the cruelty of casting such things up to her, that Sir Marmaduke was fain in his blundering way to declare that he only meant that an honest Englishman had no chance where a Frenchman once came in, and then very nearly to surrender at discretion. At any rate, he escaped from her tears by going out at the door, and calling to Lucy to mind her rose-leaves; then, as she gazed round, dismayed at the pink track along the ground, he asked her what she had been doing. Whereto she answered with bright face and honest eyes, that Mr. Mericour had been going over with her the ode 'Jam satis,' of Horatius, wherewith to prepare little Nan for him to-morrow, and then she ran hurriedly away to secure the remainder of the rose-leaves, while her companion was already on his knees picking up the petals she had dropped.

'Master Merrycourt,' said Sir Marmaduke, a little gruffly, 'never heed the flower-leaves. I want a word with you.'

Claude de Mericour rose hastily, as if somewhat struck by the tone.

'The matter is this,' said the knight, leading him from the house, and signing back the little girls who had sprung towards them—'it has been brought to my mind that you are but a youth, and, pardon me, my young master, but when lads and lasses have their heads together over one book, tongues wag.'

The colour rushed hotly into young Mericour's face, and he answered quickly, 'My rank—I mean my order—should answer that.'

'Stay, young man, we are not in France; your order, be it what it may, has not hindered many a marriage in England; though, look you, no man should ever wed with my consent who broke his word to God in so doing; but they tell me your vows are not always made at your age.'

'Nor are they,' exclaimed Mericour, in a low voice, but with a sudden light on his countenance. 'The tonsure was given me as a child, but no vow of celibacy has passed my lips.'

Sir Marmaduke exclaimed, 'Oh!—' with a prolongation of the sound that lasted till Mericour began again.

'But, sir, let tongues wag as they will, it is for nought. Your fair daughter was but as ever preparing beforehand with me the tasks with which she so kindly indoctrinates her little sisters. I never thought of myself as aught but a religious, and should never dream of human love.'

'I thought so! I said so!' said Sir Marmaduke, highly gratified. 'I knew you were an honourable man that would never speak of love to my daughter by stealth, nor without means to maintain her after her birth.'

The word 'birth' brought the blood into the face of the son of the peer of France, but he merely bowed with considerable stiffness and pride, saying, 'You did me justice, sir.'

'Come, don't be hurt, man,' said Sir Marmaduke, putting his hand on his shoulder. 'I told you I knew you for an honourable man! You'll be over here to-morrow to hear the little maids their *Jam satis*, or whatever you call it, and dine with us after to taste Lucy's handiwork in jam cranberry, a better thing as I take it.'

Mericour had recovered himself, smiled, shook the good Sir Marmaduke proffered hand, and, begging to excuse himself from bidding good night to the ladies on the score of lateness, he walked away to cross the downs on his return to Combe Walwyn, where he was still resident, according to the arrangement by which he was there to await Berenger's return, now deferred so much beyond all reasonable expectation.

Sir Marmaduke, with a free heart, betook himself to the house, dreading to find that Lucy had fallen under the objurgations of her step-mother, but feeling impelled to stand her protector, and guided to the spot by the high key of Dame Annora's voice.

He found Lucy—who, on the race occasions when good-natured Lady Thistlewood was really angry with her, usually cowered meekly—now standing her ground, and while the dame was pausing for breath, he heard her gentle voice answering steadily, 'No, madam, to him I could never owe faith, nor troth, nor love, save such as I have for Philip.'

'Then it is very unfeeling and ungrateful of you. Nor did you think so once, but it is all his scars and——'

By this time Sir Marmaduke had come near enough to put his arm round his daughter, and say, 'No such thing, dame. It had been unseemly in the lass had it been otherwise. She is a good girl and a discreet; and the Frenchman, if he has made none of their vows, feels as bound as though he had. He's an honest fellow, thinking of his studies and not of ladies or any such trumpery. So give me a kiss, Lucy girl, and thou shalt study *Jam satis*, or any other jam he pleases, without more to vex thee.'

Lucy, now that the warfare was over, had begun to weep so profusely that so soon as her father released her, she turned, made a mute gesture to ask permission to depart, and hurried away; while Lady Thistlewood, who disliked above all that her husband should think her harsh to her step-children, began to relate the exceeding tenderness of the remonstrance which had been followed with such disproportionate floods of tears.

Poor Sir Marmaduke hoped at least that the veil of night had put an end to the subject which harassed him at a time when he felt less capable than usual of bearing vexation, for he was yearning sadly after his only son. The youths had been absent ten months, and had not been heard of for more than three, when they were just leaving Paris in search of the infant. Sir Francis Walsingham, whose embassy had ended with the death of Charles IX., knew nothing of them, and great apprehensions respecting them were beginning to prevail, and, to Sir Marmaduke especially, seemed to be eating out the peace and joy of his life. Philip, always at his father's side ever since he could run alone, was missed at every visit to stable or kennel; the ring of his cheery voice was wanting to the house; and the absence of his merry whistle seemed to make Sir Marmaduke's heart sink like lead as he donned his heavy boots, and went forth in the silver dew of the summer morning to judge which of his cornfields would soonest be ready for the sickle. Until this expedition of his sons he had, for more than fourteen years never been alone in those morning rounds on his farm; and much as he loved his daughters, they seemed to weigh very light in the scale compared with the sturdy heir who loved every acre with his own ancestral love. Indeed, perhaps, Sir Marmaduke had deeper, fonder affection for the children of his first marriage, because he had barely been able to give his full heart to their mother before she was taken from him, and he had felt almost double tenderness to be due to them, when he at length obtained his first and only true love. Now, as he looked over the shinning billows of the waving barley, his heart was very sore with longing for Philip's gladsome shout at the harvest-field, and he thought with surprise and compunction how he had seen Lucy leave him struggling with a flood of tears. While he was still thus gazing, a head appeared in the narrow path that led across the fields, and presently he recognized the slender, upright form of the young Frenchman.

'A fair good morrow to you, Master Merrycourt! You come right early to look after your ode?'

'Sir,' said Mericour, gravely saluting him, 'I come to make you my confession. I find that I did not deal truly with you last night, but it was all unwittingly.'

'How?' exclaimed Sir Marmaduke, recollecting Lucy's tears and looking much startled. 'You have not——' and there he broke off, seeing Mericour eager to speak.

'Sir,' he said, 'I was bred as one set apart from love. I had never learnt to think it possible to me,—I thought so even when I replied to you last evening; but, sir, the words you then spoke, the question you asked me set my heart burning, and my senses whirling——' And between agitation and confusion he stammered and clasped his hands passionately, trying to continue what he was saying, but muttering nothing intelligible.

Sir Marmaduke filled up the interval with a long whistle of perplexity; but, too kind not to pity the youth's distress, he laid his hand on his shoulder, saying, 'You found out you were but a hot-blooded youth after all, but an honest one. For, as I well trust, my lass knows nought of this.'

'How should she know, sir, what I knew not myself?'

'Ha! ha!' chuckled Sir Duke to himself, 'so 'twas all Dame Nan's doing that the flame has been lighted! Ho! ho! But what is to come next is the question?' and he eyed the French youth from head to foot with the same considering look with which he was wont to study a bullock.

'Sir, sir,' cried Mericour, absolutely flinging himself on his knee before him with national vehemence, 'do give me hope! Oh! I will bless you, I will——'

'Get up, man,' said the knight, hastily; 'no fooling of this sort. The milkmaids will be coming. Hope—why, what sort of hope can be given you in the matter?' he continued; 'you are a very good lad, and I like you well enough, but you are not the sort of stuff one gives one's daughter to. Ay, ay, I know you are a great man in your own country, but what are you here?'

'A miserable fugitive and beggar, I know that,' said Mericour, vehemently, 'but let me have but hope, and there is nothing I will not be!'

'Pish!' said Sir Marmaduke.

'Hear me,' entreated the youth, recalled to common sense: 'you know that I have lingered at the chateau yonder, partly to study divinity and settle my mind, and partly because my friend Ribaumont begged me to await his return. I will be no longer idle; my mind is fixed. To France I cannot return, while she gives me no choice between such doctrine and practice as I saw at court, and such as the Huguenots would have imposed on me. I had already chosen England as my country before—before this wild hope had awakened in me. Here, I know my nobility counts for nothing, though, truly, sir, few names in France are prouder. But it shall be no hindrance. I will become one of your men of the robe. I have heard that they can enrich themselves and intermarry with your country *noblesse*.'

'True, true,' said Sir Marmaduke, 'there is more sense in that notion than there seemed to be in you at first. My poor brother Phil was to have been a lawyer if he had lived, but it seems to me you are a long way off from that yet! Why, our Templars be mostly Oxford scholars.'

'So it was explained to me,' said Mericour, 'but for some weeks past the Lady Burnet, to whose sons, as you know, I have been teaching French, has been praying me to take the charge of them at Oxford, by which means I should at least be there maintained, and perchance obtain the means for carrying on my studies at the Temple.'

'Not ill thought of,' said the knight; 'a fair course enough for you; but look you, you must have good luck indeed to be in a state to marry within ten or fifteen years,—very likely not then—having nothing of your own, and my wench but little, for Lucy's portion cannot be made equal to her sisters', her mother having been no heiress like Dame Nan. And would you have me keep the maid unwedded till she be thirty or thirty-five years old, waiting for your fortune?'

Mericour looked terribly disconcerted at this.

'Moreover,' added the knight, 'they will all be at me, so soon as those poor lads come home—Heaven grant they do—to give her to Berenger.'

'Sir,' said Mericour, looking up with a sudden smile, 'all that I would ask is, what you are too good a father to do, that you would not put any force on her inclinations.'

'How now? you said you had never courted her!'

'Nor have I, sir. But I see the force of your words. Should she love another man, my dream were, of course, utterly vain, but if not——' He broke off.

'Well, well, I am no man to force a girl to a match against her will; but never trust to that, man. I know what women are; and let a fantastic stranger come across them, there's an end of old friends. But yours is an honest purpose, and you are a good youth; and if you had anything to keep her with, you should have Lucy to-morrow, with all my heart.'

Then came the further question whether Mericour should be allowed an interview with Lucy. Sir Marmaduke was simple enough to fancy that she need not be made aware of the cause of Mericour's new arrangement, and decided against it. The young man sorrowfully acquiesced, but whether such a secret could be kept was another thing. To him it would have been impossible to renew their former terms of intercourse without betraying his feelings, and he therefore absented himself. Lady Thistlewood triumphed openly in Sir Marmaduke's having found him out and banished him from the house; Lucy looked white and shed silent tears. Her father's soft heart was moved, and one Sunday evening he whispered into her ear that Dame Nan was all wrong, and Mericour only kept away because he was an honourable man. Then Lucy smiled and brightened, and Sir Duke fondly asked her if she were fool enough to fancy herself in love with the man.

'Oh no, how should she, when he had never named love to her? She was only glad her father esteemed him.'

So then foolish, fond Sir Marmaduke told her all that had passed, and if it had not been too late, he would have sent for Mericour from Lady Burnet's; but his own story did almost as well in bringing back Lucy's soft pink color. She crept up into Cecily's room one day, and found that she knew all about it, and was as kind and sympathizing as she could be—when a vocation had been given up, though no vows had been taken. She did not quite understand it, but she would take it on trust.

CHAPTER XXXIII
THE SCANDAL OF THE SYNOD OF MONTAUBAN

O ye, wha are sae guid yourself,

   Sae pious and sae holy,

Ye've naught to do but mark and tell

   Your neebour's fauts and folly.

                    —*BURNS*

The old city of Montauban, once famous as the home of Ariosto's Rinaldo and his brethren, known to French romance as '*Les Quatre Fils Aymon*,' acquired in later times a very diverse species of fame,—that, namely, of being one of the chief strong-holds of the Reformed. The Bishop Jean de Lettes, after leading a scandalous life, had professed a sort of Calvinism, had married, and retired to Geneva, and his successor had not found it possible to live at Montauban from the enmity of the inhabitants. Strongly situated, with a peculiar municipal constitution of its own, and used to Provencal independence both of thought and deed, the inhabitants had been so unanimous in their Calvinism, and had offered such efficient resistance, as to have wrung from Government reluctant sanction for the open observance of the Reformed worship, and for the maintenance of a college for the education of their ministry.

There then was convoked the National Synod, answering to the Scottish General Assembly, excepting that the persecuted French Presbyterians met in a different place every year. Delegated pastors there gathered from every quarter. From Northern France came men used to live in constant hazard of their lives; from Paris, confessors such as Merlin, the chaplain who, leaving Coligny's bedside, had been hidden for three days in a hayloft, feeding on the eggs that a hen daily laid beside him; army-chaplains were there who had passionately led battle-psalms ere their colleagues charged the foe, and had striven with vain endeavours to render their soldiers saints; while other pastors came from Pyrenean villages where their generation had never seen flames lighted against heresy, nor knew what it was to disperse a congregation in haste and secrecy for hear of the enemy.

The audience was large and sympathizing. Montauban had become the refuge of many Huguenot families who could nowhere else profess their faith without constant danger; and a large proportion of these were ladies, wives of gentlemen in the army kept up by La Noue, or widows who feared that their children might be taken from them to be brought up by their Catholic relations, elderly dames who longed for tranquillity after having lost husbands or sons by civil war. Thickly they lodged in the strangely named *gasches* and *vertiers*, as the divisions and subdivisions of the city were termed, occupying floors or apartments of the tall old houses; walking abroad in the streets in grave attire, stiff hat, crimped ruff, and huge fan, and forming a society in themselves, close-packed, punctilious and dignified, rigidly devout but strictly censorious, and altogether as unlike their typical country folks of Paris as if they had belonged to a different nation. And the sourest and most severe of all were such as had lived farthest south, and personally suffered the least peril and alarm.

Dancing was unheard-of enormity; cards and dice were prohibited; and stronger expletive than the elegant ones invented for the special use of the King of Navarre was expiated either by the purse or the skin; Marot's psalmody was the only music, black or sad colour the only wear; and, a few years later, the wife of one of the most distinguished statesmen and councilors of Henri of Navarre was excommunicated for the enormity of wearing her hair curled.

To such a community it was a delightful festival to receive a national assembly of ministers ready to regale them on daily sermons for a whole month, and to retail in private the points of discipline debated in the public assembly; and, apart from mere eagerness for novelty, many a discreet heart beat with gladness at the meeting with the hunted pastor of her native home, who had been the first to strike the spiritual chord, and awake her mind to religion.

Every family had their honoured guest, every reception-room was in turn the scene of some pious little assembly that drank *eau sucree*, and rejoiced in its favourite pastor; and each little congress indulged in gentle scandal against its rival coterie. But there was one point on which all the ladies agreed,—namely, that good Maitre Isaac Gardon had fallen into an almost doting state of blindness to the vanities of his daughter-in-law, and that she was a disgrace to the community, and ought to be publicly reprimanded.

Isaac Gardon, long reported to have been martyred—some said at Paris, others averred at La Sablerie—had indeed been welcomed with enthusiastic joy and veneration, when he made his appearance at Montauban, pale, aged, bent, leaning on a staff, and showing the dire effect of the rheumatic fever which had prostrated him after the night of drenching and exposure during the escape from La Sablerie. Crowded as the city was, there was a perfect competition among the tradesfolk for the honour of entertaining him and the young widow and child of a St. Bartholomew martyr. A cordwainer of the street of the Soubirous Hauts obtained this honour, and the wife, though speaking only the sweet Provencal tongue, soon established the most friendly relations with M. Gardon's daughter-in-law.

Two or three more pastors likewise lodged in the same house, and ready aid was given by Mademoiselle Gardon, as all called Eustacie, in the domestic cares thus entailed, while her filial attention to her father-in-law and her sweet tenderness to her child struck all this home circle with admiration. Children of that age were seldom seen at home among the better classes in towns. Then, as now, they were universally consigned to country nurses, who only brought them home at three or four years old, fresh from a squalid, neglected cottage life: and Eustacie's little moonbeam, *la petite Rayonette*, as she loved to call her, was quite an unusual spectacle; and from having lived entirely with grown people, and enjoyed the most tender and dainty care, she was intelligent and brightly docile to a degree that appeared marvellous to those who only saw children stupefied by a contrary system. She was a lovely little thing, exquisitely fair, and her plump white limbs small but perfectly moulded; she was always happy, because always healthy, and living in an atmosphere of love; and she was the pet and wonder of all the household, from the grinning apprentice to the grave young candidate who hoped to be elected pastor to the Duke de Quinet's village in the Cevennes.

And yet it was *la petite Rayonette* who first brought her mother into trouble. Since her emancipation from swaddling clothes she had been equipped in a little gray woolen frock, such as Eustacie had learnt to knit among the peasants, and varied with broad while stripes which gave it something of the moonbeam effect; but the mother had not been able to resist the pleasure of drawing up the bosom and tying it with a knot of the very carnation colour that Berenger used to call her own. That knot was discussed all up and down the Rue Soubirous Hauts, and even through the Carriera Major! The widow of an old friend of Maitre Gardon had remonstrated on the improprieties of such gay vanities, and Mdlle. Gardon had actually replied, reddening with insolences, that her husband had loved to see her wear the colour.

Now, if the brethren at Paris had indulged their daughters in such backslidings, see what had come of it! But that poor Theodore Gardon should have admired his bride in such unhallowed adornments, was an evident calumny; and many a head was shaken over it in grave and pious assembly.

Worse still; when she had been invited to a supper at the excellent Madame Fargeau's, the presumptuous little *bourgeoise* had evidently not known her place, but had seated herself as if she were a noble lady, a *fille de qualité*, instead of a mere minister's widow and a watchmaker's daughter. Pretend ignorance that precedence was to be here observed! That was another Parisian piece of impudence, above all in one who showed such ridiculous airs as to wipe her face with her own handkerchief instead of the table-cloth, and to be reluctant to help herself from the genera dish of *potage* with her own spoon. Even that might have been overlooked if she would have regaled them with a full and particular account of her own rescue from the massacre at Paris; but she merely coloured up, and said that she had been so ill as to know scarcely anything about it; and when they pressed her further, she shortly said, 'They locked me up;' and, before she could be cross-examined as to who was this 'they,' Maitre Gardon interfered, saying that she had suffered so much that he requested the subject might never be mentioned to her. Nor would he be more explicit, and there was evidently some mystery, and he was becoming blindly indulgent and besotted by the blandishments of an artful woman.

Eustacie was saved from hearing the gossip by her ignorance of the Provencal, which was the only languages of all but the highest and most cultivated classes, the hostess had very little *langue d'oui*, and never ventured on any complicated discourse; and Isaac Gardon, who could speak both the *oc* and *oui*, was not a person whom it was easy to beset with mere hearsay or petty remonstrance, but enough reached him at last to make him one day say mildly, 'My dear child, might not the little one dispense with her ribbon while we are here?'

'Eh, father? At the bidding of those impertinents?'

'Take care, daughter; you were perfect with the tradesfolk and peasants, but you cannot comport yourself as successfully with this *petite noblesse*, or the pastors' wives.'

'They are insolent, father. I, in my own true person, would treat no one as these petty dames treat me,' said Eustacie. 'I would not meddle between a peasant woman and her child, nor ask questions that must needs wring her heart.'

'Ah, child! humility is a bitter lesson; and even this world needs it now from you. We shall have suspicions; and I heard to-day that the King is in Dauphiny, and with him M. de Nid de Merle. Be not alarmed; he has no force with him, and the peace still subsists; but we must avoid suspicion. There is a *preche* at the Moustier to-day, in French; it would be well if you were to attend it.'

'I understand as little of French sermons as of Provencal,' murmured Eustacie; but it was only a murmur.

Maitre Gardon had soon found out that his charge had not head enough to be made a thorough-going controversial Calvinist. Clever, intelligent, and full of resources as she was, she had no capacity for argument, and could not enter into theoretical religion. Circumstances had driven her from her original Church and alienated her from those who had practiced such personal cruelties on her and hers, but the mould of her mind remained what it had been previously; she clung to the Huguenots because they protected her from those who would have forced an abhorrent marriage on her and snatched her child from her; and, personally, she loved and venerated Isaac Gardon with ardent, self-sacrificing filial love and gratitude, accepted as truth all that came from his lips, read the Scriptures, sang and prayed with him, and obeyed him as dutifully as ever the true Esperance could have done; but, except the merest external objections against the grossest and most palpable popular corruptions and fallacies, she really never entered into the matter. She had been left too ignorant of her own system to perceive its true clams upon her; and though she could not help preferring High Mass to a Calvinist assembly, and shrinking with instinctive pain and horror at the many profanations she witnessed, the really spiritual leadings of her own individual father-like leader had opened so much that was new and precious to her, so full of truth, so full of comfort, giving so much moral strength, that, unaware that all the foundations had been laid by Mere Monique, the resolute, high-spirited little thing, out of sheer constancy and constitutional courage, would have laid down her life as a Calvinist martyr, in profound ignorance that she was not in the least a Calvinist all the time.

Hitherto, her wandering life amid the persecuted Huguenots of the West had prevented her from hearing any preaching but good Isaac's own, which had been rather in the way of comfort and encouragement than of controversy, but in this great gathering it was impossible that there should not be plenty of vehement polemical oratory, such as was sue to fly over that weary little head. After a specimen or two, the chances of the sermon being in Provencal, and the necessity of attending to her child, had been Eustacie's excuse for usually offering to attend to the *menage*, and set her hostess free to be present at the preachings.

However, Rayonette was considered as no valid excuse; for did not whole circles of black-eyed children sit on the floor in sleepy stolidity at the feet of their mothers or nurses, and was it not a mere worldly folly to pretend that a child of sixteen months could not be brought to church? It was another instance of the mother's frivolity and the grandfather's idolatry.

The Moustier, or minster, the monastic church of Montauban, built on Mont Auriol in honour of St. Theodore, had, twelve years before, been plundered and sacked by the Calvinists, not only out of zeal for iconoclasm, but from long-standing hatred and jealousy against the monks. Catherine de Medicis had, in 1546, carried off two of the jasper columns from its chief door-way to the Louvre; and, after some years more, it was entirely destroyed. The grounds of the Auriol Mountain Monastery have been desolate down to the present day, when they have been formed into public gardens. When Eustacie walked through them, carrying her little girl in her arms, a rose in her bosom to console her for the loss of her bright breast-knot, they were in raw fresh dreariness, with tottering, blackened cloisters, garden flowers run wild, images that she had never ceased to regard as sacred lying broken and defiled among the grass and weeds.

Up the broad path was pacing the municipal procession, headed by the three Consuls, each with a serjeant bearing a white rod in front and a scarlet mantle, and the Consuls themselves in long robes with wide sleeves of quartered black and scarlet, followed by six halberdiers, likewise in scarlet, blazoned with the shield of the city—gules, a golden willow-tree, pollarded and shedding its branches, a chief azure with the three *fleur-de-lys* of royalty. As little Rayonette gleefully pointed at the brilliant pageant, Eustacie could not help saying, rather bitterly, that these *messieurs* seemed to wish to engross all the gay colours from heaven and earth from themselves; and Maitre Isaac could not help thinking she had some right on her side as he entered the church once gorgeous with jasper, marbles, and mosaics, glowing with painted glass, resplendent with gold and jewels, rich with paintings and draperies of the most brilliant dyes; but now, all that was, soiled, dulled, defaced; the whole building, even up to the end of the chancel, was closely fitted with benches occupied by the 'sad-coloured' congregation. Isaac was obliged by a strenuous effort of memory to recall 'Ne-hushtan' and the golden calves, before he could clear from his mind, 'Now they break down all the carved work thereof with axes and with hammers.' But, then, did not the thorough going Reformers think Master Isaac a very weak and back-sliding brother?

Nevertheless, in right of his age, his former reputation, and his sufferings, his place was full in the midst of the square-capped, black-robed ministers who sat herded on a sort of platform together, to address the Almighty and the congregation in prayers and discourses, interspersed with psalms sung by the whole assembly. There was no want of piety, depth, force, or fervour. These were men refined by persecution, who had struggled to the light that had been darkened by the popular system, and, having once been forced into foregoing their scruples as to breaking the unity of the Church, regarded themselves even as apostles of the truth.

Listening to them, Isaac Gardon felt himself rapt into the hopes of cleansing the aspirations of universal re-integration that had shone before his early youth, ere the Church had shown herself deaf, and the Reformers in losing patience had lost purity, and disappointment had crushed him into an aged man.

He was recalled by the echo of a gay, little inarticulate cry—those baby tones that had become such music to his ears that he hardly realized that they were not indeed from his grandchild. In a moment's glance he saw how it was. A little bird had flown in at one of the empty window, and was fluttering over the heads of the congregation, and a small, plump, white arm and hand was stretched out and pointing—a rosy, fair, smiling face upturned; a little gray figure had scrambled up on the knee of one of the still, black-hooded women; and the shout of irrepressible delight was breaking on the decorum of the congregation, in spite of hushes, in spite of the uplifted rod of a scarlet serjeant on his way down the aisle to quell the disturbance; nay, as the bird came nearer, the exulting voice, proud of the achievement of a new word, shouted '*Moineau, moineau.*' Angered by defiance to authority, down came the rod, not indeed with great force, but with enough to make the arms clasp round the mother's neck, the face hide itself on in, a loud, terrified wail ring through the church, and tempestuous sobbing follow it up. Then uprose the black-hooded figure, the child tightly clasped, and her mantle drawn round it, while the other hand motioned the official aside, and down the aisle, even to the door, she swept with the lofty carriage, high-drawn neck, and swelling bosom of an offended princess.

Maitre Gardon heard little more of the discourse, indeed he would have followed at once had he not feared to increase the sensation and the scandal. He came home to find Rayonette's tears long ago dried, but her mother furious. She would leave Montauban that minute, she would never set foot in a heretic conventicle again, to have her fatherless child, daughter of all the Ribaumonts, struck by base *canaille*. Even her uncle could not have done worse; he at least would have respected her blood.

Maitre Gardon did not know that his charge could be in such a passion, as, her eyes flashing through tears, she insisted on being taken away at once. No, she would hear nothing. She seemed to fell resentment due to the honour of all the Ribaumonts, and he was obliged peremptorily to refuse to quit Montauban till his business at the Synod should be completed, and then to leave her in a flood of angry tears and reproaches for exposing her child to such usage, and approving it.

Poor little thing, he found her meek and penitent for her unjust anger towards himself. Whatever he desired she would do, she would stay or go with him anywhere except to a sermon at the Moustier, and she did not think that in her heart her good father desired little infants to be beaten—least of all Berenger's little one. And with Rayonette already on his knee, stealing his spectacles, peace was made.

Peace with him, but not with the congregation! Were people to stalk out of church in a rage, and make no reparation? Was Maitre Isaac to talk of orphans, only children, and maternal love, as if weak human affection did not need chastisement? Was this saucy Parisienne to play the offended, and say that if the child were not suffered at church she must stay at home with it? The ladies agitated to have the obnoxious young widow reprimanded in open Synod, but, to their still greater disgust, not a pastor would consent to perform the office. Some said that Maitre Gardon ought to rule his own household, others that they respected him too much to interfere, and there were others abandoned enough to assert that if any one needed a reprimand it was the serjeant.

Of these was the young candidate, Samuel Mace, who had been educated at the expense of the Dowager Duchess de Quinet, and hoped that her influence would obtain his election to the pastorate of a certain peaceful little village deep in the Cevennes. She had intimated that what he wanted was a wife to teach and improve the wives of the peasant farmers, and where could a more eligible one be found than Esperance Gardon? Her cookery he tasted, her industry he saw, her tenderness to her child, her attention to her father, were his daily admiration; and her soft velvet eyes and sweet smile went so deep in his heart that he would have bought her ells upon ells of pink ribbon, when once out of sight of the old ladies; would have given a father's love to her little daughter, and a son's duty and veneration to Isaac Gardon.

His patroness did not deny her approval. The gossip had indeed reached her, but she had a high esteem for Isaac Gardon, believed in Samuel Mace's good sense, and heeded Montauban scandal very little. Her *protege* would be much better married to a spirited woman who had seen the world, than to a mere farmer's daughter who had never looked beyond her cheese. Old Gardon would be an admirable adviser, and if he were taken into the *menage* she would add to the endowment another arable field, and grass for two more cows. If she liked the young woman on inspection, the marriage should take place in her own august presence.

What! had Maitre Gardon refused? Forbidden that the subject should be mentioned to his daughter? Impossible! Either Mace had managed matters foolishly, or the old man had some doubt of him which she could remove, or else it was foolish reluctance to part with his daughter-in-law. Or the gossips were right after all, and he knew her to be too light-minded, if not worse, to be the wife of any pious young minister. Or there was some mystery. Any way, Madame la Duchesse would see him, and bring him to his senses, make him give the girl a good husband if she were worthy, or devote her to condign punishment if she were unworthy.

CHAPTER XXXIV
MADAME LA DUCHESSE

He found an ancient dame in dim brocade.——TENNYSON

Madame la Duchesse de Quinet had been a great heiress and a personal friend and favourite of Queen Jeanne d'Albret. She had been left a widow after five years' marriage, and for forty subsequent years had reigned despotically in her own name and that of *mon fils*. Busied with the support of the Huguenot cause, sometimes by arms, but more usually by politics, and constantly occupied by the hereditary government of one of the lesser counties of France, the Duke was all the better son for relinquishing to her the home administration, as well as the education of his two motherless boys; and their confidence and affection were perfect, though he was almost as seldom at home as she was abroad. At times, indeed, she had visited Queen Jeanne at Nerac; but since the good Queen's death, she only left the great chateau of Quinet to make a royal progress of inspection through the family towns, castles, and estates, sometimes to winter in her beautiful hereditary *hotel* at Montauban, and as at present to attend any great assembly of the Reformed.

Very seldom was her will not law. Strong sense and judgment, backed by the learning that Queen Marguerite of Navarre had introduced among the companions of her daughter, had rendered her superior to most of those with whom she came in contact: and the Huguenot ministers, who were much more dependent on their laity than the Catholic priesthood, for the most part treated her as not only a devout and honourable woman, an elect lady, but as a sort of State authority. That she had the right-mindedness to respect and esteem such men as Theodore Beza, Merlin, &c., who treated her with great regard, but never cringed, had not become known to the rest. Let her have once pronounced against poor little Esperance Gardon, and public disgrace would be a matter of certainty.

There she sat in her wainscoted walnut cabinet, a small woman by her inches, but stately enough to seem of majestic stature, and with gray eyes, of inexpressible keenness, which she fixed upon the halting, broken form of Isaac Gardon, and his grave, venerable face, as she half rose and made a slight acknowledgment of his low bow.

'Sit, Maitre Gardon, you are lame,' she said, with a wave of her hand. 'I gave you the incommodity of coming to see me not openly discuss *en pleine sale.*'

'Madame is considerate,' said Isaac, civilly, but with an open-eyed look and air that at once showed her that she had not to deal with one of the ministers who never forgot their low birth in intercourse with her.

'I understand,' said she, coming to the point at once, 'that you decline the proposals of Samuel Mace for your daughter-in-law. Now I wish you to know that Mace is a very good youth, whom I have known from his birth'—and she went on in his praise, Isaac bowing at each pause, until she had exhausted both Mace's history and her own beneficent intentions for him. Then he said, 'Madame is very good, and the young man appeared to me excellent. Nevertheless, this thing may not be. My daughter-in-law has resolved not to marry again.'

'Nay, but this is mere folly,' said the Duchess. 'We hold not Catholic tenets on merit in abstaining, but rather go by St. Paul's advice that the younger widows should marry, rather than wax wanton. And, to tell you the truth, Maitre Gardon, this daughter of yours does seem to have set tongues in motion.'

'Not by her own fault, Madame.'

'Stay, my good friend; I never found a man—minister or lay—who was a fair judge in these matters. You old men are no better than the young— rather worse—because you do not distrust yourselves. Now, I say no harm of the young woman, and I know an angel would be abused at Montauban for not wearing sad-coloured wings; but she needs a man's care—you are frail, you cannot live for ever—and how is it to be with her and her child?'

'I hope to bestow them among her kindred ere I die, Madame,' said Isaac.

'No kindred can serve a woman like a sensible husband! Besides, I thought all perished at Paris. Listen, Isaac Gardon: I tell you plainly that scandal is afloat. You are blamed for culpable indifference to alleged levities—I say not that it is true—but I see this, that unless you can bestow your daughter-in-law on a good, honest man, able to silence the whispers of malice, there will be measures taken that will do shame both to your own gray hairs and to the memory of your dead son, as well as expose the poor young woman herself. You are one who has a true tongue, Isaac Gardon; and if you can assure me that she is a faithful, good woman, as poor Mace thinks her, and will give her to him in testimony thereof, then shall not a mouth open against her. If not, in spite of all my esteem for you, the discipline of the Reformed must take its course.'

'And for what?' said Isaac, with a grave tone, almost of reproof. 'What discipline can punish a woman for letting her infant wear a coloured ribbon, and shielding it from a blow?'

'That is not all, Master Isaac,' said the Duchess, seriously. 'In spite of your much-respected name, evil and censorious tongues will have it that matters ought to be investigated; that there is some mystery; that the young woman does not give a satisfactory account of herself, and that the child does not resemble either her or your son—in short, that you may be deceived by an impostor, perhaps a Catholic spy. Mind, I say not that I credit all this, only I would show you what reports you must guard against.'

'*La pauvre petite!*' said Isaac, under his breath, as if appalled; then collecting himself, he said, 'Madame, these are well-nigh threats. I had come hither nearly resolved to confined in you without them.'

'Then there is a mystery?'

'Yes, Madame, but the deception is solely in the name. She is, in very truth, a widow of a martyr of the St. Barthelemy, but that martyr was not my son, whose wife was happy in dying with him.'

'And who, then, is she?'

'Madame la Duchesse had heard of the family of Ribaumont.'

'Ha! M. de Ribaumont! A gay comrade of King Henry II., but who had his eyes opened to the truth by M. l'Amiral, though he lacked courage for an open profession. Yes, the very last pageant I beheld at court, was the wedding of his little son to the Count de Ribaumont's daughter. It was said that the youth was one of our victims at Paris.'

'Even so, Madame; and this poor child is the little one whom you saw wedded to him.' And then, in answer to the Duchess's astonished inquiry, he proceeded to relate how Eustacie had been forced to fly from her kindred, and how he had first encountered her at his own lurking-placed, and had accepted her as a charge imposed on him by Providence; then explained how, at La Sablerie, she had been recognized by a young gentleman whom she had known at Paris, but who professed to be fleeing to England, there to study the Protestant controversy; and how she had confided to him a letter to her husband's mother, who was married in England, begging her to send for her and her daughter, the latter being heiress to certain English estates, as well as French.

'Madame,' added Gardon, 'Heaven forgive me, if I do the Youth injustice by suspecting him, but no answer ever arrived to that letter; and while we still expected one, a good and kindly citizen, who I trust has long been received into glory, sent me notice that a detachment of Monsieur's army was on its way from La Rochelle, under command of M. de Nid de Merle, to search out this poor lady in La Sablerie. He, good man, deemed that, were we gone, he could make terms for the place, and we therefore quitted it. Alas! Madame knows how it fared with the pious friend we left. Little deeming how they would be dealt with, we took our way along the Sables d'Olonne, where alone we could be safe, since, as Madame knows, they are for miles impracticable for troops. But we had another enemy there—the tide; and there was a time when we truly deemed that the mercy granted us had been that we had fallen into the hand of the Lord instead of the hand of cruel man. Yes, Madame, and even for that did she give thanks, as she stood, never even trembling, on the low sandbank, with her babe in her bosom, and the sea creeping up on all sides. She only turned to me with a smile, saying, 'She is asleep, she will not feel it, or know anything till she wakes up in Paradise, and sees her father.' Never saw I a woman, either through nature or grace, so devoid of fear. We were rescued at last, by the mercy of Heaven, which sent a fisherman, who bore us to his boat when benumbed with cold, and scarce able to move. He took us to a good priest's, Colombeau of Nissard, a man who, as Madame may know, is one of those veritable saints who still are sustained by the truth within their Church, and is full of charity and mercy. He asked me no questions, but fed, warmed, sheltered us, and sped us on our way. Perhaps, however, I was over-confident in myself, as the guardian of the poor child, for it was Heaven's will that the cold and wet of our night on the sands—though those tender young frames did not suffer therefrom—should bring on an illness which has made an old man of me. I struggled on as long as I could, hoping to attain to a safe resting-place for her, but the winter cold completed the work; and then, Madame—oh that I could tell you the blessing she was to me!—her patience, her watchfulness, her tenderness, through all the long weeks that I lay helpless alike in mind and body at Charente. Ah! Madame, had my own daughter lived, she could not have been more to me than that noble lady; and her cheerful love did even more for me than her tender care.'

'I must see her,' ejaculated the Duchesse; then added, 'But was it this illness that hindered you from placing her in safety in England?'

'In part, Madame; nay, I may say, wholly. We learnt that the assembly was to take place here, and I had my poor testimony to deliver, and to give notice of my intention to my brethren before going to a foreign land, whence perhaps I may never return.'

'She ought to be in England,' said Madame de Quinet; 'she will never be safe from these kinsmen in this country.'

'M. de Nid de Merle has been all the spring in Poland with the King,' said the minister, 'and the poor lady is thought to have perished at La Sablerie. Thus the danger has been less pressing, but I would have taken her to England at once, if I could have made sure of her reception, and besides——' he faltered.

'The means?' demanded the Duchess, guessing at the meaning.

'Madame is right. She had brought away some money and jewels with her, but alas, Madame, during my illness, without my knowledge, the dear child absolutely sold them to procure comforts for me. Nay'—his eyes filled with tears—'she whom they blame for vanities sold the very hair from her head to purchase unguents to ease the old man's pains; nor did I know it for many a day after. From day to day we can live, for our own people willingly support a pastor and his family; and in every house my daughter has been loved,—everywhere but in this harsh-judging town. But for the expense of a voyage, even were we at Bordeaux or La Rochelle, we have nothing, save by parting with the only jewels that remain to her, and those—those, she says, are heirlooms; and, poor child, she guards them almost as jealously as her infant, around whom she has fastened them beneath her clothes. She will not even as yet hear of leaving them in pledge, to be redeemed by the family. She says they would hardly know her without them. And truly, Madame, I scarce venture to take her to England, ere I know what reception would await her. Should her husband's family disown or cast her off, I could take better care of her here than in a strange land.'

'You are right, Maitre Gardon,' said the Duchess; 'the risk might be great. I would see this lady. She must be a rare creature. Bear her my greetings, my friend, and pray her to do me the honour of a visit this afternoon. Tell her I would come myself to her, but that I understand she does not wish to attract notice.'

'Madame,' said Isaac, rising, and with a strange manner, between a smile and a tear of earnestness, 'allow me to bespeak your goodness for my daughter. The poor little thing is scarcely more than a child. She is but eighteen even now, and it is not always easy to tell whether she will be an angel of noble goodness, or, pardon me, a half-petulant child.'

'I understand:' Madame de Quinet laughed, and she probably did understand more than reluctant, anxious Isaac Gardon thought she did, of his winning, gracious, yet haughty, head-strong little charge, so humbly helpful one moment, so self-asserting and childish the next, so dear to him, yet so unlike anything in his experience.

'Child,' he said, as he found her in the sunny window engaged in plaiting the deep folds of his starched ruffs, 'you have something to forgive me.'

'Fathers do not ask their children's pardon,' said Eustacie, brightly, but then, with sudden dismay, 'Ah! you have not said I should go to the Moustier again.'

'No, daughter; but Madame de Quinet entreats—these are her words—that you will do her the honour of calling on her. She would come to you, but that she fears to attract notice to us.'

'You have told her!' exclaimed Eustacie.

'I was compelled, but I had already thought of asking your consent, and she is a true and generous lady, with whom your secret will be safe, and who can hush the idle tongues here. So, daughter,' he added restlessly, 'don your hood; that ruff will serve for another day.'

'Another day, when the morrow is Sunday, and my father's ruff is to put to shame all the other pastors',' said Eustacie, her quick fingers still moving. 'No, he shall not go ill-starched for any Duchess in France. Now am I in any haste to be lectured by Madame de Quinet, as they say she lectured the Dame de Soubrera the other day.'

'My child, you will go; much depends on it.'

'Oh yes, I am going; only if Madame de Quinet knows who I am, she will not expect me to hurry at her beck and call the first moment. Here, Rayonette, my bird, my beauty, thou must have a clean cap; ay, and these flaxen curls combed.'

'Would you take the child?'

'Would I go without Mademoiselle de Rambouillet? She is all her mother is, and more. There, now she is a true rose-bud, ready to perch on my arm. No, no *bon pere*. So great a girl is too much for you to carry. Don't be afraid, my darling, we are not going to a sermon, no one will beat her; oh no, and if the insolent retainers and pert lacqueys laugh at her mother, no one will hurt her.'

'Nay, child,' said Maitre Gardon; 'this is a well-ordered household, where contempt and scorn are not suffered. Only, dear, dear daughter, let me pray you to be your true self with the Duchess.'

Eustacie shrugged her shoulders, and had mischief enough in her to enjoy keeping her good father in some doubt and dread as he went halting wearily by her side along the much-decorated streets that marked the grand Gasche of Tarn and Tarascon. The Hotel de Quinet stretched out its broad stone steps, covered with vaultings, absolutely across the street, affording a welcome shade, and no obstruction where wheeled carriages never came.

All was, as Maitre Isaac had said, decorum itself. A couple of armed retainers, rigid as sentinels, waited on the steps; a grave porter, maimed in the wars opened the great door; half a dozen—*laquais* in sober though rich liveries sat on a bench in the hall, and had somewhat the air of having been set to con a lesson. Two of them coming respectfully forward, ushered Maitre Gardon and his companion to an ante-room, where various gentlemen, or pastors, or candidates—among them Samuel Mace—were awaiting a summons to the Duchess, or merely using it as a place of assembly. A page of high birth, but well schooled in steadiness of demeanour, went at once to announce the arrival; and Gardon and his companion had not been many moments in conversation with their acquaintance among the ministers, before the grave gentleman returned, apparently from his audience and the page, coming to Eustacie, intimated that she was to follow him to Madame le Duchesse's presence.

He conducted her across a great tapestry-hung saloon, where twelve or fourteen ladies of all ages—from seventy to fifteen—sat at work: some at tapestry, some spinning, some making coarse garments for the poor. A great throne-like chair, with a canopy over it, a footstool, a desk and a small table before it, was vacant, and the work—a poor child's knitted cap—laid down; but an elderly minister, seated at a carved desk, had not discontinued reading from a great black book, and did not even cease while the strangers crossed the room, merely making a slight inclination with his head, while the ladies half rose, rustled a slight reverence with their black, gray or russet skirts, but hardly lifted their eyes. Eustacie thought the Louvre had never been half so formidable or impressive.

The page lifted a heavy green curtain behind the canopy, knocked at a door, and, as it opened, Eustacie was conscious of a dignified presence, that, in spite of her previous petulance, caused her instinctively to bend in such a reverence as had formerly been natural to her; but, at the same moment, a low and magnificent curtsey was made to her, a hand was held out, a stately kiss was on her brow, and a voice of dignified courtesy said, 'Pardon me, Madame la Baronne, for giving you this trouble. I feared that otherwise we could not safely meet.'

'Madame is very good. My Rayonette, make thy reverence; kiss thy hand to the lady, my lamb.' And the little one obeyed, gazing with her blue eyes full opened, and clinging to her mother.

'Ah! Madame la Baronne makes herself obeyed,' said Madame de Quinet, well pleased. 'Is it then a girl?'

'Yes, Madame, I could scarcely forgive her at first; but she has made herself all the dearer to me.'

'It is a pity,' said Madame de Quinet, 'for yours is an ancient stem.'

'Did Madame know my parents?' asked Eustacie, drawn from her spirit of defiance by the equality of the manner with which she was treated.

'Scarcely,' replied the Duchess; but, with a smile, 'I had the honour to see you married.'

'Ah, then,'—Eustacie glowed, almost smiled, though a tear was in her eyes—'you can see how like my little one is to her father,—a true White Ribaumont.'

The Duchess had not the most distinct recollection of the complexion of the little bridegroom; but Rayonette's fairness was incontestable, and the old lady complimented it so as to draw on the young mother into confidence on the pet moonbeam appellation which she used in dread of exciting suspicion by using the true name of Berangere, with all the why and wherefore.

It was what the Duchess wanted. Imperious as some thought her, she would on no account have appeared to cross-examine any one whose essential nobleness of nature struck her as did little Eustacie's at the first moment she saw her; and yet she had decided, before the young woman arrived, that her own good opinion and assistance should depend on the correspondence of Madame de Ribaumont's history of herself with Maitre Gardon's.

Eustacie had, for a year and a half, lived with peasants; and, indeed, since the trials of her life had really begun, she had never been with a woman of her own station to whom she could give confidence, or from whom she could look for sympathy. And thus a very few inquiries and tokens of interest from the old lady drew out the whole story, and more than once filled Madame de Quinet's eyes with tears.

There was only one discrepancy; Eustacie could not believe that the Abbe de Mericour had been a faithless messenger. Oh, no! either those savage-looking sailors had played him false, or else her *bele-mere* would not send for her. 'My mother-in-law never loved me,' said Eustacie; 'I know she never did. And now she has children by her second marriage, and no doubt would not see my little one preferred to them. I will not be HER suppliant.'

'And what then would you do?' said Madame de Quinet, with a more severe tone.

'Never leave my dear father,' said Eustacie, with a flash of eagerness; 'Maitre Isaac I mean. He has been more to me than any—any one I ever knew—save——'

'You have much cause for gratitude to him,' said Madame de Quinet. 'I honour your filial love to him. Yet, you have duties to this little one. You have no right to keep her from her position. You ought to write to England again. I am sure Maitre Isaac tells you so.'

Eustacie would have pouted, but the grave, kind authority of the manner prevented her from being childish, and she said, 'If I wrote, it should be to my husband's grandfather, who brought him up, designated him as his heir, and whom he loved with all his heart. But, oh, Madame, he has one of those English names! So dreadful! It sounds like Vol-au-vent, but it is not that precisely.'

Madame de Quinet smiled, but she was a woman of resources. 'See, my friend,' she said, 'the pursuivant of the consuls here has the rolls of the herald's visitations throughout the kingdom. The arms and name of the Baron de Ribaumont's wife will there be entered; and from my house at Quinet you shall write, and I, too, will write; my son shall take care that the letters be forwarded safely, and you shall await their arrival under my protection. That will be more fitting than running the country with an old pastor, *hein?*'

'Madame, nothing shall induce me to quit him!' exclaimed Eustacie, vehemently.

'Hear me out, child,' said the Duchess. 'He goes with us to assist my chaplain; he is not much fitter for wandering than you, or less so. And you, Madame, must, I fear me, still remain his daughter-in-law in my household; or if you bore your own name and rank, this uncle and cousin of yours might learn that you were still living; and did they claim you——'

'Oh, Madame, rather let me be your meanest kitchen-girl!'

'To be—what do they call you?—Esperance Gardon will be quite enough. I have various women here—widows, wives, daughters or sufferers for the truth's sake, who either are glad of rest, or are trained up to lead a godly life in the discipline of my household. Among them you can live without suspicion, provided,' the old lady added, smiling, 'you can abstain from turning the heads of our poor young candidates.'

'Madame,' said Eustacie, gravely, 'I shall never turn any one's head. There was only one who was obliged to love me, and happily I am nor fair enough to win any one else.'

'*Tenez*, child. Is this true simplicity? Did Gardon, truly, never tell you of poor Samuel Mace?'

Eustacie's face expressed such genuine amazement and consternation, that the Duchess could not help touching her on the cheek, and saying, 'Ah! simple as a *pensionnaire*, as we used to say when no one else was innocent. But it is true, my dear, that to poor Samuel we owe our meeting. I will send him off, the poor fellow, at once to Bourge-le-Roy to preach his three sermons; and when they had driven you a little out of his head, he shall have Mariette there—a good girl, who will make him an excellent wife. She is ugly enough, but it will be all the same to him just then! I will see him, and let him know that I have reasons. He lodges in your house, does he? Then you had better come to see me at once. So will evil tongues best be silenced.

'But hold,' the Duchess said, smiling. 'You will think me a foolish old woman, but is it true that you have saved the Pearls of Ribaumont, of which good Canon Froissart tells?'

Eustacie lifted her child on her knee, untied the little gray frock, and showed them fastened beneath, well out of sight. 'I thought my treasures should guard one another,' she said. 'One I sent as a token to my mother-in-law. For the rest, they are not mine, but hers; her father lent them to me, not gave: so she wears them thus; and anything but HER life should go rather than THEY should.'

'*Hein*, a fine guardian for them!' was all the Duchess said in answer.

CHAPTER XXXV
THE ITALIAN PEDLAR

This caitiff monk for gold did swear,

That by his drugs my rival fair

A saint in heaven should be.—SCOTT

A grand cavalcade bore the house of Quinet from Montauban—coaches, wagons, outriders, gendarmes—it was a perfect court progress, and so low and cumbrous that it was a whole week in reaching a grand old castle standing on a hill-side among chestnut woods, with an avenue a mile long leading up to it; and battlemented towers fit to stand a siege.

Eustacie was ranked among the Duchess's gentlewomen. She was so far acknowledged as a lady of birth, that she was usually called Madame Esperance; and though no one was supposed to doubt her being Theodore Gardon's widow, she was regarded as being a person of rank who had made a misalliance by marrying him. This Madame de Quinet had allowed the household to infer, thinking that the whole bearing of her guest was too unlike that of a Paris *bourgeoise* not to excite suspicion, but she deemed it wiser to refrain from treating her with either intimacy or distinction that might excite jealousy or suspicion. Even as it was, the consciousness of a secret, or the remnants of Montauban gossip, prevented any familiarity between Eustacie and the good ladies who surrounded her; they were very civil to each other, but their only connecting link was the delight that every one took in petting pretty little Rayonette, and the wonder that was made of her signs of intelligence and attempts at talking. Even when she toddled fearlessly up to the stately Duchess on her canopied throne, and held out her entreating hands, and lisped the word '*nontre*,' Madame would pause in her avocations, take her on her knee, and display that wonderful gold and enamel creature which cried tic-tic, and still remained an unapproachable mystery to M. le Marquis and M. le Vicomte, her grandsons.

Pale, formal stiff boys they looked, twelve and ten years old, and under the dominion of a very learned tutor, who taught them Latin, Greek and Hebrew, alternately with an equally precise, stiff old esquire, who trained them in martial exercises, which seemed to be as much matters of rote with them as their tasks, and to be quite as uninteresting. It did not seem as if they ever played, or thought of playing; and if they were ever to be gay, witty Frenchmen, a wonderful change must come over them.

The elder was already betrothed to a Bearnese damsel, of an unimpeachably ancient and Calvinistic family; and the whole establishment had for the last three years been employed on tapestry hangings for a whole suite of rooms, that were to be fitted up and hung with the histories of Ruth, of Abigail, of the Shunammite, and of Esther, which their diligent needles might hope to complete by the time the marriage should take place, three years later! The Duchess, who really was not unlike 'that great woman' the Shunammite, in her dignified content with 'dwelling among her own people,' and her desire to 'receive a prophet in the name of a prophet,' generally sat presiding over the work while some one, chaplain, grandson, or young maiden, read aloud from carefully assorted books; religious treatises at certain hours, and at others, history. Often, however, Madame was called away into her cabinet, where she gave audience to intendants, notaries from her estates, pastors from the villages, captains of little garrisons, soldiers offering service, farmers, women, shepherds, foresters, peasants, who came either on her business or with their own needs—for all of which she was ready with the beneficence and decision of an autocrat.

The chapel had been 'purified,' and made bare of all altar or image. It was filled with benches and a desk, whence Isaac Gardon, the chaplain, any pastor on a visit, or sometimes a candidate for his promotion, would expound, and offer prayers, shortly in the week, more at length on Sunday; and there, too, classes were held for the instruction of the peasants.

There was a great garden full of medicinal plants, and decoctions and distilleries were the chief variety enjoyed by the gentlewomen. The Duchess had studied much in quaint Latin and French medical books, and, having great experience and good sense, was probably as good a doctor as any one in the kingdom except Ambroise Pare and his pupils; and she required her ladies to practise under her upon the numerous ailments that the peasants were continually bringing for her treatment. 'No one could tell,' she said, 'how soon they might be dealing with gun-shot wounds, and all ought to know how to sew up a gash, or cure an argue.'

This department suited Eustacie much better than the stitching, and best of all she liked to be sent with Maitre Isaac to some cottage where solace for soul and body were needed, and the inmate was too ill to be brought to Madame la Duchess. She was learning much and improving too in the orderly household, but her wanderings had made her something of a little gipsy. She now and then was intolerably weary, and felt as if she had been entirely spoilt for her natural post. 'What would become of her,' she said to Maitre Isaac, 'if she were too grand to dress Rayonette?'

She was not greatly distressed that the Montauban pursuivant turned out to have only the records of the Provencal nobility, and was forced to communicate with his brethren at Bordeaux before he could bring down the Ribaumont genealogy to the actual generation; and so slow was communication, so tardy the mode of doing everything, that the chestnut leaves were falling and autumn becoming winter before the blazoned letter showed Ribaumont, de Picardie—'Gules, fretty or, a canton of the last, a leopard, sable. Eustacie Berangere, m. Annora, daughter and heiress of Villiam, Baron of Valvem, in the county of Dorisette, England, who beareth, azure, a siren regardant in a mirror proper.' The siren was drawn in all her propriety impaled with the leopard, and she was so much more comprehensible than the names, to both Madame de Quinet and Eustacie, that it was a pity they could not direct their letters to her rather than to 'Le Baron de Valvem,' whose cruel W's perplexed them so much. However, the address was the least of Eustacie's troubles; she should be only too glad when she got to that, and she was sitting in Maitre Isaac's room, trying to make him dictate her sentences and asking him how to spell every third word, when the dinner-bell rang, and the whole household dropped down from *salon*, library, study, or chamber to the huge hall, with its pavement of black and white marble, and its long tables, for Madame de Quinet was no woman to discard wholesome old practices.

Then, as Eustacie, with Rayonette trotting at her side, and Maitre Isaac leaning on her arm, slowly made her way to that high table where dined Madame la Duchess, her grandsons, the ministers, the gentlemen in waiting, and some three or four women besides herself, she saw that the lower end of the great hall was full of silks, cloths, and ribbons heaped together; and, passing by the lengthy rank of retainers, she received a bow and look of recognition from a dark, acute-looking visage which she remembered to belong to the pedlar she had met at Charente.

The Duchess, at the head of her table, was not in the best of humours. Her son had sent home letters by a courier whom he had picked up for himself and she never liked nor trusted, and he required an immediate reply when she particularly resented being hurried. It was a *galimafre*, literally a hash, she said; for indeed most matters where she was not consulted did become a *galimafre* with her. Moreover, under favour of the courier, her porters had admitted this pedlar, and the Duchess greatly disliked pedlars. All her household stores were bought at shops of good repute in Montauban, and no one ought to be so improvident as to require dealings with these mountebank vagabonds, who dangled vanities before the eyes of silly girls, and filled their heads with Paris fashion, if they did not do still worse, and excite them to the purchase of cosmetics and love-charms.

Yet the excitement caused by the approach of a pedlar was invincible, even by Madame la Duchess. It was inevitable that the crying need of glove, kerchief, needle, or the like, should be discovered as soon as he came within ken, and, once in the hall, there was no being rid of him except by a flagrant act of inhospitality. This time it was worst of all, for M. le Marquis himself must needs be the first to spy him, bring him in, and be in want of a silver chain for his hawk; and his brother the Vicomte must follow him up with all manner of wants inspired by the mere sight of the pack.

Every one with the smallest sum of money must buy, every one without inspect and assist in bargaining; and all dinner-time, eyes, thoughts, and words were wandering to the gay pile in the corner, or reckoning up needs and means. The pedlar, too, knew what a Calvinist household was, and had been extremely discreet, producing nothing that could reasonably be objected to; and the Duchess, seeing that the stream was too strong for her, wisely tried to steer her bark through it safely instead of directly opposing it.

As soon as grace was over, she called her maitre d'hotel, and bade him look after that *galimafre*, and see that none of these fools were unreasonably cheated, and that there was no attempt at gulling the young ones with charms or fortune-telling, as well as to conclude the matter so as to give no excuse for the Italian fellow lingering to sup and sleep. She then retired to her cabinet to prepare her dispatches, which were to include a letter to Lord Walwyn. Though a nominal friendship subsisted between Elisabeth and the French court, the Huguenot chiefs always maintained a correspondence with England, and there was little danger but that the Duke de Quinet would be able to get a letter, sooner or later, conveyed to any man of mark. In the course of her letter, Madame de Quinet found it necessary to refer to Eustacie. She rang her little silver handbell for the hall. There, of course, Master Page had been engulfed in the *galimafre*, and not only forming one of the swarm around the pedlar, but was actually aping courtly grimaces as he tried a delicate lace ruffle on the hand of a silly little smirking maiden, no older than himself! But this little episode was, like many others, overlooked by Madame de Quinet, as her eye fell upon the little figure of Rayonette standing on the table, with her mother and two or three ladies besides coaxing her to open her mouth, and show the swollen gums that had of late been troubling her, while the pedlar was evidently expending his blandishments upon her.

The maitre d'hotel was the first to perceive his mistress, and, as he approached, received a sharp rebuke from her for allowing the fellow to produce his quack medicines; and, at the same time, she desired him to request Madame Esperance to come to her immediately on business. Eustacie, who always had a certain self-willed sense of opposition when the Duchess showed herself peremptory towards her, at first began to make answer that she would come as soon as her business was concluded; but the steward made a gesture towards the great lady sailing up and down as she paced the *dais* in stately impatience. 'Good fellow,' she said, 'I will return quickly, and see you again, though I am now interrupted. Stay there, little one, with good Mademoiselle Perrot; mother will soon be back.'

Rayonette, in her tooth-fretfulnes, was far from enduring to be forsaken so near a strange man, and her cry made it necessary for Eustacie to take her in arms, and carry her to the *dais* where the Duchess was waiting.

'So!' said the lady, 'I suspected that the fellow was a quack as well as a cheat.'

'Madame,' said Eustacie, with spirit, 'he sold me unguents that greatly relieved my father last spring.'

'And because rubbing relieved an old man's rheumatics, you would let a vagabond cheat drug and sicken this poor child for what is not ailment at all—and the teeth will relieve in a few days. Or, if she were feverish, have not we decoctions brewed from Heaven's own pure herbs in the garden, with no unknown ingredient?'

'Madame,' said Eustacie, ruffling into fierceness, 'you are very good to me; but I must keep the management of my daughter to myself.'

The Duchess looked at her from head to foot. Perhaps it was with an impulse to treat her impertinence as she would have done that of a dependant; but the old lady never forgot herself: she only shrugged her shoulders and said, with studied politeness, 'When I unfortunately interrupted your consultation with this eminent physician, it was to ask you a question regarding this English family. Will you do me the honour to enter my cabinet?'

And whereas no one was looking, the old lady showed her displeasure by ushering Madame de Ribaumont into her cabinet like a true noble stranger guest; so that Eustacie felt disconcerted.

The Duchess then began to read aloud her own letter to Lord Walwyn, pausing at every clause, so that Eustacie felt the delay and discussion growing interminable, and the Duchess then requested to have Madame de Ribaumont's own letter at once, as she wished to inclose it, make up her packet, and send it without delay. Opening a secret door in her cabinet, she showed Eustacie stair by which she might reach Maitre Gardon's room without crossing the hall. Eustacie hoped to find him there and tell him how intolerable was the Duchess; but, though she found him, it was in company with the tutor, who was spending an afternoon on Plato with him. She could only take up her letter and retreat to Madame's cabinet, where she had left her child. She finished it as best she might, addressed it after the herald's spelling of the title, bound it with some of the Duchess's black

- 319 -

floss silk—wondering meanwhile, but little guessing that the pedlar knew, where was the tress that had bound her last attempt at correspondence, guessing least of all that that tress lay on a heart still living and throbbing for her. All this had made her a little forget her haste to assert her liberty of action by returning to the pedlar; but, behold, when she came back to the hall, it had resumed its pristine soberness, and merely a few lingering figures were to be seen, packing up their purchases.

While she was still looking round in dismay, Mademoiselle Perrot came up to her and said, 'Ah! Madame, you may well wonder! I never saw Maitre Benoit there so cross; the poor man did but offer to sell little Fanchon the elizir that secures a good husband, and old Benoit descended on him like a griffin enraged, would scarce give him time to compute his charges or pack his wares, but hustled him forth like a mere thief! And I missed my bargain for that muffler that had so taken my fancy. But, Madame, he spoke to me apart, and said you were an old customer of his, and that rather than the little angel should suffer with her teeth, which surely threaten convulsions, he would leave with you this sovereign remedy of sweet syrup—a spoonful to be given each night.'

Eustacie took the little flask. She was much inclined to give the syrup by way of precaution, as well as to assure herself that she was not under the Duchess's dominion; but some strong instinct of the truth of the lady's words that the child was safer and healthier undoctored, made her resolve at least to defer it until the little one showed any perilous symptom. And as happily Rayonette only showed two little white teeth, and much greater good-humour, the syrup was nearly forgotten, when, a fortnight after, the Duchess received a dispatch from her son which filled her with the utmost indignation. The courier had indeed arrived, but the packet had proved to be filled with hay and waste-paper. And upon close examination, under the lash, the courier had been forced to confess to having allowed himself to be overtaken by the pedlar, and treated by him to a supper at a *cabaret*. No doubt, while he was afterwards asleep, the contents of his packet had been abstracted. There had been important documents for the Duke besides Eustacie's letters, and the affair greatly annoyed the Duchess, though she had the compensation of having been proved perfectly right in her prejudice against pedlars, and her dislike of her son's courier. She sent for Eustacie to tell her privately of the loss, and of course the young mother at once turned pale and exclaimed, 'The wicked one! Ah! what a blessing that I gave my little darling none of his dose!'

'*Hein*? You had some from him then!' demanded the Duchess with displeasure.

'No, Madame, thanks, thanks to you. Oh! I never will be self-willed and naughty again. Forgive me, Madame.' And down she dropped on her knee, with clasped hands and glistening eyes.

'Forgive you, silly child, for what?' said Madame de Quinet, nearly laughing.

'Ah! for the angry, passionate thoughts I had! Ah! Madame, I was all but giving the stuff to my little angel in very spite—and then——' Eutacie's voice was drowned in passion of tears, and she devoured the old lady's hand with her kisses.

'Come, come,' said the Duchess, 'let us be reasonable. A man may be a thief, but it does not follow that he is a poisoner.'

'Nay, that will we see,' cried Eutacie. 'He was resolved that the little lamb should not escape, and he left a flask for her with Mademoiselle Perrot. I will fetch it, if Madame will give me leave. Oh, the great mercy of Heaven that made her so well that I gave her none!'

Madame de Quinet's analytic powers did not go very far; and would probably have decided against the syrup if it had been nothing but virgin honey. She was one who fully believed that her dear Queen Jeanne had been poisoned with a pair of gloves, and she had unlimited faith in the powers of evil possessed by Rene of Milan. Of course, she detected the presence of a slow poison, whose effects would have been attributed to the ailment it was meant to cure; and though her evidence was insufficient, she probably did Ercole no injustice. She declined testing the compound on any unfortunate dog or cat, but sealed it up in the presence of Gardon, Eutacie, and Mademoiselle Perrot, to be produced against the pedlar if ever he should be caught.

Then she asked Eutacie if there was any reason to suspect that he recognized her. Eutacie related the former dealings with him, when she had sold him her jewels and her hair, but she had no notion of his being the same person whom she had seen when at Montpipeau. Indeed, he had altered his appearance so much that he had been only discovered at Nid-de-Merle by eyes sharpened by distrust of his pretensions to magic arts.

Madame de Quinet, however, concluded that Eutacie had been known, or else that her jewels had betrayed her, and that the man must have been employed by her enemies. If it had not been the depth of winter, she would have provided for the persecuted lady's immediate transmission to England; but he storms of the Bay of Biscay would have made this impossible in the state of French navigation, even if Isaac Gardon had been in a condition to move; for the first return of cold had brought back severe rheumatic pains, and with them came a shortness of breath which even the Duchess did not know to be the token of heart complaint. He was confined to his room, and it was kneeling by his bedside that Eutacie poured out her thankfulness for her child's preservation, and her own repentance for the passing fit of self-will and petulance. The thought of Rayonette's safety seemed absolutely to extinguish the fresh anxiety that had arisen since it had become evident that her enemies no longer supposed her dead, but were probably upon her traces. Somehow, danger had become almost a natural element to her, and having once expressed her firm resolution that nothing should separate her from her adopted father, to whom indeed her care became constantly more necessary, she seemed to occupy herself very little with the matter; she nursed him as merrily as ever, and left to him and Madame de Quinet the grave consultations as to what was to be done for her security. There was a sort of natural buoyancy about her that never realized a danger till it came, and then her spirit was roused to meet it.

CHAPTER XXXVI
SPELL AND POTION

Churl, upon thy eyes I throw

All the power this charm doth owe

MIDSUMMER NIGHT'S DREAM

Her rival lived! The tidings could not but be communicated to Diane de Selinville, when her father set out *en grande tenue* to demand his niece from the Duke de Quinet. This, however, was not till spring was advancing; for the pedlar had not been able to take a direct route back to Nid-de-Merle, since his first measure had necessarily been to escape into a province where the abstraction of a Huguenot nobleman's despatches would be considered as a meritorious action. Winter weather, and the practice of his profession likewise, delayed Ercole so much that it was nearly Easter before he brought his certain intelligence to the Chevalier, and to the lady an elixir of love, clear and coloured as crystal, and infallible as an inspirer of affection.

Should she administer it, now that she knew her cousin not to be the lawful object of affection she had so long esteemed him, but, as he persisted in considering himself, a married man? Diane had more scruples than she would have had a year before, for she had not so long watched and loved one so true and conscientious as Berenger de Ribaumont without having her perceptions elevated; but at the same time the passion of love had become intensified, both by long continuance and by resistance. She had attached herself, believing him free, and her affections could not be disentangled by learning that he was bound—rather the contrary.

Besides, there was plenty of sophistry. Her father had always assured her of the invalidity of the marriage, without thinking it necessary to dwell on his own arrangements for making it invalid, so that was no reasonable ground of objection; and a lady of Diane's period, living in the world where she had lived, would have had no notion of objecting to her lover for a previous amour, and as such was she bidden to rank Berenger's relations with Eutacie. And there was the less scruple on Eutacie's account, because the Chevalier, knowing that the Duchess had a son and two grandsons, had conceived a great terror that she meant to give his niece to one of them; and this would be infinitely worse, both for the interests of the family and of their party, than even her reunion with the young Baron. Even Narcisse, who on his return had written to Paris a grudging consent to the experiment of his father and sister, had allowed that the preservation of

Berenger's life was needful till Eutacie should be in their power so as to prevent such a marriage as that! To Diane, the very suggestion became certainty: she already saw Eutacie's shallow little heart consoled and her vanity excited by these magnificent prospects, and she looked forward to the triumph of her own constancy, when Berenger should find the image so long enshrined in his heart crumble in its sacred niche.

Yet a little while then would she be patient, even though nearly a year had passed and still she saw no effect upon her prisoners, unless, indeed, Philip had drunk of one of her potions by mistake and his clumsy admiration was the consequence. The two youths went on exactly in the same manner, without a complaint, without a request, occupying themselves as best they might—Berenger courteously attentive recovered his health, and the athletic powers displayed by the two brothers when wrestling, fencing, or snow-balling in the courtyard, were the amazement and envy of their guard. Twice in the course of the winter there had been an alarm of wolves, and in their eagerness and excitement about this new sport, they had accepted the Chevalier's offer of taking their parole for the hunt. They had then gone forth with a huge posse of villagers, who beat the woods with their dogs till the beast was aroused from its lair and driven into the alleys, where waited gentlemen, gendarmes, and game keepers with their guns. These two chases were chiefly memorable to Berenger, because in the universal intermingling of shouting peasants he was able in the first to have some conversation with Eutacie's faithful protector Martin, who told him the incidents of her wanderings, with tears in his eyes, and blessed him for his faith that she was not dead; and in the second, he actually found himself in the ravine of the Grange du Temple. No need to ask, every voice was shouting the name, and though the gendarmes were round him and he durst not speak to Rotrou, still he could reply with significative earnestness to the low bow with which the farmer bent to evident certainty that here was the imprisoned Protestant husband of the poor lady. Berenger wore his black vizard mask as had been required of him, but the man's eyes followed him, as though learning by heart the outline of his tall figure. The object of the Chevalier's journey was, of course, a secret from the prisoners, who merely felt its effects by having their meals served to them in their own tower; and when he returned after about a month's absence though him looking harassed, aged, and so much out of humour that he could scarcely preserve his usual politeness. In effect he was greatly chagrined.

'That she is in their hands is certain, the hypocrites!' he said to his daughter and sister; 'and no less so that they have designs on her; but I let them know that these could be easily traversed.'

'But where is she, the unhappy apostate child?' said the Abbess. 'They durst not refuse her to you.'

'I tell you they denied all present knowledge of her. The Duke himself had the face to make as though he never heard of her. He had no concern with his mother's household and guests forsooth! I do not believe he has; the poor fellow stands in awe of that terrible old heretic dragon, and keeps aloof from her as much as he can. But he is, after all, a *beau jeune home*; nor should I be surprised if he were the girl's gay bridegroom by this time, though I gave him a hint that there was an entanglement about the child's first marriage which, by French law, would invalidate any other without a dispensation from the Pope.'

'A hard nut that for a heretic,' laughed the Abbess.

'He acted the ignorant—knew nothing about the young lady; but had the civility to give me a guide and an escort to go to Quinet. *Ma foi!* I believe they were given to hinder me—take me by indirect roads, make me lose time at chateaux. When I arrived at the grim old chateau—a true dungeon, precise as a convent—there was the dame, playing the Queen Jeanne as well as she could, and having the insolence to tell me that it was true that Madame la Baronne de Ribaumont, as she was pleased to call her, had honoured her residence for some months, but that she had now quitted it, and she flatly refused to answer any question whither she was gone! The hag! she might at least have had the decorum to deny all knowledge of her, but nothing is more impertinent that the hypocritical sincerity of the heretics.'

'But her people,' exclaimed the Abbess; 'surely some of them knew, and could be brought to speak.'

'All the servants I came in contact with played the incorruptible; but still I have done something. There were some fellows in the village who are not at their ease under that rule. I caused my people to inquire them out. They knew nothing more than that the old heretic Gardon with his family had gone away in Madame la Duchesse's litter, but whither they could not tell. But the *cabaretier* there is furious secretly with the Quinets for having spoilt his trade by destroying the shrine at the holy well, and I have made him understand that it will be for his profit to send me off intelligence so soon as there is any communication between them and the lady. I made the same arrangement with a couple of gendarmes of the escort the Duke gave me. So at least we are safe for intelligence such as would hinder a marriage.'

'But they will be off to England!' said the Abbess.

'I wager they will again write to make sure of a reception. Moreover, I have set that fellow Ercole and others of his trade to keep a strict watch on all the roads leading to the ports, and give me due notice of their passing thither. We have law on our side, and, did I once claim her, no one could resist my right. Or should the war break out, as is probable, then could my son sweep their whole province with his troops. This time she cannot escape us.

The scene that her father's words and her own imagination conjured up, of Eustacie attracting the handsome widower-duke, removed all remaining scruples from Madame de Selinville. For his own sake, the Baron must be made to fulfil the prophecy of the ink-pool, and allow his prison doors to be opened by love. Many and many a tender art did Diane rehearse; numerous were her sighs; wakeful, languishing, and restless her nights and days; and yet, whatever her determination to practise upon her cousin the witcheries that she had learnt in the *Escadron de la Reine-mere*, and seen played off effectually where there was not one grain of love to inspire them, her powers and her courage always failed her in the presence of him whom she sought to attract. His quiet reserve and simplicity always disconcerted her, and any attempt at blandishment that he could not mistake was always treated by him as necessarily an accidental error, as if any other supposition would render her despicable; and yet there was now and then a something that made her detect an effort in his restraint, as if it were less distaste than self-command. Her brother had contemptuously acquiesced in the experiment made by herself and her father, and allowed that so long as there was any danger of the Quinet marriage, the Baron's existence was needful. He would not come to Nid-de-Merle, nor did they want him there, knowing that he could hardly have kept his hands off his rival. But when the war broke out again in the summer of 1575 he joined that detachment of Guise's army which hovered about the Loire, and kept watch on the Huguenot cities and provinces of Western France. The Chevalier made several expeditions to confer with his son, and to keep up his relations with the network of spies whom he had spread over the Quinet provinces. The prisoners were so much separated from all intercourse with the dependants that they were entirely ignorant of the object of his absence from home. On these occasions they never left their tower and its court, and had no enlivenment save an occasional gift of dainties or message of inquiry from the ladies at Bellaise. These were brought by a handsome but slight, pale lad called Aime de Selinville, a relative of the late Count, as he told them, who had come to act as a gentleman attendant upon the widowed countess. The brothers rather wondered how he was disposed of at the convent, but all there was so contrary to their preconceived notions that they acquiesced. The first time he arrived it was on a long, hot summer day, and he then brought them a cool iced sherbet in two separate flasks, that for Philip being mixed with wine, which was omitted for Berenger; and the youth stood lingering and watching, anxious, he said, to be able to tell his lady how the drinks were approved. Both were excellent, and to that effect the prisoners replied; but no sooner was the messenger gone than Berenger said smilingly, 'That was a love potion, Phil.'

'And you drank it!' cried Philip, in horror.

'I did not think of it till I saw how the boy's eyes were gazing curiously at me as I swallowed it. You look at me as curiously, Phil. Are you expecting it to work? Shall I be at the fair lady's feet next time we meet?'

'How can you defy it, Berry?'

'Nay, Phil; holy wedded love is not to be dispelled by a mountebank's decoction.'

'But suppose it were poisonous, Berry, what can be done?' cried Philip, starting up in dismay.

'Then you would go home, Phil, and this would be over. But'—seeing his brother's terror—'there is no fear of that. She is not like to wish to poison me.'

And the potion proved equally ineffective on mind and body, as indeed did all the manipulations exercised upon a little waxen image that was supposed to represent M. le Baron. Another figure was offered to Diane, in feminine form, with black beads for eyes and a black plaster for hair, which, when stuck full of pins and roasted before the fire, was to cause Eustacie to peak and pine correspondingly. But from this measure Diane shrank. If aught was done against her rival it must be by her father and brother, not by herself; and she would not feel herself directly injuring her little cousin, nor sinking herself below him whom she loved. Once his wife, she would be good for ever, held up by his strength.

Meantime Berenger had received a greater shock than she or her father understood in the looking over of some of the family parchments kept in store at the castle. The Chevalier, in showing them to him, had chiefly desired to glorify the family by demonstrating how its honours had been won, but Berenger was startled at finding that Nid-de-Merle had been, as it appeared to him, arbitrarily and unjustly declared to be forfeited by the Sieur de Bellaise, who had been thrown into prison by Louis XI. for some demonstration in favour of the poor Duke de Berri, and granted to the favourite Ribaumont. The original grant was there, and to his surprise he found it was to male heirs—the male heirs alone of the direct line of the Ribaumont—to whom the grant was made. How, then, came it to Eustacie? The disposal had, with almost equal injustice, been changed by King Henry II. and the late Count de Ribaumont in favour of the little daughter whose union with the heir of the elder line was to conclude all family feuds. Only now did Berenger understand what his father had said on his death-bed of flagrant injustice committed in his days of darkness. He felt that he was reaping the reward of the injuries committed against the Chevalier and his son on behalf of the two unconscious children. He would willingly at once have given up all claim to the Nid-de-Merle estate—and he was now of age; two birthdays had passed in his captivity and brought him to years of discretion—but he had no more power than before to dispose of what was the property of Eustacie and her child; and the whole question of the validity of his marriage would be given up by his yielding even the posthumous claim that might have devolved on him in case of Eustacie's death. This would be giving up her honour, a thing impossible.

'Alas!' he sighed, 'my poor father might well say he had bound a heavy burthen round my neck.'

And from that time his hopes sank lower as the sense of the justice of his cause left him. He could neither deny his religion nor his marriage, and therefore could do nothing for his own deliverance; and he knew himself to be suffering in the cause of a great injustice; indeed, to be bringing suffering on the still more innocent Philip.

The once proudly indifferent youth was flagging now; was losing appetite, flesh, and colour; was unwilling to talk or to take exercise; and had a wan and drooping air that was most painful to watch. It seemed as if the return of summer brought a sense of the length and weariness of the captivity, and that the sunshine and gaiety of the landscape had become such a contrast to the captives' deadness of spirit that they could hardly bear to behold them, and felt the dull prison walls more congenial to their feelings than the gaiety of the summer hay and harvest-fields.

CHAPTER XXXVII
BEATING AGAINST THE BARS

My horse is weary of the stall, And I am sick of captive thrall.—LADY OF THE LAKE

Letters! They were hailed like drops of water in a thirsty land. No doubt they had been long on the way, ere they had reached the hands of the Chevalier de Ribaumont, and it was quite possible that they had been read and selected; but, as Berenger said, he defied any Frenchman to imitate either Lord Walwyn's style or Sir Marmaduke's, and when late in the autumn the packet was delivered to him, the two captives gloated over the very outsides before they opened them.

The first intelligence that greeted them made them give a cry of amusement and surprise. Lady Thistlewood, whose regrets that each of her girls was not a boy had passed into a proverb, had at length, in Dolly's seventh year, given birth to a son on Midsummer Day.

'Well,' said Philip, sighing, 'we must drink his health tonight! It is well, if we are to rot here, that some one should make it up to them!'

'And join Walwyn and Hurst!' said Berenger; and then both faces grew much graver, as by these letters, dated three months since, they understood how many they must have missed, and likewise that nothing had been heard of themselves since they had left Paris sixteen months ago. Their letters, both to their relations and to Sir Francis Walsingham, had evidently been suppressed; and Lord North, who had succeeded Walsingham as ambassador, had probably been misled by design, either by Narcisse de Nid-de-Merle himself, or by some of his agents, for Lord Walwyn had heard from him that the young men were loitering among the castles and garrisons of Anjou, leading a gay and dissipated life, and that it was universally believed that the Baron de Ribaumont had embraced the Catholic faith, and would shortly be presented to Henry III. to receive the grant of the Selinville honours, upon his marriage with his cousin, the widow of the last of the line. With much earnestness and sorrow did good old Lord Walwyn write to his grandson, conjuring him to bethink himself of his some, his pure faith, his loving friends, and the hopes of his youth: and, at least, if he himself had been led away by the allurements of the other party, to remember that Philip had been intrusted to him in full confidence, and to return him to his home. 'It was grief and shame to him,' said the good old man, 'to look at Sir Marmaduke, who had risked his son in the charge of one hitherto deemed trustworthy; and even if Berenger had indeed forgotten and cast away those whom he had once seemed to regard with love and duty, he commanded him to send home Philip, who owed an obedience to his father that could not be gainsaid.' Lord Walwyn further bade his grandson remember that the arrangements respecting his inheritance had been made in confidence that his heir was English in heart and faith, and that neither the Queen nor his own conscience would allow him to let his inheritance pass into French of Papist hands. There was scarcely a direct reproach, but the shaken, altered handwriting showed how stricken the aged man must be; and after his signature was added one still more trembling line, 'An ye return not speedily, ye will never see the old grandsire more.'

Berenger scarcely finished the letter through his burning tears of agony, and then, casting it from him, began to pace the room in fierce agitation, bursting out into incoherent exclamations, grasping at his hair, even launching himself against the massive window with such frenzied gestures and wild words that Philip, who had read through all with his usual silent obtuseness, became dismayed, and, laying hold of him, said, 'Prithee, brother, do not thus! What serves such passion?'

Berenger burst into a strange loud laugh at the matter-of-fact tone. 'What serves it! what serves anything!' he cried, 'but to make me feel what a miserable wretch I am? But he will die, Philip—he will die—not having believed me! How shall we keep ourselves from the smooth-tongued villain's throat? That I should be thus judged a traitor by my grandfather——'

And with a cry as of bodily anguish, he hid his face on the table, and groaned as he felt the utter helplessness of his strong youth in bonds.

'It can't be helped,' was the next of the unconsolatory platitudes uttered by Philip, who always grew sullen and dogged when his brother's French temperament broke forth under any sudden stroke. 'If they will believe such things, let them! You have not heard what my father says to it.'

'It will be all the same,' groaned Berenger.

'Nay! now that's a foul slander, and you should be ashamed of doing my father such wrong,' said Philip, 'Listen;' and he read: 'I will believe no ill of the lad no more than of thee, Phil. It is but a wild-goose chase, and the poor young woman is scarce like to be above ground; but, as I daily tell them, 'tis hard a man should forfeit his land for seeking his wife. My Lord North sends rumours that he is under Papist guiding, and sworn brother with the Black Ribaumonts; and my Lady, his grandmother, is like to break her heart, and my Lord credits them more than he ought, and never a line

- 330 -

as a token comes from you. Then there's Dame Annora, as proud of the babe as though neither she nor woman born ever had a son before, and plains over him, that both his brothers should be endowed, and he but a younger son. What will be the end on't I cannot tell. I will stand up for the right as best man may do, and never forget that Berry is her first-born, and that his child may be living; but the matter is none of mine, and my Lord is very aged, nor can a man meddle between his wife and her father. So this I tell you that you may make your brother lay it to heart. The sooner he is here the better, if he be still, as I verily believe and maintain him to be, an honest English heart that snaps his fingers at French papistry.' 'There,' conclude Philip triumphantly, 'he knows an honest man! He's friend and good father to you as much as ever. Heed none of the rest. He'll never let this little rogue stand in your light.'

'as if I cared for that!' said Berenger, beginning his caged-tiger walk again, and, though he tried to repress his anguish, breaking out at times into fierce revilings of the cruel toils that beset him, and despairing lamentations over those beloved ones at home, with sobs, groans, and tears, such as Philip could not brook to witness. Both because they were so violent and mourn-full, and because he thought them womanish, though in effect no woman's grief could have had half that despairing force. The *fierte* of the French noble, however, came to his aid. At the first sound of the great supper-bell he dashed away his tears, composed his features, washed his face, and demanded haughtily of Philip, whether there were any traces in his looks that the cruel hypocrite, their jailer, could gloat over.

And with proud step and indifferent air he marched into the hall, answered the Chevalier's polite inquiry whether the letter had brought good tidings by coolly thanking him and saying that all at home were well; and when he met the old man's inquiring glance out of the little keen black bead in the puckered, withered eyelid, he put a perfectly stony unmeaningness into his own gaze, till his eyes looked like the blue porcelain from China so much prized by the Abbess. He even played at chess all the evening with such concentrated attention as to be uniformly victorious.

Yet half the night Philip heard suppressed moans and sobs—then knew that he was on his knees—then, after long and comparatively silent weeping, he lay down again, and from the hour when he awoke in the morning, he returned no more to the letters; and though for some little time more sad and dispirited, he seemed to have come to regard the misjudgment at home as a part of the burthen he was already bearing.

That burthen was, however, pressing more heavily. The temperaments of the two brothers so differed that while the French one was prostrated by the agony of a stroke, and then rallied patiently to endure the effects, the

English character opposed a passive resistance to the blow, gave no sign of grief or pain, and from that very determination suffered a sort of exhaustion that made the effects of the evil more and more left. Thus, from the time Philip's somewhat tardy imagination had been made to realize his home, his father, and his sisters, the home-sickness, and weariness of his captivity, which had already begun to undermine his health and spirits, took increasing effect.

He made no complaint—he never expressed a wish—but, in the words of the prophet, he seemed 'pining away on his feet.' He did not sleep, and though, to avoid remark, he never failed to appear at meals, he scarcely tasted food. He never willingly stirred from cowering over the fire, and was so surly and ill-tempered that only Berenger's unfailing good-humour could have endured it. Even a wolf-hunt did not stir him. He only said he hated outlandish beasts, and that it was not like chasing the hare in Dorset. His calf-love for Madame de Selinville had entirely faded away in his yearnings after home. She was only one of the tediously recurring sights of his captivity, and was loathed like all the rest. The regulation rides with the Chevalier were more detestable than ever, and by and by they caused such fatigue that Berenger perceived that his strength must be warning, and became so seriously alarmed that one evening, when Philip had barely dragged himself to the hall, tasted nothing but a few drops of wine, and then dropped into an uneasy slumber in his chair, he could not but turn to the Chevalier an appealing, indignant countenance, as he said, in a low but quivering voice, 'You see, sir, how he is altered!'

'Alas! fair nephew, it is but too plain. He is just of the age when such restraint tells severely upon the health.'

Then Berenger spoke out upon the foul iniquity of the boy's detention. For himself, he observed, he had nothing to say; he knew the term of his release, and had not accepted them; but Philip, innocent of all damage to the Ribaumont interests, the heir of an honourable family, what had he done to incur the cruel imprisonment that was eating away his life?

'I tell you, sir,' said Berenger, with eyes filled with tears,' that his liberty is more precious to me than my own. Were he but restored to our home, full half the weight would be gone from my spirit.'

'Fair nephew,' said the Chevalier, 'you speak as though I had any power in the matter, and were not merely standing between you and the King.'

'Then if so,' said Berenger, 'let the King do as he will with me, but let Philip's case be known to our Ambassador.'

'My poor cousin,' said the Chevalier, 'you know not what you ask. Did I grant your desire, you would only learn how implacable King Henri is to those who have personally offended him—above all, to heretics. Nor could the Ambassador do anything for one who resisted by force of arms the King's justice. Leave it to me; put yourself in my hands, and deliverance shall come for him first, then for you.'

'How, sir?'

'One token of concession—one attendance at mass—one pledge that the alliance shall take place when the formalities have been complied with—then can I report you our own; give you almost freedom at once; despatch our young friend to England without loss of time; so will brotherly affection conquer those chivalrous scruples, most honourable in you, but which, carried too far, become cruel obstinacy.'

Berenger looked at Philip; saw how faded and wan was the ruddy sun-burnt complexion, how lank and bony the sturdy form, how listless and wasted the hands. Then arose, bursting within him, the devoted generosity of the French nature, which would even accept sin and ruin for self, that so the friend may be saved; and after all, had he not gone to mass out of mere curiosity?—did he not believe that there was salvation in the Gallican Church? Was it not possible that, with Philip free to tell his story at home, his own deliverance might come before he should be irrevocably committed to Madame de Selinville? If Eustacie were living, her claims must overthrow that which her rival was forcing upon him at her own peril. Nay, how else could he obtain tidings of her? And for those at home, did they deserve that he should sacrifice all, Philip included, for their sake? The thoughts, long floating round his brain, now surged upon him in one flood, and seemed to overwhelm in those moments of confusion all his powers of calling up the other side of the argument; he only had an instinct remaining that it would be a lie to God and man alike. 'God help me!' he sighed to himself; and there was sufficient consideration and perplexity expressed in his countenance to cause the Chevalier to feel his cause almost gained; and rising eagerly, with tears in his eyes, he exclaimed, 'Embrace me, my dear, dear son! The thing is done! Oh! what peace, what joy!'

The instinct of recoil came stronger now. He stepped back with folded arms, saying again, 'God help me! God forbid that I should be a traitor!'

'My son, hear me; these are but easily removed points of honour,' began the Chevalier; but at that moment Philip suddenly started from, or in his slumber, leapt on his feet, and called out, 'Avaunt, Satan!' then opened his eyes, and looked, as if barely recalling where he was.

'Philip!' exclaimed Berenger, 'did you hear?'

'I—I don't know,' he said, half-bewildered. 'Was I dreaming that the fiend was parleying with us in the voice of M. le Chevalier there to sell our souls for one hour of home?'

He spoke English, but Berenger replied in French.

'You were not wrong, Philip. Sir, he dreamt that the devil was tempting me in your voice while you were promising me his liberty on my fulfilling your first condition.'

'What?' said Philip, now fully awake, and gathering the state of things, as he remembered the words that had doubtless been the cause of his dream. 'And if you did, Berenger, I give you warning they should never see me at home. What! could I show my face there with such tidings? No! I should go straight to La Noue, or to the Low Countries, and kill every Papist I could for having debauched you!'

'Hush! hush! Philip,' said Berenger; 'I could not break my faith to Heaven or my wife even for your sake, and my cousin sees how little beholden you would be to me for so doing. With your leave, Monsieur, we will retire.'

The Chevalier detained Berenger for a moment to whisper, 'What I see is so noble a heart that I know you cannot sacrifice him to your punctilio.'

Philip was so angry with Berenger, so excited, and so determined to show that nothing ailed him, that for a short time he was roused, and seemed to be recovering; but in a few days he flagged again, only, if possible with more gruffness, moodiness, and pertinacity in not allowing that anything was amiss. It was the bitterest drop of all in Berenger's cup, when in the end of January he looked back at what Philip had been only a month before, and saw how he had wasted away and lost strength; the impulse rather to ruin himself that destroy his brother came with such force that he could scarcely escape it by his ever-recurring cry for help to withstand it. And then Diane, in her splendid beauty and witchery, would rise before him, so that he knew how a relaxation of the lengthened weary effort would make his whole self break its bonds and go out to her. Dreams of felicity and liberty, and not with Eustacie, would even come over him, and he would awaken to disappointment before he came to a sense of relief and thankfulness that he was still his own. The dislike, distaste, and dread that came so easily in his time of pain and weakness were less easy to maintain in his full health and forced inactivity. Occupation of mind and hope seemed the only chance of enabling either of the two to weather this most dreary desert period; and Berenger, setting his thoughts resolutely to consider what would be the best means of rousing Philip, decided at length that any endeavour to escape, however arduous and desperate, would be better than his present apathetic languor, even if it led to nothing. After the first examination of their prison, Berenger had had no thought of escape; he was then still weak and unenterprising. He had for many months lived in hopes of interference from home; and, besides, the likelihood that so English a party as his own would be quickly pursued and recaptured, where they did not know their road and had no passports, had deterred him lest should fall into still straiter imprisonment. But he had since gained, in the course of his rides, and by observation from the top of the tower, a much fuller knowledge of the country. He knew the way to the grange du Temple, and to the chief towns in the neighbourhood. Philip and Humfrey had both lost something of their intensely national look and speech, and, moreover, was having broken out again, there was hope of falling in with Huguenot partisans even nearer that at La Rochelle. But whether successful or not, some enterprise was absolutely needed to save Philip from his despondent apathy; and Berenger, who in these eighteen months had grown into the strength and vigour of manhood, felt as if he had force and power for almost any effort save this hopeless waiting.

He held council with Humfrey, who suggested that it might be well to examine the vaults below the keep. He had a few days before, while going after some of the firewood stored below the ground-floor chamber, observed a door, locked, but with such rusty iron hinges that they might possibly yield to vigorous efforts with a stone; and who could tell where the underground passages might come out?

Berenger eagerly seized the idea. Philip's mood of contradiction prompted him to pronounce it useless folly, and he vouchsafed no interest in the arrangements for securing light, by selecting all the bits of firewood fittest for torches, and saving all the oil possible from the two lamps they were allowed. The chief difficulty was that Guibert was not trusted, so that all had to be done out of his sight; and on the first day Berenger was obliged to make the exploration alone, since Humfrey was forced to engross Guibert in some occupation out of sight, and Philip had refused to have anything to do with it, or be like a rat routing in the corners of his trap.

However, Berenger had only just ascertained that the ironwork was so entirely rusted away as to offer no impediment, when Philip came languidly roaming into the cellar, saying, 'Here! I'll hold the torch! You'll be losing yourself in this wolf's mouth of a place if you go alone.'

The investigation justified Philip's predictions of its uselessness. Nothing was detected but rats, and vaults, and cobwebs; it was cold, earthy, and damp; and when they thought they must have penetrated far beyond the precincts of the keep, they heard Humfrey's voice close to them, warning them that it was nearly dinner-time.

The next day brought them a more promising discovery, namely of a long straight passage, with a gleam of light at the end of it; and this for the first time excited Philip's interest or curiosity. He would have hastened along it at once, but for the warning summons from Humfrey; and in the excitement of even this grain of interest, he ate more heartily at supper than he had done for weeks, and was afterwards more eager to prove to Berenger that night was the best time to pursue their researches.

And Berenger, when convinced that Guibert was sound asleep, thought so too, and accompanied by Humfrey, they descended into the passage. The light, of course, was no longer visible, but the form of the crypt, through which they now passed, was less antique than that under the keep, and it was plain they were beneath a later portion of the Castle. The gallery concluded in a wall, with a small barred, unglazed window, perfectly dark, so that Berenger, who alone could reach to the bottom of it, could not uses where it looked out.

'We must return by daylight; then, maybe, we may judge,' sighed Philip.

'Hark!' exclaimed Berenger.

'Rats,' said Philip.

'No—listen—a voice! Take care!' he added, in a lower tone, 'we may be close on some of the servants.'

But, much nearer than he expected, a voice on his right hand demanded, 'Does any good Christian hear me?'

'Who is there?' exclaimed Philip.

'Ah! good sir, do I hear the voice of a companion in misery? Or, if you be free, would you but send tidings to my poor father?'

'It is a Norman accent!' cried Berenger. 'Ah! ah! can it be poor Landry Osbert?'

'I am—I am that wretch. Oh, would that M. le Baron could know!'

'My dear, faithful foster-brother! They deceived me,' cried Berenger, in great agitation, as an absolute howl came from the other side of the wall: 'M. le Baron come to this! Woe worth the day!' and Berenger with difficulty mitigated his affectionate servant's lamentations enough to learn from him how he had been seized almost at the gates of Bellaise, closely interrogated, deprived of the letter to Madame la Baronne, and thrown into this dungeon. The Chevalier. Not an unmerciful man, according to the time,

- 336 -

had probably meant to release him as soon as the marriage between his son and niece should have rendered it superfluous to detain this witness to Berenger's existence. There, then, the poor fellow had lain for three years, and his work during this weary time had been the scraping with a potsherd at the stone of his wall, and his pertinacious perseverance had succeeded in forming a hole just large enough to enable him to see the light of the torch carried by the gentlemen. On his side, he said, there was nothing but a strong iron door, and a heavily-barred window, looking, like that in the passage, into the fosse within the walled garden; but, on the other hand, if he could enlarge his hole sufficiently to creep through it, he could escape with them in case of their finding a subterranean outlet. The opening within his cell was, of course, much larger than the very small space he had made by loosening a stone towards the passage, but he was obliged always to build up each side of his burrow at the hours of his jailer's visit, lest his work should be detected, and to stamp the rubbish into his floor. But while they talked, Humfrey and Philip, with their knives, scraped so diligently that two more stones could be displaced; and, looking down the widening hole through the prodigious mass of wall, they could see a ghastly, ragged, long-bearded scarecrow, with an almost piteous expression of joy on his face, at once again seeing familiar faces. And when, at his earnest entreaty, Berenger stood so as to allow his countenance to be as visible as the torch could make it through the 'wall's-hole,' the vault echoed with the poor fellow's delighted cry. 'I am happy! M. le Baron is himself again. The assassin's cruel work is gone! Ah! thanks to the saints! Blessed be St. Lucie, it was not in vain that I entreated her!'

The torches were, however, waxing so low that the sight could not long be afforded poor Osbert; and, with a promise to return to him next day, the party returned to the upper air, where they warmed themselves over the fire, and held council over measures for the present relief of the captive. Berenger grieved that he had given him up so entirely for lost as to have made no exertions on his behalf, and declared his resolution of entreating that he might be allowed to enjoy comparative comfort with them in the keep. It was a risk, but the Chevalier might fairly suppose that the knowledge of Osbert's situation had oozed out through the servants, and gratitude and humanity alike impelled Berenger to run some risk for his foster-brother's sake. He was greatly touched at the poor fellow's devotion, and somewhat amused, though with an almost tearful smile at the joy with which he had proclaimed—what Berenger was quite unaware of, since the keep furnished no mirrors—the disappearance of his scars. ''Tis even so,' said Philip, 'though I never heeded it. You are as white from crown to beard as one of the statues at Paris; but the great red gash is a mere seam, save when yon old Satan angers you, and then it blushes for all the rest of your face.'

'And the cheek-wound is hidden, I suppose,' said Berenger, feeling under the long fair moustache and the beard, which was developing into respectable proportions.

'Hidden? ay, entirely. No one would think your bald crown had only twenty-one years over it; but you are a personable fellow still, quite enough to please Daphne,' said Philip.

'Pshaw!' replied Berenger, pleased nevertheless to hear the shadow of a jest again from Philip.

It was quite true. These months of quiescence—enforced though they were—had given his health and constitution time to rally after the terrible shock they had sustained. The severe bleedings had, indeed, rendered his complexion perfectly colourless; but there was something in this, as well as in the height which the loss of hair gave his brow, which, added to the depth and loftiness of countenance that this long period of patience and resolution had impressed on his naturally fine features, without taking away that open candour that had first attracted Diane when he was a rosy lad. His frame had strengthened at the same time, and assumed the proportions of manhood; so that, instead of being the overgrown maypole that Narcisse used to sneer at, he was now broad-shouldered and robust, exceedingly powerful, and so well made that his height, upwards of six feet, was scarcely observed, except by comparison with the rest of the world.

And his character had not stood still. He had first come to Paris a good, honest, docile, though high-spirited boy: and though manly affections, cares, and sorrows had been thrust on him, he had met them like the boy that he was, hardly conscious how deep they went. Then had come the long dream of physical suffering, with only one thought pertinaciously held throughout—that of constancy to his lost wife; and from this he had only thoroughly wakened in his captivity, the resolution still holding fast, but with more of reflection and principle, less of mere instinct, than when his powers were lost or distracted in the effort of constant endurance of pain and weakness. The charge of Philip, the endeavour both of educating him and keeping up his spirits, as well as the controversy with Pere Bonami, had been no insignificant parts of the discipline of these months; and, little as the Chevalier had intended it, he had trained his young kinsman into a far more substantial and perilous adversary, both in body and mind, than when he had caged him in his castle of the Blackbird's Nest.

CHAPTER XXXVIII
THE ENEMY IN PRESENCE

Then came and looked him in the face,

An angel beautiful and bright,

And then he knew it was a fiend,

That miserable knight.

   —COLERIDGE

'Father, dear father, what is it? What makes you look so ill, so haggard?' cried Diane de Selinville, when summoned the next morning to meet her father in the parlour of the convent.

'Ah, child! see here. Your brother will have us make an end of it. He has found her.'

'Eustacie! Ah, and where?'

'That he will not say, but see here. This is all billet tells me: "The hare who has doubled so long is traced to her form. My dogs are on her, and in a week's time she will be ours. I request you, sir, to send me a good purse of crowns to reward my huntsmen; and in the meantime—one way or the other—that pet of my sister's must be disposed of. Kept too long, these beasts always become savage. Either let him be presented to the royal menagerie, or there is a still surer way."'

'And that is all he says!' exclaimed Diane.

'All! He was always cautions. He mentions no names. And now, child, what is to be done? To give him up to the King is, at the best, life-long imprisonment, yet, if he were still here when my son returns—Alas! alas! child, I have been ruined body and soul between you! How could you make me send after and imprison him? It was a mere assassination!' and the old man beat his head with grief and perplexity.

'Father!' cried Diane, tearfully, 'I cannot see you thus. We meant it for the best. We shall yet save him.'

'Save him! Ah, daughter, I tossed all night long thinking how to save him, so strong, so noble, so firm, so patient, so good even to the old man who has destroyed his hope—his life! Ah! I have thought till my brain whirls.'

'Poor father! I knew you would love him,' said Diane, tenderly. 'Ah! we will save him yet. He shall be the best of sons to you. Look, it is only to tell him that she whom he calls his wife is already in my brother's hands, wedded to him.'

'Daughter,'—and he pushed back his gray hair with a weary distressed gesture,—'I am tired of wiles; I am old; I can carry them out no longer.'

'But this is very simple; it may already be true—at least it will soon be true. Only tell him that she is my brother's wife. Then will his generosity awaken, then will he see that to persist in the validity of his marriage would be misery, dishonour to her, then——'

'Child, you know not how hard he is in his sense of right. Even for his brother's sake he would not give way an inch, and the boy was as obstinate as he!'

'Ah! but this comes nearer. He will be stung; his generosity will be piqued. He will see that the kindest thing he can do will be to nullify his claim, and the child——'

The Chevalier groaned, struck his brow with his fist, and muttered, 'That will concern no one—that has been provided for. Ah! ah! children, if I lose my own soul for you, you——'

'Father, my sweet father, say not these cruel things. Did not the Queen's confessor tell us that all means were lawful that brought a soul to the Church? and here are two.'

'Two! Why, the youth's heresy is part of his point of honour. Child, child, the two will be murdered in my very house, and the guilt will be on my soul.'

'No, father! We will—we will save him. See, only tell him this.'

'This—what? My brain is confused. I have thought long—long.'

'Only this, father, dear father. You shall not be tormented any more, if only you will tell him that my brother has made Eustacie his wife, then will I do all the rest.'

Diane coaxed, soothed, and encouraged her father by her caresses, till he mounted his mule to return to the castle at dinner-time, and she promised to come early in the afternoon to follow up the stroke he was to give. She had never seen him falter before,—he had followed out his policy with a clear head and unsparing hand,—but now that Berenger's character was better known to him, and the crisis long delayed had come so suddenly before his eyes, his whole powers seemed to reel under the alternative.

The dinner-bell clanged as he arrived at the castle, and the prisoners were marched into the hall, both intent upon making their request on Osbert's behalf, and therefore as impatient for the conclusion of the meal, and the absence of the servants, as was their host. His hands trembled so much that Berenger was obliged to carve for him; he made the merest feint of eating; and now and then raised his hand to his head as if to bring back scattered ideas.

The last servant quitted the room, when Berenger perceived that the old man was hardly in a state to attend to his request, and yet the miserable frost-bitten state of poor Landry seemed to compel him to speak.

'Sir,' he began, 'you could do me a great kindness.'

The Chevalier looked up at him with glassy eyes.

'My son,' he said, with an effort, 'I also had something to say. Ah! let me think. I have had enough. Call my daughter,' he added, feeling helplessly with his hands, so that Berenger started up in alarm, and received him in his arms just in time to prevent his sinking to the floor senseless.

'It is a stroke,' exclaimed Berenger. 'Call, Phil! Send the gendarmes.'

The gendarmes might be used to the sight of death of their own causing, but they had a horror of that which came by Nature's hand. The purple face and loud gasps of the stricken man terrified them out of their senses. 'C'est un coup,' was the cry, and they went clattering off to the servants. These, all men but one old crone, came in a mass to the door, looked in, beheld their master rigid and prostrate on the floor, supported by the prisoner, and with fresh shrieks about 'Mesdames! a priest! a doctor!' away they rushed. The two brothers were not in much less consternation, only they retained their senses. Berenger loosened the ruff and doublet, and bade Philip practice that art of letting blood which he had learnt for his benefit. When Madame de Selinville and her aunt, with their escort, having been met half-way from Bellaise, arrived sooner than could have been expected, they found every door open from hall to entrance gateway, not a person keeping watch, and the old man lying deathlike upon cushions in the hall, Philip bandaging his arm, and Berenger rubbing his temples with wine and the hottest spices on the table. 'He is better—he is alive,' said Berenger, as they entered; and as both ladies would have fallen on him with shrieks and sobs, he bade them listen, assured them that the only chance of life was in immediate care, and entreated that bedding might be brought down, and strong essences fetched to apply to the nose and temples. They obeyed, and the sister infirmarer had arrived from the convent, he had opened his eyes, and, as he saw Berenger, tried to murmur something that sounded like 'Mon fils.'

'He lives!—he speaks!—he can receive the sacraments!' was the immediate exclamation; and as preparations began to be made, the brothers saw that their presence was no longer needed, and returned to their own tower.

'So, sir,' said the gendarme sergeant, as they walked down the passage, 'you did not seize the moment for escape.'

'I never thought of it,' said Berenger.

'I hope, sir, you will not be the worse for it,' said the sergeant. 'An honourable gentleman you have ever proved yourself to me, and I will bear testimony that you did the poor old gentleman no hurt; but nobles will have it their own way, and pay little heed to a poor soldier.'

'What do you mean, friend?'

'Why, you see, sir, it is unlucky that you two happened to be alone with M. le Chevalier. No one can tell what may be said when they seek an occasion against a person.'

To the brothers, however, this suggestion sounded so horrible and unnatural, that they threw it from them. They applied themselves at every moment possible to enlarging Osbert' hole, and seeking an outlet from the dungeon; but this they had not been able to discover, and it was necessary to be constantly on their guard in visiting the vaults, lest their absence from their apartment should be detected. They believed that if Narcisse arrived at the castle, they should find in him a far less gentle jailer than the poor old man, for whose state their kindly young hearts could not but grieve.

They heard that he had recovered consciousness enough to have made a sort of confession; and Pere Bonami brought them his formal request, as a dying man, for their pardon for all the injuries he had done them; but his speech was too much affected for any specification of what these were. The first thing they heard in early morning was that, in the course of the night, he had breathed his last; and all day the bells of all the churches round were answering one another with the slow, swinging, melancholy notes of the knell.

In the early twilight, Pere Bonami brought a message that Madame de Selinville requested M. le Baron to come and speak with her, and he was accordingly conducted, with the gendarme behind him, to a small chamber opening into the hall—the same where the incantations of the Italian pedlar had been played off before Philip and Diane. The gendarme remained outside the door by which they entered the little dark room, only lighted by one little lamp.

'Here, daughter,' said the priest, 'is your cousin. He can answer the question you have so much at heart;' and with these words Pere Bonami passed beneath the black curtain that covered the entrance into the hall, admitting as he raised it for a moment a floor of pure light from the wax tapers, and allowing the cadence of the chanting of the priests to fall on the ear. At first Berenger was scarcely able to discern the pale face that looked as if tears were all dried up, and even before his eyes had clearly perceived her in the gloom, she was standing before him with clasped hands, demanding, in a hoarse, breathless whisper, 'Had he said anything to you?'

'Anything? No, cousin,' said Berenger, in a kind tone. 'He had seemed suffering and oppressed all dinner-time, and when the servants left us, he murmured a few confused words, then sank.'

'Ah, ah, he spoke it not! Thank Heaven! Ah! it is a load gone. Then neither will I speak it,' sighed Diane, half aloud. 'Ah! cousin, he loved you.'

'He often was kind to us,' said Berenger, impelled to speak as tenderly as he could of the enemy, who had certainly tortured him, but as if he loved him.

'He bade us save you,' said Diane, her eyes shining with strange wild light in the gloom. 'He laid it on my aunt and me to save you; you must let us. It must be done before my brother comes,' she added, in hurried accents. 'The messengers are gone; he may be here any moment. He must find you in the chapel—as—as my betrothed!'

'And you sent for me here to tempt me—close to such a chamber as that?' demanded Berenger, his gentleness becoming sternness, as much with his own worse self as with her.

'Listen. Ah! it is the only way. Listen, cousin. Do you know what killed my father? It was my brother's letter saying things must be brought to an end: either you must be given up to the King, or worse—worse. And now, without him to stand between you and my brother, you are lost. Oh! take pity on his poor soul that has left his body, and bring not you blood on his head.'

'Nay,' said Berenger, 'if he repented, the after consequences to me will have no effect on him now.'

'Have pity then on yourself—on your brother.'

'I have,' said Berenger. 'He had rather die with me than see me a traitor.'

'And least of all,' she exclaimed, with choking grief, 'have you compassion on me!—on me who have lost the only one who felt for me— on me who have loved you with every fibre of my heart—on me who have lived on the music of your hardest, coldest word—on me who would lay my life, my honour, in the dust for one grateful glance from you—and whom you condemn to the anguish of—your death! Aye, and for what? For the mere shadow of a little girl, who had no force to love you, or whom you know nothing—nothing! Oh! are you a crystal rock or are you a man? See, I kneel to you to save yourself and me.'

There were hot tears dropping from Berenger's eyes as he caught Diane's hand, and held it forcibly to prevent her thus abasing herself. Her wild words and gestures thrilled him in every pulse and wrung his heart, and it was with a stifled, agitated voice that he said—

'God help you and me both, Diane! To do what you ask would—would be no saving of either. Nay, if you will kneel,' as she struggled with him, 'let it be to Him who alone can bring us through;' and releasing her hand, he dropped on his knees by her side, and covered his face with his hands, in an earnest supplication that the spirit of resistance which he almost felt slipping from him might be renewed. The action hushed and silenced her, and as he rose he spoke no other word, but silently drew back so much of the curtain that he could see into the hall, where the dead man still lay uncoffined upon the bed where his own hands had laid him, and the low, sweet requiem of kneeling priests floated round him. Rest, rest, and calm they breathed into one sorely tried living soul, and the perturbed heart was quelled by the sense how short the passage was to the world where captivity and longing would be ended. He beckoned to Pere Bonami to return to Diane, and then, protected by his presence from any further demonstrations, kissed her hand and left her.

He told Philip as little as possible of this interview, but his brother remarked how much time he spent over the Psalms that evening.

The next day the brothers saw from their upper winder the arrival of Narcisse, or, as he had called himself for the last three years, the Marquis de Nid-de-Merle, with many attendant gentlemen, and a band of fifty or sixty gendarmes. The court was filled with their horses, and rang with their calls for refreshment. And the captives judged it wise to remain in their upper room incase they should be called for.

They were proved to have been wise in so doing; for about an hour after their arrival there was a great clanging of steel boots, and Narcisse de Ribaumont, followed by a portly, heavily-armed gentleman, wearing a scarf of office, by two of the servants, and by two gendarmes, entered the room. It was the first time the cousins had met since *le baiser d'Eutacie* had been hissed into Berenger's ear. Narcisse looked older, sallower, and more worn than at that time; and Philip, seeing his enemy for the first time, contrasted him with the stately presence of Berenger, and felt as if a rat were strangling a noble steed.

Each young man punctiliously removed his hat, and Nid-de-Merle, without deigning further salutation, addressed his companion. 'Sir, you are here on the part of the King, and to you I deliver up these prisoners, who, having been detained here on a charge of carrying on a treasonable correspondence, and protected by my father out of consideration for the family, have requited his goodness by an attempt to strangle him, which has caused his death.'

Philip actually made a leap of indignation; Berenger, better prepared, said to the officer, 'Sir, I am happy to be placed in charged of a King's servant, who will no doubt see justice done, and shelter us from the private malice that could alone devise so monstrous an accusation. We are ready to clear ourselves upon oath over the corpse, and all the household and our own guards can bear witness.'

'The witnesses are here,' said Narcisse, pointing to the servants, ill-looking men, who immediately began to depose to having found their master purple-faced and struggling in the hands of the two young men, who had been left alone with him after dinner.

Berenger felt that there was little use in self-defence. It was a fabrication the more easily to secure his cousin's purpose of destroying him, and his best hope lay in passing into the hands of persons who were less directly interested in his ruin. He drew himself up to his full height, saying, 'If there be justice in France, our innocence will be proved. I demand, sir, that you examine the abbess, the priest, the steward, the sergeant of gendarmes: they are impartial witnesses, and will serve the King's justice, if justice be his purpose. Or, if this be but M. de Nid-de-Merle's way of completing the work he left unfinished four years ago, I am ready. Only let my brother go free. He is heir to nothing here.'

'Enough, sir. Words against the King's justice will be reckoned against you,' said the officer. 'I shall do myself the honour of attending the funeral the day after to-morrow, and then I shall convey you to Tours, to answer for this deed at your leisure. Monsieur le Marquis, are the prisoners secure here, or would you have them *garde a vue.*'

'No need for that,' said Narcisse, lightly; 'had there been any exit they would have found it long ago. Your good fellows outside the door keep them safe enough. M. le Baron de Ribaumont, I have the honour to wish you a good morning.'

Berenger returned his bow with one full of defiance, and the door was again locked upon the prisoners; while Philip exclaimed, 'The cowardly villain, Berry; is it a hanging matter?'

'Not for noble blood,' said Berenger. 'We are more likely to be brought to no trial, but to lie prisoners for life;' then, as Philip grew white and shivered with a sick horror, he added bravely, 'But they shall not have us, Philip. We know the vaults well enough to play at hide and seek with them there, and even if we find no egress we may hold out till they think us fled and leave open the doors!'

Philip's face lighted up again, and they did their best by way of preparation, collecting wood for torches, and putting aside food at their meals. It was a very forlorn hope, but the occupation it caused was effectual in keeping up Philip's spirits, and saving him from despondency.

CHAPTER XXXIX
THE PEDLAR'S PREDICTION

But if ne'er so close you wall him,

Do the best that you may;

Blind Love, if so you call him,

Will find out his way.

—OLD SONG

'Too late,' muttered Berenger to himself, as he stood by the fire in his prison-chamber. Humfrey and Philip were busy in the vaults, and he was taking his turn in waiting in the sitting-room to disarm suspicion. 'It is too late now, and I thank God that so it is.'

'Do you indeed, M. le Baron?' said a low voice close beside him; and, as he turned in haste, he beheld, at the foot of the turret-stair, the youth Aime de Selinville, holding a dark lantern in his hand, and veiling its light.

'Ha!' and he started to his feet. 'Whence come you?'

'From my Lady,' was the youth's answer. 'She has sent me to ask whether you persist in what you replied to her the other day. For if not, she bids me say that it is not too late.'

'And if I do persevere?'

'Then—ah! what do I know? Who can tell how far malice can go? And there are towers and bastilles where hope never enters. Moreover, your researches underground are known.'

'Sir,' said Berenger, the heart-sinking quelled by the effort of resistance, 'Madame de Selinville has my answer—I must take the consequences. Tell her, if she truly wishes me well, the honourable way of saving us would be to let our English friends know what has befallen us.'

'You forget, M. le Baron, even if she could proclaim the dishonour of her family, interference from a foreign power might only lead to a surer mode of removing you,' said Aime, lowering his voice and shuddering.

'Even so, I should thank her. Then would the bitterest pang be taken away. Those at our home would not deem us faithless recreants.'

'Thank her!' murmured the lad in an inward voice. 'Very well, sir, I will carry her your decision. It is your final one. Disgrace, prison, death—rather than freedom, love, wealth!'

'The semblance of dishonour rather than the reality!' said Berenger, firmly.

The light-footed page disappeared, and in a few moments a very different tread came up from below, and Philip appeared.

'What is it, Berry? Methought I heard a voice.'

'Forgive me, brother,' said Berenger, holding out his hand; 'I have thrown away another offer.'

'Tush, the thing to pardon would be having accepted one. I only wish they would leave us in peace! What was it this time?'

'A messenger through young Selinville. Strange, to trust her secrets to that lad. But hush, here he is again, much sooner than I thought. What, sir, have you been with your lady again?'

'Yes, sir,' the young said, with a trembling voice, and Berenger saw that his eyes were red with weeping; 'she bids me tell you that she yields. She will save you eve while you have and despite her! There is only one thing—_'

'And what is that?'

'You must encumber yourself with the poor Aime. You must let me serve you instead of her. Listen, sir, it cannot be otherwise.' Then with a brisker, more eager voice, he continued: 'Monsieur knows that the family burial-place is Bellaise? Well, to-morrow, at ten o'clock, all the household, all the neighbourhood, will come and sprinkle holy water on the bier. The first requiem will be sung, and then will all repair to the convent. There will be the funeral mass, the banquet, the dole. Every creature in the castle—nay, in all the neighbourhood for twenty miles round—will be at the convent, for the Abbess has given out that the alms are to be double, and the bread of wheat. Not a soul will remain here, save the two gendarmes on guard at that door, and the poor Aime, whom no one will miss, even if any person could be distinguished in their black cloaks. Madame la Comtesse has given him this key, which opens a door on the upper floor of the keep, unknown to the guards, who, for that matter, shall have a good tankard of spiced wine to console and occupy them. Then is the way clear to the castle court, which is not over looked by their window, the horses are in the stables, and we are off,—that is if M. le Baron will save a poor youth from the wrath of M. de Nid-de-Merle.'

'You are and honest fellow!' cried Philip, shaking him vehemently by the hand. 'You shall go with us to England, and we will make a brave man of you.'

'We shall owe you our lives,' said Berenger, warmly, 'and be ever bound to you. Tell your lady that THIS is magnanimity; that now I truly thank her as our preserver, and shall bless her all the days of the life she gives us. But my servants?'

'Guibert is a traitor,' said Aime; 'he has been so ever since you were at Paris. Breathe no word to him; but he, as a Catholic, shall be invited to the funeral. Your stout Englishman should by all means be with us.'

'My Norman also,' added Berenger,—'my dear foster-brother, who has languished in the dungeon for three years;' and when the explanation had been made, Aime assented, though half-unwillingly, to the necessity, and presently quitted them to bear back their answer to his lady. Philip shook his hand violently again, patted him on the back, so as almost to take away his breath, and bade him never fear, they would be sworn brothers to him for ever; and then threw up his hat into the air, and was so near astonishing the donjon walls with a British hurrah, that Berenger had to put his hand over his mouth and strangle the shout in his very throat.

The chief of that night was spent in enlarging the hole in Osbert's wall, so as to admit of his creeping through it; and they also prepared their small baggage for departure. Their stock of money, though some had been spent on renewing their clothes, and some in needful gratuities to the servants and gendarmes, was sufficient for present needs, and they intended to wear their ordinary dress. They were unlikely to meet any of the peasants in the neighbourhood; and, indeed, Berenger had so constantly ridden out in his black mask, that its absence, now that his scars were gone, was as complete a change as could be effected in one whose height was of unusual.

'There begins the kneel,' said Philip, standing at the window. 'It's our joy-bell, Berry! Every clang seems to me to say, "Home! home! home!"'

'For you, Phil,' said Berenger; 'but I must be satisfied of Eutacie's fate first. I shall go first to Nissard—whither we were bound when we were seized—then to La Rochelle, whence you may——'

'No more of that,' burst out Philip. 'What! would you have me leave you now, after all we have gone through together? Not that you will find her. I don't want to vex you, brother, on such a day as this, but you conjurer's words are coming true in the other matter.'

'How? What mean you, Phil?'

'What's the meaning of Aime?' asked Philip. 'Even I am French scholar enough for that. And who sends him?'

Meantime the court was already filling with swarms of persons of every rank and degree, but several anxious hours had passed before the procession was marshaled; and friars and monks, black, white, and gray,—priests in rich robes and tall caps,—black-cloaked gentlemen and men-at-arms,—all bearing huge wax tapers,—and peasants and beggars of every conceivable aspect,—filed out of the court, bearing with them the richly-emblazoned bier of the noble and puissant knight, the Beausire Charles Eutache de Ribaumont Nid-de-Merle, his son walking behind in a long black mantle, and all who counted kindred of friendship following two and two; then all the servants, every one who properly belonged to the castle, were counted out by the brothers from their windows, and Guibert among them.

'Messieurs,' a low, anxious voice sounded in the room.

'We will only fetch Osbert.'

It was a terrible only, as precious moments slipped away before there appeared in the lower chamber Berenger and Humfrey, dragging between them a squalid wretch, with a skin like stained parchment over a skeleton, tangled hair and beard, staring bewildered eyes, and fragments of garments, all dust, dirt, and rags.

'Leave me, leave me, dear master,' said the object, stretching his whole person towards the fire as they let him sink down before it. 'You would but ruin yourself.'

'It is madness to take him,' said Aime, impatiently.

'I go not without him,' said Berenger. 'Give me the soup, Philip.'

Some soup and wine had been placed by the fire, and likewise a shirt and a suit of Humfrey's clothes were spread before it. Aime burst out into the yard, absolutely weeping with impatience, when, unheeding all his remonstrances, his three companions applied themselves to feeding, rubbing, and warming Osbert, and assuring him that the pains in his limbs would pass away with warmth and exercise. He had been valiant of heart in his dungeon; but his sudden plunge into upper air was like rising from the grave, and brought on all the effects of his dreary captivity, of which he had hardly been sensible when he had first listened to the voice of hope.

Dazzled, crippled, helpless, it seemed almost impossible that he should share the flight, but Berenger remained resolute; and when Aime returned from his fourth frantic promenade, he was told that all was ready.

But for the strength of Berenger and Humfrey the poor fellow could never have been carried up and up, nearly to the top of the keep, then along a narrow gallery, then down again even to the castle hall, now empty, though with the candle-sticks still around where the bier had been. Aime knelt for a moment where the head had been, hiding his face; Osbert rested in a chair; and Philip looked wistfully up at his own sword hung over the chimney.

'Resume your swords, Messieurs,' said Aime, observing him; 'Madame desires it; and take pistols also.'

They gladly obeyed; and when, after this short delay, they proceeded, Osbert moved somewhat less painfully, but when they arrived at the stable only four horses stood there.

'Ah! this miserable!' cried Aime, passionately, 'he ruins all my arrangements.'

'Leave me,' again entreated Landry. 'Once outside, I can act the beggar and cripple, and get back to Normandy.'

'Better leave me,' said Humfrey; 'they cannot keep me when you are out of their clutches.'

'Help me, Humfrey,' said Berenger, beginning to lift his foster-brother to the saddle, but there the poor man wavered, cried out that his head swam, and he could not keep his seat, entreating almost in agony to be taken down.

'Lean on me,' said Berenger, putting his arms round him. 'There! you will be able to get to the Grange du Temple, where you will be in safe shelter.'

'Sir, sir,' cried Aime, ready to tear his hair, 'this is ruin! My lady meant you to make all speed to La Rochelle and there embark, and this is the contrary way!'

'That cannot be helped,' said Berenger; 'it is the only safe place for my foster-brother.'

Aime, with childish petulance, muttered something about ingratitude in crossing his lady's plans; but, as no one attended to him, he proceeded to unfasten his horse, and then exclaimed, half crying, 'Will no one help me?'

'Not able to saddle a horse! a pretty fellow for a cavalier!' exclaimed Philip, assisting, however, and in a few minutes they were all issuing from a low side gate, and looking back with bounding hearts at the drooping banner on the keep of Nid-de-Merle.

Only young Aime went with bowed head and drooping look, as though pouting, and Berenger, putting Osbert's bridle into Humfrey's hand, stepped up to him, saying, 'Hark you, M. de Selinville, I am sorry if we seemed to neglect you. We owe you and your lady all gratitude, but I must be the judge of my own duty, and you can only be with me if you conform.'

The young seemed to be devouring his tears, but only said, 'I was vexed to see my lady's plan marred, and your chance thrown away.'

'Of that I must judge,' said Berenger.

They were in a by-lane, perfectly solitary. The whole country was at the funeral. Through the frosty air there came an occasional hum or murmur from Berenger, or the tinkle of a cow-bell in the fields, but no human being was visible. It was certain, however, that the Rotrous, being Huguenots, and no vassals of Nid-de-Merle, would not be at the obsequies; and Berenger, walking with swift strides, supporting Osbert on his horse, continued to cheer him with promises of rest and relief there, and listened to no entreaties from Philip or Humfrey to take one of their horses. Had not Osbert borne him on his shoulders through the butchery at Paris, and endured three years of dungeon for his sake?

As for Philip, the slow pace of their ride was all insufficient for his glee. He made his horse caracole at every level space, till Berenger reminded him that they might have far to ride that night, and even then he was constantly breaking into attempts at shouting and whistling as often repressed, and springing up in his stirrups to look over the high hedges.

The Grange was so well concealed in its wooded ravine, that only when close upon the gate the party became aware that this farm-yard, usually so solitary, formed an exception to the general desertion of the country. There was a jingle and a stamp of horses in the court, which could hardly be daylight echoes of the Templars. Berenger feared that the Guisards might have descended Rotrou, and was stepping forward to reconnoiter, while young De Selinville, trembling, besought him not to run into danger, but to turn and hasten to La Rochelle. By this time, however, the party had been espied by two soldiers stationed at the gate, but not before Berenger had had time to remark that they did not wear either the gold *fleur-de-lys* like his late guards, or the white cross of Lorraine; nor had they the strange air of gay ferocity usual with the King's mercenaries. And almost by instincts, at a venture, he made the old Huguenot sign he had learnt form his father, and answered, 'For God and the Religion.'

The countersign was returned. 'Bearn and Bourbon is the word to-day, comrade,' replied the sentinel. '*Eh quoi!* have you had an encounter, that you bring a wounded man?'

'Not wounded, but nearly dead in a Guisard prison,' said Berenger, with an unspeakable sense of relief and security, as the sentries admitted them into the large walled court, where horses were eating hay, being watered and rubbed down; soldiers snatching a hasty meal in corners; gentlemen in clanking breastplates coming in and out of the house, evidently taking orders from a young man in a gray and silver suit, whose brown eagle face, thin cheeks, arched nose, and black eyes of keenest fire, struck Berenger at once with a sense of recognition as well as of being under a glance that seemed to search out everybody and everything at once.

'More friends!' and the tone again recalled a flood of recollections. 'I thank and welcome you. What! You have met the enemy—where is he?'

'My servant is not wounded, Sire,' said Berenger, removing his hat and bending low. 'This is the effect of long captivity. We have but just escaped.'

'Then we are the same case! Pardon me, sir, I have seen you before, but for once I am at fault.'

'When I call myself De Ribaumont, your Grace will not wonder.'

'The dead alive! If I mistake not, it was in the Inferno itself that we last met! But we have broken through the gates at last! I remember poor King Charles was delighted to hear that you lived! But where have you been a captive?'

'At Nid-de-Merle, Sire; my kinsmen accused me of treason in order to hinder my search for my wife. We escaped even now during the funeral of the Chevalier.'

'By favour of which we are making our way to Parthenay unsuspected, though, by my faith, we gather so like a snowball, that we could be a match for a few hundreds of Guisards. Who is with you, M. de Ribaumont?'

'Let me present to your Majesty my English brother, Philip Thistlewood,' said Berenger, drawing the lad forward, making due obeisance, though entirely ignorant who was the plainly-dressed, travel-soiled stranger, so evidently a born lord of men.

'An Englishman is ever welcome,' was his gracious reception.

'And,' added Berenger, 'let me also present the young De Selinville, to whom I owe my escape. Where is he, Philip?'

He seemed to be busy with the horses, and Berenger could not catch his eye.

'Selinville! I thought that good Huguenot house was extinct.'

'This is a relation of the late Count de Selinville, my cousin's husband, Sire. He arranged my evasion, and would be in danger at Nid-de-Merle. Call him, Philip.'

Before this was done, however, the King's attention was otherwise claimed, and turning to one of his gentlemen he said, 'Here, d'Augigne, I present to you an acquaintance made in Tartarus. See to his entertainment ere we start for Parthenay.'

Agrippa d'Aubigne, still young, but grave and serious-looking greeted M. de Ribaumont as men meet in hours when common interests make rapid friendships; and from him Berenger learnt, in a few words, that the King of Navarre's eyes had been opened at last to the treachery of the court, and his own dishonourable bondage. During a feverish attack, one night when D'Aubigne and D'Armagnac were sitting up with him, his resolution was taken; and on the first hunting day after his recovery, he, with these two, the Baron de Rosny and about thirty more of his suite, had galloped away, and had joined the Monsieur and the Prince of Conde at Alencon. He had abjured the Catholic faith, declared that nothing except ropes should bring him back to Paris, and that he left there the mass and his wife—the first he could dispense with, the last he meant to have; and he was now on his way to Parthenay to meet his sister, whom he had sent Rosny to demand. By the time Berenger had heard this, he had succeeded in finding honest Rotrou, who was in a state of great triumph, and readily undertook to give Osbert shelter, and as soon as he should have recovered to send him to head-quarters with some young men who he knew would take the field as soon as they learnt that the King of Navarre had set up his standard. Even the inroads made into the good farmer's stores did not abate his satisfaction in entertaining the prime hope of the Huguenot cause; but Berenger advanced as large a sum as he durst out of his purse, under pretext of the maintenance of Osbert during his stay at the Grange. He examined Rotrou upon his subsequent knowledge of Isaac Gardon and Eutacie, but nothing had been heard of them since their departure, now nearly three years back, except a dim rumour that they had been seen at the Synod of Montauban.

'Well, my friend,' said Philip, when about to remount, 'this will do rather better than a headlong gallop to Rochelle with Nid-de-Merle at our heels.'

'If M. le Baron is safe, it is well,' said Aime shortly.

'Is Selinville there?' said Berenger, coming up. 'Here, let me take you to the King of Navarre: he knew your family in Lauguedoc.'

'No, no,' petulantly returned the boy. 'What am I that he should notice me? It is M. de Ribaumont whom I follow, not him or his cause.'

'Boy,' said Berenger, dismayed, 'remember, I have answered for you.'

'I am no traitor,' proudly answered the strange boy, and Berenger was forced to be thus satisfied, though intending to watch him closely.

CHAPTER XL
THE SANDS OF OLONNE

Is it the dew of night

That on her glowing cheek

Shines in the moonbeam?—

Oh, she weeps, she weeps,

And the good angel that abandoned her

At her hell baptism, by her tears drawn down

Resumes his charge... and the hope

Of pardon and salvation rose

As now she understood

Thy lying prophecy of truth.—SOUTHEY

'M. de Ribaumont,' said Henry of Navarre, as he stood before the fire after supper at Parthenay, 'I have been thinking what commission I could give you proportioned to your rank and influence.'

'Thanks to your Grace, that inquiry is soon answered. I am a beggar here. Even my paternal estate in Normandy is in the hands of my cousin.'

'You have wrongs,' said Henry, 'and wrongs are sometimes better than possessions in a party like ours.'

Berenger seized the opening to explain his position, and mention that his only present desire was for permission, in the first place, to send a letter to England by the messenger whom the King was dispatching to Elisabeth, in tolerable security of her secret countenance; and, secondly, to ride to Nissard to examine into the story he had previously heeded so little, of the old man and his daughter rescued from the waves the day before La Sablerie was taken.

'If Pluto relented, my dear Orpheus, surely Navarre may,' said Henry good-humouredly; 'only may the priest not be more adamantine than Minos. Where lies Nissard? On the Sable d'Olonne? Then you may go thither with safety while we lie here, and I shall wait for my sister, or for news of her.'

So Berenger arranged for an early start on the morrow; and young Selinville listened with a frown, and strange look in his dark eyes. 'You go not to England?' he said.

'Not yet?' said Berenger

'This was not what my Lady expected,' he muttered; but though Berenger silenced him by a stern look, he took the first opportunity of asking Philip if it would not be far wiser for his brother to place himself in safety in England.

'Wiser, but less honest,' said Philip.

'He who has lost all here, who has incurred his grandfather's anger,' pursued Aime, 'were he not wiser to make his peace with his friends in England?'

'His friends in England would not like him the better for deserting his poor wife's cause,' said Philip. 'I advise you to hold your tongue, and not meddle or make.'

Aime subsided, and Philip detected something like tears. He had still much of rude English boyhood about him, and he laughed roughly. 'A fine fellow, to weep at a word! Hie thee back to feed my Lady's lap-dog, 'tis all thou art fit for.'

'There spoke English gratitude,' said Aime, with a toss of the head and flash of the eye.

Philip despised him the more for casting up his obligations, but had no retort to make. He had an idea of making a man of young Selinville, and his notion of the process had something of the bullying tendency of English young towards the poor-spirited or cowardly. He ordered the boy roughly, teased him for his ignorance of manly exercises, tried to cure his helplessness by increasing his difficulties, and viewed his fatigue as affectation or effeminacy. Berenger interfered now and then to guard the poor boy from a horse-jest or practical joke, but he too felt that Aime was a great incumbrance, hopelessly cowardly, fanciful, and petulant; and he was sometimes driven to speak to him with severity, verging on contempt, in hopes of rousing a sense of shame.

The timidity, so unusual and inexplicable in a youth of eighteen or twenty, sowed itself irrepressibly at the Sands of Olonne. These were not misty, as on Berenger's former journey. Nissard steeple was soon in sight, and the guide who joined them on a rough pony had no doubt that there would be ample time to cross before high water. There was, however, some delay, for the winter rains had brought down a good many streams of fresh water, and the sands were heavy and wet, so that their horses proceeded slowly, and the rush and dash of the waves proclaimed that the low of the tide had begun. To the two brothers the break and sweep was a home-sound, speaking of freshness and freedom, and the salt breeze and spray carried with them life and ecstasy. Philip kept as near the incoming waves as his inland-bred horse would endure, and sang, shouted, and hallooed to them as welcome as English waves; but Aime de Selinville had never even beheld the sea before: and even when the tide was still in the distance, was filled with nervous terror as each rushing fall sounded nearer; and, when the line of white foamy crests became more plainly visible, he was impelled to hurry on towards the steeple so fast that the guide shouted to him that he would only bury himself in a quicksand.

'But,' said he, white with alarm, and his teeth chattering, 'how can we creep with those dreadful waves advancing upon us to drown us?'

Berenger silence Philip's rude laugh and was beginning to explain that the speed of the waves could always be calculated by an experienced inhabitant; and his voice had seemed to pacify Aime a little, when the spreading water in front of a broken wave flowing up to his horse's feet, again rendered him nearly frantic. 'Let us go back!' he wildly entreated, turning his horse; but Berenger caught his bridle, saying, 'That would be truly death. Boy, unless you would be scorned, restrain your folly. Nothing else imperils us.'

Here, however, the guide interposed, saying that it had become too late to pursue their course along the curve of the shore, but they must at once cut straight across, which he had intended to avoid, because of the greater depth of a small river that they would have to cross, which divided further out into small channels, more easily forded. They thus went along the chord of the arc formed by the shore, and Aime was somewhat reassured, as the sea was at first farther off; but before long they reached the stream, which lost itself in many little channels in the sands, so that when the tide was out there was a perfect network of little streams dividing low shingly or grassy isles, but at nearly high tide, as at present, many of these islets were submerged, and the strife between river and sea caused sudden deepenings of the water in the channels.

The guide eagerly explained that the safest place for crossing was not by the large sandbank furthest inland and looking firm and promising—it was a recent shifting performance of the water's heaping up, and would certainly sink away and bury horse the channels on either side had shingly bottoms, and were safe.

'This way,' called Berenger, himself setting the example, and finding no difficulty; the water did not rise above his boots, and the current was not strong. He had reached the shingly isle when he looked round for his companions; Humfrey and Philip were close behind him; but, in spite of the loud 'gare!' of the guide, Aime, or his horse,—for each was equally senseless with alarm,—were making inwards; the horse was trying to tread on the sandbank, which gave way like the water itself, under its frantic struggles—there was a loud cry—a shrill, unmistakable woman's shriek—the horse was sinking—a white face and helpless form were being carried out on the waves, but not before Berenger had flung himself from his horse, thrown off his cloak and sword, and dashed into the water; and in the lapse of a few moments he struggled back to the island, where were Philip and Humfrey, leg-deep in water: the one received his burthen, the other helped him to land.

'On, gentlemen, not a moment to lose,' cried the guide; and Berenger, still panting, flung himself on his horse, held out his arms, gathered the small, almost inanimate figure upon the horse's neck before him, and in a few minutes more they had crossed the perilous passage, and were on a higher bank where they could safely halt; and Philip, as he came to help his brother, exclaimed, 'What a fool the boy is!'

'Hush!' said Berenger, gravely, as they laid the figure on the ground.

'What! he can't have been drowned in that moment. We'll bring him to.'

'Hands off!' said Berenger, kneeling over the gasping form, and adding in a lower voice, 'Don't you see?' He would his hand in the long drenched hair, and held it up, with cheeks burning like fire, and his scar purple.

'A woman!—what?—who?' Then suddenly divining, he exclaimed, 'The jade!' and started with wide eyes.

'Stand back,' said Berenger; 'she is coming to herself.'

Perhaps she had been more herself than he knew, for, as he supported her head, her hand stole over his and held it fast. Full of consternation, perplexity, and anger as he was, he could not but feel a softening pity towards a creature so devoted, so entirely at his mercy. At the moment when she lay helpless against him, gasps heaving her breast under her manly doublet, her damp hair spread on his knees, her dark eyes in their languor raised imploring his face, her cold hand grasping his, he felt as if this great love were a reality, and as if he were hunting a shadow; and, as if fate would have it so, he must save and gratify one whose affection must conquer his, who was so tender, so beautiful—even native generosity seemed on her side. But in the midst, as in his perplexity he looked up over the gray sea, he seemed to see the picture so often present to his mind of the pale, resolute girl, clasping her babe to her breast, fearless of the advancing sea, because true and faithful. And at that thought faith and prayer rallied once again round his heart, shame at the instant's wavering again dyed his cheek; he recalled himself, and speaking the more coldly and gravely because his heart was beating over hotly, he said, 'Cousin, you are better. It is but a little way to Nissard.'

'Why have you saved me, if you will not pity me?' she murmured.

'I will not pity, because I respect my kinswoman who has save our lives,' he said steadying his voice with difficulty. 'The priests of Nissard will aid me in sparing your name and fame.'

'Ah!' she cried, sitting up with a start of joy, 'but he would make too many inquiries! Take me to England first.'

Berenger started as he saw how he had been misunderstood.

'Neither here nor in England could my marriage be set aside, cousin. No; not priest shall take charge of you, and place you in safety and honour.'

'He shall not!' she cried hotly. 'Why—why will you drive me from you—me who ask only to follow you as a menial servant?'

'That has become impossible,' he answered; 'to say nothing of my brother, my servant and the guide have seen;' and, as she remembered her streaming hair, and tried, in dawning confusion, to gather it together, he continued: 'You shrank from the eye of the King of Navarre. You cannot continue as you have done; you have not even strength.'

'Ah! have you sailed for England,' she murmured.

'It had only been greater shame,' he said. 'Cousin, I am head of your family, husband of your kinswoman, and bound to respect the reputation you have risked for me. I shall, therefore, place you in charge of the priest till you can either return to your aunt or to some other convent. You can ride now. We will not wait longer in these wet garments.'

He raised her from the ground, threw his own dry cloak round her shoulders and unmanageable hair, and lifted her on his horse; but, as she would have leant against him, he drew himself away, beckoned Philip, and put the bridle into his hands, saying, 'Take care of her. I shall ride on and warm the priest.'

'The rock of diamond,' she murmured, not aware that the diamond had been almost melting. That youthful gravity and resolution, with the mixture of respect and protection, imposed as usual upon her passionate nature, and daunted her into meekly riding beside Philip without a word—only now and then he heard a low moan, and knew that she was weeping bitterly.

At first the lad had been shocked beyond measure, and would have held aloof as from a kind of monster, but Madame de Selinville had been the first woman to touch his fancy, and when he heard how piteously she was weeping, and recollected where he should have been but for her, as well as all his own harshness to her as a cowardly boy, he felt himself brutally ungrateful, and spoke: 'Don't weep so, Madame; I am sorry I was rude to you, but you see, how should I take you for a woman?'

Perhaps she heard, but she heeded not.

'My brother will take good care to shield you,' Philip added. 'He will take care you are safe in one of your nunneries;' and as she only wept the more, he added, with a sudden thought, 'You would not go there; you would embrace the Protestant faith?'

'I would embrace whatever was his.'

Philip muttered something about seeing what could be done. They were already at the entrance of the village, and Berenger had come out to meet them, and, springing towards him, Philip exclaimed, in a low voice, 'Berry, she would abjure her Popish errors! You can't give her up to a priest.'

'Foolery, Philip,' answered Berenger, sternly.

'If she would be a convert!'

'Let her be a modest woman first;' and Berenger, taking her bridle, led her to the priest's house.

He found that Pere Colombeau was preaching a Lent sermon, and that nobody was at home but the housekeeper, to whom he had explained briefly that the lady with him had been forced to escape in disguise, had been nearly drowned, and was in need of refreshment and female clothing. Jacinthe did not like the sound, but drenched clothes were such a passport to her master's house, that she durst not refuse. Berenger carried off his other companions to the cabaret, and when he had dried himself, went to wait for the priest at the church door, sitting in the porch where more than one echo of the exhortation to repentance and purity rang in his ears, and enforced his conviction that here he must be cruel if he would be merciful.

It was long before Pere Colombeau came out, and then, if the scar had not blushed for all the rest of his face, the sickly, lanky lad of three years since would hardly have been recognized to the good cure. But the priest's aspect was less benignant when Berenger tried to set before him his predicament; he coldly asked where the unhappy lady was; and when Berenger expressed his intention of coming the next morning to ask his counsel, he only bowed. He did not ask the brothers to supper, nor show any civility; and Berenger, as he walked back to the cabaret, perceived that his story was but half believed, and that, if Diane's passion were still stronger than her truth or generosity, she would be able to make out a terrible case against him, and to willing ears, naturally disposed against a young cavalier and a heretic.

He sat much dispirited by the fire of the little wine shop, thinking that his forbearance had been well-nigh thrown away, and that his character would never be cleared in Eustacie's eyes, attaching, indeed, more importance to the blot than would have been done by a youth less carefully reared.

It was quite dark when a knock came to the door: the cure's white head appeared in the lamplight; he nodded kindly to all the guests, and entreated that M. de Ribaumont would do him a favour to come and speak with him.

No sooner were they outside the house, than the cure held out his hand, saying 'Sir, forgive me for a grievous injustice towards you;' then pressing his hand, he added with a voice tremulous with emotion, 'Sir, it is no slight thing to have saved a wandering sheep by your uprightness and loyalty.'

'Have you then opened her eyes, father?' said Berenger, relieved from a heavy load.

'You have, my son,' said the old man. 'You have taught her what truth and virtue are. For the rest, you shall heard for yourself.'

Before Berenger knew where he was, a door was opened, and he found himself in the church. The building was almost entirely dark; there were two tall lights at the altar in distance, and a few little slender tapers burning before certain niches and shrines, but without power to conquer with the gloom more than enough to spread a pale circle of yellow light beneath them, and to show mysteriously a bit of vaulting above. A single lamp hung from an arch near the door, and beneath it, near a pillar, knelt, or rather crouched, on the floor, a female figure with a dark peasant cloak drawn over her head.

'The first token of penitence is reparation to the injured,' said the priest.

Berenger looked at him anxiously.

'I will not leave you,' he added. 'See, I shall pray for you yonder, by the altar,' and he slowly moved up the aisle.

'Rise, cousin, I entreat you,' said Berenger, much embarrassed, as he disappeared in the darkness.

'I must speak thus,' she answered, in a hoarse, exhausted voice. 'Ah! pardon, pardon!' she added, rising, however, so far as to raise clasped hands and an imploring face. 'Ah! can you pardon? It was through me that you bear those wounds; that she—Eustacie—was forced into the masque, to detain you for THAT night. Ah! pardon.'

'That is long past,' said Berenger. 'I have been too near death not to have pardoned that long ago. Rise, cousin, I cannot see you thus.'

'That is not all,' continued Diane. 'It was I—I who moved my father to imprison you.' Then, as he bent his head, and would have again entreated her to rise, she held out her hand as if to silence him, and spoke faster, more wildly. 'Then—then I thought it would save your life. I thought——' she looked at him strangely with her great dark eyes, all hollow and cavernous in her white face.

'I know,' said Berenger, kindly, 'you often urged it on me.'

There was a sort of movement on the part of the kneeling figure of the priest at the altar, and she interrupted, saying precipitately. 'Then—then, I did think you free.'

'Ah!' he gasped. 'Now——!'

'Now I know that she lives!' and Diane once more sank at his feet a trembling, shrinking, annihilated heap of shame and misery.

Berenger absolutely gave a cry that, though instantly repressed, had the ring of ecstasy in it. 'Cousin—cousin!' he cried, 'all is forgiven—all forgotten, if you will only tell me where!'

'That I cannot,' said Diane, rousing herself again, but speaking in a dull, indifferent tone, as of one to whom the prime bitterness was past, 'save that she is under the care of the Duchess de Quinet;' and she then proceeded, as though repeating a lesson: 'You remember the Italian conjurer whom you would not consult? Would that I had not!' she added, clasping her hands. 'His prediction lured me? Well, he saw my father privately, told him he had seen her, and had bought her jewels, even her hair. My father sent him in quest of her again, but told not me till the man returned with tidings that she was at Quinet, in favour with the Duchess. You remember that he went from home. It was to demand he; and, ah! you know how long I had loved you, and they told me that your marriage was void, and that all would be well upon the dispensation coming. And now the good father there tells me that I was deceived—cruelly deceived—that such a dispensation would not be granted save through gross misrepresentation.' Then, as Berenger began to show tokens of eagerness to come at tidings of Eustacie, she continued, 'Ah! it is vain to seek to excuse one you care not for. My father could learn nothing from the Duchess; she avowed that she had been there, but would say no more. However, he and my brother were sure she was under their protection; they took measures, and—and the morning my poor father was stricken, there had been a letter from my brother to say he was on her track, and matters must be ended with you, for he should have her in a week;' and then, as Berenger started forward with an inarticulate outburst, half of horror, half of interrogation, she added, 'Where, he said not, nor did I learn from him. All our one interview was spend in sneers that answered to my wild entreaties; but this I know—that you would never have reached Tours a living man.'

'And now, now he is on the way to her!' cried Berenger, 'and you kept it from me!'

'There lay my hope,' said Diane, raising her head; and now, with glittering eyes and altered voice, 'How could I not but hate her who had bereaved me of you; her for whose sake I could not earn your love?'

The change of her tone had, perhaps, warned the priest to draw nearer, and as she perceived him, she said, 'Yes, father, this is not the way to absolution, but my heart will burst if I say not all.'

'Thou shalt not prevail, foul spirit,' said the priest, looking earnestly into the darkness, as though he beheld the fiend hovering over her, 'neither shall these holy walls be defiled with accents of unhallowed love. You have made your reparation, daughter; it is enough.'

'And can you tell me no more?' said Berenger, sadly. 'Can you give me no clue that I may save her from the wolf that may be already on her track? Cousin, if you would do this, I would bless you for ever.'

'Alas! I would if I could! It is true, cousin, I have no heart to deceive you any longer. But it is to Madame de Quinet that you must apply, and if my brother has though me worth pursuit, you may be in time! One moment,'— as he would have sprung away as if in the impulse to fly to the rescue,— 'cousin; had you gone to England as I hoped, I would have striven to deserve to win that love of yours, but you have conquered by your constancy. Now, father, I have spoken my last save as penitent.'

She covered her head and sank down again.

Berenger, bewildered and impelled to be doing something, let the priest lead him out before he exclaimed, 'I said nothing to her of pardon!'

'You do pardon?' said the priest.

He paused a moment. 'Freely, if I find my wife. I can only remember now that she set me on the way. I would ease her soul, poor thing, and thinking would make me hard again.'

'Do the English bring up their sons with such feelings?' asked the cure, pausing for a moment.

'Of course,' said Berenger. 'May I say that one word, sir?'

'Not now,' said the priest; 'she had better be left to think of her sin towards Heaven, rather than towards man.'

'But do you leave her there, sir?'

'I shall return. I shall pray for her true penitence,' said the priest, and Berenger perceived from his tone that one without the pale might inquire no further. He only asked how safe and honourable shelter could be found for her; and the cure replied that he had already spoken to her of the convent of Lucon, and should take her there so soon as it could safely be done, and that Abbess Monique, he trusted, would assist her crushed spirit in finding the path of penitence. He thought her cousin had better not endeavour to see her again; and Berenger himself was ready to forget her very existence in his burning anxiety to outstrip Narcisse in the quest of Eustacie.

CHAPTER XLI
OUR LADY OF HOPE

Welcome to danger's hour,

Brief greeting serves the time of strife.

—SCOTT

As soon as it was possible to leave Nissard, Berenger was on his way back to head-quarters, where he hoped to meet the Duke de Quinet among the many Huguenot gentlemen who were flocking to the Bourbon standard; nor was he disappointed in the hope, for he was presented to a handsome middle-aged gentleman, who told him, with much politeness, that his mother had had the honour to receive and entertain Mme. de Ribaumont and that some months ago he had himself arranged for the conveyance of her letters to England, but, he said, with a smile, he made a point of knowing nothing of his mother's guests, lest his duties as a governor might clash with those of hospitality. He offered to expedite M. de Ribaumont's journey to Quinet, observing that, if Nid de Merle were, indeed, on the point of seizing the lady, it must be by treachery; indeed he had, not ten days back, had the satisfaction of hanging an Italian mountebank who had last year stolen a whole packet of dispatches, among them letters from Mme. de Ribaumont, and the fellow was probably acting as a spy upon her, so that no time was to be lost in learning from his mother where she was. On the next morning he was about to send forward twenty men to reinforce a little frontier garrison on the river Dronne, and as M. le Baron must pass through the place, it would be conferring a favour on him to take the command. The men were all well mounted, and would not delay; and when once across the frontier of Guyenne, no escort would be needed.

Berenger gladly accepted the proposal. It did not occur to him that he was thus involved in the civil war, and bearing arms against the sovereign. In spite of Queen Elisabeth's alliance with the French court, she connived at her youthful subjects seeking the bubble reputation in the mouths of Valois cannon; and so little did Henry III. seem to Berenger to be his king, that he never thought of the question of allegiance,—nay, if the royal officers were truly concerned in his arrest, he was already an outlaw. This was no moment for decision between Catholic and Calvinist; all he wanted was to recover his wife and forestall her enemies.

Henry of Navarre gave his full consent to the detachment being placed under charge of M. de Ribaumont. He asked somewhat significantly what had become of the young gentleman who had attended M. de Ribaumont, and Philip blushed crimson to the ears, while Berenger replied, with greater coolness than he had given himself credit for, that the youth had been nearly drowned on the Sable d'Olonne, and had been left at Dom Colombeau's to recover. The sharp-witted King looked for a moment rather as Sir Hugh the Heron did when Marmion accounted for his page's absence, but was far too courteous and too INSOUCIANT to press the matter further, though Berenger saw quite enough of is expression to feel that he had been delivered from his companion only just in time.

Berenger set forth as soon as his impatience could prevail to get the men into their saddles. He would fain have ridden day and night, and grudged every halt for refreshment, so as almost to run the risk of making the men mutinous. Evening was coming on, and his troop had dismounted at a cabaret, in front of which he paced up and down with Philip, trying to devise some pretext for hastening them on another stage before night, when a weary, travel-stained trooper rode up to the door and was at once hailed as a comrade by the other men, and asked, 'What cheer at Pont de Dronne?'

'Bad enough,' he answered, 'unless you can make the more speed there!' then making obeisance to Berenger he continued his report, saying that Captain Falconnet was sending him to M. le Duc with information that the Guisards were astir, and that five hundred *gens d'armes*, under the black Nid de Merle, as it was said, were on their way intending to surprise Pont de Dronne, and thus cut the King of Navarre off from Guyenne and his kingdom beyond it. After this Berenger had no more difficulty with his men, who were most of them Quinet vassals, with homes south of the Dronne, and the messenger only halted for a hasty meal, hastening on to the Duke, that a more considerable succour might at once be dispatched.

'Is she there whom they call the Lady of Hope?' asked one of the soldiers, a mercenary, less interested than most of his comrades, as he had only a fortnight since transferred his services from Guise to Quinet.

'Our Lady of Sadness just now,' replied the messenger; 'her old father is at the point of death. However, she is there, and at our last siege twenty wine-skins would not so well have kept up men's hearts.'

'And the little one, the white fairy, is she there too? They say 'tis a spirit, a changeling that could not brook the inside of a church, but flew out of the Moustier at Montauban like a white swan, in the middle of a sermon.'

'I only know I've seen her sleep like a dormouse through prayers, sermon, and all at Pont de Dronne. *Follette* is she be, she belongs to the white elves of the moonlight.'

'Well, they say bullets won't touch her, and no place can be taken where she is,' replied the trooper. 'Nay, that Italian pedlar rogue, the same that the Duke has since hung, has sold to long Gilles and snub-nosed Pierre silver bullets, wherewith they have sworn to shoot the one or the other next time they had a chance.'

These words were spoken at not great distance from Berenger, but passed by him as mere men-at-arms' gossip, in his eagerness to expedite the start of his party; and in less than an hour they were *en route* for Pont de Dronne; but hasten as he would, it was not till near noon the next day that he came in sight of a valley, through which wound a river, crossed by a high-backed bridge, with a tall pointed arch in the middle, and a very small one on either side. An old building of red stone, looking like what it was—a monastery converted into a fortress—stood on the nearer, or northern bank, and on the belfry tower waved a flag with the arms of Quinet. Higher up the valley, there was an ominous hum, and clouds of smoke and dust; and the *gen d'armes*, who knew the country, rejoiced that they were come just in time, and exchanged anxious questions whether the enemy were not fording the river above them, so as to attack not only the fortress on this northern side, but the bridge tower on the southern bank of the river.

Spurring down the hill, the party were admitted, at the well-guarded gateway, into a large thickly-walled yard, where the soldiers and horses remained, and Berenger and Philip, passing through a small arched doorway into the body of the old monastery, were conducted to a great wainscoted hall, where a pulpit projecting from the wall, and some defaced emblematic ornaments, showed that this had once been the refectory, though guard-room appliances now occupied it. The man who had shown them in left them, saying he would acquaint Captain Falconnet with their arrival, and just then a sound of singing drew both brothers to the window. It looked out on what had once been the quadrangle, bounded on three sides by the church, the refectory, and the monk's lodgings, the cloistered arcade running round all these. The fourth side was skirted by the river, which was, however, concealed by an embankment, raised, no doubt, to supply the place of the wall, which had been unnecessary to the peaceful original inhabitants. What attracted Berenger's eyes was, however, a group in the cloister, consisting of a few drooping figures, some of men in steel caps, others of veiled, shrouded women, and strange, mingled feelings swept over him as he caught the notes of the psalm sung over the open grave—

'Si qu'en paix et seurte bonne

Coucherai et reposerai—

Car, Seigneur, ta bonte tout ordonne

Et elle seule espoir donne

Que seur et sain regnant serai.'

'Listen, Philip,' he said, with moistening eyes; then as they ended, 'It is the 4th Psalm: "I lay me down in peace and take my rest." Eustacie and I used to sing it to my father. It was well done in these mourners to sing it over him whom they are laying down to take his rest while the enemy are at the gates. See, the poor wife still kneels while the rest disperse; how dejected and utterly desolate she looks.'

He was so intently watching her as not to perceive the entrance of a tall, grizzled old man in a steel cap, evidently the commander of the garrison. There was the brief welcome of danger's hour—the briefer, because Captain Falconnet was extremely deaf, and, taking it for granted that the new-comers were gentlemen of the Duke's, proceeded to appoint them their posts without further question. Berenger had intended to pursue his journey to Quinet without delay, but the intelligence that the enemy were on the southern as well as the northern side of the river rendered this impossible; and besides, in defending this key of Guyenne against Narcisse, he was also defending Eustacie.

The state of affairs was soon made known to him. The old monastery, covering with its walls an extensive space, formed a fortress quite strong enough to resist desultory attacks, and protect the long bridge, which was itself strongly walled on either side, and with a barbican at the further end. In former assaults the attacks had always been on the north, the Catholic side, as it might be called; but now the enemy had crossed the river above the fort, and were investing the place on both sides. Long foreseeing this, the old commandant had guarded the bank of the river with the earthwork, a long mound sloped irregularly on either hand, over which numerous little paths had since been worn by the women within, when on their way to the river with their washing; but he had been setting every one to work to destroy and fill up these, so that the rampart was smooth and slopping, perfectly easy indeed to cross, but high and broad enough to serve as an effectual protection against such artillery as the detached troops of the Guise party were likely to possess; and the river was far too wide, deep, and strong in its main current to be forded in the face of a hostile garrison. The captain had about fifty *gen d'armes* in his garrison, besides the twenty new-comers whom he persisted in regarding as Berenger's charge; and there were, besides, some seventy peasants and silk spinners, who had come into the place as a refuge from the enemy—and with these he hoped to hold put till succour should come from the Duke. He himself took the command of the north gate, where the former assaults had been made, and he instructed to his new ally the tower protecting the bridge, advising him to put on armour; but Berenger, trying on a steel cap, found that his head could not bear the weight and heat, and was forced to return to his broad-brimmed Spanish hat, while Philip in high glee armed himself as best he could with what Captain Falconnet could lend him. he was too much excited to eat of the scanty meal that was set before them: a real flight seemed like a fair-day to him, and he was greatly exalted by his brother's post of command—a post that Berenger felt a heavy responsibility only thrust upon him by the commandant's incapacity of hearing how utterly inexperienced he was.

The formal summons to surrender to the King, and the refusal, had duly passed, and it became evident that the first attack was to be on the bridge-gate. Captain Falconnet hurried to the place, and the fighting was hot and desperate. Every assailant who tried to throw his fagot into the moat became a mark for arquebus or pistol, and the weapons that had so lately hung over the hearth at Nid de Merle were now aimed again and again at the heads and corslets of Guisards, with something of the same exulting excitement as, only higher, more engrossing, and fiercer than, that with which the lads had taken aim at a wolf, or ridden after a fox. Scaling-ladders were planted and hurled down again; stones were cast from the battlements, crushing the enemy; and throughout Berenger's quick eye, alert movements, and great height and strength, made him a most valuable champion, often applauded by a low murmur of commendation from old Falconnet, or a loud shout of 'Ha, well done, the Duke's Englishman,' from the *gen d'armes*—for English they would have him to be—on the presumptions afforded by his companions, his complexion, and his slow speech. Nor did Philip and Humfrey fail to render good service. But just as the enemy had been foiled in a sharp assault and were dragging away their wounded, Philip touched his brother, and saying, 'I can hold out no longer,' showed blood trickling down his right side.

Berenger threw an arm round him, and Captain Falconnet, seeing his case, said, 'You are hit, *petit Anglais*; you have done gallantly. There will be time for you to take him to his quarters, sir; these fellows have had enough for the present, and you can tarry with him till you hear the bugle. Whither, did you ask? Let me see. You, Renaud, take him to the chapel: the old chancel behind the boarding will be more private; and desire Madame to look to him. Farewell! I hope it may prove slight; you are a brave youth.' And he shook hands with Philip, whose intense gratification sustained him for many steps afterwards.

He hardly remembered receiving the hurt, and was at first too busy to heed it, or to call off any one attention, until a dread of falling, and being

- 369 -

trodden on, had seized him and made him speak; and indeed he was so dizzy that Berenger with difficulty kept him on his feet over the bridge, and in the court lifted him in his arms and carried him almost fainting into the cloister, where by the new-made grave still knelt the black-veiled mourner. She started to her feet as the soldier spoke to her, and seemed at first not to gather the sense of his words; but then, as if with an effort, took them in, made one slight sound like a moan of remonstrance at the mention of the place, but again recollecting herself, led the way along a stone passage, into which a flight of stairs descended into the apsidal chancel, roughly boarded off from the rest of the church. It was a ruinous, desolate place, and Berenger looked round in dismay for some place on which to lay down his almost unconscious burthen. The lady bent her head and signed towards the stone sedilia in the wall; then, after two ineffectual essays to make her voice audible, choked as it was with long weeping, she said, low and huskily, 'We will make him more comfortable soon;' and added some orders to the soldier, who disappeared up the stairway, and Berenger understood that he was gone to fetch bedding. Then taking from under her heavy mourning cloak a large pair of scissors, she signed to Berenger how to support his brother, while they relieved him of his corslet, sword-belt, and doublet. The soldier had meantime returned with an old woman, both loaded with bedding, which she signed to them to arrange in one of the little bays or niches that served to form a crown of lesser chapels around the chancel. She flung aside her muffling cloak, but her black hood still hung far over her face, and every now and then hand or handkerchief was lifted as if to clear her eyes from the tears that would not cease to gather and blind her; and she merely spoke when some direction to an assistant, some sympathetic word to the patient, was needed. Even Philip in his dizzy trance guessed that he was succeeding to the bed whence one much dearer had gone to his quieter rest in the cloister. Before he was laid there, however, the bugle sounded; there was a loud shout, and Philip exclaimed, 'Go, brother!'

'Trust him to me, sir,' said the sunken, extinguished voice; 'we will do our best for him.'

He was forced merely to lift Philip to the bed, and to hurry away, while the soldier followed him saying, consolingly, 'Fear not, sir, now our Lady of Hope has him. Nothing goes ill to which she sets her hand.'

Another growl of artillery was not heard, and it was time for the warriors to forget the wounded in the exigencies of the present. An attack was made on both gates at once, and the commandant being engaged at his own post, Berenger had to make the utmost of his brief experience, backed by the counsel of a tough old sergeant; and great was his sense of exhilaration, and absolute enjoyment in this full and worthy taxing of every power of mind or body. The cry among the enemy, 'Aime at the black plume,' attested his prominence; but he black plum was still unscathed when spring twilight fell. The din began to subside; recalls were sounded by the besiegers; and Berenger heard his own exploit bawled in the ear of the deaf commandant, who was advancing over the bridge. The old captain complimented him, told him that he should be well reported of to M. le Duc and Sieur la Noue, and invited him to supper and bed in his own quarters. The supper Berenger accepted, so soon as he should know how it was with his brother; but as to bed, he intended to watch his brother, and visit his post form time to time.

The captain entered by the main door of the chapel, where ten or twelve wounded were now lying, tended by peasant women. Berenger merely passed through, seeing as he went the black hood busy over a freshly-brought-in-patient. He found a door which admitted him through the rough screen of boards to the choir where he had been in the earlier part of the day. The moonlight came through the shivered eastern windows, but a canvas curtain had been hung so as to shelter Philip's vaulted recess from the cold draught, and the bed itself, with a chair beside it, looked neat, clean, and comfortable. Philip himself was cheery; he said the bullet had made a mere flesh-wound, and had passed out on the other side, and the Lady of Hope, as they called he, was just such another as Aunt Cecily, and had made him very comfortable, with clean linen, good cool drinks, and the tenderest hand. But he was very sleepy, so sleepy that he hardly cared to hear of the combat, only he roused himself for a moment to say, 'Brother, I have seen Dolly.'

'Dolly!'

'Our sister Dolly.'

'Ah, Phil! many a strange visitor has come to me in the Walnut Chamber at home.'

'I tell you I was in my perfect senses,' returned Philip; 'there she was, just as when we left her. And, what was stranger still, she talked French.'

'Sleep and see her again,' laughed Berenger.

CHAPTER XLII
THE SILVER BULLET

I am all wonder, O my son, my soul

Is stunned within me; powers to speak to him

Or to interrogate him have I none,

Or even to look on him.

                  —*Cowper's ODYSSEY*

In his waking senses Philip adhered to his story that his little sister Dolly had stood at the foot of his bed, called him '*le pauvre*' and had afterwards disappeared, led away by the nursing lady. It seemed to Berenger a mere delusion of feverish weakness; for Philip had lost a great deal of blood, and the wound, though not dangerous, permitted no attempt at moving, and gave much pain. Of the perfections of the lady as nurse and surgeon Philip could not say enough, and, pale and overwept as he allowed her to be, he declared that he was sure that her beauty must equal Mme. De Selinville's. Berenger laughed, and looking round this strange hospital, now lighted by the full rays of the morning sun, he was much struck by the scene.

It was the chancel of the old abbey church. The door by which they had entered was very small, and perhaps had led merely to the abbot's throne, as an irregularity for his own convenience, and only made manifest by the rending away of the rich wooden stall work, some fragments of which still clung to the walls. The east end, like that of many French churches, formed a semicircle, the high altar having been in the centre, and five tall deep bays forming lesser chapels embracing it, their vaults all gathered up into one lofty crown above, and a slender pillar separating between each chapel, each of which further contained a tall narrow window. Of course, all had been utterly desolated, and Philip was actually lying in one of these chapels, where the sculptured figure of St. John and his Eagle still remained on the wall; and a sufficient remnant of his glowing sanguine robe of love was still in the window to serve as a shield from the *bise*. The high altar of rich marbles was a mere heap of shattered rubbish; but what surprised Berenger more than all the ruined architectural beauty which his *cinque-cento* trained taste could not understand, was, that the tiles of the pavement were perfectly clean, and diligently swept, the rubbish piled up in corners; and here and there the relics of a cross or carved figure lay together, as by a tender, reverential hand. Even the morsels of painted glass had been placed side by side on the floor, so as to form a mosaic of dark red, blue, and green; and a child's toy lay beside this piece of patchwork. In the midst of his observations, however, Captain Falconnet's servant came to summon him to breakfast; and the old woman appearing at the same time, he could not help asking whether the lady were coming.

'Oh yes, she will come to dress his wound in good time,' answered the old woman.

'And when? I should like to hear what she thinks of it,' said Berenger.

'How?' said the old woman with a certain satisfaction in his disappointment; 'is our Lady of Hope to be coming down among you gay gallants?'

'But who is this Lady of Hope?' demanded he.

'Who should she be but our good pastor's daughter? Ah! and a brave, good daughter she was too, abiding the siege because his breath was so bad that he could not be moved.'

'What was his name?' asked Berenger, attracted strangely by what he heard.

'Ribault, Monsieur—Pasteur Ribault. Ah! a good man, and sound preacher, when preach he could; but when he could not, his very presence kept the monks' REVENANTS from vexing us—as a cat keeps mice away; and, ah! The children have been changed creatures since Madame dealt with them. What! Monsieur would know why they call her our Lady of Hope? Esperance is her true name; and, moreover, in the former days this abbey had an image that they called Notre-Dame de l'Esperance, and the poor deceived folk thought it did great miracles. And so, when she came hither, and wrought such cures, and brought blessing wherever she went, it became a saying among us that at length we had our true Lady of Hope.

A more urgent summons here forced Berenger away, and his repetition of the same question received much the same answer from deaf old Captain Falconnet. He was obliged to repair to his post with merely a piece of bread in his hand; abut, though vigilance was needful, the day bade fair to be far less actively occupied than its predecessor: the enemy were either disposed to turn the siege into a blockade, or were awaiting reinforcements and heavier artillery; and there were only a few desultory attacks in the early part of the morning. About an hour before noon, however, the besiegers seemed to be drawing out in arms, as if to receive some person of rank, and at the same time sounds were heard on the hills to the eastward, as if troops were on the march. Berenger having just been told by the old sergeant that probably all would be quiet for some time longer, and been almost laughed at by the veteran for consulting him whether it would be permissible for him to be absent a few minutes to visit his brother, was setting out across the bridge for the purpose, his eyes in the direction of the rampart, which followed the curve of the river. The paths which—as has been said—the feet of the washerwomen and drawers of water had worn away in quieter times, had been smoothed and scarped away on the outer side, so as to come to an abrupt termination some feet above the gay marigolds, coltsfoot, and other spring flowers that smiled by the water-side. Suddenly he beheld on the rampart a tiny gray and white figure, fearlessly trotting, or rather dancing, along the summit and the men around him exclaimed, 'The little moonbeam child!' 'A fairy—a changeling!'—'They cannot shoot at such a babe!' 'Nor could they harm her!' 'Hola! little one! *Gare!* Go back to your mother!' 'Do not disturb yourself, sir; she is safer than you,' were the ejaculations almost at the same moment, while he sprang forward, horrified at the peril of such an infant. He had reached the angle between the bridge and rampart, when he perceived that neither humanity nor superstition were protecting the poor child; for, as she turned down the remnant of one of the treacherous little paths, a man in bright steel and deep black had spurred his horse to the river's brink, and was deliberately taking aim at her. Furious at such brutality, Berenger fired the pistol he held in his hand, and the wretch dropped from his horse; but at the same moment his pistol exploded, and the child rolled down the bank, whence a piteous wail came up, impelling Berenger to leap down to her assistance, in the full face of the enemy. Perhaps he was protected for the moment by the confusion ensuing on the fall of the officer; and when he reached the bottom of the bank, he saw the little creature on her feet, her round cap and gray woolen dress stripped half off in the fall, and her flaxen hair falling round her plump, white, exposed shoulder, but evidently unhurt, and gathering yellow marigolds as composedly as though she had been making May garlands. He snatched her up, and she said, with the same infantine dignity, 'Yes, take me up; the naughty people spoilt the path. But I must take my beads first.' And she tried to struggle out of his arms, pointing therewith to a broken string among the marshy herb-age on which gleamed—the pearls of Ribaumont!

In the few seconds in which he grasped them, and then bore the child up the embankment in desperate bounds, a hail of bullets poured round him, ringing on his breastplate, shearing the plume from his hat, but scarcely even heard; and in another moment he had sprung down, on the inner side, grasping the child with all his might, but not daring even to look at her, in the wondrous flash of that first conviction. She spoke first. 'Put me down, and let me have my beads,' she said in a grave, clear tone; and then first he beheld a pair of dark blue eyes, a sweet wild-rose face—Dolly's all over. He pressed her so fast and so close, in so speechless and over powering an ecstasy, that again she repeated, and in alarm, 'Put me down, I want my mother!'

'Yes, yes! your mother! your mother! your mother!' he cried, unable to let her out of his embrace; and then restraining himself as he saw her frightened eyes, in absolute fear of her spurning him, or struggling from him, 'My sweet! my child! Ah! do you not know me?' Then, remembering how wild this was, he struggled to speak calmly: 'What are you called, my treasure?'

'I am *la petite Rayonette*,' she said, with puzzled dignity and gravity; 'and my mother says I have a beautiful long name of my own besides.'

'Berangere—my Berangere—'

'That is what she says over me, as I go to sleep in her bosom at night,' said the child, in a wondering voice, soon exchanged for entreaty, 'Oh, hug me not so hard! Oh, let me go—let me go to her! Mother! mother!'

'My child, mine own, I am take thee!—Oh, do not struggle with me!' he cried, himself imploring now. 'Child, one kiss for thy father;' and meantime, putting absolute force on his vehement affection, he was hurrying to the chancel.

There Philip hailed them with a shout as of desperate anxiety relieved; but before a word could be uttered, down the stairs flew the Lady of Hope, crying wildly, 'Not there—she is not—' but perceiving the little one in the stranger's arms, she held out her own, crying, 'Ah! is she hurt, my angel?'

'Unhurt, Eustacie! Our child is unhurt!' Berenger said, with an agonized endeavour to be calm; but for the moment her instinct was so entirely absorbed in examining into the soundness of her child's limbs, that she neither saw nor hear anything else.

'Eustacie,' he said, laying his hand on her arm, she started back, with bewildered eyes. 'Eustacie—wife? do you not know me? Ah! I forgot that I am changed.'

'You—you—' she gasped, utterly confounded, and gazing as if turned to stone, and though at that moment the vibration of a mighty discharge of cannon rocked the walls, and strewed Philip's bed with the crimson shivers of St. John's robe, yet neither of them would have been sensible of it had not Humfrey rushed in at the same moment, crying, 'They are coming on like friends, sir!'

Berenger passed his hand over his face. 'You will know me WHEN—IF I return, my dearest,' he said. 'If not, then still, thank God! Philip, to you I trust them!'

And with one kiss on that still, cold, almost petrified brow, he had dashed away. There was a space of absolutely motionless silence, save that Eustacie let herself drop on the chancel step, and the child, presently breaking the spell, pulled her to attract her notice to the flowers. 'Mother, here are the *soucis* for the poor gentleman's broth. See, the naughty people had spoilt all the paths, and I rolled down and tore my frock, and down fell the beads, but be not angry, mother dear, for the good gentleman picked them up, and carried me up the bank.'

'The bank!' cried Eustacie, with a scream, as the sense of the words reached her ears. 'Ah! no wonder! Well might thy danger bring thy father's spirit;' and she grasped the little one fervently in her arms, murmuring, 'Thank, thank God, indeed! Oh! my precious one; and did He send that blessed spirit to rescue thee?'

'And will you tie up my frock? and may I put the flowers into the broth?' chattered Rayonette. 'And why did he kiss me and hug me so tight? and how did he know what you say over me as we fall asleep?'

Eustacie clasped her tighter, with a convulsive, shudder of thankfulness; and Philip, but half hearing, and barely gathering the meaning of her mood, ventured to speak, 'Madame——'

As if touched by an electric shock, Eustacie started up, as recalled to instant needs, and coming towards him said, 'Do you want anything, sir? Pardon one who has but newly seen a spirit from the other world—brought by his child's danger.' And the dazed, trance-like look was returning.

'Spirit!' cried Philip. 'Nay, Madame, it was himself. Ah! and you are she whom we have sought so long; and this dear child—no wonder she has Dolly's face.'

'Who—what?' said Eustacie, pressing her temples with her hands, as if to retain her senses. 'Speak; was yonder a living or dead man—and who?'

'Living, thank God! and your own husband; that is, if you are really Eustacie. Are you indeed?' he added, becoming doubtful.

'Eustacie, that am I,' she murmured. 'But he is dead—they killed him; I swathe blood where he had waited for me. His child's danger brought him from the grave.'

'No, no. Look at me, sister Eustacie. Listen to me. Osbert brought him home more dead than alive—but alive still.'

'No!' she cried, half passionately. 'Never could he have lived and left me to mourn him so bitterly.'

'If you knew—' cried Philip, growing indignant. 'For weeks he lay in deadly lethargy, and when, with his left hand, he wrote and sent Osbert to you, your kinsfolk threw the poor fellow into a dungeon, and put us off with lies that you were married to your cousin. All believed, only he—sick, helpless, speechless, as he was—he trusted you still; and so soon as Mericour came, though he could scarcely brook the saddle, nothing would hold him from seeking you. We saw only ruin at La Sablerie, and well-nigh ever since have we been clapped up in prison by your uncle. We were on the way to Quinet to seek you. He has kept his faith whole through wounds and pain and prison and threats,—ay, and sore temptation,' cried Philip, waxing eloquent; 'and, oh, it cannot be that you do not care for him!'

'Doubt not my faith, sir,' said Eustacie, proudly; 'I have been as true to him as if I had known he lived. Nor do I know who you are to question me.'

At this moment the child pressed forward, holding between her tow careful plump hands a red earthenware bowl, with the tisane steaming in it, and the yellow petals strewn over the surface. She and Philip had taken a great fancy to each other, and while her mother was busy with the other patients, she had been left to her quiet play with her fragments of glass, which she carried one by one to display, held up to the light, to her new friends; who, in his weak state, and after his long captivity, found her the more charming playmate because she so strangely reminded him of his own little sisters. She thought herself his little nurse, and missing from his broth the yellow petals that she had been wont to think the charm of tisane, the housewifely little being had trotted off, unseen and unmissed, across the quadrangle, over the embankment, where she had often gathered them, or attended on the '*lessive*' on the river's brink; and now she broke forth exultingly, 'Here, here is the tisane, with all the *soucis*. Let me feed you with them, sir.'

'Ah! thou sweet one,' gasped Philip, 'I could as soon eat them as David could drink the water! For these—for these——!' and the tears rushed into his eyes. 'Oh! let me but kiss her, Madame; I loved her from the first moment. She has the very face of my little sweeting, (what French word is good enough for her?) didst run into peril for me, not knowing how near I was to thee? What, must I eat it? Love me then.'

But the boarded door was thrown back, and 'Madame, more wounded,' resounded. The thrill of terror, the elastic reaction, at the ensuing words, 'from the north gate,' was what made Eustacie in an instant know herself to be not widow but wife. She turned round at once, holding out her hand, and saying with a shaken, agitated voice, '*Mon frere*, pardon me, I know not what I say; and, after all, he will find me *bien mechante* still.' Then as Philip devoured her hand with kisses, and held it fast, 'I must go; these poor men need me. When I can, I will return.'

'Only let me have the little one,' entreated Philip; 'it is almost home already to look at her.'

And when Eustacie next looked in on them, they were both fast asleep.

She, poor thing, the only woman with brains among the many scared females in the garrison, might not rest or look the wonder in the face. Fresh sufferers needed her care, and related gallant things of 'the Duke's Englishman,' things of desperate daring and prowess that sent the blood throbbing to her heart with exultation, but only to be followed by a pang of anguish at having let him go back to peril—nay, perhaps, to death— without a word of tenderness or even recognition. She imaged him as the sunny-faced youth who had claimed her in the royal castle, and her longing to be at his side and cling to him as his own became every moment more fervent and irresistible, until she gladly recollected the necessity of carrying food to the defenders; and snatching an interval from her hospital cares, she sped to the old circular kitchen of the monastery, where she found the lame baker vainly trying to organize a party of frightened women to carry provisions to the garrison of the bridge-tower.

'Give some to me,' she said. 'My husband is there! I am come to fetch his dinner.'

The peasant women looked and whispered as if they thought that, to add to their misfortunes, their Lady of Hope had become distracted by grief; and one or two, who held the old faith, and were like the crane among the sparrows, even observed that it was a judgment for the profane name that had been given her, against which she had herself uniformly protested.

'My husband is come,' said Eustacie, looking round with shining eyes. 'Let us be brave wives, and not let our men famish.'

She lifted a loaf and a pitcher of broth, and with the latter poised on her erect and graceful head, and elastic though steady step, she led the way; the others following her with a sort of awe, as of one they fancied in a superhuman state. In fact, there was no great danger in traversing the bridge with its lofty parapet on either side; and her mind was too much exalted and moved to be sensible of anything but a certain exulting awe of the battle sounds. There was, however, a kind of lull in the assault which had raged so fiercely ever since the fall of the officer, and the arrival of the reinforcements. Either the enemy had paused to take food, or were devising some fresh mode of attack; and as the line of women advanced, there started forth from under the arch a broad-shouldered, white-faced, golden-

- 378 -

bearded personage, who cried joyously, 'My dearest, my bravest! this for me!' and lifted the pitcher from her head as he grasped her hand with a flesh and blood clasp indeed, but the bright-cheeked, wavy-haired lad of her dream withered away with a shock of disappointment, and she only looked up with wistful puzzled earnestness instead of uttering the dear name that she had so long been whispering to herself. 'Dearest,' he said, 'this is precious indeed to me, that you should let me feast my eyes once more on you. But you may not tarry; the rogues may renew the attack at any moment.'

She had thought of herself as insisting on standing beside him and sharing his peril. Had he been himself she must have don so, but this was a stranger, whose claiming her made her shrink apart till she could feel the identity which, though she believed, she could not realize. Her hand lay cold and tremulous within his warm pressure, but he was too much wrought up and too full of joy and haste to be sensible of anything but of the brave affection that had dared all to come to him; and he was perfectly happy, even as a trumpet-call among the foe warned him to press her fingers to his lips and say, as his bright blue eye kindled, 'God grant that we may meet and thank Him tonight! Farewell, my lost and found! I fight as one who has something to fight for.'

He might not leave his post, but he watched her with eyes that could not be satiated, as she recrossed the bridge; and, verily, his superabundant ecstasy, and the energy that was born of it, were all needed to sustain the spirits of his garrison through that terrible afternoon. The enemy seemed to be determined to carry the place before it could be relieved, and renewed the storm again and again with increasing violence; while the defenders, disheartened by their pertinacity, dismayed at the effects of the heavy artillery, now brought to bear on the tower, and direfully afraid of having the bridge destroyed, would have abandoned their barbican and shut themselves up within the body of the place, had not Berenger been here, there, and everywhere, directing, commanding, exhorting, cheering, encouraging, exciting enthusiasm by word and example, winning proud admiration by feats of valour and dexterity sprung of the ecstatic inspiration of new-found bliss, and watching, as the conscious defender of his own most beloved, without a moment's respite, till twilight stillness sank on the enemy, and old Falconnet came to relieve him, thanking him for his gallant defence, and auguring that, by noonday tomorrow at latest, M. le Duc would succour them, unless he were hampered by any folly of this young Navarre.

Too blissful for the sense of fatigue, Berenger began to impart to the Commandant his delight, but the only answer he got was 'Hope, yes, every hope;' and he again recognized what he had already perceived, that the indistinctness of his utterance made him entirely unintelligible to the deaf Commandant, and that shouting did but proclaim to the whole garrison, perhaps even to the enemy's camp, what was still too new a joy not to be a secret treasure of delight. So he only wrung the old Captain's hand, and strode away as soon as he was released.

It was nearly dark, in spite of a rising moon, but beneath the cloister arch was torchlight, glancing on a steel head-piece, and on a white cap, both bending down over a prostrate figure; and he heard the voice he loved so well say, 'It is over! I can do no more. It were best to dig his grave at once here in silence—it will discourage the people less. Renaud and Armand, here!'

He paused for a few minutes unseen in the shadow while she closed the eyes and composed the limbs of the dead soldier; then, kneeling, said the Lord's Prayer in French over him. Was this the being he had left as the petted plaything of the palace? When she rose, she came to the arch and gazed wistfully across the moonlit quadrangle, beyond the dark shade cast by the buildings, saying to the soldier, 'You are sure he was safe?'

'My Eustacie,' said Berenger, coming forward, 'we meet in grave times!'

The relief of knowing him safe after the sickening yearnings and suspense of the day, and moreover the old ring of tenderness in his tone, made her spring to him with real warmth of gladness, and cry, 'It is you! All is well.

'Blessedly well, *ma mie*, my sweetheart,' he said, throwing his arm round her, and she rested against him murmuring, 'Now I feel it! Thou are thyself!' They were in the dark cloister passage, and when he would have moved forward she clung closer to him, and murmured, 'Oh, wait, wait, yet an instant—thus I can feel that I have thee—the same—my own!'

'My poor darling,' said Berenger, after a second, 'you must learn to bear with both my looks and speech, though I be but a sorry shattered fellow for you.'

'No, no,' she cried, hanging on him with double fervour. 'No, I am loving you the more already,—doubly—trebly—a thousand times. Only those moments were so precious, they made all these long years as nothing. But come to the little one, and to your brother.'

The little one had already heard them, and was starting forward to meet them, though daunted for a moment by the sight of the strange father: she stood on the pavement, in the full flood of the moonlight from the east window, which whitened her fair face, flaxen hair, and gray dress, so that she did truly look like some spirit woven of the moonbeams. Eustacie gave

- 380 -

a cry of satisfaction: 'Ah! good, good; it was by moonlight that I saw her first!'

Berenger took her in his arm, and held her to his breast with a sense of insatiable love, while Philip exclaimed, 'Ay, well may you make much of her, brother. Well might you seek them far and wide. Such treasures are not to be found in the wide world.'

Berenger without answering, carried the little one to the step of the ruined high altar, and there knelt, holding Eustacie by the hand, the child in one arm, and, with the moon glancing on his high white brow and earnest face, he spoke a few words of solemn thanks and prayer for a blessing on their reunion, and the babe so wonderfully preserved to them.

Not till then did he carry her into the lamplight by Philip's bed, and scan therein every feature, to satisfy his eyes with the fulfilled hope that had borne him through those darkest days, when, despairing of the mother, the thought of the child had still sustained him to throw his will into the balance of the scale between life and death. Little Berangere gazed up into his face silently, with wondering, grave, and somewhat sleepy eyes, and then he saw them fix themselves on his powder-grimed and blood-stained hands. 'Ah! little heart,' he said, 'I am truly in no state to handle so pure a piece of sugar as thou; I should have rid myself of the battle-stains ere touching thee, but how recollect anything at such a moment?'

Eustacie was glad he had broken the spell of silence; for having recovered her husband, her first instinct was to wait upon him. She took the child from him, explaining that she was going to put her to bed in her own rooms up the stone stair, which for the present were filled with fugitive women and children who had come in from the country, so that the chancel must continue the lodging of Berenger and his brother; and for the time of her absence she brought him water to wash away the stains, and set before him the soup she had kept warm over her little charcoal brazier. It was only when thus left that he could own, in answer to Philip's inquiries, that he could feel either hunger or weariness; nay, he would only acknowledge enough of the latter to give a perfect charm to rest under such auspices. Eustacie had dispatched her motherly cares promptly enough to be with him again just as in taking off his corselet he had found that it had been pierced by a bullet, and pursuing the trace, through his doublet, he found it lodged in that purse which he had so long worn next his heart, where it had spent its force against the single pearl of Ribaumont. And holding it up to the light, he saw that it was of silver. Then there returned on him and Philip the words they had heard two days before, of silver bullets forged for the destruction of the white moonlight fairy, and he further remembered the moment's shock and blow that in the midst of his wild amaze on the river's bank had made him gather his breath and strength to bound desperately upwards, lest the next moment he should find himself wounded and powerless.

For the innocent, then, had the shot been intended; and she running into danger out of her sweet, tender instincts of helpfulness, had been barely saved at the extreme peril of her unconscious father's life. Philip, whose vehement affection for the little one had been growing all day, was in the act of telling Berenger to string the bullet in the place of the injured pearl, as the most precious heirloom of Ribaumont bravery, when Eustacie returned, and learning all, grew pale and shuddered as danger had never made her do before: but this strange day had almost made a coward of her.

'And this is has spared,' said Berenger, taking out the string of little yellow shells. 'Dost know them, sweet heart? They have been my chaplet all this time.'

'Ah!' cried Eustacie, 'poor, good Mademoiselle Noemi! she threaded them for my child, when she was very little. Ah! could she have given them to you—could it then not have been true—that horror?'

'Alas! it was too true. I found these shells in the empty cradle, in the burnt house, and deemed them all I should ever have of my babe.'

'Poor Noemi! poor Noemi! She always longed to be a martyr; but we fled from her, and the fate we had brought on her. That was the thought that preyed on my dear father. He grieved so to have left his sheep—and it was only for my sake. Ah! I have brought evil on all who have been good to me, beginning with you. You had better cast me off, or I shall bring yet worse!'

'Let it be so, if we are only together.'

He drew her to him and she laid her head on his shoulder, murmuring, 'Ah! father, father, were you but here to see it. So desolate yesterday, so ineffably blest today. Oh! I cannot even grieve for him now, save that he could not just have seen us; yet I think he knew it would be so.'

'Nay, it may be that he does see us,' said Berenger. 'Would that I had known who it was whom you were laying down "*en paix et seurte bonne!*" As it was, the psalm brought precious thoughts of Chateau Leurre, and the little wife who was wont to sing it with me.'

'Ah!' said Eustacie, 'it was when he sang those words as he was about to sleep in the ruin of the Temple that first I—cowering there in terror—knew him for no Templar's ghost, but for a friend. That story ended my worst desolation. That night he became my father; the next my child came to me!'

'My precious treasure! Ah! what you must have undergone, and I all unknowing, capable of nothing wiser than going out of my senses, and raging in a fever because I could convince no one that those were all lies about your being aught but my true and loving wife. But tell me, what brought thee hither to be the tutelary patron, where, but for the siege, I had over-passed thee on the way to Quinet?'

Then Eustacie told him how the Italian pedlar had stolen her letters, and attempted to poison her child—the pedlar whom he soon identified with that wizard who had talked to him of 'Esperance,' until the cue had evidently been given by the Chevalier. Soon after the Duke had dispatched a messenger to say that the Chevalier de Ribaumont was on the way to demand his niece; and as it was a period of peace, and the law was decidedly on his side, Madame de Quinet would be unable to offer any resistance. She therefore had resolved to send Eustacie away—not to any of the seaports whither the uncle would be likely to trace her, but absolutely to a place which he would have passed through on his journey into Guyenne. The monastery of Notre-Dame de l'Esperance at Pont de Dronne had been placed there, as well as a colony of silk-spinners, attracted by the mulberry-trees of the old abbey garden. These, however, having conceived some terror of the ghosts of the murdered monks, had entreated for a pastor to protect them; and Madame la Duchesse thought that in this capacity Isaac Gardon, known by one of the many aliases to which the Calvinist ministers constantly resorted, might avoid suspicion for the present. She took the persecuted fugitives for some stages in an opposite direction, in her own coach, then returned to face and baffle the Chevalier, while her trusty steward, by a long *detour*, conducted them to Pont de Dronne, which they reached the very night after to Chevalier had returned through it to Nid de Merle.

The pastor and his daughter were placed under the special protection of Captain Falconnet, and the steward had taken care that they should be well lodged in three rooms that had once been the abbot's apartments. Their stay had been at first intended to be short, but the long journey had been so full of suffering to Isaac, and left such serious effects, that Eustacie could not bear to undertake it again, and Madame de Quinet soon perceived that she was safer there than at the chateau, since strangers were seldom admitted to the fortress, and her presence there attracted no attention. But for Isaac Gardon's declining health, Eustacie would have been much happier here than at the chateau; the homely housewifely life, where all depended on her, suited her; and, using her lessons in domestic arts of nursing and medicine for the benefit of her father's flock, she had found, to her dismay, that the simple people, in their veneration, had made her into a sort of successor to the patroness of the convent. Isaac had revived enough for a time to be able to conduct the worship in the church, and to instruct some his flock; but the teaching of the young had been more and more transferred to her, and, as he ingenuously said, had taught her more than she ever knew before. He gradually became weaker through more suffering, and was absolutely incapable of removal, when an attack by the Guisards was threatened. Eustacie might have been sent back to Quinet; but she would not hear of leaving him; and this first had been a mere slight attack, as if a mere experiment on the strength of the place. She had, however, then had to take the lead in controlling the women, and teaching them to act as nurses, and to carry out provisions; and she must then have been seen by some one, who reported her presence there to Narcisse—perhaps by the Italian pedlar. Indeed Humfrey, who came in for a moment to receive his master's orders, report his watch, and greet his lady, narrated, on the authority of the lately enlisted men-at-arms, that M. de Nid de Merle had promised twenty crowns to any one who might shoot down the heretics' little white *diablesse*.

About six weeks had elapsed since the first attack on Pont de Dronne, and in that time Gardon had sunk rapidly. He died as he lived, a gentle, patient man, not a characteristic Calvinist, though his lot had been thrown with that party in his perplexed life of truth-seeking and disappointment in the aspirations and hopes of early youth. He had been, however, full of peace and trust that he should open his eyes where the light was clear, and no cloud on either side would mar his perception; and his thankfulness had been great for the blessing that his almost heaven-sent daughter had been to him in his loneliness, bereavement, and decay. Much as he loved her, he did not show himself grieved or distressed on her account; but, as he told her, he took the summons to leave her as a sign that his task was done, and the term of her trials ended. 'I trust as fully,' he said, 'that thou wilt soon be in safe and loving hands, as though I could commit thee to them.'

And so he died in her arms, leaving her a far fuller measure of blessing and of love than ever she had derived from her own father; and as the enemy's trumpets were already sounding on the hills, she had feared insult to his remains, and had procured his almost immediate burial in the cloister, bidding the assistants sing, as his farewell, that evening psalm which had first brought soothing to her hunted spirit.

There, while unable, after hours of weeping, to tear herself from the grave of her father and protector, had she in her utter desolation been startled by the summons, not only to attend to the wounded stranger, but to lodge him in the chancel. 'Only this was wanting,' was the first thought in her desolation, for this had been her own most cherished resort. Either the *bise*, or fear of a haunted spot, or both, had led to the nailing up of boards over the dividing screen, so that the chancel was entirely concealed from the church; and no one ever thought of setting foot there till Eustacie, whose Catholic reverence was indestructible, even when she was only half sure that it was not worse than a foible, had stolen down thither, grieved at its utter desolation, and with fond and careful hands had cleansed it, and amended the ruin so far as she might. She had no other place where she was sure of being uninterrupted; and here had been her oratory, where she daily prayed, and often came to hide her tears and rally her spirits through that long attendance on her fatherly friend. It had been a stolen pleasure. Her reverent work there, if once observed, would have been treated as rank idolatry; and it was with consternation as well as grief that she found, by the Captain's command, that this her sanctuary and refuge was to be invaded by strange soldiers! Little did she think——!

And thus they sat, telling each other all, on the step of the ruined chancel, among the lights and shadows of the apse. How unlike to stately Louvre's halls of statuary and cabinets of porcelain, or the Arcadian groves of Montpipeau! And yet how little they recked that they were in a beleaguered fortress, in the midst of ruins, wounded sufferers all around, themselves in hourly jeopardy. It was enough that they had one another. They were so supremely happy that their minds unconsciously gathered up those pale lights and dark fantastic shades as adjuncts of their bliss.

CHAPTER XLIII
LE BAISER D'EUSTACIE

No pitying voice, no eye, affords

One tear to grace his obsequies.

—GRAY

Golden sunshine made rubies and sapphires of the fragments of glass in the windows of Notre-Dame de l'Esperance, and lighted up the brown face and earnest eyes of the little dark figure, who, with hands clasped round her knees, sat gazing as if she could never gaze her fill, upon the sleeping warrior beside whom she sat, his clear straight profile like a cameo, both in chiseling and in colour, as it lay on the brown cloak where he slept the profound sleep of content and of fatigue.

Neither she nor Philip would have spoken or stirred to break that well-earned rest; but sounds from without were not long in opening his eyes, and as they met her intent gaze, he smiled and said, 'Good morrow, sweet heart! What, learning how ugly a fellow is come back to thee?'

'No, indeed! I was trying to trace thine old likeness, and then wondering how I ever liked thy boyish face better than the noble look thou bearest now!'

'Ah! when I set out to come to thee, I was a walking rainbow; yet I was coxcomb enough to think thou wouldst overlook it.'

'Show me those cruel strokes,' she said; 'I see one'—and her finger traced the seam as poor King Charles had done—'but where is the one my wicked cousin called by that frightful name?'

'Nay, verily, that sweet name spared my life! A little less spite at my peach cheek, and I had been sped, and had not lisped and stammered all my days in honour of *le baiser d'Eustacie!*' and as he pushed aside his long golden silk moustache to show the ineffaceable red and purple scar, he added, smiling, 'It has waited long for its right remedy.'

At that moment the door in the rood-screen opened. Captain Falconnet's one eye stared in amazement, and from beneath his gray moustache thundered forth the word 'Comment!' in accents fit to wake the dead.

Was this Esperance, the most irreproachable of pastor's daughters and widows? 'What, Madame, so soon as your good father is under ground? At least I thought ONE woman could be trusted; but it seems we must see to the wounded ourselves.'

She blushed, but stood her ground; and Berenger shouted, 'She is my wife, sir!—my wife whom I have sought so long!'

'That must be as Madame la Duchesse chooses,' said the Captain. 'She is under her charge, and must be sent to her as soon as this *canaille* is cleared off. To your rooms, Madame!'

'I am her husband!' again cried Berenger. 'We have been married sixteen years.'

'You need not talk to me of dowry; Madame la Duchesse will settle that, if you are fool enough to mean anything by it. No, no, Mademoiselle, I've no time for folly. Come with me, sir, and see if that be true which they say of the rogues outside.'

And putting his arm into Berenger's, he fairly carried him off, discoursing by the way on *feu* M. l'Amiral's saying that 'over-strictness in camp was perilous, since a young saint, an old devil,' but warning him that this was prohibited gear, as he was responsible for the young woman to Madame la Duchesse. Berenger, who had never made the Captain hear anything that he did not know before, looked about for some interpreter whose voice might be more effectual, but found himself being conducted to the spiral stair of the church steeple; and suddenly gathering that some new feature in the case had arisen, followed the old man eagerly up the winding steps to the little square of leaden roof where the Quinet banner was planted. It commanded a wide and splendid view, to the Bay of Biscay on the one hand, and the inland mountains on the other; but the warder who already stood there pointed silently to the north, where, on the road by which Berenger had come, was to be seen a cloud of dust, gilded by the rays of the rising sun.

Who raised it was a matter of no doubt; and Berenger's morning orisons were paid with folded hands, in silent thanks-giving, as he watched the sparkling of pikes and gleaming of helmets—and the white flag of Bourbon at length became visible.

Already the enemy below were sending out scouts—they rode to the top of the hill—then a messenger swan his horse across the river. In the camp before the bridge-tower men buzzed out of their tents, like ants whose hill is disturbed; horses were fastened to the cannon, tents were struck, and it was plain that the siege was to be raised.

Captain Falconnet did his ally the honour to consult him on the expedience of molesting the Guisards by a sally, and trying to take some of their guns; but Berenger merely bowed to whatever he said, while he debated aloud the PROS and CONS, and at last decided that the garrison had been too much reduced for this, and that M. le Duc would prefer finding them drawn up in good order to receive him, to their going chasing and plundering disreputable among the enemy—the Duke being here evidently a much greater personage than the King of Navarre, hereditary Governor of Guyenne though he were. Indeed, nothing was wanting to the confusion of Berenger's late assailants. In the camp on the north side of the river, things were done with some order; but that on the other side was absolutely abandoned, and crowds were making in disorder for the ford, leaving everything behind them, that they might not have their retreat cut off. Would there be a battle? Falconnet, taking in with his eye the numbers of the succouring party, thought the Duke would allow the besiegers to depart unmolested, but remembered with a sigh that young king had come to meddle in their affair!

However, it was needful to go down and marshal the men for the reception of the new-comers, or to join in the fight, as the case might be.

And it was a peaceful entrance that took place some hours later, and was watched from the windows of the prior's rooms by Eustacie, her child, and Philip, whom she had been able to install in her own apartments, which had been vacated by the refugee women in haste to return home, and where he now sat in Maitre Gardon's great straw chair, wrapped in his loose gown, and looking out at the northern gates, thrown open to receive the King and Duke, old Falconnet presenting the keys to the Duke, the Duke bowing low as he offered them to the King, and the King waving them back to the Duke and the Captain. Then they saw Falconnet presenting the tall auxiliary who had been so valuable to him, his gesture as he pointed up to the window, and the King's upward look, as he doffed his hat and bowed low, while Eustacie responded with the most graceful of reverences, such as reminded Philip that his little sister-in-law and tender nurse was in truth a great court lady.

Presently Berenger came up-stairs, bringing with him his faithful foster-brother Osbert, who, though looking gaunt and lean, had nearly recovered his strength, and had accompanied the army in hopes of finding his master. The good fellow was full of delight at the welcome of his lady, and at once bestirred himself in assisting her in rectifying the confusion in which her guests had left her apartment.

Matters had not long been set straight when steps were heard on the stone stair, and, the door opening wide, Captain Falconnet's gruff voice was heard, 'This way, Monseigneur; this way, Sire.'

This was Madame la Baronne de Ribaumont's first reception. She was standing at the dark walnut table, fresh starching and crimping Berenger's solitary ruff, while under her merry superintendence those constant playfellows, Philip and Rayonette, were washing, or pretending to wash, radishes in a large wooden bowl, and Berenger was endeavouring to write his letter of good tidings, to be sent by special messenger to his grand-father. Philip was in something very like a Geneva gown; Eustacie wore her prim white cap and frill, and coarse black serge kirtle; and there was but one chair besides that one which Philip was desired to retain, only two three-legged stools and a bench.

Nevertheless, Madame de Ribaumont was equal to the occasion; nothing could have been more courtly, graceful, or unembarrassed than her manner of receiving of King's gallant compliments, and of performing all the courtesies suited to the hostess and queen of the place: it was the air that would have befitted the stateliest castle hall, yet that in its simplicity and brightness still more embellished the old ruinous convent-cell. The King was delighted, he sat down upon one of the three-legged stools, took Rayonette upon his knee, undertook to finish washing the radishes, but ate nearly all he washed, declaring that they put him in mind of his old hardy days on the mountains of Bearn. He insisted on hearing all Rayonette's adventure in detail; and on seeing the pearls and the silver bullet, 'You could scarcely have needed the token, sir,' said he with a smile to Berenger; 'Mademoiselle had already shown herself of the true blood of the bravest of knights.'

The tidings of the attack on Pont de Dronne had caused the Duke to make a forced march to its relief, in which the King had insisted on joining him; and they now intended to wait at Pont de Dronne till the rest of the troops came up, and to continue their march through Guyenne to Nerac, the capital of Henry's county of Foix. The Duke suggested that if Philip were well enough to move when the army proceeded, the family might then take him to Quinet, where the Duchess would be very desirous to see Madame; and therewith they took leave with some good-humoured mirth as to whether M. le Ribaumont would join them at supper, or remain in the bosom of his family, and whether he were to be regarded as a gay bridegroom or a husband of sixteen year's standing.

'Nay,' said the King, 'did his good Orpheus know how nearly his Eurydice had slipped through his fingers again? how M. de Quinet had caught the respectable Pluto yonder in the gray moustache actually arranging an escort to send the lady safe back to Quinet *bon gre malgre*—and truly a deaf Pluto was worse than even Orpheus had encountered!'

So laughing, he bowed again his compliments; but Eustacie demanded, so soon as he was gone, what he meant by calling her by such names. If he thought it was her Christian name, it was over-familiar—if not, she liked it less.

'It is only that he last saw you in the Infernal Region, *ma mie*,' said Berenger; 'and I have sought you ever since, as Orpheus sought Eurydice.'

But her learning did not extend so far; and when the explanation was made, she pouted, and owned that she could not bear to be reminded of the most foolish and uncomfortable scene in her life—the cause of all her troubles; and as Berenger was telling her of Diane's confession that her being involved in the pageant was part of the plot for their detention at Paris, Osbert knocked at the door, and entered with a bundle in his arms, and the air of having done the right thing.

'There, sir,' he said with proud satisfaction, 'I have been to the camp across the river. I heard there were good stuffs to be had there for nothing, and thought I would see if I could find a coat for Monsieur Philippe, for his own is a mere ruin.'

This was true, for Eustacie had been deciding that between blood and rents it had become a hopeless case for renovation; and Osbert joyfully displayed a beautifully-embroidered coat of soft leather, which he had purchased for a very small sum of a plunderer who had been there before him. The camp had been so hastily abandoned that all the luggage had been left, and, like a true valet, Osbert had not neglected the opportunity of replenishing his master's wardrobe. 'And,' said he, 'I saw there on whom M. le Baron knows,—M. de Nid de Merle.'

'Here!' cried Eustacie, startled for a moment, but her eyes resting reassured on her husband.

'Madame need not be alarmed,' said Osbert; 'M. le Baron has well repaid him. Ah! ah! there he lies, a spectacle for all good Christians to delight in.'

'It was then he, *le scelerat?*' exclaimed Berenger; 'I have already thought it possible.'

'And he fell by your hands!' cried Eustacie. 'That is as it should be.'

'Yes, Madame,' said Osbert; 'it did my very heart good to see him writhing there like a crushed viper. M. le Baron's bullet was mortal, and his own people thought him not worth the moving, so there he lies on the ground howling and cursing. I would have given him the *coup de grace* myself, but that I thought M. le Baron might have some family matters to settle with him; so I only asked what he thought now of clapping guiltless folk into dungeons, and shooting innocent children like sparrows; but he grinned and cursed like a demon, and I left him.'

'In any one's charge?' asked Berenger.

'In the field's, who is coming for him,' said the descendant of the Norseman. 'I only told Humfrey that if he saw any one likely to meddle he should tell them he was reserved for you. Eh! M. le Baron is not going now. Supper is about to be served, and if M. le Baron would let me array him with this ruff of Spanish point, and wax the ends of his belle moustache——'

'It is late,' added Eustacie, laying her hand on his arm; 'there may be wild men about—he may be desperate! Oh, take care!'

'*Ma mie*, do you not think me capable of guarding myself from a wild cat leap of a dying man? He must not be left thus. Remember he is a Ribaumont.'

Vindictiveness and revenge had their part in the fire of Eustacie's nature. Many a time had she longed to strangle Narcisse; and she was on the point of saying, 'Think of his attempts on that little one's life—think of your wounds and captivity;' but she had not spent three years with Isaac Gardon without learning that there was sin in giving way to her keen hatred; and she forced herself to silence, while Berenger said, reading her face, 'Keep it back, sweet heart! Make it not harder for me. I would as soon go near a dying serpent, but it were barbarity to leave him as Osbert describes.'

Berenger was too supremely and triumphantly happy not to be full of mercy; and as Osbert guided him to the hut where the miserable man lay, he felt little but compassion. The scene was worse than he had expected; for not only had the attendants fled, but plunderers had come in their room, rent away the coverings from the bed, and torn the dying man from it. Livid, nearly naked, covered with blood, his fingers hacked, and ears torn for the sake of the jewels on them, lay the dainty and effeminate tiger-fop of former days, moaning and scarcely sensible. But when the mattress had been replaced, and Berenger had lifted him back to it, laid a cloak over him, and moistened his lips, he opened his eyes, but only to exclaim, 'You there! As if I had not enough to mock me! Away!' and closed them sullenly.

'I would try to relieve you, cousin,' said Berenger.

The answer was a savage malediction on hypocrisy, and the words, 'And my sister?'

'Your sister is in all honour and purity at the nunnery of Lucon.'

He laughed a horrible, incredulous laugh. 'Safely disposed of ere you cajoled *la petite* with the fable of your faithfulness! Nothing like a Huguenot for lying to both sides;' and then ensued another burst of imprecations on the delay that had prevented him from seizing the fugitives—till he—till he felt as if the breath of hell were upon him, and could not help vindicating himself, vain though he knew it to be: 'Narcisse de Ribaumont,' he said gravely, 'my word has never been broken, and you know the keeping of it has not been without cost. On that word believe that Madame de Selinville is as spotless a matron as when she periled herself to save my life. I never even knew her sex till I had drawn her half drowned from the sea, and after that I only saw her in the presence of Dom Colombeau of Nissard, in whose care I left her.'

Narcisse's features contorted themselves into a frightful sneer as he muttered, 'The intolerable fool; and that he should have got the better of me, that is if it be true—and I believe not a word of it.'

'At least,' said Berenger, 'waste not these last hours on hating and reviling me, but let this fellow of mine, who is a very fair surgeon, bind your wound again.'

'Eh!' said Narcisse, spitefully, turning his head, 'your own rogue? Let me see what work he made of *le baiser d'Eustacie*. Pray, how does it please her?'

'She thanks Heaven that your chief care was to spoil my face.'

'I hear she is a prime doctress; but of course you brought her not hither lest she should hear HOW you got out of our keeping.'

'She knows it.'

'Ah! she has been long enough at court to know one must overlook, that one's own little matters may be overlooked.'

Berenger burst out at last, 'Her I will not hear blasphemed: the next word against her I leave you to yourself.'

'That is all I want,' said Narcisse. 'These cares of yours are only *douceurs* to your conceited heretical conscience, and a lengthening out of this miserable affair. You would scoff at the only real service you could render me.'

'And that is——'

'To fetch a priest. Ha! ha! one of your sort would sooner hang me. You had rather see me perish body and soul in this Huguenot dog-hole! What! do you stammer? Bring a psalm-singing heretic here, and I'll teach him and you what you MAY call blasphemy.'

'A priest you shall have, cousin,' said Berenger, gravely; 'I will do my utmost to bring you one. Meanwhile, strive to bring yourself into a state in which he may benefit you.'

Berenger was resolved that the promise should be kept. He saw that despair was hardening the wretched man's heart, and that the possibility of fulfilling his Church's rites might lead him to address himself to repentance; but the difficulties were great. Osbert, the only Catholic at hand, was disposed to continue his vengeance beyond the grave, and only at his master's express command would even exercise his skill to endeavour to preserve life till the confessor could be brought. Ordinary Huguenots would regard the desire of Narcisse as a wicked superstition, and Berenger could only hurry back to consult some of the gentlemen who might be supposed more unprejudiced.

As he was crossing the quadrangle at full speed, he almost ran against the King of Navarre, who was pacing up and down reading letters, and who replied to his hasty apologies by saying he looked as if the fair Eurydice had slipped through his hands again into the Inferno.

'Not so, Sire, but there is one too near those gates. Nid de Merle is lying at the point of death, calling for a priest.'

'*Ventre Saint-Gris!*' exclaimed the King, 'he is the very demon of the piece, who carved your face, stole your wife, and had nearly shot your daughter.'

'The more need of his repentance, Sire, and without a priest he will not try to repent. I have promised him one.'

'A bold promise!' said Henry. 'Have you thought how our good friends here are likely to receive a priest of Baal into the camp?'

'No, Sire, but my best must be done. I pray you counsel me.'

Henry laughed at the simple confidence of the request, but replied, 'The readiest way to obtain a priest will be to ride with a flag of truce to the enemy's camp—they are at St. Esme—and say that M. de Nid de Merle is a prisoner and dying, and that I offer safe-conduct to any priest that will come to him—though whether a red-hot Calvinist will respect my safe-conduct or your escort is another matter.'

'At least, Sire, you sanction my making this request?'

'Have you men enough to take with you to guard you from marauders?'

'I have but two servants, Sire, and I have left them with the wounded man.'

'Then I will send with you half a dozen Gascons, who have been long enough at Paris with me to have no scruples.'

By the time Berenger had explained matters to his wife and brother, and snatched a hasty meal, a party of gay, soldierly-looking fellows were in the saddle, commanded by a bronzed sergeant who was perfectly at home in conducting messages between contending parties. After a dark ride of about five miles, the camp at the village of St. Esme was reached, and this person recommended that he himself should go forward with a trumpet, since M. de Ribaumont was liable to be claimed as an escaped prisoner. There was then a tedious delay, but at length the soldier returned, and another horseman with him. A priest who had come to the camp in search of M. de Nid de Merle was willing to trust himself to the King of Navarre's safe-conduct.

'Thanks, sir,' cried Berenger; 'this is a work of true charity.'

'I think I know that voice,' said the priest.

'The priest of Nissard!'

'Even so, sir. I was seeking M. de Nid de Merle, and had but just learnt that he had been left behind wounded.'

'You came to tell him of his sister?'

And as they rode together the priest related to Berenger that M. de Solivet had remained in the same crushed, humiliated mood, not exactly penitent, but too much disappointed and overpowered with shame to heed what became of her provided she were not taken back to her brother or her aunt. She knew that repentance alone was left for her, and permitted herself to be taken to Lucon, where Mere Monique was the only person whom she had ever respected. There had no doubt been germs of good within her, but the crime and intrigue of the siren court of Catherine de Medicis had choked them; and the first sense of better things had been awakened by the frank simplicity of the young cousin, while, nevertheless, jealousy and family tactics had led her to aid in his destruction, only to learn through her remorse how much she loved him. And when in his captivity she thought him in her power, but found him beyond her reach, unhallowed as was her passion, yet still the contemplation of the virtues of one beloved could not fail to raise her standard. It was for his truth and purity that she had loved him, even while striving to degrade these quantities; and when he came forth from her ordeal unscathed, her worship of him might for a time be more intense, but when the idol was removed, the excellence she had first learnt to adore in him might yet lead that adoration up to the source of all excellence. All she sought NOW was shelter wherein to weep and cower unseen; but the priest believed that her tears would soon spring from profound depths of penitence such as often concluded the lives of the gay ladies of France. Mere Monique had received her tenderly, and the good priest had gone from Lucon to announce her fate to her aunt and brother.

At Bellaise he had found the Abbess much scandalized. She had connived at her niece's releasing the prisoner, for she had acquired too much regard for him to let him perish under Narcisse's hands, and she had allowed Veronique to personate Diane at the funeral mass, and also purposely detained Narcisse to prevent the detection of the escape; but the discovery that her niece had accompanied his flight had filled her with shame and furry.

Pursuit had been made towards La Rochelle, but when the neighbourhood of the King of Navarre became known, no doubt was entertained that the fugitives had joined him, and Narcisse, reserving his vengeance for the family honour till he should encounter Berenger, had hotly resumed the intention of pouncing on Eustacie at Pont de Dronne, which had been decided on upon the report of the Italian spy, and only deferred by his father's death. This once done, Berenger's own supposed infidelity would have forced him to acquiesce in the annulment of the original marriage.

It had been a horrible gulf, and Berenger shuddered as one who had barely struggled to the shore, and found his dear ones safe, and his enemies shattered and helpless on the strand. They hurried on so as to be in time. The priest, a brave and cautious man, who had often before carried the rites of the Church to dying men in the midst of the enemy, was in a secular dress, and when Berenger had given the password, and obtained admittance they separated, and only met again to cross the bridge. They found Osbert and Humfrey on guard, saying that the sufferer still lingered, occasionally in a terrible paroxysm of bodily anguish, but usually silent, except when he upbraided Osbert with his master's breach of promise or incapacity to bring a priest through his Huguenot friends.

Such a taunt was on his tongue when Pere Colombeau entered, and checked the scoff by saying, 'See, my son, you have met with more pardon and mercy even on earth than you had imagined possible.'

There was a strange spasm on Narcisse's ghastly face, as though he almost regretted the obligation forced on him, but Berenger scarcely saw him again. It was needful for the security of the priest and the tranquillity of the religious rites that he should keep watch outside, lest any of the more fanatical of the Huguenots should deem it their duty to break in on what they had worked themselves into believing offensive idolatry.

His watch did not prove uncalled for. At different times he had to plead the King's safe-conduct, and his own honour, and even to defend his own Protestantism by appealing to his wounds and services. Hearts were not soft enough then for the cruelty of disturbing a dying man to be any argument at all in that fierce camp; but even there the name of Pere Colombeau met with respect. The saintly priest had protected too many enemies for any one who had heard of him to wish him ill.

Nearly all night was Berenger thus forced to remain on guard, that the sole hope of Narcisse's repentance and salvation might not be swept away by violence from without, renewing bitterness within. Not till towards morning was he called back. The hard, lingering death struggle had spent itself, and slow convulsive gasps showed that life was nearly gone; but the satanic sneer had passed away, and a hand held out, a breathing like the word 'pardon' seemed to be half uttered, and was answered from the bottom of Berenger's kind and pitying heart. Another quarter of an hour, and Narcisse de Ribaumont Nid de Merle was dead. The priest looked pale, exhausted, shocked, but would reveal nothing of the frame of mind he had shown, only that if he had been touched by any saving penitence, it was owing to his kinsman.

Berenger wished to send the corpse to rest in the family vault at Bellaise, where the Chevalier had so lately been laid; and the priest undertook to send persons with a flag of truce to provide for the transport, as well as to announce the death to the sister and the aunt. Wearied as he was, he would not accept Berenger's earnest invitation to come and take rest and refreshment in the prior's rooms, but took leave of him at the further side of the fortress, with almost reverent blessings, as to one not far from the kingdom of heaven; and Berenger, with infinite peacefulness in his heart, went home in the silence of the Sunday morning, and lay sleeping away his long fatigue through the chief part of the day, while Pastor Merlin was preaching and eloquent sermon upon his good brother Isaac Gardon, and Eustacie shed filial tears, more of tenderness than sorrow.

CHAPTER XLIV
THE GALIMAFRE

Speats and raxes, speats and raxes, speat and raxes

Lord Somerville's billet

Never wont to let the grass grow under his feet, Henry of Navarre was impatient of awaiting his troops at Pont de Dronne, and proposed to hasten on to Quinet, as a convenient centre for collecting the neighbouring gentry for conference. Thus, early on Monday, a party of about thirty set forth on horseback, including the Ribaumonts, Rayonette being perched by turns in front of her father or mother, and the Duke de Quinet declaring that he should do his best to divide the journey into stages not too long for Philip, since he was anxious to give his mother plenty of time to make preparations for her royal guest.

He had, however, little reckoned on the young King's promptitude. The first courier he had dispatched was overtaken at a *cabaret* only five leagues from Pont de Dronne, baiting his horse, as he said; the second was found on the road with a lame horse; and the halt a day's journey remained beyond it. The last stage had been ridden, much to the Duke's discontent, for it brought them to a mere village inn, with scarcely any accommodation. The only tolerable bed was resigned by the King to the use of Philip, whose looks spoke the exhaustion of which his tongue scorned to complain. So painful and feverish a night ensued that Eustacie was anxious that he should not move until the Duke should, as he promised, send a mule litter back for him; but this proposal he resented; and in the height of his constitutional obstinacy, appeared booted and spurred at the first signal to mount.

Nor could Eustacie, as she soon perceived, annoy him more than by showing her solicitude for him, or attracting to him the notice of the other cavaliers. As the only lady of the party, she received a great deal of attention, with some of which she would gladly have dispensed. Whether it were the King's habit of calling her '*la Belle Eurydice*,' or because, as she said, he was '*si laid*' and reminded her of old unhappy days of constraint, she did not like him, and had almost displeased her husband and his brother by saying so. She would gladly have avoided the gallantries of this day's ride by remaining with Philip at the inn; but not only was this impossible, but the peculiar ill-temper of concealed suffering made Philip drive her off whenever she approached him with inquiries; so that she was forced to leave him to his brother and Osbert, and ride forward between the King and the Duke, the last of whom she really liked.

Welcome was the sight of the grand old chateau, its mighty wings of chestnut forest stretching up the hills on either side, and the stately avenue extending before it; but just then the last courier was discovered, reeling in his saddle under the effects of repeated toasts in honour of Navarre and Quinet.

'We are fairly sped,' said the Duke to Eustacie, shrugging his shoulders between amusement and dismay.

'Madame la Duchesse is equal to any *galimafre*,' said Eustacie, demurely; at which the Duke laughed heartily, saying, 'It is not for the family credit I fear, but for my own!'

'Nay, triumph makes everything be forgiven.'

'But not forgotten,' laughed the Duke. 'But, *allons*. Now for the onset. We are already seen. The forces muster at the gateway.'

By the time the cavalcade were at the great paved archway into the court, the Duchess stood at the great door, a grandson on either side, and a great burly fresh-coloured gentleman behind her.

M. de Quinet was off his horse in a second, his head bare, his hand on the royal rein, and signing to his eldest son to hold the stirrup; but, before the boy had comprehended, Henry had sprung down, and was kissing the old lady's hand, saying, 'Pardon, Madame! I trust to your goodness for excusing this surprise from an old friend's son.'

Neither seeing nor caring for king or prince, the stranger gentleman at the same moment pounced upon Eustacie and her little girl, crying aloud in English, 'Here she is! My dear, I am glad to see you. Give her to me, poor Berenger's little darling. Ah! she does not understand. Where's Merrycourt?'

Just then there was another English exclamation, 'My father! Father! dear father!' and Philip, flinging himself from the saddle, fell almost prone on that broad breast, sobbing convulsively, while the eyes that, as he truly boasted, had never wasted a tear on his enemies, were streaming so fast that his father's welcome savoured of reproof: 'What's all this? Before these French too.'

'Take care, father,' cried Berenger, leaping from his horse; 'he has an ugly wound just where you are holding him.'

'Wounded! my poor boy. Look up.'

'Where is your room, sir?' said Berenger, seeing his hosts entirely occupied with the King; and at once lifting the almost helpless Philip like a little child in his strong arms, he followed Sir Marmaduke, who, as if walking in his sleep, led the way up the great stone staircase that led outside the house to the upper chambers.

After a short interval, the Duchess, in the plenitude of her glory at entertaining her dear Queen's son, came up *en grande tenue*, leading the King by the hand, the Duke walking backwards in front, and his two sons each holding a big wax candle on either side.

'Here, Sire, is the chamber where the excellent Queen did me the honour to repose herself.'

The Duke swung open the door of the state bed-chamber. There on the velvet-hung bed sat *le gros Chevalier Anglais*, whom she had herself installed there on Saturday. Both his hands were held fast in those of a youth who lay beside him, deadly pale, and half undressed, with the little Ribaumont attending to a wound in his side, while her child was held in the arms of a very tall, bald-headed young man, who stood at the foot of the bed. The whole group of interlopers looked perfectly glorified with happiness and delight. Even the wounded youth, ghastly and suffering as he was, lay stroking the big Englishman's hand with a languid, caressing air of content, almost like that of a dog who has found his master. None of them were the least embarrassed, they evidently thought this a visit of inquiry after the patient; and while the Duchess stood confounded, and the Duke much inclined to laugh, Eustacie turned eagerly, exclaiming, 'Ah! Madame, I am glad you are come. May I beg Mademoiselle Perrot for some of your cooling mallow salve. Riding has sadly inflamed the wound.'

'Riding—with such a wound! Are we all crazed?' said Madame la Duchesse, absolutely bewildered out of her dignified equanimity: and her son, seeing her for once at a loss, came to her rescue. 'His Grace will condescend to the Andromeda Chamber, Madame. He kindly gave up his bed to our young friend last night, when there was less choice than you can give him.'

They all moved off again; and, before Eustacie was ready for the mallows, Madame de Quinet, for whom the very name of a wound had an attraction, returned with two hand-maidens bearing bandages and medicaments, having by this time come to the perception that the wounded youth was the son of the big Englishman who had arrived with young Mericour in search of her little *protegee*, and that the tall man was the husband so long supposed to be dead. She was curious to see her pupil's surgery, of which she highly approved, though she had no words to express her indignation at the folly of traveling so soon. Indeed, nothing but the passiveness of fatigue could have made her despotism endurable to Philip; but he cared for nothing so long as he could see his father's face, and hear his voice—the full tones that his ear had yearned for among the sharp expression of the French accent—and Sir Marmaduke seemed to find the same perfect satisfaction in the sight of him; indeed, all were so rejoiced to be together, that they scarcely exerted themselves to ask questions. When Berenger would have made some explanation, Sir Marmaduke only said, 'Tell me not yet, my dear boy. I see it is all right, and my head will hold no more yet but that I have you and the lad again! Thank God for it! Never mind how.'

When, however, with some difficulty they got him away from Philip's bedside down to supper, the King came and made him high compliments upon the distinguished bravery of his sons, and Mericour interpreted, till Sir Marmaduke—though answering that of course the lads must do their duty, and he was only glad to hear they had done it—became more and more radiant and proud, as he began to gather what their trials and what their steadfastness and courage had been. His goodly face, beaming with honest gladness, was, as Henry told the Duchess, an absolute ornament to her table.

Unable, however, to converse with any one but Berenger and Mericour, and pining all the time to get back to his son, the lengthy and ceremonious meal was a weary penance to him; and so soon as his release was possible, he made his way up-stairs again, where he found Philip much refreshed by a long sleep, and only afraid that he should find the sight of his father merely a dream; then, when satisfied on that head, eager to hear of all at home— 'the sisters, the dogs, my mother, and my little brother?' as he arranged his inquiry.

'Ha! you heard of that, did you?'

'Yes,' said Philip, 'the villains gave us letters once—only once—and those what they thought would sting us most. O father, how could you all think such foul shame of Berry?'

'Don't speak of it, Phil; I never did, nor Aunt Cecily, not for a moment; but my Lord is not the man he was, and those foes of yours must have set abroad vile reports for the very purpose of deceiving us. And then this child must needs be born, poor little rogue. I shall be able to take to him now all is right again; but by St. George, they have tormented me so about him, and wanted me to take him as a providence to join the estates together, instead of you and Berry, that I never thought to care so little for a child of my own.'

'We drank his health at Nid de Merle, and were not a little comforted that you would have him in our place.'

'I'd rather—Well, it skills not talking of it, but it just shows the way of women. After all the outcry Dame Annora had made about her poor son, and no one loving him or heeding his interest save herself, no sooner was this little fellow born than she had no thought for any but he, and would fain have had her father settle all his lands on him, protesting that if Berry lived, his French lands were enough for him. Out of sight, out of mind, is the way with women.'

Womanhood was already made accountable for all Lady Thistlewood's follies, and Philip acquiesced, asking further, 'Nay, but how came you hither, father? Was it to seek us or Eustacie?'

'Both, both, my lad. One morning just after Christmas, I rid over to Combe with my dame behind me, and found the house in commotion with a letter that young Sidney, Berry's friend, had just sent down by special messenger. It had been writ more than a year, but, bless you, these poor foreigners have such crooked ears and tongues that they don't know what to make of a plain man's name, and the only wonder was that it ever came at all. It seems the Duke here had to get it sent over by some of the secret agents the French Protestants have in England, and what do they do but send it to one of the Vivians in Cornwall; and it was handed about among them for how long I cannot say, till there was a chance of sending it up to my Lord of Warwick; and he, being able to make nothing if it, shows it to his nephew, Philip Sidney, who, perceiving at once whom it concerned, sends it straight to my Lord, with a handsome letter hoping that it brought good tidings. There then it was, and so we first knew that the poor lady had not been lost in the sack of the town, as Master Hobbs told us. She told us how this Duchess had taken her under her protection, but that her enemies were seeking her, and had even attempted her child's life.'

'The ruffians! Even so.'

'And she said her old pastor was failing in health, and prayed that some trusty person might be sent to bring home at least the child to safety with her kindred. There was a letter to the same effect, praising her highly too, from the Duchess, saying that she would do her best to guard her, but the kinsmen had the law on their side, and she would be safer in England. Well, this was fair good news, save that we marveled the more how you and Berry should have missed her; but the matter now was who was the trusty person who should go. Claude Merrycourt was ready——'

'How came he there?' demanded Philip. 'I thought he had gone, or been sent off with Lady Burnet's sons.'

- 401 -

'Why, so he had; but there's more to say on that score. He was so much in favour at Combe, that my Lord would not be denied his spending the holiday times there; and, besides, last summer we had a mighty coil. The Horners of Mells made me a rare good offer for Lucy for their eldest son, chiefly because they wanted a wife for him of my Lady Walwyn's and Mistress Cecily's breeding; and my wife was all for accepting it, having by that time given up all hope of poor Berry. But I would have no commands laid on my girl, seeing that I had pledged my word not to cross her in the matter, and she hung about my neck and prayed me so meekly to leave her unwedded, that I must have been made of stone not to yield to her. So I told Mr. Horner that his son Jack must wait for little Nancy if he wanted a daughter of mine—and the stripling is young enough. I believe he will. But women's tongues are not easy to stop, and Lucy was worn so thin, and had tears in her eyes—that she thought I never marked—whenever she was fretted or flouted, and at last I took her back to stay at Combe for Aunt Cecily to cheer up a bit; and—well, well, to get rid of the matter and silence Dame Nan, I consented to a betrothal between her and Merrycourt—since she vowed she would rather wait single for him than wed any one else. He is a good youth, and is working himself to a shadow between studying and teaching; but as to sending him alone to bring Berry's wife back, he was over-young for that. No one could do that fitly save myself, and I only wish I had gone three years ago, to keep you two foolish lads out of harm's way. But they set up an unheard-of hubbub, and made sure I should lose myself. What are you laughing at, you Jacksauce?'

'To think of you starting, father, with not a word of French, and never from home further than once to London.'

'Ah! you thought to come the traveled gentleman over me, but I've been even with you. I made Dame Nan teach me a few words, but I never could remember anything but that "mercy" is "thank ye". However, Merrycourt offered to come with me, and my Lord wished it. Moreover, I thought he might aid in tracing you out. So I saw my Lord alone, and he passed his word to me that, come what would, no one should persuade him to alter his will to do wrong to Berenger's daughter; and so soon as Master Hobbs could get the THROSTLE unladen, and fitted out again, we sailed for Bordeau, and there he is waiting for us, while Clause and I bought horses and hired a guide, and made our way here on Saturday, where we were very welcome; and the Duchess said she would but wait till she could learn there were no bands of the enemy at hand, to go down with me herself to the place where she had sent the lady. A right worthy dame is this same Duchess, and a stately; and that young King, as they call him, seems hard to please, for he told Berry that his wife's courtliness and ease in his reception were far above aught that he found here. What he means is past a plain man, for as to Berry's wife she is handy, and notable enough, and 'tis well he loves her so well; but what a little brown thing it is, for a man to have gone through such risks for. Nothing to look at beside his mother!'

'If you could only see Madame de Selinville!' sighed Philip; then—'Ah! sir, you would know the worth of Eustacie had you seen her in yonder town.'

'Very like!' said Sir Marmaduke; 'but after all our fears at home of a fine court madam, it takes one aback to see a little homely brown thing, clad like a serving wench. Well, Dame Nan will not be displeased, she always said the girl would grow up no beauty, and 'tis the way of women to brook none fairer than themselves! Better so. She is a good Protestant, and has done rarely by you, Phil.'

'Truly, I might be glad 'twas no court madam that stood by me when Berry was called back to the fight: and for the little one, 'tis the loveliest and bravest little maid I ever saw. Have they told you of the marigolds, father?'

'Why, the King told the whole to the Duchess, so Berry said, and then drank the health of the daughter of the bravest of knights; and Berry held her up in his arms to bow again, and drink to them from his glass. Berry looked a proud man, I can tell you, and a comely, spite of his baldness; and 'tis worth having come here to see how much you lads are thought of— though to be sure 'tis not often the poor creatures here see so much of an Englishman as we have made of Berry.'

Philip could not but laugh. ''Tis scarce for that that they value him, sir.'

'Say you so? Nay, methinks his English heart and yours did them good service. Indeed, the King himself told me as much by the mouth of Merrycourt. May that youngster's head only not be turned! Why, they set him at table above Berenger, and above half the King's gentlemen. Even the Duchess makes as if he were one of her highest guests—he a poor Oxford scholar, doubting if he can get his bread by the law, and flouted as though he were not good enough for my daughter. 'Tis the world topsy turvy, sure enough! And that this true love that Berenger has run through fire and water after, like a knight in a pedlar's run through turn out a mere little, brown, common-looking woman after all, not one whit equal to Lucy!'

Sir Marmaduke modified his disappointment a little that night, when he had talked Philip into a state of feverishness and suffering that became worse under Madame de Quinet's reproofs and remedies, and only yielded to Eustacie's long and patient soothing. He then could almost have owned that it was well she was not like his own cherished type of womanhood, and the next day he changed his opinion still more, even as to her appearance.

There was a great gathering of favourers of the Huguenot cause on that day; gentlemen came from all parts to consult with Henry of Navarre, and Madame de Quinet had too much sense of the fitness of things to allow Madame de Ribaumont to appear at the ensuing banquet in her shabby, rusty black serge, and tight white borderless cap. The whole wardrobe of the poor young Duchess de Quinet was placed at her service, and though, with the thought of her adopted father on her heart, she refused gay colours, yet when, her toilette complete, she said into Philip's room, he almost sprang up in delight, and Sir Marmaduke rose and ceremoniously bowed as to a stranger, and was only undeceived when little Rayonette ran joyously to Philip, asking if *Manan* was not *si belle, si belle*.

The effects of her unrestful nights has now passed away, and left her magnificent eyes in their full brilliancy and arch fire; the blooming glow was restored to her cheek; and though neck, brow, and hands were browner than in the shelter of convent or palace, she was far more near absolute beauty than in former days, both from countenance and from age. Her little proud head was clustered with glossy locks of jet, still short, but curling round her brow and neck, whose warm brunette tints contrasted well with the delicate, stiffened cobweb of her exquisite standing ruff, which was gathered into a white satin bodice, with a skirt of the same material, over which swept a rich black brocade train open in front, with an open body and half-sleeves with falling lace, and the hands, delicate and shapely as ever, if indeed a little tanned, held fan and handkerchief with as much courtly grace as though they had never stirred broth nor wrung out linen. Sir Marmaduke really feared he had the court madam on his hands after all, but he forgot all about his fears, as she stood laughing and talking, and by her pretty airs and gestures, smiles and signs, making him enter into her mirth with Philip, almost as well as if she had not spoken French.

Even Berenger started, when he came up after the counsel to fetch her to the banqueting-hall. She was more entirely the Eustacie of the Louvre than he had ever realized seeing her, and yet so much more; and when the Duchess beheld the sensation she produced among the *noblesse*, it was with self-congratulation in having kept her in retirement while it was still not known that she was not a widow. The King of Navarre had already found her the only lady present possessed of the peculiar aroma of high-breeding which belonged to the society in which both he and she had been most at home, and his attentions were more than she liked from one whose epithet of Eurydice she had never quite forgiven; at least, that was the only reason she could assign for her distaste, but the Duchess understood her better than did Berenger, nay, better than she did herself, and kept her under the maternal wings of double form and ceremony.

Berenger, meanwhile, was in great favour. A command had been offered him by the King of Navarre, who had promised that if he would cast in his lot with the Huguenots, his claims on all the lands of Ribaumont should be enforced on the King of France when terms were wrung from him, and Narcisse's death removed all valid obstacle to their recognition; but Berenger felt himself bound by all home duties to return to England, nor had he clear convictions as to the absolute right of the war in which he had almost unconsciously drawn his sword. Under the Tudors the divine right of kings was strongly believed in, and it was with many genuine misgivings that the cause of Protestant revolt was favoured by Elisabeth and her ministers; and Berenger, bred up in a strong sense of loyalty, as well as in doctrines that, as he had received them, savoured as little of Calvinism as of Romanism, was not ready to espouse the Huguenot cause with all his heart; and as he could by no means have fought on the side of King Henry III. or of the Guises, felt thankful that the knot could be cut by renouncing France altogether, according to the arrangement which had been defeated by the Chevalier's own supper-subtle machinations.

At the conference of gentlemen held at Quinet, he had been startled by hearing the name of the Sieur de Bellaise, and had identified him with a grave, thin, noble-looking man, with an air of high-bred and patient poverty. He was a Catholic but no Guisard, and supported the middle policy of the Montmorency party, so far as he possessed any influence; but his was only the weight of personal character, for he had merely a small property that had descended to him through his grandmother, the wife of the unfortunate Bellaise who had pined to death in the dungeon at Loches, under Louis XI. Here, then, Berenger saw the right means of riding himself and his family of the burthen that his father had mourned over, and it only remained to convince Eustacie. Her first feeling when she heard of the King's offer, was that at last her ardent wish would be gratified, she should see her husband at the head of her vassals, and hear the war-cry motto '*A moi Ribaumont.*' Then came the old representation that the Vendeen peasants were faithful Catholics who could hardly be asked to fight on the Calvinist side. The old spirit rose in a flush, a pout, a half-uttered query why those creatures should be allowed their opinions. Madame la Baronne was resuming her haughty temperament in the *noblesse* atmosphere; but in the midst came the remembrance of having made that very speech in her Temple ruin—of the grave sad look of rebuke and shake of the head with which the good old minister had received it—and how she had sulked at him till forced to throw herself on him to hinder her separation from her child. She burst into tears, and as Berenger, in some distress, began to assure her that he would and could do nothing without her consent, she struggled to recover voice to say, 'No! no! I only grieve that I am still as wicked as ever, after these three years with that saint, my dear father. Do as you will, only pardon me, the little fierce one!'

And then, when she was made to perceive that her husband would have to fight alone, and could not take her with him to share his triumphs or bind his wounds, at least not except by bringing her in contact with Henry of Navarre and that atmosphere of the old court, she acquiesced the more readily. She was a woman who could feel but not reason; and, though she loved Nid de Merle, and had been proud of it, Berenger's description of the ill-used Sieur de Bellaise had the more effect on her, because she well remembered the traditions whispered among the peasants with whom her childhood had been passed, that the village crones declared nothing had gone well with the place since the Bellaise had been expelled, with a piteous tale of the broken-hearted lady, that she had never till now understood.

For the flagrant injustice perpetrated on her uncle and cousin in the settlement on Berenger and herself she cared little, thinking they had pretty well repaid themselves, and not entering into Berenger's deeper view, that this injustice was the more to be deplored as the occasion of their guilt; but she had no doubt or question as to the grand stroke of yielding up her claims on the estate to the Sieur de Bellaise. The generosity of the deed struck her imagination, and if Berenger would not lead her vassals to battle, she did not want them. There was no difficulty with Sir Marmaduke; he only vowed that he liked Berenger's wife all the better for being free of so many yards of French dirt tacked to her petticoat, and Philip hated the remembrance of those red sugar-loaf pinnacles far too much not to wish his brother to be rid of them.

M. de Bellaise, when once he understood that restitution was intended, astonished Sir Marmaduke by launching himself on Berenger's neck with tears of joy; and Henry of Navarre, though sorry to lose such a partisan as the young Baron, allowed that the Bellaise claims, being those of a Catholic, might serve to keep out some far more dangerous person whom the court party might select in opposition to an outlaw and a Protestant like M. de Ribaumont.

'So you leave us,' he said in private to Berenger, to whom he had taken a great liking. 'I cannot blame you for not casting your lot into such a witch's caldron as this poor country. My friends think I dallied at court like Rinaldo in Armida's garden. They do not understand that when one hears the name of Bourbon one does not willingly make war with the Crown, still less that the good Calvin left a doctrine bitter to the taste and tough of digestion. Maybe, since I have been forced to add my spoon to stir the caldron, it may clear itself; if so, you will remember that you have rights in Normandy and Picardy.'

This was the royal farewell. Henry and his suite departed the next morning, but the Duchess insisted on retaining her other guests till Philip's cure should be complete. Meantime, Claude de Mericour had written to his brother and arranged a meeting with him. He was now no boy who could be coerced, but a staid, self-reliant, scholarly person, with a sword by his side and an English passport to secure him, and his brother did not regard him as quite the disgrace to his family he had at first deemed him. He was at least no rebel; and though the law seemed to French eyes infinitely beneath the dignity of a scion of nobility, still it was something not to have him a heretic preacher, and to be able at least to speak of him as betrothed to the sister of the Baron de Ribaumont. Moreover, that Huguenot kinsman, whose extreme Calvinist opinions had so nearly revolted Mericour, had died and left him all his means, as the only Protestant in the family; and the amount, when Claude arranged matters with his brother, proved to be sufficient to bear him through his expenses handsomely as a student, with the hope of marriage so soon as he should have kept his terms at the Temple.

And thus the good ship THROSTLE bore home the whole happy party to Weymouth, and good Sir Marmaduke had an unceasing cause for exultation in the brilliant success of his mission to France.

After all, the first to revisit that country was no other than the once homesick Philip. He wearied of inaction, and thought his county neighbours ineffably dull and lubberly, while they blamed him for being a fine, Frenchified gentleman, even while finding no fault with their old friend Berenger, or that notable little, lively, housewifely lady his wife, whose broken English and bright simplicity charmed every one. Sorely Philip needed something to do; he might have been a gentleman pensioner, but he had no notion, he said, of loitering after a lady to boat and hunt, when such a king as Henry of Navarre was in the field; and he agreed with Eustacie in her estimate of the court, that it was horribly dull, and wanting in all the sparkle and brilliancy that even he had perceived at Paris.

Eustacie gladly retreated to housewifery at Combe Walwyn, but a strenuous endeavour on Lady Thistlewood's part to marry her stepson to a Dorset king's daughter, together with the tidings of the renewed war in France, spurred Philip into writing permission from his father to join the King of Navarre as a volunteer.

Years went by, and Philip was only heard of in occasional letters, accompanied by presents to his sisters and to little Rayonette, and telling of marches, exploits, and battles,—how he had taken a standard of the League at Coutras, and how he had led a charge of pikemen at Ivry, for which he received the thanks of Henry IV. But, though so near home, he did not set foot on English ground till the throne of France was secured to the hero of Navarre, and he had marched into Paris in guise very unlike the manner he had left it.

Then home he came, a bronzed gallant-looking warrior, the pride of the county, ready for repose and for aid to his father in his hearty old age, and bearing with him a pressing invitation from the King to Monsieur and Madame de Ribaumont to resume their rank at court. Berenger, who had for many years only known himself as Lord Walwyn, shook his head. 'I thank the King,' he said, 'but I am better content to breed up my children as wholly English. He bade me to return when he should have stirred the witch's caldron into clearness. Alas! all he has done is to make brilliant colours shine on the vapour thereof. Nay, Phil; I know your ardent love for him, and marvel not at it. Before he joined the Catholic Church I trusted that he might have given truth to the one party, and unity to the other; but when the clergy accepted him with all his private vices, and he surrendered unconditionally, I lost hope. I fear there is worse in store. Queen Catherine did her most fatal work of evil when she corrupted Henry of Navarre.'

'If you say more, Berry, I shall be ready to challenge you!' said Philip. 'When you saw him, you little knew the true king of souls that he is, is greatness, or his love for his country.'

'Nay, I believe it; but tell me, Philip, did you not hint that you had been among former friends—at Lucon, you said, I think?'

Philip's face changed. 'Yes; it was for that I wished to see you alone. My troop had to occupy the place. I had to visit the convent to arrange for quartering my men so as least to scandalize the sisters. The Abbess came to speak to me. I knew her only by her eyes! She is changed—aged, wan, thin with their discipline and fasts—but she once or twice smiled as she alone in old times could smile. The place rings with her devotion, her charity, her penances, and truly her face is'—he could hardly speak—'like that of a saint. She knew me at once, asked for you all, and bade me tell you that NOW she prays for you and yours continually, and blesses you for having opened to her the way of peace. Ah! Berry, I always told you she had not her equal.'

'Think you so even now?'

'How should I not, when I have seen what repentance has made of her?'

'So!' said Berenger, rather sorrowfully, 'our great Protestant champion has still left his heart behind in a French convent.'

'Stay, Berenger! do you remember yonder villain conjurer's prediction that I should wed none but a lady whose cognizance was the leopard?'

'And you seem bent on accomplishing it,' said Berenger.

'Nay, but in another manner—that which you devised on the spur of the moment. Berenger, I knew the sorcerer spake sooth when that little moonbeam child of yours brought me the flowers from the rampart. I had speech with her last night. She has all the fair loveliness that belongs of right to your mother's grandchild, but her eye, blue as it is, has the Ribaumont spirit; the turn of the head and the smile are what I loved long ago in yonder lady, and, above all, she is her own sweet self. Berenger, give me your daughter Berangere, and I ask no portion with her but the silver bullet. Keep the pearls for your son's heirloom; all I ask with Rayonette is the silver bullet.'

THE END

CPSIA information can be obtained
at www.ICGtesting.com
Printed in the USA
BVHW071104180821
614612BV00009B/627